COVERT DECISIONS

DONALD PETERS

WORKBOOK PRESS LLC
187 E Warm Springs Rd,
Suite B285, Las Vegas, NV 89119, USA

Website: https://workbookpress.com/
Hotline: 1-888-818-4856
Email: admin@workbookpress.com

Ordering Information:
Quantity sales. Special discounts are available on quantity purchases by corporations, associations, and others. For details, contact the publisher at the address above.

Library of Congress Control Number:

ISBN-13:   978-1-958176-91-7 (Paperback Version)
                978-1-958176-92-4 (Digital Version)

REV DATE: 08/31/2022

COVERT DECISIONS

First Book of 'The Mark Taylor' Series

Donald Peters

By the same author :

The Gatekeeper

The Iran Affair

Donald Peters
www.donaldpetersbooks.nz

Chapter 1

Trouble

In a democracy, people should have the right to live in peace. They should be able to get up in the morning, do honest days' work, and then go home to their loved ones to watch TV or whatever else people do to unwind.

Unfortunately – not everyone thinks that way.

One event that shattered the peaceful dreams of people in the western world – and countless others – occurred on September 11th, 2001, in the United States. On that day, militant terrorists from the Islamic extremist group al Qaeda highjacked four airplanes and used them as weapons to attack. The resulting carnage saw almost three thousand people killed. These people were just going about their regular daily routines and had no idea that this would be their last day on this earth.
Subsequent analysis of what had happened revealed that several of these terrorists had lived in the United States for over a year. Unbeknown to the authorities and the public, they appeared to be normal people going about their lives in the country that had welcomed thousands, if not millions, of immigrants with similar backgrounds to share the land of the free. In retrospect they had come to the United States on a mission which would remain undetected until that horrible day when they executed it.

Amongst the group of would-be terrorists, four of them were provided with flying lessons at American commercial flight schools. Those lessons could have been obtained at any flying school, anywhere in the world. But such was the confidence of al Qaeda that they registered and went to school in the land of the infidels.

The rest of the terrorists who were to have various roles to play had easily slipped into the country in the months before the attack. On the day of the attacks, these terrorists had smuggled knives and box-cutters through US domestic airport security without any of them being either questioned or apprehended.

Why anyone would want to take over an airplane loaded with 20,000 gallons of jet fuel and fly it into a building is beyond the comprehension of most sane people. But that is exactly what they did. Well – in three out of the four cases.

An American Airlines Boeing 767 crashed into the north tower of the World Trade Center – in the heart of New York City. While first responders tried to evacuate both north and south towers, they genuinely believed that they had witnessed a freak accident. Such was the impact of the resulting explosion, and its awful aftermath CNN and other new agencies had the world enthralled, as the scene was broadcast around the globe. And everyone was riveted to the pictures of this carnage as they came through - gasping as they tried to comprehend what had happened.

And then a second airplane appeared in the sky.

United Airlines Flight 175 turned towards the World Trade Center and smashed into the south tower. All dutifully recorded in real time for all to see. This was no accident. This was a deliberate act carried out by a group of mad men.

Only then did it become clear. America was under attack on an unprecedented scale. That had occurred without any warning. And the United States security and intelligence services had no clue of what had happened, who was responsible, or why?

The world was watching as the horror of the World Trade Center was unfolding when there was another incident. This time further south in the capital Washington. American Airlines Flight 77 crashed into the west side of the Pentagon military headquarters in Arlington, Virginia, killing 125 military and civilian personnel. This was no accident or coincidence. This was also a deliberate act carried out by someone who had to be aware of the destruction caused in New York City.

Then came the fourth airplane involved in the operation. United Flight 93 had been delayed at take-off. Once the flight was in the air, some of the passengers had got word of what was happening in New York and quickly realized that their airplane was about to suffer a similar fate.

They had nothing to lose. Their fate was sealed once the flight had left the ground. So, they attacked the terrorists but could not save themselves. The flight crashed upside down into a rural field in Shanksville, Western Pennsylvania killing everyone on board.

The number of lives saved because Flight 93 did not find the intended target was unknown. Based on where the other three flights originated and where they terminated, the fourth flight was intended to land somewhere in Pennsylvania. And to cause some severe damage.

Was it intended that the flight crash into the White House or Camp David? Or the Capital building?

We know that George W. Bush the 43rd President of the United States was not in Washington on this day. He was attending a reading demonstration at the Emma E. Brooker Elementary School, Sarasota Florida. The question would be asked – had the terrorists made a mistake? Had the terrorists assumed that the President would be in residence and was the White House one of the targets? We may never know!

One thing is known.

The United States changed forever on that day.

Within one month of these attacks on American soil, US forces were in Afghanistan to smash the terrorist network set up there by Osama bin Laden. The United States launched Operation Enduring Freedom with the fury of a wounded nation and chased the Taliban out of Kabul.

A new department was created – The Department of Homeland Security – to ensure that such a tragic event could not occur again. The vast security and intelligence services which had collectively failed to identify the threat were given a massive shake-up. Air travel security throughout the world was overhauled to ensure that weapons could not be taken on board airplanes.

These, and other measures - some planned some merely a knee-jerk to circumstances - should have fixed the problem.

But did they?

Yes – it is possible that steps to prevent a repeat of the events on that fateful day – September 11, 2001 – may be successful.

Is it possible that someone else would try to emulate the events on another day?

Chapter 2

The Augem Group

Meetings of the Board at the Augem Group were not typically events involving tension. Well, there was no point, was there? Any likely cause of stress, or trouble, had long since been dealt with. And those who were unhappy with the way the Group was being run had long since resigned to their, or the Company's, fate. The Board Room had only recently been constructed, and the members of the Board had previously been accustomed to the more informal atmosphere of either the Chief Executives' or the General Managers' office. But today, things would be different. The Augem Group was, unwittingly to some of the members, about to commence a chain of events that would lead to violence and the death of at least one of their members. And the reasons were quite insane.

There were only five people who comprised the Board. Rob Augem was the company's founder and was still, at least theoretically, the Chairman. But his shareholding had been reduced to the point that only his seniority, and his extraordinary knowledge of the business that they were in, kept him in that job. He was well into his seventies. While that showed in his physical appearance, when you looked into his eyes, you could see that he was still one of the sharpest and shrewdest men around. He was tall and dapper and gave the unfortunate impression of being arrogant, but he was a very considerate and kindly man.

The company had suffered in the share market crash of 1987, and Rob had struggled, primarily on behalf of his clientele, to keep the company afloat while many in the Finance and Insurances industries had simply folded and gone off to find other ways of making money – or not losing any more money – well not theirs.

The saviour of the Company had been John Dubois. Dubois knew nothing about the Finance and Insurance business that the Augem Group was in. But he did understand money. He just saw a company that had potential – at least that is what he told the then Board – and he poured in enough money to save the company – and of course, to ensure he had a very secure controlling interest. So, he became the Chief Executive Officer, replacing Rob Augem. John was a big, overweight, bald man with piercing, but otherwise lifeless, grey eyes, thick rubbery lips, and a prominent chin that seemed to thrust out challenging anyone he met. He was over six feet in height, but when seated, he seemed to shrink. Very few people in the Company knew any details of John's background except that he had been born, raised, and educated in Beirut before moving further afield. Eventually, he ended up in the United States of America, a well-known but not particularly well-respected resident of New York City.

The other three members of the Board, if they could stay awake long enough to participate in decision-making, the other three members of the board were there to make sure that whatever Dubois proposed to do was passed with at least a four to one majority. Anything that Rob Augem suggested, and that Dubois did not like was voted down by the same margin. Of the three, one who went by the name Silas Weatherspoon had been with the organization since its' formation in the 1970s and had initially been, at least by his actions, supported Augem. The other two were brought onto the Board by Dubois. For no apparent reason other than self-preservation, Weatherspoon switched his allegiance from Augem to Dubois, and from that point onwards he became a rubber stamp for the new CEO.

Hence Rob was alone.

It was rare for any matter to be raised at Board meetings that concerned anything other than the procedural issues of the Company. Occasionally the discussions ventured into technical matters, but only those connected with the business of making money. The three members came to collect their directors' fees, have lunch, and then go off to their other appointments. Even by the end of this particular meeting, where the discussions would be more robust than usual, they would be no wiser. And could have cared even less.

Dubois, on the other hand, certainly worked hard for the company. There was no slacking just because he was the boss, and he did not have the ostentatious and glamorous habits of his peers. Well – he did have a Bell Jet Ranger helicopter that was parked at the Heliport in East 34th Street, which he took great pride in taking some important clients for a spin. But that was work, wasn't it? He took even greater pride in always being the first person into the office in the morning – that is on the mornings that he was in town. Many of the staff had tried to beat him into the office, but they gave up trying when even starting at six o'clock in the morning failed to make an impression.

But no one knew why he started so early. There was

just nothing much to get all that excited about. The company had very few international accounts where their clients would be working in different time zones, so there was no need to provide a service twenty-four hours per day, seven days per week. Even if they had, Dubois was hardly a person qualified to provide it.

They were, after all, heavily into a combination of insurance and funds management, and that business just carried on with the usual mix of nothing happening – the normal – and everything happening – the abnormal—like the horrific events of September the 11th 2001. In that episode, Rob Augem had lost several friends of many years standing. And it was fair to say, the Augem group had lost several competitors. Not that Rob thought in those terms, but some others did. For example – John Dubois did.

It was part of the company practice that the General Manager, Matt Reynolds, always attended the Board meetings. Reynolds was not the brightest general manager on the planet. But he had the height and the physical build of a quarterback, and an air of aggression and good humour that made him a good fit for his role. Although a senior executive of the company, he could not vote at Board meetings. Not that he alone would have made much difference. But Reynolds did know the finance and insurance business. More importantly, he knew the systems and procedures that they had put in place. Therefore, he could get Dubois out of any hole he might— and often did—dig for himself.

Also attending the meetings was Debbie Peterson —the Secretary to the Board, secretary to John Dubois, and office receptionist. While Reynolds had an easy relationship with the Board, Debbie did not. She was a petite, impeccably dressed, attractive lady, very loyal, attentive to detail, and afraid.

Occasionally other members of the staff would be invited into Board meetings to advise on technical matters, but they did not participate in decision making. Today was no different in that regard. At the beginning of the meeting, Dubois had introduced two other people to the Board. From their demeanour and body language, they would not be leaving the meeting anytime soon. Dubois did not say why these people were at the meeting which, to Rob Augem, the three silent members, and Debbie, did seem rather strange.

Rob Augem had a particularly good idea why they were there, hence the tension in the Board Room. Asid Dal, obviously the higher in the pecking order of the two, and Mohammed Pradesh, sat through the introductory and more formal part of the meeting without saying a word or appearing to be the least bit interested in what was being discussed. But, when Rob Augem announced that the next item on the agenda would be the computer system, they became fully awake and attentive, sitting forward in their seats in anticipation. Augem noticed their interest, and he could not control the body language that said he hated their very presence. He knew why they were interested, and there was nothing that he, as Chairman of the company, could do about what would transpire.

'We have to take control of our computer systems. We cannot carry on leaving ourselves vulnerable to an outside organization, and we have to do it now.'

Dubois delivered these three statements like the President giving the State of the Nation address. He ignored Rob Augem but could not have missed the glare emanating from the older man. He continued 'Reynolds has been more involved with that Taylor character so I will let him explain how we might achieve these objectives.'

'Well,' Matt began, 'we need to purchase the software

outright, and we need to terminate the contract that we have with Taylor Software for the monitoring service, maintenance, and support that they provide. That is not a trivial matter because there is an existing contract between us and Taylor Software that has some years to run. And then of course, since we want to continue using the systems, we have to be sure we can also continue to maintain and support them.'

'That is where these gentlemen come in.' John interrupted, nodding his head in the direction of Asid and Mohammed.

Matt did not seem surprised by the interruption, nor was he surprised by its' meaning. He did however change his tone of voice to one which could be interpreted as cynical.

'We should not terminate our contract with Taylor Software unless or until we are confident that we can continue to run and maintain the systems. So how confident are we?'

Asid, who was also the older of the two, nodded to Dubois and then replied to Reynolds.

'We are very confident. There is nothing clever that Taylor has. But we must have the documentation. Get these for us, have Mr. Taylor locked out, and we can then have our plans.'

Reynolds grimaced at the choice of words used by Asid. More so he cringed at the arrogance with which they had been delivered. Matt Reynolds had only been partly involved in the recruitment of these two men who came from India. At least that is where they had claimed that they came from. They were introduced to Dubois and Reynolds on a visit to Los Angeles some six months earlier, by a recruitment consultant who looked of equally dubious origin. At that first meeting, although Reynolds suspected it was not Dubois' first meeting with either the Consultant or the two 'Indian" gentlemen, they had been charming, polite, and smiling. They had displayed an attitude and an aptitude of due deference and Matt could not help but be impressed with their obvious knowledge of the computer and communications business. More importantly, they still appeared eager and wanted to learn new things.

Most computer 'experts' become 'expert' by knowing more than those around them – and then they become a pain up the ass – you cannot tell them anything! But these two were different. They had come to the United States to advance their knowledge of computers, electronics, and communications technology. Dubois, Reynolds, and the Augem Group were extremely fortunate to find such qualified, clever, yet humble, men.

'How wrong can you be?' Reynolds thought to himself. It was probably a difference in cultures that caused him to have some concerns about these people. But since they had moved from prospective employees to actual employees without, as far as he could recall, very much input from anyone other than Dubois, something had changed in these two people. It was the way the older guy spoke—with an air of absolute invincibility – and the way he said things—that got up his nose. Had these gentlemen no respect for anyone else and had they not heard of the legal processes that must be gone through?

Mark Taylor, the owner of Taylor Software, and the man who had developed the Augem Group's computer software was a brilliant guy in anyone's language. He would take one of Taylor for a dozen of these guys if only he had the chance. Taylor was a man of integrity, a characteristic absent in many of the people in the computer business, yet he had an easy-going nature that Reynolds' enjoyed. It was a pity that there was the likelihood that Mark Taylor would soon be out of the picture – but if only?

'You should not dismiss Taylor Software quite so easily' Reynolds began. 'Mark's system – and I stress that at this stage it is His system – is very professional, very clever, amazingly easy to use, and extremely efficient. But – these things aside—he never undertook to supply a system with documentation of the kind that we now have in mind. We asked for, and we got, operating stuff – but design stuff, especially the source code, is an entirely different matter. Therefore, we are headed for a legal battle – or at least I believe we are – unless we can make Mark an offer that he cannot refuse.'

Reynolds addressed Dubois directly and did not bother to acknowledge Asid. However, Asid was not used to the protocol of the Board room – or he simply did not give a rat's fart about the niceties of the situation.

'This system, he writes for you, so you demand what he does' re-joined Asid, while Mohammed sitting beside him nodded wisely in affirmation.

Reynolds almost lost it. He was already concerned that Dubois' plan involved these two taking over the work currently being done very professionally and competently by Mark Taylor and the people at Taylor Software. The Augem Group depended on their reputation for integrity and professionalism to do business, and they were looking after other people's money. These new guys had very little respect for the law, very little respect for business ethics, even less respect for other people, and even less command of the English language! Reynolds was about to try to put this delicate matter another way, when Rob Augem, who could restrain himself no longer, joined in the conversation.

'John, so far you have not explained to the Board why

we are at risk and why we need to change anything' Rob began. 'I do not doubt that your friends Asid and Mohammed are very capable' although his body language raised serious doubts about his views on that issue, 'but refresh my memory. Why change a situation that has worked, and is continuing to work, very well for us? You have yet to explain what it is about our systems or Taylor Software that would make us vulnerable, and vulnerable to what?'

Now the situation was starting to get messy. Dubois had certainly not articulated any coherent reason for this action to the Board. Well, there was no need to—was there? But in John Dubois' simplistic view the situation should have been clear. He, and therefore the Augem Group, should have absolute control of their systems. For no simpler reason than that is what he wanted, and a slightly more complex reason—he had his agenda. He had no intention of enlightening the Board about the latter. Again, there was no need.

There was the issue of emails coming through the system that appeared to have little to do with insurance, finance, or the Augem Group. But who cared about those?

The security part of the software let them through so that was an end to that part of the puzzle. The security on the operational side of the system was there to protect the funds – their funds – from someone trying to gain access from outside the company. It also sought to prevent anyone from inside the company from messing around with their clients' funds. And surely Dubois was not planning to mess around in that area. There was such an array of corporate laws at the state level that specified how such funds were to be administered.

That is not to say that the various laws were consistent, or even understandable to the average layman like, for example, John Dubois, But, even if you could circumvent the security and do something that was not quite legal, you would get nabbed – eventually. And you would end up serving a long stretch in a penitentiary far from the comfort of the office – and the money. The Federal Bureau of Investigation and the Justice Department took a dim view of company executives playing around with other people's money. And as the majority shareholder, John Dubois, had more to lose than anyone else – didn't he?

Therefore, it did not take a rocket scientist to work out that Dubois planned to use the system for something else or to take the Augem group into a business that was different from what they were in at present. Dubois did not want anyone who was not under his direct control to have any knowledge of it – it was a dog-eat-dog market. So, unfortunately, they could not afford their computer systems to be poked and prodded by any outside organization – thereby gaining crucial knowledge of what they were up to.

Rob Augem was not a rocket scientist, but he was a brilliant man and had been through the hoops a few times over many years in the business. Therefore, he would have worked out what, in his opinion, Dubois was up to. Many Finance and Insurance companies, similar to the Augem Group, had thrived in the market for years by simply doing the bidding of their clients and not asking too many serious questions about what they did. The finance company just collected money and hoped that they did not have to give any of it back – which was usually the case. The fact that billions of dollars passed through the Augem accounts meant they could make a tidy profit on each transaction. After all, it was only money – wasn't it? But cash for – What? or from—Where?

Rob Augem had a suspicion that he knew the from where part of the scheme that Dubois had in mind. And he also suspected that the US Drug Enforcement Agency would be more than a little interested if they were able to find out. He also had a suspicion that Mark Taylor had spent some time before becoming a supplier of computer software chasing drug bosses in different parts of the world. And Mark Taylor's reaction would also be interesting should he find out that the Augem Group were laundering drug money. Therefore, his question was not about where the money originated —but about why and how Dubois was intending to use the Augem Group and its' systems?

Dubois was not about to enlighten him.

'Rob, I have had my people working on a new range of products but, until we have all the loose ends tidied up, it is just too early to discuss it or to announce it, even at the Board level. You of all people should know how sensitive these things are. And we certainly cannot allow an outside organization to have access to anything concerning this.'

If Dubois' explanation was meant to appease the Chairman of the board it was not evident.

Rob Augem lost it.

'I have been through all manner of things in this business over more years than you have been alive. And now, I am not even privy to what is happening in my own company!' he shouted. 'If some new product is to be introduced I, and the rest of this Board, have every right to know.

Unfortunately, there was too much emphasis on the "my own company" part of the rhetoric.

'Rob – it is not your company. Now, where were we?' Dubois asked of no one in particular, before turning his attention back to Matt Reynolds.

The fact that a part of the Dubois plan was that Asid and Mohammed were to take over the system was a bit of an irritation to both Augem and Reynolds. It would have been far better to buy Taylor Software and have done with it. After all, the cost of such a move would hardly make a dent in the current and foreseeable financial position of the Augem Group. But Dubois had expressed the view that Mark Taylor could not be bought. And he was possibly correct in that opinion. But was there some other reason? Was it personal? Did Dubois, quite simply, want Taylor out of the picture?

Unfortunately, Reynolds did not think along similar lines to Rob Augem. He was not concerned about what was being done, only about how—because that was his job. In his innocence, Matt Reynolds still thought it was worth trying to retain Mark Taylor in the loop. For just one more time, in the best interests of the company – well, really his own best interests – he tried one more time.

'Well, let's look at our legal position. Mark Taylor owns the software – that is the source code that is his intellectual property. And he is not obliged to sell it. Therefore, we have to make him an offer that would more than encourage him to sell us the intellectual property rights. As far as I am aware, he is the only shareholder in his company. He has no dependents, and only the Bank to worry about. So, I say again, make him such an offer that he cannot refuse. It would be brilliant if we could also take his right-hand man, that nerd Brad Morgan, and Mark Taylor, as part of the deal. That may interfere with other plans that you have, but from a system point of view, it does make sense.'

Reynolds thought he had summed up the situation reasonably well. He was not prepared to push his preference too far. He was being more than well paid, and at the end of the day, they were spending their money, and not his. But if Taylor and Morgan came on board as part of the deal then there would be no need for Asid and Mohammed. That killed two birds with one stone would it not?

Reynolds knew or thought he knew that Taylor had a scary past. But that had nothing to do with the Augem Group – did it?

The reaction he got from Rob Augem was a look of pride. From Dubois, he got a look of complete indifference. From the two Indian gentlemen, a look of absolute hostility.

John managed to start speaking before the two Indian gentlemen could say anything else, otherwise, the meeting could have turned nasty.

'Mark would not come across for sure and Brad is too much of a nerd to want to work in the Finance or Insurance industry. That is why we have recruited these two gentlemen. In the opinion of Asid, Mark's software, while it does a brilliant job for us, is nonetheless fairly simple to someone who knows what they are doing. There are several issues and faults that they want to deal with. Fixing such problems would be difficult if we had either Mark or Brad on board. I do not know much about computer software, but we should not have any bugs in the system. So - our next step would be to talk to Taylor about the faults to put him on the defensive. And then offer him a price that is fair given our dissatisfaction with the software. He cannot refuse.'

Dubois sat back and surveyed the assembly almost daring anyone to challenge the logic of what he had just said.

This presented problems for the other Board members. For his part, Rob Augem did not know enough about computers—and even less about the software. While he had every faith in Taylor Software and even more faith in Mark Taylor, he did not know how complicated or simple the system was. Matt Reynolds equal faith in Mark, and he did know some of the technical characteristics of the software. Which was of several orders of magnitude greater than anything that Dubois knew. But was it enough to challenge anything Dubois had said? Or to question any advice that Dubois had received from the Indian gentlemen?

The other three Board members, while fascinated by the interplay, could not have cared less. Debbie did not know anything except that something was not being said, and something was not right. Nobody, including Dubois, knew how much Asid and Mohammed knew, except that it was assumed to be more than anyone else in the meeting knew.

Matt Reynolds sighed.

'Well, let us get Mark to come in for a chat and see how we go'.

John Dubois smiled.

'Do it today.'

Chapter 3

Taylor Software

It started very much like any other day. Well, it was Friday—so that made it different in a way. This week Mark Taylor had been determined to achieve some major objectives and to reach some significant milestones before the week ended—just like he had been determined to do so last week, and every other week since he had first formed the Company five or so years ago.

It was 7:30 am, and he was alone in the office. As far as he was concerned that was the good news. Many of Mark's clients thought that the office, which was providing round the clock service, was staffed 24/7. In reality, which was not necessary. In the age of modern communications, and Mark's heavy involvement with all the paraphernalia that was entailed in that, the office itself was largely unnecessary. Still, he had an office to house the computer systems, there was an expectation in the minds of his clients that he would have an office, and so that is where he now was.

He liked to be in the office before the rest of the team arrived. At least, that is how he justified it to anyone who cared to listen. If he did not leave his apartment before 6:00 am, he could add a few hours to the trip – and take a few hours off his life from the stress. And that would make him the last to arrive.

The other point was—he had nothing else to do. Mark was one of the many lonely individuals in the City of New York who was too shy to do anything about it except bury himself in his work. The fact that there were almost two million people in Manhattan, and ten million people in New York City, for some strange reason made him seem more alone.

Mark Taylor owned the Company as a sole shareholder and Director. But the truth of the matter was that the company was owned by the bank. He had started Taylor Software after leaving the armed services—much to the apparent horror and disbelief of his then-wife Helen. She thought that the Armed Forces would be his lifelong career, following in her father's footsteps. The Army had been the chosen career of the males in her family for generations—and in his own father's footsteps – a government employee serving his country in all parts of the world – almost, but not quite, the same thing. But the first Gulf war, followed by many covert excursions on behalf of his country that few knew about, into parts of the world no one had ever heard of or cared about, Mark felt that it was time to get out. It was not that he wasn't good as a serving officer. He was extremely good. He just did not see the sense in continually putting himself in harm's way, for an organization that did not seem to know what was going on.

Maybe the criticism was a little bit strong when that organization was headed by the undisputed leader of the free world, but that was how he felt. The military could give out purple hearts, and Mark had a few. They would be worn with pride by the living. But if you were dead that was a different story. And if the operations in which you were engaged were so covert, not to mention ill-conceived and planned, that no one had any idea what the expected outcome was supposed to be – well at least on a need-to-know basis—and no one appeared to care a rat's ass whether you came back alive or dead—then it was time to get out.

His ex-wife Helen saw things differently. She always appeared pleased to see him on the infrequent and irregular occasions that he escaped from the Special Forces for some Rest and Recreation. And she was very good in bed – or anywhere else for that matter. Mark had begun to suspect that her undoubted sexual appetite was well catered for while he was away and that was a subject that he had intended to raise with her when the time was opportune. But he never got the opportunity. When he quit the service and decided that his future lay in the computer business, then that was the end of their marriage. There was no animosity in the break-up. He suspected that Helen did not want him around to interfere with her boyfriends or girlfriends, and that was the reason why the marriage was at an end. Consequently, he moved to New York City, and the powerhouse that was Manhattan, there to make his mark in the computer and communications business.

He did know about computers having studied them, first in New Zealand while his father had been on assignment to Wellington, and then later through the use of computers and other electronic gadgetry in the armed services. His father was now back in Wellington, off on some other bizarre project that only the United States foreign services could invent, but that again was another story. Both of these experiences told him that the vast majority of people knew next to nothing about computers. Consequently, he had started to build some software that could make computers do what businesses wanted, instead of the rubbish that programmers, salespeople, and consultants said that people wanted them to do. It is not generally realized that the things salespeople say you need in a computer system are generally misleading, inaccurate, incorrect, or just plain lies. What they are saying is that, if you adopt the system that 'we' present to you, our support problems will go away – but not yours. Mark had a very commendable plan to fix this, except for one thing. He did not have the capital, nor for that matter, the particular skills, inclination, and drive, to market it as aggressively as the product required.

He got himself an office in the Upper East Side of New York City. It was a building that used to belong to an Automotive Mechanic. From what the property people had to say after he had signed the papers, the previous residents spent most of their time running drugs into Harlem. In the early days of his tenure, unsavoury characters would come calling unaware that their source of drugs had moved on, or unaware that the people they wanted to beat up on were no longer there.

Eventually, they got the message and they also moved on, but there was always that uneasy feeling that the drug underworld was not very far away. Still, the big advantage of the premises was that they were cheap – and built to withstand an attack by a nuclear bomb – well not quite—but relatively safe from outside predators.

So here he was five years later, a broken marriage, in debt to the bank, short of customers – at least those who would pay on time—and the same problems that he had experienced at the start. Where do you find people who can think about what customers want—rather than making a quick buck—and people who care about what customers are presented with? And it was not as though he was particularly happy in his role.

Many people assume that, if you are in the computer business, you live a high life. But in fact, Mark was lonely, and like many in his industry and his position, he was just too busy to do anything about it.

Probably because of his upbringing by very 'old school' and strict parents, and also because of his time in the Special Forces, Mark was very particular about his appearance and personal hygiene. While away fighting for his country it was not always the norm for him to be clean. It was no use hiding in a jungle smelling like an advert for cosmetics. And it was no use trying to shower in the middle of a desert where there was no water. What water there was would probably be more dangerous than the guns they carried.

When he returned from such adventures, he reverted to being immaculately clean. The computer software industry he was in almost demanded that he wore casual clothes, but that did not mean they had to be scruffy, dirty, or untidy. Mark made an imposing figure, about six feet four, well-built and proportioned, an unassuming and ready smile, and no hang-ups that could interfere with his daily business or his personal life – such as it was.

He had other reasons for wanting to appear so, as would become evident when a certain person turned up for work in about one hour.

As far as the plan for the week was concerned, he had known exactly what he had to do and how long each task would take. At least he told himself that he knew that much. He logged his computer workstation into the network, fired up the Scheduler, and looked at the plan that the computer laid out for him for the next week. The problem with using the scheduling system was that in addition to a start time and date, it also wanted a finish time and date. That was the hard part. Although he had designed the Scheduler himself—in the euphoria of design it seemed like a good idea at the time—but in the computer software business, it does not work that way. The old saying was—think of how long a job should take, then double it, and even taking this calculation into account you will still be wrong – usually by a factor of at least two.

His plan, however brave and well thought out, included many clients who had things that they wanted to be done, in times that were impossible to achieve, and at a price, they were not prepared to pay. He knew that some would soon be on the telephone and that some, but by no means all, would make it into his schedule. That meant that the overall plan would not be met in the planned timescale, but you had to at least try.

'Why did I ever get into this crazy software business?' he asked the computer.

He got a response, but not from the machine. In his usual way, Brad Morgan, who made arriving at work the most silent event of the decade, slipped into his chair, and said 'Because you are what you are, and you do what you do.'

It was the longest sentence that Brad had uttered since joining the company two or so years previously.

'Good morning, Brad, and how was your evening?' he asked of the Afro-American man who could have passed for Eddie Murphy if only he spoke! That question just brought a smile and a shrug.

How Brad survived was a mystery to the entire office. His partner – Honey—but her real name was a more appropriate Felicity – appeared to have all the personality of a wet cabbage. They lived in a tiny apartment that was due to be demolished, but the owner was hoping that it would fall first and save him the cost. Brad lived and breathed computers – a brilliant programmer, but also an expert on networks large and small. And an expert at hacking into any computer and any application. Mark thought of Brad as a 'geek' because that is what he looked like – thin and gangly and not much bothered about his physical appearance, although he was very fit and athletic. But behind the glasses, there was a very clever guy and a real thinker. And he was good – exceptionally good. And he came cheap.

Most of the other people who worked for Taylor Software would be making their way out to client sites around various parts of the city and beyond. There did not seem any point in their coming into the office and then going out again. The traffic in New York City dictated how many times you went out in a day. Usually once was more than enough.

The other person who did come into the office every day, and without fail, and always at the same time, was Annette Covic.

Mark was infatuated with her. He had to admit to being deeply in love. He desperately tried to hide his feelings and not let them interfere with his work. Although Mark had insisted that he would never get personal with anyone in or near the business, Annette was the exception. She did things to him that no other person could do. He believed that Annette would be at least receptive to any advances he may make. But shyness prevented that.

She had been introduced to Mark by a business associate who had suggested that he needed a Personal Assistant. 'Bull Shit!' had been his initial reaction. But then there were other considerations. One – the business associate was about to become a significant client of Taylor Software, so he had to be listened to and any comment taken seriously and treated with respect. Two – the client was very much into the corporate thing and expected related—well dependent—companies to be of a similar disposition. Three – Mark was grossly overworked and overstressed and did need someone to help him to get organized. Four – the company desperately needed business – any business – and this new client was talking millions of dollars in long term – so a PA was a small price to pay. But most of all—Five – she was stunningly beautiful!

And so, she got the job, whatever she cared to call herself.

And the price was not too bad.

Mark had never met anyone quite like her. She was about five feet nine, with long brown hair if anyone cared to notice anything beyond her gorgeous figure. And the way she dressed—she always looked like a million dollars, even though the clothes were – well – smart but nothing too flashy. That was because, although she modestly seemed to go to some lengths to hide it, her figure was perfectly proportioned. And her body seemed to float. But it was her smile that captivated everyone she met and in particular Mark. But even more than just her stunning looks—she was efficient in the extreme. She did not seem to be affected by the weather, time of the month, headaches, or any of the other well-known female disorders which he had endured when married to Helen. Mark and Annette had their disagreements of course. Well, Mark would ask for a file, or a progress report, or a few telephone calls to be made, or a little white lie to be told excusing him from a meeting, or any of the other paraphernalia that went with running a small understaffed and undercapitalized business. He would not get what he asked for, but the uncanny thing was that the business just ran as smooth as anyone could have wished. More so because of her manner on the telephone, and her straightforward way with people, which turned troublesome complaints from angry customers into apologies.

The even stranger thing was that when she did arrive at eight-thirty in the morning Brad Morgan did not seem to notice her. Whether he did not want to embarrass Mark or wanted to avoid any blatantly obvious comparison with what he had left at home, no one knew.

Mark tried to look busy as she entered his workspace but could not avoid the engaging smile and inevitably of being dragged into a spluttering description of what had been a fairly uneventful night – on his own and lonely – yet again. Yet no matter how he tried to turn the conversation around, he never found out what Annette had been doing.

Before long on this particular morning, she was into the Scheduler, rearranged it entirely, and advised him what he had to do next.

Well, it was not quite like that. He did have some say in what was and was not to be done. Yet before long things would start to go downhill rather rapidly in any case and the schedule would be long forgotten. But he did not know that. Yet.

The coffee arrived unasked for, black and weak in Mark's case, creamy, strong, and sweetened in Brad's case. Brad got a cheerful smile and hello that would have caused most able-bodied men to faint. He did not thought Mark, because Brad did not exactly look like an able-bodied anything. He just waved, which Annette seemed to interpret as a warm thank-you and she cheerfully set off to attack the mail—her term—bills—Mark's more correct term.

Just then the telephone started ringing. 'Here we go

again!' groaned Mark. Someone would have arrived at work, somewhere in the city, and found their machine 'hung' and needed to yell at someone. Not that it usually had anything to do with the Software. But when a man in a dark blue suit, white shirt, red tie, and with a screwdriver stuck where it belonged, says only software can hang a machine, telephones started ringing. Well fair enough – the solution is always the same – reboot the machine, the software reignites itself – and everything is back to near normal. Except that the first telephone call of the day was not from one of these cretins.

Annette took the call and became engrossed in a fairly frank disagreement with the caller, which was unusual for her. Eventually, she walked over to Mark telephone in hand, and for the first time he noticed – was it anger, or embarrassment – at least a definite undertone that said she was not happy. It came as more of a surprise when she announced the name of the caller.

Over two years before today, Mark had been approached by a firm that was in the Finance and Insurance business—The Augem Group—who he had only vaguely heard of previously. They were into everything that had anything to do with money, short of printing it, and they wanted to replace their computer system. It transpired that they made money from money rather than from things. Computers are exceptionally good at quickly adding numbers and they do not get confused with too many zeros. And subtracting large numbers too, but that rarely, if ever, seemed to happen in the Augem business.

The software they were using at the time was not that old, but they wanted more than it was capable of delivering. The software system, which Mark through Taylor Software had developed, could on the other hand easily meet their criteria. The funny thing was they just rang—

no tender process – no apparent evaluation – no concerns with the price – no jostling over details and specifications – they just ordered it.

The software itself had proven to be more difficult to install, not because of any technical requirements of the system, but because of the need to demonstrate at each step of the installation process what was happening to their data, and then to modify the security access to meet their stringent requirements. By the time the initial project was complete, it is doubtful whether any of the big number-crunching machines held by the National Security Agency (NSA), the Federal Bureau of Investigation (FBI), or the Central Intelligence Agency (CIA) could have hacked into it—that is if they cared to try – and why should they?

At the time, because all of Taylor Software invoices were paid promptly and in full by the Augem Group – sometimes even before Mark had the time to raise an actual invoice – Mark's company was more than happy, and things were looking as though the company was going to get out of the financial mire. Slowly however the cheerful enthusiasm that gripped the company began to wane as the Augem Group became almost paranoid about their security.

Mark, and in particular Brad, became almost bereft of ideas of how they could make the system more secure. The documentation of the security arrangements for the software alone was enough to fill a building if anybody had ever cared to print it out. And then there was the email traffic. After the initial shock at the realization of just how easily even college students – well in particular college students—could hack into their system, and alarmed by the usual concoction of viruses, worms, Trojans, and spam, they asked Mark to design and implement a series of firewalls that would make even Bill Gates and his Microsoft Empire envious.

One of the problems of the modern age is that technology has placed a ridiculous amount of computer power in the hands of ordinary people. The fact that few of those people understand the power they have at their fingertips was beside the point. Armed with a conventional personal computer, individuals could create systems – and chaos—that was unheard of only a few years before. More to the point, they could encrypt their work, hide their source of transmission, and hide their identity, making it almost impossible for the average punter to understand what was happening or what had happened. This gave the likes of the National Security Agency, the people who felt that they had a legitimate reason to pry into the affairs of anyone without their knowledge, a real headache. Even more to the point, the Internet gives access to all manner of inconsequential and innocuous information such as— how to make a nuclear bomb. The critical point is that people in any occupation, either with intent or just for fun, can break into anywhere, anytime, and make all kinds of mischief. And in many cases, the user of the target computer would be unaware of anything untoward.

The Augem system specified that it had to filter every internal and external message, without the originator or the recipient being aware of it. Then there was the delicate question of who would be exempt from these checking procedures. John Dubois would naturally be exempt as the Chief Executive Officer of the Augem Group, since he was paying the bills. Mark thought otherwise and, therefore, so did the software.

All this required constant checking and proofing, and part of Brad Morgan's routine was to periodically try to bypass the Taylor Software installed security and try to infiltrate the system. Part of Mark's routine was to convince the client that they were doing some work, when according to Brad, no matter how he tried, he could not break-in. At least—not by any conventional means.

Annette put the call on hold and said 'It is Matt Reynolds. He needs you to go to a meeting with the Augem Board this afternoon. There is an issue on their security which has to be thrashed out, and in his words—your input is crucial.'

'Then I do not seem to have much choice, but why the urgency?'

That question just brought a shrug from Annette, and for the first time that Mark could remember, she did not smile. He took the telephone.

'Hi, Matt – how was your week?' Mark asked, easing into the conversation. The question and the levity with which it was delivered were ignored.

'The Augem Group Board is meeting again at 2:00 pm this afternoon. We would like you to attend and discuss some rather important, matters that have cropped up. Because the traffic is as it is, and you do not need the hassle of finding a park, I will have one of my staff drive by and pick you up – about 1:00 pm – ok?'

Mark was quite used to clients who think that software people sit on their butts waiting and hoping, for clients to ring. He was also aware that he had little choice in the matter, being that this particular client was by far his biggest. And therefore, one for which he could quite readily and easily jump through rings backward. He was clean and tidy. But the facts were that he would have to shave to remove the partial growth that he had for some insane reason felt could impress Annette. He was dressed in jeans, the oddest jersey that he owned, and a pair of running shoes were minor considerations. These things would need to be addressed for him to attend The Board of the Augem Group. Not that he knew who was on the Board. This was the first time the existence of a "Board" had even been mentioned.

'I will have to try to rearrange a few meetings—otherwise, we may have to make it early next week?' Mark countered.

But he knew there was no conviction in his voice. For one thing, he was not a particularly good liar when it came to simple matters of fact. His ex-wife Helen had worked that out—unfortunately—long before he did. And he did not have any meetings scheduled, apart from the inevitable monthly meeting at the bank to justify, or not, the continuation of their understanding .

Well, that was how the Bank put it. It did not seem to matter whether you had money or not, the Bank was always wanting to do a 'review' – bureaucracy gone mad. But then, they had all the money!

As far as Mark was concerned the review could wait until he retired. For another Mark knew, that Matt knew, that Annette would be the one doing the rearranging . And she was good at that kind of thing and had probably already done it. Since Matt Reynolds had been the one who introduced him to Annette, he knew how the cards were stacked. In this case, she did not need her persuasive powers.

Mark thought for one moment he detected hesitation in Matt's voice. On reflection, he sensed – heard – felt—that someone was impatiently telling Matt to get on with it.

Mark asked, 'Who is on the Board?'

Then he knew someone was pulling the strings. After a sharp muttered oath, Reynolds, as he was referred to by everyone Mark spoke to—the Chief Executive to the janitor – said rather stiffly.

'Soon enough for that Mark. My car will pick you up at 1:00 pm' and he just disconnected the call without any further comment.

'Could you please rearrange my schedule for this afternoon?'

Mark limply asked his PA and wandered off down to the bathroom to find a razor and a change of clothes. The office was an old two-story building that had been used as a mechanics workshop until that business dried up as the area gradually became more run down, and the few people who could or would pay for repairs moved away. But it was ideal for Mark because it did not matter where your office was in the computer business. With modern communications equipment and software, you could be in outer Mongolia for all that it mattered. And it was cheap.

For some reason, the previous owner had built a huge bathroom on the first floor and that is where Mark went now, knowing that he had more clothes at the office than he did at his apartment.

After shaving and freshening up, Mark felt better. He still had a couple of hours to spare before he would need to get changed into something more appropriate for a Board meeting, and that gave him the time to review the Augem account.

Looking on the positive side, the monthly income from the Augem Group was sixteen thousand dollars. The software business is no different from any other business when it came down to cash flow. The same rules apply, call them Murphy's law, Parkinson's law, or anyone else's law. And when a client called and wanted to discuss 'things' the owner of the supplying business immediately thought of the worst possible scenario.

If the cash flow from the Augem account was maintained, they would be ok. If, on the other hand, the client no longer needed support for the Taylor Software, then those sixteen thousand dollars would have to be replaced by – what? However, this was mere speculation. Mark did not know what the 'issues' were that the board wanted to discuss.

One of the strange things about being the boss of a computer software company is that you do not own anything other than a collection of ideas known as intellectual property—sometimes coordinated, more usually not so, even more usually an absolute shambles – but held together in a way that few understand so that they comprise a solution. Those people who regard computer software as a Product were dreaming. Especially of the type of solution that Mark was involved in. You build the ideas and experience of your clients into the solution, and you continue to do so as their business needs change – must change – to stay at least one step ahead of their competition.

But the techniques of the software business were a bit flaky. The owner of the company was dependent on his staff, for he could not know, or keep up with, all the tricks of the trade. When you had to talk to one of the nerds who holds these mystical powers you are lucky if they deem to convey much, even though you sign the payroll, and when they do you might understand every fourth or fifth word. Mark was fortunate in being technically competent, but he still had to depend on others. And the 'other' in this case was Brad who was not exactly the best communicator in the world. Well – right now Mark could not concentrate on anything else so why not give it a go?

As it transpired, Brad Morgan almost made sense.

'What was the outcome of your latest test of the Augem system? Was there anything different from previous tests?' looking for at least a positive "No" Mark began?

Brad almost came to life. 'Yes'

'Well—what?' asked Mark.

'They have been messing around with the email security.'

'What do you mean by messing around?'

Mark was used to this type of question/answer session – he did not understand why he tolerated it – but he was quite used to it.

'They have added a couple more terminals' Brad replied.

'But they can't just add terminals without our being involved.' Mark began to sit up – he should have read about the changes in Brad's daily reports – but they were boringly repetitive – and as usual, other things were demanding his attention.

'Yes—but they are not using the conventional – sorry 'our' – security system.'

'Why would they want to do that?'

The question asked but with no thought of an answer – well one that made any sense. He was not disappointed.

Brad just shrugged 'I have no idea.'

And Brad returned to his machine, having twice in as many hours exceeded his longest recorded sentence. Mark was thinking more about the financial implications as far as the software was concerned.

If Augem did want to terminate their arrangement, then the next meeting with the Bank should be attended by his ex-wife. That would at least keep them occupied.

The risk to a small business was always – what do you do if you lose your main client? You had to rapidly find another client to take their place. Hence the telephone call had unsettled Mark more than a little and both Brad and Annette sensed it. If Augem were not going to continue using the software – Mark was certain that no other company, at least on this planet, would ever want it. Mark was convinced that businesses had to get real about computer system security, sooner rather than later, but he did not have the marketing skills to get that message across and did not have the money to pursue it.

In the end, Taylor Software, and therefore Mark, would be the big loser. You quoted for development work on the basis that other people could do the job, so you had to be competitive. You considered your prior knowledge, your competitive edge that arose from that, and then what knowledge you would gain from this particular job. You then planned, or hoped, that the client would continue paying for support long enough for you to recover first your actual costs, then to a break-even point, and then into profit. And they were barely at a break-even point yet. Cash flow is one thing—the books of the company were another.

'Having spent heavens knows how much money on security, why would they want to bypass it? And more to the point, why were we not consulted?' Mark directed the question at no one in particular.

Again, did not expect an answer.

And again, he was not disappointed.

Within the next twenty-four hours, he would be.

But for other reasons.

Chapter 4

New York City

Although the majority of the male population would prefer to drive themselves, Mark liked to be driven around the city. New York City, and in particular the lower part of Manhattan, was always so very much alive, although the yellow cabs tried to make it not so for anyone who tried to cross the street.

Mark was a courteous, careful, and patient driver and he could not understand the stupid risks that people took in getting from point A to point B. Risk to the vehicles they were driving, risk to themselves, and risk everyone and everything in their proximity.

Latterly Mark had to lease cars rather than buy them outright, but no one knew that did they? And he treated his leased car like he owned it.

But being driven by someone else, in a vehicle where he had no responsibility for what went wrong, was simply great. One of the major advantages of New York City was that many of the streets were numbered rather than named. That made navigation a whole lot easier – that is until you reached Greenwich Village, an area just to the north of the financial district – then they reverted to names which confused no one – except tourists. The mad rush from one set of traffic lights to the next made absolutely no sense, consumed about twice as much gas as was necessary, wore out tires at twice the speed of normal use – and that was just the cars. What about the human cost? But it was the thrill of the chase that had always appealed to man's basic instincts.

He was aroused from his daydreaming by the man seated next to him who indicated that he should get out. They had arrived at the office of the Augem Group in Chambers Street.

Not Wall Street but close enough to it.

When Matt Reynolds had said that one of "his staff" would drop by and pick him up, Mark had expected that it would be the Augem secretary/receptionist – Debbie Peterson. He hoped it would be Debbie for a simple reason. Not only was she an incredibly attractive lady, but also, she loved to talk. If something was happening, she would know, and she would tell, at least as much as she knew. Mark was available , and quite good-looking. She was single – and becoming desperate. And anyway, Mark was now part of the family – wasn't he?

Mark had noticed, on more than one occasion, that when he had been in Matt Reynolds' office or thereabouts, she was always hovering somewhere nearby and eager to meet his every requirement. And to attract his attention. And to talk.

Had she come to pick him up, Mark would have been able to go into the meeting of the Augem Board at least with a clue as to what it was all about. As it was, he had only his thoughts and ideas, which would turn out to be partially right and partially wrong. He would get no help from his escorts. If he had known the outcome of what this trip would lead to, he would have been better off to stay at the office – at least while he still had one.

For whatever reason, he had been collected from the

office of Taylor Software by two guys who had failed finishing school. When they had arrived at Mark's office they had pointed to the car as though Mark would not have realized this was the mode of transport. He had been more or less manhandled into the rear seat. Neither of the men made any attempt to speak or to introduce themselves. The back seat was cut off from the driver by what looked like bullet-proof glass. Not that it mattered. The driver never reacted to his passengers. Probably the glass was to prevent bullets from hitting the driver if one of his passengers happened to have a gun.

But why would such a person let into the car in the first place?

There was little doubt from the bulge under the right armpit, and the bulge at the ankle of the left leg, that at least one of the passengers was armed and appeared too dumb to understand any other form of communication.

There was little doubt from the bulge under the right armpit, and the bulge at the ankle of the left leg, that at least one of the passengers was armed and appeared too dumb to understand any other form of communication.

The guy sitting on Mark's left also had the annoying habit of sucking on toothpicks. It was not as though the exercise would achieve much. His teeth were a mess. Mark assumed that his continual picking, examining the results of his labours, and then sucking again was some insane animal ritual. When he had achieved an unknown goal, he snapped the pick in two, dropped it on the floor, and started the same insane ritual over again with a new toothpick.

What was this type of person doing working for a respectable finance and insurance company like the Augem Group? Mark had no idea, but it did seem out of character. Except - What?

Mark had a suspicion that John Dubois was into something other than just insurance and funds management. But what other things he did not know. This was the first time he had met any questionable characters who were apparently on the Augem payroll – other than your normal crook who, because they wore a collar and tie, could claim to be just doing their job. Mark had in another life, had met characters of a similar type to his two "transporters" and he knew what "other" things they were into – namely drugs.

At first, this whole scene was like a comic opera to Mark. However, as the car had got closer to its' destination, the tension in the car mounted for no reason that Mark was aware of.

Mark began to worry.

The office of The Augem Group was nestled in one of the smaller buildings just off Chambers Street. His escorts went to great pains to show that they were on legitimate business, entering the building's carpark, which was below the street level and going to the reserved space alongside that of the Chief Executive Officer – John Dubois.

Mark exited the car in very much the same fashion as he had entered it. And then the transporters just left him and took off with a squeal of tires looking for someone else to scare. They were pleased to have nothing more to do with whatever was about to eventuate.

On entering the lobby of the building, Mark automatically walked to the bank of three elevators and pressed the button to go up. Since he was early for his 2:00 pm "appointment" there seemed to be little point in selecting the express elevator which bypassed the first nine floors. But old habits die hard and so he did. Which seemed like a mistake.

Standing in the group of people waiting for the elevators, and to Marks left, were two extremely attractive ladies. Since they kept glancing in his direction Mark assumed that they were looking at him! Their body language said that they knew who he was!

He looked to his right, and there, also waiting for the elevators, were two men who were also looking in Marks' direction. To describe them as serious probably did not do justice to their unsmiling faces and their body language. Still, if you had to look full of purpose and intent on serious business, they would hardly go around grinning. Mark was not into racial discrimination of any kind, but he was particularly good at reading body language. While you could expect all sorts of people to be transacting financial business, and many may be nervous about it because money tended to do that to people, these two looked both hyped up and out of place.

The two foreign gentlemen of either Indian or Pakistan origin brought a whole new meaning to appearing nervous and aggressive at the same time. And they did seem to have taken a non-trivial interest in Mark's presence.

An elevator arrived and, since the two girls headed that way, so did Mark. The two foreign gentlemen remained rooted in their particular space waiting for their elevator.

But Mark was intrigued by the ladies – well girls really—and turned his attention to them. They were of the same height and shape. They wore identical clothes – more a uniform than normal clothes. But the way they wore them merited attention. They moved with the easy grace of people who were full of confidence. They knew exactly where they were going and what they were about, without being aware of just how beautiful they looked. And they moved together as though choreographed.

As Mark followed them into the elevator, he subconsciously christened them Ebony and Ivory.

The only discernible difference between them was in the colour of their skin.

'And where do we go for a drink when you stop work?' the white girl asked him playfully.

The look in her eyes said that she was full of confidence and not the least bit concerned about her appearing either assertive or pushy. Mark on the other hand was a naturally shy person and was taken aback by this frank question. And Mark was sufficiently wound up with his thoughts of what would happen at the Augem meeting to see the otherwise obvious signs of a setup.

'Well, I think I will need a drink after my meeting' replied an embarrassed Mark, but with a smile partly from amusement and partly from how he was feeling about the way this day was unfolding.

'I will probably go over to PJs he added not sure where this would lead, and how or if he would get out of the conversation.

He could not easily say, in present company, that he intended to simply return to his office like a wimp. Still, it was quite some time since he had practiced any of his few pick-up lines. And there was no harm done - was there?

The girls seemed young enough to be his daughters. He did not care really! Just to contact a human being again after the ride in the car with the two gorillas was enough. The girls turned as one, smiled as one, and in a microsecond decided who should speak. Ebony replied with a knowing wink.

'Well – We will see you there!'

'Ok. I will look forward to that.' Mark replied.

The elevator doors opened, and the girls were gone.

He had four more stops and a good deal of coming and going before he reached his destination on the 14th floor.

Well, it was the 13th but someone who had either designed or owned the building did not want to test their luck.

Nor did Mark.

That was the only good news.

As soon as the doors opened, Debbie Peterson came running across from the reception desk to greet him. She began by apologizing for the fact that Mark was early. The meeting had started without him, but that was the intention. He was not to worry. She would organize coffee.

Mark just smiled and said she was not to worry — being secretary to John Dubois and company was enough to worry about for anyone.

It was then that Mark felt a chill. For one thing, although Debbie had greeted him with her usual enthusiasm, she was steering him away from the Board Room. For another, the two foreign gentlemen he had seen down in the elevator lobby were there. They had beaten him to the office by using another express elevator. They were standing to one side but close to the Meeting Room door. For another, Debbie was obviously in a state of stress far more than anything that Mark had witnessed before.

To Mark's surprise, the foreign gentlemen entered the Board room before he did. He had to sit on his own in the reception area waiting and contemplating what was to follow.

Eventually, Debbie came out and invited him into the board room as he had expected.

The Board Room was new. It was only a couple of weeks before this day that the area had been the open-plan workspace to at least half a dozen brokers. Now it was very impressive if a rather odd, room. The main table was made of solid mahogany and was immaculately polished. The chairs were in matching wooden frames and upholstered in rich burgundy leather. Sitting on the table before each chair was a leather-bound writing pad also in burgundy and a pen and a pencil neatly laid out threatening anyone who dared use them. The table and the setup would have looked more at home in a Victorian-era board room belonging to an old-fashioned financial institution.

That was only one of the odd things about the room. The walls were white and hung with a diverse collection of the works of a modern artist. To Marks's untrained eye, you could not tell whether they were original or copies, and there was not one painting that merited a second look unless you were picky and thought one might be upside down.

It was as though the room had not been planned at all and furnished with whatever was available at short notice. Mark had that bit right but did not know it.

Even odder was that the room had no windows even though it would have had a very passable view of lower Manhattan and the financial district.

Seated at the head of the table was John Dubois, looking as ever totally relaxed, dressed as always in a dark grey suit which must have cost more than the average, and very much the man in charge.

Mark had seen him on several occasions but could not recall hearing him speak. He was obviously of middle eastern origin, so it came as quite a surprise to Mark when he did speak in a very cultured New England accent-less voice, welcoming Mr. Taylor, and apologizing, not exactly with any degree of sincerity, for the inconvenience and the delay. If Dubois's body language was of calm, relaxed indifference, Matt Reynolds' was off the other end of the scale. He had discarded his jacket, undone his tie, half rolled up his sleeves, and rearranged his hairstyle to resemble a kitchen mop. He was not a happy man, and the

2:00 pm meeting, which had started well before, was not going well.

Rob Augem sat across the table, as usual impeccably dressed, but still looking as though he was in a similar state of stress.

Mark knew that Rob had been the founder of the Augem Group all those many years ago. He also knew that the company had suffered in the share market crash in the 1980s. He suspected that Dubois had come to the rescue like a knight in shining armour. He had retained Rob as Chairman and Consultant, in name if not in fact. Not that Rob had much to consult on. Nor for that matter could he reasonably be expected to stay switched on long enough to hear the question, never mind give a considered response given the degree to which he was stressed. He was well into his seventies and high blood pressure at that age is not a clever idea. At least he would have the right Insurance for it, was Mark's passing thought. But Mark did get an acknowledgment from Rob Augem, and he did notice a gleam in the old man's weary eyes.

And he could not miss the slight raise of the eyebrows and the resumed glare as Rob looked down along the table at John Dubois.

There were several other people at the table by the time Mark Taylor made his entrance. Three gentlemen looked as though they were part of the Board – they were immaculately dressed in Finance industry uniforms – dark blue pin-striped suits, white shirt, blue tie, white hair, and careworn expressions.

Then there were the two gentlemen who had been waiting for the elevator and then waiting at the reception – who were unlikely to be Board members. They were introduced to Mark as Asid and Mohammed. He did not catch their other names.

Mark also did not catch the names of the other three members. He was busy focusing on these two Indian or Pakistani gentlemen. 'Pull the other one!'—thought Mark. They were obviously of southeast Asian origin so there was no point in calling them, Smith, and Jones. They were both wearing grey suits and brown shirts which to Mark's unskilled eyes seemed an unlikely combination.

Marks' previous experience in dealing with people of similar origin still left him quite unable to distinguish whether a particular name fitted a person or not. But he did know when a name did not suit, especially when the name was not in any way acknowledged by the bearer. Dubois made the mistake of not indicating the men as he introduced them, so they did not react to their names. Either that or they were not the least bit interested in who Mark Taylor was. Or, for that matter, who anyone was. The arrogance may have been a cultural thing or a cover for the fact that they were out of their comfort zone. He had his doubts about both options.

'Good afternoon, Mr. Dubois, Rob, Matt.'

Mark thought he had them in the correct order of seniority if not the correct order of merit.

'Nice to meet you!' was his nodded acknowledgment of the other five, although there was no visible sign that the two eastern gentlemen were on planet earth.

The other three board members just smiled weakly and resumed contemplating their fingernails.

Matt Reynolds got the meeting underway.

'Thanks for coming in at such short notice Mark. We have three subjects that we need to discuss with you urgently, and hence our reason for asking you to come in. Firstly - we believe our security has been breached. Secondly - we need you to explain the system to these two gentlemen, Asid, and Mohammed so that we can be sure that nothing they are responsible for in any way impinges on what you do and vice versa. If it does, then we may have to reorganize our security. Thirdly - we need to review the contractual agreement that we have between the Augem Group and Taylor Software and see if we cannot come to a better arrangement.'

Well, that was just dandy, thought Mark. What was it with these people? Firstly - they had not had a security "breach" otherwise Matt Reynolds, Mark, and Brad would all know about it. At least Mark did not know. And Brad had said he did not know. The security system was strictly controlled so that very few – like not anyone of the people in this particular room except Mark – knew about the mechanism of detecting any breach, so what had a suspected breach got to do with the Board? Surely, to bring this matter up at a Board level, it would need to be something serious.

But - nothing had happened!

Secondly - what were these two eastern gentlemen doing that in any way could impinge on the work of Taylor Software and the security of the system? More to the point, the main security system, as far as Augem was concerned, related to effectively preventing theft, by someone in the house, from the Trust Accounts. The system was about protecting other people's money which Augem invested or managed on their behalf. That is apart from the odd couple of hundred million that Augem managed to siphon off and then invest on its' own account.

Thirdly - Mark was not aware of any better arrangement than the present one. No doubt the meeting would get around to discussing that at the proper time.

Since a response was expected from Mark, he replied.

'We were not aware of any security breach, so perhaps

we could start there. From our monitoring systems, we have had no report that would indicate that there has been any breach and nothing that would indicate that there have been any problems. Could you elaborate on exactly what the problems are that you have experienced?'

Mark was in something of a spot. He had never revealed to anyone in the Augem Group the full extent to which his company monitored the system. Nor, in his view, did they need to know. Nor could they have found out, unless they had some very clever people now working for them. Security of Internet traffic was the easy part. There are always people trying to send spam, Trojans, spyware, ransomware, viruses, and other nonsense, both harmless and traumatic, across the internet. Most of these and other rubbish were filtered out by Internet Service Providers known as ISPs. Then you had to have anti-virus software and a Firewall in case something slipped in, or out. And that had to be smarter than something just checking for spam, but it was still nonetheless simple in principle.

The multi-level security system, that Mark and Brad had designed, built, and maintained, was fool proof. Well to all intents and purposes except Mark's intents and purposes. It was encrypted in such a way that it was very doubtful that anyone could break it. And, certainly, none of the known personnel of the Augem Group would even know where to start. The Eastern gentlemen Mark began to suspect may take a crack at it, but their chances of any real success were about zero, without access to some real computing power. At least that was his view after many years in his industry and knowing what he did of encryption.

The security of the Trust Accounts was another matter entirely. Mark had installed the software and then had the Augem Group pay extra for a monitoring system and a regime that attempted to stop someone in-house from playing around with someone else's money. Of course, it still prevented people from outside the organization from doing the same thing, and in Mark's view, which should be the most critical part. If Augem wanted to rip their clients off, he was sure they could do so. No amount of computer wizardry could prevent that. Well to a point.

The idea of a good security system aiming at preventing internal or external threats is to treat every keystroke as a potential risk. Therefore, you treated everyone as a potential crook. That applied equally to everyone who tried to access the system from either outside or inside the organization. Especially to the people in this room right here and right now. They had potentially more to gain – if for no other reason than that they made investment decisions whereas other lesser mortals merely followed instructions which may or may not have revealed what those decisions were based upon. The people in this room also had much more to lose.

Reynolds looked to Dubois but got no response, and his look towards the eastern gentlemen drew no more response than a look of arrogant disregard. His conclusion from that situation was that no one wanted to speak for fear of being made to look foolish. So – he spoke on behalf of the Augem group.

'We installed a couple of new machines a week ago. These machines were standard devices and then when we connected them to the network, we managed to breach our security. What we would like to know is—what is the point of having your security systems if anyone can simply connect a new machine and gain access, albeit with several errors and other issues?'

Mark had always got along well with Matt Reynolds. Reynolds knew his limitations and invariably left matters that were outside his level of expertise or experience to others – in the case in point to Taylor Software. Well really to Brad Morgan. But Brad was not at this meeting.

He was uncomfortable with the line the meeting was taking and he certainly appeared unsure of himself. It sounded as though he had erred into an area where he was hardly competent to even discuss any form of error. He may have completely lost the plot.

Mark was becoming increasingly suspicious of the line the meeting was taking. The matters Reynolds had raised were both inaccurate and trivial. They pointed to an area in which the Augem Group had breached the agreement and if Reynolds had cared to read it, he would find that that action meant that Taylor Software was absolved of any liability. Since this was a simple explanation that had nothing whatsoever to do with the work of Taylor Software, he would have been better to move on!

Mark considered his response carefully. The Augem group was still his client, so his instinct was to ignore the breach. He felt as though he should call Matt's bluff, but that would let everyone know that Matt did not know what he was talking about. In deference to Matt Reynolds, he stated the obvious.

'We became aware that you had acquired two additional machines and that there was an attempt to connect them to your network. That is something we would have expected Taylor Software to have been involved with. It is possible that these machines were a source of some corruption. But neither the machines nor their users would have had any access rights to the areas of your system that we were asked to protect. So, while they may have appeared to have breached your security, I would doubt that they did. They may have generated error messages, but that is to be expected. In my view, they presented no significant threat to your data or the security. They are just not allowed to connect. We would therefore have expected you to have asked Taylor Software for them to be set up properly. As yet we have no record of such a request.'

That comment certainly got the attention of at least two people in the room.

What Mark did not add was that his contract stated that Taylor Software supplied all computer equipment to the Augem Group. It had just been easier for all concerned to have the one source of supply—and no other equipment should even have made it through the Augem front door.

So, where had these two machines come from and why?

It would not take a rocket scientist to work out part of the answer – they would be machines with login names something like Asid and Mohammed. The problem that Augem had encountered was not a breach of security. Their problem was more likely to be that they could not attach them at all. They would interpret the chaos that resulted from their attempt to connect them as a form of breach.

Rob Augem stepped in before Mark was asked to explain further, and to take the discussion down a path that would lead nowhere other than one that involved acrimony.

'Why don't we stop beating about the bush and tell Mark what we want to do?'

The outburst came from Rob in a style that was reminiscent of a child who was about to be told that there were no cookies left in the jar.

'Ok.' Dubois quickly joined the conversation.

'The breach of security is a minor matter, and will no doubt require some further investigation that is beyond the understanding of some of the people here.'

That comment got a glare from Augem, a look of apprehension from Reynolds, and an increase in the arrogance – and did Mark detect frustration—on the faces of the two eastern gentlemen. Well - at least one. The senior one did not seem to be at all interested in the discussion – he was waiting for his chance to speak. The fact that the statement had been delivered in a tone that suggested that John Dubois was one of the few who could understand the security was perplexing to Mark, but he did not show any reaction. Dubois continued.

'What we are looking to do is buy out your contract. The question is—How do we do that and at what price?'

Apart from the shock of the abrupt way in which Dubois had introduced this subject, Mark noticed more than a slight difference in the body language of the two main players. Rob Augem was not wanting to do something. John Dubois was going to do something.

Did that mean that Rob Augem was opposed to what was involved?

Did it mean that Dubois did not care?

At least the cards were on the table now. Mark's worst fears had been realized, but he was not about to lose his biggest client, at least without a fight.

'That is not a simple matter' Mark began, trying to keep the rising anxiety and stress out of his voice.

'There is the question of the original terms of our agreement. Taylor Software may have sold you a software system, but we did not sell you the intellectual property rights. We could work out something I suppose but we would have to involve the legal boys. What are you after exactly?' enquired Mark more in hope because he thought he knew what the answer was going to be.

Intellectual property rights were one thing, the price

was another. People who purchase software with source code – which is in effect the intellectual property of the originator—do not appreciate the value that they acquire. Nor do they understand the risk that the vendor takes – being placed in a situation where the purchasing organization could become a competitor in the market with access to all the Vendors secrets. All matters which were of little concern to John Dubois.

Before John Dubois could continue with his abrupt style, Reynolds stepped into the discussion to ease the pain he had correctly sensed.

'We need to change our approach to the security of our computers. We simply want to have control of our systems.' Reynolds said with a total lack of conviction but mimicking the stated policy of Augem – well John Dubois – which appeared to amount to the same thing.

'Well, that's fine' replied Mark, 'but there are a few loose ends that need to be tied up, and the matters are far from trivial. First - we have a contract that still has the best part of three or so years to run. Second - if you are going to continue to use the software, there is the question of ownership of the intellectual property, and particularly who is going to be making changes to the software. And third—who is going to provide the support, maintenance, and monitoring of the system?'

Matt Reynolds again looked uncomfortably towards Dubois, but in the absence of a response from that source, he muttered, half answering the question.

'Those matters are best left to the legal people, but they tell us that will not be a problem. These two gentlemen will be responsible for the system' he concluded, nodding his head towards Asid and Mohammed.

'Like Hell!' thought Mark. Just as with the actual security and their paranoid approach to that, they had originally got so tangled up with terms and conditions of the agreement that Mark had to have his legal team involved. Not that it had cost him anything. The Augem Group paid for everything. And not that the Taylor Software legal team amounted to very much. Mark had used an ex-Special Forces guy who had left the military service at about the same time as Mark had, but who had turned his talents to law – Archibald Thomas Miller LLB – otherwise known as Dusty. Not that anyone would want to tangle with Dusty.

The Augem legal team was huge and in this business money and size count for a lot. But Mark's 'team' had made sure that it was very clearly understood what they were getting into, there was no simple get-out clause for the Augem Group. And Taylor Software was absolved of any liability if things went off the rails. The Augem legal team, if they were earning their money, would have been equally aware of that.

So, had they been consulted on the legal aspects of this latest twist? On balance, Mark considered that it was obvious that they had not. As for the efforts of Asid and Mohammed, Mark cringed at the thought of having to train them in the support and maintenance of the system. In the software business, imparting knowledge by the trainer was one thing – retaining knowledge by the trainee was another.

Mark however could see the writing on the wall. The "Board" – well John Dubois—had made up its' – well his – mind, long before Mark got involved in this meeting. Matt Reynolds was left with the problem of somehow making this work, with help from "others" who Mark assumed included the 'silent' two foreign gentlemen. Rob was forced to go along with whatever had been decided – by sheer weight of numbers—and was spitting tacks. He doubted whether John had even the remotest idea what the niceties of the law involved and could have cared even less. Consequently, he conceded.

'What kind of price are we talking about?' Mark asked, raising the question with much more confidence in his voice than he felt.

'How about five million – dollars that are—upfront and another five million dollars when you have sorted out a few of our issues and when Reynolds is satisfied that the revised support system is bedded in.' Dubois dangled a pen over the pad in front of him, as he leered down the table, waiting for Mark to respond.

Mark tried to look as though he was considering the offer as he paused. After all, this was a Board meeting, and important decisions were to be made, and he was – at least temporarily – part of those decisions. It required people to be diplomatic and reserved.

But holy mother of God – the five million dollars alone was more than ten times the value that Mark could have dreamt up at his most optimistic, and another five million dollars to follow. Well, shit happens! Mark thought about a bluff. However, the look on John's face—well he could call him John if they were talking that kind of money —said no. So, he answered.

'That is a pretty fair offer. I do not know all the details—like what the issues are – and we will need to involve the legal people again – but I could accept that as a basis on which to start negotiations.'

'Ok. It is a done deal.' John abruptly replied. 'Talk to our legal people about the details. We will deposit the first five million dollars in your bank immediately.'

With that said, Dubois jumped to his feet, as an afterthought shook hands with Mark, turned with a nod to the rest of the assembly, and left, followed in silence by the two eastern gentlemen and the three equally silent members, whose contribution to this meeting of the Board had been absolutely nil.

Rob Augem came across the room and shook hands with Mark, looking him straight in the eyes and wished him luck, then turned and with a tired wave to Reynolds, shuffled out of the room, ushering Debbie before him. Reynolds then closed the door nodding his head at the CCTV video cameras that were festooned around the walls.

'There is no need to get down to the details now of what has to be done. Better leave it to the legal people. I assume you will be using Mr. Miller's team. Thanks for your understanding, and now let us go for a drink. I sure need one. Oh, by the way, the first five million dollars should already be in your bank – John knew that you would accept, so the money was set up to transfer before the bank closed for business.'

'I have just one question.' Mark said. 'Why doesn't this Board Room have any windows?' He was surprised, not so much by the answer, but by the look on the face of Matt Reynolds.

'This is the room that Asid and Mohammed are going to use.' Reynolds replied. 'They were worried about someone peering in the window at their work. Although how someone could achieve that on the fourteenth floor of a building is a mystery to me. John said that we were to just meet their needs so here we have it' Matt concluded with a shrug and a cynical laugh.

What neither of them knew was that it would not be for long. And in any case, why should Mark care.

Mark was still stunned by the figure he had negotiated.

Well, he had not exactly done anything. Other than to express the opinion that it was a fair offer.

Chapter 5

Lust

Mark and Matt Reynolds made their way across to PJ's Bar and Brassiere which was a popular watering hole in the financial district of New York City. Mark had not realized just how much time had been taken up with the meeting at the Augem Group. What seemed like only a couple of minutes had taken the best part of four hours.

It was now approaching 6:00 pm and the city was starting to change its' mood from one that reflected the stresses of work to one of the more relaxed social activities. The main bar at PJ's was already fairly crowded and they had to elbow their way through to the back before they found an uncluttered seating area.

At first, they just sat there in silence for a while drained from the drama and stress of what they had just been a part of.

Mark was still shaking his head but after half downing the glass of beer he had to ask.

'Well—what was that all about?'

Matt Reynolds could not help but smile. But it was a

tired smile, almost forced. When he looked at Mark there was a sadness in his eyes.

'We have both been taken on a rollercoaster ride, the end of which was never in doubt. Why all that bullshit about security, I do not know if that was necessary? I do know what the intention was but why go to the trouble? As you would know, I do not know jack shit about computer security, and John Dubois knows even less. The whole discussion was meant to put you off and to make you feel uncomfortable presumably to gain fuck knows what. But Rob Augem and I knew it was a waste of time. John does not understand the system, but he had to act the part. That is why Rob cut in on John. You should thank him later. He was probably responsible for getting you the second five million dollars. Not that the odd couple of million dollars means that much to John – or should I say the Augem Group' he concluded.

Although Mark had quite a good working relationship with Matt—well Mark liked to think he had a good working relationship with most people, particularly his clients, provided, that is, that they talked straight – he was beginning to feel both let down and somehow conned. Sure, the ten million dollars would make a difference. And sure, Mark would come out of the deal far better off than he could ever have hoped for. But the way the deal had been done grated on him.

Mark had the feeling that something was not right.

Reynolds must have known the value of the software. At least he must have known of a value closer to being a realistic figure! So why had the 'deal' been done?

As with the original acquisition of the system, it had been done without any negotiation.

That negotiation should have started somewhere near a couple of hundred thousand dollars. Instead, the starting and finishing point was ten million!

Surely the five or ten million was not the starting offer, and surely, they would have expected Mark to attempt a negotiation that would have involved some kind of a counteroffer. And they had not answered the question of intellectual property rights. So, they either did not know of the significance of those rights. Or they had been advised by their lawyers not to bother. Or they were plain dumb.

On the other hand, Mark could not help but laugh.

'They just want one hell of a handover for that kind of money.' Mark mused. And he did not add, with an outright purchase of software – not the company – they would not get the source code or the intellectual property. That was embedded in Mark's head. And they had not offered to purchase him! That is unless their legal people were going to produce some serious terms that had not thus far been revealed.

'You and your company have done a far better job than you realize Mark.' Reynolds responded.

'While all the fuss has been about the security, the real worth is in the system itself. It is so fast and efficient and has so many good features. The Augem group can make a couple of million dollars extra a day just because they have a smarter system than our competition does. You do not know what that means in our business. And other than the executives of Augem, you and your people are the only ones who know what we have. By the time the competition realizes what we have, it will be too late. Getting our heads around the security – to keep it in the house – should be a breeze.'

What kind of an idiot did Matt Reynolds think he was, Mark pondered? While Matt's explanation made sense – yes, the system was good, and yes it certainly gave the Augem Group an edge over their competitors – you would have to have shit for brains to believe that drivel as a reason for the deal that had just been done. Mark and his company were free to move on, and indeed any of the people in the Augem Group were free to move on. Or at least they should be. While Mark had committed at the onset of his dealings with Augem, not to replicate the system for another customer who could be construed as a competitor – that was his method, and it was strictly enforced – he still retained the knowledge. Similarly, people at Augem must know what the system did, and if they moved on, you could hardly prevent them at least observing that their "new" systems did not do what they were used to having access to. That is assuming they were still alive when they left,

Mark laughed to himself. But then thought better of it. There could be a more serious side to this business. Mark was assuming he was allowed to go about his business with all his faculties intact. Mark did laugh aloud this time, but it was an extremely nervous laugh.

Mark continued.

'The security system uses encryption, and you know from our original agreement that you can never have access to the encryption algorithm. You can try to break the algorithm that the encryption is based on, but you will get no help from Taylor Software on that score. Just monitoring the system may seem trivial compared to that, but it nonetheless requires particular skills so that you do not cause serious trouble. Do you have the people with those skills, and can they continue to run the system?' Mark asked.

'You do not think we can do that?'

Reynolds almost sounded offended. But Mark detected in his body language that there was else going on.

Matt did not believe that they could either.

'I have every confidence in you Matt, but I have not got the same confidence in your foreign friends. Apart from the fact that they give me the creeps, they do not seem to be prepared to listen. No! Let me put it more bluntly – they are arrogant—and in the computer business, and more so in the software business that usually means they do not know jack shit.'

That comment brought a sigh from Reynolds.

'You must know that John Dubois was born and raised in the middle east – Beirut to be exact. And he has a different perception of people from the East. Our foreign friends as you described them are very capable with computers and communications. So – we will do all right!'

That statement made sense and was made with some conviction. What did not match that was again the body language. Matt Reynolds was a very worried man. Matt must have read Mark's reaction. He just shrugged and nodded in resignation, or the beers must have started to have an effect.

'Well look who we have here!' said Reynolds, appearing both surprised and immensely relieved to be changing the subject.

The Who turned out to be Ebony and Ivory – the girls that Mark had a conversation with earlier in the afternoon while riding up in the elevator. Mark's initial reaction was one of surprise and pleasure. That was until the introductions were completed. Ivory turned out to be the daughter of Matt Reynolds and Ebony turned out to be the daughter of John Dubois!

Mark should have realized that their turning up like this was just too much of a coincidence but that thought escaped him, as indeed the prospect had earlier in the day.

The presence of the two girls was nonetheless a welcome relief at the end of a stressful day. And they did not seem to be the least bit interested in talking about business.

And did not seem to be the least bit interested in where millionaires got their wealth.

While Ivory was soon engrossed in a deep conversation with her father, about her latest boyfriend, Ebony - whose real name was "Charlie" - turned her attention to Mark and playfully tried to find out his whole life story.

The beers and cocktails kept coming and Mark soon became aware that Charlie could foot it with the best of them when it came to her capacity for drink. And she could certainly beat them all when it came to entertainment value. The looks Mark was getting from the other males in the bar certainly suggested extreme jealousy. Charlie ignored them all and Mark began to feel rather pleased with himself. The day was not turning out too bad – ten million dollars and now he had one of the most attractive girls in the bar – no in New York City – no in the whole World! – hanging onto his arm and did not appear to be about to let go anytime soon.

But deep inside Mark could not let himself go entirely.

Although his days on covert and clandestine operations were well behind him, when women – especially beautiful young women – got involved, warning bells went off.

He began to have a suspicion that what was happening on this day was too good to be true and maybe it was a setup. If it sounded too good to be true, the odds were, it usually was and there had to be a twist. But what could anyone gain by pairing him off with this beautiful young lady, even if she were the daughter of the man who had just made him extraordinarily rich? Well – rich by Marks's standards? He was not involved in any way in anything even remotely illegal or that required subterfuge or that required this kind of influence. Since Charlie was related to John Dubois, John may very well know what she was up to now. But surely, having done the deal, gotten Mark drunk, and probably laid, would achieve nothing. Charlie made no mention of the Augem Group, or the work that the firm did, or of her father, or the software, or ten million dollars, or any other minor matter. Mark was puzzled but for some reason, he just did not care.

Charlie snapped him out of his thought process – he realized that he had been daydreaming and staring at nothing.

'Hey – look who is here now – it is Anna!'

Charlie leaped to her feet and hugged the approaching Annette Covic. Then she did a very strange thing. She ushered Annette into the seat that she had previously occupied beside Mark Taylor. Then she proceeded to ignore Mark, as though the last couple of hours had simply not happened and turned her undivided attention to Ivory.

Mark was even more puzzled by this turn of events. But he was beyond caring. He now had Annette with him!

And that had to be better news, at the end of an otherwise normal day.

'You look as though you have had a few too many.' said Annette with a laugh. Mark blushed. Did she mean beers, or was she referring to Charlie? Mark had no reason to feel guilty, so how come he did? Annette had no reason to be jealous – they were very much in a working relationship – nothing more, nothing less. But, for some reason, Mark felt that she was. He was almost spoilt for choice between these two ladies who had suddenly become the focus of his undivided attention.

Annette had intrigued and tantalized him since the day they first met. And now, while Mark had been infatuated with Charlie, Annette was in an entirely different league. She was a very sophisticated lady, impeccably dressed and presented, but at the same time almost demure. It was as though she simply did not know what effect she had on the people around her. The fact that she leaned over and kissed him full on the lips came as a surprise but by no means an unpleasant one.

'I thought I had better come to town and make sure you could get home. Your SUV is still at the office, but you don't appear to be in any fit condition to drive.' She laughed again.

'The meeting at Augem must have gone well considering the state you and Matt are in.'

It was more of a question than an observation which Mark was about to answer when Reynolds interrupted them.

'We must get away – you know how it is – the wife will be mad if I am any later. Do you want a lift Mark or are you ok?' he said with a laugh and a wink at Annette, which Mark failed to see.

He was about to say he would take a cab, but Annette just smiled and said that she would look after him. Which was fine with Mark or at least he thought it was. He got a kiss from both Ebony and Ivory, shook hands with Matt, and watched as they left the bar with not a care in the world.

Mark did not know why. But something appeared false about this whole episode. While they had had a few drinks, it was unusual for Mark to feel so disoriented.

He began to worry about that. He felt as though someone had slipped him a Mickey, and in the fuzzy world that he found himself in, he at least was able to decide that he would have no more to drink. Shit! He was getting paranoid – just enjoy yourself! Something was going on, but he could not see how it involved him. But be careful Mark – the warning bells were ringing.

As if on cue Annette ordered two coffees, and as usual his was exactly as he liked it. Annette hung onto his arm, and this time almost whispered in his ear 'So, what happened at the Augem meeting to make you so happy?'

Mark thought about the question for a moment, and then he shrugged 'The unwelcome news is that the Augem Group are no longer going to be using the services of Taylor Software. The good news is they are going to pay for the privilege.' Mark almost choked 'ten million dollars!' and he turned to look directly into Annette's eyes, expecting her to be as pleased and as shocked as he had been.

He was disappointed.

She did not say whether she believed him or not. Annette just giggled and said, 'it is about time I took you home.'

Annette and Matt linked arms as they walked to her car. If they had not done so it was probable that Mark would have fallen over. He was sufficiently sober to enjoy the closeness of this beautiful young lady and sufficiently drunk to be a little more amorous than was appropriate for a boss/PA relationship. If Annette noticed anything inappropriate it did not show.

They had never, as a couple, been to Mark's apartment – or anywhere else for that matter. In a show of gallantry, Mark navigated Annette through the streets by a less direct, but easier to follow, route than he would normally have driven himself. Nevertheless, they took a couple of wrong turns, more due to Marks' lack of concentration than any errors on Annette's part. They both laughed as the journey took them a good fifteen minutes longer than would have otherwise been the case. Neither of them seemed to be in any hurry, even though it was now approaching midnight on a day that had just become a blur.

As usual Mark's cat was waiting by the door of his apartment. It was another one of the great mysteries of life. The cat obviously did not spend all day parked at the door, but whatever time Mark arrived home the cat was there. He had not arrived home with a companion before but that did not seem to disturb the cat at all. It was not his cat – it had just turned up at his door one day and had stayed. They entered directly into the lounge and Mark said he would find some coffee leaving Annette to secure the door. The first task of course was to feed the cat which had taken up station in front of the fridge. He would have been mortified if Annette had thought for one moment that the cat came first, but she again did not appear to notice, and the cat was a more permanent resident.

'What do you call her?' she asked crouching down to stroke the cat. Down near the floor, she leaned forward as she knelt, and her blouse opened slightly revealing more of her breasts than she realized. Her thighs, which had an olive tan that Mark found so seductive, were revealed as her skirt rode up in the process of her squatting down. Mark was momentarily immobilized and could only stare. He knew that he was attracted to Annette but just for a moment it was lust that he felt. In the office, he had managed to avoid such emotional confrontations by quite simply looking the other way. But not now. Fortunately, he recovered some of his composure before Annette looked up to him.

'She is a He, and I call him Fridge because that is his only interest. He just happened by one day and this is where he stayed.' was his stumbling reply.

She laughed in a way that only she could. Mark knew that if only she gave him the come on, his office rules about getting into relationships with the staff would take a dive. There was still something hovering at the back of his mind about this whole situation that did not feel quite right. However, in his own home, he began to feel more relaxed, and rules could be broken. And Annette's next comment did nothing to deter him.

'I would prefer something a little stronger than coffee if that is ok with you. While you have been out enjoying yourself, some of us have been working and have yet to have a drink' she said with more than a twinkle in her eyes.

'Ok. I have some Vodka and plenty of mixes—so how will that do?'

'As long as I can taste the Vodka!' Annette replied with a playful smile. He did not know whether it was just his interpretation, but he began to feel that Annette was making a move, and he felt even more relaxed, but excited at the same time. The way she smiled at him made him weak at the knees. Something was happening.

'Where do I find the bathroom?' was her next question, as he again realized this was the first time that Annette had been to his apartment – yet it seemed so natural.

'Left past the bedroom – second door on the right is the bathroom, first on the right is the other half' he replied as he grappled with a tin of cat food – then a bottle of vodka from which he poured one for Annette and an exceptionally light one for himself – very light. While Fridge chewed and purred, Mark went across to his CD player, selected a couple of his favourite Celine Dion tracks and turned them on, walked across and turned on a couple of lamps, turned off the overhead light that he had switched on as they entered the apartment, and then walked across to settle on the couch.

Annette came out of the bathroom and came across to the couch and seated herself close to Mark – closer than she had ever done before. But Mark was not interested in where she sat. It was the how. Mark felt a warm glow come over him as he just could not take his eyes off her. That she was beautiful was never in doubt. Now though she had transformed into an object of intense sexual desire. Gone were the ribbons and clips that had held her hair in that strict Secretary configuration. Gone were the pantyhose, and the high-heeled shoes. Gone was the bra. Her small but well-rounded breasts fought to escape from what remained of the blouse that sought to contain them. Her nipples stood erect.

As if sensing his embarrassment, Annette reached over and held his hand, smiled, and said, 'After all the time we have known each other, do you realize we have never been alone together?'

Mark heard the question, but he could not reply. He was transfixed. The beautiful thing about Annette was that she carried herself so modestly and she kept her distance out of respect for Mark and his position.

The sad thing about Mark was that he was very shy. It would normally have taken something of the magnitude of a major earthquake to get one of them to make the first move if there was indeed ever to be one. But then she kissed him, and his hands slowly caressed her body, but careful not to travel where his desire said to go but his conscience said not to go. Annette recognized the reluctance for what it was – Mark was terrified that this thing could end abruptly should he overstep an imaginary line. He wanted her so much, but could he have her?

Annette slowly leaned forward and kissed him again full on the lips, while her hand, which was still holding his, moved to rest inside her blouse and gently caressed her left breast. Mark immediately felt a warm flush come over him and found himself becoming even more aroused than he already was. He returned the kiss, initially tentatively, but that just turned her on. For his part, he was now out of control, and he no longer cared. Before long, the blouse fell to one side and then his hands were drawn down to her thighs as all his inhibitions were cast aside and he explored and caressed her whole body. Her skirt, which was short to start with, moved up and Mark realized that she had somehow removed her underwear if indeed she had any on in the first place.

She gently pushed him down and her hand slowly stroked the inside of his thigh, moving just so close to his pleasure point then drifting away again for just a moment then back again – frustrating but so pleasurable. Mark did not know whether she was doing it out of innocence and that she was also too reluctant to go the extra step, but he wished that she would. But then her hand reached for his belt and in frantic haste struggled to let him loose.

'The bed would be more comfortable.' he moaned in her ear, and quickly they both got up and rushed off into the bedroom.

The first time they reached a climax they were both still partly clothed, such was their haste – arms and legs were everywhere as they were thrust together in a passionate embrace. The second time, Mark lay on his back, now both of them completely naked, while Annette slowly brought him to another climax that he would never forget. He clung to her satisfied for only the second time in something like five years and drifted off into a very deep and satisfying sleep.

The ringing of a bell was the first conscious sign that he was waking up. In his mind, he visualized that Annette was holding a small bell in front of his face and moving it slowly backward and forwards so that it rang at each change of direction. He saw her look over the length of her beautiful body and groaned. She was exquisite – and at last, she was his! And then with a start, he recovered to full consciousness. He looked at the bed – Annette was sleeping soundly and at peace – and dragged his mind back to focus on the insistent ringing of the telephone.

He wanted to ignore the telephone and find Annette once more, but he knew he could not. For one thing, is anyone calling this late at night—or was it early morning? — must have—had better have—something rather important to say. For another, there were so few people who had his unlisted home telephone number, that he would know the caller.

'Hello – Mark Taylor.' he said answering the telephone, trying hard, and failing, to keep the frustration out of his voice.

'Hi Mister Taylor, sorry to call at such a late hour, or is it early?' the caller laughed. 'It is Diane from the Bay Ridge security monitoring company here. We have not had any acknowledgment from your mobile or office telephone, but your office alarm has not been set and we wondered if everything was, ok?'

No—everything was not ok! The alarm would normally have been set in two stages. On leaving the first floor, the alarm was set for the main office and computer room, and then, on leaving the building, another alarm was set for the first floor. Both of these alarms were monitored independently. Brad should have set the alarms when he left the building. It was most unusual for him not to have done so.

'Just a minute, I'll check.' Mark responded, now unable to keep the tension out of his voice.

He gently called out to Annette. She looked so peaceful and beautiful lying there and it seemed a shame to have to disturb her. Looking around the room, he saw a trail of his and her clothes from the door to the bed. He was hoping that Diane did not know anything about his living arrangements, otherwise she might wonder how he could check. He looked across the room and out into the lounge and the couch, and back came memories of a night he would never forget. 'What is it?' asked Annette as she reached across to cuddle up close to Mark.

He almost forgot about the call as he stroked her hair – then shook his head back to the present and said 'It is the security company checking on the alarms for the office – it appears that they were not set last night. Was Brad still at the office when you left?'

'Yes, he was—That is not like Brad.' Annette murmured still not fully awake.

'Just a minute, I'll check with Brad.' Mark muttered into the telephone. He was beginning to become more irritated. While the alarm was important in the scheme of things, it was not particularly significant if Brad had failed to set it was it? When it was originally installed, he had envisaged that the alarms and the monitoring service would give him a warning if the drug dealers came calling. As for what they were trying to protect, the software, which they kept at the office, was the operational stuff. The real source code was kept off-site and to a software company that was the important part.

The nature of Marks' business meant that they had no client data on the premises, so there was not an issue with that. And there was no money or anything else of value kept at the office. Still, not everyone was aware of that. He rummaged around the scattered clothes and finally grabbed his mobile. Why was his mobile switched off? He never switched it off! Puzzled – but he would worry about that later.

He switched it on and first rang the office number but after the allowed number of rings, he went to answer the phone. The office telephone went to answer-phone when the lines were busy or when there was just no one there. At this time of night, the latter option seemed to be the more obvious of the two. He rang Brad's cell phone number. He got the message to say that the phone was out of the area – unusual—but he guessed even Brad had to have moments of peace. Also, he could not recall ever having to ring him at such an inappropriate hour. So, he rang Brad's private land-line number. It rang and rang but there was no reply. And that was very unusual – Brad was hardly the type to be out this late – or early—and Felicity was always there!

'I will have to call you back. There seems to be a problem.' Mark offered in a resigned voice.

'Do you want us to send a patrol car around to the building?' the caller asked, trying to be helpful.

'No thank you – at least not just yet – let me check a few things first.' he replied.

'Ok. Talk to you later.' came the efficient and cheery if uncaring reply and the call ended.

Mark walked back to the bed and kissed Annette as though for the first time. Then in a voice that he hoped reflected his disappointment he had to ask.

'I do not suppose you could give me a lift back to the

office?' at least recognizing that he was still in no condition to drive himself even if he had a vehicle.

At least Annette looked similarly disappointed. She slowly rose, smiled, and said 'Just give me time for a quick shower, and you could do with one too, then we'll go.'
They clung to each other for several minutes, Mark breathing in the smell of her body, fighting his instincts to have her again, and then he finally kissed her long and hard, and reluctantly let her go.

They drove to the office in silence. It was not a silence caused by any stress – it was a silence of contentment. Mark had told Annette what the security company had said but neither of them had a clue of what the problem was. Mark had to check it out, but he did not expect that the problem would be anything other than a simple, honest mistake. He was the boss, so he had to react responsibly, but at the end of the day, it was just one more of those frustrating trivial things that come up every day and need to be dealt with.

However, he was more than a little pleased that Annette had so easily acquiesced to his request to drive him to the office. He was even more pleased about the way she had acquiesced earlier. Mark sensed that during their brief, and rudely interrupted, encounter things had changed between them. He felt close to her now and he was determined to continue where he had left off when the opportunity arose.

The office was in a part of the city where people did not normally go a night, and it was that time of night when anyone who was about was usually up to no good. He was also determined that she would not stray from his sight. He now had something worthwhile to protect. And he was exceptionally good at that. He would sort out the simple problem with the office alarms, and then return to what promised to be a good weekend – with a loving friend to keep him company for a change.

That prospect suited him fine.

Except that it would not last.

Chapter 6

Chaos

They reached the office of Taylor Software and Annette parked the car in her usual parking spot. Mark's SUV was still parked by the door – albeit in a "Visitor" marked park – Mark had never liked the idea of personalized executive car parks. It struck Mark as a little quirky that Annette chose to park where she did – in her normal park which was at the end of the series of Visitor car parks. They were hardly likely to have any visitors to the office at this time early on Saturday morning. He looked at his watch and the time was only just turned 3:30 am. Still, old habits die hard, so the saying goes, and he did not comment on this abnormality.

What was not so normal were the office lights – they were all blazing away both on the second floor and a couple of lights in the entranceway on the first floor. That would have been quite normal in the evening, except there was no one in the building as far as Mark was aware at this time in the morning. Well – in no condition to answer the telephone. At least Brad's car was still parked in its' usual spot – although the car looked as though it could barely have made it to the knackers' yard. That would also seem quite normal.

Things would shortly change quite dramatically.

The reasons would be found later and on the other side of the world.

Mark cautiously headed for the door and to his surprise, it opened to his touch. That was unusual. The first-floor entrance was always locked even when the office was working normally. It was opened either by a key – that only Mark, Brad, and a few other people who came and went at odd times, had – or by a relay switch operated from Annette's reception desk on the second floor.

As Mark walked in it soon became evident what had happened. The electronic unit that controlled the door had been smashed and would never function again. But someone had to first be inside the building to gain access to the controller.

Mark's immediate reaction was one of regret, almost panic. He had been convinced that this was a simple problem that he would fix and then return to other more pleasurable affairs. He had not bothered to arm himself. Although his training in the Marines and the Special Forces gave him some confidence that he could manage almost any situation that did not necessarily help all that much against armed thugs, and especially drugged thugs who had no concern for their own, or anyone else's safety. He was licensed to own and to use a Colt M1911 pistol – courtesy of a farewell gift from the 10th SFG. At the moment that was back at his apartment.

'It's a good job Augem did not pay me in cash.' he mused 'We have been broken into. The drug people have finally been or someone like that.'

Mark became concerned as the aura of the earlier night-time activity rapidly dissipated. He turned to Annette and told her to go back to her car and lock herself in while he investigated further. But she was having none of that. She quite reasonably explained that she felt safer with Mark than alone in the car. Mark was pleased, but now was not the time to say so.

'Ok stay close and behind me' he commanded as he moved like a cat, further into the building. He would need to be armed before he tackled the second floor, and he had a solution to that.

He quickly headed to the large bathroom on the first floor. This time it was Annette's turn to think Mark was the quirky one. Even more so when he proceeded to twist the mirror above the sink then he pushed it hard. Then she could see what he was doing. The mirror shot to the left like a door opening and revealed a small rack containing four pistols of various shapes and calibres, and what looked like boxes of ammunition. The look on Mark's face dissuaded Annette from asking why. He had a steely look in his eyes and, although she knew little of Mark's past, fear crept in as she realized his mind was back in the Special Forces frame. Without saying a word and in total silence, he loaded two of the pistols, checked that they were working, and flicked their safety catches off. He then handed the smaller of the two, a Beretta 96 which used the .40 Smith and Wesson ammunition (of limited value at more than a few meters), to Annette and retained the other one—a Smith and Wesson 99 which used the same ammunition and was heavier and far more reliable over a longer distance – not that the distance advantage amounted to much.

Unbeknown to Annette, the mirror arrangement in the bathroom was simply a leftover from the earlier occupants of the building. Mark had discovered it while he was cleaning the place when he first took up residence. Being the bathroom and changing rooms of an Automotive company, after years of use, it would have been a miracle if anyone had exited from the bathroom any cleaner than when he or she had come in. More so the mirror that revealed its' secret as Mark scrubbed to bring a semblance of respectability to the place. It was obvious what it had been used for, and initially, Mark was reluctant to also make use of it. But then he had the problem of where to store the relics from an earlier life without them being discovered by people who were in the much more innocent business of writing software, or by people in law enforcement who would be curious for more professional reasons. Mark did have a license to own a gun but these four were not in any records that he knew of. He finally figured that the previous occupants were long gone, and it was unlikely that their friends in the drug trade knew of the hiding place.

Mark motioned to Annette to remain silent and to follow him. The downstairs part of the building was little more than one large area apart from the bathroom and changing room plus a couple of storage areas. Mark rapidly crept to the bottom of the stairs, and it was amazing that he did so without making the slightest sound, and all the time scanning what was before him. Annette realized that she would have to do the same and had the sense to remove her shoes. Mark turned to her as she approached and frowned. He could not help himself – he kissed her lightly on the cheek – and then whispered in her ear.

'I do not have time to say this nicely, but I would much rather you did not point that thing straight at me. I enjoyed last night but you do not have to shoot me for it.' he said with a smile. 'Hold it in both hands pointing down. If you need to aim it at someone, bring it straight up and just point it where you want to shoot, and you will be fine – preferably though not towards me. I would also like you to cover my backside while I go up the stairs. Can you do that?'

Annette was not pleased with the reprimand. But fear is a much stronger emotion than pride, so she just nodded her head. Mark smiled again, gave her another peck on the cheek, and he was off up the stairs at an amazing speed. And again, in total silence.

When he got to the top, he crouched down to survey the scene. Fortunately, the bright lights in the office compared to the dimmer lighting of the stairwell gave him a slight advantage. What he saw made him feel as though he had been kicked in the guts. The place was an absolute mess with papers scattered everywhere, drawers pulled out of desks, phones ripped from the walls, and chairs upturned.

The place was silent.

While working in the office environment it went unnoticed, but there was usually the constant hum of computers – well the fans that kept the air circulating. Now he could hear nothing – there was total, absolute silence.

Mark rose to his feet and motioned to Annette to come up the stairs. 'There is no one here – if there was you would be able to hear them breathing' he said matter-of-factly. While Annette did not like to question Mark, she wondered how he could be so sure. However, when she got to the top of the stairs, she let out an involuntary gasp and immediately mouthed an apology to Mark. He just put an arm around her and stared at the mess thinking. They had been on these premises for several years, so why would the druggies suddenly decide to visit them. Or—If it was not the druggies, then who was it?

Mark took the Beretta off Annette, unloaded the weapons, and put them into his left and right-side trouser pockets. They went further into the office and over to the control console where the results of their client monitoring would normally be recorded, rather like a series of meaningless numbers and codes marching up the screen. Now the LCD screen was blank. This in itself was only a minor irritation. There would be few, if any, clients around at this time of night, and the Taylor software was smart enough to store at their origin any messages until the link was restored. The clients would be none the wiser for the interruption – which was the good news.

The unwelcome news was that this was the place where Brad would have been seated and since his vehicle was still here, where was he? His chair was at the far side of the office but across the floor and splattered over papers was a trail of red. Mark bent down with his nose close to the floor, careful not to touch anything, and then looked at Annette.

'That is blood. Who has done this and why?' he muttered more to himself. Annette looked on scared and did not reply. Mark then turned his attention to the main computer rack that was further down the office. At first glance, it looked as though nothing there had been touched until he looked at the Raid-5 disk rack. Normally there were four removable disks in the stack but now there was a gap. There was nothing especially unusual about that. The system could keep running – that was the general idea of the Raid-5 system. Mark looked at the bench where they would place components awaiting repair or other action and the fourth disk was not there. Again, there was nothing especially unusual about that either. Except that as far as he was aware there had been no maintenance scheduled, and the disk would have been left for the maintenance people to deal with. But it was not there.

He looked at the whiteboard where Brad would have written up a maintenance note if anything would require attention, but there was nothing aside from an innocuous note of Brad's next dental appointment. He turned to retrace his steps and went to check the office safe. This was a fireproof type where they kept various backups from client systems, but no money and nothing of any value, so the safe was not normally locked. But the door was open, which was unusual, and the contents had been rifled through and scattered around the floor. However, at first glance, nothing seemed to be missing. It began to look to Mark as though whoever had done this had been either looking for drugs or money, or they had a specific goal in mind. People looking for money or other valuables usually smashed things up out of sheer frustration at not being able to find anything of value and certainly were unlikely to wander off with a computer hard disk drive. Sure, there were a lot of papers scattered around but there did not appear to be much damage – except—where was the missing disk? And why had it been taken?

And what had happened to Brad?

'We had better not touch anything and call the police, but first, we will get rid of these.' Mark said, indicating the two pistols. He headed back towards the stairs, with Annette racing behind him, obviously in a state of confusion and shock, but not about to be left alone. He paused at the top as something caught his eye. He was about to say something, then thought better of it. But at that moment he had a suspicion that he knew the 'Who' part of this riddle – a broken toothpick was not that significant an item except that he had only seen one person using them – recently that is. The 'Why' part of the riddle was another question entirely because finding the toothpick suggested a scenario that Mark did not want to contemplate in his present state of mind.

Mark headed, not to the bathroom, but to his SUV where he unlocked the vehicle and secured the guns under the front seat. He then returned to the bathroom where he replaced the mirror to its original position and then returned up the stairs to the office. Annette followed him like a pet dog and then sat on a chair looking lost amongst the shambles. But Mark had work to do.

He first called the Security company on his mobile telephone to tell them what they did not want to hear, and then he called the police.

Mark was not in a mood to suffer fools easily and it was rather late, or early, depending on your perception of time. He rapidly began to lose some of his control. It is generally accepted that the most serious crimes – murders, rapes, and the like– occur at night-time. This is not because criminals, like most people, drink in the evening and when sufficiently intoxicated go out and commit their chosen crime. It is simply a matter of it being dark and there are fewer people around, the two factors taken together meaning that there are fewer witnesses. Yet most burglaries, on the other hand, at least statistically, tend to occur during daylight hours. And burglary, again statistically by far the largest occupation amongst the criminal fraternity, is not considered a sufficient priority by the majority of police forces around the world to warrant instant action.

The advice that the police force gives to people who have been the target of a bunch of thieves is to not disturb the crime scene and that is understandable lest they interfere with potential evidence. But people who have been a target of a burglary still have lives to lead, and things have to get back to normal as quickly as possible— the world moves on.

'What do you mean, no one can deal with this scene for four hours?' Mark's voice grated into the phone. 'I have to get my machines up and running now and the office back to normal – I have important clients who pay me good money to monitor their systems 24/7 and right now they are getting nothing. I cannot answer your question of whether anything has been stolen, because I have not yet looked. For all I know, you could be investigating a murder here because one of my men has disappeared. And you tell me not to disturb things and wait for four hours. What do you expect me to do?'

'Are you now reporting a murder, sir?' came the monotone response.

Mark was about to explode. Annette took the phone from Mark before he threw it into the wall.

'Hello, it is Mr. Taylor's secretary here. Could you just clarify what has been said? You are saying that you will attend here in about four hours. Is that the best you can do?'

'Lady, we have every officer tied up with other matters – of a higher priority than a burglary. If we had the workforce fine, but we don't, so what else can I do?' The guy sounded harassed but reasonable. Annette, ever the professional secretary, gave the officer their address and mobile telephone number, thanked him and said they would await the arrival of the police, and terminated the call.

For something to do, and in a forlorn attempt to vent his frustration, Mark tried once again to contact Brad, both on his mobile and his landline. Again—nothing.

They walked out to Mark's SUV and climbed into the back, locking the doors. At least they would feel safe in the car and with the two guns that Mark had earlier stowed under the seat. Whatever Mark had been drinking the night before, plus the enjoyable but exhausting exercise, plus the adrenaline rush of activity at this ridiculous time of the morning, was beginning to take its' toll and he just had to close his eyes and lie down. Annette sat on the edge of the seat and stroked his hair. For a brief moment, he began to feel aroused again with Annette sitting so close and touching him so intimately. How did women manage to appear so calm yet able to become objects of lust at all times of day or night? But while these thoughts cruised through his mind, tiredness won the day and he soon drifted off into a fitful sleep.

It seemed only minutes, but it was over four hours later that Mark awoke to the gentle prodding.

'The police should be here shortly' Annette whispered. He smiled, putting his arm around her, and holding her close, wondering again why women always managed to smell so seductive despite the conditions. Again, he had the urge to make love to her again—and to hell with the police—but eventually reality took control. They alighted from the SUV and made their way back into the building, holding hands like kids on their first date. Mark headed for the bathroom to relieve himself and was surprised to find Annette close behind. But she just stayed by the door, close enough, but modest enough, to give him some privacy. After a quick wash, more to wake himself up, they headed to the stairs and sat there again holding hands. If ever there was someone Mark would wish to be with in a crisis it was Annette, however illogical that may sound. It had the effect of calming him down, which was not such a bad thing given what was to follow.

Why the New York Metropolitan police force, known around the world as the NYPD, act the way they do is often a mystery to the average person in the street. It could have had something to do with a change of shifts, and this was the first job that this particular group of officers had for the day. They arrived with lights flashing and sirens wailing, and all the fanfare normally associated with the assassination of a President – albeit well more than four hours after the perpetrators had long since departed.

Even though the car park was neatly laid out, they haphazardly parked their vehicles at all angles and rushed towards the door as though attending a spring sale.

Once through the door, they were confronted with Mark and Annette sitting quietly on the bottom of the stairs. The Officer in charge came bristling up to them and asked where the crime scene was. Fortunately, Annette beat Mark before he exploded. 'Upstairs.' was all she said pointing behind her, and in moves reminiscent of the Keystone cops, they flooded up to the main office, closely followed at a more sedate pace by the victims.

'Who is in charge here?' demanded the officer leading the charge. The man was about six feet tall. The hair was becoming both thin and grey and only his moustache retained a semblance of his original colouring. At some stage in the past, he had been very fit and into his gym work. But those days were long gone. Now he was grossly overweight and puffing from the exercise—clearly a smoker and not pleased at having rushed up the stairs in time to find – nothing.

'I own the business if that's what you mean.' answered Mark. Who did he think was in charge? The police officer introduced himself as Sergeant McGuire but strangely did not ask to whom he was talking. McGuire grabbed one of the chairs off the floor and sat himself down at the nearest desk, pushed aside the papers which were scattered around, leafing through his notebook until he found a blank page. The rest of the force rapidly gave up their cursory look around the office and retired from this crime scene. All except two of them returned to their cars and left having got more interesting matters to deal with.

It soon became evident to Mark that McGuire knew a lot more than he was letting on. It became clearer still when his mobile telephone rang before he could start writing his notes. He answered it with a grunt and provided not much else to the conversation other than to state that he was having a chat with Mr. Taylor and Ms Covic. Now was not that interesting? – at no stage had Mark been asked or had mentioned either of their names. McGuire ended the apparent conversation with another grunt and then informed Mark that they were not to touch anything until the FBI had a look at things.

'So that was the FBI on the telephone?' Mark asked of no one in particular. That just got a look of irritation from McGuire, who then proceeded to ask never-ending, and at times irrelevant, questions in an officious but disinterested tone.

'Has anything unusual occurred here recently.' was his opening and mindless question.

'No – nothing unusual had occurred in the recent past until last night that is – and this is the result.' was Mark's reply indicating the shambles that had once been his office—well five million dollars in the bank, with five more to come, and a night with Annette that he would not forget in a hurry were "things" that were unusual – but these two events had nothing to do with McGuire or the New York Police Department, or the Federal Bureau of Investigation, or anyone else – Mark did not say.

'You run a computer company from here?' was McGuire's next question, the answer to which would have been obvious to even the most casual observer.

'Yes – this is a computer company. This is the office of Taylor Software – we design computer and communication systems and software.' answered Mark in the same disinterested tone that the question was asked.

'Do you know why anyone would want to break in? Do you keep anything here of value?' McGuire asked in his monotone voice.

'No – I cannot think of why someone should break in.'

Well, they had not, had they? It looked as though they had broken out! Mark continued. 'I understand that these premises in a previous life were used by the drug trade – they used to run drugs into Harlem—but there are no drugs here now and there was nothing of any monetary value in the safe, or anywhere else for that matter.'

'Does the data that you have here have any value at all?' This question was accompanied by a raised eyebrow and a shrug that more-or-less dismissed Mark's response as irrelevant small-talk before he had answered.

'Yes – you could say that the data is valuable – but anyone wishing to steal it would get a better result by breaking into the clients' system – that is where all the useful stuff is.'

'Do you owe anybody any money? Any arguments with employees? Any debts that could cause people to look to recover them in this way?' McGuire was at last alluding to the occupation of the previous tenants, and he certainly looked old enough and wise enough to have been well aware of what they had been up to.

'No – I do not owe anyone any money, other than to the Bank – I do not argue with my staff—I am not in debt to anyone – again other than the Bank.' And that would end soon Mark did not add.

'Who was in charge here last night?'

'Brad Morgan, an employee of mine, was in charge.' Not that there was much to be in charge of, Mark again did not add, but continued for the benefit of a disinterested McGuire. 'And I assume that he was present when our perpetrators had called.'

'Do you suspect that this is an in-house job?' McGuire showed some signs of life, but Mark's reply soon caused him to revert to his normal.

'No – I could not imagine that this was any of Brad's handiwork.'

McGuire changed the subject and tried a different tack. 'Is it not unusual for the computers to be switched off?'

'Yes, it is – the computers appear to have been switched off by someone – but who? They are never switched off this is the first time they have been switched off, apart from the odd power failure, since they were installed.'

'Do you have any idea why they were switched off?'

'No – I have no idea why – unless Brad switched them off.' Mark let that answer hang in the air. He would have to ask Brad. That is, if he could ever find him.

'Yes?' McGuire, at last, seemed to take a serious note of at least the tone of Mark's reply.

'Well – if someone wanted something from the computer – the best way to deny them that would be to switch the machines off. No one can switch them on again and gain access to anything without the passwords. So, if Brad were here, and he thought that the system was being threatened, it would be a quite straightforward way of protecting them. In Brads' case, it would be his natural reaction, although I would imagine that the visitors would have been more than a little angry!'

'Has any equipment been taken?' asked McGuire, once again oblivious to anything Mark had to say. Or was this the way the police were taught to ask questions? Mark had some limited experience of interrogation techniques – if you could call a five-day course at the 'Farm' experience – and the apparent random questions were designed to detect evasion. Not that Mark was seeking to evade, but McGuire could not know that. Or McGuire could have been just playing for time until someone else turned up to take over this onerous task. Mark had this one right but did not know that yet.

'Well—Yes – a hard disk is missing from the rack.

However, you do not need the system to be switched off to remove one. Until I can talk to Brad, I do not know yet if it has been stolen. It may have been taken away for repair. Who knows?'

McGuire changed tack once more – he either did not have a great attention span, or he was disappointed with Marks' replies, or he just did not care. The body language said the latter.

'Do you know if any damage has been caused?'

'No – but how would I know if anything has been damaged – because the officer who we spoke to earlier when we reported the break-in said not to touch anything – so how would I know without switching the machines back on again?'

'Are the systems themselves important?'

'Yes – of course, the systems are important – at least to me and my clients.' the frustration starting to get into Mark's voice. 'But hardly worth thieving.'

'But surely there must be stuff here to attract thieves!'

'No – there is nothing that would interest the average burglar.' Mark could not imagine a New York crook running around the city trying to sell bits of computers, or software, or any information that they contained, but what did he know?

'Have you tried to contact Mr. Morgan – the Brad you referred to?'

'Yes – I have tried to contact Brad, several times, on his landline and his mobile telephone but I do not get a reply. What worries me more is that his car is still in the parking area!'

Again, McGuire raised his eyebrows. 'There can be a quite innocent explanation for the car – it looks as though it would be ready for scrapping anytime soon. And you can hardly expect him to answer the telephone at night or the weekend – that is surely ridiculous!'

McGuire was beginning to irritate Mark. He had a suspicion that McGuire knew why Brads' car was still there, but he did not have a clue why that would be. He decided to stick with the matter of him being non-contactable.

'No – that is not ridiculous – Brad is usually contactable 24/7.'

'Does Brad have access to everything on the computers and in the office?'

'Yes – Brad has access to everything'—although Mark knew but did not say – well not exactly everything.

'Have you had an argument with Brad that may have caused him to feel aggrieved about anything?'

'No – I have never had an argument or disagreement with Brad – how can you argue with someone as clinical as Brad? He never communicated much – it was hard enough to have a normal conversation never mind an argument.'

'He is quite a guy – this Brad – or was quite a guy.'

'Yes—he certainly is.' Mark ignored the inference in the was.

And then McGuire asked the question that Mark had been waiting for.

'Where were you last night?'

Mark still had to think about how to answer that question for a second or two while holding the un-flickering stare of McGuire, and conscious of the bemused look on the face of Annette. He continued to think that the events of yesterday were business matters which had nothing to do with the police and nothing to do with the break-in—well that was apart from the toothpick – but that was hardly a riveting piece of evidence.

So he told McGuire the raw details—that he had a business meeting with a client in the afternoon, after which he had a few drinks with the client, then was taken home by Annette, then been awoken by a telephone call from the security company—his mobile telephone had been switched off by a person unknown—then he had come to the office, then had to wait for more than four hours for McGuire and his Keystone cops to arrive. That about summed up the essentials.

McGuire ignored the jibe about the keystone cops and turned his attention to Annette, who Mark observed had a smile on her face for the first time since – well earlier in the day.

'Why did you go into the city to meet up with Mr. Taylor?' McGuire asked. The question seemed a little stupid to Mark. Was Annette supposed to work the crazy hours that Brad did? What was wrong with her going for a drink with the boss?

Annette did not even blink.

'I had a call from the secretary of the company that Mr. Taylor had the meeting with to say that Mr. Reynolds' and Mr. Taylor were going for a drink, so it would be best if I came in and gave him a lift back to the office since Mark's car was still here at the office and since Mr. Reynolds' transport was otherwise occupied.'
Annette's reply came out smooth but with a hint of sarcasm.

'Was Brad still here when you left?'

'Yes – Mr. Morgan was still here at the office when I left at about 7:00 pm and he was expecting to be here for a further four or five hours.'

'Is it not unusual to look after your boss – sorry Mister Taylor—in this way – surely you have your own life to live?'

'No – It is not unusual to as you say, "look after the

boss in this way" – we are a small company, and we care about our boss.' she said with a giggle. To Mark's recollection, such caring had never happened before but what the hell. 'As for my life outside of the office – that has nothing to do with you, Mr. McGuire.'

'Sergeant – Sergeant McGuire!' was the response. That comment was rewarded with a shrug and a disarming smile from Annette. But Annette was starting to get to McGuire, Mark observed with an inner smile.

'So, you know this secretary of Mr. Reynolds' well enough to just do what she says that you should do – is that about it?'

'Yes – I know Ms Peterson very well – We discussed the situation and the action I took seemed appropriate at the time. Do you not agree?'

McGuire was having difficulty staying in control of himself, such was the disarming way that Annette managed the questioning, but he persevered.

'Did you know what Mr. Taylor's meeting was about?'

'No – I had no idea what the meeting was about, and I still don't – what has that to do with anything?' Mark was surprised at Annette's outburst but thought it justified because that was what he was thinking. The way she was manipulating the conversation with McGuire was quaint. But her meaning was obvious. Keep your nose out of matters that do not concern you, even though they might interest you!

'You knew that Taylor would be found at PJ's – you have been there before yourself?'

'Yes – I heard from Debbie – Miss Peterson that is —that they would be at PJs, and Yes I have been there before.'

This little exchange caused Mark to freeze – as far as he was aware this was the first mention of PJ's. So,

McGuire knew much more about the night's activities. But from whom? Or from where?

This McGuire character had been fully briefed by someone on the events he was investigating. Someone had forgotten or did not know; how dumb the police sergeant was. Something was not right about this picture. Mark decided to keep his thoughts to himself.

'Is it your normal practice for you to take Mr. Taylor home?'

'No – it is not the normal procedure to take Mr. Taylor home, we would normally have come back here to the office – but he had been drinking so there was no point – was there? There was no way I would have allowed him to drive—would you?' Annette asked with yet another disarming smile.

McGuire ignored the questions. He still had a job to do, and it was reasonable to ascertain where these two people had been at the time of the alleged break-in. Even if that may infringe on matters that others nay regard as private or sensitive. 'And you stayed at Mr. Taylor's place?'

'Yes – I stayed at Mr. Taylor's place. How was he to get his car back if I weren't there to give him a lift?' Annette replied with almost a challenge to McGuire to dig further—as though it was quite the natural thing to do – and stated so matter-of-factly and with that smile – McGuire seemed uncomfortable.

'Did you switch off Mr. Taylor's mobile telephone?'

'No – I did not, and I have no idea how Mark's cell phone came to be turned off.'

That was the question that Mark had in his mind. It struck him as too coincidental that his mobile had been switched off on the one occasion that the security company could have alerted him far earlier to the fact that the alarm was not set. And on the one occasion in their five-year occupation that the office had been broken into. He could not recall, at any stage, leaving his mobile unattended, except when he got back to his apartment. But surely, the alarm monitoring company would have tried to contact him before then! Before that, he had been at a meeting with the Augem Group who had instigated the drinking session. There was also the issue of his spiked drink. Then there was the issue of why Annette had suddenly switched from Mr. Taylor to Mark. A lapse perhaps? And then there was the issue of the toothpick. Maybe?

'You have something you want to add.' McGuire's growl brought Mark back to the present, as his body language must have shown him to be lost in thought. But Mark's subconscious told him to back off. He was fairly rapidly forming an opinion that someone at Augem had orchestrated the whole evening's events so that he had been otherwise occupied while someone from the Augem Group – yes it had to be Augem—had a look around his office. The 'Why' was still to be worked out, but one thing was for sure. There was no future in having the New York police department climb all over a company that had already paid him five million dollars, with another five million to come.

What Augem would gain from raiding his office was in Mark's estimation about zero. So, they had expected to gain – well something – but would have got nothing – so they would now have to try a more subtle approach to get what they wanted. It was becoming clear that someone had told the NYPD, or the FBI, who had then told the NYPD, what had happened. But who? And how much had they been told? It was too early to involve someone as dumb as McGuire – Mark would manage this in his own way.

The sooner he had a chat with his lawyer Dusty Miller the better.

The testy atmosphere was made more so when two men wearing charcoal grey pin-striped suits entered the office. They did not exactly announce that they would be taking over the investigation.

They just said that they were Damien O'Connell, a thin and very effeminate man, and Clive Henderson who was the dead opposite, from the local office of the FBI. McGuire immediately gave up his interviews and vacated the chair. The FBI men also gave the impression that they knew exactly what they were about and would resolve any outstanding matters quickly. That was the good news, except that in Mark's view they either knew jack shit or else they knew everything and could not have cared less.

Henderson, who was the senior of the two FBI agents, sat down facing Mark and Annette, while his colleague set about assisting the NYPD brushing for fingerprints and taking blood samples in a manner that struck Mark as pretty haphazard.

'Tell me exactly what happened here.' he said in the manner of a teacher addressing two errant pupils.

Mark decided that he would not be intimidated or distracted by the change of personnel. He also felt that any territorial or jurisdictional dispute there might be between the FBI and the NYPD would be a matter for someone else to worry about. He was also beginning to enjoy the process because he knew what he was not going to tell them. They would no doubt find out in due course that Mark was worth a little more – well ten million dollars was a little more—than he had been worth yesterday, but that was irrelevant in this investigation. As for the toothpick, that was insignificant, at least until Mark had established who the bozo on that trip into town had been.

There seemed little point in risking five million dollars on an obscure hunch. His night-time activity with Annette was also not their concern, but he would enjoy any further attempt to pursue the question, particularly because Annette was enjoying it too – and that was good.

'As you can see, our office has been broken into, probably by druggies, and our man – Brad Morgan—is missing, which I assume is the reason the FBI is here!' Mark said sarcastically but trying to keep his tone as neutral as he could.

'Have you tried to contact this missing person?' came the response, to which Mark repeated his advice to the NYPD that they had tried both the landline and mobile telephone of Brad Morgan, several times, but had got no reply.

At that stage, Henderson merely nodded his head to O'Connell, who immediately gave up his trying to look busy and left.

'Nothing unusual has happened in the most recent past?' was Henderson's next question.

'You have to be joking! Why don't you talk to Sergeant McGuire of the NYPD? We have already been through the wringer with him and covered what we know and what we do not know. What I do not know is—when can I get the computers in this place up and running again? Without them, we do not know if there is any message left on the network that might give us a clue as to what happened here. What we do know is that neither I nor Ms Covic had any part to play in this disruption. I also know that the NYPD, and now apparently the FBI, seems more than a little bit interested in the role of Brad Morgan. So why don't you just find him and ask him?'

It was not that Mark had anything but respect for the

FBI, and for that matter, for the NYPD. In an earlier life, he had some concerns with the CIA and others in the spook business, but never with the federal police. The problem was that they were getting nowhere and seemed disinterested in the entire event. Except that the FBI was now involved. And for no apparent reason.

A person was not officially missing for quite some time after they were last seen, so who had alerted the FBI so early, and why? That did not make a whole heap of sense when considered in the context of the timing of events. As far as anyone knew Brad may have decided to have his way with Felicity and therefore was deliberately out of communication while he was merrily bonking away. Although that did stretch the imagination! While Brad was normally available 24/7, Mark had to admit that he had little cause to check this out all that regularly and it might also just be pure coincidence. He was under no obligation to be at the office. He may not have been in the office when the night-time visitors had called. There had not been time to get an analysis of the blood so any assumption that it was Brad's was pure speculation.

The FBI's involvement was only required if there was a missing person and they had hardly had time to establish that there was, and by their definition, he was not yet missing, was he? Marks' conclusion from all of this was that the FBI involvement was because they knew that Brad was missing long before this haphazard interview process had even begun. So, they also did not know where he was, and they wanted to find him. Now was not that interesting?

The remarks that Mark had made about the computers did however have an impact on Henderson and all his arrogance seemed to dissipate. 'How long would it take you to get the computers up and running?' he asked with an unusual spark of interest.

'That depends on what has happened. In the worst case, they may have been damaged so then it is anyone's guess. In the best case, a couple of minutes should do the trick.' Mark summarised the position.

'Well let us give it a go!' said Henderson, getting to his feet and moving towards the main console. Mark immediately stood in his way.

'I think is best if I do this. You do not know the start-up sequence. Nor do you know the passwords. And FBI or not, I am not about to tell you anytime soon, if ever.'

For a few seconds, Henderson looked as though he may push the issue. However, with Mark's imposing figure and obvious intent, he dropped any ideas he had of intervening and logic prevailed. He sullenly accepted what Mark had said and sat back down. Annette stayed at the table and did not attempt to help, for the simple reason that she had never been around when the computers were started up. So, for something to do, Henderson started asking her questions to which McGuire already had the answers.

One thing about Annette was that she had an exceptionally good memory so that in the unlikely event that Henderson and McGuire compared notes, they would end up with just one story.

Meanwhile, Mark went about the process of starting the machines.

Mark first checked the cabling to each machine and that was fine. Next, he went around behind the main rack and checked everything visually to make sure nothing had been damaged. The missing disk would not affect the system at all – other than that they cost a few dollars – but that was for the insurance company to worry about. For the time being, that was not an issue. Finally, he went to the uninterruptible power supply system, and there he found the reason the machines were down. The equipment power cables had been disconnected from the UPS and the mains power to the UPS had also been disconnected. Which was an interesting if brutal, way to take the equipment down.

Each machine on the network had its' own power switch, but if you wanted to take the lot down in a hurry, the UPS was the answer.

Unlike many office network environments where individual machines each had their own UPS device, at Taylor Software they were all fed through one device. This was a more expensive way of doing things, but the benefit came in greater stability. The loss of power to the network controller would mean that it could not be restarted until power was restored and only then could each machine be restarted. Switching a machine off was not particularly difficult but it did have a sequence that could take a few minutes to properly close down each machine.

Now, Mark had the answer. It must have been Brad who took the system down. The only reason he would have done so would be because the system was under threat. And once down no one could bring it back up – that is except Brad or Mark – or someone with the cooperation of Brad.

There must have been some pretty pissed-off people here last night, mused Mark. And pissed off people do pretty drastic things. Like they beat the shit out of the origin and source of their problem. So, what had happened to Brad? And where was he?

For the first time Mark began to seriously worry about Brad – but still, that would have to wait for at least a minute or two.

He reconnected the UPS to the mains power and the

unit came to life. Mark patiently waited while the equipment spent a minute or so going through its' cycle of checks. He then connected the equipment cables to the UPS. He hit the power switch on the main computer rack and to his relief, the network came up all ok. At least it was doing all the normal things.

Systems, particularly Servers, get their knickers in a twist if they are not shut down in the correct sequence, but Microsoft had got the method of recovery from such events organized (at last), and with the usual checking the system recovered and eventually produced the login prompt.

After checking that no one could see what he was doing he entered login and password, not as the Administrator, but just as an ordinary user. He would check the Administrator and Supervisor functions when there were fewer eyes around. The system came up fine.

'Well, now let us see what we can see' Mark said more to himself than anyone in particular. Henderson had been on his mobile telephone. As soon as Mark spoke, he rapidly terminated the call and joined Mark at the console that Brad would have been working at. Mark activated that workstation and used the same login procedure that he had used on the main system. He smiled to himself as he saw that Henderson took a note of what he keyed in while pretending to be writing down something related to his telephone conversation. A fat lot of use that would be! The clever stuff was only accessible by the Supervisor with the correct password, and, to a lesser extent, the Administrator again with the correct password.

While many people, the FBI included, had access to quite clever password-finding techniques, it was doubtful that they would be of any use in this case. Taylor Software was in the software security business and knowing what the FBI and their fellow spooks did they had devised very clever methods themselves. These were frighteningly simple and therefore remarkably effective.

Mark next went into the log of what had been happening to the system and soon found the last message timed at 11.14 pm but that message was innocuous. There would be another log that only someone with Supervisor rights could access, which may reveal some more interesting details. Mark was not about to let the FBI or anyone else into that area. He scrolled through the log, and then went to another message area and scanned through that, but there was nothing significant, or out of the ordinary, in that area either.

Messages from the client systems were numbered and flagged with a time of transmission and time of receipt which explains why computers 'date stamp' things with ridiculous hundredths of seconds. Nothing after 11:14:09:03 pm the previous day would be received until the landlines were restored.

Mark pushed the chair away from the console. He announced that although the time the system lost power was approximately 11:15 pm there were no messages recorded by Brad, so there was not even a hint of what had happened.

Body language is a strange thing and consequently in his earlier days as a mad keen Marine Mark had studied it in depth. It was not that he needed to. It was just that when the military had to work with other government agencies, particularly intelligence agencies, they often had to deal with people who in a sense used a lot of spin to avoid telling things straight. In other words, they lied – even though they were supposed to be on the same side. Many people in the military are so brainwashed they would believe anything if it were represented as the wishes or direction of their Commander-in-Chief. But not Mark. He had become cynical, to the point of paranoia.

No one else noticed. But Mark did. Henderson was visibly relieved that no message had been left by Brad. Well, wasn't that interesting? What was going on?

Neither Henderson nor McGuire, who had for all this time been leaning against the wall seemingly disinterested, were about to tell him.

'Well, I guess we have done all we can for now. We have prints and samples. Nothing seems to have been stolen or damaged. It was a professional job and I do not hold out any hope of the prints providing anything. All we need do now is the blood and then onto the question of what happened to your friend Brad.' Henderson almost muttered as he walked towards the stairs.

'Are we free to clean up the mess and return things to normal?' Mark asked expecting McGuire at least to have objections.

But no. He just shrugged, exchanged looks with Henderson, and they both said 'Ok' simultaneously.

'If you want a guard on the door until you can get it repaired, we can get someone around.' McGuire offered. Mark was not about to accept the offer.

'We can repair that ourselves and do it now so there is no need to worry yourselves about that.'

Mark's response irritated Henderson more than it did McGuire but again the shrug and they were on their way.

'What do you want me to do now?' Annette asked, sensing the relief that they both felt with the departure of Henderson, McGuire, and the few police officers who had stayed around.

'You do not have to do anything. You have done enough for me already. Why not just go home and have the weekend off like any other normal person?'

Mark's heart was not in it but that is what he had to say. The body language thing again came into play. At first, Annette looked a little hurt. Then she came to him and put her arms around his neck, and for not the first time today, he noticed a tear in her eyes. The words she came out with brought a tear to Mark's eyes as well.

'Mark, don't you understand what is happening? I love you. You are in a mess, so I am here to help you. I do not want to go home and spend the weekend alone. I want to be here with you. That is if you want me.' Mark held her tight. Yes – that was what he so desperately wanted to hear. After too long being almost afraid to show any emotion in the presence of women, particularly after his experience with Helen. Especially after his experience with his mother. He felt a surge of emotion. But in that brief moment, Mark knew that this was the girl with who he wanted to spend the rest of his life.

He gently moved her away from him and held both of her hands in his and smiled.

'You have no idea how much I have wanted you since I first saw you. I do not want you to go anywhere. But this is the office, and I am the boss. If we can agree on that, let us get to work, and then I will take you to dinner. I will let you choose what we do after that.'

Annette laughed and again hugged him.

'Yes, boss. But can I please make one minor change? Dinner at my place. By the time we have finished cleaning up this mess, you will not want to go out. Ok?'

'Ok. It is a deal, provided I get to choose the desert.'

She knew what that meant, hugged him again. Annette then changed her personality and immediately became the efficient Personal Assistant again. She did not need any instruction. She just started to pick up and stack the papers back where they had come from, making order out of chaos.

But with a smile on her face.
And this time the smile was—different.

Chapter 7

Recovery

The first thing that Mark had to do was to fix the main door into the building. It was unlikely that he could get the electronic locking mechanism fixed at such short notice and on a Saturday morning. He could revert the door to a normal key lock and this he achieved fairly quickly.

One of the things not normally realized by civilians was the amount of training that went on in the armed services. In the military people were trained to work as a team. In the Special Forces Group, they were also trained to be self-sufficient. And, in any case, they had to do something instead of killing people, especially in times of peace.

Such training had its' limits. Had Mark been asked to install the door in the first place it may have opened upwards rather than sideways, but once there he could deal with it. He locked the door, collected what remained of the door control unit, and then returned upstairs.

On re-entering the office, he was amazed at how much progress Annette had made. The place was almost back to normal although she had in front of her four massive piles of papers through which she was methodically sorting. She smiled at him as he entered and then, quieter than normal, she asked him.

'There are some of your personal papers amongst these. What do you want me to do with them?'

He glanced at the piles and saw a mixture of office documents, letters from his mother – which were often more business-like and interesting than office papers. Then he saw papers relating to his divorce from Helen, his ex-wife, that for some reason he had filed in the office, probably under 'Legal.'

The look on Annette's face was enquiring. Despite the body language angle, he was not sure if he detected animosity, jealousy, or other emotion. Or whether the two of them were only tired.

He quickly moved to dispel any potential problem that may arise between them. He had nothing to hide. At the same time, he did not understand women. Maybe he was reading something into the situation that was just not there! He had long since forgotten about his previous marriage, both the good and the bad but women seemed to assume that he would never forget.

'Annette, you have been here for a while. You know that, even before last night, I have had no reason to keep any secrets from you. Just sort them out if you can.'

She seemed relieved and again the smile returned if a little weaker than it had been. 'Ok—You're the boss.'

With this minor distraction still hovering in the back of his mind, Mark then set about restoring their landlines. Whoever had ripped the telephones from the wall had done so crudely and obviously did not know about, or care about, the finer points of communication systems. The broadband link on the computer, which after all was just a part of their telephone system, was the first that he tackled. The cable for that had been separated from its' plug. It would have been far easier to simply unclip the plug, so whoever was responsible for that had used brute force, but it was easy for someone with Mark's particular skills to fix. While the fixes that Mark made would have to be made more secure by the telecommunications company technician, they would at least be operational for the near future.

Having done that, he went to the main console and logged on as the Supervisor. He did the same on Brad's console and then downloaded the electronic traffic looking for clues as to what had happened the night before. He was disappointed. It was all routine traffic reporting that all was well, and most of the messages would again be consigned to the rubbish bin – well Microsoft's version of the rubbish bin.

He then, with a certain amount of trepidation, logged into the Banking System and called up his company current account – Yes! – the 5 million dollars that Matt Reynolds had promised would be in the account had been transferred. He realized he would have to explain what had happened to the Bank Manager. For once in his short life as sole Director of his company, he would enjoy that meeting.

As Mark understood his position in the company, he could quite simply take the money himself. By the use of tricky wording when the company document was drawn up, Mark Taylor and not Taylor Software owned the software systems. The Company made its' money by providing the service on that intellectual property.

He was unsure of the tax implications. It was a fair bet that there would be tax implications, none of them particularly favourable to either Mark or the company. That was a subject that was best left to others. Consequently, he resisted the temptation of transferring money into his account and instead transferred the bulk of the money into an interest-bearing company account, leaving sufficient in the current account to more than offset the overdraft. For the first time in a long time!

Mark then fired up the monitoring programs which included a link to the Augem Group system. That would have to change once the final agreement was in place. Meanwhile, he still had responsibility, so he set in motion the download routines which captured any problems and other issues that occurred on-site in the client systems since the last connection. That would keep all the clients happy – not that they would know that the system had been down – and the systems were now more or less back to their normal state. And despite all the trials and tribulations of the last twelve or so hours, everything was fine.

He also fired up a special monitoring program that just linked into the Augem Group's system and set in motion the download routines that captured a variety of other matters that occurred on-site in the Augem system since the last time it was run. That would not keep Augem at all happy if they knew what kind of information it sought – not that they would know that the system even existed. And just for now, Mark intended to keep that running, at least until he had answers on who had broken into their office, and why.

He then restored one of the telephones to as near normal a condition as his crude connections would allow and dialled the answering service. Surprisingly, there were no messages, meaning that no disasters had occurred while the telephone system had been down.

The next job he had to do was to call the Bay Ridge security firm and request a twenty-four-hour guard for the rest of the weekend. He got the same cheerful Diane that he had talked to earlier in the day. She seemed quite happy with Mark's assurance that it was all the assistance he needed, and that everything was fine. Of course, everything was far from fine, but Diane was hardly the person who could do anything about that.

That is why his next call was to Dusty Miller.

As was to be expected on a Saturday morning, Dusty would have been drinking the night before. Mark knew that he would be at home nursing a hangover. He, therefore, knew that his friend would be grumpy. Dusty was always grumpy.

'How are you, Dusty? It is Mark here.' he started, trying to talk as quietly as possible.

'What the fuck do you want? It is Saturday morning for heaven's sake!' came the reply.

There was nothing unusual about Dusty's use of the 'f' word. He always managed to include the word in every sentence he uttered no matter what the time of day or day of the week, and no matter to whom he was talking. But he had calmed down in recent years. They had been together in the Special Forces and although Mark had been the senior, Dusty had always treated him like a younger brother, and one who was very much in need of looking after.

They came from vastly different backgrounds, Mark from a typical American middle-class family. Dusty from the other side of the tracks from a family riddled by violence and drugs. And with issues about race and discrimination. Dusty had turned his back on his family, and their gripes. but he still harboured a degree of resentment at the apparent unfairness of life. His sheer size – he was one of the few men who made Mark feel small—meant that in any company he could say whatever he liked, even in the respectable business environment in which he had made his living. As part of his marketing of legal services, such as it was, he said that his services were available 24/7.

Dusty spoke to all his clients the same way and grumbled no matter what time of day or night it was. Mark was not put off in any way by the response he had got.

Mark laughed. He had a job that needed solid legal expertise. And the man he was talking to would provide that.

'Dusty, we have to talk. And sooner rather than later. There have been a couple of events in the last twenty-four hours that have changed a few things. Not the least of which—Brad Morgan has gone missing. The FBI and the NYPD have been crawling around the office, but they seem either incompetent or disinterested – but something should be happening, and it is not, so we need your help on that one.'

'What do you mean – Brad has gone missing? When did you find this out? Where has he gone?'

Dusty, for all his faults, had taken a liking to Brad, and they were after all both Afro-American – albeit from widely diverse backgrounds. And Mark knew that the mere mention of Brads' disappearance would get Dusty's attention. He also knew that Dusty had a soft spot for Annette as well. Whether he found her attractive he had never said. For some reason, Mark got the impression that Dusty would protect her like she was his own. Mark had yet to figure out that Dusty had read the situation that existed within the company. In particular the relationship between the various players, long ago. Dusty was patiently waiting for Mark to get off his ass and make a move on the girl he was so obviously infatuated with. So again, it was Mark who Dusty was protecting.

'I do not know where Brad has gone otherwise, why would I say that he was missing?' Mark replied. 'But he has vanished and is not answering his calls. Annette and I are at the office and all we know is that Brad did not set the alarms when he left the office last night. And the NYPD and the FBI have come up blank so far.'

'What has this to do with the NYPD and how did the FBI come to be involved?' Dusty growled into the phone.

'Well, our office was broken into last night. The NYPD eventually came around this morning to investigate. They called in the FBI presumably because Brad is missing. They seemed a little quick on the draw with that one.'

'I'll be with you in thirty minutes.'

Dusty hung up without any further preamble or comment.

Mark went down the stairs to let him in about twenty minutes later, having seen him arrive in the car park from the second-floor window. 'What the hell is wrong with the door?' was Dusty's first observation. It is funny how, when faced with a man who does nothing but swear, other men seem to stop swearing.

'Look at the switch – it has been smashed, so the relay in the office no longer works.' Mark replied with a shrug.

They went up to the office where Annette made them a much-needed coffee while Mark recounted the recent events. Well - the events that mattered. Missing out how he had arrived at the office – at least for the time being.

Dusty sat throughout with a puzzled but interested look on his face. He did not even flinch when Mark mentioned the price that the Augem Group had offered for the software. And Mark knew better than to try to bullshit

Dusty about his negotiating skills that had resulted in the sum. When he had finished, he looked expectantly at Dusty awaiting some kind of response. The response he got was not what he expected. And he did not swear, which meant that Dusty was taking things seriously.

'Are you sure that nothing was taken except for a disk?' Dusty asked.

'That is all we have been able to find that is missing – that is apart from Brad.' Mark replied.

'So that excludes Brad from being the villain – he would never take a disk that would be useless to him. So, the person who took it thought that it was worth something. What exactly was on it?'

'Nothing more than compiled code and operating stuff – as I say – it is not of much use to anyone. All the source code is safely stored off the premises.' replied Mark, really telling him something he already knew. Dusty, for all his faults, was a key part of Mark's security arrangements, for several reasons. Firstly, if Dusty decided to get involved in the computer business, he had more than the necessary skills to cope. So, he knew all about source code and its security. Secondly, his business was sufficiently remote and different from Mark's that the additional backing up to Dusty's computer system on a daily basis would be difficult to trace because it was implausible. Thirdly, no one messed with Dusty – he was big, muscular, and had that intimidating manner that kept people in their place. And because of their history together in Special Forces, there was a tremendous amount of mutual respect and trust between them.

Dusty looked around the room, lingered a little when his eyes came into contact with Annette.
'It looks like the Drug people came calling, but it does seem a little too late for that. They would find nothing here to interest them.' Dusty mused. And then he said to

Mark in a quiet voice that belied his size.

'Are you thinking what I am thinking?'

Mark answered straight away.

'You think that this was the work of someone from the Augem Group?'

Dusty nodded.

'Have you been monitoring something that they did not want you to have access to?'

This time it was Mark's turn to swear.

'How the fuck should I know?'

'I do not know Mark. It seems to me that your friends at the Augem Group – if it was them – expected to find something on that disk. If it is only normal systems, then you may have information that they do not want you to see. Or there must be something that monitors a part of their system that they do not want you to look at. If it was the Augem Group, they may have expected that their taking the disk may enable them to find out what you were looking at. Maybe they just want assurance. I must say they have a funny way of getting such assurance.'

'Why would I be interested in what they do apart from legitimately monitoring their systems?' Mark asked, not following where Dusty's questions were leading. Not that this was a surprise. As a lawyer, Dusty was quite used to questioning people and leading them on until he found out what he wanted to know. Mark could have become irritated by being treated as a suspect. He knew Dusty. Eventually, he would reveal his conclusions.

Dusty was not bothered by cash-flow issues. He had lasered in on the real issue.

Because they are up to no good. And typical of all crooks, they like to keep their little secrets secret. They are in the finance business. If the people who work in the finance industry went out of business or never needed any legal help, I would be out of a job. Look where the money is! There you will find the world's biggest and best crooks. What I think is, they are already into or are about to get into, something a bit shady. Probably drugs, money laundering, or a combination of both. The last thing they need is someone like you. You are ex-Special Forces, as honest as the day is long and incorruptible. The last thing they need is you poking around their system.'

Dusty seemed to have summed up the situation pretty well, except that he was not up with the play on what the monitoring system did.

So, Mark told him. The system monitored everything. There were parts of the monitoring system that the Augem Group would never know about – even if those parts had revealed nothing that Mark could perceive as being the least bit dodgy.

'Ok – so you have access to everything. The position still is that they do not want you in there. My first guess was right. Now your position is that they have made an offer to buy the software, and you have accepted that – Yes?'

Mark just nodded, so Dusty continued.

'I advise you to get the whole deal finalized as quickly as possible. Then get the hell out of there. I will draw up an agreement, which is in effect a deed of sale, and we will go and present it to the Augem Group on Monday. If my reading of the situation is accurate, I believe they will accept it without question – Ok?'

'That is fine with me Dusty. I do not know what they are up to, but you are the one that understands the law. You know far more than I do about these things. If that is what you recommend – let us do it.'

'Ok – that is out of the way.' said Dusty. 'Now we have to look at the question of your insurance. The actual damage is limited to the door and the disk. What is the excess on your insurance?'

Seeing the blank look on Mark's face, he looked to Annette, and she produced the appropriate document as if by magic. After a glance at the document, he cast it to one side. 'Not worth worrying about. Any claim that you may have would be well under your excess – do you agree?'

Again, Mark just nodded.

'Right—Now – what are we going to do about the break-in?' Since no one else was in the room save for Annette, Mark assumed that the question was directed at him, although Dusty seemed to have already made up his mind.

'Why don't you tell me what you suggest? – could save time and my brain is too scrambled at the present.' Mark opined, which drew an instant reaction.

'Ok – leave it to me – you are too soft – it looks as though I will have to kick asse to find out what the police are up to. As for the FBI – they should be onto Brad's case although he has not been missing long enough to be legally classified as missing. Do we know or suspect anything?'

'Nothing' replied Mark with a shrug of the shoulders.

'Ok – leave that to me as well. Best if I deal with those arrogant pricks. Now is there anything else you need me for, or can I go home and continue suffering from last night? I have work to do, but not before I have a sleep!'

Mark smiled. He had known Dusty for a long time and knew he was at his best when he had something to complain about. Dusty's hangover was beginning to take its' toll, but Mark knew that he could rely absolutely on Dusty Miller doing exactly what he had said he would do, hangover or no hangover. Although he had been a rough and tumble, hardnosed soldier when their paths had first crossed, Dusty was a very clever and intelligent man. Mark suspected that Dusty still maintained the persona of the gruff, "man from the other side of the tracks" as a tactic to tempt people into underestimating what they were up against. If that tactic failed, he was big enough and ugly enough to impose himself.

Mark said goodbye at the door, then made his way back up the stairs into the office. Annette was still busy sorting through papers but stopped when Mark put his arms around her and kissed her gently on the neck. Slowly she stood and turned around to face him and held him – their bodies close and warm.

'You have had one hell of a day!' she said, half expecting some form of emotional response to the events of the day. So far Mark had shown no response, other than to deal with each of the events as they unfolded. While Annette was just an employee—the hired help—she was a woman. She expected him to be upset and to display it. But she was beginning to develop Mark's ability to read body language. Not that you needed much imagination to read Mark's body language at the moment. She smiled.

'Let us stop for the day – and have time to ourselves. Your place or mine? There is not enough for a decent meal in your fridge, and I did promise you a dinner. I do not care as long as I can have you – and this time I will let you have control.' she said with a laugh.

'That is ok with me.' he said as he kissed her gently on the lips, and his hands moved up her body, He felt again the proud thrust of her breasts against his chest, and he remembered—something. The problem was his memory of last night was a little vague. He knew that they had made love and knew that he had enjoyed it. But this time he was fully aware of what he was about, and he could hardly wait to get her home. Nonetheless, he would wait just a little while – and enjoy the anticipation.

On the way to Annette's apartment, Mark decided to cruise by the place where Brad and 'Honey' had their pad. It was in an apartment building on West 145th Street at the northern end of the area known as Morningside Heights. The area was, on reflection, a little upmarket for someone at Brad's level of income. That was more than made up for in the run-down condition of the apartment block.

He parked the SUV about fifty yards down the street and told Annette to wait in the car with the doors locked. Rather than alarm Annette, he did not take a weapon. He just tapped on the area where he had earlier stored the pistols. This time she did not object.

He approached what he assumed to be the main entrance and there on his right were the mailboxes. He searched methodically through the names looking for the name Morgan. But there was no one with the name of Morgan.

He pressed the button for the building manager. The Manager was either on drugs or was making a very good impression of someone who was. Mark had first to convince this guy that his reasons for trying to locate Brad were legitimate. Even his driver's license and business card did not register with the Manager.

It was clear to Mark that no one from either the NYPD or the FBI had been around to check, otherwise, the Manager would surely have mentioned it. Mark struggled to get anything out of the man, except for one thing.

No one by the name of Brad Morgan lived, or in recent history had lived, in the apartments.

Chapter 8

Millionaire

The New York traffic was again a problem as Mark and Dusty made their way into the office of the Augem Group on Monday morning. The good news was that they had the use of one of the Augem Groups visitor car parks. That at least meant that they did not have to fight for a park or do battle with more traffic getting into and out of a public parking building.

On the fourteenth floor, they were greeted by Debbie Peterson who was her usual efficient self while appearing both anxious and caring. She glanced at Dusty and smiled warmly. Her attention was focused on Mark. 'Mr. Reynolds will see you immediately. Could you please come into the Board Room? He will be with you in a moment. Now I know how you have your coffee, Mr. Taylor. Could I bring one for you, Mr. Miller?'

Peterson fussed around them like a mother hen. Mark had a suspicion that she must have been advised either that something important was about to take place, or that Mark was no longer to be treated as part of the Augem family. He was not used to being referred to as a Mister, especially by Miss Peterson. But they both just nodded and smiled, and Debbie disappeared towards the galley.

'This crowd certainly know how to pick their ladies' remarked Dusty. 'She is a beauty!'

Mark looked sharply at Dusty as he felt as though he had strayed into a sensitive area. But for reasons that Mark did not understand, a cold shudder ran through his body.

Matt Reynolds came into the room at that moment.

'Hey – you are here to take our money, not our staff' he laughed as he shook hands with both of his visitors. Mark was a regular visitor. Dusty had not been to the Augem office for about two years. Yet Reynolds still greeted Dusty as though it were only yesterday.

'No offense intended Matt' said Dusty in the most disarming way 'Pleased to see you again. Now—what is the format of the meeting, or can we dispense with the jackets and get down to business?'

'That's the way to do it!' said Reynolds waving both men into chairs and taking off his jacket. 'John will join us if he is needed, but I believe I can handle most of what has to be done. I understood from our conversation that you have a document for us to look at?'

Since Mark had not spoken to Reynolds since the previous Friday night, the question was directed at Dusty. While Dusty pulled the documents out of his briefcase, Debbie arrived with a tray carrying three coffees and biscuits and placed the tray on the table. Mark looked at Debbie somewhat differently than he had done previously. Yes—she was a beauty. But there was something else – what it was he did not know. It was almost as though he had a sixth sense that told him that they would meet again. That thought disturbed him for no apparent reason.

'Thank you, Debbie – that will be all.' The words from Reynolds aroused Mark from his daydreaming as he realized that he had been staring – as had Debbie. This was no way to conduct himself at what was supposed to be a meeting of some not inconsiderable importance. But no one else appeared to be even remotely as concerned as Mark. Reynolds just shook his head. Dusty just laughed. Mark was embarrassed.

The Board Room had not changed much from the previous Friday. Everything was very neat and tidy, except for a couple of desks that had been backed into a corner together with a couple of computers. A cursory glance at them by Mark revealed that they were connected to a telephone, which had to be a broadband link. According to the Taylor monitor, they were not connected to the office network. Now wasn't that strange.

If these machines were for use by Asid and Mohammed, and these two gentlemen were taking over from Taylor Software, they would need to be connected to the internal network. Of course, the machines may have been connected via a VPN, or Virtual Private Network, link, but that did seem to be rather a dumb way to do it. If you were in the same building as the fileserver, where a simple plug and cable would do the trick. It did seem a bit strange to connect via the internet.

If they thought that such a link would bypass the security that Taylor Software had installed, weren't they in for a surprise? They also would not know that Taylor Software could still monitor their traffic irrespective of how they gained access to the Augem system. But what Taylor could not do, without the serious risk of detection, was find out what they had on their actual machines. Mark had in his pocket a flash drive from which he could download some very interesting software onto these machines. It would have saved a lot of time and effort if he had. Unfortunately, he did not know that this kind of subterfuge would be necessary.

Dusty handed out copies of the documents he had prepared. The room lapsed into silence as they each read their copy. Mark, who was not concentrating on the job in hand, was less than a half-hour into, and less than halfway through, reading his copy when Reynolds sat back. He announced that he was quite happy with the document. He then asked to see the system documentation which Mark had provided. These were also distributed, although now it was Reynolds' turn to show a lack of concentration, as he only flicked through his copy, Dusty barely glanced at his copy, while Mark continued reading the deed of sale that Dusty had prepared. Once again it was Reynolds who took the initiative – much to Mark's surprise.

'I can see no problem with these' he commented. 'Do you mind if I take these through to John? – I expect he will want to sight the documents and sign the agreement, and I am sure that you would want him to?' Reynolds added with a chuckle.

Dusty and Mark exchanged looks. Dusty replied in the affirmative.

Reynolds got to his feet, retrieved his jacket, and left the room.

As soon as he was gone Dusty made to speak.

He was instantly silenced by a signal from Mark – signals they had used to good effect while on Special Forces business in an earlier life and a different country. They were both aware of the CCTV cameras in the room, but Dusty was not aware of any sound recording device. Neither was Mark. But he was not about to take any chances. An organization that they suspected of being involved in some illegal business and were prepared to pay big money to protect that business, was not likely to skimp on minor surveillance costs. They certainly would not be likely to miss the chance of picking up any idle gossip from their friends, depending on how they viewed the friends, currently in the Augem Board room.

Mark continued reading the deed of sale while Dusty busied himself casting his eyes over the system documentation that Mark had prepared, which he found to be about as interesting as watching grass grow.

Eventually, Reynolds returned and announced that John Dubois was happy with the arrangement. And he was also happy for Matt to sign the papers on behalf of the Augem Group.

It was difficult for the two visitors to disguise their surprise. So why had Matt made the point that Mark would want John to sign, and yet had then dismissed it so offhandedly? But at the end of the day, the only issue was going to be – Who signed the check?

The deed of sale was watertight as far as Taylor Software was concerned. That left the onus on the Augem Group to counter the terms that Dusty had come up with.

Reynolds and Dubois either did not understand the fine print – which was unlikely – or did not give a rats' fart – which was beginning to appear the most likely.

The papers were signed by Matt on behalf of the Augem Group with Debbie signing as his witness. Mark signed on behalf of Taylor Software with Dusty signing as his witness.

In very short order it was all done.

Of an even greater surprise was what Matt went on to say after the rather unseemly rapid and informal signing of the documents.

'I see no point in dragging this business out any longer than we need to. We recognize that the whole matter could be somewhat disruptive to both of our businesses, so we are anxious to conclude it as soon as possible. The additional five million dollars are being transferred into your account now. The documentation you have provided meets our conditions so there is no need for any further delay.'

Mark was stunned by the speed with which, what he regarded as a major deal, had all been finalized. While Dusty had said on Saturday that they should try to conclude everything as rapidly as was possible, he did not expect the Augem Group to be equally keen on rapid action. Within little more than half of a working day, Mark had acquired more money than he had ever known. It was hard to comprehend what possible delay Matt had alluded to. Reynolds, on the other hand, seemed to be quite oblivious to any reaction from Mark.

'So – what is on the cards now for Taylor Software?' Reynolds asked, once more removing his jacket.

'Well – we first have to recover from the burglary that we suffered last Friday night' said Mark, seeing the chance to embark on a fishing expedition to see what reaction he might get.

And he was not disappointed.

Just for a second Matt Reynolds froze. A person with less experience than Mark, and Dusty, at reading body language would have missed it. Matt recovered himself well, but the damage was done.

Reynolds already knew about Friday night!

'I didn't know!' Matt lied, and then added 'What happened, and when did this happen?'

'I wish I knew' began Mark. 'They were probably looking for drugs – I have told you previously of the history of the building we are in—and they made one hell of a mess to achieve next to nothing. As far as I can tell nothing was taken or damaged, apart from a broken front door.' Mark shrugged. 'We could have lost one of our disks – but there were five eights of bugger all data on it – and it is of no use to anyone else. Probably looking for money since they were hardly likely to find drugs. The police are onto it. I don't hold out much hope of them finding anything. And the Federal Bureau of Investigation – the infamous FBI— seemed equally devoid of ideas, or disinterested.'

The latter point got a reaction.

'What have the FBI got to do with things – they don't usually get involved in break-ins and burglary?' asked Reynolds.

Again, his body language was wrong. It struck Mark as strange that Matt would raise the issue of the involvement of the FBI. Most people accept that the FBI gets involved in all manner of things, and rarely if ever does it seem logical – at least at the time.

'Well - that is equally confusing' replied Mark. 'Brad Morgan seems to have gone missing. We know that he was probably in the office at the time of the break-in. But we have not heard anything from him. We reported him as missing, and along came the FBI. We still have heard nothing.' Mark concluded with a shrug.

'What about his partner – the lady he referred to as Felicity? Can't she shed some light on where he is?' Matt asked.

'Well, that's another funny thing – she appears to have vanished as well.

Mark did not add that there was no record of Brad Morgan or Felicity at the address where they were supposed to have lived. He already had a suspicion that Reynolds knew more than he was saying. What he did not know was – why?

If there were things that Matt knew about the activities on Friday night, and he was not prepared to say what they were, it was best that Mark also says nothing. It certainly did not seem appropriate to talk about what Mark had been up to on that night while the "burglary" was taking place. It seemed even less appropriate, if less colourful, to talk about what he suspected Matt Reynolds or someone else from the Augem Group might have been up to at the time.

'That must be very worrying for you. What are you going to do?' Matt asked, showing real concern. Or rather attempting to appear to be showing real concern.

Thankfully, Dusty cut in on Mark before he could respond.

'We are all concerned, but Mark still has a business to run. I am working with the FBI and the Metropolitan Police, and I expect that they will report some progress soon. We all liked Brad, so we hope he has just gone AWOL. There is no evidence of foul play so on that front thing are looking ok. Now I am sure you are busy, so we will not take any more of your time' said Dusty – rising from his chair and gathering up his papers and jacket.

Reynolds did not seem to be too busy and had plenty of time. He seemed reluctant to let them go. But the momentum was with Dusty. Mark felt obliged to follow.

They shook hands again and made their way out into reception. As the lift arrived Mark turned to Matt and said, 'Thank you – I have enjoyed working with the Augem Group – maybe we can get together again sometime soon – socially that is – meanwhile good luck.'

Matt still seemed reluctant to let them go and had a puzzled look on his face, but he had to accept that they were leaving.

Debbie sat at the reception desk, and Mark was sure that there were tears in her eyes.

As the doors of the elevator closed, it was as though

the final curtain had come down on the final act of a play. Mark was not overly upset. After all, he was now a very rich man – at least by his standards.
And it had all happened at an almost unreal speed.

It was not until Dusty and Mark were in the car, making their way back through the traffic, that either of them talked. Dusty was his usual laid-back self as he commented.

That seemed to go ok – if a little on the faster side of bloody quick. Something is going on that you have not been told about, and I think you are better off getting the fuck right out of there.'

At least he was back to his normal self. Mark could not remember, ever, in the long time they had known each other, Dusty not swearing. During the time they had been in the Augem office, Dusty had not once sworn and there was not even a hint of him doing so. That meant he was not happy. Mark pondered.

'I was very surprised at how rapidly they signed and paid the balance of the money. The document you produced was spot on but even you are not that good. What the hell is going on?'

'I'll tell you what was going on' replied Dusty. 'For starters, Matt knew about the break-in at your office without you telling him. He also knew that a disk had been stolen. What we don't know is whether he knew that it was of absolutely no use. And I would also guess that he knew of the FBI's involvement. But for different reasons than we thought. I think that they are up to their armpits in the drug trade or money laundering, or some combination of both. And you want to know the scary part? I think that the FBI was there because the FBI representatives are on the Augem payroll – to make sure that any inquiries that you make go nowhere – at least anywhere near the truth'.

'Do I want to be involved in receiving money from the Augem Group in those circumstances?' asked Mark, beginning to see the end of his millionaire status before he even got there.

Dusty laughed.

'You are not involved, and if you read the agreement, the money that has been, or is about to be, transferred into your Bank account was for your computer software. Nothing more, nothing less. Despite what you may think, the price pales into insignificance compared with what many companies normally pay for their computer systems and software. So, you are in the clear.'

Mark was still not convinced but switched his attention to another part of the morning's conversation that had disturbed him.

'I was surprised that Matt referred to Brad's partner as Felicity – Brad always referred to her as 'Honey' and I do not recall either of us ever using her real name in Matt's presence – now what was that about?'

'Do you want to know what I think?' Dusty replied. 'I think that Brad—that son of a bitch – was in on the deal the whole time. He hasn't gone missing – he has completed his job and just left. The whole thing looks like a setup. Just maybe he took your disk, not because there may be something on it, but because we would conclude, as we did, that it was useless. And therefore, draw the reasonable conclusion that Brad could not be involved. Real smart! You were worried about his car being left at the office. It is just another part of a big con. What is Brad's car worth? You would get more money renting out his parking spot. He is probably off somewhere now driving a Lamborghini'.

Mark had to think about that. He recalled his feelings of the previous Friday night – well some of them.

He was now sure that there had been a very successful attempt to keep him otherwise occupied. Ebony had shown an inordinate amount of interest in him and had kept him well supplied with drinks. Yet, when Annette had turned up, Ebony had lost all interest in Mark. Therefore—was Annette involved?

Her reasons for turning up appeared perfectly logical. She was the one who decided he had had enough to drink. But was the damage already done? Then she had taken him home. That was logical since he was in no condition to drive. One sure way to keep him occupied would be to seduce him. But who had seduced who?

Mark decided to embellish the story he had so far told Dusty – omitting only the details of his seduction and then an amorous affair with Annette.

Dusty laughed as Mark concluded his dissertation. To Mark's relief, he did not press for further details of his night-time activity.

'The money has got to your head. You have been conned. Now—just how much did Brad know? All of it? Or have you in your usual way retained some key bits of information?'

Mark had to smile at that. Dusty knew how he operated.

'Well – he was not supposed to know about some aspects of the system. Some access is restricted. Some are so unusual that even Brad would not suspect they existed. But Brad is – was – a very clever guy. Who knows what he could have found out? But the source code for that kind of stuff is not stored at the office. On balance, I would say that he could not know much more than he had the right to. He knew that we were monitoring things that we omitted to tell Augem about. That is just normal practice in the computer business, and no one at the Augem Group has ever raised the matter as a cause for concern to them'.

'Well – we had better hope that you are right,' said Dusty. 'Otherwise, the reason why Augem is so smug is – they have got all they needed from your own man'.

Mark slumped in his seat. He had spent quite some time when in the Special Forces doing battle with Drug barons and he knew how they worked.

Money was no object – they had more than enough to make the Gross National Product of most countries pale into insignificance. People were no problem. They could afford to buy, sell, cajole, or bribe anyone and anything that they needed. Compliance was not a problem – for the quite simple reason that they could afford to pay to have anyone removed who did not comply with their wishes – no matter how trivial those wishes may appear to be.

Now Mark had been paid ten million dollars for something that was in his view worth less than a twentieth of that figure at best and less than a fiftieth if Mark wanted to be more realistic. With that kind of money, anything was possible. In his earlier discussions with Matt, it had been suggested that money was no object to Dubois or the Augem Group.

Putting things into perspective, when you considered the rather low pay rate that Brad had been on, a tax-free pay rise, or a donation, which could more than double his take take-home That would barely make a dent in someone else's petty cash account.

This whole scenario was something that Mark had not even thought about – that is, until now.

So much for Mark's assessment of people.

Had he been too trusting?

Chapter 9

Trapped

The second day of the week at the office of Taylor Software, after the dramas of the weekend, was very tiring and equally trying. Following their remarkable experience at the office of the Augem Group on Monday, Mark and Dusty had called in at the 119 Bar & Grill in Greenwich Village. Another five million dollars in the Bank for little more than a half day's work – if you could call it work—was worth a celebration.

Mark now had the money, and he could plan on an expansion of the business that he could only have previously thought about in his wildest dreams. There were many organizations in the business of designing and running virus checks, Trojan hunting, spam protection, firewalls, and all that kind of stuff that had come to prominence in the computer world since the advent of the Internet. Mark had extended his systems to produce a very sophisticated in-house security system, and that is where he believed the future lay.

If only he could convince the Chief Executive Officers of business that there was a very real threat and a very real risk. To achieve that was quite simply a matter of marketing. Now he could afford to employ someone with those skills and could afford to expand what he had created into a commercial product and start to make some real money. Who could begrudge him a few hours in the bar before commencing to implement his plans?

He did call the office and invited Annette to join them.

She had just laughed and declined.

'You deserve a break – so enjoy yourself – the business is under control. Ring me later and we will see about going out to dinner.

He did call her later in the afternoon. He was in no condition to go anywhere.

Mark tried to convince Annette that he was ok, but she very firmly told him to stay where he was. When she arrived to pick them up shortly after 6:00 pm both Mark and Dusty were very happy. But also, very drunk. She piled them into her car, dropped Dusty off at his apartment, and then took Mark home.

This time she put him straight to bed and on his own.

Annette did remove his shoes but that was all.

When Mark finally awoke on Tuesday morning it was well after his normal wakeup time. And he was very much the worse for wear.

Annette had stayed the night. She was showered, dressed, fed, and ready for another day. While she felt sorry for Mark, she could not help but be amused by his reaction to his condition.

But there was still a lot of work to be done. She gently coaxed him back to life. By the time he had spent a half-hour under a cold shower, and then five minutes under a warm one, he began to feel better.

He searched out Annette, and for a brief moment, he had ideas of returning to bed. This time with her as company. She laughingly pushed him away.

'You behave yourself today and we will make up for it tonight. Right now, we have to get to the office. You have work to do.'

Eventually, they made it into the office. And she was correct. In the rush to get the documentation organized for the meeting with the Augem Group he had left a bit of a mess. Annette had been reluctant to clean it up. She just did not know whether any of the various drafts scattered around the place was the genuine article or not. The fact that Mark scooped the lot up and headed for the shredder just brought another smile to her face. Computers were meant to reduce paper, but that rarely, if ever, happened.

Not quite so easy to deal with were the telephone and email messages. Several email messages were from clients wanting help, clarification, or odd fixes most of which Mark would have expected another member of his team, or even Brad to handle. He dealt with those by sending out a general message to say Brad was sick and that Jonathan would be in touch shortly to sort them out.

Jonathan Fullwell was what was known in the trade as Mister Reliable. A bit of a plodder but attentive and logical, and he was very reliable. That was fine with both Mark and the clients.

The calls that Mark had to return were to the Metropolitan police, the FBI, his insurance company, and his Business Manager from the Bank. He decided to handle them in reverse order, and not quite as the callers had intended.

The Business Manager at his Bank could best be

described in the politest of terms as an arrogant piece of shit. Mark rang the Bank's general number which meant he had to deal with the button-pushing required by the emotionless female digital voice. But it did bypass his Business Manager, and he eventually asked for—and got a human being—the real Manager.

It was amazing what a few zeroes added to the balance on a bank statement could achieve – even if his account was relatively small compared to some. The Manager was going to come uptown from his Broadway branch to see Mark—immediately! There was a first time for everything! Whether the Bank Manager was anxious to help or inquisitive of the newfound wealth would be decided later.

Mark then rang the insurance company. A casual listener to the Insurers' side of the conversation would have thought Mark had suffered a break-in of the size and significance of the removal of all the gold from Fort Knox. Insurance organizations are always your friends until that is, you make a claim. But Mark had not made a claim – so how did they know that a claim was being considered? He told the broker to get in touch with Dusty Miller. That should cause a few ripples. Dusty would be in his prime, nursing a hangover and so early in the day.

The calls from the FBI were next. Strangely, these calls were from cell phone numbers, but he did not immediately call those numbers. Instead, he called the FBI New York Field Office in Federal Plaza. Again, having grappled with digital voices who never seem to have available the actual option required, asked for agent Henderson.

The Henderson that he spoke to was not the Henderson he had met on Saturday morning and seemed annoyed that Mark had been on a first-name basis with Clive. For a start, this Henderson was female, and, while he had some doubts about the agent who had accompanied Henderson on Saturday morning, there was no doubt he had the wrong person. Not that Mark regarded himself as being in any way privileged. And Miss or Mrs. Henderson was not exactly helpful in trying to transfer Mark to the correct Henderson, so that approach was abandoned.

Mark then called the cell phone number and spoke to Clive Henderson's mailbox, leaving a message to the effect that they were playing some kind of telephone tag.

He then rang the NYPD, asked for and eventually got, the correct Sergeant McGuire. That conversation added nothing to Mark's already limited knowledge of the events of Friday night. McGuire had nothing to report except to say that Mark should contact Henderson at the FBI for an update. Mark's comment about going around in circles and playing games of telephone tag did not sit well with an irritated McGuire. The NYPD was not exactly well known for it's ability to communicate with the public helpfully. McGuire took that art to another level.

The Bank Manager arrived before Mark could change gear, at about the same time that Dusty appeared, surprisingly appearing none the worse for wear from their escapades of the day before.

The Bank of New York was founded in 1784 and was reputed to be the oldest bank in the USA. The Manager must have been one of the original founders. He looked well beyond the age of retirement and did not seem to be the right kind of guy to be talking to someone like Mark who was, after all, in an industry that was at the leading edge of technology. But the Manager's mind was surprisingly as sharp as a tack.

It was soon obvious that Dusty's observation of yesterday about the price companies usually paid for computer software was right on the button. The whole discussion revolved around how to get the best use out of 10 million dollars and the subject of how and where such a sum came from was not an issue. That question was simply not raised.

Dusty handled the paperwork. By the time the Manager left, Mark no longer had an overdraft facility and instead had several investments that would see Taylor Software significantly more stable than it had been at any time since its' formation. There was some talk from the Manager about investing in higher-risk opportunities, but Mark was in the software business and knew all about opportunities. Dusty was in the legal business – as well as a friend – and knew all about risks. Mark was not sure whether Dusty's subsequent proposal that they go out and have a few beers to celebrate the achievement of yet another milestone in the affairs of Taylor Software, was genuine or not. It did not matter because Annette firmly said 'No!' and they both knew that was an end to the matter.

Mark was about to get back to what he was supposed to be doing – reorganizing his company—when the return call came from Henderson. For no reason other than that Dusty was there, Mark switched his telephone onto speaker.

'Thanks for returning my call, returning your calls of yesterday' began Mark. He did not hold out much hope of getting anything useful from the conversation and was rapidly losing interest in Friday's events. But he still added 'I have spoken to the NYPD and McGuire suggested you may be able to bring me up to date.'

Henderson's report was at least predictable.

'We have been unable to turn up anything on your man Brad Morgan – he seems to be a bit of a mystery man. And the NYPD has got nowhere in finding out who did the break-in. On Saturday morning you were adamant that your man would have had nothing to do with the alleged break-in. Are you still so sure?'

Mark was not so sure, given Dusty's comments about the possible involvement of Brad. However, he did not see any point in telling Henderson that. Since Dusty was also convinced that the FBI, or at least Henderson and his cronies, were on the payroll of the Augem Group, there did not seem any point in telling him anything. So, he replied, 'It would be completely out of character if Brad Morgan had had anything to do with it – he would have no logical reason' and left it at that.

'Are you certain? His timing could be a clue. Wasn't he tied up with the system that you monitor at the Augem Group?' Henderson asked.

'Yes, he was – but what has that got to do with anything? Besides, there is no way he could have known that our relationship with the Augem Group was about to change' Mark countered. But Henderson's response surprised him.

'That is unless he was told by someone that things were about to change, and he decided it was time he got out. Is that a possibility?

The conversation was traveling down the same path that Mark and Dusty had gone along the day before. In the end, it was going nowhere because, in the absence of Brad in the flesh, this was mere speculation. Mark exchanged glances with Dusty – it was time to terminate.

'Well - we would only be speculating. We have had no contact with Brad, so until you guys can come up with something, we are as in the dark as you people appear to be' concluded, Mark.

Henderson hesitated.

'Have you tried to contact Morgan since our discussion on Saturday?' he asked.

When Mark replied in the negative, he hurriedly finished the conversation with a noncommittal 'We'll look into it.'

The line went dead.

Dusty seemed unimpressed.

'Ok – it now seems certain that Henderson knows that you have cut a deal with the Augem Group. It would not surprise me in the least that he knows all the details. The question is—who told him?'

'Well - he did not get it from me!' replied Mark. 'You were right. Henderson is on the Augem payroll. And what other reason could there be but drugs? What a mess! But thank God we are out of it.'

Annette interrupted them – and she looked worried.

'It is a call from New Zealand – from your mother. She sounds pretty upset!'

Now that would have to be unusual. His mother never got upset. And as for displaying any emotion, that was unheard of!

'Ok – put her through' Mark said, not looking forward to the conversation. It was not that he did not love his parents. He did – and that was ok, provided that is they stayed as far away as was possible from Mark's personal and business life.

'Mark – it is your mother' the conversation commenced. It sounded to Mark as though mother was her normal self. Then what Mark was used to as normal was aloof and arrogant in anyone else's language. He had no idea how Annette could get the impression that his mother was upset unless that is it was a women's thing. She was so cold and emotionless.

'I am afraid that I have some unwelcome news for

you. Father is in hospital. And it is serious. He wants you to come down to New Zealand immediately.'

The immediate part of his mother's message was delivered to leave no doubt that she expected Mark to comply. She prattled on about how serious he was, but in the same breath told Mark not to worry. How could his father be in a serious condition, and still be able to issue an edict that Mark stops everything and see him? It was not as though they were in the same town! He had requested Mark to travel to the bottom of the world. But his mother's view was 'not to worry? However, there was a finality in the way his mother delivered messages that other people would find either disturbing or amusing. The inference that 'Father' had requested Mark's attendance was of doubtful reliability – unless he was close to death. What was certain was that she had issued a virtual order. It was expected that Mark would carry it out.

Mark thought about further discussion but knew that it would be futile. In any case, he could now easily afford the trip. And, apart from the odd hiccup – the 10-million-dollar deal, the break-in, the missing Brad, his having to reallocate people and resources, his newfound relationship with Annette, and a million and one other things that were reliant on him – there was not anything to stop him going was there?

Mark had forgotten to switch off the speakers after his talk with Henderson. Dusty and Annette were well aware of what was going on. Dusty knew all about his mother and therefore knew that Mark could choose to ignore the command. Annette was a woman and therefore would expect Mark to comply with the command, simply because firstly his father was ill, and secondly his mother had requested his presence. Mark had to make a decision.

The first of many that over the next few weeks would lead him to some interesting places.

And into no end of trouble.

'**Ok – I** will arrange to be on the first flight I can. Give father my best regards' replied Mark.

Most other families would have shown more emotion. Not the Taylor family.

Mark's comment 'I will see you in Wellington' was met with his mother's reply, 'Be as quick as you can!' The connection was then terminated without any apology for disturbing Mark's otherwise mundane life or any display of anything that could be even remotely construed as emotion.

Dusty had to say something.

'Can you afford to do that? I am not talking about the money. You are needed here! You know what your mother is like!'

But, knowing the Taylor's, Dusty knew that he was pushing shit uphill with a fork.

Mark just shrugged before replying.

'I will just go down and come straight back. I would rather the word came directly from my father, but he is incapacitated. And you do know my mother. She would not ask if it was not serious.'

He had a visitor's Visa to get into New Zealand which was still current from a previous trip. Consequently, there were no worries on that score – were there?

'Annette could you please check on flights to connect with Air New Zealand or Qantas International out of Los Angeles. I will leave New York in the morning' he added, rather more forcefully than was necessary. Annette understood and smiled.

Dusty did not understand but still smiled. He had to ask.

'Ok – so Mr ten times millionaire – who is going to run things while you are away?'

'I thought you could' Mark replied, knowing that Dusty would.

Dusty let out a big sigh, but he also knew what the answer would be. He could continue his own business from anywhere. Not that he had that much on at present that could not be deferred, as was the way with lawyers arguing money issues. He quite enjoyed the variety that Taylor Software provided.

And there was always Annette to keep him company.

'Ok – let us just sort out what we have got. Do you want the NYPD and FBI to continue poking around, or should we call it quits?' Dusty asked, in a tone of voice that suggested he had already made up his mind on the subject.

'What do you think?' Mark asked, but with his mind already on other things.

'As if what I think matters!' Dusty responded, obviously not exactly in agreement with Marks' travel plans. He continued talking having realized that this was one argument that he could not win.

'Ok – I'll tell you what I think. I think you have just escaped from a drug cartel with yourself, your company, and your bank account intact. I still think that one of your staff—Brad Morgan—was involved and took off before he got caught. The FBI has now inferred that they don't know anything and that will remain their position, The reason that? They have no interest. I think – if you keep your head down and ass up just doing what you are good at— you will do well. Therefore, I think the sooner we get rid of the FBI and the NYPD the better we will be. The sooner we forget about the Augem Group, and particularly that John

Dubois who I haven't met, and don't particularly want to, so much the better.'

Mark was not sure that he agreed with his lawyer's assessment of the involvement of Brad Morgan. However, there was nothing to be gained by pursuing that riddle. And he had a plane to catch.

'Ok – I agree. So, I can leave you to get on with it? I will need Annette to help me pack and get my flights organized. Can you manage without her for the rest of the day?'

'As long as there is a beer in the fridge, I will survive.'

Dusty was a pushover.

'Off you go – and give my best wishes to your father.'

Mark did work at the office for a couple of hours getting things into some sort of order. Then it was time for him to go.

Mark and Annette drove through the city to Mark's apartment in Annette's car in an atmosphere of both tension and expectation. When they got there, the first thing that they did was to have some time out.

This time they went through an almost ritualistic and slow removal of each other's clothes – slowly uncovering their bodies, their hands fluttering over places as though for the first time. When eventually they were both naked, they initially stood just there just looking at each other, as though neither was willing to break the initial spell.

Slowly and carefully, Mark lowered her onto the bed. He made love to her, as passionately and caring as he could ever remember being with a woman. It was nothing like his lovemaking with his ex-wife Helen. That was like running a marathon at the pace of a hundred yards dash. And Annette clung to him passionately for some time after her orgasm. It was as if she did not want this to ever end.

But it would.

The following morning, Mark and Annette said their goodbyes at John F Kennedy International Airport. Mark was as apprehensive as any international traveller flying over the United States in the post 9/11 era. But he now had someone to come back to, so that apprehension went to the back of his mind. The sooner this trip was done and dusted, the sooner he would be back and into her arms.

He knew that working and living with someone you loved could have its problems. That was something he would have to deal with when he returned from New Zealand.

Maybe they would have children. That would solve two problems. It would be a reason to get Annette out of the office. It would also provide him with the security of a home-life that he had never looked like getting in his marriage to Helen.

As for the business, they might have been close to involvement in the drug trade, but they had escaped any harm. Brad may have disappeared but there was nothing that Mark could do about that. Even if Brad had been somehow involved in the break-in, there would be no lasting harm. Things were starting to look good.

They kissed goodbye and then Mark headed for the Departure gate. He turned one last time, wishing he could stay.

He waved and then was gone.

There was a deep sadness in Annette's eyes as she watched Mark disappear through the departure gate. She knew that she had so little time left with him.

Neither of them had any idea what fate had in store for them. Neither of them knew that Mark was heading off into an unknown that would turn his life upside down. Neither of them knew that Dusty had misread the situation – if not in terms of the seriousness of the situation – at least in terms of who had been doing what.

Only Annette had good reason to know that things would be quite different. She feared that she would never see Mark again.

The problem was that she just did not yet know how much different things could be. She had a fundamental problem. Now that she had established a very personal relationship with the Boss, at last, she had someone who she could talk to about it.

But now was not the time.

He had problems of his own.

She would talk to him when he returned.

That would not be too late.

Chapter 10

Wellington – New Zealand

The long flight down to New Zealand allowed Mark to have a well-earned rest. On reflection, he had had no more than a couple of periods of uninterrupted sleep. That was from two alcohol-induced periods of sleep—since that meeting with the Augem Group Board on the previous Friday.

It seemed like a lifetime had elapsed since then. There was so much going on in his life at the present that he hardly had the time to catch his breath. He now felt that he had things under control, despite the apparent chaos, and now this! The last thing he needed was an unscheduled trip down-under to the bottom of the world.

At least it would give him time to reflect on his newfound wealth – monetary and otherwise.
Things would only get better from here on – or so he thought.

His experience in the military forces had taught him to take sleep whenever the place and the time presented itself, and so he did. The other two rules – never miss the opportunity to take a leak, and never trust a fart – did not apply at this time.

The problem was that, while the crew on the aircraft were used to the constantly changing of time zones, very few of the passengers that they were supposed to be caring for were. The otherwise delightful flight attendant seemed to be constantly waking him up. With a cheerful smile, she would tell him that breakfast, lunch, or dinner was being served. But what the flight plan said was never in agreement with what the passengers anticipated.

It reminded him of the time he had spent in a hospital in Panama. After one of his excursions into South America, he had sickness with some unprintable name that caused the body's excretions services to go ballistic. Mark was sent into the hospital to get him away from the other members of his platoon. His commanding officer just felt sorry for all the not-so-light-hearted banter that his so-called mates heaped upon him. The fact that a brute of a nurse woke him up from the deepest sleep at midnight to give a sleeping pill was the basis of countless jokes in his unit. The unit was disbanded many years later but not before the story became folklore. Whatever the case, on board this aircraft, if the food was worth the interruption, that fact escaped Mark.

He ate mechanically, skipped the coffee, and settled back to rest. The guys on either side of him seemed to be far too preoccupied with their laptops and paperwork to want to participate in any meaningful conversation. And that was fine with Mark. For a brief moment, he thought of pointing out to the guy on his left that he was doing things to his spreadsheet that would render it useless. That may have involved either a rebuke (hey – everyone was an expert right!), or a long conversation to unscramble the mess.

If either of the men had seen Mark loading his carry-on baggage into the overhead locker, they could not have missed that he also had a laptop computer. They would have been more than a little surprised at what he had on it and even more than a little surprised at just how powerful it was. But right now, he wanted to forget about computers. His concern was what awaited him when he got to Wellington, New Zealand and that was more than enough for him to think about.

His mind wandered to thinking about his father – Harry or Harold Taylor depending on the mood that he was in. Harold Taylor had always stressed the duty of the provision of service to your country. And that was something Harold certainly did himself to the letter.

Unfortunately, unlike Mark, his father believed that the higher the rank of a person giving the orders or instructions the more right he or she had to be. Orders were to be followed to the letter – no ifs, no buts, and no maybes. Even if that meant placing yourself in danger, with no visible sign of hope or help from those providing the orders from above. If no new orders were forthcoming, you stayed focused on the last order. Heaven forbids that you should use any initiative, particularly of the type that caused you to stray from the stated objective.

Ironically, it was his father's drive and dedication to duty that had led Mark to join the military. And the same drive and dedication that made Mark seek to excel at whatever he tried.

That was why he had ended up amongst the elite of the United States fighting forces. First in the Marines, then Special Forces and the Delta Force. But that drive, and because Mark was good at everything that he tackled, led him into places where he had some serious doubts that Uncle Sam had any right to be.

Much of the intelligence, and many of the orders, he

received in the field were often totally out of context and bore little resemblance to the reality of the situation that Mark found himself in. Orders like Take him alive when the only way to save your ass was in a firefight where there could only be one winner. Did they want or expect the enemy to stay alive until they produced a better plan? Probably.

Mark chose to ignore the more obvious flaws in the intelligence data and the orders that he received. He did his job as best he could and as he saw it – dealing with what was in front of him. That at least ensured that he could stay alive. And that he could write a report that matched reality.

After all, dead people draft terrible reports.

But not his father. Now lying in a Wellington hospital bed, supposed to be fighting for his life and about to die. But until the order came down from on high, patiently waiting for the order to do so.

The sad thing was that his mother had got caught up in the same insane attitude – she got increasingly like her husband as she got older. Consequently, there were few outward signs of affection in the Taylor family. Just a duty.

Now his father was critically ill, described by Mother as He is not too good – could soon die – but in the absolute best of hands.

Mark was concerned, hence he had dropped everything and taken off down-under. But he was dreading his arrival. While he loved his father and mother, he was happy that they stayed as far away from him as possible – and Wellington New Zealand certainly qualified on that score.

The flight finally landed at Auckland International

Airport at 2:40 pm, or so the passengers were informed by the still cheerful crew. He could understand their cheer. They would shortly go off duty. Off for a cool beer and – well whatever off-duty airlines crew did when they have a break in a foreign but friendly land.

Mark had work to do. He was still at the wrong end of the North Island of New Zealand. The flight centre back in New York had cheerfully told him that he would be wait-listed on a more-or-less connecting flight from Auckland to Wellington. At the time of receiving this information, he was not overly concerned. Partly because getting to the same country was the number one priority. And partly because – well New Zealand was a friendly enough place, someone would find him a seat. And there were not that many people down there.

He was rudely awakened to the reality of the situation he found himself in when he presented himself to the New Zealand immigration counter. Mark had been into several countries, some with the knowledge of the local officialdom, some without that knowledge. The latter did not require him to pass through immigration. When he had met with officials, his body language was such that there was rarely a problem.

This time he had stated on his entry form that he was visiting relatives, and that was true. The immigration official was very polite but wanted to know more. So, he told him his father was in Wellington hospital, seriously ill, and that was also true. He had a current visitor's visa so what was the problem?

The ability to read body language was a pre-requisite for the officials – it was also an ability that Mark had. The immigration official seemed to want to believe him, so why did the guy continue to indicate that he did not believe him? But he finally let Mark through after what seemed like a very long and very pointless discussion.

Then it was the turn for New Zealand Customs. Although Mark had nothing to declare and therefore should have gone through the green lane, the first Customs official he met politely asked him to go down the red lane. There his bags were examined, and particular interest was shown in his laptop computer. The question that was asked was quite simple and logical.

'Why – if you are visiting relatives – do you need a laptop?'

Mark's answer was, quite reasonable. That he was in the software business and liked to be in touch with his office via email.

No – he could not use Internet Cafes because he had software on the machine that he might, in fact probably would need to refer to if one of his clients back in the US had a problem.

No – he was not planning on selling any software in New Zealand. And – Yes – he had more than enough funds via his business and personal credit cards to survive without becoming a burden on the New Zealand taxpayers.

They eventually let him pass, but again – Why did the guy want to believe him but still had to ask these questions? It was all very pleasant and friendly – not like the treatment that would be meted out to a visitor to the United States.

Mark found it difficult to understand, and more than a little frustrating.

The only thing that the two sets of officials seemed to have achieved was to delay Mark's entry and to waste his time. Marks' reading of their body language was that they were very pleased with their efforts. But why?

However, the weather can also be even less friendly.

Mark found that out when he rolled up to the Air New Zealand transfer/information desk. There was no seat available until tomorrow morning because Wellington had been closed by fog. And the airline was trying to clear the backlog. Fog in Wellington? From its reputation as being one of the windiest places on the planet, the fog seemed to be something of an enigma! He patiently and quite reasonably explained that his father could be dead by the time he got there. Again, the girl was very friendly and appeared to sympathize with his predicament. Nonetheless, she ignored his plea. Would he like to be booked on tomorrow morning's 11:35 am flight or would he like to be wait-listed on tomorrow's 9:20 am flight?

Mark decided that neither option suited his purpose.

He went off in search of a telephone.

He rang his mother's mobile telephone but all he got was her answering service. Obviously to his mother, in a crisis, the telephone was not an important instrument. She was probably sitting dutifully by her husband's deathbed, not wishing to be disturbed (correction—his father to be disturbed) so she would have switched the telephone off. Mark thought that this was just plain dumb. However, there would be little point in saying anything to his mother when or if he was eventually able to speak to her. He disconnected the call.

Next, he went to the Hertz counter and arranged to hire a rental car. Yes—he had driven on the left-hand side of the road before (but omitted to say where).

No—he did not want the top of the range automatic (he had an eight-hour drive and wanted something to do – and on New Zealand roads the power was wasted anyway).

Yes—he would pay by Credit card – take your pick – would 10 million dollars be enough?

No—he did not require a travel guide for the City of Sails.

No—he did not need a map – rental firms provide maps, but he remembered when flying into Manchester England. He asked for a map to get out of the car park. They gave him a map of Europe!

The lady making out the paperwork was in no hurry and that was unusual for the Hertz operation. And the questions just kept coming. He did not normally require full insurance cover, but it seemed that was the only way the lady would let him go. Since money was not an issue—what the hell! It was almost as though she did not want him to have the car.

Eventually, he managed to prise a set of keys out of her hand, and he was on his way.

The next stop was at the local telecommunications dealer – Telecom—to get a SIMM card that would enable people ringing his US cellular number to get patched through to his telephone. He had not planned to purchase Telecom, but it appeared that way – the SIMM was more expensive than a new phone!

He called his office in New York, knowing that he would only get voice mail at that time of day – or rather night the day before – but he would leave a message for Annette to say he had arrived safely. It seemed strange to be leaving a message for Annette – he rarely left messages for his ex-wife in case she picked up the phone and he had to talk directly to her. But now Annette was important to him, and he was actually more than a little disappointed, and unrealistically so, when she did not answer. He left a message, and immediately regretted what he had to say when he disconnected. It seemed so impersonal and inadequate and did not say what he was feeling.

'Hi, I have just arrived in New Zealand, and now have to drive down to Wellington. If anything is happening that I need to know about, you can call me on my cell phone. Talk to you later.'

It was all so business-like and impersonal, yet their relationship had now become very personal.

Next, he purchased a couple of cans of drink, some fruit, and a knife to cut it up with, made a last visit to the toilet, and then, at last, he was on his way.

He maneuvered out of the Auckland Airport traffic which, even by Auckland standards, was diabolical, and eventually made it onto the main highway heading south. He settled back for the long drive. It was now 5:15 pm and it would not be very long before the sunset. Under normal driving conditions, he could expect to arrive in Wellington at about 2:00 am, so he planned to stop on the way and have a sleep since the whole country would also be asleep. Driving four hundred and fifty-odd miles in New Zealand on roads that you hardly knew was not such a daunting task, apart from their winding nature. There is after all only one highway which, in a more developed country, would be described as something less.

Well, there are three ways to get from Auckland to the centre of the North Island of New Zealand. Once there, there is only one road to Wellington. He elected to travel through Te Kuiti and Taumaranui which would lead him around the west side of Lake Taupo and Mount Ruapehu.

As he began to approach the central plateau where volcanoes were the main feature, there was virtually no traffic around. That is except for one car that seemed to be keeping a discrete distance between itself and Mark's car. No matter whether he sped up or slowed down, the vehicle just kept coming inexorably on maintaining the same distance between them.

After a while, the monotony of the following vehicle began to irritate Mark. He pulled off into a rest area and got out for a stretch. And waited. He was, after all, not in any hurry. But nothing came. It was as if the other vehicle had simply disappeared.

He pulled out onto the road and carried on. And before long, there was the 'other' vehicle following at the same discrete distance. Mark was confused. Very few people knew where, or even who, he was. He was only visiting the country for his father's sake. It was not like he was once more off on a deployment with the Special Forces on some covert service mission that would require other people to take a genuine interest in his movements. Then he would have had to take evasive measures. And he was very good at that.

Mark initially thought that he was being paranoid. But he convinced himself that he was not, and he could not let the matter rest.

The following distance seemed to be about a half-mile. Whether Mark sped up or slowed down, the gap remained the same. He had taken the National Park route to get through to Wellington and he had a vague recollection of a long passing uphill lane that led up to the National Park village on the volcanic plateau. He bided his time until the hill came up, and then accelerated. In the distance, he could now see the other vehicle approaching the hill. He knew that there was no way the other car could be hidden – short of driving off the road. And in this terrain that was certainly not recommended.

Making sure that there was no other traffic, Mark executed a near-perfect high-speed reverse and ended up heading back down the hill. He doubted whether the other driver was aware of what had just happened, but the other vehicle seemed to slow initially, and then speeded up again. But Mark was having none of that. He veered right and headed directly for the other vehicle. The driver then seemed to get the message, but unlike the reaction of someone being car-jacked, the driver pulled up as Mark's car nudged the car onto the roadside.

The driver, whoever he or she was, was very confident of their ability to handle the situation. Mark was confident too.

Both drivers shot out of their respective cars, one with an indignant look at being stopped in this strange way, the other with a confident smile on his face.

'Now tell me why you are following me? – and more to the point how?' Mark demanded to know. The smile was genuine. So was the implied threat.

The other driver was a young male – maybe in his late twenties – but he was not lacking in self-confidence. He was impressively dressed in a grey suit, white shirt, and a tie. That did not seem to be the recommended attire for a long drive, especially at this time in the evening, and more especially in New Zealand. He was however all innocent as he replied that he was not following anyone, just driving south.

Mark's response would have left no doubt that this reply was not to be believed.

'I have been followed before, by experts. While you are no expert, you are following me. I would like to know how and with what in mind?' The young man hesitated, and then seemed to make a decision. All the time watching Mark's face for some tell-tale sign.

'We were expecting a guest on your flight into Auckland. You were the most likely candidate. So, we decided to follow you to find out where you were going.'

Mark did a quick assessment. There could be no issue with this visit. Unfortunately, immigration services had access to all sorts of information, some good, and some bad. Countries defending their borders sometimes turned people away who had questionable backgrounds. Sometimes they let them enter their country in the hope that they would lead the powers that be onto other much larger and more important "fish". Mark had been into some strange places where the border control people would have no idea that he had even come or gone. On other occasions, he had gone into places with their knowledge. In the first case places like Colombia and Iran. In the second case places like Pakistan, Afghanistan, and Iraq to mention a few. It was therefore not unreasonable that the Kiwis would be suspicious but in a friendly sort of way.

He tried to bluff, but with knowledge on his side.

'What on earth would the New Zealand Security Intelligence Service want with me? I left the military five years ago, and now run a little computer software company in New York City. I thought I had left all this cloak-and-dagger stuff behind. I am just going to see my father in Wellington – who incidentally is lying critically ill in hospital. So, if you don't mind, leave me be. You've got the wrong guy pal'.

The other man could not help but look embarrassed. He was fairly new at the game and did not like being sprung so early in his career. But that was good news to Mark. This was a low-level, low-priority, operation. For all that he knew, the tail had been set up to give the locals something to practice on—no more no less. So, Mark shrugged his shoulders.

'Ok, if you must follow me try to make it less obvious!'

He turned to leave and then added.

'I will be having a sleep soon so try not to wake me when you search my car' and with a wink, he returned to his car and proceeded up the hill.

Mark could not help but smile at the idiosyncrasies that were bugging him on this trip. A trip that should have been free of all the nonsense normally associated with more clandestine or covert operations. He could now see why he was delayed in immigration, customs, and at the Hertz counter. Every bureaucracy, be it secretive or otherwise, had to go through the same ritual. Unlike in the movies where agents were plentiful, and they all of them magically knew the plot - someone had to decide first what had to be done. Then they had to decide what resources were required. Then they had to assemble the resources. Finally, someone had to be briefed on what was expected of them.

This all takes time to get set up. And that is where the secretive nature of the exercise gets a little mixed up. The person doing the actual job had to report to someone. They were government servants and they worked reasonably standard hours. So, with the guy on a night-time mission and traveling the length of the North Island, there had to be at least two, and possibly three people he reported to depending on the time of day or night. They also had to report to someone, who also was part of the bureaucratic jungle. So as far as Mark could tell probably the whole New Zealand Security Intelligence Service was in on this one.

The SIS was by no means large and New Zealand was not exactly the kind of place where security and intelligence matters were big news.

The problem with New Zealand is that if you are driving from A to B any two people can do it on the same road, at approximately the same time of day or night, and never actually see one another. That is unless they stop for gas, or a feed at the same place.

When Mark pulled into the Shell service station at Waiouru for petrol, a visit to the toilet and a snack, the representative from the New Zealand SIS could do nothing but go to a competing Caltex service station on the opposite side of the road, do the same things, and watch. The only reason that Waiouru exists is that the New Zealand Army has a base there. Otherwise, it would be too cold and remote for even hardened Kiwis to bother.

Mark got back into his car and drove off, waving to the SIS man as he did so. He only went a couple of miles down the road and pulled into a rest area, switched off the engine, got into the back seat, locked the doors, and curled up apparently for a sleep.

But he did not sleep.

He watched.

The following car did not appear despite their earlier encounters, which suited Mark's purposes admirably. Eventually, a four-wheel-drive vehicle pulled into the rest area and the driver got out for a rest, a stretch, and a smoke. This presented Mark with a chance to do some mischief.

He carefully got out of the car on the left side, went around the back, and felt behind the bumper until he found what he was after. The device that someone had attached during his "processing" at Auckland was being used to track him. It was a fairly crude device but effective. A simple magnet held it in place. It would have had a detectable range of several miles.

Mark then walked over to the man who was having a smoke, said hello, and then gave him some bad news.

'When you pulled in, I think I noticed that one of your rear lights was not working. Would you like to check it out?'

The man looked as if he had a few drinks too many and did not seem overly concerned. That was not Mark's problem.

'Which one?' was his response.

'Well, if you just turn the lights on for a minute we will see.'

The man dutifully got in the cab and turned the lights on.

'Ok, it seems to be alright now, must be a loose connection or something. Better have it looked at when you get home. Anyway, no harm done, I'll see you around.'

Mark did a plausible imitation of a kiwi accent and waved goodbye. He then got into his car and drove out of the rest area back onto the road south and was on his way.

If the man in the 4WD noticed that Mark did not have any lights on as he drove away, he did not appear to notice.

He would not have noticed the device now connected to the rear bumper of his 4WD either.

Mark drove on to the south. As soon as he saw the lights of vehicles coming in the opposite direction, he put his lights on again and continued on his way. After a while, he came to another rest area, this time on the right-hand side of the road. He pulled into it, made sure that his car was well hidden from the road by bushes, and then settled down for real sleep, setting the alarm on his wristwatch for 5:30 am.

He was awake before this time. Something going on outside had disturbed him. With him being bundled on the back seat, someone looking in could have assumed the car was empty. And because it was cold outside the inside of the windows had misted up somewhat.

The person outside appeared to be endeavouring to peer through and at the same time gently trying each door presumably stealing the car or its' contents. Mark waited until his new visitor came to the right rear passenger door, unlocked the door, and then crashed it open with his feet to get maximum impact on the would-be thief. He then leaped out himself and landed on top of the would-be intruder.

The look of fear on the young boy – Mark doubted if he was more the fourteen or fifteen-year-old—was not faked. He was petrified by this sudden attack and the sheer size of the so-called victim. But his slightly bigger and older friend was not so shocked and grabbed a knife from his pocket and made to move towards Mark. He did not get far. He was tackled from behind by another man and very rapidly and efficiently dispossessed of the knife and rendered immobile.

'It's you again!' Mark exclaimed.

The SIS man shrugged.

'I knew the training would come in handy one day' he grinned.

'Don't you ever give up? – but thanks for that pal' Mark mused. But he could see the funny side.

The SIS man had followed the 4WD vehicle to a farmhouse just north of the central North Island town of Taihape before he had realized the ruse. He had then spent the best part of the night, first heading south, looking for Mark's car, and then backtracking until he had found him. You had to give the guy full marks for his application, and all things considered, his logic was not too bad. But Mark had had enough of playing games.

He knew that people in this part of the world, even those on counter-espionage duties, did not normally carry guns. Nonetheless, he was somewhat embarrassed at having been "saved" by this young man. Saved that is from leaving two young boys very much the worse for wear.

'So – what do we do with these two?' asked Mark.

The SIS guy did his best imitation of a cop and read the riot act, taking careful note of the names and addresses that they gave. The boys innocently explained that they were merely checking out an abandoned car. A plausible story, which did not however explain what they were doing out so early in the morning, and at such a young age. Suitably reprimanded, they took off. The bemused look and shake of the head from the SIS man indicated that he would not be following up on the fictitious names that he had recorded.

Mark however was not so impressed He removed the knife that he had purchased at Auckland Airport to cut his fruit from his pocket, grabbed the SIS man, and slammed him hard against the side of the car. He placed the blade of the knife against the man's throat and gave him his last opportunity to explain. The words came from the SIS man both out of fear and out of frustration. Mostly the latter.

'I honestly do not know what I am doing. I work for the Government and at short notice, I was told to follow you and report anything that you did that was unusual.'

'What have you reported so far?' Mark asked.

'Nothing' was the reply.

'So, you do not regard my first driving you off the road, and then sending you on a wild goose chase in the middle of the night, and in the middle of nowhere, as unusual?' The sarcasm in Marks's voice was almost masked by the involuntary laughter.

'No.' came the reply.

Mark relaxed. Either this guy was a complete idiot, or he was being extremely clever. But whichever of the two, he did not appear to be in any way a threat. He had would have reported in. And, equally obviously, had been told to stay on the case – whatever that was.

'What is your name?' Mark asked, not expecting an honest reply. It beat the shit out of referring to the guy as 'You' even if the 'You' refused to acknowledge that he was from the SIS. The Security Intelligence Service was the closest thing that New Zealand had to a Central Intelligence Agency, but more a mixture of the United Kingdom Security Service – commonly known as MI5, and the British Secret Intelligence Service – commonly known as MI6 or Box 850 after a post office box number. He was unlikely to be from any other Government agency – the New Zealand Government only had one organization in the spook business. Well, it did have one other group in the security business – the Government Communications Security Bureau. If anything, that group was more secretive than the SIS. And was extremely unlikely to be found careering around the country in the dead of night on a mad-cap exercise like this one.

'Carl' was the reply

'Well listen to me—Carl. I am driving to Wellington to see my father who is in hospital. With a bit of luck, I will get there before he dies. If you want to follow me, I cannot stop you so you can. But I can save you the trouble. Simply ring your boss and tell him to meet me on the steps of Wellington hospital – and I will tell him what a good boy you have been.'

All the time Mark was pressing the knife against Carl's and some blood was starting to trickle around his neck. Just enough to make the man unsure of what came next.

But Carl was a practical man. There was no point in being killed just because this visitor had told a lie to the immigration people – about his reason for coming to New Zealand.

'But your father's not in hospital' came the sputtered reply. 'We monitor comings and goings from the US Embassy—especially Mr. Taylor and his associates. He is and always was, alive and well.'

Mark was stunned.

It was not so much that Carl knew who he was and seemed to know much more about his father. The New Zealand SIS had every right to keep track of people working in foreign embassies – even friendly ones. And of course, they would know if anyone did or did not end up in hospital. It would not however surprise Mark if his mother, at his father's behest, had tricked him into coming to New Zealand. If she had called to say father was not well, Mark would have recommended he take a couple of Aspirin tablets and have a good night's sleep. But she had stressed that Harold Taylor was close to death.

What reason could they possibly have for wanting Mark to come to New Zealand? He racked his brain through birthdays, anniversaries, and the like but could come up with nothing. What on earth was going on? Mark hesitated and then removed the blade from Carl's throat.

'We will find out then. Do not move or you are as good as dead. If you know me—and you do know something about me—I am quite comfortable with a knife. And I know that you are unarmed.'

Mark could never understand the New Zealand aversion to carrying guns, even for their local police, and yet again the look on Carl's face told him that he had guessed correctly.

Mark reached into the car and pulled out his laptop. This he connected to his mobile phone. After a few seconds, it was up and running and he went to the Web. Keying in a couple of queries he soon found what he wanted and wrote a number down on a scrap of paper. Then he switched off the laptop and entered the number into his cellular phone. After another few seconds, he got an answer in a very efficient military voice, but a recording.

'You have reached the Embassy of the United States. If your requirement is urgent, please dial 04 555 9999 now.'

Mark cut that one off and entered the new number. This one was answered by a similar military-styled voice, and this time it was not a recorded message. This time it did not say as much.

'How can I assist?' was all the voice said.

'It is urgent that I reach Mr. Taylor. Could you please tell me what time he will be in the Embassy in the morning?'

The voice was true to his word.

He did assist.

'He should be in his office by 8:00 am.'

No mention of dead or dying people. The voice did not even know who it was talking to.

That did not seem to matter. There was no hesitation.

Harold Taylor was very much alive and well.

Chapter 11

The Embassy

Mark drove to the residence that his parents inhabited in Woburn. They had lived in the same property years before and, in true Taylor style, once again had returned to familiar surroundings, Woburn was one of the plusher suburbs of Lower Hutt, a small town on the banks of the Hutt River which wound its way down the valley to end up in the Wellington harbour. New Zealand was often referred to as 'The Shaky Isles' because it was situated on several faults, rather similar to Los Angeles and San Francisco. One such major fault ran roughly south to north straight through the centre of the city of Wellington, up the side of the harbour, and on up the west side of the Hutt Valley.

The residents seemed unconcerned.

The time was just after 7:00 am he preferred if there were to be words exchanged on the subject of his father's illness, that they would be in the privacy of the Taylor family home rather than at the United States Embassy.

From what he had learned on the trip down from Auckland, he was none too pleased with the fact that it appeared that he had been misled. At least for now he would let matters take their natural course and see what happened. While the SIS attempt to follow Mark was amusing, there was a serious question still to be answered. What was it about the Taylor family that had attracted so much attention?

As he pulled into the drive his progress was obstructed by what was a rental car parked by the front door. The garage doors were closed but the garage was usually reserved for his father's car and a small runabout dinghy that his father used for infrequent fishing trips. There was no sign of his mother's car, so he surmised that she had had yet another accident and was using a rental. He was wrong.

He got out of the car, strode to the front door, and rang the bell. It was answered by his mother. The greeting was not exactly warm for her favourite son. Mark did not expect anything different. His mother was not the warmest person on the planet.

She was quite tall for a woman, being about five feet ten, but she carried it well. Her hair was short and if it were not for the colourful blouse and the long black skirt she could quite easily pass as a man. The sternness of her face did nothing to kill that impression. There was no sign of makeup to hide the grim lines that rimmed her pale blue eyes and her mouth. There was not even a smile.

'Mark! – Well, hello – you must be very tired after your trip. You look as though you are not looking after yourself again. But do come in – a friend of yours is waiting to see you in the drawing-room.'

It was rather like the greeting from an old, discarded aunt. Cold, a matter of fact, business-like – not a hint of affection – though deep-down Mark knew something close to that was probably there.

'Hi, Mother. How is Father?'

'Mark, we can talk about your father later. He has gone to the Embassy early and that is where he wants to see you, but first your friend!' She turned around and briskly walked towards what Mark assumed was the drawing-room.

To say that his old friend Paul Williams looked like a drowned rat was an understatement. But there was no mistaking the body language. He was pissed off.

Paul was not as tall as Mark but had the appearance of being strong and wiry. The time that he had spent with Mark, and others, in places left unsaid, had left a face that was permanently scarred, and one that now looked worried. The soft blue eyes held a much gentler look. Mark knew that was only when he was amongst friends. From the look on his face, he did not regard the present company as his friends. Which Mark found curious.

'How are you, Paul? What are you doing on this side of the world?' Mark enquired of his buddy from way back.

'I would love a beer' was Paul's immediate reply. 'I've never liked flying but having to fly all this way Economy Class just sucks.'

Mark laughed. He had not seen Paul since they had left the Special Forces at the same time five or so years ago. Unlike Mark, Paul was not particularly muscular, although they were of a similar build, and like all men who had served in the elite of the US armed services. He had about him an air of strength and purpose. He was not the kind of guy you would like to get on the wrong side of. Mark had heard through mutual friends that Paul had joined the Central Intelligence Agency. That he also found rather curious.

Paul did not like bureaucracy or red tape, and he

certainly did not like the intelligence morons of which the US government had more than its' fair share. More of an issue with Paul though was the number of times they had gone into the field with what turned out to be faulty intelligence. Paul often swore that, if he ever met the bastard who supplied it, he would kill him.

Now he appeared to be working for that very organization that supplied it! At least, after a few years, Paul had begun to realize that it was not the fault of field agents, but rather the reporting and analysis systems that completely fucked up what was otherwise good data.

Strange, but then it was hard for men who left the armed services to find a job. There was not much demand in the civilian world – well the law-abiding part of that world—for people, whose Curriculum Vitae placed a major emphasis on the skills and ability to kill people.

Mark had been lucky. He had an interest in and was skilled in computers. Paul was first and foremost a soldier. So, for him, it was either work for a security company or find work with some federal agency that would understand and need his particular skills. In that case, the CIA seemed about the only reasonable choice that Paul could make.

Paul, like Mark, had kept up his fitness, though his hair was greying and the expression on his face looked like he carried half the world on his shoulders. In different circumstances, Paul could be good company – affable and with a sense of humour and always ready to talk – but now he was far from happy.

They walked into the drawing-room and selected a couple of seats well away from Mother who had gone off to make some coffee.

'Well—are you going to tell me what you are doing

here and what this is all about, or are you just going to sulk?'

Mark asked anticipating that there was more to Paul's foul mood than he had expected.

'Yes – I suppose you deserve an explanation' Paul began with a sigh. 'That is why your father is waiting for you at the Embassy. My job for the moment is to let you know a little of the background, and then your father will fill in the gaps. But we have got some real problems. Your father seems to think that we need some outside help – and specifically your help.'

'Well, that is nice' Mark began.

'It would perhaps help me if there was not so much of the cloak and dagger stuff to get me out to New Zealand in the first place. You, or whoever you are working for, did not choose the ideal way or the time to be assured of getting help from anyone. I would describe lying about my father's health as deceitful and obnoxious and that is being kind. Against that background, you are assuming that I am prepared to help. Why me? I have a business to run these days, and you have not exactly picked the most convenient time to drag me away from it.'

The fact that Paul never questioned why Mark had concluded that someone had been lying struck Mark as strange, but he would not pursue that question just yet.

Paul looked a little embarrassed.

'That is a matter that you will have to take up with your father – it was his idea. But I have to admit I probably pushed him a little.' he added with a laugh. 'If we can dispense with the theatrics for now and explain what is going on, you will begin to understand.'

'I can't wait' said Mark without a lot of enthusiasm. 'But what has, whatever it is, got to do with my father and then with me? Since when did the business of running an office in our foreign service, and in—of all places—New Zealand, require people to be deceitful. He, or you. could have said that you wanted some help in New York and I could have saved a lot of time, effort, and money by saying "No" to you there! Haven't you people heard of the telephone?'

Paul still looked embarrassed, but this time his response caused a cold chill.

'Your father does not just run an office at the United States Embassy Mark. He is the head of the Central Intelligence Agency in this part of the world.'

Mark just stared and then quietly mouthed a question that he now knew the answer to.

'Since when has he been working for the CIA?'

Did Mark sense sympathy in Paul's attitude?

He looked at Mark and with a sigh replied.

'Since before you were born.'

Paul got no response from his friend, who just stared at him. Not in disbelief. But from someone who had realized his worst nightmare. His father had listened to Mark recounting stories of his exploits as a marine and had never as much as hinted that he would have – could have – should have known about. Mark would not have commented on the faulty intelligence that affected those exploits because he was bound by the code of silence that he had sworn to as a Marine.

Mark's voice went very cold.

'You had better tell me what this is all about.'

The two retired Marines sat just looking at each other for several moments. The trust that there was between the two friends, which had been built up over many years and in many long forgotten, and some never to be forgotten, places, prevented any anger or animosity from emerging. But that was a close call.

'Ok—let me start at the beginning' Paul began.

'During the cold war in particular, but also at other times, we had quite a number of companies in the finance business through which we channelled funds to finance various intelligence operations. They handled money to pay people to buy things that would have raised a few eyebrows if we had put them through, shall I say, more conventional government programs. Of course, those companies that we selected had to be genuine operators in the financial markets. They had to have valid business interests and had to have a proven track record. But control of the whole operation was somewhat loose.'

'You mean that money went missing?' Mark asked.

He had heard stories of such operations. And it was not just from Hollywood. If the Government was into clandestine operations that involved handing out money, then some very smart businesspeople would be in on the deal. But for all the wrong reasons.

'Partly that' Paul replied. 'But also, some operations that were funded in this way were completely off the record. And some companies were using the funding to finance operations of their own.'

'What do you mean operations of their own?' Mark asked. 'Surely, they were not able to use intelligence assets, as you people call the men in the field, for non-government work?'

'No!' Paul replied. 'As far as we know there was none of that. Although we have a suspicion that some agencies and agents may have been double-dealing. We had to assume that the finance companies would not risk being caught double-dipping. But there are always exceptions. Some operations that were not in the best interests of the good Ole USA we believe were funded through the same financial services that we were using.'

'Surely the selection and choice of companies, and the people selected to be in the know on such a scheme, should have prevented that.'

Mark was beginning to get the picture. Few people would be able to resist the chance of getting their hands on government funds. Especially funds where the controls were, by necessity, not too strict. And there was naturally a system in place to cover all the tracks to obliterate them. An ideal environment for crooks and the USA, and in particular the finance industry, had its' fair share of those. But although it did not sound good, Mark had no idea what it all had to do with him.

That was unless Dusty's opinion that drugs were involved was closer to the point than Mark had given him credit for. Why not use such a funding system to launder money. Keep the clean, albeit secret, government money and pass on the money you wanted to launder? In that case, if you got caught out, or something went wrong, you could always point the finger back at the Government!

'It was not quite so simple Mark. You know what it is like in any business. You cannot control everything. People talk, especially between the sheets. And the personnel change or the people themselves change over time. The process was designed to be well disguised but there were inevitable leaks. The people we chose were very clever, in ways I am afraid that the government could never be and failed to appreciate. As new people joined the various companies, some became aware of what was going on. We ended up not knowing who we could trust and what was going on, so we had to get out. But the networks that we had set up had to be dismantled as carefully as we had set them up. The whole thing was a nightmare.'

Paul took a long swallow of the coffee that Mother had produced and had just as quietly and unobtrusively disappeared once more. He glared across the table at Mark as though it was his entire fault.

'So, I still do not know—what has all that got to do with me?' Mark asked.

'The Augem Group was one of those companies.'

'The Augem Group was one of the better ones' Paul continued, his tone and his body language almost adopting the guise that they were conspirators. 'At least we thought so—and we continued to use them through the Eighties and Nineties and even today.'

'Hang on!' Mark objected. 'During the share market crash in the eighties, Rob Augem had to go to the market begging someone, anyone, to bail him out. Why didn't the government help him then? You must have known what was going on, and if the company was reliable, and you still needed a front, why did no one help him?'

'You might recall that at the time you and I were barely out of our nappies. So, this had nothing to do with me! For fuck's sake let me give you the background!' roared Paul. But, just as quickly, he calmed down. 'As I said, the controls were a bit loose, and it's all very well to have the benefit of hindsight. We – and we I am talking about is the entire United States security and intelligence service, let what happened happen – we could not get too involved otherwise the cover would be blown—and the result seemed ok.'

'What do you mean – seemed?' Mark asked.

'Well, this is where we have to go off the record. But – Shit—we need some help.'

Paul waved at the doorway with a gesture that could have been misinterpreted, but since two more coffees arrived in double quick time, the gesture was not. Mother once again vanished as quickly as she came, but Mark now had the message that she was not too far away – and listening to every single word. She must have heard some strange conversations over the years, and heaven knows what she thought of – or did with—that information.

'I had been doing a little bit of research into some related matters. I stumbled onto the Augem situation quite by chance, I can't even remember how, but that doesn't matter. It seems that someone higher up the ladder in the Intelligence community wanted Augem to continue and ask for my opinion and that is why I did my research. And that is where you come in – who should pop up in the scheme of things but one Mark Taylor.'

'What are you talking about?' Mark exploded. 'I would have thought that having an ex-Special Forces guy providing security services to a company that was effectively on the CIA payroll would give you or your masters some degree of confidence!'

'That's the whole point! When you surfaced to provide the Augem Group with a system that had enough security features to look after Fort Knox and make even Bill Gates and his Microsoft operation blush, we should have leaped at the chance to tighten the screws. Except for one thing. Someone in the CIA decided that you – Mark— had been turned and, shall we say, were working against the best interests of the United States.'

'You can't be serious!' Mark responded. But from the look on Paul's face, he realized that he very definitely was.

'Well, let me continue, so you can get totally pissed off. The Augem Group didn't raise their heads out of the bushes until sometime after 9/11. Then they got really serious about security.

'There was nothing unusual about that. The whole world got serious!' Mark retorted.

'Yes, but at the time we suspected the Augem Group

of some involvement with the funding of terrorist organizations. That as you well know is only a small step away from funding terrorist operations. Although they were only small players – at least we thought so – there was a chance they could lead us up the chain to other more important players. When they started looking at security, we were, shall I say interested, because that could have had an impact on what we were planning.'

'Which was?' Mark asked.

'Come on Mark. You know how the system works. We wanted to take a peep into their computer and communications systems.'

Mark couldn't help laughing. The Augem Group had hired Taylor Software to set up a security system to make sure that no one could get in, and that would include the CIA, the FBI, the NSA, and God knows who else! Was that the reason why Augem had seemed in such a hurry to have their security enhanced? And consequently, why they did not go through what is euphemistically termed the due process of seeking a supplier?

'So - because I get a job from some company that I had hardly heard off, let alone all this shit that you people conjure up from the past, which I also could hardly be expected to have even dreamt of, never mind know about, some arsehole decides that I am part of some plot to siphon off government funds. You must be – you are— nuts!'

'I did say you would be pretty angry. But there is some more if you'll let me go on.'

Mark was annoyed.

'Be my guest. I can hardly wait.'

'Think back to how you got the job. At the time the Augem Group approached you, you had the software and know-how to do the job. But you didn't have the people apart from yourself who could stand up to any kind of scrutiny. You had to find someone with at least half your knowledge, and in a hurry, and that's why you recruited Brad Morgan.'

For a moment Mark thought he was going to throw up. He still blamed himself for what had happened back in New York. According to Dusty, he had been conned by Brad. And he was still angry that the NYPD and the FBI had turned up absolutely nothing on what had happened to Morgan. Paul wasn't to know that, was he? So, it was unfair to sound off at him. But how did Paul know anything about Brad Morgan and more to the point, how much did he know?

'How do you know about Brad Morgan? How much do you know about my company and its' employees? What has – or had—Brad got to do with any of this? He was very bright and knew his stuff, but you're surely not about to confirm Dusty's opinion that he was working for them!'

'No. Brad Morgan was working for us.'

Mark almost jumped out of the chair.

'It certainly is a great organization you work for Paul. All you had to do was ask me and I would have done whatever you wanted. You know me. You and I have been to hell and back for this country. And your organization pulls that one. But more to the point, Brad, for all his idiosyncrasies and irritations, was a good guy. But he just disappears, and for all I know, he could be dead! And I thought he was working for me. I get told by Dusty that he was probably working for the Augem Group. And now you tell me he was working for you and the CIA. Bloody brilliant!'

'Well, you know how the system works' Paul said with a smile. 'But I have some good news for you. Brad is alive and well.'

Mark could hardly believe what he had just heard. He couldn't resist a jest.

'You'll be telling me next that his partner Honey – sorry Felicity – or whatever her name was—was on your payroll too!'

'Yes - she was, and she still is on our payroll.'

'No wonder we are losing so many battles and losing the war on the criminals, drug dealers, and terrorists of this world. If you cannot trust someone with my background, there is no hope. And then you put me through all sorts of hell, first with Brad, and then with my father. You let me live with all the lies and deceit. And then you get me to New Zealand on the pretext that you want some help. You and your organization need a psychiatrist. I need a visit to the toilet.'

Mark thought about what he had just heard as he wandered off to the bathroom. From his point of view the CIA – a department of state and a, if not the major player in the security and intelligence business that should have known Mark's background—had screwed up big time. How on earth could they conclude that he of all people had been turned? And on what possible grounds?

Mark knew that he had done nothing wrong. But he had to admire them for one thing. Nobody in his right mind would have picked Brad and Felicity as being CIA.

What had he said, or done, that would cause Brad, or any of the CIA's so-called experts, to reach such a crazy conclusion that Mark was a risk?

It was almost unthinkable that it was the CIA that had raided his office and made Brad disappear. If Brad had been involved—why had they not taken Mark's "personal" backup rather than a useless Raid 5 disk? But then, if the Augem Group had been behind the raid, had they become aware of Brad's involvement with the CIA? That did not matter, did it? Why should they care?

By the time Mark got back to the table he was more confused than ever.

Paul had been thinking it through as well. He smiled as Mark sat down.

'Let me see if I can't put this into some kind of perspective. When you were looking to recruit a technical guy to help you ensure that you could pull the Augem system off, our intelligence services saw the opportunity to insert one of their own people. Never mind how we found out, but you can take my word for it – it was pure luck. At the time, the plan was to take you into our confidence if the intelligence guy got the job. He did in a roundabout way, but before we could get to you and let you know what was going on, you did a stupid thing.'

'Oh, thanks – for a while I thought I was just doing everything the CIA required – not that any of this has anything to do with the CIA. Correct me if I am wrong, but isn't this the area normally the province of the FBI?'

'I will get around to that but first, let me finish. You went and hired a Personal Assistant, probably because you wanted to get into her pants. Not that that's a bad idea from what I hear of her. You should be more careful who you take your advice from. An Augem plant and you fell for it!'

Mark went very cold. He had, since leaving Auckland, pushed his thoughts about Annette to the back of his mind.

'Now hang on. I presume you are talking about Annette Covic. Are you telling me that Annette is working for them – or is she another CIA double agent? She is just my Personal Assistant and hardly knows a thing about what we do. You guys are paranoid.'

Mark felt his face begin to redden – the next thing he expected was a comment on his recent night-time activity. He began to feel somewhat uneasy. Annette knew a ton of things about what they did – although not a lot about how – at least Mark did not think that she did. The critical thing was that he had trusted her. And to do that, he had relied on his ability to read body language. Surely – he could not have misread the situation so badly?

Paul recognized the dilemma. He could do nothing about that.

'Mark, it doesn't matter what she looks like, or what you think she knows or doesn't know. The facts are that she's probably working for them – the Augem Group'.

'This is all too much for me to take in. We are not exactly running the National Security Agency mainframe. We were just doing a simple security system, for a small-time finance and insurance company. And now we are not even doing that because we just been fired. And Annette is still working for me. Apart from the odd sort out, she now has nothing to do with the Augem Group. Have your knuckleheads put a spin on that too and decided that we're going into partnership to set up our own drug or terrorist network funded from heaven knows where?'

'It was just necessary for me to explain to you how it looked from the CIA's perspective. We are tracking the Augem Group, who have an operation whose aims we have reason to question – seriously—and you enter the scene and fowl it up just as we were, or thought we were, about to get lucky.'

'Okay – so someone decided I was bad news. But I think you can now stop this crap because presumably, that same someone has decided that now I am not bad news – never mind whether it is CIA, FBI, DEA, or any other three-lettered fuck-wit organization in Washington. So, why get my father to pretend to be dying, to get me to come all this way, to tell me that I am one of the good guys after all?'

Paul sighed.

'There are some things that I cannot tell you. I have probably told you more than I was supposed to. Best we get into the Embassy and your father can finish off the story. If I have another one of these coffees, I won't be able to sleep for a week. Also, best if, when the Intelligence head tells you the story again, you pretend that it is all new.'

'Okay I'll go with that – but just one more thing. Why the CIA involvement and not the FBI?'

'We have a mole pretty high up at the FBI.'

'You don't say!' Mark sounded surprised, but not by the mere fact. Moles in high places were not exactly rare. But hearing it from Paul did put it into a slightly different perspective.

'You have not brought me to New Zealand just to get away from the FBI. You will next be telling me that you have also got a mole high up in the CIA!'

Mark looked at Paul's face.

Paul could lie with the best of them. But he was exhausted and did not have his usual self-control. They did have a mole in the CIA as well as one in the FBI. Wasn't this getting interesting – and what a fucked-up world we live in!

'So how come I was followed down from Auckland? I suppose that was one of your agents, even though the guy implied he worked for the New Zealand SIS.'

That got Paul's attention.

'Shit! Those guys are smarter than I thought!'

Paul was almost talking to himself.

'They must have got the tip-off from someone stateside but that is not necessarily something to worry about.'

Mark told him briefly what happened on his trip down from Auckland. And he had to laugh because in the light of what Paul had just told him the story sounded like something from a comic book. In a few years, the story would be told countless times over a few beers and would simply get increasingly sillier with each telling. But right now, Paul was not laughing.

'Did he let you know anything about how they had got onto you?' Paul asked, seriously but not overly worried.

'He just said that they got the tip-off from my saying that I was coming in to visit my sick father' Mark replied, and his voice made it obvious what he thought of that.

'What he did not say was—why he was waiting at the airport in the first place. That was the only time I had mentioned to anyone outside my office why I was coming to New Zealand. And you will recall that your man Brad was not around—and it all happened too fast. Unless that was the reason for my slow progress through the airport!'

What Mark did not say was—who he had told in the office. There were only two people – Dusty and Annette – and he was certain that Dusty would have told no one.

'Well, we will find out.' Paul replied.

'They got a DPS from your name, so they could have been tipped off by someone stateside – one of ours or one of theirs or some third party is the question?'

Paul was still talking to himself.

'What is a DPS?' Mark had to ask. 'I thought I knew all the three-letter acronyms.'

'That is a Direct and Positive Sighting.' Paul answered, but he was not interested in Mark's question.

'This is getting to be a pain up the ass. We had better get to the Embassy – your father will be pissed off if you have been rumbled even before he gets to talk to you.'

'He will not be on his own' said Mark, although he still did not know why it mattered.

Paul was all concentration.

'There is one other problem I have to tell you before we go. From your reactions I think you are right – you're on our side – so now I can tell you. We cannot go to the Embassy.'

Mark was now beginning to lose it, but simply asked 'Why ever not?'

'Because we do not know who we can trust at the Embassy. We have rented an apartment which we are using as a safe house for a couple of weeks – it is just around the corner in Tinakori Road—and a couple of weeks are all we need it for. We will meet your father there.'

'A couple of weeks? Are you sure you can root out all the people you cannot trust in both the CIA, the FBI and not to mention the Embassy, in so short a time?'

'That is not what determines our timeframe. They can go fuck themselves for all I care. I will leave it to your father to talk about the timing – the timing is determined from what he wants you to do – that is all I can say.'

'Ok – there is nothing like a bit of intrigue to spice things up. We may as well go in your car – I have done enough driving for one day.'

'No!' Paul responded. 'We should go separately. That way we can check to see if either one of us is followed. I presume you can still remember all we were taught about stalking and being stalked. You have to watch your tail and if anyone looks suspicious you must lose them before you go to the house. Should someone follow you, and you cannot shake them, don't go to the safe house.'

'You cannot be serious!' Mark exploded, but just as quickly calmed down. 'Ok I will play at being a spook, but the story my father has to tell had better be good.

The drive from Woburn to the so-called rented safe house was at the morning peak hour for traffic. While Wellington traffic is nothing like New York City in terms of volume – there is infinitely less – the road structure is made for less traffic and so you get the same result—chaos.

The United States Embassy was located on Fitzherbert Terrace in Thorndon and with the traffic, at this time of the morning, it would have been a problem to get to. The road where they had rented the apparent safehouse was worse. After the long night, it took all of Mark's concentration to drive, remember once again to stay on the left, and to check for tailing spooks. But the tailing issue proved not to be a problem. Following someone and keeping a reasonable distance so as not to alert suspicion in the Wellington traffic, at this hour of the day, would have been next to impossible, no matter how good they may be.

Nonetheless, the pressure was starting to take its toll.

Mark had left the military to get away from all the politics and heaven alone knows what else that made life so rat-shit, and into a new business where at least, he was his own boss. Then the CIA had just stepped in, as if they owned the whole world, and decided who were the good guys and who were the bad guys. And then they had decided that one of their own, and probably many more than one, was bad. So then to make matters right, you fly off one of the good guys, who was previously one of the bad guys – at his own expense no less – to the other side of the world, to meet a father he thought was dying, but is apparently in perfectly good health, for – what?

He finally located the safe house in Tinakori Road and after driving around the side streets he found a parking space. It was so far removed from the house that it was extremely doubtful that anyone could have associated either the car or its occupant and the safe house. He was just another Wellington motorist looking for a park. In any case, once he had parked the vehicle, he was quite adept at slipping into the place without any fuss or bother – playing the spook game is like riding a bike.

Mark was quite satisfied that no one had observed him arrive.

The front door of the house was open, and he was met by a man who made looking ill and being serious into an art form. He was probably the thinnest man, and one of the tallest men, Mark had ever met. He wore glasses that seemed precariously balanced on his nose and because of the imbalance, with every second stride he had to touch them to keep them in place. His hair – not that there was much of it—looked as though it had not seen a comb in years. He carried in his hand a bunch of papers that looked as though they had already been through the shredder. Although the way he clutched them meant he was not about to let go of them any time soon. An altogether untidy individual – but to be at this house he must be trusted – so at least he had something in his favour – or so Mark thought. Incorrectly as things turned out.

They entered a lounge area in which three men sat surrounded by bits of paper. One of them was Paul Williams and another was his father, Harold Taylor. The third man he did not know.

Harold could pass in any learning institution as a

professor, such was his academic look. Like Mark he was tall, but he was leaner. Dressed in a dark grey suit with an immaculate white shirt and dark blue tie he was presented as Mark would have always known him – the bureaucrat.

'Hello Mark' Harold said as he stood to greet his son.

'I am sorry to put you to all this trouble, but all will become clear shortly. Mark—I would like you to meet our ambassador – William McCormick.'

Mark shook the hand that was extended towards him. Rather like shaking hands with a dead fish. The Ambassador was a typical product of the US foreign service that Foggy Bottom still churned out. Looking arrogant and cool, and totally out of his depth. The other man who had met Mark at the door was introduced as Forester and was an assistant to the Assistant Deputy Director of Intelligence of the CIA, whatever that would mean. But since the ADDI - Stephen Rodriguez - was effectively Harold's boss that would have made him fairly important in the scheme of things. Mark was not about to let his father off the hook by these distractions.

'This had better be good –I can hardly wait. I still have no idea what this has to do with me. Anyway—how are you? –enjoying playing CIA games.'

Mark could barely restrain himself from punching his old man but managed to hold himself in check. If any offense was taken at Mark's words, or his obvious demeanour, it did not show itself in any reaction from his father. The old man was all business. He seemed so at ease you would think he was in his own office. He turned to the twig and barked an order, that almost caused spectacles and papers to scatter.

The man called Forester briefly left the room and returned with what had to be a much younger man. And he was an Afro-American.

'Is this a meeting of the presumed dead or dying?' asked Mark of no one in particular.

'How are you, Brad? I suppose you are in this because you have come to collect your final paycheck.

Mark shook his hand.

It was hard not to like the guy. Sure – he had come into Taylor Software as a plant and then disappeared. He was just doing his job and Brad could not be blamed for that. But Mark could not resist having a dig.

'How is Honey?'

And that question got a surprising instant, and innocent, response.

'Fine – she is still in the States but may be involved later.'

Brad seemed more at ease, more confident, less of a geek than Mark could recall, and Mark could understand that. He had to give Brad full marks for his acting ability – and he had carried it out for so long! Now he was all business, and back to a role that did not involve acting.

Or so it seemed to the only amateur present.

The elder Taylor was bored by this small talk and quickly brought the meeting to some sort of order. A nod of the head was a signal for no less a person than the Ambassador himself to take his leave.

It was briefly explained that he had some other more urgent matter to attend to. From the way Harold Taylor looked at him as he left, Mark thought there was more to it than that. Reading body language could be a pain-up-the-arse at times.

'Mark, I need your help—we need your help. But before this meeting can go any further, we need your we need your assurance that anything you hear in this room will remain strictly off the record and go no further. It is of the utmost secrecy and God only knows there have been enough leaks so far and we cannot afford anymore.'

'Well, isn't that nice?' responded Mark. 'I know that my balls will be in the grinder if I do not say Yes. And I also know that the warning hardly matters. You have got me involved in heaven knows what. My life will hardly be worth living no matter what I do now if I do not accede to whatever it is that you want. And before I can pretend to do that, there are a few minor matters that I need to know. Like why I thought that Brad had disappeared or was dead. Why I thought you were dying. Why the CIA has fucked with my business. Why you tricked me into flying halfway around the world at my own expense – just to name a few.'

Mark struggled to keep the sarcasm out of his voice. But he could sense that the level of his voice had risen perceptibly.

'Well, yes, there are a few things that you might find hard to understand.' Harold replied in a voice that indicated he could not have cared less. Or that there were far more important things to worry about than the trivia that Mark had mentioned. He continued.

You can take my word for it that there are valid explanations for them—all of them.'

'Like I believed the call from Mother to say you were dying? What are you playing at Dad? You are sick in the head if you think I can trust you now. Of all people - the one person I should be able to trust.'

He had intended to have this conversation with his father back in the solitude of the Woburn house. Now he was having it in, of all places a Safe House. And in front of others. He had never before spoken to his father in this tone, and he was somewhat taken aback at the reaction.

His old man seemed to crumble.

The others in the room sat as though frozen in time, and there followed what was probably only a few seconds, but seemed like hours, of total silence. Then Harry Taylor looked at Mark and with a shrug commenced a long rambling monologue, the original qualification forgotten.

'You are in a unique position to do a job that we believe no one else can do. We – the CIA that is—have been penetrated and God knows how high, wide, or deep it goes. We are meeting on this side of the world because no one else, other than Brad, has accepted that there is a connection between the issues that we have identified. That position will not last. But, let me start at the beginning.'

Mark was stunned by the candour of his father and sat down without saying another word. As did the others, except that is for Forester. He stood there with his eyes glued to Mark.

'As you know, the NSA monitors all communications to and from the United States – well all over the world for that matter. Of particular concern is the internet, for two reasons. Firstly - it is so big we have an exceedingly difficult job getting a handle on it. Secondly - because of the first, it is the chosen method of communication for every criminal on the planet. We can skip the debate on the rights or wrongs of monitoring—we have to know if someone is planning any activity against our people, our country, our military, or our allies. We have to track every hint of trouble and to follow down every blind alley and hope that we do not find anything that is sufficiently suspicious to warrant further investigation.'

His father detected the raised eyebrows, not only from Mark.

'Yes – although the public may think otherwise, we do not have the time or the resources to read every email. What is more, we do not want to. Those who believe they are protecting civil liberties by raving about our eavesdropping have got it all wrong. A cop standing on a street corner watching the world go by is not invading anyone's privacy. He may be just waiting for an old lady to help to cross the road. But listen to the screams of indignation, and from the same people, if he is not there when someone else invades their privacy – by raping them or making them a victim of some other crime. No – you can believe it—we are not interested in your everyday correspondence and communications. We set flags – you of all people should know about flags Mark – that is how all good systems work. If nothing is happening, there is no flag. When something happens, a flag is raised. And, depending on the nature of that flag, you make something happen.'

'Well, a flag was raised within the FBI when John Dubois took over a company called the Augem Group. The original flag mostly concerned his background – not that we knew all that much about him. He was born and raised in Beirut in a well-to-do family and went to the University of Beirut where he graduated with a degree in accounting. There was nothing unusual about him, except that he travelled widely—to Afghanistan and later to Pakistan. And later even to the country that was formerly called Yugoslavia. Someone in the CIA made a note in the intelligence database to check on him if he ever came to the USA. And of course, he did, but at the time no one had reason to deny him entry and he dropped off the radar.'

'At the time of 9/11, the FBI was too busy chasing other phantoms to worry about him. But in the aftermath, when they were going through what they may have missed, they noticed that there had been an increase in communication involving John Dubois and various other people just before the event. This gave the FBI reason to put another flag on his file – with the intention of investigating when someone had some time.'

Mark had to interrupt—the story was getting interesting – but he had to get something straight.

'You are implying that back at the time of 9/11 John Dubois was sending emails – you have to be joking – John would not know one end of a computer from the other.'

His father's face creased in a brief smile.

'Is that just an opinion or have you got some proof? I am afraid John is more resourceful than you give him credit for. But he even fooled Brad so you should not be terribly upset that you have been conned.'

The news came as more than a surprise to Mark, and he did not miss the barb. He held his peace, and let his father go on.

'When the Augem Group decided to install some new software nothing untoward seemed to happen. That is until we found out that neither the CIA via the NSA nor the FBI could get into their system shall we say as easily as had been the case. We made some inquiries and who should now pop up on the radar but one Mark Taylor the CEO of Taylor Software. Paul has probably filled you in on what we did then.'

Paul and Mark exchanged glances. That just got a shrug from Harold.

'You had better go back a bit.' Mark interrupted. 'You are starting to lose me. Paul has told me a few things. However, if you want me to help you with whatever crazy scheme you are now planning, I must fully understand the position. From what you have said so far, just go out and arrest John Dubois.'

Mark's cryptic comments brought a sigh from his

father. The rest of them sat there in silence, engrossed in what was going on. Mark could feel drawn into his days with the Delta force when he had to put up with "briefings" by an assortment of CIA and other intelligence people. He did not accept them at their word then, and he was certainly not going to do that now unless or until he fully understood. He was now a civilian and he could just turn his back and walk away.

'Ok – I suppose I asked for that.' Harold replied. 'But it is not so simple. We cannot just go arresting people without just cause and without getting approval from a judge. Getting such authorization is not so easy. I have to tell you some more of the background.'

Forester moved around the room filling everyone's cup, and then sat down still looking at Mark, this time with a sort of reprimand. Mark did not miss the look or miss the body language – who was this guy? In the opinion of Mark, if Forester was one of his father's trusted aides, they were heading for trouble.

Mark held his peace—unfortunately.

Chapter 12

Briefing

Harold Taylor searched through the briefing papers that had been handed to him by Forester and selected those that he wanted. Then Mark, Paul, and Brad all sat there in silence as he read selected items from the briefs that recounted the history of the events that led to their sitting in a room half a world away from where Mark had started on this journey.

The papers were all stamped Top Secret—US Eyes Only so it was not surprising that he did not hand out copies to the others in the room. Although who qualified as meeting the Eyes-Only classification no one asked or said. It struck Mark as a little strange that Forester, and not his father, was the one who had access to the entire story.

In Mark's simplistic view – aided by his assessment of the body language—if you were looking for someone in an organization that was a mole – look at the person who has access to all the data. Now that was something to think about.

His father commenced reading the papers as though he was seeing the story in this amount of detail for the first time. And yet Mark felt certain that he – the only person who was not on the governments' payroll—was the only person in the room who did not know what this was all about. So that meant that the sole purpose of the briefing was to convince Mark – of what?

It also meant, therefore, that the rest of them had already agreed on a plan of action. What plan and what action? Now that was indeed curious.

Harold read from the brief in a steady monotone but no one in the room seemed to notice.

'During the Cold War as it was known the Americans participated in a full range of operations that the authorities did not want the public to know about.'

He looked up from the papers.

'Well, that was only part of the story. There were some operations that the CIA and others, but the CIA more particularly, did not want the authorities to know about. That included other security and intelligence organizations which were supposed to be on the same— that is their—side. Part of the business had something to do with deniability. It was questionable whether the main drive was such deniability, politics, or just self-interest. If you were to be pedantic you could say it was self-preservation. Whatever the semantics, it was agreed that there had to be a mechanism that enabled the security apparatus to support operations out in the field without being under constant scrutiny. That, in particular, relates to the required funding.'

That snippet of information caused Harold to again pause.

'The idea that we have a whole army of dedicated personnel working for the cause without fear or trepidation and all alone in the world always was false. Without a network of support personnel and finance and plenty of it, field operations just would not happen. If the US public knew how few actual field operators the CIA has for the dollars we appear to spend on such matters, they would scream for someone's head!'

'The answer was to set up several organizations within existing the existing business structure. The role of these was to receive money by the bucket load from various funds duly authorized by Congress. Then they would disperse the money to people they never knew, for purposes they never knew, or for that matter, cared about. It is not strictly true to say that the funds were duly authorized. Congress rarely has any idea what it was authorizing. The House Intelligence Committee oversees the mechanics of our operations. The Congress and the Senate is effectively a rubber stamp.'

Again, Harold paused.

'If the Congress or the American public ever found out how much money was shaved off various 'funds' they would again scream for someone's head. Luckily, they would be unlikely to ever be able to find out whose head they should lop off. That is unless they regard our Commander in Chief – the President—as ultimately responsible.'

Harold laughed at what he obviously thought was something funny. And it probably was. The joke escaped the rest of them. Except for Mark. He had, in a previous life, first-hand experience of executive decisions which could only have emanated from the President. Or so he thought.

From this point onwards Harold seemed to be half reading, half adlibbing.

'One such organization that had a dual purpose was the Augem Group, which in the dim distant past was headed by Rob Augem. Rob was a true-blue American boy. Shrewd and recognized amongst his peers as one of the best in the business. Because the guy had ethics – a rare commodity in any business, especially within the finance community – he kept a low profile. His company quietly made millions without being noticed. This was the ideal situation for the CIA and a deal was done that enabled Augem to become one of the chosen few. The company has since the 1960s funnelled millions of dollars to a variety of countries, agents, and other non-describable entities. The system was so good that even Rob Augem would not have known about many of the transactions. Unlike some other organizations, there was no attempt by the Augem Group to cream off anything from the funds. The money came in, the money went out, and that was an end to the matter.'

'The audits of such companies and their—well not actually their—funds, were a bit obscure. Augem, being a trusted agency, was one company over which there was only a very loose form of monitoring. Then came the share market crash, and that put a scare up the CIA and other agencies that used this kind of funding arrangement. Some of the companies simply folded. Others folded and then reconvened with new titles and carried on where they had left off none the worse for wear. Except of course for the odd millions of dollars that unsecured clients and unsecured creditors lost and committed suicide over. Some money was lost in that process, by regular means— meaning that transactions were in progress but never got completed, and by irregular means – meaning that some saw the opportunity to take a slice off the funds that no one else could ever trace.'

'Even if the authorities had been able to trace where the money had gone, it was extremely hard to distinguish between the not-so-legal things that the CIA was doing, and the not-so-legal things that the businessmen were doing. To admit such goings-on even existed was to invite some very nasty and messy Congressional, Court or 'off the radar' type action. So, the decision was made to forget it. Of course, the real reason was to save face by those who had dreamed up the scheme in the first place, but that is not our concern.'

'Amongst all this, the Augem Group was in some trouble. However, being a relatively small player, and never having caused the CIA much grief in the past, they were overlooked in the scheme of things. When the dust settled Augem had a new boss by the name of John Dubois, who no doubt fronted with his own money. The same Rob Augem, who for some reason known only to Dubois, remained Chairman of the Board – albeit a different Board. They carried on as though nothing had happened and as far as the CIA was aware there was nothing other than the minor discrepancies that occur with transactions of this nature. The CIA had no reason to be concerned – although John Dubois was a person of interest so were thousands of others. And he had become an American citizen so why worry?'

Harold paused for effect.

'And then came the events of September 11th, 2001.'

But there was no emotion.

He had not been in New York or Washington on that terrible day. Others – including Mark – had been. Harold continued as if this was merely preliminary information that he needed to get through before – what?

'Putting aside the loss of life and everything that such a shocking and terrible event encompasses, the financial markets recovered surprisingly rapidly. The business carried on, and the CIA's clandestine operations carried on, stressed to the maximum. But people still needed funds. Because of the pressure then being applied to the whole security and intelligence network, every agency had to examine what it was doing. Another organization was created to which the previous structure reported. It is doubtful whether this had any effect on the shambles that already existed, and continues to exist, in the US security services.'

'Since the bean-counters at organizations such as the CIA probably outnumbered field staff by at least one hundred to one, most attention – misguided attention—was paid to following the money. But that was hard to do. In an organization like the Augem Group, a couple of transactions are made to receive money from someone who was not supposed to be supplying it. The identity of the supplier was lost at that point – well erased. A couple of transactions are made to disperse money to someone who was not supposed to be receiving it, so therefore the identity of the receiver – if it was ever known – was lost at that point – again erased at that point. The fact that anything at all had happened was lost, erased, and gone forever.'

'There followed a bit of an argument. The people in the field had to have access to funds quickly and preferably without the bureaucratic nonsense that usually accompanies such access. And what is more, with everyone who could get within a bull's roar of a microphone demanding better intelligence, there was a need for more funding and quickly. The people who had, or thought they had or claimed that if they had known they would have, authorized funds, wanted to know where their—well, not actually their—money went, in case it was found out that some went where it should not have. But no one knew.'

'The answer to this nightmare was to take steps to follow the money more closely than had been the past practice. According to the bean-counters in the intelligence community that was quite simple to do – that is assuming someone knew where it was coming from and for what purpose. The theory was that you simply went to the agency set up to handle cases of this nature – that is assuming someone knew who that agency was. Then in turn you simply went to the recipient and made sure they got the funds and used them for the purpose that someone meant them to be used for – that is assuming that you knew who the recipient was and what crazy purpose they had. But no one knew.'

Harold took a drink and surveyed his audience. No one spoke. He had gotten their attention. He seemed oblivious to the fact that he had been talking in sentences that included so many qualifications that it would have been difficult to follow. But clearly, everyone was following the story. Or they already knew. Or, in Mark's case, he was more interested in where it would lead. Harold pulled another piece of paper from the bundle, but it was by now clear at least to Mark that he was probably not reading from them at all. But he continued talking with his head buried in the papers.

'So, having more or less failed to get any traction with this approach – in simple terms the operational side refused to cooperate—they reverted to the use of technology. After 9/11 the FBI, working in conjunction with the National Security Agency—the NSA—and various other organizations, sought to extend its monitoring of all communications both internal and external in an endeavour to trace patterns of behaviour or keywords that appeared as a risk or a threat to the USA and its allies. The NSA had this capability through its massive computer resources at Fort Meade Maryland where it has been in residence in 1957. The internet, and the massive increase in traffic that this media involved, caused a bit of a headache. But the job was quite simple. All you had to do was nominate certain words which in context were suspicious, and then observe increased activity, and bingo you had Osama bin laden by the balls. And you might at at the same time be able to find where the funds for terrorist training and planning were coming from, or at least to find out how the various terrorist operations were being funded.'

'Apart from the fact that the bad guys were on to this in a couple of nanoseconds., They could change their vocabulary so that a Boeing 767 loaded with passengers (and not to forget the tons of fuel) being used as a missile could be referred to as a fly on the wall. Nonetheless, the monitoring system did have some benefits and did, after a fashion, work. While the internet, being the preferred method of communication for most organizations on this planet, is notoriously difficult to obtain audit trails from, you can trace some communications provided you have at least a clue as to who the sender or receiver was. Then it is simply a matter of carefully sorting out specific transactions from the billions that occur. This is why electronic intelligence gathering is studying history. And why spies emphasize, and politicians for their own peculiar reasons ignore, the need for real intelligence gathering by humans.'

'The answer to the problem of simply handling the sheer volume of data is to be selective. There is still a minefield to navigate. There are smart-arse politicians— who have their unrelated agenda and could not care less about the facts of any situation. And there are equally smart-arse media types who would not know an agenda if it were stapled to their forehead. They will twist the facts to suit any situation. Comments that certain 'intelligence' information was in the hands of the authorities but not acted upon. They are deluding themselves and the public. And by the way, by the sheer volume of noise, they are deluding the rest of the world at the same time. Targeted intelligence gathering, using the available technology, and using undercover resources—some call them underhand resources but never mind—is the only way to make progress and try to keep one step ahead. That is if you know which way you or "they" are headed, and if you know who the "they" are.'

'But that is how we at the CIA got lucky if you want to call it that. The Augem Group was just a small player that the NSA and FBI systems monitored from time to time. Someone at the NSA, who had nothing better to do, took a peek at their system, and – whoops – some words popped out. Someone in Augem was communicating with someone and using language that raised issues. So, a flag was placed on their communications. Nothing too serious, not a repeat of 9/11, but issues that someone with nothing better to do could look at. These messages seemed to follow a pattern. And it was the pattern that raised another flag. The situation continued for some time – a flag was on the file, so the NSA continued monitoring. Nothing substantial came of it. They just monitored traffic and passed the information on to analysts.'

'Then, all of a sudden, the NSA could no longer get into the system, and all attempts to get around the security failed. So - they panicked. Forget for the present how we found out, but it became evident that the Augem Group was setting up a security system that even the NSA, with all its knowledge and expertise, could not penetrate. That is not in itself suspicious. People are always trying to improve their security systems, and since they are usually oblivious to what the NSA was up to, they may inadvertently disrupt the NSA monitoring systems. But since someone in the security organization had hit the panic button, something had to be done.'

'What followed this was a mixture of unparalleled inter-agency cooperation—almost unknown in the history of the US intelligence network—and unparalleled stupidity – which is much more common. The actual sequence of the events is now lost in the rabble of history, but we will try to get the order correct. The FBI pointed out that Taylor Software was the company responsible for developing the security system for Augem. Therefore, they had to be suspected of working in collusion with the Augem Group. Further investigation revealed that they had taken on a personal assistant who coincidently was also on the list of persons of interest. She was of questionable origin and certainly appeared to be more connected to the Augem Group than to the Taylor company. Digging deeper they found that Taylor Software was owned and operated by Mark Taylor. Because Mark had been in the military and had been involved in some of the more nefarious of our clandestine operations, the FBI reached the obvious conclusion that he had set his company up with funds obtained during those operations—unauthorized from authorized funds. In other words, the Augem Group had creamed off funds, originally earmarked for some obscure CIA operations, to help Mark set up his business so that they could use him for their own endeavours.'

At this point, he stopped pretending to read and looked at Mark.

'I have to say Mark that the CIA thought that the FBI's conclusion was a bit out of the leftfield, to say the least. We checked with the Pentagon intelligence people and they just scoffed at the idea and wrote it off as bureaucracy gone mad. But the fact that the Augem Group did not appear to be overly diligent in looking around the market or at the competition – they just went straight to Taylor Software – did give the FBI conclusion some merit.'

Mark merely nodded. He had wondered about that. Why the Augem Group had picked Taylor Software seemingly unexpectedly from all the computer software companies available – and many of them, at least on paper, were far better qualified? But the funding part of the story was quite laughable. Mark's Bank manager would have had some fundamental questions to ask, like – why do you need an overdraft when you have all this money coming from unknown sources to do unknown work? But more to the point, the FBI could have, and without anyone having to know should have, looked through his company's official records. They would have been able to see for themselves that the company's funding was quite legitimate. If not grossly inadequate.

The FBI conclusion had to be based on a lie. But it was reached and accepted by someone who must be quite high up the tree. This was pointing to the mole that Paul Williams had alluded to.

Mark filed that piece of information away for future reference.

The elder Taylor continued.

'Since Mark was on the lookout for technical staff, and the particular qualifications that he required were rare, the FBI came up with a brilliant solution. They would have one of their people apply for the position. That solution would kill two birds—in fact, several birds—with one stone. They could find out what Taylor Software was up to. They could find out the history of the company's financial arrangements. They could find the link between their "persons of interest" and Mark Taylor and the Augem Group. They could get back into the Augem system and find out what Augem were really up to.'

'And that is where they got even more cunning. Whoever at the FBI was orchestrating this charade rang a colleague at the CIA. That person asked if they could also provide an "applicant" for the position so that the FBI "applicant" did not seem too good to be true. The CIA in a spirit of unprecedented cooperation duly did just that.'

'Unfortunately, someone forgot to tell Mark about

whom he was supposed to select. And this was an understandable oversight given the FBI's suspicions. They also forgot to tell the FBI guy to let down his air of arrogant superiority—that is to first get the job. And this was so fundamental they probably never thought—and forgot to tell the CIA ring-in to not be so nice. That is not to seriously try to get the job. They forgot it was Brad Morgan who the CIA put forward. When Mark rang and informed Brad that the job was his if he wanted it, there followed scenes normally reserved for a comic opera. The FBI was warned by Morgan that he had a job offer. That caused the FBI guy to ring Mark to ask what was happening with his application. He got the distinct impression from Mark's tone that his application was not being further considered, even if the selected candidate refused the job. The net result was that rather than risk missing out altogether on this rare opportunity, the FBI and the CIA agreed to let Brad run with it.'

'It soon became evident to Brad that there was no truth in the FBI suspicions. Mark was not working either for or with, the Augem Group on any illegitimate or undercover activities—as had been concluded by the FBI. Mark's association with his Personal Assistant – Miss Annette Covic—while in some respects comical, was not a risk. Trust her though he might, Mark had a clear view of what need-to-know meant. There was no evidence that she was anything other than a normal Personal Assistant. It also soon became evident that there was no financial tie between Taylor Software and the Augem Group other than that of a supplier and a client. Every invoice was carefully scrutinized before it was submitted, and Mark's casual method of handling the account made it simple to conclude that everything was legitimate.'

'It also became evident that Mark was a very clever guy. The software would do exactly what it was supposed to do. It would stop anyone from inside or outside the organization, first of all, penetrating the security of the system, and second hiding anything by doing things that were not recognizable or traceable by the software. It also became evident—and this was the clincher—that the system had a pinhole through which only someone at the monitoring end—that is in Taylor Software—could take a peek at what was happening beyond the strict criteria laid down by the Augem Group.'

'Augem were unaware of this pinhole and did not look like being able to detect it. Mark was taking no chances with the Augem account and had a fall-back position of which they were also totally unaware. Conclusion – Mark was clean if a little devious. This information was fed through the CIA to the FBI. However, that failed to convince the FBI – at least whoever was driving the Taylor file—that their original suspicions were unfounded.'

'The monitoring of the Augem systems became Brad's responsibility. Mark only occasionally questioned Brad on what was happening, leaving Brad to inform him if anything outside the ordinary occurred. This put Brad in the position where he could carry out his duties of monitoring their system—what Augem were paying for and what Mark was paying Brad for—and could monitor all incoming and outgoing traffic additional to the more routine stuff—what the CIA and the FBI were paying Brad for.'

'In the course of monitoring the email traffic in his CIA/FBI role, it became evident to Brad that something was not quite right. Some transactions were going through the Augem system which, although having all the appearance of being legitimate, were connected to organizations that had nothing to do with the core business of the Augem Group – finance, insurance, and funds management. These organizations were, of all places, in the South Pacific and, even more surprising, in the former Yugoslavia. Further investigation of this email traffic pointed to a similar range of keywords and targets of messages which occasionally came onto the radar of the anti-terrorist watch list.'

'Careful analysis of the traffic, its points of origin, and keywords was then cross-checked with the NSA, and that confirmed our suspicions. Something was being planned offshore and was going to eventually lead to some kind of terrorist activity in the USA. Coupled with our tagging certain people as persons of interest, all the evidence pointed to a terrorist plot being hatched at least with the knowledge of certain people at the Augem Group. Further, the terrorist cell appeared to be of Indonesian origin but skilfully had its source of communications buried somewhere in the islands in the southwest Pacific which as we all know is not exactly at the top of the list of suspect countries.'

'Up to this point the entire process had been handled in a fairly routine manner. The normal procedure would then be that the FBI would assemble a team to follow up the threat, and the CIA would assemble a team to track down the overseas parties. But first, there has to be a meeting at the National Counterterrorism Centre feeding off the information provided by the relevant people from the FBI and the CIA. All the information was fed through to the CIA and the FBI. But nothing happened.'

At last, Taylor paused. He looked as though he had aged ten years while recounting the story. He glanced around the room resting for a moment on each face. Mark was the only one who did not quite understand the massive significance of what had just been said, but he was rapidly catching on. After a moment Taylor senior carried on.

'No meeting took place anywhere in the office of the Director of National Intelligence, no team has been assembled at the FBI and no team has been assembled at the CIA. The conclusion would have to be that several people in the security intelligence service – and yes—there had to be more than one – got together and either did not believe that a threat exists, or they simply killed the story. The problem this presented to those of us who were on the inside of the story was quite simple. If someone at the DNI had got together with someone at the FBI, had got together with someone at the CIA – where could you go in any of the three organizations to have the matter reviewed? One of the problems is that we have at least three pyramids of bureaucracy—which have never exactly danced to the same tune—in which decision making is done at a quite senior level based on papers – and options —submitted from below. Here our very own security does not help.'

'Until the threat is accepted as a clear and present danger, very few know anything at all about the story, its sources, or the field staff involved. If you go into any one of the three pyramids of bureaucracy involved in all of this at too low a level the story again gets killed. If you go into any one of the three pyramids at too high a level, you have the massive problem of all bureaucracies. Who the hell are you to question decisions made at the appropriate, but higher level than you? If, on the other hand, you go into any one of the three pyramids at precisely the level at which the decision to kill the story was made in the first place, then that is equivalent to committing suicide. What is worse, the true story, and the people who claim to know what that story is, are likely to be made to disappear.'

'So, gentlemen that is where we are at. We are the one small group of people on the planet, outside of the perpetrators of an apparent plot, and the intelligence people who killed it, who know of the existence of the story. We are not necessarily a known quantity at this stage and, as long as we do not tip them off, then we should be ok. And we should be able to implement a strategy that can at least attempt to recover the situation.'

'But the FBI or the CIA did react in one respect to the story. And it was not a reaction of the type we expected. Someone told the Augem Group.'

'What followed was again at times comical, at other times bizarre. The Augem Group was informed that Mark was clean and was not aware of the information that the FBI had acquired. They were also informed that Mark was unaware of Brad's connections to the CIA and the FBI. So, they made an immediate decision to do away with Mark's services as quickly and amicably as could be arranged and cut the link that the FBI and the CIA had established. They made an offer to purchase the system and paid a price that some would say, with all due respect to Mark, was a bit over the top. But then they had other things to attend to and the amount of money was not an issue. They knew, and accepted, that Mark and Brad had access to their systems, but wanted to be sure that they knew how.'
'While Mark was busy celebrating his newfound wealth, they planned to raid his offices to get copies of absolutely everything before Mark had the opportunity to edit out the bits, he did not want them to know about.'

'Unfortunately, there was a foul-up in communications. Someone overlooked the fact that a CIA official by the name of Brad Morgan would be working late at the time of the raid. When they did realize their mistake our friends at the FBI put the idea in Brad's mind that Mark was after all up to no good, but that can wait. Entry to the building was relatively easy. They rang the bell and announced that they had returned from a meeting and had brought back Mark in a drunken state. Brad found that hard to believe and could see no sign of Mark on the video, but when he saw a couple of FBI jackets there, he pushed the button and let them in any way.'

'When they came up the stairs it was obvious that something was very wrong, so Brad immediately shut down the systems. That made some Pakistani livid, so he pulled out a gun, but was calmed down by the FBI. In the shambles that followed, while they were distracted trying to get the system up and running again, Brad escaped but was lucky to get out alive. He had to get out when he overheard some bloke called Mohammed to describe how he was going to kill him. Funnily enough, the guys were talking about Mark as though he was one of them, which merely served to confirm the information he had been fed by the FBI. This presented Brad with a serious dilemma, so he thought his best bet was to disappear back into the bowels of the CIA.'

'So now let me summarise our position. We appear to have identified a threat to the security of the USA. That threat has been notified to both the FBI and the CIA. However, both organizations have someone fairly high up in the pecking order who has killed the story. Therefore, we cannot get approval to have the resources that we would need to investigate the matter further. Consequently, at this stage, we are on our own. That is unless we go to a higher authority. While there are some obvious people we could go to, what we do not know is how far the disease has spread. If for example, we go to Foggy Bottom, they will check with their own security people. They will in turn check with their connections at both the CIA and FBI, and therefore we have a problem. If we as much as hint at who "we" are and where "we" are, and the "connections" just happen to be the story killers, we are as good as dead. Therefore, while it is a bit over the top to visualize this scenario as a World War III in the making, the people in this room form the only team available who can follow through with this investigation. It has taken about two years to get us to this stage.'

Harold Taylor once more looked at each face and then concluded. 'However, the real problem is that our information suggests that we have two weeks to sort it out, or a lot of people are going to die.'

Chapter 13

Decision Time

The people seated around the table seemed stunned by the enormity of the last statement. Since Mark was the one who was the least informed of the five men present, and probably the one who this whole story had been framed around, he was the only one to react.

'What do you mean by—two weeks before a lot of people die?' Mark asked, looking first at Paul who was studying his feet, then at Brad who was chewing his fingers, before riveting his attention back on his old man.

His father let out a long sigh and then replied.

'In 3 days, we will be into September. And 11 days after that will be the anniversary of 9/11. Our analysis of the data we had before Brad's source was cut off indicated that a plot was being hatched for some major, and unsavoury, event for that anniversary. The target for that event in New York City.'

No one else in the room seemed to be the least bit surprised, while Mark was flabbergasted. But this would not be the last of his shocks.

The meeting was interrupted at that stage by a cell phone call and an embarrassed, and agitated, Forester answered it. He then quickly apologized to Harold Taylor and without a word or acknowledgment of the others, left the meeting in something of a hurry.

Mark was at first again shocked by this weird turn of events. Then his father's body language told him a different story.

'Do I take it that you are not overly impressed with Mr. Forester?' Mark enquired, not expecting an answer. But the reply he got from his father came as another surprise.

'That call would have come from the Embassy, albeit a little later than planned. All that stuff I was talking about was filling in time. I am glad that Forester will not be with us for the final part of our discussion' his father replied. 'Don't be fooled by his mincing around looking like the hired help. He is one step down from ADDI – sorry Assistant Deputy Director of Intelligence – of the CIA in Washington. And don't let the combined Assistant and Deputy words fool you, or even the "one step down from" words. He is an enormously powerful and influential man, and incidentally, he is one of the best analysts that the CIA has. But he is a pain up the ass!'

'The same could be said for any number of members of the CIA' Paul said joining the conversation. 'But while he may be a bit of a pain in the ass, don't we need him on our side?'

Again, Harold sighed.

'I do not know that I can trust him. I discussed the overall situation with the authorities in Washington – Stephen Rodriguez the ADDI among others—and because of that, they sent Forester and Brad Morgan to assist in this exercise – assist being a relative term. I did not explain to Washington exactly what I had in mind, and ever since his arrival in Wellington Forester has been prodding around trying to find out. While ranking in the bureaucracy places him above me, in New Zealand, I am the boss. But – and this is the reason I don't trust him – he has not asked me directly what I plan to do, which I find strangely out of character. This means that he already knows – though God knows how. Or he does not care – which is a little scary. Or that he does not want to appear too inquisitive for fear of being rolled.'

To Mark, this was all in house politics. If someone in Washington needed to find out what was happening, there would be little need to ask Forester to prod. Why did the people pulling Forester's strings not just come straight out and ask Harold Taylor?

This seemed like another example of a bureaucracy gone mad and Mark was beginning to get very impatient with all the crap. He still was no closer to finding out what on earth this whole business had to do with him, apart from his obvious, and now terminated, association with one of the players – the Augem Group. So, he asked.

'Ok – so you still have not told me what I am supposed to be able to do to help.'

After all, Mark was not a spook. And from what he had heard so far, he did not want to become one anytime soon. His best bet was to high tail it back to the United States. Except that he would be going to New York City. And New York City was to be the target.

'Mark – I would like you and Brad to take a trip up to Rabaul.' his father answered, rather too casually.

'Where is Rabaul?' Mark asked.

'Rabaul is in East New Britain – in Papua New Guinea' Harold answered, throwing a set of maps onto the table. A couple were normal touristy maps, the others were satellite photos in a variety of resolutions.

'I believe that someone in Rabaul – the most unlikely

of places – is running a terrorist network' his father said with some intensity. 'I think the answers lie in Rabaul. But neither we at the CIA nor the Australians who are responsible in that part of the world – have any proof, or indeed even a glimmer of proof. What we – sorry I – need is someone there to find out and if possible, gather the proof. Mark, I know your service record. I know that I can trust you. I know that you understand computers and communications. If you were a CIA agent on the ground, you would be remarkably qualified for the task. But you have one quality that exceeds all of that. You are unknown to the intelligence communities. That means you can get into and out of Papua New Guinea without being noticed.'

'I thought you said that you wanted Brad and me to go. What about Brad? Doesn't he count amongst your so-called intelligence community?' replied Mark, starting to get a little irritated by his father's logic. But his reply did make some sense.

'Brad Morgan can disappear into Papua New Guinea as easily as he could disappear in the Bronx. Also, he is with the CIA's Directorate of Science and Technology, not with Operations. So, he does not appear on any watch list of known spooks – at least that we know of. Add to that, as you pointed out yourself earlier, Brad has officially disappeared. The FBI is supposedly trying to find him in the States. If they are, unless they contact Interpol or the CIA – which our information is that they haven't—they are unlikely to look for him overseas. And certainly not in the South Pacific. So, time is on our side. At least for the present.'

'So, why the need for experience in computers and communications?' Mark asked, probably already knowing the answer. He was not wrong.

'The Internet!' was all Harold had to say.

Mark was about to ask who was going to pay for this little excursion, but then he remembered that he had about 10 million reasons not to care.

Instead, he raised a more significant issue.

'How am I supposed to be able to find a terrorist cell in this place called Rabaul, when I would not know what one looks like?' he asked with a shrug.

'I have thought of that. We will fly you to Rabaul via Sydney—Australia. In Sydney, you will meet a guy called Peter who will give you an outline of the kind of people we are up against and give you a clue of what to look for' replied his father, with a flourish of his hands as though it were a done deal.

Mark still did not think so.

'I thought you said earlier that we were a tight group. This guy – Peter whatever his name is – who is he?'

His father looked a little bit ill at ease but nonetheless, he replied.

'He is tied up with the intelligence and counter-terrorist people in Australia. You do not need to know his real name; I cannot tell you his second name or who he works for – other than that he is tied up with the Australian Intelligence Service. He is supposed to be their expert in terrorists and their cell culture. And we don't have the same problem with the Australian intelligence services that we have with our CIA' he concluded with a certain amount of bitterness.

Mark sighed. His father was too much of a professional to try to appeal to the goody-goody instincts that would see him march off into battle on behalf of the good old Uncle Sam. Harold had planned the whole thing and was supremely confident that his plan would work, and – more to the point – who his players would be.

There was also a weird logic to it all. Agency employees were restricted to where they could go—well within reason –

either by government intervention or by the simple fact that they were known. And they were restricted in what they could do when they got there. In Marks' case, those restrictions simply did not apply. He had to admire the old man for his sheer audacity.

'Ok – When do we go?' Mark asked in a resigned voice.

The chance to travel to somewhere as remote as Rabaul did have a certain element of excitement and adventure attached to it. This was going to take some explaining, especially to Dusty back in New York. He would not be pleased that Mark was wandering off on a CIA trip. And more especially to Annette given what he had just heard about the official interpretation of his hiring techniques or aspirations.

Harold was oblivious to any concerns Mark may have had.

'Tomorrow morning. Brad is booked on a direct flight to Brisbane. You are booked on a flight to Sydney. You will meet up again in Brisbane. You are traveling independently. You must watch your tails. Brad has been trained in counter-surveillance techniques and from your time in Special Forces you should be able to handle it. It is also important that you say nothing to anyone in the United States about the trip. When I last heard you were still single – Is that still the case?'

Now that was a hard one.

He would need to talk to Annette, as well as Dusty. And he would have to tell them the same story. Annette, he could handle. Now that there was some doubt about her background and involvement with the Augem Group. But would he lie? He was apprehensive, but deep down he still loved her. He could not lie to Dusty. Dusty was like a mind reader, and they had known each other for too long for Mark to risk lying to him.

There was also the question of his friendship. It was too important, even relative to the events that his father had alluded to, to place at risk a friendship that had lasted for most of Mark's adult life. He would tell them both as near to the truth as possible. But his father was a different story.

'Yes – that is still the case – I have no ties.' Mark replied.

'Good. No one else knows where you are going except Paul and me. Some at the Embassy already know that you are somehow involved, and they may be snooping around. Therefore, it is extremely important to avoid any chance of your movements becoming known to anyone from the Embassy. Or any CIA agent or other operative. Once you get into Papua New Guinea that will not be quite the same problem. You will be observed as a foreigner but so will everyone else of similar ethnicity, whether they are in the spook business or not. You need to be as covert as possible.'

'Wouldn't we need visas to get into Papua New Guinea?' asked Mark, knowing that would indeed be the case, but feeling that the question was pointless. It was.

'All taken care of. If you could let me have your passports for a couple of hours, I will have the visas attached. The High Commission of PNG is just up the road in Willis Street.'

'We could go to the High Commission ourselves – it will give us something to do' said Mark, again wondering what kind of negative answer he would get this time. It was negative, but again it made some sense.

'No – we do not want you anywhere near the PNG High Commission. For that matter anywhere near our Embassy. I have booked you into separate hotels overnight and I would like you to go to them now and lay low. I do not want you to talk to anyone other than Paul or myself about where you are going or what you are going to be doing. Anything you need for your trip – just ask – and we will get it for you. Use taxis to get to the Hotel and the airport. And we will not be using this house again' his father concluded.

'Why?' This time the question came from Paul.

'Because I suspect that our small group may have been penetrated.' Harold replied with the now inevitable sigh.

Paul Williams appeared a little upset.

'But there are only six people – you, me, Brad, Mark, Forester, and the Ambassador' Paul said, stating the obvious. 'You can count the first four out because they are all here. Who of the other two that you do not trust?'

For some reason or another, Harold smiled as he replied 'Both!'

Mark and Paul let out a simultaneous 'Shit!'

Brad looked pensive but not in the least bit surprised.

Harold let out another sigh.

'Forester may be a brilliant and a very competent analyst, but he and I have never got on. He is devious and I find him irritating. When people irritate me, I find I cannot trust them. He is probably fine, and his prodding around is probably his natural instinct. But that is the way I view him.'

'As for the Ambassador – he is probably fine too. The problem is, he reports to people at Foggy Bottom. I would not trust a diplomat to do anything except organize cocktails parties and make speeches at official diplomatic dinners. They have no sense of secrecy. If it suits their particular needs at the time, they will exchange any information with anyone and not worry that they may place someone else's life in danger. They spend most of their time playing word games and exchanging favours.'

'The Embassy does not officially know anything of this

plan, although it involves our entering another sovereign state. And that is the way it will stay, at least until after the event. There is always a risk that the Papua New Guinea High Commission people may talk to our ambassador, but I think it is a small risk and there is nothing we can do about that in any case. I will know if anyone at the Embassy starts snooping around and will deal with that when it happens.'

It never ceased to amaze Mark how his father managed to avoid swearing. He seemed to take the idiosyncrasies of the various organizations he had to deal with as fact, and just dealt with them for what they were. He had to admire his resolution, and he was beginning to understand, after all these years, that there was much more to his old man than he had previously thought.

The most amazing thing was – Harold had been certain that Mark would accept his plan and be the one heading for PNG. Everything was planned and arranged beforehand. The only thing that could have happened, if Mark had not agreed to this crazy scheme, is that Harold would have been out of pocket by a few thousand dollars.

On the positive side, Harold had access to numerous accounts from which he could extract funds for any clandestine projects that he might engineer. Mark had at least learned that much today!

It was also a good job Harold had a map.

Mark had not a clue of where he was going.

Brad shook hands with Mark and said goodbye – again – and said that he would see him again in a couple of days. The look said more than the words. Mark turned to his father.

'How I am supposed to pull this off, when I don't know how to be a spook, and enter another country unsanctioned, and without a clue of what to look for?'

The exasperation that Mark was feeling whether caused by the enormity of the task or caused by the worry of how he was going to explain it to Dusty and Annette, was evident. Again – if his father was in any way put out by the reaction, it failed to show.

'I have every confidence in you Mark. I have seen your military file and it is very impressive if we ignore the obvious flaws, you have occasionally displayed when receiving orders. Going into another country I thought would be the least of your worries. As for being a spook – well you are not really. And as for spotting anyone who may be following you, it is common sense really.'

His father rambled on telling him what to expect and how to deal with it, as though it were a walk in the park. Mark thought of interrupting and asking why it took many years at the Farm to train the CIA field agents to be at least competent. That was followed by many years in the field to become proficient. Yet a five-minute chat was all that was needed in Mark's case.

He didn't interrupt and this omission would bite him in the ass later. Not that it mattered in the overall scheme.

Having exchanged handshakes they said their goodbyes, Mark decided to walk to the Hotel. It was not the Hotel that Harry had booked for him. He needed time to clear his head and to think. He wanted to get away from the whole drama that was the CIA and the recent revelation that his father was part of that.

He had plenty of time. And the question was, from what his father had said – who, if anyone, was still on their side?

There were supposed to be six people who were, one

way or another, involved in the scheme. Taking them in the order that Mark had perceived as least—trusted to most trusted—the devious Forester had raised Mark's antenna early on. The fact that Harold Taylor did not like or trust him was sufficient for Mark to have him top of the list of the untrusted. The question now was whether Forester had been sent out to New Zealand by someone at the CIA who wanted to thwart Harold's plans or if it had just happened by chance?

That had to raise a question mark over Brad's role. After all—the powers that be had sent Forester and Brad together. So, if Forester was not to be trusted, the same should equally apply to Brad.

As for the Ambassador, Mark did not know the man. But Harold's view that he should not be trusted was a cause for concern. Although Mark had no doubts of the man's integrity – he would not be in the position he was unless he was a solid citizen. There had been in Mark's own experience numerous occasions in which the careful art of diplomacy had wreaked havoc with the lives of other people. The fact that the greater or long-term goals may have justified an exchange of otherwise secret information was little comfort to those in the firing line. And the same insane ritual was carried on by all sides in the diplomatic game and yet they never seemed to learn.

That left Paul and Harold since Mark knew that he could at least trust himself. And the surprising choice for the fourth was Harold. It was not that the old man was anything but loyal to the CIA. His loyalty was the problem. It would take just one word spoken to one person to cause the whole house-of-cards to tumble down. While Harold had talked about moles and was sensitive to the damage they could do, he still had his loyalty to someone back at headquarters that he would assume that he could trust.

The question therefore was could they trust Harold's

circle of confidants. Harold had to trust his boss, the ADDI Stephen Rodriguez. However, what filters did the ADDI have to sort out the myriad of subjects that he had to deal with.

People in bureaucracies had at some stage to delegate, or nothing got done. So how seriously was Rodriguez taking this minor episode down in the South Pacific? As for Paul – Mark had no doubts. He had been to hell and back with Paul and it was incomprehensible that he could be a risk. So, at this early stage, Paul was the one who Mark could trust. But Paul was not the person chosen to go with him to PNG.

Mark would not only need to watch his back. He also had to keep a wary eye on his companion.

The James Cook Hotel was not far away, and that was as good as any Hotel in the city of Wellington. That was if one ignored the fact that the Hotel was built right on a fault line such that, in the event of a major earthquake, the Hotel would simply cease to exist.

It had turned out to be a nice day – if a little breezy. He walked down to Lambton Quay and stopped at Starbucks for a coffee, positioning himself at the back of the shop so that he could observe the comings and goings. Not that he was aware of anyone following or observing him – the territory was unfamiliar to him, so what would he know? But there were no obvious observers, and he was the only one who ordered a refill. He could conclude that he was not at this stage being followed. But any spook worth his salt would be aware that Mark would be awake to that. So, if one was there, he or she would take some alternative action. Mark was quite good at second-guessing people in business. But this spook craft was another game entirely. He would have to play the game by a set of rules that he made up as he went along.

He checked in to the James Cook, making sure as far as he could that he did so when no one else was around. He went up to his room, placed the "Do Not Disturb" sign on the outside of the door, and then immediately got back into the lift and went in search of a taxi.

He got a ride to a place that was a couple of blocks away from where he had parked his rental car. As far as he could tell no one took any notice of him but he did not care. He drove the rental car to the City Life Hotel where his father had arranged his booking and left it there in the hotel car park. He called in at reception and asked if any messages had been left for a Mr. Taylor. Sure enough, a courier pack was there containing his passport complete with the necessary PNG visa and other things. The package included enough hard cash to make anyone drool – United States, Australian, and New Zealand dollars, plus Kina, the currency of Papua New Guinea.

All of the cash was in used notes and divided roughly into equal amounts, While Mark had few ideas of what lay in store in PNG, he doubted whether there would be a need for more than two thousand dollars per day. Mark's immediate reaction was to call Harold and ask whether he was required to account for what he spent, as is the way with bureaucratic organizations, but he thought better of it. He felt quite confident that he could handle any situation where someone might try to relieve him of his newfound wealth, but not too sure that he could handle the paperwork. So that task he would delegate – to his father.

The receptionist had been instructed to book him in, so he went through the ritual of filling in the hotel booking form and giving her his Visa details. He then smiled at the girl, said he would look at his room later, and returned to the James Cook.

He rang the car rental firm telling them where they would find the car and then lay down on the bed and was soon asleep. He awoke with a start several hours later – someone was at the door! He rushed to the door and peered through the peephole.

There was no one there.

Mark shook his head. It was probably just someone who was coming to turn down the bed. Or he was becoming paranoid. He determined that he would not take this business quite as seriously as he had done so far. He just needed to be careful.

He had a shower, changed into some clean clothes, and made his way out of the room to go to the restaurant. The elevator arrived to take him down, but then he had another thought. He went back into his room and placed everything that could identify him, where he had come from and where he was headed to, into his bag. Then he carefully clipped a few hairs from his head and placed them strategically around the room. He wasn't exactly qualified in forensics but at least if they were not there when he returned it would tell him all he wanted to know.

He then left the room again taking the bag with him. The waiter in the restaurant was quite used to paranoid Americans and never offered to stow the bag elsewhere. Not that Mark would have let him.

His cell phone rang as he was about to start his main course. It was Harold checking that he had received his passport and visa. His father made no mention of which hotel he was at, and Mark did not volunteer that piece of information. His father however would not be a very good spook if he did not already know. Mark was not a spook and could not have cared less.

When Mark returned to his room it was evident that someone had been snooping. And that was good. It proved that he at least was not being paranoid. It was clear that someone had been there and done a very professional job of searching it. Nothing was out of place. All that was missing were the tell-tale hairs that Mark had placed, he thought strategically, in various positions.

Fortunately, Mark had not done a very professional job of preparing it, not knowing how to do so. The person who had accessed the room would have assumed that he had done nothing. But a couple of hairs were not where they were supposed to be. Again, it may have been some innocent person going about their normal business of making sure that his stay was comfortable. But Mark did not think so. The "Do Not Disturb" sign was still on the door.

Mark could only chuckle to himself. Someone had followed him even though he was in the wrong hotel and his car was at another—and there was nothing he could do about that. They had not found anything, because there was nothing to find. His father was right – whoever "they" were, wanted to know more about Mark's movements. They could be CIA – either good guys or bad guys—the local New Zealand SIS, one of his father's crew of ever-diminishing resources, someone from the Augem Group, or even someone with ties to al Qaeda. Or anyone else with an axe to grind. Since he had no idea which of these or other options could be responsible, there was no point in worrying about it.

His rational assumption was that it had to have been the local SIS. They were the only people who knew Mark outside of the few he had met at the so-called safe house. It was doubtful if anyone else would risk being exposed. The only question was – who was the local Security Intelligence Service working with or for? If it was the CIA—which side of that organization, did they think was the correct one? It seemed unlikely that they would be working with Harold Taylor because his father had inferred that there was no diplomatic knowledge of his plans. That did not mean that the SIS were not acting on their own – did it! Mark gave up working out all the possible combinations of events and players and went to sleep.

The following morning, Mark had a leisurely breakfast in the Hotel restaurant observing the various coming and goings of people. No one stood out as an obvious spook.

But then that was the whole point, wasn't it? He was beginning to enjoy the game. It certainly gave him something to do. If they were onto him, they were certainly well disguised as men just going about their business, as indeed Mark was.

Eventually, he checked out of the James Cook and took a taxi to the Airport. Whoever was following him would have had a hard job in the morning traffic typical of Wellington City. However, did not doubt that they were there. And he was in no doubt that they would learn nothing from their efforts.

The question that he could not know the answer to was - who they were? And how far they would be prepared to go?

He was not of course armed and that was a bit of a worry. He would rectify that as soon as he arrived in PNG. Being followed in a civilized country like New Zealand was one thing. Being followed in somewhere as remote and wild as Rabaul PNG was another matter entirely. His father had briefed him on his counter-surveillance strategies. From this, and his earlier years traveling into foreign countries with Special Forces, he was confident that he could eventually give them the slip. He was also confident he could handle any physical confrontation. He was also aware that spooks rarely, contrary to the Hollywood versions, got caught in such matters.

Still, if the need arose, he was confident in his ability to handle himself in a fight.

He just had no idea what he would do with the bodies.

Chapter 14

Sydney—Australia

Before departure, Mark called his New York office from Wellington Airport.

Annette answered the telephone.

'Hi – How are things going?' he began, still unsure how he was going to handle this.

Annette's credibility had been questioned by Paul Williams and his father, so he was both suspicious and cautious. He did not want to believe the doubts that had been expressed. But years of training had taught him to be careful, especially where affairs of the dick were concerned. And—what were the stakes?

She was pleased to hear his voice, and there was no hint of anything untoward, but it was work time, so she was still at her efficient best. And she laughed.

'Fine—Dusty is in—Would you like to talk to him?' she asked, while Mark detected in her voice the hope that he would want to speak more with her. While reading body language over the telephone could be full of disappointments Mark also detected sincerity and no hint of deception. Conversations on the telephone could be full of misconceptions.

Mark decided to play it safe.

'I wish I was home with you – I miss you—but I am afraid I will have to stay for a few more days. My father needs me to stay down here for a little longer. Can you manage without me?' Mark asked, hoping that she did not ask too many questions. She did not.

'Yes – we are fine—but I miss you too. I had better put you through to Dusty – he is about to leave. I love you!' And she was gone.

'Hi, Dusty – How are you getting along?'

'Oh – that guy Jonathan Fullwell knows his stuff – so we are fine. How about you? More to the point how is your dad?'

That was the question Mark did not want him to ask. But he had asked. So, he had to answer.

'Cantankerous as ever which means that he will survive. I don't think I can take much more of it. I might catch the next plane back to the States.

Dusty's response was immediate.

'Now listen to me fuckwit! We are doing quite alright without your presence, so you stay down there as long as it takes, you hear me! There are times when you Taylor's need to get real – your father is more important than anything we have going on. You do hear me?'

Mark had to smile. Dusty had a way with words, and he loved him for it. Dusty had unwittingly let Mark off the hook. No lies were necessary – at least not yet. He answered as calmly as he could.

'Thanks, Dusty – I will owe you one when I get back.'

'Yes, you will. Now can I go and have a beer?'

But at least Dusty was laughing when he added.

'I suppose you want to say goodbye to the girlfriend – take care' and the phone was switched back to Annette. There was no laughing from her.

'What did Dusty mean? – "Take care" – Is everything

alright?' she asked, sounding both anxious and, did he detect, tiredness in her voice?

Mark just laughed at her concern.

'That's just the way Dusty talks – I am fine. I just must stay down here for a few more days. Now, why don't you go with him for a drink? It sounds like you could both do with one or two.'

'You don't mind?'

The question hung in the air. Yes, Mark certainly did mind. He should be the one taking her out for a drink. But there was one thing you could rely on where Dusty was concerned. No one would get within a mile of Annette while she was Mark's beau and Dusty's loyalty as a friend was beyond reproach. She could not be in better or safer company.

'Of course, I mind – but only because I am not there too. Dusty will look after you until I get back. So off you go. I love you. Bye!'

Mark reluctantly cut the connection.

Had he known what was happening back in New York he would not have been quite so confident.

That morning, the Wellington airport was open because there was no fog. Well, there may have been, but with the wind backing to more than forty-five miles per hour, there was not much chance of the fog hanging around.

Mark had been advised to keep an eye out for anyone who appeared to be acting suspiciously or taking an inordinate interest in him. He suspected someone was on his tail. But what did that mean?

Because the check-in time was two hours before the flight left, he had more than ample time to view everyone who was lining up to board the flight.

Then a curious thing happened as he was about to settle down for a coffee. A guy in the uniform on an Air New Zealand steward came over carrying a coffee and the local newspaper and took a seat at the next table. Then as soon as an announcement was made over the speakers concerning a flight, he stood up smiling at Mark and gave him the newspaper saying he had to go and would not have time to read it. That was fine with Mark, but he soon discovered that there was more to this little play. Folded inside the newspaper were copies of the loading schedule and passenger list for flight QA86. The same flight that Mark was booked on.

The Australian airline Qantas – the Flying Kangaroo—flight, had come from Los Angeles, via Honolulu, and into Wellington New Zealand. It was going to end up in Sydney Australia.

It would be too much of a coincidence if anybody on a flight from the States was interested in someone who had booked to join the flight after that flight had left LA. Or so he thought. Therefore, Mark could concentrate on people who were boarding the flight in Wellington. That meant that he had about seventy people to be concerned about.

A fair number of the seventy were families, either going to Sydney and then on to God knows where, or Australians returning home. He could reject them. Parents had enough trouble controlling kids on an international flight to have the time to worry about Mark Taylor and the game he was playing. That left about thirty passengers.

Some of these thirty people were so old that he had serious doubts about whether they would still be alive when the flight got to Sydney. That left twenty-three.

Mark was traveling Economy Class because that was the only seat available at short notice. Of the twenty-three, two were traveling first class and seven were traveling business class. At least they went to the Qantas Club lounge—and if their task was to watch Mark that was not such a good idea. That left fourteen.

Of these fourteen, five were just too young. They had possibly been visiting or were going to visit, one or the other of estranged parents on either side of the Tasman Sea. That left nine.

Having reached this conclusion, during which he had shown an extraordinary amount of interest in all of them, and they, in turn, had shown no interest whatsoever in him, he decided that the whole exercise was pointless. Nevertheless, someone had gone to extraordinary lengths to ensure that he at least had the opportunity to check them out.

That person had to be his father.

Flight QA86 proved uneventful, if a little rough, flying into the teeth of the predominantly westerly winds which hammer the coast of New Zealand. The passengers seemed unconcerned.

The Sydney airport was as busy as any international terminal would be at that time of the morning so Mark had not a clue as to how Peter, the person he was to meet, would find him, let alone recognize him. The plane had parked at Gate 31, so he had a fair walk to get through to immigration, baggage claim, and customs. That process took about a half-hour to complete. There was nothing like the painstaking dramas that Mark had experienced entering New Zealand not so long ago.

When Mark finally got to the exit gate, he looked around just like any other visitor would on entering a foreign country for the first time. do but did not see anyone he recognized or anyone that had appeared to recognize him. He went off to the side and parked himself on a bench and waited.

Mark was dressed in a pair of slacks and an open-neck shirt and had on his feet a pair of trainer shoes that were both comfortable and in keeping with his casual appearance. Although it was almost September, and early morning, the temperature was still about 70 degrees—over 20 degrees Celsius. He had been assured that his casual dress would be perfectly acceptable in Australia. Judging by the presentation of people busily coming and going around the airport, that advice was correct. If anything, he was over-dressed.

However, he was not as casual as Peter.

A man just appeared from nowhere and sat down on the bench next to Mark and introduced himself. He was so casually dressed he could be described as scruffy, slightly shorter, and about the same age as Mark but much thinner. He had not shaved for a few days and Mark guessed he had not had a change of clothes during the recent past. But he was pleasant enough.

And his body language told Mark that he was an ok guy.

'So how did you find me?' Mark asked.

That brought a genuine smile from Peter.

'Just a process of elimination mate. Most people who came off the flight knew where they were going. You did not. And you are probably the tallest and fittest-looking guy on the plane. This is obviously your first time in Sydney?'

'Yes, it is. And I guess I still have some catching up to do in the spook business.' replied Mark with a grin, still unsure of whether this guy Peter had told him the absolute truth. And unsure what truths Peter had been told about him.

'So, what do we do? They told me you are the expert in terrorist culture and all that kind of stuff.'

Peter laughed again.

'No mate—no one is an expert in that game. I have had some success in keeping a track of people suspected of being involved with terrorist groups here in Australia Would-be terrorists vary so much that I cannot claim to be an expert. What is more, I simply do not understand them. Anyway, why don't we go into town and have a coffee and I will tell you what I can? I understand you have an early evening flight to Brisbane. We will be back in plenty of time for that.'

Peter was well informed.

Mark did not know whether his knowledge came from a simple examination of flight plans or someone in Wellington. If it was the latter, he hoped it was from Harold. Otherwise, the whole plan of being covert was looking shaky before it even started.

They got to the short-term car park where there was every make of car most of them fairly new. But nothing like the car they got into. It was a Holden VH Commodore station wagon, well over twenty years old, and it looked like it. The engine however roared into life and was well maintained.

'We will go to Surry Hills – it is fairly close and should serve our needs.' opined Peter and Mark just nodded. He had no idea where he was, less idea where Surry Hills was or were, so any place was as good as any other.

They arrived in what was a suburb not too far from the centre of the city. Sydney, with a population of over four million, was surprisingly quiet. Peter parked the car and they wandered to a coffee shop where chairs and tables spilled out onto the sidewalk.

Peter was immediately greeted like a member of the

family by a man who was the owner of the coffee shop. He was a middle eastern-looking man who was short, bald, and fairly rotund and looked to be in his early fifties.

'Hi Omar, I would like you to meet a friend of mine – Mark – he is from the United States, but not everyone can choose their friends.' he added with a laugh,

Omar reached across the table and shook hands with both of them. The body language was fine. Mark smiled and added 'he normally calls me mate – I am surprised he remembered my real name!' The comment was understood by Peter and Omar. With a nod to Peter, Omar took off inside to get coffees.

'We can talk here.' said Peter 'Omar is one of us. Surry Hills is an area where immigrants from the middle east tend to concentrate. Originally most of them were Lebanese, but latterly they come from all over the place, and in a coffee bar, a lot of people talk probably more than they should. I understand you are off to Papua New Guinea?'

The sudden change of tack took Mark by surprise, but he managed to retain his composure. His father had said that very few people knew of his planned trip, so how had this "Peter" come to know? Either he was one of the trusted few and Harold had told him, or he had extremely good intelligence, or he was told by someone else, or he was guessing. Mark discounted the "guess" option as just too farfetched, so the worry was that he had found out unofficially—but how?

Mark decided to play dumb. Which he was finding fairly easy to do. 'I do not know – I go to Brisbane, and they will tell me where I go next when I get there.'

Peter just grinned.

'Well, you can take my word for it. That's where you're

headed, mate. Now, where should we begin? They say you are fairly new to this game. You had a life before?'

Those words, and change of subject, told Mark that the word had come through Harold. He hoped he was right.

'Yes – I used to be in the Marines – well Special Forces Group' answered Mark, without wishing to go into detail. He did not say – 'Yes, I am one day into this life and haven't a clue what I am up against.' He decided to return the compliment.

'What organization pays your wages?'

Surprisingly, Peter answered without hesitation.

'ASIO – that's the Australian Security Intelligence Organisation – the other half or overseas part is ASIS – the Australian Secret Intelligence Service.'

'So, ASIO is like our Federal Bureau of Investigation and ASIS like our Central Intelligence Agency?' Mark asked.

That brought a huge laugh from Peter.

'Shit I sincerely hope not! Probably the CIA part is ok. Well, you're CIA so you know how it works – but no, not the FBI.'

He burst out laughing again. So, now Mark knew what he was supposed to be, but still had only a rudimentary understanding of who or what Peter was. He had a faint suspicion that Peter was at a far higher level in ASIO, or whatever Australian outfit paid his wages than he would have assumed from his appearance.

It was rather nice of his father not to have told him. There was an outside chance that Peter was testing him, but the body language said otherwise.

'Ok – so tell me how these terrorist cells work.'

Peter knew his stuff and chatted away in a manner

reminiscent of a guy discussing the local rugby league. While he talked, his eyes constantly scanned the passers-by, and occasionally he would exchange a greeting. Mark watched the body language and could usually tell that all the greetings were not necessarily friendly. The difficult part was that with people from different cultures that Peter was on at least nodding acquaintance with you had to look at the eyes. But Peter continued and Mark never lost track of the story.

'Al Qaeda tends to be the organization most often mentioned in the same breath as terrorism. But the problems go back way before Osama bin Laden had got into the act with his training camps in Afghanistan. There has long been a view—some would say extreme view—held by followers of Islam, that the world is dominated by Jews and Christians. Add to this a militant interpretation of Islamic doctrine and you have justification for doing something about it. And you have a powder keg waiting for a fuse. One problem of such extreme views is that you have a no-compromise position – that is what the Koran tells us to do so we do it. The interpretation in the western world, especially following 9/11, is that anyone with a beard and a turban is working for al Qaeda. The good news is – that is not so. The bad news is – how do you find the ones who are?'

Peter paused while Omar placed coffees on the table, and after a few comments about a gentleman by the name of Mustafa Sharrouf, the drift of which Mark could not follow, Omar went back inside.

'Muslims, like everyone else on the planet, move around and many of them have settled here in Australia. Many of the more peaceful types came to escape the problems in their lands. Some hot-headed extremists came too. While extremists are not always terrorists, terrorists are always extremists. We have no way of knowing whether the bad guys amongst these people came to form sleeper cells and then we do not know whether the focus of their extremism is overseas or domestic. Add to that the younger generation without jobs or ostracised from the society that they were trying to join, get marginalized, and become influenced by rhetoric. And, funnily enough, the very freedom that they were supposed to enjoy has an effect. Being free and able to express themselves the rhetoric is often extreme. People get upset by that – Australians who just want them to go away, and other more rational Muslims – the vast majority I might add—who just want to live in peace.'

'But we are in a situation where any event which we may regard as irrelevant – because it usually is—can cause unrest. For example, many of our Muslim friends were annoyed by the West's apparent failure to protect Bosnian Muslims during the war in Yugoslavia. But there are valid questions to be asked. Did the West – meaning the United States and Europe – have any responsibility for what happened, and could they or should they have done anything about it? And the answer is – No!'

'What do you mean?' asked Mark – remembering the messages he had heard about between the Augem Group and someone in the former Yugoslavia.

'I would never have linked that part of the world with terrorist activity.'

Peter again laughed, but his response was serious.

'You have to understand a little more about Islam. While we tend to treat various conflicts as regional and localized, they tend to treat them as something different. They are religious and global. It does not matter where they are. If Muslims are involved that is reason enough for the extremists to get angry, and to take their anger to the streets. That part of the world is complex. Albania is a Muslim country but under Yugoslavia, some of them moved north to find work. The Muslims have spilled over into Bosnia, Serbia, and Kosovo. Whatever else people may say, the trouble in the Adriatic is based on religion. When there are conflicts, people tend to divide along the lines of religion or race.'

'Here the cultures of the West do not help. The USA likes to project itself as the leader of the free world and that means the democratic world. But, leading the world about what? One obvious distinction is democratic cultures versus non-democratic cultures. To some eyes that are equivalent to Christian and Jew versus Islam. Hence you have a conflict. The real confusing factor in all of this is economics. Just look where the oil reserves are! Most of the oil is controlled by Muslim nations. The main markets are non-Muslim. Economics and Religion! The two major reasons for all historical conflicts as far back in history as you care to go!'

Mark began to feel a little out of place. Was Peter implying that the United States of America—Mark's own country—was the cause of the terrorist problem rather than a victim of terrorism? But then again, looked at from a dispassionate point of view, he may be right! Mark changed the subject.

'You are saying that everywhere that you have Muslim communities, you have the potential for trouble?'

'That's right!' said Peter. 'The goings-on overseas, especially in Madrid and London, caused the locals here in Australia to believe that they too could blow something up as well. In Australia recently we had nine Muslim men go on trial suspected of a terrorist conspiracy. There is ample evidence that they had acquired substantial amounts of industrial chemicals – hydrochloric and citric acids, glycerine, and acetone. All the sort of stuff that could be used to make bombs to blow up half of Sydney. They also had detonators which are not much use unless you want to trigger an explosion. They also had laboratory equipment, all sorts of literature about bomb-making, and videos of al-Qaeda beheadings which just about confirms their terrorist affiliations. They can make, and have made, all sorts of excuses and explanations for their possessions. But you and I both know what they were up to.

'However, we have a fickle justice system. Even to be called a terrorist organization under Australian law is not so simple. In 2002 courtesy of our democratic process and our bureaucrats, a whole range of offenses spelled out in a thing called the Security Legislation Amendment (Terrorism) Act. But you have to convince the politicians or a court or some combination of both before you can call someone a Terrorist – even if they have enough explosives to start World War III. Under our weird laws, we currently have about twenty groups listed as terrorist organizations. The vast majority of them are based overseas. However, we just do not know the extent to which they have infiltrated local communities.'

'So how do you recognize a terrorist cell?' Mark asked.

He, like anyone else who had an interest in international affairs, not to mention some experience in foreign lands, knew all the stuff that Peter was talking about. But he kept his tone akin to that of a student, and Peter continued as the teacher.

'We do not have cells as such. We have networks. The local guys are pretty harmless really. They tend to be amateurs merely repeating what is reported in the press. The thing we fear most is the external groups. That requires communications. What we have to do then is work out who is talking to who, then we have to find out what they are talking about. Hopefully, someone in the network will make a mistake, and so far, we have been lucky.'

That comment caused Mark to raise his eyebrows. But he did not interrupt. He was at last learning something.

'The problem with homegrown terrorists, or would-terrorist groups, is that they do not have the organization of their overseas counterparts. In this part of the world an organization called Jemaah Islamiyah – JI for short—is the main cause for concern. They are theoretically based in Indonesia. They use one country for training. In another, they raise the money. And in yet another, they hide the real terrorists until they are ready to make their move. The JI has obvious links to al Qaeda which they brutally demonstrated in Bali not so long ago. The international network is what concerns us most. They could strike anywhere, at any time, and from anywhere. Like you, we have all the acronyms AIC, ASIO, ASIS, ONA, DIO, DSD, and DIGO chasing around, hopefully not getting in each other's way. And hopefully all dancing to the same tune on gathering and analysing intelligence. It must be a pain in the ass when you get a couple of moles amongst that lot – I sympathize with you.'

Again, the sudden inclusion of that final comment brought Mark down to earth with a jolt. He was learning that this was how discussions were carried out between countries, friendly and not so friendly. But he had neither the time nor the experience to match it with this Australian. Mark shrugged.

'So, you know about our problem?'

The look of concern on Peter's face said that he did.

'Well, your contact in Wellington said this meeting was to be kept secret from your local Company officers. So, I put two and two together, and your reaction confirms what we thought,' he replied.

'Spooks spying on spooks' he added with a laugh.

'You know how it works – I will go back to my office and file a report on our meeting. Once that is done it is out of my control. It goes into the system either to be filed away un-read in some irrelevant file, or some bureaucrat takes an interest – who can tell? What do you want me to do?'

Mark was beginning to feel even more out of his depth and did not know how to handle this one. Suppose he asked Peter to keep it quiet? Peter could say 'yes' – and he could still file a report – saying that he had said Yes. But Mark had to try, first to appear as though he knew what the game was all about, and second that he knew what Peter and his Australian Security Intelligence Service was capable of. So, he tried. He got the guidance for what he was going to say from Peters' own words – his concern about the international networks.

'We worry that the mole or moles in our intelligence network are more widespread than we at first thought – maybe even as far as Australia.'

That certainly grabbed Peter's attention, and, for the first time, the smile left his face. 'Shit!' was all he said.

His attention had been grabbed by something else. Walking down the street in their direction was a couple of men dressed very much as Mark and Peter were, except they both had long beards. He called out to Omar pretending to be ordering something from him and almost whispered. 'That is Mustafa – I do not know who is with him.'

The two men took up seats at the opposite side of the coffee bar and Omar went across to take their order. Just at that moment, a car cruised by, with three men inside – at least the driver had a similar beard to the two new customers – they could not make out the other two – and the car looked as though it was about to stop. Then another car cruised by this time with only one man – and this time the driver was a Caucasian. This second car slowed perceptibly when the driver saw something at the coffee bar and it was clear his interest was in Mustafa or his colleague, and then both cars drove on, apparently taking no notice whatsoever of Mark and Peter.

The whole episode lasted barely a few seconds and would have gone completely unnoticed but for Peter's reaction – and Mark's ability to read body language.

'Well, this is getting interesting' said Peter 'Do you know that guy who was driving that second car?'

'No – should I?' asked Mark.

'Well maybe you should—he is Bernard Frost—a Cultural Attaché at the US Embassy here in Sydney – or so the staff list says.'

The car had been very unimpressive, but Peter recognized it and the Terrorist wannabes also probably knew who and what it was. It was all part of a charade. Peter looked at Mark expectantly but still did not get the result he was expecting. He looked concerned.

'The Deputy Chief of Mission is a guy called Martin Quinton – you're going to tell me you don't know him either?'

Mark had a hollow feeling in the pit of his stomach. He began to see the connection. The guy driving the car was CIA and no doubt he reported to Quinton who, therefore, was also CIA. But the damage was already done. Any CIA person, whether covert or otherwise, would know who his local people were, especially in a foreign country – Australia in this case. But Mark did not know. Even entering a country covertly – meaning without the local Embassy being informed—as Mark had done, he should have at least been briefed on who he could contact in the case of things turning pear-shaped. But he hadn't. So, he didn't.

Fortunately, it appeared as though the local CIA did not know or recognize him either – which was hardly surprising in the circumstances.

'Who are you?' Peter asked – and this time there was an edge to his voice. 'All that stuff that I told you about al Qaeda and JI you can read anytime, anyway by doing a little research on the Internet, so there is no harm done. But you seem remarkably unprepared for what you are into. What is your game, Mark?'

'Let's take a drive. I think there are a couple of things that you should know, and I don't like to talk in the present company.'

They got back into the car after Peter had exchanged a couple of words with Omar. Mark had no way of knowing what was said, but the body language in the car was now far from friendly. Peter muttered about heading out to Penrith and said nothing while he made his way through endless sets of traffic lights until they ended up on the Freeway and the traffic eased somewhat. Finally, Peter broke the silence.

'I should probably dump you and leave you to your own devices – but we have about a half-hour drive from here to Penrith – so talk.'

And so, Mark told him as briefly as possible what he was doing in Australia – well almost. 'Shit!' was Peter's immediate reaction.

'Here we go again! The CIA thinks they can use people, any people, to do their bidding. What happened to international cooperation? They are going to send you, an amateur, un-briefed and unprepared, into another foreign and alien country, and I suppose they expect you to single-handedly dismantle the whole network and return with Osama bin laden in chains.'

Peter was not too happy. What had seemed to Mark like a reasonable plan back in Wellington, seemed like a crazy plan now when analysed by this rather down-to-earth

Australian. There were a few things that Mark had not told Peter. That he would be accompanied by a real spook. Well, Brad Morgan is half qualified. And that Mark did have computer skills which at least Harold felt could be critical in patching together the plot. That suspected plot was to hit New York City in a couple of weeks, and as far as Mark could tell, a fair amount of the responsibility for finding out about that plot rested on his seemingly inadequate shoulders.

Peter eventually calmed down and almost to himself said 'If the mole is high enough up the chain, I could understand why the Wellington CIA Chief would want to keep the whole thing well below the radar. Therefore, it could make sense to use someone who would never appear on anyone's radar. And you certainly qualify for that. But what are they hoping to achieve? Unless!' He almost pulled off the road as he turned to Mark.

'Unless the timing is so critical—when and where are they expecting some kind of plot to eventuate?'

'New York City on September 11th' was all Mark said.

'Shit – you don't say!' Peter pulled into a lay-by deep in thought. 'Why would anyone in their right mind who works for the CIA, or the FBI want to screw the investigation into that. Unless that is, they are terrorists or fully paid-up members of some group and they have infiltrated the organization. But the CIA alone does not make decisions on the assessment of threats. So, there must be a network in the whole intelligence organization – and that means the NSA and probably the DNI. The lessons of the original 9/11 have not been learned. Your intelligence organization is sick!' The latter came out as an accusation and directly levelled at Mark.

Mark held up his hands in supplication.

'I am just doing my best to help – my father is the one

pulling the strings.'

That got a reaction. 'Shit – you are the son of – you are Harold Taylor's son?'

'You know my father?' asked Mark.

'Yes, I know him – Harry Taylor. A stuffy old prick who does everything by the book. But he certainly knows his stuff. If he has got his son involved that places a different emphasis on things – it must be serious.'

Peter remained deep in thought for some time, and then he drove back onto the road and continued their journey towards Penrith. Eventually, he seemed to come to a decision. The body language now said he trusted Mark and that seemed to come from Peter's knowledge of his father. At least the old man had a use after all. The description of him as a stuffy old prick described him to a tee but he had the respect of at least one Australian. And this Australian was one that Mark felt he could respect and was feeling increasingly confident in.

'So, here's the deal.' Peter said eventually. 'I will keep quiet about most aspects of your trip in exchange for your telling me what you discover up in Papua New Guinea. We have never suspected any connection with any terrorist activity in that part of the world – the PNG economy has been struggling –it is fucked—and they have enough problems of their own. I tend to think the connection is a little farfetched. If it is not, we need to know about it and quickly. While we can sympathize with you guys, PNG is in our backyard, and an attack on the States could mean only one thing – Australia is next. '

Mark thought about that for a moment. He still had not said that he was on the way to PNG, but Peter seemed so well informed that it was pointless to deny it.

'That is fair enough – but I have not got the time to come back via Sydney. How can we arrange that?'

Peter just smiled. 'You let me worry about that. Do we

have a deal?'

'Ok.' Was all Mark could, or had, to say.

There was just no point in shaking hands on their deal because Mark was rapidly coming to the view that deals did not stand for much in the security and intelligence business.

They drove on into Penrith, turned off the Freeway onto Northern Road, and then turned left into the car park of the Penrith RSL Club. They went inside and Peter ordered them a schooner each of the local low-alcohol beer and a meat pie. They then walked outside where they sat looking out across a road and into the grounds of the University. They talked about a few things, each lost in his thoughts, probably reluctant to broach the subject, waiting for the other to get back to the real issue. They talked about PNG during which Peter warned Mark to expect something less than third world conditions – which Mark could handle. They talked in general terms about the spook business – which Mark could not even comprehend. They talked about cooperation, or lack of it, between the world's various security and intelligence services.

Mark began to understand which countries could be trusted and which could not and gained a whole new understanding of the problems that his country faced in dealing with so-called friendly countries. And dealing with not-so-friendly intelligence services. In particular, Peter was not at all impressed with Pakistan which was supposed to be one of the United States' closest allies – at least as far as dealing with and fighting al Qaeda was concerned. They talked about what Peter described as the CIA's "sister" organization the FBI and their post 9/11 problems. Mark was aware that the FBI had taken on a new counter-terrorism role but was not aware of how that was perceived by outsiders looking in. Sure, the FBI had no choice but to change, but if Peter's description of terrorism from an Australian perspective were to be applied to the United States, which would tend to increase the conflict with the CIA. After all, it was the CIA that gathered most of the data, and they tended to pass that on to others in an analyzed form. The FBI would not like that, nor did the FBI exactly have a reputation for taking advice from anyone. The motto Fidelity, Bravery, and Integrity, corresponding to the initials of the FBI, did not appear to extend to the acceptance of the meaningful change. Such is the nature of all bureaucracies.

But then they had to get back to the reason they were meeting.

'How does Osama bin Laden manage to control such a vast network of terrorists and have such an influence on something the size and sophistication of the CIA?' Mark finally asked almost of himself. That brought another laugh from his colleague.

'You should not come down too hard on the old boy. Sure, he is a thorn in the side of many, but look at things from his point of view. Al Qaeda is all about a global jihad – they have as much interest in punishing Muslim leaders who don't see things their way as they have in attacking western targets. They want to unite the Muslim world under one leader.' Peter took another swig of beer and looked to Mark challenging him to respond. Which he did.

'No global jihad that results in events like the 9/11 debacle in New York and Washington can be justified by any religious teachings.' Mark retorted. 'The guy is sick.'

'Well, if you think Osama bin Laden is sick, you should try his friend and deputy, Ayman al-Zawahiri. Zawahiri is, or was, an Egyptian doctor, about five years older than bin Laden. He has been tied up with the jihad for almost forty years, and he is the chief organizer. He has about a dozen aliases and is generally referred to as either The Doctor or The Teacher. This guy prefers to use suicide bombers against what we in the trade call soft targets. His Egyptian Islamic Jihad, which was originally looking to overthrow the Egyptian Government, has merged with al Qaeda, and that happened a couple of years before 9/11. You have a fanatical organizer hell-bent on killing Americans and he doesn't care who, how, or where. Who do you think organized 9/11?'

That was all new to Mark, and he had to ask the question.

'What kind of a doctor is Zawahiri?'

'Well, there you have it. He is a medical doctor – actually a surgeon. How would you like him to be the one responsible for performing lifesaving, or rather a life-threatening, surgery on your loved ones? But my point is, bin Laden, who after all founded al Qaeda, gets all the publicity, but the organization is now so diverse and vast that you have to be wary of other people. Osama could be killed or captured tomorrow, and we estimate that it would make not one iota of difference. So, what are you going to do in Rabaul?'

Again, the switch in the conversation took Mark by surprise. In this case, he at least could see where it was leading. Before long Peter would be telling him what he would have for breakfast. Peter had gone from talking about the country of PNG to talking about the town of Rabaul – a place that barely 24 hours before Mark had never even heard of.

'I hope you are not telling me I am going to meet al-Zawahiri?' said Mark. That brought another laugh, but this time the body language did not quite fit.

'I sincerely hope for your sake you don't.' Peter replied, taking the shrug from Mark to mean what he thought it meant – This Yank hasn't got a clue what he is up for! Peter put his thoughts into words.

'Let's think about what could be going on in Rabaul. The clue to having an effective terrorist cell is communications. If I was running a cell out of a place as remote as Rabaul I would need to communicate with someone. Hell – the place is so remote. There is just nothing in the town. So, if there is a cell, it can only be a conduit for someone or something. That would need equipment.'

'Have you been to Rabaul? How sure are you that it is so remote? The maps that I was shown in Wellington indicated that it was a tourist destination. That would make it an ideal spot with people able to come and go without attracting attention from the authorities.'

Peter smiled at that.

'Some years ago, the place blew up. If you do not already know, it has more than its' share of highly active volcanoes. That put a stop to tourism for now and probably forever. However, the United States and Australian governments poured money into monitoring what was going on. That may be a clue – data is collected from around Rabaul, and it has to be coordinated and then transmitted to Port Moresby or even direct to overseas.'

Mark could use all the help he could get, and this analysis was the first indication he had of where he could start looking. He filed away that information for future reference.

Little did Mark know that Peter was alluding to a critical part of the whole setup of a terrorist's cell. However, neither of them could know who was involved. Not that it would make any difference.

Mark was pensive for a few moments. There was another subject that had been bothering him for a while and which he felt helpless to deal with. On the spur of the moment, he decided to raise the subject with the Australian.

'I suspect that I have been followed since before I had the meeting with my father in Wellington.' He proceeded to tell him of the comical experience with the New Zealand SIS, but also the strange happening at the Wellington airport. He concluded with an admission.

'What I do not know is—who by? As far as I can tell they have not followed me in Sydney – but what would I know?'

Peter looked at Mark as though he were a child and then shook his head.

'Poor bastard! Get used to it! I would guess that you are being followed by two groups. One group would be your father's people to make sure you got on your flight ok and to find out who else was taking an interest in you. The other group would be people who were trying to find out which flight you were on and where you were going. The latter could have been New Zealand's SIS but could also have been your own government's CIA agents or even Embassy people. You are probably aware, at least you should be, that your foreign diplomats also have their own intelligence service. What they get up to is anyone's guess. Because your father's people would have been around it is unlikely that you were followed by other CIA people. Two people at Kingsford airport were taking an interest in you. That is a small contingent, so the odds are they were not particularly expecting you to turn up in Sydney. Anyway, we either lost them or they lost interest' he added with the inevitable smile.

'I won't ask how you knew or how we lost them. This whole business is getting too complicated for me.' Mark responded. But at least Peter had some good news.

'I will do my best to make sure you do not get hassled

while you are in Australia – but you're doing ok. It goes with the territory. Just keep a sensible lookout and avoid contact with people. It pays in this game not to socialize. If you are unsure of anyone, pretend you don't speak their language'.

Eventually, Peter dropped him back at the airport. By this time Mark felt quite exhausted but he was nonetheless grateful for the advice he had received.

'Thank you for your time and help – I appreciate it' Mark said as they said goodbye.

'That's ok mate – good luck in Rabaul' replied Peter.

'Poor bastard!' he did not say.

Mark would need all the luck he could get.

Chapter 15

Rabaul – Papua New Guinea

After his talks with Peter in Sydney, Mark was determined that he would lift his game and begin to take the spook business much more seriously than he had done so far. He would make a conscious effort to implement the counter-surveillance procedures that his father had vainly and vaguely tried to get him to adopt in Wellington, and he would endeavour to remain below the radar.

The flight from Sydney to Brisbane passed without incident.

He had spent the night in the Airport Hacienda Motel, which turned out to be not as close to the airport as he would have thought, during which he consumed a couple of beers over dinner with the only person he met – Mike Simpson the Manager of the Hacienda. The Motel had been chosen at random and quite by chance, and the manager was everything a spook should not be. Apart from the fact that he was over seventy-five years old—he looked as though he had held a bottle of some kind in his hand for at least the last sixty of those years.

Early the following morning, Mark made his way back to the international airport to catch his flight to PNG. The Brisbane Airport terminal was relatively small by international standards and was therefore relatively easy to observe – and to be observed.

He did the usual things that people do in airport terminals – wandering around the shops looking at the various products and their crazy prices. And looking at everyone else that appeared to be doing the same thing. He had a drink of coffee at the bar—and watched – just like everyone else was doing. Unlike the majority who had nothing better to do in the mind-numbing boredom of waiting, Mark took a genuine interest in what he was watching.

He thought that he knew enough of the tradecraft of undercover, or underhand, operators to be able to spot anything odd. After about an hour he was fairly certain either that no one in the airport was the least bit interested in Mark Taylor. Or that they were just being too clever for him to spot.

He did however form a very definite opinion on who was being watched and who the watchers were. During his surveillance, he had spotted Brad Morgan. He seemed to be doing the same thing as Mark was. But Brad was not alone. There were two people – a very officious-looking businessman and a young lady—who were both showing an extraordinary amount of interest in Brad. The lady was about thirty years of age and was almost the complete opposite of the businessman in appearance. She was dressed in a baggy jean jacket and trousers that were deliberately patched, a thin girl with long unruly hair, and the most outrageously colored shoulder bag. She looked like any other young female traveller who had done it all before and was just waiting for her next adventure to start.

But she was not like any other traveller. The book she was reading was either not particularly good or was written in a language that she did not understand. Or she was the slowest reader on the planet. The book was of no interest to her. She was watching.

Mark caught up with her in a refreshment area while she was nibbling on a bun, drinking an orange juice, and had the inevitable book from which she was reading. He smiled at her as he took an adjacent seat and casually asked her where she was headed. This probably wasn't the smartest thing for Mark to say or do, but he needed to get some reaction. He was not disappointed. She replied that she was headed to Singapore. He reciprocated by telling her he was headed back to PNG. There seemed to be little point in both lying, otherwise, the conversation would go nowhere. She was pleasant and appeared genuine, but it was her eyes that most interested Mark.

Mark had deliberately positioned himself roughly between the girl and where Brad was sitting. She had very deep brown, highly intelligent eyes, and she appraised Mark with a once-over look, and she was not displeased with what she saw. After all, Mark was quite good-looking, well-built, and had a pleasant easy-going nature that many women would find attractive. But her eyes flickered from time to time over Marks's broad shoulders – watching. Soon her eyes flickered in a different direction. Mark casually surveyed the terminal and saw that Brad had moved – as had the businessman – in the direction of her gaze. So, he knew. What he did not know was who she was, and he also did not know that Brad knew that he was being watched.

At another time, and in another place, Mark could have quite enjoyed the company of the young lady. But he was there to do a job. He finished his drink, cheerfully said goodbye to the girl, and walked towards the shops in the opposite direction. She did not turn around so he either had failed to impress her or she had other interests.

Later he came across the girl again in one of the shops rummaging through some jerseys but looking around the stand to where Brad was quietly reading a newspaper.

'Hi – You're still here! Your plane is boarding now. Better not miss it eh!' Mark said, giving the girl his most disarming smile. She returned the smile, but it was the eyes – it is always the eyes.

'Oh—just some last-minute shopping then I am on my way was the words that came out. Her body language said something different. 'Why doesn't this American smart-ass just go away and let me do my job?' The accent was Australian and, from what little Mark could know of such matters, appeared to be from Sydney. That may have been part of an act. Mark speculated that she was a part of the ASIS, although whether she was part of Peters' flock or some other surveillance team, he had no idea. His main concern was that she was watching Brad and he could not see how she could have latched on. Unless, of course, it was a double play. Had Mark been watching Brad? And then the lady was watching Mark. There were so many possibilities in the spook games.

Fun though it was to speculate, Mark need not have worried. The girl did not get on the plane for Singapore, but fearing that her cover was blown, or maybe it was just time for her to go and observe someone else, she changed places with a young man of equally rough appearance, and she disappeared. Mark eventually wandered to the boarding gate for the Qantas flight to Port Moresby, but Brad played it cool.

So as not to alert anyone to his plans he had deliberately waited in the main concourse. Unless whoever was observing him had checked with immigration, they would not know which flight he was booked on. You could not discount that because they had after all at least gained access to the area restricted to actual passengers. That was not unusual in the spook business, but the odds were about 70/30 in Brad's favour that they had not got tickets for the same flight. Brad waited until the final call for the flight, and the very last minute before he rushed to the departure gate. That did cause some consternation in the terminal because it was far too late for anyone to get on the flight, and it was not as though they simply had to wait for the next flight. Today was Thursday. The next flight was on Sunday.

Papua New Guinea is not high on the list of preferred destinations.

While the CIA had some limited resources in Port Moresby—the capital of PNG—two factors were working against them there. Firstly, PNG is a third-world country where smart-assed surveillance techniques were out of the question – those doing the surveillance would stand out like dogs' balls. Secondly, it was unlikely that the moles that had infected the CIA in the United States, probably New Zealand, and possibly Australia, would have made it to PNG. There was just nothing to do in PNG, and contrary to widely held belief, the CIA did not have a surplus of field operators in all parts of an admittedly shrinking world. If they had, then Mark and Brad could be in real trouble and the whole trip could be a waste of time unless they found some way of giving their followers the slip. If the CIA, or whoever was interested in Mark and Brad, knew that their target was Rabaul then the CIA was in an even worse position because Rabaul was about as remote as you could get. So, on balance, the odds were that Mark and Brad would be on their own until they completed their mission and returned to Australia.

The flight arrived on time at Jackson Airport in Port Moresby and then the passengers had to contend with customs and immigration procedures. The officials had no concept of time and that was refreshing after the hustle and bustle of the States and, to a lesser extent, Australia. But they were equally diligent.

Mark's laptop proved an item of interest. Strangely enough, Brad simply walked straight through, although he had similar equipment. When Mark finally got out of the immigration and customs procedures at the International Terminal, he had less than five minutes to catch his connecting Air Niugini flight to Rabaul – at least according to what was written on his ticket.

The trip from Port Moresby to Rabaul was something of an adventure. For a start, and fortunately for Mark, it did not leave on time. That gave him time to call at the local telecommunications airport office to get yet another SIMM card for his cell phone. The staff was extremely helpful. However, they omitted to tell him that the SIMM card would be useless where he was headed.

While some of the foreign passengers were distressed by the delay in the flight time and adopted an air of arrogant displeasure, the locals had an air about them of complete indifference. Mark adopted the attitude of an ex-pat returning to his job in Rabaul and accepted the situation as normal. He trusted that he would not get involved in any conversations that would have him admit to anything and so he avoided everyone by burying his head in a couple of magazines that were of doubtful literary value as well as being hopelessly out of date. Brad had the easier role.

Brad was able to blend in with the locals, although not quite as black, and apart from his height – he was much taller than the average local—he adopted the guise of someone fascinated by volcanoes and going to Rabaul to witness first-hand what was happening in this strange and remote land. As they patiently waited for the call to board the aircraft, they independently scanned the crowd for any signs that could indicate any interest in their travel plans. None was immediately obvious apart from four gentlemen who looked so nervous that Mark thought they would bolt out of the terminal waiting area at any moment. But they were Pakistani, and Mark remembered what had been said to him while talking to the Australians. Peter had said, while admittedly laughing, that the easiest way to get a message to al Qaeda was to inform the ISI – the Directorate for Inter-Services Intelligence—in Pakistan. Mark knew that the problem was much more complex than that. But he remembered Harold's advice – treat everyone as suspicious until you knew otherwise.

There was a wide variety of other nationalities booked on the particular flight but since they were to travel on a Fokker aircraft, Mark knew that once onboard there would be nowhere for anyone to hide. First Class on Air Niugini flights meant that you had two more inches of legroom, but apart from that, you sat with the rest of the rabble. So, he could assess each passenger at his leisure and if he decided that anyone was a potential threat there was plenty of time to take appropriate action when the flight landed. That was of course if they landed and did not get blown out of the sky by some mad bomber.

Mark could not help but smile. Despite the somewhat ramshackle way in which the PNG locals seemed to carry on their functions of preparing an aircraft for take-off, there was certain confidence generated by the simplicity of it all. The gentleman manning the airport's only x-ray machine was one of the smallest and ugliest men that Mark had ever met. But, when he smiled, he seemed to generate a field around him that made everyone else smile. And he knew exactly what he was doing, as some of the passengers, and some who were no longer passengers on this particular aircraft, soon found out. He had a simple philosophy – if someone lied to him once they were a liar, so they are no longer on this aircraft – go and explain or complain to someone else! All done with a broad smile. And that got rid of one at least one of the people that Mark had previously regarded as suspicious.

When the call finally came to board their aircraft, they all trooped out of the air-conditioned terminal building and into the oppressive heat of the concrete runway and clambered aboard and into their seats. Mark had a seat at the right rear of the plane, while Brad was about midway forward and on the left-hand side.

Eventually, the flight took off and headed northeast towards the storm clouds that were gathering. The Fokker was surprisingly quiet for an aircraft that was getting old. Although the maintenance on Air Niugini aircraft was carried out by Qantas, the Australian airline, PNG was not exactly flush with funds, and there must have been the temptation to cut corners on service and more so on the purchase of new parts. But the pilot, who was also Australian, seemed to know what he was doing. He did not sound at all worried when he came to greet the passengers and announce the flight details.

Even when things started to get a little rough the pilot still sounded as though he was in control. The weather in PNG is very warm and humid any time of the year is situated just south of, but awfully close to, the equator. Therefore, it was not unusual to run into the odd tropical storm. And they did.

The Fokker people certainly knew how to build an aircraft. What they did not know is how to get them to fly with people standing or moving around the cabin. It was fine for the steward because he—at least "he" was dressed as a male—gave up on handing out biscuits and drinks and strapped in tight to his seat. However, his instructions, backed by a stern but friendly warning from the pilot to passengers to remain seated with their seatbelts fastened, were ignored by one of the Pakistani men.

While he struggled to extricate something from his bag in the overhead locker, he first went sideways and then upwards banging his head on the locker, and then crashed to the deck in a crumpled heap. In the confusion that followed, a couple of pieces of paper slipped from his grasp and were retrieved by Brad. From his position at the back of the plane, Mark observed the action and noted that Brad had made no attempt to return the papers to their unsuspecting owner. Not that the Pakistani appeared to care. He seemed more relieved to crawl back to his seat and strap himself in. The Steward gave a toss of the head, rather like a mother watching her children doing something stupid and returned to looking out the window at the passing storm with an air of contemptuous disregard.

The flight information provided by Air Niugini was that the flight was from Port Moresby to Rabaul. It came as a surprise to Mark that the plane, first of all, landed at Lae in the province of Morobe on the northern side of the island. Well, you cannot refer to this part of Papua New Guinea as an island because the western half of it was actually in Indonesia. At Lae airport there was the usual exchange of passengers. They were on the ground for little more than ten minutes, and they were off again.

Another surprise was in store. They next landed at Hoskins, a place that can best be described as an airstrip, and a town that could hardly be described as a village at the western end of the island of New Britain. There they were able to stretch their legs while some passengers disembarked, and new passengers climbed on board. Mark took the opportunity to exchange a few words with Brad, and amongst the chit-chat about the weather he was able to ascertain that the papers that the Pakistani had dropped were simply an exchange of emails. They were concerning a replacement disk drive. The papers indicated that the man could have been called Khan which was not significant. The reason Brad had hung onto them was that he recognized the email address and that was significant. It was info@augemgroup.com.

Brad also surprised Mark by commenting briefly on their experience at Brisbane airport international terminal. Brad had noticed the two people who were taking an interest in him, but he had also noticed a lady following Mark! He was sure that she was friendly, but it impressed Mark that he had picked it up. He was sure as hell he had not. What Brad lacked in experience he certainly made up for in the application of spook craft. Mark began to feel more confident. But still realized he had a lot to learn about this business in a short time.

Time was one thing they did not have a lot of.

Since Mark had no prior knowledge of the stopover at Lae and Hoskins, he did not know what to expect. The new passengers were greeted in a way that suggested they were known to at least some of those on board, and they were either locals just traveling or ex-pats just visiting. Mark had no reason to suspect any of them and concentrated on the Pakistanis. With a wave from a guy sitting in a World War II jeep, which Mark took to be the control tower, the Fokker took off once more and continued to head east.

The three Pakistani gentlemen had remained seated and belted during the fifteen-minute stay. Which made Mark begin to feel uneasy. Not that they yet posed any obvious threat. They were by now so terrified that it would be hard not to feel sorry for the trio. But they rarely spoke and appeared to be doing what Mark and Brad had agreed to do—travel alone and do not acknowledge the other. That was simple for Mark and Brad since they could not be more different in appearance. But the Pakistanis were almost identical, and they sat in adjacent seats.

They may not know each other, but that was unlikely. Or they may have argued and were not speaking —which seemed improbable. Or they did not expect anyone to take any notice – which in the confines of the plane beggared belief. Or they were amateurs at the game – which seemed to be the most likely.

The thought of them being amateurs almost made Mark laugh out loud. If anyone was an amateur, he was. But he was learning fast and would keep an eye on these men. Brad would keep a closer eye on Khan, the one who had lost the papers. This had given them an unexpected but very welcome lead.

The town of Rabaul was situated at the eastern end of the island of New Britain which placed it conveniently in one of the most explosively sensitive places on the planet – on a major junction between two of the earth's tectonic plates. On one side of the major fault line was the Pacific Plate, which was shifting northwest. On the other side was Rabaul sitting on the Bismarck Plate which was shifting southeast. The whole area was a mess of faults and volcanic activity that made it volatile. It did not surprise many that the airport at Rabaul had been destroyed – well buried under meters of volcanic dust— in

September 1994 by a volcanic eruption. Two simultaneous eruptions caused the problem. The previously well-known volcano called Tavurvur was joined by the lesser-known Vulcan on the other side of the harbour (otherwise known as the Rabaul Caldera). The result was to cover the airport in enough volcanic ash to render it useless and for it to remain so, probably permanently.

Before this event, Rabaul had been a popular destination for holidaymakers from Australasia and further afield. Even after the event, there was still a mixed collection of ex-pats, mostly Australians, who ran local businesses. And these people still needed to travel, either on holiday back to Australia, or Thailand, or the Philippines – anywhere to get a break. So, there was still a need to get into – and out of—Rabaul.

Therefore, flights had to land at an airport somewhere nearby. The closest was an airstrip at Tokua just east of Kokopo. This airstrip was originally built by the Japanese during World War II. Its location meant that you had an hour's drive once you landed at Tokua to get to Rabaul since no one was going to rebuild the Rabaul airport anytime soon, if ever.

The Tokua airstrip had benefited from a recent infusion of money from Japan such that it had all the trappings of a modern airport. To the west of Tokua was the Kokopo township, which had replaced Rabaul as the business centre in this part of the world. Kokopo had a similar (in nature but not in size) infusion of assistance from New Zealand to get the roads attended to. However, the economy of Papua New Guinea was such that not much was spent on maintenance and the capital improvements were rapidly deteriorating.

The aircraft carrying Mark and Brad had finally landed,

and the passengers wandered into the baggage claim area. It was there that Brad approached the Pakistani assumed to be called Khan and asked if he had lost some papers and flourished the papers which he had secured on the flight. How Brad knew which one to approach, Mark had no idea. They were all three dressed in the same shade grey suits and, apart from the sweat stains, were identical. But the gentleman seemed first surprised, then flustered, and then grateful, even offering to pay for their return, obviously mistaking Brad for a local. If Brad was in any way offended —after all he was proud of his African American heritage — he did not show it. He laughed, rejected the offer of payment, resumed his attitude of total indifference, and went in search of his bags.

There were no obvious signs that Khan placed any significance on the event. It may have been different if Mark had approached him, but that is the way the world works.

From Port Moresby Mark and Brad had independently confirmed the booking of rental cars from the agent at Kokopo, and he had assured them that they would be awaiting their arrival at the airport. And they were. They had taken the agent's word for it that they needed four-wheel-drive vehicles, the make of vehicle to be decided when they landed, on the assumption that they would get the best then available. What greeted them outside the airport terminal building came as a mild surprise. The fact that the vehicles did not appear to have been cleaned in anything like the recent past was the least of their worries.

In the United States, or for that matter anywhere else on planet Earth, the vehicles would have long since been confined to the scrap heap. Nevertheless, the vehicles seemed to go and that was all Mark and Brad cared about.

It was somewhat fortunate that, during the stopover at Hoskins, Mark and Brad had agreed that Brad would follow the Khan fellow as far as possible to find out where he went. When they came out of the terminal Khan immediately went to a four-wheel-drive vehicle which was in infinitely worse condition than either Marks' or Brads' and issued a string of instructions to the local driver. The other two of his companions headed for what appeared to be the local bus and consequently Mark lost interest in them and concentrated his attention on the activities of Khan.

He tried to understand the instructions Khan had given to his driver, but they were given in the pidgin language that the locals used, and in any case, were delivered too fast for Mark to follow. The driver was quite obviously a local native, and equally obviously did not appreciate being spoken to in the way that Khan had delivered the message. Whether it was the actual words, which Mark did not understand, or the tone, which Mark did understand, did not matter to the outcome. The driver simply left the vehicle and walked back into the terminal building.

Mark pretended to have forgotten something and walked back inside, to find the driver ordering a drink, and going nowhere for the time being. This was followed a couple of minutes later by a now irate Khan and a couple of seconds later by a bemused Brad.

The refreshment area at the Tokua airport is not large by any standards, so you had the comical situation of all four men standing literally within a couple of feet of each other. Khan let forth another tirade at his would-be driver, and that caused Brad to do a curious thing. He proceeded to give Khan a dressing down and at the same time apologized to the driver for the way Khan was treating him – all done in fluent Pidgin! During all this, he did another curious thing. He gave the driver a ten kina note – which by American standards was equivalent to a small tip – by PNG standards would be about one normal week's pay.

After a furious exchange, Khan seemed to calm down and spoke to his driver in passable English and a much more acceptable tone. The driver motioned to his drink and indicated that he would follow him when he was finished. An exasperated Khan stormed out of the terminal, and after Brad had drawn the driver's attention to the cell phone number, he had written on the ten kinas note, he followed Khan outside. Mark ordered a soft drink and engaged in small talk with the driver which did not elucidate much other than that he would be extremely glad to see the back of Khan once he had delivered him to his destination. That piece of trivia was nonetheless of considerable importance to Mark, so he shook hands with the smiling driver, and they left the terminal together, to then go their separate ways. Or so Mark thought.

The drive to Rabaul had everything to it that his briefing by the Australian would have had him believe, and then some. The road from the airport to the Kokopo township was relatively smooth. Although narrow and it had most of the larger potholes filled. As long as you followed at a reasonable distance behind any vehicle in front, and you kept an eye out for debris flying around from vehicles traveling in the opposite direction, you could navigate without incident.

The road through Kokopo was the part that had been attended to by the Kiwis, and apart from the fact that the locals treated the sealed road as a walking path, was relatively luxurious. But from there on the conditions rapidly deteriorated.

Most of the road repair gangs in this part of PNG had little to work with by way of materials but they did the best they could. That 'best' meant filling potholes with earth and stones and simply thumping that into place. The result was no match for vehicles driving over them at speed and the result was that most of the stones used for filling the holes ended up as missiles. The situation got even worse when the road came to circumnavigate the Vulcan volcano. During the now not so recent eruption the original road had disappeared under tons of volcanic ash and debris. In true PNG spirit, the locals had simply bulldozed a path through the ash, and although not sealed, you had a new road.

Then it rained.

Volcanic soil is fairly porous, but the dust is not. Consequently, each time it rained the water made its' own path, so the bulldozer went through again and reformed the road. Over time the road ended up more like a fairground big dipper. Now Mark began to understand why the rental vehicles looked so dilapidated. You could take a brand-new vehicle through the Vulcan Road and come out the other side with – well—what he had for a vehicle.

The township of Rabaul was somewhat subdued in comparison. But the consequences of the eruptions were very plain to see. Over half of the town had been flattened by the volume of ash, and since Tavurvur was still belching smoke, ash, gas, and noise, the government had decided not to recover that part of the town. Which led to yet another curious situation. In most towns, the Hotels are usually located close to airports, and this had been the situation in Rabaul. The airport had been adjacent to the end of the town that had been destroyed. The locals had simply dug the hotels out of the debris, fashioned a road along the original main street, albeit several feet higher than the original, and complete with undulations and in the absence of any close neighbours, the hotels were back in business.

Nothing else, just three hotels. Isolated from everything.

Each is like an oasis in the middle of a desert.

Mark had booked into the Tavurvur hotel which turned out to be the closest to the erupting volcano. The hotel which Brad had booked – the Hamamas—was at the end of the road on the borderline between what the government had allowed being recovered and what should not be recovered.

That was the least of Mark's worries. If he had been expecting to use his mobile cell phone to contact Brad, and Brad certainly was expecting to use his, he would have been hugely disappointed. There were no mobile telephone facilities in this backwater.

There were no Internet Cafes in Rabaul either, but for different reasons. No one could afford to use them. The only form of communication was the local telephone service. Given the condition of the telephone lines and the power network, which could prove both cumbersome and unreliable. But after a fashion, it worked.

Mark settled into his hotel room, and set up his laptop computer, to make sure that it had not suffered from the various X-ray machines it had been subjected to during his journey into the unknown. Then he rang and left a message at the Hamamas for Brad to contact him as soon as possible. But he had no sooner sent the message when his phone rang, and it was Brad.

'We need to talk. Your place or mine?'

Since Mark's hotel was more remote – if that was possible—and as far as he had been able to tell there had been no new arrivals other than himself, he immediately responded.

'Mine – see you in the bar.'

The problem for Mark was communicating to the locals that he would have expected to have access to a fridge.

In the absence of one in his room, he had gone along to the communal fridge at the end of the corridor. That fridge had a notice on it saying that if it was found to be empty, residents should go to the bar. The fridge was empty, and there was no evidence that it had been switched on in the last decade. That left the bar. And in these temperatures' hydration was essential - even though Mark had no recollection of Brad ever drinking.

Mark disconnected the laptop, put it into the carry bag, and placed his passport and other items which could identify who he was in the side pocket. Then he headed off for the bar which was on the same first floor as his room. He was just about to enter the bar when a thought occurred to him. Remembering the lessons that he had picked up in Wellington and reinforced by Peter in Sydney, he returned to the room and placed a couple of his hairs in the drawers and then in the door, just as he had done in Wellington to beneficial effect. He then closed the door once again and locked it.

Was he was getting paranoid? Who would be snooping around in this God-forsaken place? But there was a certain common sense in it all, and he was starting to enjoy the thrill and adrenalin that tripping around to strange unfamiliar places involved – especially as a spook. That is apart from the fact that in a couple of weeks' someone - well a fair number of people - would die if he did not do something. What he was doing about it so far away from where that would happen, he did not yet know.

Now the problem was quite simple. They had made the trip up to Rabaul relatively easily, even though it had taken the best part of two days. Now their task was to find out – What?

In Wellington, Harold had inferred that the key lay in

Rabaul PNG. And Rabaul was hardly a big place even by the standards of a third-world country. But where to start looking for something that even remotely looked like what they were supposed to be looking for was the problem. Having got to the place, reality set in.

They had at least got two hints. The first one came from Peter in Sydney when he had said that any terrorist cell would need some form of communications. And there could be very few places with that kind of capability in this out-of-the-way place. The other hint that they had so far had been somewhat luckily provided by their Pakistani friends – the slip of paper that Brad had purloined on the flight tied something in Rabaul to the Augem Group. That something had to be a computer since there is not much else that has a use for a hard drive.

There was a tenuous link provided by the fact that it was reasonable to assume that the man Khan was a Muslim. As Peter had said in Sydney – how do you find the ones who are involved? The Khan fellow may have been delivering the hard drive to a friend. Unless they got exceptionally lucky, the slip of paper could be all they got. Not a lot to show for a trip into the third world. And flights into PNG were not exactly cheap. But it was better than nothing.

The enormity of the task that they faced, now that they had arrived in Rabaul, began to worry Mark as he strolled towards the hotel bar. He could take the view that this wasn't his fight. If they failed to find anything— well so be it.

However, that was not in Marks' nature. His father had given him a job to do although it was doubtful if he had provided him with all the necessary tools. That was typical of his father. Harold also knew Mark very well, despite the irritation in their father and son relationship. Mark had to admit that he had inherited several characteristics from his father – once you were given a job and you had accepted it – finish it.

Mark did not share his father's stubbornness and his belief in orders from above. He was quite used to taking the initiative, but were the two unrelated clues that they had going to lead them down a tunnel with no light at the end? There is a view that, in such a tunnel, the successful people of this world keep going until they find a light. The other view – held probably by the vast majority of people – is that there is no point, so quit while you are behind. Their problem was that they had yet to find the tunnel.

He would soon, but it would be of dubious help.

Chapter 16

Tavurvur

The Bar at the Tavurvur tavern was the local watering hole for the relatively large number of ex-pats who still managed to remain employed in Rabaul. This was despite the diminishing returns businesses in and around the area were experiencing since the near destruction of their town.

As Mark walked into the main bar, the conversation suddenly ceased as everyone turned to survey the recruit to their drinking fraternity. Mark nodded to the large group of fairly intoxicated men and women gathered around a table at the centre of the room, went to the serving area, and quietly asked for a beer. There was no point in asking for a bottle of Budweiser – the Tavurvur bar only had one beer – and that was the local PNG brew produced by the South Pacific Brewery, Port Moresby. The only distinction between the three options was the colour of the label - green, brown, or blue. It was still the same local beer and the barmaid answered Mark's question of the difference between the colours with just a smile and shrug – and not much else.

From Mark's observation, the men in the bar were

drinking from green bottles, which is what he got. He thanked the local lady who served him with the customary smile, and he wandered off to the far end of the room. This area was not so crowded. And where he could be alone with his thoughts.

Through the large window of the bar, facing to the east, was a stunning view of the Tavurvur volcano. In the darkness, he could see the sparks that the volcano emitted. It did not seem to be that far away. But no one in the bar seemed to be the least bit concerned. If this was the mountain behaving itself, Mark sure did not want to be around when it did not!

The babble of conversation rapidly returned to its' previous level and Mark hoped that the local drunks had forgotten about him. But no such luck. One of the women in the group strolled over with the clear intention of finding out who this new stranger was. She was obviously the wife or partner of one of the men at the centre table. Which one Mark could not tell? No one took the slightest bit of notice of her departure from the group.

She had once been an extremely attractive lady. But age had not been kind. She was well into her late thirties, she was a little overweight, she was a smoker. And showing the signs of many days and nights in a bar. The amount of make-up she wore could only be described as excessive.

Mark did not want to offend the lady but try as he might distance himself from her advances, she was not about to leave him alone any time soon. A couple more of the ladies moved across to join them, and very soon the whole crowd seemed to be at Mark's end of the room. It was all very sociable and friendly. Mark's problem was that he had not prepared himself to answer questions from the curious.

Rabaul was a small town. The ex-pat community was

even smaller. And they had little else to do but gossip. He tried to cover his reluctance to divulge anything about himself by talking about the volcano and Rabaul and the ladies seemed only too pleased to babble on about the exciting times they had experienced in this god-forsaken hole. He knew this situation would not last. The questions kept coming back to – Who are you and what are you doing here?

Fortunately, before he was able to dig himself too far into the shit, Brad Morgan came through the door. Now the crowd had another target – and this one was black. This did not seem to rest too easily with some of the assembled, particularly the men. But Brad seemed to be far more adept at handling the situation than had Mark. Firstly, he issued a general greeting in Pidgin to which no-one seemed the least bit surprised, and they acknowledged and replied in kind. Secondly, he did an Eddie Murphy type exclamation at the size of the crowd that had assembled there to greet him, which everyone found so funny. Then he greeted Mark with 'You must come to see these photographs of the mountain!' and whisked him out the door before anyone had time to react.

Mark was not sure whether Brad's action was to save him from having to drink, but he did not mind leaving his beer behind. The stuff was bloody awful. He made a mental note to make sure the green bottle was cold the next time so at least it would have no taste!

They went down to Mark's room.

'If you are going to pull that again, it might pay to have a camera' Mark laughed as he closed and locked the door to his room behind them. At which point Brad pulled a very expensive-looking Cannon from his pocket and placed it on the table. He was all business and ignored Mark's comment.

'We have a problem. We cannot use our cell phones' complained Brad. 'Here in Rabaul it would be a miracle if the ordinary fixed lines work!' he said as he cycled through the images in his digital camera. He finally stopped at the photograph he was trying to locate and thrust the camera to Mark before he continued.

'I could not follow our man Khan any further, because I did not know the lie of the land. Take a look and see what you think.'

The photograph showed the vehicle, in which their friend Khan was a passenger, disappearing up a dirt road and alongside it was a large sign which read Rabaul Volcano Observatory.

'What the hell is going on?' Mark asked. 'The last thing the Augem Group would be the least bit interested in is a Volcano!'

But Mark was starting to see that Peter's ramblings in Penrith were not that wide of the mark. The United States and Australian contributions to any monitoring program would surely be linked to a Volcanic Observatory, and there they would find communications and other gear. They would have all sorts of telemetric measuring equipment and since no one was likely to voluntarily sit on top of a volcano there would be transmission and receiving devices. Also, telemetry was of no use unless they could transmit their finding to the outside world.

They needed to find out some more about the Rabaul Volcanic Observatory.

Brad continued, unaware of the thoughts passing through Mark's mind.

'Yes, but all the signs are that the messages monitored from New York and traced through New Zealand have their origin here in Rabaul as Harold Taylor said.

They could of course come from any one of several computers, but I am sure our friend Khan is the key. If not that, then he at least is the only lead we have. I am also equally sure that he would not be engaged in a site-seeing trip. Therefore, the computer, based on what we know so far, would appear to be on top of that hill. And what better place to hide an operation? Where the rest of his team, or teams, resides is anyone's guess but first I think we have to find out what is at that Observatory. There will be computers. And there will be communications systems.'

'Ok. I agree' said Mark, reaching the same conclusion, albeit a tenuous one.

'It looks like you may have solved one of our problems. We cannot hope to search the whole town either in the time we have available or with our limited resources' continued Mark scratching his head.

'The best way to get started is to go back into that bar and get people to talk. You are here looking at Volcanoes so it seems fair enough that you should have a desire to go to this Observatory at some stage, so raising that as an issue does not create problems. I have so far only muttered to people about having a look around, so there is no harm done there either. But then our only problem is that you don't drink and sitting around a bar with everyone else half cut, would not seem the smartest thing to do.'

'Who said I do not drink?' asked Brad with a grin.

'Shit! What would I know?' Mark said, grinning in response.

This was turning out to be an interesting trip. He checked the hairs were still in place, replaced the hair on the door, and locked it again.

'Let's go and see what we can find out.'

They could both see that this was going to be fun.

Initially, it would be.

They made their way back to the Tavurvur Bar which seemed much the same as it had when they had left it. Apart from the noise which had increased by several decibels.

Immediately on entering, Mark was accosted once again by the thirty or so years old woman as though she was greeting a long-lost friend and one who she had claimed as her own. She steered him back to the table where his warm bottle of beer was still standing half drunk. It turned out that the lady's name was Sandra. She was the partner of the guy called Mario Tudjman who, in turn, seemed to be the centre of attention at the main table.

Mark's antenna was raised. The name Tudjman did ring a bell – somewhere in another life, and the vague memory did not appear to be pleasant. Mario, so Sandra informed Mark, was the head of the ex-pat group in Rabaul. It was his fiftieth birthday the following day and they had started celebrating early. From the condition that Mario appeared to be in at present, he seemed to have little chance of making it through to tomorrow. But that was not Mark's problem. The whole group seemed hell-bent on out-drinking each other so the situation seemed ideal for what Mark and Brad had in mind.

Brad made his way from the serving area through the group at the centre of the bar and towards the back of the room, when he was stopped by Mario who demanded to know what right Brad had to be buying drinks. The gentleman named Tudjman seemed a strange choice to be head of the ex-pat group. Most of the ex-pats were Australians whereas this guy was clearly of east-European descent from his accent and his appearance. He had the craggy face and colouring that Mark recognized from the time he had spent in Yugoslavian during the conflicts in the Adriatic country. Tudjman had been quite fit at some stage in his life, although the drinking had caused his stomach to balloon out and overhang his trouser belt. His ruddy complexion could have been explained by the sun but was more likely to have been caused by the booze.

For a couple of moments, Brad went tense, thinking that the challenge was related to the colour of his skin. But Mario quickly informed everyone who cared to listen that "He" was the only one buying drinks tonight. He burst out laughing, thumping Brad on the back which almost resulted in Mark wearing the two bottles that Brad was carrying. Brad just smiled pleasantly.

Only Mark would have detected that the smile did not travel to his eyes.

Mark's memory of the Tudjman name slowly came back to him. He remembered. Franco Tudjman was one of the leaders involved in the so-called ethnic cleansing that went on in and around Bosnia, Croatia, and Serbia in the 1990s. And it was still going on today in one form or another wherever the Serbs were involved. While Mario was much younger than Franco, the name Tudjman was not all that common. What Mario was doing in this part of the world was anyone's guess. It could quite simply mean that he had had enough of the Yugoslavian conflicts and bailed out. It may be that this piece of information was irrelevant. Mark was worried that there was something else to this encounter, and, like any ex-Marine and now an undercover field operator with no less an organization than the Central Intelligence Agency, he filed it away for future reference.

Like many ex-pats in this almost forgotten outpost, Mario Tudjman was a racist. He had done a commendable job of recovering the situation, but Brad would take note, and so did Mark. Brad had eye contact with Mark and got the message to say nothing. They were not in town to do battle with the likes of Tudjman. But Brad was on a different agenda.

'So, who is the pisshead who thinks he owns the fucking place?' Brad asked Mark, at a voice level that left little doubt that he would be overheard by everyone in the room. Mark was a little stunned by the question coming from Brad. Firstly, because the partner of the "who" was leaning on the table almost climbing into Marks' pants. Secondly, because he had never heard Brad swear!

To Mark's surprise, the answer came from Sandra.

'That piss-head who thinks he is God-all-fucking mighty is the guy who shares my bed.' She then proceeded to laugh uncontrollably until tears started to come, and she wiped her eyes on Mark's shirt. What followed stunned both Brad and Mark. One of the other men at the table, who turned out to be called Derek, told Mario to back off in no uncertain terms and whacked him over the head. That caused the whole bar to erupt in further spontaneous laughter, and the crowd moved from the central table to the table where Mark and Brad were, leaving Mario on his own and looking a little put-out. Derek, who it turned out was British and had the unlikely hyphenated name of Carson-Hobson, assured Brad that Mario was not normally like that and signalled to the bar for another round of 'green' bottles.

Brad smiled to himself and exchanged a glance with Mark. He had achieved what he wanted. They were now a part of the crowd. But they would need to keep an eye on Tudjman. There was something about this Mario that made them both suspicious.

It had to happen. Although the conversation could best be described as idle banter, someone finally asked what Mark did for a real job. He had to think hard about that. Mark and Brad had begun to wonder why they had even bothered to book into separate hotels. On the map, there was half of the town and quite some distance between them so back in the comfortable surroundings of Wellington New Zealand it had seemed like a good idea at the time. The problem was – the "half of the town" was a volcanic wasteland. And in this God-forsaken place, there was just no point in trying to maintain any guise of their not knowing each other. Mark decided to tell the truth.

'I run a Computer Software company in New York City – Brad has done some work with me in the past, so we decided to get away from it all and come here for a break.'

That set everyone off in another round of uncontrolled laughter. Between New York City and Rabaul, there would have to be many other places that were preferable to Rabaul, at least to this assembly of drunkards. In any case, no one was the least bit interested in what Mark did, or his reasons for being in this remote place. With the exchange of this piece of trivia, Mark and Brad were readily accepted into the PNG ex-pat drinking community.

The conversation drifted both in terms of the subject and the participants until eventually, Tudjman came across to their table. He muttered an apology to Brad and asked what he was planning to do in Rabaul. By this time, while Mark was still managing to keep Sandra at bay, the chatter around the table seemed to be about Australian Rules football and the Australian Rugby league. No one took any particular notice of Brad and Mario.

It turned out that Tudjman knew a fair bit about the history of Rabaul. Under careful prodding from Brad and between quaffs of beer, was able to tell him about the Rabaul Volcano Observatory, or the RVO as it was known to the locals.

The RVO was part of the World Organisation of Volcano Observatories. It was established after the eruption of Tavurvur in 1937 and had the task of monitoring the activity of fourteen active and twenty-three dormant volcanoes in the area. These are spread along three volcanic arcs through PNG and have been responsible for over one hundred and forty eruptions in the last two hundred years. The Observatory itself was located on the northern rim of the Rabaul cathedra. But in addition to volcano monitoring, it was responsible for various other functions including geological reconnaissance, tephratratigraphic studies, and other matters of concern. These "other matters" were what interested Brad. He had not even the faintest idea what tephratratigraphic studies were about and he did not think that Tudjman, whether drunk or sober, was about to enlighten him. He had no idea either.

'Is the Observatory open to the public at some time? I would like to have a look around.' Brad prodded.

'Certainly is—I'll take you up there tomorrow' replied Tudjman as though he owned the place. 'The view is great.'

They were making progress.

The following morning Tudjman arrived at about 11:00 am, about an hour later than he had originally planned, and about an hour earlier than Mark's guess as to what time he would turn up. Mario looked surprisingly well, bearing in mind the state that he had appeared to have been in the night before.

The previous night Mark and Brad had excused themselves from the group to go and get a feed, but when they returned to the bar, Tudjman was still knocking drinks back despite appearing almost incapable of standing up straight. His condition had led to Sandra proposing that she, and not Mario, would take Brad sightseeing, and she was even keener on this arrangement since Mark had agreed to join in. As it transpired, all four of them turned out, Mario back to the centre of attention, and Sandra, a little put out, but keen to spend more time with her newfound friends.

That arrangement suited Mark and Brad just fine because there would be less attention drawn to them in the presence of their hosts and their guise as tourists.

When Brad was asked where he would like to go first, Brad left the matter entirely in the hands of their hosts and did not express any particular desire to go to any particular place or the observatory. The four of them cruised around for hours looking at the destruction caused by the volcanic eruptions. They went to see the caves that held the rusting hulks of Japanese landing barges from World War II.

During this visit to the caves, Mark noticed how the locals seemed to drift in and out of the bush silently and without any prior warning. They would make better recruits to the US Special Forces than some of the buffoons who had tried and failed in Mark's earlier life. Tudjman even managed to borrow a powerboat and they went on the harbour to take a closer look at Tavurvur, this time from the harbour. Well, in most other places in the world the vessel that they were in would not be called a boat. It barely stayed above the water, which resulted in constant bailing to retain buoyancy, and the seats were just strips of wooden planking. The motor sputtered and

and farted, and Mark and Brad were sure that they would be left marooned out on the water. Neither of their hosts seemed to be the least bit concerned.

Eventually, and without any prodding by Brad or Mark, they ended up on the top of the hill where the Rabaul Volcanic Observatory was located. Mark, from all his years with the Special Forces, was well equipped to surreptitiously make a mental note of the layout. Brad with his CIA experience was able to note the potential logistics of the area. All done while keeping up a continuous conversation with their hosts as they gazed in wonder at the various magnificent views. They could not have wished for a better cover for their observations.

However, for this exercise to be of any use to Mark and Brad they would need to get inside the buildings of the RVO and take a look around. And as it transpired that would be no easy task. They were able to establish that the Observatory worked some irregular hours because, apart from the ongoing volcanic activity at Tavurvur, there was some activity going on at the Turanguna vent – only a couple of miles to the east – and at the Ulawun volcano – a hundred miles or so to the south-west.

While their hosts and their guests were not the least bit concerned about these unrelated events, along with the rest of the population of the town, the people who were manning the observatory were very excited. So, they stayed at work. In reality, there was not much else to do in and around Rabaul. But, once again, luck was on the side of the two tourists.

By what seemed to be pure chance, Tudjman knew one of the senior guys working at the RVO—Bill McKee— and he happened to come out to have a chat while they were admiring the views. As strange as it may seem, Bill was Scottish but had been born and raised in Indonesia. He was a pleasant enough fellow even if he seemed to find it difficult to lower his conversation to a level that mere mortals could understand. One thing Mark and Brad were able to understand – Saturday would be their one chance because that was the day that the Observatory would close early. Bill explained that the members of the staff were going to play Golf, but where or how was beyond anything that Mark had observed in this part of the world. At least that was the plan and Bill seemed very excited about that as well.

They took their leave as Bill tried to convince his guests to join in the Golf. They each declined in their own way and for their own reasons. Brad because he never participated in any sport that did not involve computers, Mark because he thought the game was a stupid waste of time, Sandra because it was too far to walk, laughing and explaining that she would spend most of the time zigzagging through the course. And Tudjman because he said that he was going to be too busy to join in their drunken game.

The only one of the four who caused any apparent disappointment to Bill was Mario. The other three were just stunned that Mario would decline the opportunity to participate in what was an excuse to get drunk. The most stunned was Sandra.

While the banter carried on, Mark began to plan their next move. This little exchange meant that from Marks' point of view they would need to try to make a clandestine visit to the Observatory on Saturday night. He did not see much future in trying to break into the place in broad daylight. Even though they were not exactly in the middle of town and were as close to the end of civilization as we know it, Mark had already witnessed how the natives could silently appear in the middle of nowhere. He did not rate their chances of satisfactorily explaining what they were about, should they be discovered. His training had given him all the skills necessary to creep around silently and undetected, but that was fine if you were allowed to kill anyone who happened to get in the way.

The real problem was that Saturday was September 1st. They were rapidly running out of time.

What had not been factored into their plans was that they only had one plan. While Mark had gone along with the conclusion that Khan was involved in something, and that Khan was involved in the RVO, and that something involved the Augem Group, it was hardly riveting evidence. There was a credible gap between this tenuous link and the type of terrorist organization and activity that he had learned about courtesy of Peter and the Australian Security Services. The most threatening things that they had encountered so far were Sandra, the beer, and the Volcano in about that order from most threatening to least threatening. If it turned out that the Rabaul Volcano Observatory was a dead end, then what?

Harold Taylor, for one, would be unimpressed, not to mention the people who were about to die.

Chapter 17

Rabaul Volcano Observatory

The Friday evening went very much like the evening before. Mark had no idea whether there was anything in Rabaul that could have entertained Mario Tudjman any differently on his fiftieth birthday. From the response he got from everyone that he spoke to on the subject, he assumed not. They drank at the Tavurvur bar just like they had done the night before, it was pretty much the same crowd. The evening was interspersed with moments of jollity, arguments, back to jollity, and endless green bottles.

While Mario was in the middle of yet another argument, the origins of which escaped the two visitors from the United States completely, Mark raised the matter of firearms. In any other bar that Mark had been in over the years, in many different parts of the world, the mere mention of the subject of firearms would have immediately sent everyone scurrying to get out of there. The answer he got was a simple one.

'Go and see Hans.'

So, he did just that.

At about 10:00 pm, Mark and Brad made their escape

from the bar amid an argument that threatened to turn into World War III. The argument was assumed to be about who won an obscure game of league football many years before, but no one was sure of the facts. Neither Mark nor Brad could not help. Neither could Tudjman.

Not that Mark did not enjoy the company. He just had more important things to think about and to plan for. On re-entering his room, he had checked the traps that he had set, and it appeared that nothing had been tampered with.

They seemed to be alone in Rabaul.

The following day the two of them just wandered around the town, ostensibly trying to find out whether there was anything else of significance in Rabaul – significance that is to the planning of a major terrorist strike in another place, at another time. They came up empty – their casual inquiries revealed absolutely nothing. They spent most of their time talking to the Papuan locals, visiting the markets, and trying a few of the local delicacies. It was all very low-key and very relaxed as they pretended to be tourists while thinking about the drama that was likely to follow. They were dressed in shorts and tee-shirts and they each wore a pair of "thongs" – a strange flip-flop type sandal—that Sandra had presented to them with much fanfare but for no particular reason that Mark could see. They spent a considerable amount of time sitting on a log facing the cliff face at the top of which the Rabaul Volcanic Observatory was situated and wondering what secrets if any, it held.

At one stage a group of people came to the market and that raised their alertness somewhat. This was a group of Pakistanis and included amongst them was their friend Khan. Khan's group looked like and were treated like, outsiders, but otherwise, the locals showed no concern whatsoever. They purchased some fruits and left just as quickly as they had arrived. Mark and Brad blended in, enjoying the casual and laid-back atmosphere, spent hours chatting to the friendly locals, asking endless questions about the local goings-on.

Nothing was going on, or about to go on, in this peaceful town, in this remote location, forgotten by the World.

At least Mark, in the peace and tranquillity of Rabaul afternoon, had the opportunity to clear his mind of something that had been worrying him for some time. How had Brad managed to escape from the office on that fateful Friday night back in New York City?

This was the first opportunity they had had since that time for a simple one-on-one conversation. Brad thought the whole escapade was a bit of a joke, and his body language said that he was telling the truth.

It appeared that when the men descended on the office—there were six of them – two Pakistani men who Mark assumed were Asid and Mohammed from the Augem Group, two men wearing FBI jackets who Mark assumed to be Henderson and his girlfriend, and two thugs who Mark assumed to be the people who had escorted him to the Augem office earlier on that day.

What followed was bizarre. When Brad killed the machines, he ripped his hand on the edge of the UPS, which gave the impression to Mark that someone had been up to some mischief. While Brad tried to stem the flow of blood, which no one else seemed to be the least bit concerned about, there followed an argument between the Pakistanis and the FBI agents about who was best qualified to attempt to get the machines back online. It was reasonable to assume that the sextet had arrived with some sort of plan and some sort of designation of who was responsible for what. But the problem when there is a mixture of professionals and amateurs is that everyone assumes something about the other group. The professionals would assume that the amateurs would do what they were told to do. The amateurs would assume that the professionals had everything under control and would tell them what to do.

As it turned out the least professional of the groups – the two thugs – became fascinated with the computer problem—a subject that they were not even remotely qualified to even have an opinion on—and Brad simply just walked out.

When Brad got out of the building, he did the only sensible thing that he could do in the circumstances. He vanished. There was no point in taking his car. The car had been just a prop supplied by his CIA masters and did not appear on anyone's list of assets to be accounted for. It was extremely unreliable, and he did not see the point of chancing his luck any further by making a noise but going nowhere. So, he walked or ran into the night.

He did call Mark on his cell phone and got no answer. He rang his home landline and got no answer even though it was after 11:30 pm. As it transpired this timing was just bad luck. The thought of Brad calling his fixed-line later and having Annette answer the telephone brought a smile to Mark's face. Brad could not have known about the nocturnal activities – could he?

Brad then called his CIA case officer, or minder, for instructions, and that resulted in his being told to close down the entire operation. So, he did just that.

Mark also took the opportunity to find out how Brad had been funded for the trip, and as it turned out that Brad had received about the same amount of money that Mark had. It did not seem to be a matter of great concern to his young friend that he would have to account for everything he spent, and he also did not seem at all surprised that the amount was grossly more than anything they could ever require. Mark was just not used to thinking like a millionaire. But he could get used to it.

Back in Rabaul, by Saturday evening it was time for serious business. Mark drove from the Tavurvur Hotel where he was staying down the road to the Hamamas Hotel. It was not actually a road. The ash from the volcanic eruptions had settled on what used to be the road and was about two to three meters deep except where rain had washed gullies, and as is the way with such things, going various ways apparently at random. The net result was that the road was more like a rollercoaster ride since no one bothered to tidy it up. It was a good job the vehicle was a four-wheel-drive although from the sounds emanating from the rear it was not too long for this world. By this time, it was dark and had become so very quickly, being as they were near the equator.

He parked in the Hamamas car park and Brad came out to meet him. They were both dressed entirely in black clothing and were wearing black rubber-soled shoes. It was going to be an interesting night and the less attention they attracted to themselves so much the better. For this reason, they left both of their vehicles at the Hotel and proceeded through the town on foot.

They had agreed earlier that it was now best if they continued the role of friends on holiday, so there was no point in trying to move around independently. At least not yet, as they had neither seen nor heard anything, which would indicate that anyone was interested.

Since Rabaul is close to the equator the sun goes down rapidly, and since Rabaul was only a shell of its former self there were few streetlights to worry anyone. They had been told before coming into PNG that it was dangerous to move around at night – at least that would have applied in the capital—Port Moresby. However, they had a couple of things in their favour.

Firstly, they were both well trained in unarmed combat and Rabaul was nothing like as rough a place as it was on the mainland. Secondly, they each had a Glock 37 pistol. This was not their weapon of choice, being, of Austrian design rather than American, but it was light and for reliability, it was second to none. In any case, which was all that Hans—the German friend that they had been introduced to in the Tavurvur bar—could offer with sufficient ammunition and with a minimum amount of explanation.

Mario Tudjman had, true to his word, taken Mark and Brad on the sight-seeing tour during the previous day. He did not appear to be much the worse for wear from the night before. He remembered that Brad was interested in volcanoes. And he remembered that Brad had been a little negative towards him because of Mario's attitude.

Consequently, he had endeavoured to play the perfect host. When they eventually came down off the hill Brad was happy to share a few more beers at the Hamamas but declined anymore in favour of an evening nap. Mario was quite happy – if not relieved—to let him go.

Later they had reconvened at the Tavurvur where Mario proceeded to drink himself into apparent oblivion. Mark and Brad had not seen either Mario or Sandra on Saturday and did not expect to do so.

Now it was Saturday evening and Mark and Brad set

off towards their goal which was at the other end of the town. They kept off the main road, moving along a street that ran parallel to it – not that there was much to distinguish the two apart. The only cost was that they seemed to attract the attention of every dog in town, although all the houses were surrounded by fences and the dogs were inside those fences. Fortunately, the residents seemed quite used to the continuous cacophony of noise, and the passage of the two intruders, apart from the odd person who came out and just waved when they saw the cause of the noise, was largely ignored.

At the end of the town, the road turned right and started to climb the hill, and then on the right of this road, they came to the track that was the entrance up to the observatory that Mark recognized from the photograph that Brad had shown him earlier.

The notice that announced that they were to enter the property of the Rabaul Volcano Observatory, which was surprisingly printed in English, told them that the road was closed from 6:00 pm until 6:00 am. There was only a single bar gate and there was a padlock on the bar. That was all the security there was. They stepped easily around the bar and set off up the track. They decided that there was no point in tramping through the woods on either side of the track because they were unlikely to meet anyone at this time of night—so they kept to the track. Another reason was that they did not wish to risk injury tripping on the volcanic rocks that littered the ground and were difficult to see.

They trudged on in the eerie silence. After New York City, where the closest you ever got to nature was to step in a dog-turd on the sidewalk, this was almost unbelievable. It was the same sky but so full of stars in the absence of the distortion of the lights of the city, and the sound of the occasional vehicle faintly in the distance just emphasized the remoteness and peacefulness of the place. The only other sounds to be heard were noises from animals going about their business in the undergrowth, and the occasional squawk for native birds disturbed by the presence of the intruders.

Suddenly the evening peace was shattered when a very noisy four-wheel drive vehicle came racing up the hill. Both tourists threw themselves into the bushes and it was only the angle of the road with its winding twisting track that saved them from being seen in the glare of the headlights. They were unable to see who was in the 4WD, but they did recognize the vehicle. They had seen it before at the Tokua airport – carrying their Pakistani friend Khan.

Mark was about to recover from his abrupt plunge into the undergrowth when Brad pulled him back down. Another vehicle went racing past going up the hill at a quite ridiculous speed, but this time they had no idea of the origin of the vehicle, or who the driver and any passengers were. Mark was becoming more than a little concerned. This Saturday night was planned to be quiet, and he had been led to believe that they would have the RVO to themselves! But they needed to proceed and complete their surveillance – even if that meant that they were in for a very long night and in the company of others.

They patiently waited until the noise of the vehicles had subsided. Then they dragged themselves out of the undergrowth not sure whether this part of PNG had any snakes or poisonous insects that they should have been concerned about.

After this encounter, they would need to be more cautious. They now walked on the side of the track that was shaded from the moonlight, swapping back and forth as the track twisted and turned up the hill. The vegetation thinned as they came close to the top of the road.

They heard another noise sounding as though someone or something was coming down towards them through the undergrowth on the opposite side of the track. Mark motioned with his fingers, using signals he had used when on assignment with the Special Forces, but which Brad seemed to understand. They again moved off the track into the undergrowth which they did with a good deal more decorum than they had on the previous occasion. They crept in as quietly as possible, well hidden in the gloom, and waited.

Nothing moved or made a sound for several seconds and then Mark heard the noise again – closer this time. They both automatically drew their Glock, not wishing to use them, but they certainly gave them some assurance. A wild pig burst out of the undergrowth and for a moment it stopped on the track, with eyesight superior to theirs. The pig was surprised at meeting two human beings in this terrain and at this time of the night. However, the pig did not seem frightened at all, just curious. But that moment's hesitation cost the pig its' life.

All Mark heard was a slight whooshing noise. The pig jolted and then tried to run back into the woods. It dragged its' back legs and then fell as though it had been shot.

A couple of Papuan locals appeared silently out of the woods on the far side of the track from which the pig had earlier emerged. While one of the men went to check on the pig, the other one walked directly over towards where Mark and Brad thought that they were hidden.

The man was less than five feet tall and was wearing only a bark-type skirt, but his body was all muscle. He was chewing something and occasionally spitting out a blood-like substance. Mark guessed that it was Betel nut juice—and he understood why people said it looked so scary with the almost luminous red around the man's mouth. Like the pig, the man had very good eyesight and did not seem to be the least bit frightened, as he looked at them in the shadows.

'Yu mekim wanem?' he asked, addressing them in pidgin. When he got no response, he reverted to barely passable English.

'What you do here?'

As far as Mark could tell they were well hidden in the undergrowth, but this guy was talking as though they were out there in broad daylight. And that meant the presence of their Glock pistols was a known fact, yet still, the man easily stood his ground quite unperturbed. On the spur of the moment, Brad took control of the situation and made a decision.

Stepping out of the bushes and putting the Glock in his belt, Brad said pleasantly.

'We are with the security services trying to find out what is happening at the observatory. We did not mean to disturb your hunt.'

The man smiled and nodded and then surprised them with some crucial information.

'Tu man' he said pointing up the hill 'Nogat gut' – there were two men and that was not good.

'What? They are there now?' Brad asked.

The man nodded and repeated 'Ya—tu man,' and then as though they were never there, turned his attention to the pig and his friend and seemed to forget the presence of the two interlopers.

Mark had not counted on there being anyone present when they looked at the Observatory. They already knew that there were two men ahead of them – at least there were two vehicles and now there were at least two Papuans, and probably more. There did not seem to be much future in trying to engage the Papuans in any further conversation. While Mark had a reasonable understanding of Pidgin, it was another matter to try to speak it, and these men, it appeared, could not speak much English. Still, they had delivered a warning so Mark and Brad would now be even more cautious in their approach.

Of some concern was that Mark was certain that he had seen a passenger in the first vehicle, so that meant that there had to be at least three people – but the Papuan had said two. Either the guy could not count or there was something else going on about which Mark so little point in speculating. They had to get on.

They started back up the track while the Papuans slipped away as silently as they had appeared taking the now dead pig with them.

At the top of the track, the ground dropped away into a clear area. To the right, they had a good view of the whole of the Rabaul Caldera and the harbour. In the distance to their left was the rumbling volcano of Tavurvur which they could just make out in the moonlight, and far to their right was the eerily silent volcano called Vulcan. At least the Tavurvur was relatively quiet tonight.

They were at an altitude of about 2 thousand feet at top of an almost sheer cliff, below which was the Rabaul township. To the left of the area in which they were standing were the offices of the observatory and there were lights on in at least two of the windows. Parked at the side of the largest building were an old Mitsubishi utility and a Toyota 4WD. This told Mark that at least one of the men present had access to the key to the single bar gate. Therefore, whatever he was doing, he had every right to be here. In the worst case, he could be using a stolen key, but that had nothing to do with Mark. But why at night and why now? There was hardly a code red state of an emergency as had been the case back on September 18th, 1994, when the volcano had exploded, even though some volcanic activity was still going on.

Volcanic activity, while spectacular and often fiercely dramatic, is not likely to be affected by someone working a bit of overtime on any given day. Mark whispered to Brad that he should stay in the shadows and keep a lookout back down the hill while he took a closer look at who the people were who had so unexpectedly interrupted their plans.

Mark was too experienced at this kind of thing, from his earlier life in the Special Forces, to go creeping around the way they do in the movies. Whoever was inside the building was in a lighted area and Mark was outside in the darkness. There was the risk that there was someone else outside the building, but Mark decided that the chances were slim and, if there was, he would just have to handle it. They were wasting too much time. So, he just walked up to the nearest lighted window and peered inside.

What he saw was a Papuan local sitting there looking through a variety of magazines and looking completely bored. In front of him were an array of monitoring-style equipment and a computer that was doing what all computers often do when switched on – absolutely nothing. Mark was certain that the Papuan was not the same guy that had been driving Khan's at the Tokua airport a couple of days before. He was not paying attention to anything and was either waiting for something to happen or was waiting for someone. It looked like the latter.

Mark then moved to the next window and peered in. This time there was some activity. Two Pakistani men were sitting in front of another computer, chatting away in their language. One of the men was typing furiously on the keyboard. The second Pakistani was the one they had referred to as Khan on the trip from Port Moresby and again at Tokua airport.

So, the Papuan reference to "tu man" must have meant these two. But what of the other man who was in the room plus the Papuan. The third man was unimportant to the Papuans but very important to Mark.

It was Mario Tudjman from the Tavurvur bar and their host of the previous day!

What was he doing there?

And were there any others?

Tudjman knew more about the Observatory than he had alluded to earlier. And, since he had not mentioned it to Bill McKee, was he supposed to be here now?

At least Mark had established several facts. Firstly, there was no monitoring equipment either volcanic or seismic in the room where the two Pakistanis and Mario Tudjman were chatting. Secondly, they were not playing computer games. Thirdly, it seemed likely that they were using the internet and probably sending email traffic. Fourthly, since the mysterious Khan was involved, it seemed likely that they had traced the place where the hard drive was intended to go.

That meant that the Augem Group was involved and that in turn meant that Mark and Brad had stumbled onto something at their first attempt. The assessment by the Australian Peter, coupled with their lucky encounter on the flight into Rabaul, was beginning to look about right.

Now they had to find out what their host from the previous day had to do with this. Mark's immediate fear that Tudjman was far smarter than he had at first appeared. And what if he had worked out exactly what Mark and Brad were doing in Rabaul?

From the body language in this group of three, Tudjman appeared to be the one in charge! Again, in Mark's inimitable way, he saw little point in speculating.

They had to find out much more about the goings-on in Rabaul.

Mark made his way back to where Brad was waiting and joined him at the edge of the bushes. They had no choice but to wait and the frustration started to take its toll on the two of them. Mark told Brad what he had discovered, and then they just sat there watching and waiting.

In an earlier life, Mark would have been ok with that. Patience was the name of the game. But time was also a name, and this was not a game.

Eventually, after about an hour of apparent inactivity, the light in the room in which Tudjman and the Pakistanis had been, was extinguished. Then there was a bustle of activity in the other room and then that light was also extinguished, and the four men came out of the building together. The Papuan was the last one to emerge and Mark assumed from the digital countdown that began, that he had set some form of an alarm inside the door.

Tudjman headed to the Mitsubishi while the others headed to the Toyota. The Pakistanis were still chattering away in a language that Mark could not understand, but he assumed was Urdu. The Papuan jumped into the driver's seat and coaxed the engine into life. It was some time since the vehicle had any attention, particularly in maintenance to the exhaust system – the noise was deafening in the quiet tranquil night. The two vehicles took off down the track at a similar speed to that which they had come up. The noise from their engines slowly faded into the distance.

It appeared to Mark that the place was now empty. Brad cautioned that they should be taking no chances. They were now at the place where, if their assumptions were correct, and the conference that they had at the safe house in Wellington was correct, was the centre of a plot that was to cause serious damage in a place many time zones away. Mark looked at their surroundings and mused that it was probably about the best place on earth to run such an operation. There was a valid reason for having telemetric, communications, electronic, and computer equipment in this place. There was no apparent or obvious reason why anyone should suspect a Papua New Guinea government, and the United States sponsored, facility as being used in plotting or planning terrorist activity. Rabaul and PNG were close enough to the country – Indonesia—that had the world's largest Muslim population.

Rabaul was remote enough, and sufficiently damaged by natural causes, that few people would consider ever going there. And there was only a small police force in the town that was more concerned with local issues and was hardly up with the play when it came to international terrorist activity or the use of modern forms of communication. From all of this, the one thing that Mark and Brad might have in their favour was that this organization was so unlikely and remote that the people responsible for its' operation may have become complacent. As it transpired, they were quite correct.

They cautiously approached the door and examined the lock. They were not particularly concerned about being approached from the track because there was really only one way in and that was in full view on this fine moonlight night. They were concerned that someone may be left as a watchman somewhere within the building complex, but there were no lights on anywhere, so that possibility was unlikely.

The lock was not exactly designed to beat the more determined of crooks and they soon had the lock beaten with the help of a Bump Key that Brad had produced from his pocket. Then they looked around for a security alarm system and Mark found the control panel behind the door. Again, it was somewhat crude. Although it would no doubt make one hell of a racket if the alarm was set off, there was unlikely to be any monitoring. In any case, it was sufficiently remote from any other residence to render any alarm quite pointless. Still, old habits die hard – security was part of someone's plan. But that person had never been to Rabaul. Mark quickly disabled the alarm and they both moved inside the building locking the door behind them.

Although it was unlikely that they would be observed they did not put on any lights. A diesel generator hummed away in another part of the building to provide constant power to the various pieces of electronic gadgetry in the observatory. The Rabaul mains power supply was both unreliable and unstable and was turned off at various times, sometimes with, sometimes without, warning. So, the generator made sense. Both Mark and Brad each had a torch and they set off down the corridor towards the room where Tudjman and the Pakistanis had been, and where they should be able to find out what had been going on with the email traffic.

The Pakistanis had left the computer switched on but not the display. Mark switched that on, and the operating system was asked for a username and a password. He pulled a flash drive out of his pocket. This might seem a strange piece of equipment for Mark to be carrying in such a remote and technologically backward place as Rabaul. To Mark flash drives are like a blanket was to Snoopy.

He placed the flash drive in the USB port and rebooted the computer. The machine came up ok and this time did not ask for either a username or a password. They would still need to find out the password security which protected the data. Mark then connected a second USB flash drive, copied a couple of routines to the hard disk, and fired them up. Within a few minutes he had the passwords – computer encryption software does not care too much whether passwords are created in English, Swahili, or Urdu. They now had control of the entire computer and, as far as Mark could tell, they now had access to all the data on it.

At this stage, he then handed the machine over to Brad. Mark prided himself at being able to beat any security system, but he was no match for Brad when it came to following data trails and analysing what he found along the way.

Mark whispered to Brad that he would take a look around the place while Brad performed his magic, and he went out of the door into the corridor. The offices were more or less as one would expect for a Volcanic Observatory. One office was dedicated to measurements of seismic activity and was littered with graphs that showed a surprising amount of activity in the greater Rabaul region. Another office was the radio room where the staff could make contact with the various outstations but there was nothing of any interest there. A third room seemed to be dedicated to the storage of documents, maps, and photographs. As far as Mark could tell they were all concerned with the volcanic eruptions, earthquakes, and other scary events that were after all the purpose of the RVO.

There was nothing that indicated any activity of the

type he had been led to expect of a terrorist cell. Or of the type that would interest a Finance Company such as the Augem Group far away in New York. From what he had learned in Sydney, there should be something that indicated, either training, planning, communication, or a financial facility. There was just nothing.

But then he entered the fourth room.

This room did not seem specific particular purpose having several desks and filing cabinets but nothing electronic and looking largely unused. That is apart from a laptop computer which was sitting in its' carry case on the floor. Then the purpose of this room began to become clear.

As an observatory, it was part of a worldwide network involved with volcanic monitoring and particularly with the United States Geological Service (USGS) and the Australian Geological Survey Organisation (AGSO). Because Rabaul had had more than its' fair share of extreme volcanic activities in recent years, many scientists from around the world would want to visit Rabaul and the surrounding stations. This was the visitor room.

Was this the place that terrorists had used to get one facility buried within another?

The RVO got on with the business of monitoring volcanoes and other forms of explosions and general mayhem caused by things of that nature. The visitors got on with their business of planning and creating them caused by mankind – all under one roof.

After the 1994 eruption of Tavurvur and Vulcan, most of the cost of the restoration of the monitoring equipment was met by the United States. Not that the US government was being particularly generous. They had monitoring equipment, for legitimate and other reasons, all over the world. Any chance to get involved in a foreign country was just that. Now it was possible that, although a major investment had also been made by the Australian government, the facilities could be used in terrorist activities against the USA of which Australia was a not insignificant partner. Neither of these governments would be pleased if someone else was being devious, but that was just the way the world works.

Mark moved further into the room and scanned the row of filing cabinets. They were a variety of sticky labels that had been marked with a pen to denote the names of the various temporary owners. There was nothing to indicate that any name was of more interest than any other, so Mark made a mental note of the names, and turned his attention to the laptop computer.

He was about to unpack it from its carry case when he heard the distant sound from outside of an approaching vehicle, and it was rapidly getting closer. He rushed back to the office in which Brad was working. Brad had heard the noise as well. He quickly restored the machine he was working with back to the icon display it had been in originally then turned off just the screen, doused his torch, and followed Mark out of the door. They scanned the rear of the building and found a door that was bolted from the inside, and which led into an area of the bush where there would be enough cover in which they could hide.

Mark was taking a chance but rushed to the front door and reset the alarm. It began beeping on a digital countdown. Mark thought that the resetting would normally take exactly sixty seconds which seemed about the time taken when originally set by the Papuan. But they had no real way of knowing. They had to just assume that they had that much time to get out, and to hope that it took whoever was coming up the track more than that time to approach the building. If the new visitors approached and heard the beeping, they would be more than a little suspicious.

The noise of the engine of the approaching vehicle would initially drown out the beeping. However, if the arriving driver switched the engine off before the sixty, or however many, seconds had expired, they would know that something was wrong. The only good news that Mark could think of was that whoever the visitor or visitors were, they were unlikely to be able to call on a battalion of troops for support in this remote place. In the peaceful air of the night, the beeping sounded like a ship's foghorn. The seconds seemed like hours. And they could do nothing about locking the rear door.

They hurried into the undergrowth and waited.

Eventually, a van lumbered from the track into the parking area. It looked like a security vehicle and another Toyota, although it was hard to tell given the mud-splattered condition. The question now was - was the security visit caused by Mark's disabling the alarm – in other words, the alarm was, in fact being monitored from elsewhere. Failing that, – was the security company simply making either one of their scheduled visits or a random visit.

The countdown on the alarm had gone for fifty seconds when the vehicle came to a halt. Mark and Brad held their breath. As far as they could tell there was only one person in the vehicle. He was unlikely to have the firepower that was a match for that of their two Glocks. He would certainly be armed as were most of the police and security people in this part of the world. But the last thing Mark wanted was to get into a firefight. There could only be one outcome and the prospect of that was frightening given that their operation was supposed to be covert and was certainly unsanctioned by anybody other than the dubious link to Harold Taylor. And in any case, the security guard was only doing his routine, monotonous and mind-numbingly boring job.

The engine of the Toyota was killed with fifty-five seconds gone on the alarm, but the guard did not get out immediately. He appeared to be talking on his radio to someone presumably at his base. Was he merely reporting in or was he reporting that something was wrong? It was the time spent on the radio that could have saved them—the beeping had ceased. Were they in luck once again?

The guard got out of the vehicle and for a moment just looked around and stretched. He was of similar build to the Papuans that they had earlier met on the track. He was dressed in a rough-looking uniform, very similar in colour – a dark blue—to that worn by the local police. He switched on a powerful torch which he flashed over the building and then, to the astonishment of Mark and Brad, selected a key from a huge bundle that he carried on his belt. He then entered the building and turned the alarm off. Mark began to worry. He had been told that the locals had an extreme sense of smell and therefore could detect that a foreigner had been in the place.

They need not have worried. Possibly because so many different people had been in the office, the guard seemed unconcerned. A light came on in the room that from memory Mark thought to be the toilet. Then it went out, to be followed by a light in the kitchen and cafeteria area. The light stayed on.

Mark signalled to Brad that he was going to investigate and silently made his way to the window. The guard had helped himself to a drink and was sitting down thumbing through a couple of old magazines that lay on the table.

Again, they patiently waited. After what seemed like

hours, but was probably only about fifteen minutes, the guard stirred, switched off the light, reset the alarm, and locked the building. He was just about to get back into the van when he suddenly caught a glimpse of something or someone in the undergrowth just by the top of the track.

Out of the woods came what looked like the two men that Mark and Brad had met before – there was no definitive way to tell.

'I gat wok welpig' one of the men said with a smile. To which the guard replied 'naisela wok.' As far as Mark could make out this was a conversation about a pig hunt and no mention seemed to be made of 'narapela' – the other men on the mountain. Finally, the two Papuans disappeared back down the track and the guard got into his vehicle and drove off following the two men.

This brief encounter caused Mark and Brad to have a chat before they got back to what they had come for. They felt that the locals had simply been attracted by the sound of the vehicle, but that did not explain why nothing had been said about their presence on the mountain. The fact that the guard had not appeared to be the least bit surprised to find the Papuans there meant that it was quite normal for the locals to wander around the mountain at night. Of more concern to Mark was the insurmountable fact that no matter where you were the locals seemed to silently observe and be aware of the various comings and goings. An idea was forming in Mark's mind that body language played a large part in Papuan culture.

In their earlier meeting on the track, the Papuans had not attempted to hide what they were doing on the mountain. Maybe—just maybe—they had stumbled upon someone who they could trust. Not that it mattered. But it did Mark the assurance that the natives were friendly.

After waiting for a further five minutes to make sure that all was clear, they approached the door again. While the door through which they had exited the building was open, there was still the problem of the alarm. They had to re-enter through the original door. Mark defeated the lock more quickly this time, disabled the alarm, and they returned to their original tasks.

Very quickly Brad was making some headway in sorting through the email messages of interest. Some had been deleted but not cleared from the deleted folder. The person doing the deletion was not aware that to Microsoft Delete meant store somewhere else. This suited Brad just fine. He had established folders on the flash drive to store them, and although it was relatively slow, this meant that he could simply detach the drive at once, rather than store them on the hard disk and attempt to copy them all in one hit.

Mark concentrated his attention on the laptop. He went through the same routine as they had done on the desktop and was quickly into the system and had access to all the folders. What he discovered both surprised and shocked him. He was surprised that the machine that had been left behind, happened to be the one that contained the very information that they sought. This was either a coincidence or the person that had left it behind thought that it was safer here than elsewhere. Or had it been deliberately left there so they would find it? Or did they just not care?

In the game of 'hide and seek' that all security services play you could very quickly lose your marbles trying to guess and second guess in every event. Mark just got on with the job in hand and left it to others to worry about the ifs, buts, and maybes.

He was shocked at the information. It seemed to

contain a wealth of data on the terrorist networks throughout Indonesia including names, places, strategies, and plans. This information, in the hands of the Central Intelligence Agency, in fact, any agency that was in the business of tracking terrorist organizations, would be priceless.

He pulled a couple of flash drives out of his pocket and proceeded to make backup copies of all the relevant folders. He could have set the machine to do them all in one hit. However, as Brad was doing with the email traffic, it was better to be sure of getting it bit by bit, and if need be, getting out if someone else should come calling. He smiled at the thought of how many movies he had seen where the copy process was always just a nano-second longer than when the bad – or good—guys were due to appear. Still, some folders took longer than he would have liked. He went to see how Brad was doing and to fill him in on what he had found, rather than die from the boredom of watching the copy process.

Brad was a very worried man, and the news that Mark had brought did nothing to improve that. The good news was that they were getting far more information than what they had expected to and at relatively low risk of discovery, either before, during, or afterward. The bad news was that everything seemed to confirm what the CIA and the FBI had refused to accept. There was a serious threat emanating from here that was going to bite someone in the ass. It seemed to confirm everything that Harold Taylor had alluded to in Wellington.

Why had the CIA, in all its' wisdom, and its' brilliance in the art of analysis, chosen to ignore the information?

Mark had his own worries, which he kept to himself for the time being. This whole exercise, with all its twists and turns, seemed to be going too well. The email traffic that had been at least identified by someone in the CIA had been traced to the South Pacific. Mark's father had further narrowed this down to Rabaul. That itself was complex but not beyond the trap and trace technologies that were readily available to anyone with the time and inclination. The US government had more than enough of both. That was provided that they decided to use them.

And provided they targeted the right places and right people.

There was, of course, a more fundamental question.

Why had the originator of the emails not used a Remailer? There are many available on the web - well beyond the jurisdiction of the United States law enforcement system – to hide the origins? This could be explained by naivety. But in these days, when terrorist organizations were becoming more and more sophisticated, this seemed highly unlikely. That aside, the laptop computer that Mark had "found"—was it just too good to be true? The very things that the team was looking for and needed appeared to be all neatly stored on one hard disk drive! The protection that ordinary computer security systems provided could mean that there was no perceived risk if the computer was found. But just suppose that someone had left it behind in the knowledge that Mark and Brad would have the necessary skills to break the security? And if this scenario proved to be a correct assumption, it had far more serious implications.

Who else knew that they were in Rabaul, and more to the point, what their purpose was in being here? The only logical answer to the riddle that Mark could think of was Tudjman, but how could he have known anything? Unless that was, he or someone was far better informed than he would have thought.

Mark shuddered. He would firm up his thoughts before he bounced them off Brad. Much as he trusted the Afro-Americans it appeared that someone was playing silly games. It was just that they are not so silly when lives are at stake. Or was it just that time of the night when the mind plays silly games? Was it that in reality, they had just been plain lucky? No – there were too many coincidences, and coincidences worried people in the security and intelligence business. There were also assumptions, and the entry-level course at spook school said – never to assume anything.

Mark shook his head to clear it of these crazy thoughts. They were in Rabaul to find information, and they seemed to have been successful. Let someone else worry about its' origins! That was a job for the CIA. And if the CIA fucked up again then that was their problem.

He went back into the room and set up the laptop to take a copy of another folder. While that was copying, he put the task in the background and began to search through the files looking for clues of the name of the person who owned the laptop. That also turned out to be relatively easy.

The laptop computer appeared that belonged to Doctor Abdul Jabbar. That was one of the names that appeared on at least two of the filing cabinets. Mark walked over to the first cabinet but found that it was locked. The standard locking mechanism on cabinets of the four-drawer type was a bar lock that locked all four drawers at once, and this one appeared to be no different. That meant that the other unknown users of this set of drawers all had access. So, Mark reasoned that a key would be kept somewhere in the office, rather than have several sets of keys which would keep a locksmith in business for quite some time. That also proved to be correct. He found sets of keys in the bottom drawer of one of the desks and soon had the correct key. He was then able to look at the doctor's files.

The Doctors' section of the drawers – the top two—were only about one-third full. The filing system was somewhat haphazard with files located at random, so he quickly skipped through them. Most of them were just notes on geophysical matters and were of little interest to Mark. He was just about to give up his search when something triggered his thinking. A couple of the papers had figures with dollar signs on them and dollars had little to do with geophysics. And he belatedly realized that a couple of the maps were not of Papua New Guinea. They were of islands – but the geographical coordinates indicated they were well to the west of Rabaul.

They were in Indonesia.

Further examination revealed a computer file reference on the documents.

He rushed back to the laptop. No folder bore any resemblance to the file references. Mark began talking to himself. 'Come on baby – I know you are there – show me!'

All computer systems can 'hide' files and hidden files can be notoriously difficult to find. That is if you do not know where or how to look. Mark did. He changed the flash drive from the one he was copying onto and inserted another and copied down another program. In a standard operating system, some functions enable a search for hidden files. That function required Administrator rights and another higher-level password. Mark's program bypassed this problem. Again, he had the files.

Most of the files in the folders that he found were encrypted. Breaking that encryption would be far easier than searching further through filing cabinets. He again swapped the flash drives and started the copy process. While that was going on, he locked the drawers and returned the keys to their original hiding place. There was not much chance of their movement being spotted, but there was no point in taking that risk. He replaced them exactly as he had found them. When the copy process was complete, he deleted the programs he had copied from his flash drives and deleted any evidence that he had been there.

Brad had finished his copying at about the same time, and he also returned everything on the computer to the state that it had been in originally. Then they locked the back door through which they had made their earlier escape, reset the alarm, and exited the building through the front door.

Walking back down the hill Mark had a feeling of achievement and began to consider what they would do with the information that they had gathered and how best they could get it through to the United States. That was a mistake, but as it transpired not an irreparable one.

Mark was alone with his thoughts when he just about died of fright when the two Papuans who they had met earlier appeared on the track in front of them.

Brad said 'mipela go nau' but the locals just smiled and replied, 'Yu gut man – kam brata dring' and ushered the two of them off the track. At first, Mark was wary but received a reassuring smile from Brad – and the reassuring touch of the Glock. Although they were now off the main track, there was nonetheless evidence that people had walked this ground before. Mark then heard another – or was it the same – vehicle slowly climbing its' way up the track.

The leading Papuan turned around to Mark and said in perfect English 'That will be Billy returning with his girlfriend', laughed, and continued on his way.

Mark could only laugh too. What a strange place and even stranger people!

Soon they came to a group of huts. They were in the middle of a native village. An even greater surprise for Mark and Brad was the identity of the person who stepped out to greet his visitors. He looked a little different in his native dress but did not seem at all surprised to be receiving visitors that late at night – well early in the morning.

It was Khan's driver that they had met on Thursday at the Tokua airport.

'Welcome to my humble abode.' he said, in near perfect, but heavily accented, English, as he extended his hand to each of them in turn.

'Come and have a drink – you have been busy tonight and you must be bloody thirsty' he continued with a wink and the inevitable grin. He could have been a fair dinkum Australian were it not for the blackness of his skin and the harsh facial features of a Papuan.

It turned out that he had spent a few years playing in the NRL—Australian Rugby league – that is where he had picked near-perfect English – before returning to the peace of Rabaul.

The five of them sat down around a rough table and out came the inevitable green bottles. As it turned out the two who they had met up by the Observatory both also spoke perfectly good English. A funny old world thought Mark.

'So – you have now found out that this cell phone number you gave me is no good. And what else have you found out about in Rabaul?' the man who was referred to as 'Lucky' asked with a laugh.

There was no pressure, no animosity, just five men from two very different worlds having a chat over a few beers. But Mark did not want to give anything away. Their experience with the cellular telephones was just plain dumb on their part, so he laughed as well. But, as for their other activities, he would not be imparting much information – for two reasons. Firstly, his story would have sounded quite preposterous to these hosts so remote and far away from the real world. Secondly, he felt insecure in the knowledge that Lucky was, for all his good nature, still Khan's driver. As Mark was well aware from an earlier life, casual, often off-the-cuff innocuous comments could get people killed. Not that these people were as well educated or as well connected as the diplomats who came readily to mind, but the principle still holds.

Mark decided to reverse the question.

'What is going on at this Observatory of yours? There seem to be a lot of things happening that have nothing to do with volcanoes.'

Mark was again surprised – more at the honesty of the response that he got from Lucky.

'Ever since that bloody Doctor arrived things have not been good. And his bloody black friends have made things worse.'

Brad grinned at Lucky's description of the Pakistanis. They were, after all, of the same colour. Mark Taylor was the only white man at this particular meeting.

'What do you mean?' Mark asked, probing further, and oblivious to the apparent anomaly. He was not disappointed by the reply.

'They keep all their information on that bloody computer of theirs and spent many a night emailing backward and forwards. They have nothing to bloody do with the rest of the staff – the arrogant bastards!'

'We saw an ex-pat up there tonight – what has he got to do with the Observatory?' Mark asked, not sure whether to mention that they had previously met the European gentleman. This time he was even more surprised by the reply.

'That would be Mario Tudjman. He is not an Australian. He comes from Europe.' Lucky replied with a laugh. The latter description said as though there were something to be guilty about.

'He thinks he runs the show in Rabaul, but actually, he knows nothing. When the Doctor first came to Rabaul he befriended Mario and has since sort of kept him, shall I say, employed. He is paid to keep an eye on anyone who comes snooping around. I am surprised you did not know him?'

Mark and Brad exchanged glances. It was no use pretending that they did not know who they had seen. And it was probable that the locals would know about Mario's drinking habits, and therefore his companions. And therefore, his tourism efforts on the previous day. Mark answered with a disarming smile.

'Oh – we know Mario. I just did not think that you would. He appears to spend most of his time drinking at the Tavurvur tavern. That is where we met him a couple of days ago.'

Lucky just smiled.

'If you have met him, you will know that he is not very bright. He burst out laughing and then became very serious.

'Our coloured friends are however a different matter.'

Now that was interesting. Although Mark was confident that the Papuans had a reasonable idea of what went on, and who was what in the small town of Rabaul, he was not so sure that they had accurately assessed their friend Mario Tudjman. But that assessment would have to wait. At least it confirmed that Mark and Brad had homed in on the correct source of information. Mark glanced at Brad, who shrugged.

'We are going to do something about them.' Mark said, and again he was surprised by the reaction. Lucky got to his feet, rushed into his hut, and returned with some glasses and a bottle of what looked like the Kava that Mark had drunk in Fiji years ago - with disastrous results. It was warm to the taste, but Mark was careful to drink only sparingly. He knew what these local brews could do.

Eventually, they took their leave of Lucky's hospitality. 'Gut nait – yu gut man' was the final comment. One of the men who had been hunting pigs earlier in the evening led them about one hundred yards through the trees and they were on the road that led back into the Rabaul township just a little further up the hill from where they had entered the RVO land. Again, the exchange of handshakes was accompanied by 'Gut nait – yu gut man' and then he seemed to just merge into the undergrowth, and they were on their own.

'What was all that about?' Brad asked as they set off down the road. He had understood what was said in the farewell. It was the whole episode that had him confused.

Mark was looking pleased with himself as he replied. 'Don't you get the impression that the locals don't like our Pakistani friends?'

Their secrets would be safe because the locals trusted them and did not trust the people that Mark and Brad had relieved of precious information. In that sense, it was a very successful night's work. Except that is for the outstanding questions—Where was the mysterious Doctor Abdul Jabbar? And what was the role of Tudjman?

Mark would have liked to take Lucky at his word that Mario Tudjman was merely an appendage. However, there was the nagging thought that it was not quite that simple. They had the trust of the locals—the trouble was that they just did not know who was who? However, it would be much harder to gain the trust of their own people – that much they did know.

With more disastrous results than just the odd drink of Kava – that much they did not know – yet.

And it was now the early hours of September 2nd.

Chapter 18

Analysis

Brad got back to the Hamamas Hotel at 3:35 am, and Mark was in his Tavurvur room about ten minutes later.

Mark should have been able to go to sleep easily with the combination of the time, the tiring and at times stressful work that the visit to the Observatory had involved, and the Kava-like drink that they had courtesy of their Papuan hosts. But sleep would not come easily.

His mind dwelt on the things that they would need to do and the fact that—if his father was indeed right about the timing—they had so little time left in which to do it.

For the first time in a few days, he let his mind wander onto thinking about Annette Covic. He felt almost guilty. The peace and tranquillity that typified Rabaul also brought a sense of loneliness. After the rapid pace and bustle of life in New York City, to be suddenly dumped in this strange land, and you were physically so far away from everything, brought with it helplessness. Eventually, by concentrating his thoughts on Annette, and trying to forget the pressure caused by matters beyond his control. He seemed to calm down and sleep came, albeit fitfully.

Mark awoke at 7:30 am and, although he was still

tired, he realized they had some work to do. It was a beautiful day in Rabaul, and peaceful, apart from the occasional yapping of dogs and the shrill cries of the roosters who seemed to have no concept of day or night. He rang the room service, such as it was and arranged a breakfast to be served in his room.

He then fired up his laptop computer and began copying the data that he had acquired at the Rabaul observatory from the flash drive to his hard drive. He was in for a long day.

It would have made some sense to rush back to the States with the information that they had gathered at the observatory and get the Federal Bureau of Investigation, the Central Intelligence Agency, and National Security Agency, with all their computer power, at work to analyse it all. But they had discussed that, and the prospects did not look hopeful. There were at least three problems that decided to do that difficult.

The first problem was that an exercise of that kind required getting authorization to use the resources and right now, in the absence of what was termed conclusive evidence, they reckoned on having a shit show in hell of getting that authorization. The people who had quietly side-lined the intelligence they had already received in the United States from Brad, and probably from Harold, could just as easily at least delay such authorization and any subsequent investigation. There just was not the time or inclination to risk that.

The second problem was far more practical. The telephone system in Rabaul did not easily lend itself to communications of the style required – sending large volumes of data electronically. The services in Rabaul were restricted to dialup, and at that not the most reliable of connections, being old copper wire. This meant that it would be quicker and infinitely more reliable to hand carry the data to Washington, or at least as far as a civilized country.

But that presented another practical problem. There was no way – well no legitimate way—of getting out of PNG in a hurry. International flights to Australia from Port Moresby only occurred on Thursdays and Sundays – and today was Sunday – and it was too late to get from Rabaul to Port Moresby in sufficient time. There was also a risk in going to Port Moresby where there was a possibility of their coming to the attention of the security people who, as always, were no doubt there snooping around.

As far as they knew no one, other than Harold in Wellington and Peter in Australia, had the faintest idea where they were. However, in the spook business, you could never be sure. So, for now, they decided to stay in Rabaul to analyse the data they had, and if possible, build the case to the point where the evidence was irrefutable.

They had recovered so much information from the observatory that it was going to take them a couple of days to categorize and decipher it all, and then try to make some sense out of it all.

Mark had all the information from the laptop computer hard disk drive belonging to Doctor Abdul Jabber, while Brad had all the email traffic from the desktop belonging to the RVO. So, the task was at least neatly divided into two discrete areas of responsibility. They decided to cast aside any worries they may have about convincing the CIA of their conclusions until after they had reached them – if any!

Most of the email traffic was encrypted, which made Brad's task of selecting messages a little harder and more time-consuming. In simple terms that meant that he probably had a lot to analyse only to then discard it. But he would not be discarding anything just yet. Messages over the internet sometimes meant just what they said. At other times they could and did, mean something entirely different. It was a matter, as always in the analysis business, of looking for and establishing patterns. It could be time-consuming and boring, but it had to be done.

Fortunately, Brad had all sorts of software on his laptop which would assist with an exercise of this kind. It was not an ordinary laptop and Brad was not an ordinary user. And he had a powerful incentive. The CIA and the FBI, or at least someone with all the required influence in, or over, those organizations, had rejected his earlier conclusions. Now he was sure that amongst all the data there was the proof that trouble was not only brewing. Now he knew who more of the players were, he had a fair idea when their plans were to be implemented, and he had a fair idea where.

He did not know the How. But he wrongly assumed that the How did not matter.

His first task was to work out the encryption algorithm. After a certain amount of trial and error, which proved to be a relatively simple exercise. Whoever had set the encryption system for their emails at the Observatory had used an algorithm that was in fairly common commercial use. Although this changed from time to time, it was just a matter of finding the date of transmission – which was always in clear text – and relating that to a particular version of the algorithm.

The next thing he had to do was to sort out the messages into point of origin or sender and receiver address so that he built up a folder of communications relating to each person or name. Then in each folder, he stored them in date order. It would have been better to have access to an NSA computer which would have handled the

the entire task in a matter of seconds but there were a couple of problems with that solution. He could have used his contacts to sneak into a computer without getting formal permission, linked his machine, then downloaded the data to the NSA computer, done the sorting, then copied the resultant analysed data back to his machine, and then deleted the fact that he had ever been there. But the PNG telephone system did not allow that. And, even if it did, who could he trust back in the States? He settled in to do the job the slow way.

A pattern began to emerge. A fair amount of the traffic was under the name of Waseem who was one of the Pakistani men they had seen at the Observatory. The gentleman's full name might have been Waseem Khan which would tie him to the man they had encountered on the flight from Port Moresby, but that did not matter. He knew that Khan was at the observatory, and active on the computer, and the latest email with the name Waseem was date and time stamped 09:02 21:33:05 on Saturday – and that was last night when Brad and Mark had been there. Although Waseem occasionally communicated in his native language – Urdu—all of his messages that used the encryption algorithm had their origins in English.

Brad fired up a translation package just to be certain he was reaching the correct conclusion – and he was. The messages in Urdu were personal. Waseem would certainly not want his mother or his wife to have access to this folder, but they were of little interest to Brad.

The messages, which had their origin in English, also followed a set pattern. Waseem would receive a message from someone, and he would then send a message on to someone else, with very little, if any, modification to the text. This meant that Waseem was a go-between working for someone else and he did not appear to be a major player in whatever game they were playing. He was just a participant. But participating in what?

Doctor Abdul Jabbar was however a very different proposition. He frequently used the machine from which Brad had taken the data, and that appeared to indicate that this was the machine – possibly the only machine in the Rabaul Volcanic Observatory – that was connected to the internet. This conclusion was reached because a fair amount of traffic was just normal administrative communication to and from people who were part of the observatory's general staff.

The Doctors' traffic in both directions was far from normal communications – for a person who was supposed to be primarily interested in volcanoes. Of course, anyone could have used the machine in the name of the Doctor, but there was little point in worrying about that. The facts were that his involvement made him very much a "Person of Interest" and, before examining the traffic in any detail, Brad side-tracked and made some inquiries about the life and times of the good doctor.

That meant that he had to access the database of the Indonesian State Intelligence Agency – the "Badan Intelijen Negara" – otherwise known as BIN. The BIN was meant to be a civilian organization, but it was civilian in name only. It was headed by a "retired" four-star General from the Indonesian Special Forces, and it pursued its' duties with the same ruthlessness and disregard for civil rights as did the military services.

Being Indonesia, still grappling with the switch from autocracy to democracy, it also lacked the discipline and structure of other organizations in their kind of business. Some parts of the Indonesian government were not exactly well known for their integrity and ability to keep secrets, and the Badan Intelijen Negara was no exception.

In any case, the CIA and other intelligence organizations "cooperated" with the Indonesian BIN and therefore had what was termed "limited access" to their database. And Brad knew all about accessing databases, to get that extra bit of data that he could not otherwise get via a Google search. It was a slow process, but it was well worth the effort.

Abdul Jabbar grew up in the Indonesian capital of Jakarta and was conspicuously absent from any intelligence or security reports until he reached the age of eighteen and attended the University of Indonesia. He went to the University to read Geology in the 1970s and developed a fascination for volcanoes, which was fine. And other things that blow up, which was not so fine. He graduated in 1976 and then stayed on for three more years to get his Doctorate – again in Geology.

This was when he came to be noticed by the Indonesian intelligence and security people. There was nothing wrong with doing a Doctorate in Geology or having an interest in things that go bang. What was wrong, and got their attention, was the network of friends and associates he appeared to be developing during this time. Also, during his doctorate years, he spent a good deal of his time overseas. While there was nothing definite to link him to anything clandestine, there was also nothing that would logically connect his studies to, and the sites he visited, in Pakistan, Afghanistan, Malaysia, and elsewhere.

Among his associates were Abdullah Sungkar and Abu Bakar Ba'asyir. These two gentlemen had been arrested in Indonesia in 1979 as members of Dural Islam – known to the security profession as DI. The DI organization dated back to the rebellion in West Java in 1949 but became the movement that led to the emergence of the Jemaah Islamiyah terrorist organization – which in turn became known as JI.

When these two gentlemen were released in 1982, they went to Malaysia apparently to escape the attention of the Indonesian security forces. There, with a community of other Indonesian mainly Muslim exiles, they became involved in the recruitment of people to go to Afghanistan, essentially to fight the Soviets. When the Soviets finally pulled out of Afghanistan the DI and JI recruits stayed on and eventually, and inevitably, linked up with al-Qaeda.

The extent to which Doctor Abdul Jabbar himself was directly involved in any activity which involved al-Qaeda was vague and his loose associations with terrorists meant that he was a "Person of Interest" but little more. Even his communication with the cleric Abu Bakar Bashir, and one of his disciples, Hambali, barely raised an eyebrow, until after the Bali bombing in October 2002. Then, when the Indonesian police were rounding up suspects, including the cleric Bashir, the doctor simply dropped off the radar – or probably more correctly he got the hell out of the way and went underground.

There were no records of him anywhere that Brad could find until he magically reappeared at the Rabaul Volcano Observatory as just a plain and simple geologist who had expertise in pyroclastic shield volcanoes.

This presented Brad with a dilemma. Indonesia is a vast archipelago that has all the characteristics that made it a very fertile ground for terrorist and their activities. Its' maritime borders were so widespread and diverse – there are over seventeen thousand islands—and still counting— in Indonesia—as to make them almost impossible to patrol. They leaked like a sieve.

Indonesia has many varied separatist movements. There are over three hundred ethnic and linguistic groups

—each with a separate agenda. Many of them were linked to Islam and with their influence stretching from the Aceh province at the western end of Sumatra, through Java and Timor to the far eastern region of Papua. The country as a whole was a mess with corruption prevalent and the government, economy, and financial systems were all weak.

After the demise of President Suharto, during whose rule the military had squashed any kind of resistance with ruthless, and often bloody, efficiency, the country had struggled towards democracy. The same military had tried to handle all sorts of dissension but was becoming progressively impotent in handling such a vast array of groups. However, even the most wanted terrorists and their organizations, although linked to al-Qaeda, usually only operated in Indonesia and surrounding countries like the Philippines, Singapore, and Malaysia. They had never embarked on any known terrorist activity in Australia to the south, let alone had any known plans to attack the United States of America on its own soil.

What Brad was finding was evidence that this was about to change. He was finding links to people in the United States, and evidence that the doctor was by no means an insignificant player in the movement. It was beginning to look an even bet that Doctor Abdul Jabbar was the person of particular interest and was the lead that they should follow.

They just did not have much time if Brad's interpretation of the messages being sent to and received from, someone in the United States was correct.

The messages were dated from October 2004— exactly one month after the Australian Embassy in the Indonesian capital of Jakarta was bombed. This could have been due to the possibility that the beginnings of the apparent terrorist cells were not established in Rabaul until about that time, and in itself may not have been that relevant. However, there was a trail that established the fact that the doctor was communicating with Noordin Mohammed Top - probably the most wanted terrorist in Southeast Asia.

Most of the communications were to an Internet Service Provider located in Java and seemed to be about money – or the lack of it. Nonetheless, Noordin Top was probably responsible for the second Bali bombing in October 2005. And immediately before this event, there was a notable increase in the amount of email traffic both ways and for which Doctor Abdul Jabbar was either the sender or the receiver.

Brad made a note to check whether the traffic volumes with the United States had increased at about the same time. From the messages, he had scanned so far this did not appear to be the case. That it was something else to check out if he had the time.

He went on to follow the other trails. The other messages that were of interest to Brad were sent to an ISP located on the east coast of the United States and they also did follow a particular pattern. They were invariably sent from Rabaul at about 9:30 pm, which meant that they were received the same day but early in the morning at about 5:30 am. There seemed to be no particular reason for this other than the fact that they would be sent at a time when very few people would be around the Rabaul observatory. And also received at a time in the United States when it was unlikely that many would be around the receiving computer other than the intended recipient.

That being the case, it seemed a little strange that they had not been deleted. Then Brad remembered that he had retrieved many of the messages from the deleted messages folder. Surely no one could be so dumb as to leave the computer rubbish bin—which was itself a folder—un-cleared! But that was not Brad's problem – was it?

He next studied the detail of the content of the message. The earlier messages – the ones that followed the bombing in October 2004 – seemed to contain little more than advice. This was what happened. This was how it was arranged. These were the precautions that were taken to avoid detection. And this was the result.

Anyone in the world could have read about the first matter – the What, and the last matter – the Result, in any half-assed newspaper. Or simply watched CNN.

To have access to the second matter – the How it was arranged , and the third – How it was kept below the radar , the person had to have been involved. Therefore, Doctor Abdul Jabbar was involved. But, apart from the CNN or the like trying to get a scoop, who in the United States was asking for, and getting, such information and why?

He dug further.

Some of the more interesting messages used a somewhat crude method of disguising the names of places and dates. It was fairly simple for Brad to work out that cities were identified by a code that was not unrelated to the international codes used to identify airports—IATA codes – so that TSS turned out to be New York City using the airport code for a Heliport on East 34th Street. Why they should choose this obscure Heliport rather than JFK for John F Kennedy, or LGA for La Guardia was a bit of a mystery.

The answer to that question lay in one of John Dubois' ego trips, but Brad could not have been expected to make this connection.

Dates were simply numbers. The latter was resolved

when Brad worked out from a couple of assumptions that he made about relative timings of certain events. If the difference between two known numbers was seven and certain events occurred seven days apart, it was then possible to work out the base number, and from that point on it was a simple matter to convert a number to its' equivalent date. The base for the system was zero and that equated to the date December 31st, 1967, which other than it being the base, had no particular significance that Brad could see.

However, the number 13402 was quite significant to Australia. It translated to the date of September 9th, 2004 - the date that the Australian Embassy in Jakarta had been bombed. As was the number 13789. It was October 1st, 2005, the date that several people had lost their lives, or limbs, or loved ones, in the Bali bombing. It was fairly basic, but no one would take any notice of traffic that contained just numbers and letters, so it was effective. Until someone with particular skills and logic took a closer look. Brad could have done without the distraction, but it made the rest of the exercise progress more rapidly and would prove more than useful in reaching his conclusions.

The rest of the messages for the most part appeared to concern money. With the growth of various movements in Indonesia and a move by these groups to force a greater involvement of Islam in matters of state, various people in the Middle East had taken an increasing interest in Indonesia and supplied funding, particularly for schools. It made sense to spend money on breeding, educating, and indoctrinating the faithful, rather than spending money trying to convert them when they were older, and presumably, wiser.

That money was targeted and could not be used by the various factions fighting their own little wars, so it stood to reason that they would look elsewhere for funding. The extent to which any overseas funding would be made dependent on the export of the terrorist activity was a moot point. These considerations led Brad to the conclusion that there was far more to the funding arrangements than would have otherwise been assumed.

It appeared that the Al Qaeda group, and their many support organizations, were interested in stirring things up. The Indonesian groups were interested in their own little wars, albeit that their ultimate objectives were at least ambitious, and probably impossible. But when there is money on the table there can develop strange bedfellows.

And Doctor Abdul Jabbar was interested in money.

From the many names that were included in the various messages, three names of apparent Pakistani origin began to occur frequently in the later messages. The names were fairly common—Lateef, Muhammad, and Arif. And it appeared that these three were residents in the United State. They were all Muslims. And they all certainly lived in New York City.

There was nothing beyond that to indicate who or what these people were, or where they had come from. But when coupled with the advice that was being exchanged before their involvement, these three seemed to have been recruited into the network for a very specific job which seemed to involve blowing up someone, or something.

What was not so clear was the involvement of the Augem Group. That they were the recipients or the originators of a fair number of the email messages was now beyond any doubt. But what was their role, and in what? They were the first to start using the three names, so it was logical to assume that someone in the Augem Group had recruited them and introduced them through the network. Were they seeking approval from the Doctor, or whoever he represented, or were they just informing the Doctor? Augem, or whoever within the Augem Group was the originator, did not come across as an authority, yet the Doctor didn't either. Could Augem be controlling a cell or were they simply yet another relay or conduit in some complex and as yet undefined network?

Brad turned his attention to the text of any messages that were around the times that these names were mentioned to see what else he could find out. The three names were always mentioned in the same sequence, which may or may not have been relevant, but that in itself was a pattern. He soon discovered that in the very latest messages the name "Arif" had vanished and been replaced by Ano. That suggested that Arif was no longer involved in whatever it was that they were doing or going to do and that he had been replaced by someone called Ano. That was a stretch – Brad had no knowledge of any first name of Ano – at least in Pakistan.

Then he thought back to his younger days when he often had to make up teams at school and leave a few spots for people yet to be confirmed – they were always shown as A.N.Other. Was that who mister Ano was? The messages overall seemed to always involve three, in something, not as yet confirmed, that was to occur somewhere, not as yet confirmed, at some time, not as yet confirmed.

He dug further. The three "recruits" were in New York so the "somewhere" place seemed likely to be New York City – the area code for the "event" was TSS, on a certain date. Further investigation of the timings meant Brad now had enough information so that the date could at least be confirmed. They were recruited to do something related to the numbers 12308 and 14499. The first number translated to September 11th, 2001 – a very significant date in the United States. The second number translated to a date that was also September 11th, 2007 – just eight days away. Nowhere, however, did the various emails and other documents reveal what they were to be involved in.

That required an assumption.

But it did not require a rocket scientist to work that part out.

The exercise had taken two days during which Brad had had little sleep. He was mentally tired from the concentration, but now the adrenalin started to kick in. From the mass of messages, he had established beyond any doubt that there was something very specific going on, and the various messages going backward, and forwards were not just exchanging pleasantries.

He believed that his analysis had been logical and was not in any way driven to its' conclusion by prior knowledge of what Harold Taylor had said in Wellington. From his training in analysis with the CIA – everyone went through the same basic course whether they were to be a spook or just a paper clip counter – Brad knew that making assumptions could screw the whole process that he had been through.

He was also taught that coincidence had a part to play. There were just too many coincidences. He knew the date and he knew the names of two of the participants. And he knew the pseudonym of a third. He could speculate that the funding was provided in the United States, presumably through the Augem Group, and that the expertise was provided by or through Doctor Abdul Jabbar. The latest email traffic indicated that the Doctor was not currently in town, and he was particularly secretive about his whereabouts. But at least the traffic also indicated he would return shortly. He would qualify as the right kind of person for the CIA to check into Guantanamo Bay.

He quickly made up a document summarising his finding and cross-referencing it to key messages by the originator, time, and date. He then packed up his laptop computer and set off for the car park. It was time to talk to Mark and see what he had come up with. It was the evening of September the 3rd – it had taken him almost two whole days to analyse the data.

They still had plenty of time – didn't they?

Chapter 19

Digging In

Mark's task was a little easier than Brads. Also, Mark was not so concerned with the lack of access to the giant number- crunchers back in the States, for two main reasons. Firstly, he was not used to working in an environment in which you simply handed off a task to a computer or a team of geeks, waited for the result, and then simply moved on. He was used to working things out for himself – slowly, methodically, crosschecking, understanding each step. If you had to rely on someone else's logic – and even in the age of computers, it was someone, rather than something – you lost any feeling for the issue that you were trying to get a handle on.

That led to his second reason. Computers cannot think—they only think they can. To analyse documents, the programs are looking for particular words and particular sequences – albeit those sequences may be completely random in structure. The words and sequences must be first defined by a person and written into a program – warts, bugs, and all. But they were the result of someone's or some groups' experience.

Did the NSA, or whoever designed such software,

think that the world stood still while they developed and applied their analysis algorithms? In any case, based on Mark's experience with the intelligence services of his country so far, how could he put any faith in any such analysis? They were bureaucrats, after all. It would be reasonable to assume that the analysis programs had been somewhat modified since – or rather as a consequence of – 9/11. But by who? And what had they learned from the terrible events of that day and the gut-wrenching aftermath?

The initial security on the folders and files had been stripped off to gain access to the data when he copied it across onto his flash drive back at the Observatory. Mark had to smile.

The art of deciphering codes went back to the ninth century and had first been put forward by an Arab—Abu Yusuf Yaqub. And the irony was – Abu himself was a Muslim!

Doctor Abdul Jabbar thought that no one would be able to read the files because, unless they had the rights of access, they would never have known that the files even existed. Equally obvious was that the good Doctor had inherited little of Abu's logic, for that is where Mark was able to use his own logic to gain access.

The original disk size was something like 80 gigabytes. The used space was 39 gigabytes. On the folders that you could see and adding the gigabytes of space taken by the operating system, they accounted for perhaps 23 gigabytes. Therefore about 16 gigabytes was hidden which was just too much to be explained as "normal". From that point on it was just a matter of locating the hidden files, scanning through the documents in the 16 gigabytes to distinguish useful from useless data, and then storing the useful data in some kind of sequence. Once he had the data on his own computer all the encryption that remained was stripped off and he had a list of clean files to work with.

That done Mark began reading.

The various documents included detailed analysis of almost every terrorist plot that had occurred in Indonesia going back to an attack on the Philippine Ambassador to Indonesia in August 2000. That suggested that the Doctor was either a fully paid-up member of Jemaah Islamiyah, or that he had extraordinary access to information that he was not supposed to have.

The content of other documents tended to confirm the former. The files also included information about camp locations and facilities in Indonesia, Malaysia, the Philippines, Thailand, and even in Pakistan and Afghanistan.

The most significant fact was - the files had nothing whatsoever to do with his expertise in, and study of, volcanoes.

Next Mark went in search of the dollar signs. There were several instructions sheets for transferring funds between international accounts. Doctor Abdul Jabbar seemed to have a constant flow of funds passing through his system, but very few of those funds stayed in his hands. They were not particularly large sums of money, nor did they need to be.

Whatever the perception of terrorist groups, they had one major advantage over the many anti-terrorist organizations set up to counter them – they did not need complex bureaucratic structures or vast sums of the folding stuff. The largest single expense for most bureaucratic organizations was their vast overheads of which the payroll was the major contributor. On the other hand, terrorists volunteered and came together only when something specific – and often nasty – needed to be done. And in many cases – such as suicide bombers – they would not live long enough to be of any further financial drain on the available funds!

Most of the funds were on a one-way journey – from the United States. And there was a consistency in the Bank and the account remitting the funds. It was not from the Bank of New York, and that may not be significant even though that is where the Augem Groups accounts were held. It was from a Bank operating on behalf of the Novosadska Banke – and that also may not be significant —because that was a Serbian Bank. It just seemed a little strange and Mark made a mental note to check out the connection later.

The disbursements were quite another thing. Some went to an account at the Bank Negara Indonesia, and others went to an account at the Bank Bumiputera – another Indonesian bank. However, the vast majority went to the Muslim Commercial Bank in Pakistan. with instructions for them to be further passed on to accounts in the Banque du Liban in Lebanon, the Union Bank of Egypt, and the Mizrahi Bank in, of all places, Israel.

Doctor Abdul Jabbar certainly seemed to have had some interesting connections in the Banking industry. Had he retained the money flowing from the United States he would have been a very rich man.

But he did not.

Mark then turned his attention to the Doctors role. Several of the documents were either originated by Jabbar or were copied from elsewhere without any acknowledgment. Whether this was simply to hide their origin, or whether it was to hide where they had gone was a moot point, but probably not relevant.

There were analyses of various plots or scenarios that terrorist groups, particularly of Indonesian origin, had been involved in. Therefore, it could be assumed that he was a collector of information and that they were there for referral to others in his extensive network. Many of the documents were well written in a journalistic style that was enthusiastic about the achievements, and a style that sought to encourage further participation, which suggested that their originator was both an educated man and an extremist.

There was nothing in the documents that suggested any involvement in planning such events and it soon became evident that Jabbar was not in any way directly involved in the planning of any plot – in the past, at present, or at any time soon.

Could these documents have been written by a journalist? If so, who was he or she?

There was some evidence that many of the texts could have been written by Abdul Rahim and that would certainly be of interest to the Australians. Rahim was an Indonesian-born Australian who was reputed to be the head of a Jemaah Islamiyah regional cell with a particular interest in their southern neighbour. There was no evidence that the doctor himself was funding any part of this, no evidence that he was involved in any decision making, no evidence of his direct involvement in any planning—there was just nothing.

Mark began to have a suspicion that the Doctor was only involved because he was a facilitator – so deeply buried in the network to be invisible. It appeared exactly as Peter had described back in Sydney. The terrorist groups kept things in separate cells.

Had they found the paymaster. But who was he paying? And with whose money? And for what purpose?

Like Brad, Mark did some research on the Doctors background and who he might have had contact with. He took a slightly different approach. Because the timing of Jabbar's appearance in Rabaul seemed to be linked to the Bali bombing, then occurrences around that time were his interest. Although there was confidence that at least some of the operatives in the Jemaah Islamiyah cell responsible for the Bali bombings had been captured, there was also ample evidence that some had escaped, not the least of them was Noordin Mohammed Top. While Noordin Top in an earlier part of his life had been seemingly innocent mathematics and science teacher at a Malaysian school, it was apparent that he had taught several people who subsequently became members of JI.

There was no link between mathematics and membership of JI, so Noordin Top obviously taught more than just how to add or subtract - except in the latter case when you were talking about people. There was some evidence that Top, and several others of his associates, had escaped and were hiding in the southern Philippines. That of itself was not of any particular concern to Mark. What was though was the link to another suspect – Umar Patek – who went by the nickname of The Trainer – among others. Again, the name did not matter quite so much as the who Patek was working for.

He was a member of the Abu Sayyaf Group (ASG) – an Islamic terrorist organization that was effectively at war with the government of the Philippines. Patek was believed to be the "Accountant" for the ASG and where did he get his money? It looked as though it was all channelled through Doctor Abdul Jabbar in Rabaul.

The Philippines had similar problems to those encountered in Indonesia. At least in substance but fortunately not in scale. The Philippines only had just over seven thousand islands to worry about and nothing like the diversity of ethnicity and language. Their "rebel" groups could more or less be divided into four, and one of those was largely imported. They had the Moro Islamic Liberation Front, the Abu Sayyaf group, the New People Army – the military wing of the communist party, and Jemaah Islamiyah the Indonesian group that seemed to pop up everywhere in Southeast Asia. Like Indonesia, their military was constantly trying to quell these groups with some spectacular successes, the result of which was that the groups appeared somewhere else.

Mark tried another tact. Was there any significance in the name Tudjman?

The most significant Tudjman in recent history was Franco – the past President of Croatia. However, apart from the claims that he could have been charged with war crimes had he not conveniently died of cancer in 1999, there was just nothing to indicate how he could have been involved in any of this. He had two sons one called Miroslav who had been the secret service chief when his father was President, and the other Stjepan about whom nothing much was known, apart from that he, in turn, had a son named after his grandfather Franco. He was going in circles—there was just no connection, so that line of inquiry he abandoned.

In his search for names, something else gradually started to emerge. Mark came across a document that contained brief resumes of three United States citizens. One was the genuine article, the son of an old Republican family and an apparent convert to Islam. One was born in the United States to a Pakistani father and an Indian mother. Of the other one, there was no indication of where he had come from or of how he came to be in the United

States to a Pakistani father and an Indian mother. Of the other one, there was no indication of where he had come from or of how he came to be in the United States. They were identified only as recruits one, two, and three.

But recruited by whom and for what? And what had they got to do with Doctor Abdul Jabbar?

Mark tried a search based on keywords that appeared in the resumes. Nothing. It was quite by chance that he came across another document that confirmed two "participants in the global Jihad" and a third "participant" as yet unnamed.

After checking with Brad who had unscrambled the numbers, the date for the "event" was quite clearly the anniversary of another event—September the 11th.

Although not stated other than as a number, the tone of the documents suggested that the event would be sooner rather than later –just over a week away.

That document also had reference to the source of funds and that got Marks' attention. The funding was being arranged in the United States by citizens of that country. Gradually he pieced together another part of the story.

The people behind the scheme were in the business of supplying funds that were channelled through Doctor Abdul Jabbar and eventually found their way into a series of accounts in the name of Abu Dujana. Further research revealed who he was – he was a key leader of the terrorist organization Jemaah Islamiyah. In apparent exchange for the funds, JI was supplying advice and expertise to the United States originator of the funds. But it was not the kind of advice that you would normally expect from a terrorist organization. There was nothing about the 'What' or the 'How' of an operation in the documents. Nor was there anything about what precautions should be taken in any operations. There was plenty about the Results.

Now that was strange because the critical result of any terrorist event was plain for all to see – the victims would be highly pissed off. To vent their anger, people needed a name. And one name sprung to mind – readily and easily – al Qaeda.

So, what had these people – whoever they were— done? They had recruited, or were in the process of recruiting, three people who had links to various terrorist training camps in Pakistan and Afghanistan that they were going to use in an event, or events, in the United States, on September 11th. That much was certain. It was a closed operation, meaning that no other assistance was to be either sought or was necessary – financial or otherwise.

Was it possible that the motive for the plot was not based on any Jihad after all? Was it either purely bloody-minded, revengeful or to feed someone's ego? Or was it designed to achieve some commercial goal that had nothing whatsoever to do with religion?

But nothing was surer. Al Qaeda would be blamed. And in true terrorist style, that would be fine with them. That much appeared to be crystal clear.

Mark sat back almost aghast at the thought.

Unlike Brad, he had not been taught about assumption and coincidence. Marines and the Special Forces were given occasional sessions in spook witchcraft, but they were not expected to do any actual analysis. That did not mean that they could not think. Was it possible that someone had designed a plot to look like a terrorist plot, but it was nothing of the kind? Was it being funded and planned by American citizens to blow up American citizens?

But for what reason?

What worried Mark more than anything else was that

he knew the people who seemed to be behind it. Yes –
there was little doubt that Mark had been meeting the
very people in the organization who were planning and
funding the operation not so long ago. And to them,
money did not seem to be a particular problem, as Mark
himself had recently experienced.

The Augem Group.

He thought again, back over the conversations he
had with the Australian, Peter, in Sydney. The style of an
operation was to have several cells operating
independently and security would be tight so that no one
cell was aware of the whole plan. But what if in this case
there was only one cell? The rest of the setup was done by
email advice. All they needed was some recruits who were
willing to die for any cause just so long as it was part of a
Jihad - they would get their reward in the next life. Nut
cases or people who had been so brain-washed that
nothing had to make sense anymore.

But where were the weapons or the bombs? Had
Mark and Brad come all this way to find out – what? That
the so-called plot was alive and well, organized by people
with who he was on a first-name basis. And not a stone's
throw from where he had left – New York City!

Then there were the other two unknowns.

Firstly—Where was the Doctor? Mark was now
fairly certain that Abdul Jabbar was a major player but for
financial and other reasons, and he was not to be an
actual participant. However, if there was a plot, and it was
going down within the timeframe that Mark had
identified, the Doctor would surely be in communication
with the other players.

Secondly – What was the role of Mario Tudjman
in all of this? If Mark had guessed correctly Tudjman was

was either a Croat or a Serb. What on earth was he doing in an organization which, for whatever other reasons they had for being, was based on Islam?

Mark was certain of one thing. Mario Tudjman was not a Muslim. So, what was the connection with the Serbian Bank? And why were funds channelled there?

Someone else would have to fathom out that part of the puzzle. Mark had no idea, and no time.

It had taken him two whole days of searching and reading, to conclude that even his father had not alluded to in Wellington.

The result of a plot was one thing. The organization of an event was another. Someone in the United States – certainly, someone at CIA and probably also at the FBI— was at least distracting attention away from a planned event or a plot.

A cover-up of the kind that Mark suspected had occurred was not that difficult to organize. The Intelligence services received millions of bits of information daily. These bits all had to be catalogued and analysed. It was like having a huge jigsaw puzzle and no picture to relate the pieces to. If someone removed a couple of the pieces the task became impossible?

Now the people trying to assemble this particular picture had another problem. The field operatives in this particular case were an ex-Marine who in real life ran a computer company and a technician from a non-operational division of the CIA. But all that aside, was it possible that the reason the CIA or the FBI were killing the plot was that it was not a plot at all?

Now that Mark had almost absolute proof that the plot existed, what did he do with it? His next action would be to convince someone that they should take it seriously.

Then he had to convince the "someone" that it was more important than money because he now had more than a suspicion that money, rather than doctrine or religion, was at the bottom of this whole mess.

In some respects, the money angle should have made it easier. Had the people involved been driven by what they believed in then no amount of talk would deter them from their objective. That is why there is no point in pointing a gun at a suicide bomber. Having decided that, there are few actual live demonstrations during suicide bombing lessons. At least with money on the table, there was a definitive and finite measure with which you at least had a chance to compete. So – they had recruited some people who were keen to participate in a Jihad, but in reality, there was a commercial objective that had nothing to do with anyone's God. The whole thing was insane.

The knock on the door roused Mark from his thoughts. He quickly returned his laptop computer to an idle state and opened the door. It was Brad. Mark looked at his watch and just about flipped. 'Shit – is that the time!'

Brad came in carrying his laptop, but he did not attempt to take it out of the carry case. He just placed it by a chair and sat down. His body language said it all – he was very worried, and at the same time excited, about what his analysis had uncovered.

They each explained what they had discovered and concluded from their two days of work that there seemed to be a certain commonality in their findings. They had spent some time on the telephone discussing various aspects of their respective studies during the last two days, but this was the first time they had compared their conclusions.

Brad was not entirely convinced of Mark's logic that led to his conclusions about the nature of the so-called plot, but did that matter?

Mark was pleased that Brad's research was consistent and at least pointing in the same direction, and that did matter. The timing of an event was beyond question, as was where it would occur. It did not matter who was going to carry it out, or how, or why. It was decision time – and time was not something they had in abundance.

'We have to get back to Wellington, and then to the United States.' said Brad 'this is a little too hot for me to handle – but what are the chances of this story being shelved yet again?'

Mark paused then said what they were both thinking.

'There are an astonishing amount of money changing hands, and most of it seems to originate in the United States. Irrespective of the motive, you don't think that someone at the CIA, or the FBI, or both, is on the payroll of this scheme and is being paid to cover this up – do you?'

'That is exactly what I think.' was Brads' reply.

Mark's face was grim.

He could handle incompetence. He had seen more than his fair share of it in his time, first in the military, and then somewhat surprisingly in private enterprise. What he could not handle was deliberate dishonesty by people who you should have been able to trust. And then you have these people standing by watching their fellow countrymen placed in harm's way, while they made some more money. He felt sick.

'What could be the possible motive?' Mark asked, almost talking to himself.

'Drugs is my guess'

'Yes – I think you are correct' replied Mark 'but that

will involve yet another organization – the Drug Enforcement Agency. I don't know that we want to get tied up with them as well. We have enough trouble with the CIA and FBI. I have had past dealings with the DEA, and I would rate them, but do we want to get them involved now?'

Brad thought about that for a moment. The last thing that Brad wanted was to get involved in yet another turf war. The DEA was, like the FBI, part of the Department of Justice and was supposed to share "concurrent jurisdiction" with the FBI on the enforcement of drug policy – whatever that may mean. Concurrent did not mean that they always agreed with each other. Brad had a simple reply.

'We have to leave that to the powers that be. Our issue is what is going to happen on September 11th, and the DEA will have to wait while someone sorts that out.'

'Yes – I think you are right again' said Mark, starting to feel more like a member of the establishment.

They had other issues to sort through, and therefore the decision was quite simple. Let the CIA and the FBI sort that one out.

'Ok. We need to decide what we are going to do with all this data. Do we simply pass it over or what?' asked Mark.

He had a feeling that the CIA would salivate at the prospect of getting their hands on the data. But would that achieve very much at this stage?

Either Brad was showing that he also could read Mark's body language, or else he knew exactly what the CIA would do.

'I think our best plan is to say nothing. I will probably be fired for saying this, but if they take the data, they will want to analyse it, and that means that they will ignore what we have to say. There just is no time for that.

So why not just encrypt it. They will probably have a look at both laptops back in the States, but we have to present the story as we see it first. I don't think it would be a good idea to delete it.' Brad concluded with a shrug. At least he had a smile on his face.

'Ok – we will do as you say. Now I think we should go and have a beer and some food, while we work out how we get the hell out of here.'

They went to the Tavurvur bar and there, holding forth as only he could, was Mario Tudjman. He greeted Mark and Brad like long-lost friends and proceeded to tell anyone who would listen about their conducted tour of a few days ago. There was no hint that he suspected them of anything underhand, or that they had anything to do with the Rabaul Volcano Observatory. The visit by Tudjman to the observatory on the night of Saturday was not mentioned. The absence of Mark and Brad from the drinking fraternity for the past couple of days was not an issue.

It appeared that the Papuans had fairly summed up the situation – Tudjman was all talk and did not seem to be the sharpest knife in the drawer. But his body language said something different. Attempts by both Mark and Brad to drift the conversation back to the people who worked at the observatory, in an attempt to find out where they might find the Doctor, proved useless.

Mark was uneasy. It could have been the worry caused by going over and over the files during the last two days, and the thought that maybe he was becoming paranoid. Or it could have been the two Pakistani gentlemen who were standing at the table looking terribly out of their depth and staring suspiciously at Brad.

At least one of them had met Brad on two occasions

and, because of Brad's characteristics, the man who went by the name of Khan was unlikely to forget him. Despite this, they never acknowledged either Mark or Brad. They just looked on with what appeared to be arrogance or indifference.

It was extremely doubtful that they had been aware of what had transpired on Saturday night. That is unless the Papuans were just as friendly with the men from Asia. But their presence did allow Mark to make a simple decision. He would not be raising the matter of their Glock pistols in the present company. Although they had purchased the Glocks, they needed to just return them to Hans – after all the money did not matter. They could hardly take them as personal baggage. Mark decided to simply leave a parcel addressed to Hans when he checked out of the Hotel, leaving Hans to wonder about the generosity of his American friends.

The only piece of good news was that every time that Mark had left his room, he had taken steps, albeit amateurish, to leave something that would tell him if someone had been in there. On the occasions that he returned to the room, the first thing he did was to check. It appeared either that no one was checking up on them, or that no one cared.

Probably the latter.

Chapter 20

Australian Security Intelligence Service

The trip back to Australia was nothing like the trip up to Papua New Guinea. The Royal Australian Air Force C-130J Hercules was not exactly the most comfortable airplane that they had travelled in. Their discomfort was offset by the relief that Mark and Brad both felt. The places they had been to in Papua New Guinea were pleasant enough, but you could always feel the tensions and the restrictions of being in a third-world country and away from the comforts of home. And they were so remote in Rabaul on what was the island of East New Britain that communicating with the outside world was at best difficult, at worst – and that was the norm – bloody impossible.

The Australian crew took great pleasure in having their guests onboard but at no stage did they attempt to find out who their guests were or what had been the purpose of their trip to PNG. Their passage back to Australia had been arranged by Brad. Or at least Brad thought so.

When they had flown into Port Moresby from Rabaul, they had noticed the Australian Air Force C130J sitting on the tarmac. Brad had gone off in search of the crew as soon as they landed. Maybe Brads' CIA connections had some bearing on their subsequent invitation to a free flight back to Brisbane. Mark had a different view. Maybe his contact in Australia – the mysterious Peter from the Australian Security Intelligence Service – had some bearing on it. In either case, they were glad to be on their way.

The flight eventually landed at Amberley, the Australian Air Force base about forty or so miles to the west of Brisbane. The customs and immigration formalities on landing were only cursory and completed in next to no time. Then the Australians offered them a lift to the Brisbane International airport.

If they thought that Brad's request that the two of them travel separately was strange, they did not say so. The Flight Lieutenant, a petite blue-eyed pretty lady with blond hair, just smiled, said 'No worries,' and lead Mark out to an unmarked car, leaving Brad to fend for himself.

The drive was pleasant if a little on the fast side. The young lady had obviously been trained for things that went quite a bit faster than the Ford Mondeo that she was driving. But she certainly could drive. At no time did she ask Mark who or what he was. Or where he had come from. Or where he was going. Or gave him sly knowing looks – she just kept up a pleasant, almost non-stop, chatter about Australia, Brisbane, and the areas they passed through.

Mark appreciated the break and the respect that the driver displayed. At the airport, she delivered him to the Departure area, and with a smile and a wave, she was gone.

He then had the job of rearranging his flight back to New Zealand. That had its' moments until he was booked on a flight to Wellington departing at 5:25 pm that evening. That achieved he sought solitude in an area away from the main streams of passengers and tried to catch up on what had been happening in the real world by reading the Brisbane Times. Mark was in a hurry to get back to Wellington, and then the United States, with what he regarded as vital information, but the flight could not leave any earlier than scheduled so he had no choice but to relax. That did not last long, however.

'So how was Rabaul?'

He looked up from his newspaper. It was Peter from the ASIS. He had forgotten all about the arrangement made in Sydney, but Peter did not seem to be at all concerned.

'I knew you would turn up sooner or later.' he said pleasantly and sat down next to Mark.

Mark was glad to see the Australian. Mark had thought long and hard about how they were going to present their findings when they got back to Wellington.

He predicted that his father would file a report by standard CIA procedure and that he would then rely on the weight of evidence to convince the powers that be in Washington that they had a problem that was about to bite them in the ass. It would never occur to his father, even though he had for once actually got off his arse and done something covert and unauthorized, that the same fate could occur yet again – the story could be killed.

He would expect that normal service would resume. There was now a chance with Peter and the Australian intelligence community in the mix that Mark could work a way around the idiosyncrasies or incompetence of his own countrymen. Or at least work around the incompetence or intrigue of the intelligence and security people.

'Have you heard of Doctor Abdul Jabbar?' Mark asked.

Peter just shrugged.

'No – Should I have? Who is he?'

'He is the man that I think runs a very clever terrorist organization in Rabaul. Clever because he is actually a Doctor of Geophysics and operates from the Rabaul Volcano Observatory. But I got a fair amount of information from his laptop computer that I gained access to. Scattered amongst seismic and other reports I found documents that tie him to the organization that you people call Jemaah Islamiyah and to al Qaeda. Plus, I was able to access his email traffic which more than suggests he is involved in terrorist activities – at least in the funding of them.'

At first, Peter had a look of surprise on his face. That soon turned to one of suspicion.

'How did you get this information and how did you get access to his computer?'

Now it was Mark's turn to laugh.

'Well, maybe that is why Harold Taylor asked someone with my qualifications to go to Rabaul. We were able to sneak into the observatory and find his computer. I believe that it was just a question of the good Doctor being too relaxed in such a remote place as Rabaul and was not expecting anyone to be able to beat his security. I make a living out of designing computer security systems' Mark added with a wink. 'Now—what do you know of Umar Patek and Abdul Rahim?'

Peter now looked astonished, and the body language said that this look was genuine. He spoke very quietly, now very much alert, and conscious of the people around them in the international terminal.

'We know of Rahim – he is responsible in JI for the Australasian region, and we try to monitor him as best we can. As for Umar Patek, we think he is in the Philippines training Islamic terrorists, and he also does the bean-counting for the ASG – sorry the Abu Sayyaf Group. Shit! I get the connection! I am sorry – I think I may have underestimated you when we talked in Sydney!'

'Well, you may be able to shed some light on another guy who seems to be involved – Mario Tudjman – do you know him?' Mark asked, beginning to feel more confident. He certainly had Peter's attention.

A worried look appeared on Peter's face as he rubbed his chin, deep in thought.

'You may have me on that one. Unless - He is a Yugoslav?' Mark nodded. Peter paused before continuing and then he got really serious.

'A guy called Franco Tudjman was involved in the conflict in Bosnia, so we learned from the Pom's – sorry the Brits. Franco was a politician, but at the same time, a nasty piece of work – as were his two sons. Things were finally settled to no one's satisfaction. Franco died of natural causes we believe—but after that, one of the sons disappeared. Reports were that he had been murdered but the Brits thought otherwise and suspected that he had made a new life somewhere overseas. It could be that your Mario – incidentally, that may not be his real name – is the same guy. He is wanted by the Croats either dead or alive, but the Brits also have a few scores to settle with that ratbag. Shit! What other little gems did you uncover?'

Mark shrugged and laughed again.

'Well, how would I know?' And this time Peter joined in the laughter.

'I have a copy of all the information that we got – both from Abdul Jabbar's computer and from the RVO email computer. Brad and I have analyzed it as best we could, and the conclusions are fairly clear. We found what we wanted, if not what we expected. There is a plot, and the target is New York City. The date looks like September the 11th. My problem is going to be that of getting our intelligence people in Washington to accept that and to do something about it.'

'And Brad is?' Peter asked, although his body language said that he already knew at least a part of the story.

Mark again had to laugh.

'You don't think Harold would let me go running around PNG on my own, do you? Brad Morgan works for the CIA science and technology side and like me, he knows a little about computers and communications. He once worked for me, but that is another story.'

Peter saw the funny side. But he was more interested in the data than the personnel.

'Any chance of my getting a copy of the information that you have – if it is as good as you imply this could be dynamite – and something we knew absolutely nothing about – and should have known. I cannot interfere in what would be a domestic matter for the United States. But I can sure cause a few flags to be raised if I have a copy of the proof.

Mark had to think about that for a few nanoseconds. He was aware that Australia and the United States were members of the Five Eyes Intelligence Alliance, along with New Zealand, Canada, and the United Kingdom. These five countries were supposed to share intelligence but, in reality, that did not always happen. Here was the obvious opportunity to share and one in which there was more to be gained than not. At least there could be benefits to Mark and on that basis alone he made the decision. He would deal with the CIA, or whichever organization played their silly political games, later.

To ensure that they got all the information back to Wellington and then on to the United States, without mishap, there were now two copies of the data – one that Mark had on his laptop computer and the other that Brad had on his laptop. Both of these copies were encrypted by a Taylor Software algorithm before leaving Rabaul as was the analysis of data on both of their laptop. Mark was not about to give a copy of his encryption algorithms to anyone, and he was not about to let the data go anywhere in clear text, even the summation that he and Brad had drawn up.

There was encryption on the data that they had extracted – Marks encryption, and also on the original data – Doctor Abdul Jabbar encryption. He decided that it was better to give Peter the original data and let him reach his own conclusions. So that meant unscrambling the data then re-encrypting it, using an algorithm that the Aussies would have access to. This would take time. The flight was due to leave for Wellington New Zealand at 5:25 pm. The time was now 3:10 pm.

'Ok—let's see what we can do' Mark said as he began to unravel a plan of action. Although the easiest solution would have been to hand over the data that they had on flash drives, Mark could not do that. That data was raw and interspersed with copies of the Taylor Software routines that had enabled the capture of the data in the first place. While the routines were encrypted, it was just not worth the risk that some bright Aussie nerd may stumble upon a translation. And Mark still had a company to run which owned that intellectual property when all this was over!

'We need somewhere more private than we are now, and you need a couple of USB Flash Drives. There is no time to mess around with formatting CDs, nor is there time to copy everything I have, so we will copy the main items of interest. But first, we have to establish some encryption rules. I don't suppose you could find out what standard encryption your nerds can use?'

'No worries.' said Peter jumping to his feet. 'Let's go'.

They went towards the back of the terminal and through a door marked No Passengers Beyond This Point. Peter took no notice of the sign, unlocked the door with a key, and marched on through. Every door of the corridor that they found themselves in had a combination locking mechanism of a kind that was new to Mark. Not to Peter. He entered a code into one door, it unlocked, and Peter motioned Mark inside. In the room that Peter had selected there was just a plain table with four chairs. The room had no windows.

'If you set up your laptop on the table, I'll be back in a jiffy.'

Mark unpacked the laptop, plugged it into the wall socket - there was little point in risking his battery running low in the middle of an encryption process – and fired it up. Peter came back into the room accompanied by a grossly overweight bearded guy of about thirty years of age who looked as though he had just run a marathon.

'This is Skittles.' Peter said by way of introduction. 'I could not understand a word he was jabbering on about – so I brought him along.'

Between gulps of air, 'Skittles' tried to tell Mark that if he just gave him the data, in whatever form it was in, that would be fine.

Mark looked at the guy and just shook his head turning to Peter.

'We don't have time for this. We don't have time to fight this guy's ego. If you want the data, we do it my way or not at all. This guy has no idea what I have on my idea what I have on my machine and how it is encrypted. And I am not about to tell him.'

Peter did not seem at all put out by Mark's obvious aggression, but the same could not be said for Skittles. He looked offended and Mark thought for a moment he was going to reply, to burst into tears. Peter had either not noticed or did not care – probably the latter. He turned to Skittles with a patronizing look.

'So now I say again – tell me which encryption algorithm we can use – anyone will do as long as we can use it – then fuck off!'.

'Blowfish' was all that 'Skittles' said, looking at Mark with reluctant respect. Mark nodded in agreement. Then Skittles dropped a bundle of flash drives on the table and rushed off out the door.

'Why do computer types always try to control everything?' Peter asked of no one in particular.
'Ok so let me guess. You are going to give us a copy of what you have encrypted, re-encrypted using Blowfish, but first, you have to de-encrypt it from whatever form you have the data in. You want to do that because you're not going to give us your algorithm, and you want it encrypted because you don't want it falling into the wrong hands. Now I can understand all that. How long will all this take?'

It was only when he asked the final question that Mark heard anything.

'Sorry, what did you say?' Which caused Peter to groan. It was a waste of time – Mark had turned into another nerd! Peter just sat down and watched as Mark worked away on the keyboard – a study in concentration. But he obviously knew what he was doing.

Finally, he pushed one of the Australian flash drives into the machine and started the copying process. He stood up and turned to Peter. 'Ok—I have given you enough to explain why we suspect our friend Doctor Abdul Jabbar is, as you people say, a person of interest. I have also given you some of the stuff from the email machine that is of most interest to us. There may be a problem with our Yugoslavia friend Marco Tudjman, because as far as I could tell he does not feature at all. I doubt that he is much more than nuisance value – but you never know in this business.'

'Now it is your turn to do me a favour. When your people look at the data, I am sure they will reach the same conclusion that I have. If you do, can you get someone to then ring the CIA and tell him they are about to have their ass blown off – yet again?'

Mark was beginning to sound like a normal – if there was a normal – field agent! Peter just grinned, nodding his agreement, and then suggested that they went and had a coffee while the machine was working away. But there was no way Mark would agree to that. Not that Mark did not trust Peter. There was no way he was going to leave his computer unattended or within reach of anyone, while it was switched on, and in particular, while it was copying data of this significance. In any case, the Australian was a spook who worked for the Australian government. He would be remiss if he did not seek to gain some advantage if the opportunity should present itself – whether he was working with a friend or not.

Peter went out and got them a coffee and then they sat and chatted while the copy process continued.

The Australian mused – who was this man and why could all Yanks not be as straightforward as Mark was? The American mused – why did the CIA have so many people jerking themselves off, while the Australians had guys as straightforward as Peter?

They established an understanding in that time that was due to last for many years, but that is another story.

About halfway through the copy process, Mark heard a distant call for his flight to Wellington New Zealand. Peter just smiled 'Don't worry – the flight will wait for you – it has all been arranged.'

Mark did not disbelieve him, but he was curious.

'It is now my turn to ask – who are you?'

Peter laughed. 'If I told you that I'd have to kill you. Anyway, shall I just say that I am high enough in the organization and with enough influence to ensure that I can hold up a flight? I have also had you upgraded to first-class so that there will be very few people who will know that you may be responsible for delaying their flight. And I can ensure that your discovery will be acted upon at least as far as notifying the CIA that they have a problem is concerned. Give me your email address and I will try to keep you informed of what transpires at our end. There is no danger of it being buried by us. What we need to worry about is what happens at your end.'

Some comments have a habit of being prophetic. They just did not know that – yet.

It was Tuesday, September the 4th.

Chapter 21

CIA HQ—Langley

The only real good news on the journey back to the United States was that Mark gained a day. The fact that the extra time was spent in business class was also an advantage but the worries of the last week or so meant that Mark had little in the way of sleep.

No sooner had he landed at Los Angeles, than he was whisked away to another waiting airplane and this one was obviously not a commercial flight. Although Air America – an airline run by and for the CIA – had ceased operating in 1976, there was still plenty of aircraft for the exclusive use of the security services.

He did not see anything of his baggage, customs, or immigration. He was on his way to Washington DC, this time in the company of Brad and Paul both of whom had reappeared in LA as if from nowhere. He had not seen either of them on the flight from New Zealand, but now that they were back in the United States, and on a CIA-sponsored flight, they obviously could travel together.

Mark could only speculate at the strange procedures of the CIA – maybe they just did not want them to talk to each other without having the facilities to

They had in any case done all their talking in Wellington. Because Brad had chosen to take a separate flight out of Brisbane, Mark was the first to arrive back from in New Zealand. Instructions were waiting at Wellington airport for him to call a cell phone number and that he had done. His father answered almost immediately, despite the lateness of the hour, and very curtly gave him an address in the Wellington suburb of Newtown where they would meet the next morning. Harold then terminated the call without asking any questions about Mark's trip, how he was – or anything.

Mark would have thought that an inquiry as to his health and well-being would not have gone amiss. But that was not how things were done in the CIA. And were nonetheless typical of how things were done in the Taylor family.

The following morning, he arrived at the address in Lawrence Street, just by the Wellington Zoo. That trip was by taxi, as he had been instructed.

Either his fathers' budget was running a little low, or else the concept of a Safe House had changed. The house was a semi-detached unit, very old, and very much in need of some tender loving care.

He was greeted at the door by a young lady who smiled pleasantly enough and asked if she could help him. But the smile did not travel to her eyes. Mark did not know what to say, so he simply told her his name. That worked, although initially, he thought it hadn't. The young lady asked him to wait for a moment and closed the door. She spoke to someone who was clearly not so far away, and then immediately reopened the door and, if appearing somewhat reluctant, invited him in.

Mark formed the opinion that this was quite simply

not a Safe House. And he was right.

They walked into a small lounge area where Paul and Harold sat drinking coffee. Paul was first on his feet, shaking Marks' hand and introducing him to the young lady. Mark was surprised that Paul had a daughter because he had no recollection of him ever having been married. Renee seemed pleasant enough, but also very tense and seemed anxious to get the hell out of the way. She excused herself saying that she was off to the gym. She gave a curious look to Paul as she said goodbye to her 'father' and she left with a shrug of the shoulders, but a worried look on her face.

'Well, Mark. How was your trip? You must accept my apologies for the accommodation, but it is the best we could do.' His father, for once, looked ruffled but did not explain the choice of their meeting place. Nonetheless, he looked eager to hear what news Mark had. So why had he not at least ventured an inquiry the previous night?

Now Harold sat nervous and apprehensive looking at Mark as though he were some sort of prodigal son.

'Tiring – but worthwhile – I think. Do we have anything other than coffee to drink?' Mark replied while squeezing into the tiny lounge. His father fetched a glass of orange juice. There was a first time for everything – he did not normally serve things. Harold quickly sat down again expectantly waiting for what Mark had to tell.

There was no point in recounting his entire trip, particularly his Australian experience, so Mark just told them almost everything that he and Brad had discovered in Rabaul. He did not tell him about what he had arranged with the Australian in Brisbane. His father would be really pissed if or when he found out, but for professional rather than practical reasons. He also did not tell them that he and Brad had copies of the original data on their laptops. He knew how the CIA worked. They would seize the laptops regarding anything collected as theirs, and he did not want to embarrass his father by refusing to comply.

He was rapidly learning how these people worked and he was not about to start playing by their rules. Except that is, for the money. Since Brad had to account for the funds that he had received, Mark thought that the least he could do was to return the unused money – which accounted for about ninety-five percent of it. But his father refused to accept it. Body language said that he was embarrassed, but by what Mark did not have a clue.

A few weeks before Mark would have been only too pleased to receive a donation from the government – after all, he paid his taxes and did not appear to get much in return. Now the sum was merely petty cash, so he decided to forget it.

After about three hours, during which Mark was grilled about what he had found out, Brad arrived looking somewhat harassed. His flight out of Brisbane had been delayed and there was talk of it being cancelled altogether. That would have meant catching another flight but to either Auckland, which was bad enough, or Christchurch, which was even worse being in the South Island.

As it was, his baggage had gone walkabout, so all he had was his carry-on baggage. Fortunately, that carry-on baggage included his laptop computer. That also held a copy of the original data, but as he and Mark had agreed in Rabaul, that was where it would stay encrypted and hidden. What Brad did not say was why he was three hours late to the meeting, but as neither Harold nor Paul seemed at all concerned, it was not something that Mark would worry about.

If Brad had been talking to someone else, he would

have worried, but since Mark could not know there was nothing to worry about – was there?

Brad simply expanded on what Mark had said, by explaining the general content of the email traffic. Harold very rapidly reached the same conclusion that Brad, and Mark had. What Harold had suspected was that there was indeed a terrorist cell in Rabaul. He never suspected however that the Rabaul cell was a major component in a terrorist network.

The evidence that he was now presented with was that Rabaul was a significant conduit for funds and information, both critical ingredients in the terrorist game. That was very significant to the intelligence community. More to the point though, they now had ample proof from analysis of the traffic that something was about to take place in New York City – proof that Harold had been correct in his original assumptions.

The task that Harold now faced was to make sure that the information reached the appropriate people at Langley. It would need to bypass those who had been instrumental in killing it when it was first raised. And it would need to reach the office of the Director of National Intelligence in sufficient time for appropriate countermeasures to be put in place.

For years Harold had assured himself, and anyone else who cared to listen, that the CIA could move rapidly and decisively when it needed to. He now had a major case in his hands. A case on which the CIA simply had to move rapidly and decisively. But the problem he now faced was that he did not now trust the organization that he had been a dedicated and loyal servant of for the greatest part of his working life.

'Mark – I have to ask for one more favour' his father

began. 'I cannot trust our communications people. This has to be done in person. If I arrange for the three of you to fly to Washington DC, will you go to CIA Headquarters at Langley and explain what you have just told me? Paul and Brad have to go back anyway, but they belong to the Company and are quite possibly compromised.'

If either Paul or Brad took offense at the last comment, they certainly did not show it. In Mark's case, he thought that Harold was being a little paranoid. His father continued as though they were discussing a trip to the beach.

'You on the other hand are a free agent. And I know you. If people at the first level don't want to listen, you will go higher up until you find someone who will listen.'

His father was being a little cheeky with this. By his nature, Mark was just as likely to tell them all to get fucked – it was just not his fight. What his father was saying was that Mark was to do more than he normally would. That meant that Harold either did not trust Paul or Brad to achieve the same thing, or he knew more about the extent of the cover-up process than he had previously acknowledged. From all of this, the only logical assumption that Mark could make was that Paul and Brad could be overwhelmed by bureaucracy – the very organization that paid their wages.

This was becoming a real family affair!

'Well, I have to get back to the United States as well.' Mark began. 'You forget Harold that I have a business to run and have very good reasons for wanting to get back to the United States. I have so far spent quite some of my time, and your money, running around doing your or the CIA's business. But what the hell? – if you can assure me that I will not be wasting my time or end up in Guantanamo Bay?'

That comment brought a sharp rebuke from his father,

a smile from Paul, and a laugh from Brad. But Mark could see the logic of what Harold had said. And he did not envy him the task of trying to tip-toe through the organization that paid his wages as well.

'Point taken' replied Harold 'I will arrange for Forester to take care of things.'

Mark exchanged a shocked glance with Paul. Mark had to ask.

'Hang on – I thought you did not trust this fellow named Forester? – at least when we were last here in Wellington you arranged for him to be called away before you got down to the details of what you wanted me to do – What goes on?'

Harold began to look even more ruffled.

'I did not say I did not trust him. I just wanted to keep some things to the smallest group possible. But he is responsible for this part of the world. That is as high as I can go up the chain without causing some serious ripples. Forester will arrange everything at Langley and make sure that you get to see the right people in CIA HQ. He does not know where you have been, and it should stay that way for now.'

'Well – I hope you know what you are doing' Mark replied, not missing his father's comment about not saying anything about where he had been. He assumed that the comment was also directed at Brad.

They agreed that they should at least write down what they had said at this meeting. Mark and Brad were left to get that done while Harold and Paul busied themselves with other things. Because Brad was CIA and Mark was a civilian, they wrote separate reports. They had discussed their conclusions in Rabaul so their two stories should have been about the same. However, getting two people to agree on what had been said in their debrief to Harold, as well as the subjects that they were talking about, can be a nightmare at the best of times. All the people involved were the CIA and they had a way of expressing things. That is except for Mark. Mark added notes to various parts of his report to make it clear where the information had come from, and what it meant. Brad did not. Little did Mark know that the style of presentation would cause problems back at CIA headquarters in Washington for several of their analysts.

And more serious problems in New York City for several hundred innocent civilians.

When they had finished, Harold went to the Embassy and printed four copies of each report that Mark had copied onto a flash drive. He then returned to what he termed the Safe House. It was no such thing, but Mark was past caring. If Harold noticed that both reports contained verbatim extracts from email traffic he did not say.

Maybe he did not notice. Maybe he did not dare to ask. Maybe he did not care either.

There was little point in repeating the debriefing process during the long flight from Los Angeles to Washington and the only reasonable conclusion that Mark could reach for them arriving in LA separately was just to let them have a break.

In the brief half-hour that they had in LA Mark checked his emails – just for something to do. But he did get a surprise. Amongst all the usual garbage that even a sophisticated check like that employed on all Taylor Software systems failed to prevent, there was an email from Australia. It was innocuous but its meaning was very apparent:

'Thursday 6 September 2009, 10:53:30. Your Doctor flew into Brisbane from Jakarta this morning and is connecting with flight QA 86 to Port Moresby departing at 14:35 local time. Someone from our Australian office is booked on the same flight and will travel on to Rabaul if need be. He should be able to catch up with Mario. I will keep in touch. Regards. Peter.'

The sender's address gave nothing away as to who Peter was or what his Australian office was or did. Mark shut down his laptop, pleased that the Australians were active, but still unsure whether this piece of information should be revealed to his inquisitors at the CIA. The good news was that he now knew he had an ally.

Or at least thought he did.

They each lost themselves in catching up on the local news and sleeping. The US Air Force crew treated them like VIPs and at last, they began to feel as though they were going to get somewhere even if their views differed on what was happening.

Brad, ever the clinical CIA operative, had analysed the data and had the proof he needed that a plot was underway. And he had little doubt that it was orchestrated by al Qaeda.

Paul, ever the cynical CIA operative, had assessed their reports and thought that there was a plot but the organization of it was so fucked up, that they would be lucky if they could successfully blow themselves up.

Mark, who was not a CIA operative and had little – and diminishing—respect for an organization that had allowed itself to be at best distracted and at worst infiltrated, was convinced that the al Qaeda connection was a by-play and that someone else was behind the plot.

The problem for all three of them was that they did

not have a specific target. New York City is a big place. Nor did they know who the players were in the USA. New York City has a lot of people and a lot of nationalities. They knew a few first names, but apart from a reasonable assumption that the people were Pakistani, they knew nothing. They just knew a date. And that date was just five days away.

Their flight landed at the Andrews Air Force Base, and they were immediately driven from the plane to the CIA headquarters at Langley. Neither Andrews nor Langley is very far from downtown Washington, but this part of the trip was a pain up the butt. The traffic was bad. And any illusions that Mark had about the way they were being treated were very quickly dissipated. The driver simply concentrated on the delivery, and his associate just showed an arrogant disregard for the passengers.

An attempt by Paul to find out what was planned and who they were meeting at Langley, was met with a curt 'You will find out soon enough.'

The CIA headquarters at Langley is in an impressive but quite intimidating building. The security, even more so. Since Paul and Brad were part of "The Company" and had previously been to Langley at least they knew the procedure. But that did not improve things very much.

It became clear to Mark that they were not about to be let into, or rather up to, the inner sanctum. After a long process of checking, cross-checking, and double-checking records, they were eventually shown into a featureless room that had little more than a table with a dozen or so chairs lined up on either side. The room had one small window which looked out over a car park, but it could have been any supermarket car park such was the bland nature of their surroundings.

Finally, three men came into the room, all dressed in almost identical dark suits, and to Marks' surprise the youngest looking of the three introduced himself as Scott and as the head of this stage of the investigation.

They sat down and Scott, armed with the reports that Mark and Brad had prepared in Wellington, explained what was going to happen next.

Mark could hardly begin to comprehend and looked at Paul and Brad for guidance. None was forthcoming. In the end, he felt inclined to speak.

'Scott – I did not catch your second name – you are telling us that you are going to interrogate the three of us individually over the next two to three days. That means, if my mathematics is accurate, that your interrogation will end on Sunday afternoon, after which you will no doubt spend the next twenty-four hours or so writing your report or whatever you people do. I do not want to appear at all panicked by this timescale. But Tuesday is September the 11th. Monday afternoon seems a bit late to reach any logical conclusions and take action, other than "that's what we think will happen" and gives you just the time to write up your "I told you it would" story. The CIA seems to make something of a habit of doing that.'

Scott, who still did not bother to give a second name, simply smiled, and replied.

'You would be surprised at how quickly this Agency can act. You can rest assured that positive steps are being taken now to not only investigate what you claim is going on but also to protect the United States from terrorism. What we have to know is – have you got anything more specific that we can act on? I am sure you would want that investigation to be as thorough as possible.'

Mark was seething but did not know whether that was from the stated facts, or from the arrogance with which they were delivered.

'Ok – well tell me how individual interrogation is going to help that? Do you think we three might have separate agendas, or do you think we have agreed on what we should say already and that it will merely mislead you? The underlying message is still the same – it is called get off your ass and do something before some real people get hurt. Or are you guys completely paranoid?'

Again, the smile. But the body language said far more than the smile. This idiot was going to do things his way, and no one would change that. The arrogance towards Mark – the only non-CIA person in the room—was palpable. His answer when it came had a finality to it and left Mark wondering which planet he had landed on.

'We have the three of you—a CIA employee from our technical division who has spent most of his time with the company sitting around playing with computers and has never before now been out in the field. We have another CIA agent who does not exactly have the reputation for following any rules and is regarded as something of a loose cannon. Then we have a civilian who, with all due respect, knows fuck all. And all of you have a different story to tell. Now if you had been able to agree on your story beforehand, we could have moved a little quicker – but you did not – so what do you expect?'

With that said he simply signalled to Paul and Brad and their escorts that they had other business elsewhere. Mark had the distinct impression that this Scott was somewhat senior to Paul, and certainly to Brad because neither said anything nor showed any response. They promptly left the room, leaving just Mark and Scott.

With the air of someone he was talking to a schoolboy, Scott assured Mark that something was being done by the FBI, Homeland Security, and the other members of the anti-terrorist or counter-terrorist forces. They had got the message that something was planned, and they had plans of their own to deal with the situation. Every known terrorist cell was being carefully watched. Every form of communication was being monitored. All airports had stepped up surveillance. The readiness alert had been lifted, not just in New York, but in Washington as well. If anyone who was known to have, or suspected of having, any links to known terrorists' groups as much as farted, the security forces would know and would react swiftly and decisively.

So how come Mark did not believe a single word of what Scott said?

'Now tell me your story' Scott said as he switched on the recording devices that were built into the table. He still took out a notebook and pen.

Mark was on the verge of getting up and leaving, but he knew what options the CIA could exercise. He also knew that, at the end of the day, he was an outsider, and it was not his fault if half of New York City was to be blown up while these idiots went about their investigation. He was also conscious of the fact that, at least according to his father, the CIA was not fully aware of the role Mark had played. More particularly, nowhere in the report that Mark had produced was there any mention of the fact that he had reason to doubt the people he was now talking to. Mark was also aware of the risk of himself being too close to the subject – he had been in situations where someone was so close that they just could not understand why nobody else was bothered. In this case, he could blame his father. It situations where someone was so close that they just could not understand why nobody else was bothered.

In this case, he could blame his father. It might be time to start playing mind games with them, leaving the real task of convincing them of a plot to Brad and Paul.

Mark told his story while Scott scribbled on his pad. It was time for Mark to mention that he, or they, had been to a place called Rabaul. For all the effect that bit of news had on Scott, it may as well have not been mentioned. And for a while, there were few interruptions except for clarification of times and names.

There were several things that Mark did not tell him. He said nothing at this stage about his suspicion about non-al Qaeda involvement. He said nothing about his meeting with Peter from the Australian Security Intelligence Services in Sydney. He said nothing about the information that he had on his laptop. He said nothing about his subsequent meeting with Peter in Brisbane.

The story he had to tell would have gained nothing from these additions, and he did not want to lose the evidence and have it buried again. The real problem was very simple—he felt that Scott was not being as straight as he implied. Had he walked into the CIA only to repeat his story to the very same people who had killed the original? But there was the chance that either, or both, Paul Walker and Brad Morgan would have more luck.

The story should have been conclusive. Given the exchange of emails and their content, and the information about Jemaah Islamiyah and Doctor Abdul Jabbar, there was a clear and present danger to the USA. But Mark may as well have read the local weather report for all the effect that it had on Scott.

He started to slowly go through his notes and asked Mark to repeat various aspects of his story. In particular, he tried to pin down the times of the events that were supposed to happen. That was merely the result of analysis and a certain amount of conjecture. The date of September the 11th seemed to Mark to be significant enough. And today was September the 6th.

Eventually, at 6:30 pm, Scott called a halt to the debriefing. He summoned two innocuous-looking individuals and instructed them to take Mark to the "Hotel" for checking in, which came as something of a surprise to the now bemused civilian. So, he said something.

'Aren't you forgetting something?' Mark asked. 'I am finished here. I do not belong to your Company as you call it, so if you don't mind, I would like to get back to New York. I have told you everything that I know, you have told me that all the security forces are on the alert, so what is the problem now?'

Scott simply smiled yet again.

'I am afraid that will not be possible. We have to check your story with that of Brad Morgan and Paul Williams. I know it is inconvenient, but I must insist that you remain in Washington until that is done. I can get a judge to sign the paperwork if you want, but I am sure there is no need for that – is there?'

'Now your laptop computer' Scott continued 'I am sure you would not mind if we took a look at it. What have you got on it that may be of interest?'

'Nothing that would be of any interest to you people' Mark replied, hoping that his anger would mask his other thoughts. 'It has copies of stuff I took from another machine in Rabaul, but most of that has no bearing on what we are here to talk about. Other than that, it only has commercial stuff, but if you want to take a look, I don't suppose I can stop you.'

It was only Mark's training in the Special Forces that kept him under control and his face neutral. He knew what kind of persuasive power the CIA could wield. He doubted whether a judge – any judge—could sign anything that would make any difference to his present situation. Under the Constitution of the United States of America, he could in theory just walk out. The CIA had little jurisdiction over civilians and especially in the USA. But they could be a real pain up the ass if they wanted to be. The CIA had a reputation for its hospitality, especially when dealing with foreigners, but it had no such reputation or illusion for dealing with United States citizens. Mark just shrugged.

'I will stay until tomorrow morning. Then, if I am not on my way back to New York City, you had better produce your judge.'

The reaction he got was to be anticipated. Scott simply got up, said that he did not think that Mark was being reasonable, that he would see Mark at his Hotel room in the morning. He left taking the laptop with him and left Mark with the two nondescript individuals whose only means of communication seemed to be to nod their heads in whichever direction they wanted Mark to move.

He had started on what could be termed an "Adventure" in a car ride through New York City with two similar animals only a few weeks before. At least that trip had resulted in his becoming rich compared to his previous status. He had few illusions about the outcome this time.

The "Hotel" that Mark was assigned to, turned out to be nothing of the kind. The place was run by the CIA, at the CIA, for the CIA. And since he never actually left the building at Langley it was more like he was being held in a prison. The unit was fine, except that it had two bedrooms and a lounge, no windows, and only one door. Mark could not detect any alternative means of access or egress other than the short corridor that seemed to be the only connection with the world outside. The two individuals settled in the lounge area and simply pointed to one of the bedrooms indicating that it was for Mark. Apart from the odd grunt, they still appeared to be devoid of conversation. But at least the lounge area had a telephone.

No one seemed to take any notice of Mark as he picked up the telephone and proceeded to punch in a number. The hollow sound in the receiver confirmed that all calls from the room were being monitored, so Mark would need to be careful.

The CIA would hardly be interested in Mark's love life – but there were aspects of at least one of the three calls he was about to make that would arouse their interest. It was now 7:45 pm in Washington so Harold should be at work on the other side of the world. There was some consternation on the CIA switchboard when Mark punched in the number – the room was obviously not set up for international traffic. But eventually, the call was put through after Mark had explained that he was merely calling his father, who was amongst other things one of theirs. After that, their consternation would have increased somewhat.

'Hi, Dad – I am spending the night in a CIA establishment, and they have permitted me to call you. That is about the only thing that they have done that makes any sense. Brad and Paul have gone off somewhere else doing God knows what. So how are mother and yourself? Better than I am, I hope' Mark began.

His father understood.

'We are fine – thinking of taking a few days off and going skiing. How was the trip back?'

'Tiring and boring. As for the purpose of it – a complete waste of time.'

Mark was cut off in mid-sentence. Then an operator

came on the line, apologized, and asked if he would like the connection re-established, to which Mark replied, 'What is the point?' and hung up the telephone. He did not care whether the CIA understood what had just happened. His father now knew that things were not going too well, and Mark hoped that he now knew what he needed to do – in addition, that is, to watch his back.

Mark's next call was to his office in New York. He did not expect anyone to be there, and he was surprised when Dusty answered.

'Hi Dusty.' were all the words Mark could get out before Dusty exploded.

'Where have you been?' he demanded, and before Mark could reply he continued. 'Your girlfriend has now apparently abandoned me, and you have gone walkabout. Would someone please tell me what the hell is going on?'

'What do you mean Dusty? Where is Annette?' The feeling in the outburst over the phone would have made anyone listening to it blush, but that was not Mark's concern.

'I would not have a clue. You tell me!' was Dusty's reply. He certainly did not sound too pleased.

'Have you tried calling her cell phone?' Mark asked, knowing the answer before he had finished asking, and fearing the worst. For Annette to get Dusty rattled raised the question of whether she was indeed the innocent Personal Assistant that Mark thought he had fallen in love with. Or was she something else? Mark recalled the discussion he had with Paul Williams in Wellington. Was she somehow involved? Was she still involved with the Augem Group? Did Taylor Software come second – to— What? He carried on talking but Dusty gave him no answers.

'Dusty – I'm tied up overnight in Washington – but I should be back tomorrow, and I will tell you the whole story as far as I know it then.'

Dusty seemed to give up at that stage and then had an afterthought. 'You do mean Washington DC? – what are you doing in Washington?'

'I am a guest of the CIA. Just doing the old man another favour. I will try to reach Annette and call you back.'

There was a pregnant pause while Dusty absorbed the gist of what Mark had just said. There was more to Marks' visit to New Zealand than had been said, and it came as no surprise to Dusty that Harold Taylor was not just a run-of-the-mill bureaucrat. Having tangled with the CIA in an earlier life he was not about to tangle with them again. He ended their conversation.

'Well don't bother to call me here at your office – you have my cell phone number – I am off to the Bar – and I might not be back!' and this time it was Dusty, rather than the CIA switchboard, which severed the call.

The CIA operative who sat not too far away raised an eyebrow but otherwise did not react. He could not know Dusty. Mark did.

The third telephone call that Mark made was to Annette. He first rang the landline of her apartment. It was immediately answered by a message service – now that was unusual. Next, he rang Annette's cell phone number and that also was immediately answered by a similar message – that was even more unusual. This time he decided to leave a message.

'Hi, Annette – it's Mark. Just to let you know that I should be back tomorrow.' And he left it at that. Again, the raised eyebrow from the CIA operative. He surely could not know about Annette! But Mark wondered if perhaps he did! It was as though the CIA had taken control of his life. He had seen all the movies in which at every step the forces of good or evil were always one step ahead of whoever would turn out to be the hero. Or a dead man! That was until the last nano-second.

He hoped that this would not be a "last nano-second" situation and he did not feel like being a hero, or dead. What the hell was going on?

Mark turned to the CIA operative and asked.

'Do we go out to McDonald's for dinner, or have the CIA got other plans?'

At least he got a response. He was handed a piece of paper on which was a telephone extension number and a couple of choices for food. The choices looked equally unappetizing, so Mark just rang the number on the paper and asked for a fillet steak with a couple of beers. The fact that fillet steak and beer were not among the choices escaped the attention of the person answering the telephone. However, three-quarters of an hour later, the steak arrived but not the beer. At least this hotel room had a refrigerator!

After finishing the steak and a couple of soft drinks, Mark retired to his bedroom, locking the door. He had never felt so tired or so alone at any stage in his short life, but there was little else to do except getting some sleep. The CIA would be unconcerned with the locked door because they could quite simply unlock it again from outside. There was not much danger of Mark trying to escape since boring through the walls looked likely to be a major undertaking. He would be spotted anyway on one of several cameras that were installed, no doubt along with some microphones linked to a recording device in case he talked to himself or talked in his sleep.

He switched off the light and eventually fell into a restless sleep while names and events from another time and place tried to keep him awake.

It was perhaps just as well that he did get some sleep. The days that followed were like his worst nightmare.

He was not allowed to leave the apartment and he was not allowed to make any further telephone calls. His laptop computer had been taken from him on the first day but was returned a day later without any comment as to where it had been, what if anything it was used for, or why it had been taken.

For something to do Mark switched it on and did a cursory check to see what, if anything, had happened to it. He smiled at the additions to the software that someone had so carefully and lovingly installed on it. Rather like a virus that when woken up by some activity or other would transmit useful information to the installer. Mark, therefore, abandoned any plans to use the laptop until he could either remove the "virus" or modify what it could intercept to the displeasure of the CIA.

Usually, they would only be able to collect data when the machine was connected to the Internet or a network. But in the age of wireless and other electronic gadgetry, you could do almost anything if you had the time and knowledge. A multi-million-dollar budget such as that enjoyed by the CIA helped of course. And judging by the skills demonstrated by Brad from the CIA Science and Technology division there was not much hope of the laptop being of much use to Mark.

Eventually, a different guy came to see him, towards the end of his second day as the CIA's guest. He asked a few questions which indicated, along with his body language, that he was the one who had tried and failed to find out what was on the laptop.

Mark replied that yes – truthfully – that it contained his encrypted software, and no – untruthfully – that there was nothing on the machine that would be of interest to the CIA. Of course, he had no way of knowing whether the CIA had been able to break through the Taylor algorithm. But he doubted whether they would have been able to do so in the time available. Part of the logic of the encryption algorithm was that it buried data deeper in the system when someone tried to access it illegally. Not very difficult to do, but very difficult to track. And he was sure someone was still working on it – or rather the copy that they would have made. And getting more confused by the hour.

That they would eventually get through the security was never in doubt. They would work on a copy, and each time they stuffed that up they would get another copy. With some of the very best analytical minds in the country working on it, it was only a matter of time. Time, patience, and resources were things that bureaucrats had by the bucket load, even if it meant that the task would take a long time. Mark rationalized, correctly, that this was the reason for the delay, but he was prepared to wait it out and put up with his continued incarceration.

Finally, on the morning of Monday, September the 10th, he was awoken by someone hammering on the door. He looked at his watch – it was 8:15 am– he had slept for nearly ten hours!

When he opened the door, he was greeted by CIA operative number two and the news that Scott was coming over to finalize their chat.

Mark's comment of "Well wasn't that good news?" got a surprising reaction from the operative – he laughed.

Mark shaved and showered and was just about dressed when Scott came in the door, looking as arrogant as ever. And somewhat irritated. Mark came out to meet him as he sat down at the table. At least someone had decided that he would need some breakfast, and that seemed to make Scott all the more irritated.

Mark sat down opposite Scott and proceeded to eat saying 'Well what have the CIA concluded or have you got to go to another committee?'

Scott had not had much sleep, or at least he had certainly not had a change of clothes for several days. That was one possible cause of his irritability although Mark doubted that. His eyes had sunk, and his skin had paled, which made his unshaven face look even more gaunt. None of this made for much in the way of a sense of humour.

It was clear that the CIA operatives, who had spent the days in Mark's unit, had little sympathy for the guy, but he was obviously their senior, so they said nothing. Mark detected a smirk from operative number two, but he also kept his face neutral.

'Can we stop playing games?' Scott began. 'You wanted us to take your story seriously, so spare us the courtesy of respecting the way we go about our business. Now, I have a few more questions, and then you are free to go.'

He pulled out the notebook that he had used on several visits during the preceding days and another notebook that Mark had not seen before. After looking backward and forwards between the two he came to some conclusion.

'Why do you think the story you told, and the story Mr. Williams told us, should differ so much, not only in detail but also in the conclusion?' he asked, without taking his eyes off the pages.

Mark temporarily froze. This was not the way an interview should be conducted. He did not know much about the CIA's internal procedures, but he knew enough about interrogation procedures to know that you always – always – looked into the eyes when asking questions.

He decided to counter the question, more to get a shock reaction, than anything else.

'Maybe Paul Williams is your mole.'

That got a reaction.

'Answer the fucking question!' Scott shouted. No "What mole?" But this time he looked up, and Mark could see the look in his eyes. Either this Scott character was genuinely out of his depth, or he was part of the original cover-up. Or he was scared shitless. But scared of what? Mark decided to press him further.

'How does my "story" compare with Mr. Morgan's? Brad was the person who accompanied me on the trip to Rabaul in Papua New Guinea – Paul Williams has only got his information second hand.'

That also got a reaction.

'Morgan is not particularly experienced in the field so he would be expected to reach erroneous conclusions and to dramatize. No – we would place more worth on William's perspective. He seems to think this is all a storm in a teacup. So, I ask again – why do the two stories differ?'

Now Mark could feel himself getting angry. The mere fact that Scott had reverted to just surnames was not the issue. He did not know if he was angry at Brad or angry at Paul or angry at Scott. If Brad had told the CIA the story that had been recounted in Wellington, based on the facts that they had uncovered, what was there to dramatize? If Paul – ever the sceptic – had simply told the story that he had agreed was supported by the facts, it could differ only in the level of seriousness. So, someone was telling lies. Was Brad telling lies? Was Paul telling lies? Or was Scott telling lies? In Mark's opinion, someone was!

'Now listen to me' Mark said keeping his voice as even as he could. 'I have just been on a trip which was not of my choosing and at the request of a senior representative of the CIA. And I have come back with the facts. Those facts point to something not very nice happening—the date of September the 11th. In case you have lost track of time – that is tomorrow.'

Mark paused, expecting some response. He was disappointed so he continued.

'Those facts point to New York City where you may recall I have my home and my business, and a lot of my friends. Those facts point to something very nasty happening and you may recall what happened last time. I frankly don't give a rat's fart for your profiling Brad as an eccentric nerd, Paul as someone who doesn't follow your rules, and me as someone who is not part of your Company. If you don't react to this threat, then some people are going to get hurt. If that happens – if people do get hurt—I will make sure that someone in the CIA goes down, and right now you are top of my list.'

To say the atmosphere in the room had become tense was an understatement. Scott was brittle.

'Are you threatening me? Do you know what you are doing?' he asked. But there was an element of fear in his voice and his body language.

'And I suppose you do not regard my being kept here against my will – and against my better judgment – as a threat?' snapped Mark. 'You have a problem mister. It is called the Constitution. You have no jurisdiction over me. But I am sure that the FBI would be very interested in what has been going on here. Place yourself in my position – I can walk away and leave you with this mess – or I can go above your head with my story – or I can go to the media. So – Yes – I am threatening you.'

Mark's mention of the FBI brought a temporary smirk to Scott's face – the significance of which Mark could not know – yet.

'And if we decide that you are a threat to the security of the United States' countered Scott with a snarl 'we could lock you away, and you could disappear without a trace.'

Mark laughed at that.

'I don't give a rat's fart about what you or the CIA can or cannot do to me. You have less than twenty-four hours to do something about what I reported. And there are just too many people who know that I am, or was, here. So that is not a threat – it is reality.'

At least the outburst from Mark got a reaction.

Scott simply got up and exited the room without even a second glance.

Mark took the opportunity to continue his breakfast when another man entered the room. He was a man well into his sixties. He was short and somewhat rotund but was immaculately dressed in a dark grey suit, white shirt, navy blue tie, and black shoes that were polished like glass. His skin had that whiteness about it that suggested that it rarely saw the sun. But the body language and the smile indicated a kindly man, who introduced himself simply as Henry. Whether that was first or last name Mark did not have a clue. Mark assumed that he was the second half of a bad guy – nice guy approach.

Henry started off talking about Marks' laptop.

'Our technicians are a little perplexed by the content of your hard drive on your laptop' he began with an amused smile on his face – and the smile spread to his eyes.

'Of course, you will know that they have taken a copy of your hard disk, but they are just going around in circles at the moment. Do you have any comment you would like to make about that?'

Mark could have made several comments. Like he felt certain that that CIA would eventually, in fact probably already had, broken through the Taylor algorithm. So, they would know what was on the disk. So why not stop playing games. There was nothing whatsoever on the laptop, now or in the past, that Mark would have reason to deny the CIA access to, in the appropriate circumstances. But he and Brad had already done their analysis of the data so that should have been all that they needed to know.

'Sure!' replied Mark. 'They could have asked, and I may have helped them. As you will know Scott took my laptop without any indication that he would need any help. But there is nothing on that disk, other than commercial and private stuff, plus a copy of some files from Rabaul, that is likely to be of any interest to the CIA who I feel certain has far more pressing problems to worry about!'

Mark also smiled then added, more for his own satisfaction.

'I am in the business of designing computer security systems, so it is good to know that the CIA has had problems breaking into what is a relatively simple system. It would have been interesting if the system was important, and we found that the CIA in all its infinite wisdom wasn't able to break in!' Mark added, seeing the other man squirm.

For a few moments, Henry sat across the table studying Mark, and then with a sigh and a smile he said.

'On behalf of the Government of the United States, I would like to thank you for your work during what has been a very trying last couple of weeks. The information that you have reported to us is of considerable value to the intelligence services. Whatever expenses you have incurred will be reimbursed, plus an amount to cover the time you have spent away from your office.' And he again smiled.

Mark did not react – he just waited. From what Henry had said so far it looked as though Harold's funding for the trip had definitely been off the CIA radar – but where had that money come from? Henry let out another sigh and continued.

'One of the problems that the intelligence service has, especially in a democracy as we have in the United States, is this. It is one thing to record what people say or discuss. It is quite another to find them guilty if they have not done anything. To prove that a plot exists we have to show that they – whoever they may be – have taken actual steps towards realizing a crime. When there is no specific evidence, no detailed plan, no date, no weapons, what can we do? We cannot go about arresting people – we can only watch, and wait, and see.'

Mark again did not outwardly react, but inside he was again seething. It had all come down to this. It did not matter whether Mark was believed or not. The analysis that the CIA had carried out was based on whether there was sufficient conclusive evidence to arrest someone, not whether there was in fact to be a plot. The organization that was reputed to be one of the most feared in the world, was hogtied by the very democracy that they were trying to defend. When something did occur, they would defend their position by blaming the system. Therefore, they were content that people would have to die first, to give them the proof that they needed. The system was sick.

Henry adopted a more philosophical attitude and smiled yet again. 'I suppose we do tend to over-analyse things. My professor at university, all those years ago, loved to quote from Friedrich Engels – you know the one – the German who helped Karl Marx write up about communism way back in 1840 something. You would not want to believe that the CIA would ever rely on anything a communist had to say, but he did say an ounce of action is worth a ton of theory.

What that had to do with communism as we came to know it is anyone's guess, but he did have a point, don't you think?'

'Maybe that should be the CIA motto instead of Ye shall know the truth and it shall set you free or the one used in the street, which goes something like We know everything after it happens, or the Yahoo favourite This motto will self-destruct in 5 seconds. Mark replied with a smile. He could not help like the guy, but did he have any influence over what went on? Probably not.

'Maybe I should suggest a change of plan for you bureaucrats' Mark carried on in the absence of any response, not sure where his thoughts would lead.

Henry still had that calm, smiling face as he replied.

'I am sure that we could benefit from your experience. You have been to some interesting places when you were with Special Forces. Every person in the field thinks they can do a better job than the intelligence types and the bureaucrats – that is until they try it. So – what particular changes did you have in mind?'

'You want to know what I think?' Mark replied. 'I am quite happy to tell you, but I doubt whether you or anyone else in this organization will listen.'

'Well try me.' said Henry 'I have the time – and I promise to listen. If there is some logic behind what you say, we would be foolish to ignore it – Do you not agree?'

Mark ignored the first response that came into his mind. It had certainly not been his experience with the idiots at the CIA so far that they would listen to anything or anyone who was not a part of the so-called Company. Instead, he recalled a discussion which he and Paul had in the depths of a Colombian jungle – while he held the gaze of this kindly man.

'Why is it that the CIA, FBI and almost every group involved with law enforcement are obsessed with letting the bad guys run rampant in the hope that letting them run will lead to the bigger fish. In the meantime, they maim, injure, dispossess, kill, and otherwise destroy people's lives – all left to their own devices in the hope that the big guys will be revealed. But they never are – are they? Why is that? It is because they have so much money and access to so many resources that they either just stay out of the way or pay people to cover up what they do. It does not matter whether we are talking about the Mafia, about the Drug Lords, Gang leaders, Terrorists, or even white-collar criminals. What do I think? How about rounding up the small guys – any guys involved in crime – and taking them off the streets? And keep doing it, until people get the message that crime at the lower level just does not pay. Then your average John Doe will be safer. Eventually, their bosses will have to change the way they do things. They will become desperate – and desperate people make mistakes. The big boys will come out of their holes looking to see where there, money is going. Then you have the big boys where you want them.'

For a moment, Mark thought that he had finally got through. Henry's smile disappeared and he fidgeted with his pen. He was just about to respond when Scott re-entered the room and passed a piece of paper to Henry. That caused Henry to take his leave quite abruptly. But not before he had politely shaken hands with Mark and again thanked him for his help, He left with a long knowing look and said, 'I'll think about what you have said.'

Mark could only shake his head and lapsed into an air of helpless silence while Scott went through an inane repetition of what they had discussed before he met with Henry.

Mark concluded that nothing would happen. He was

right as far as the CIA was concerned.

Otherwise, he was wrong.

It was now approaching mid-day on the morning of Monday, September the 10th.

Chapter 22

Washington, DC

Mark was surprised at the ease with which he managed to get out of Langley. From the tone of the discussion with Scott, he would have expected something more. But Scott had just shrugged, said there was nothing more that they needed him for, gave him back his cell phone which they would have found as useful as his laptop, and escorted him out of the building. Any questions that Mark asked about the results of the interrogation were answered with a simple and meaningless comment.

'We are continuing with our inquiries.'

Any questions that he asked about the whereabouts of Paul and Brad were answered with a simple and unhelpful "You don't need to know that". At least he was offered a ride to wherever he wanted to go. That offer was declined, and he turned his back on an organization that had gone down in Marks' estimation – if indeed it were possible to get any lower down the scale than they already were.

To say that Mark was annoyed did not adequately

describe the situation. He could understand that an organization such as the Central Intelligence Agency would play its cards pretty close to the chest on such a sensitive matter. It was required to do so by the very laws that set the CIA up way back in 1947.

However, he had been instrumental in bringing to the organization critical information – solid information – that as far as he could tell was right on the button. In the case of Doctor Abdul Jabbar and the existence of a cell in Rabaul PNG, it was incredibly good new intelligence. Yet he had no way of knowing whether that intelligence had any effect whatsoever on their analysis of the situation and whether they would take any action as a result. He got a distinct impression that they were merely circling the wagons. In the circumstances outlined in Marks' report, which did not seem to be particularly appropriate in terms of action or timing. Still, they had plenty of time, didn't they? Twenty-one hours could be a long time.

He hailed a taxi and headed south-east towards downtown Washington which was about nine miles away and on the other side of the Potomac River. It was a nice warm day, and he could have done with a walk. But there weren't two hours to spare.

He planned to hire a car and head back to New York. He would have liked to have found out what had happened to his two friends, but that now seemed unlikely. While the rental firm was getting a vehicle of his choosing organized, he called into the Starbucks shop that was just a block from the local Hertz offices in New York Avenue for a coffee.

He was so close to the White House that he could have called in and told the President face to face what was going on. But there wasn't much hope of that happening.

It was quite pleasant to be spoken to like a human

being again as he ordered his coffee weak and black. Usually, that specification brought a grimace from the server, but the girl just gave him a huge smile, poured him a glass of cold water, and turned to attend to the coffee. He pulled out his cell phone and started to search for Paul's number.

'Make that two, if you would be so kind' said Paul Williams as he slid into the booth beside Mark.

'How did you get here? Oh, don't bother! I should be used to the way you people work by now.' said Mark as he dumped the cell phone on the table.

'That is a nice greeting. I'll go if you want me to – but I thought you might like a bit a company.' said Paul, 'and a chance to find out what the result of our little debrief was.'

'Well, that would be nice!' replied Mark. 'I got the distinct impression from agent Scot What's-his-name that we achieved absolutely nothing! He certainly said or did nothing intelligent during the three or so days I spent in the Company.'

'You got that impression too? Well, at least we are on a similar wavelength. But you should see things from the CIA's point of view. I think that the information you produced about the Doctor – Abdul whatever his name was – got them a little rattled and they are on to that one big time. And I do not think you helped much with your laptop. If you had offered to help them decipher it you could have saved several days, but then I understand that they did not ask. What is on the laptop – anything I should know about?'

'Come on Paul – you know what business I am in. Everything on my laptop is encrypted, and we seem to have proved that so far, the CIA cannot break it. Which is good. As for what it contains – I cannot imagine that anything is of any real interest to the CIA – it' just commercial and personal stuff'. Mark finished with a shrug and a grin.

Lying to Paul was something he had not tried before. Well, Paul had not exactly been honest with Mark in the past, otherwise how come he had a daughter in Wellington New Zealand? And the fact was that the CIA was not that dumb. They had most likely unravelled the content of his laptop, albeit with some difficulty, but were very unlikely to admit either they had or had not. They were also unlikely to share any information that they had acquired with Paul.

Paul held Marks' gaze for a few moments, then he also shrugged, and he also grinned. They understood each other—better things left unsaid. He continued, the diversion forgotten or at least filed away for future reference.

'But as for the rest of the story, I don't think they buy it. At least not yet. They have increased the alert level and have every known terrorist wannabe and extremist under surveillance. But that is not much different from the normal situation.'

Mark made to interrupt, but Paul held up his hand and said, 'Just hear me out.'

'They claim to have absolutely no intelligence from any other source telling them that there is anything about to happen in New York City or anywhere else in the world for that matter. And they have excellent sources here in the United States that should have alerted them if something was about to happen. They have a handle on all the serious terrorists and cells likely to be linked to al Qaeda or any of the many peripheral organizations of al Qaeda wannabes and they come up with Zippo. Despite what you may think, a lot has been happening here in Washington, we have had a lot of people working 24/7 to try to locate the likely participants in any such plot.'

'For all their efforts they can find nothing. What they have concluded from all their intelligence so far is that – yes there may be a plot in the making. But we are at least a year ahead of ourselves. They think that there may be a plot that it is to happen next year at the earliest and not this year. They would regard your information as, what is called in the trade, "Soft Intelligence" which means they have no hard facts to back it up. Can you see their logic?'

It was Marks' turn to contemplate as he looked at his friend over the rim of his water glass. He had known Paul so intimately and for so long that they had become more like brothers. Paul's words were not spoken from any Agency handout or orchestrated by their PR department. They were his own words. But there was a hesitation that suggested that even he was not fully convinced.

'Yes – I can see the logic. But now the question is – are they right?' said Mark. The disappointment he felt at the lack of action could have resulted from nothing more complicated than human nature—a natural reaction. He had rationalized all the details of a plot, and that caused the adrenalin to pump through the veins. Certainly, he had gone into the investigation with a preconceived idea, courtesy of Harold, aided by Brad and Paul. One other question therefore was – had he got too carried away with it all? The CIA was a huge bureaucracy. While the size of its' actual workforce was classified information, it was reputed to have at least twenty thousand employees, who carried with them all the trappings and idiosyncrasies typical of bureaucrats the world over. And Mark was just one more blip in their otherwise ordered day. From the CIA's point of view, having twelve months' notice of a plot was ideal, giving them more than enough time to put the pieces of the jigsaw together and round up all the participants.

As usual, they could do so without alarming the residents of the country they were ordered to protect, and life would go on.

But – were they right?

'There are some pretty clued-up analysts at the Agency who have been working on it and they have reached that conclusion.' Paul said with a finality that neither of them felt. 'But there is some good news. New York City has been put on a higher state of alert and I am going to New York this afternoon to help. Not that I can do much, but I insisted, and they agreed – more to get me out of the way I think. Unfortunately, we are again talking about being in a reactive mode rather than a proactive mode. So, it may or may not be taken as seriously as you might expect.'

'What has happened to Brad?' Mark asked. The change of subject came as a surprise to Paul, and the surprise did not go unnoticed.

'I have not seen Brad since we were split up on Thursday—not that there is anything unusual about that. But I do believe he may have been reassigned – again not that there is anything unusual about that either. I believe that the computer boffins had the same problem with Brads' laptop as they had with yours. Surely you did not encrypt Brads' machine as well?'

Mark answered that one carefully.

'Brads' machine has some Taylor software still loaded on it as a backup and that is encrypted. If they have been unable to get in, that means that Brad would have told them that the security lock is double keyed, and he would need me to activate it. That, in turn, means that Brad is on our side.'

'The laptop does contain information that could be of interest to the CIA?' said Paul, taking a logical step, which placed him not too far from the truth.

Mark laughed.

'Are you here for a chat, or are you continuing with Scott and Henrys' interrogation?'

It was meant as a joke and that is how it was taken. The fact that Paul had a different view from Mark did not in any way detract from his logic, and the whole exercise had increased, rather than decreased, the respect that they each held for the other.

Again, Paul grinned, but not about the reason for his question.

'So, you have met Henry? They must be getting desperate. Henry Michelson is the guy who they send in to talk to our most difficult customers. Usually, these guys are foreigners and not exactly dancing to the same tune. He is our top psychiatrist whose main job is to find out whether we are talking to the real thing. Or someone who is just taking us for a ride. Or just a nut case. And what was Henrys' conclusion about you?'

'At the end of our chat, he just apologized for the trouble I had been through and said that the CIA would pay my actual and reasonable expenses. We also exchanged views of the CIA motto and talked about how the CIA should change its' focus.'

'Shit!' Paul reacted. 'That means that at least one person at the CIA does believe you. It is a pity his word does not carry much weight.'

'So – what is the real story with Brad' Mark asked, determined to find out – well—something.

'Well since he left Taylor Software he had been left pretty much to his own devices. Now that everything is more or less cleaned up, he was due to be posted somewhere else. There is nothing sinister about that.'

Mark sat quietly for a minute as the coffees arrived and the girl fussed over them like an old mother. Paul did change the subject. He looked at Mark like someone caught with his hand in the cookie jar and spoke with no small amount of emotion.

'I am sorry about the confusion that you must have felt in Wellington – Harold was paranoid, even about safe houses, so we met at my daughter's place. I never talked to you about my daughter Renee.'

There was not that much that Mark could say to that. Yes, he was confused. His fathers' choice of a place to meet however was the least of his worries. He had long since ceased worrying about trying to understand his fathers' logic, and that was long before the beginning of this little adventure. Paul was a different story. For two men who had shared so much it did seem more than a little odd that one of them should have a beautiful young daughter, and the other one did not know anything about her. Mark just replied as gently as he could.

'Do you want to tell me about her now?'

It had to be told to someone, and as it all transpired, it was just as well that it was. Paul had started his working life as a rookie cop, married to his young, and very pregnant, a childhood sweetheart. Being a young rookie, he was of course indestructible. That Ais until he tried to arrest someone who had been in the game for a while and who took exception to the young upstart. Paul, his wife Caroline, and his new-born baby daughter all ended up in hospital courtesy of a traffic accident that had all the randomness associated with a NASA trip to the moon.

Caroline did not survive after the accident. Paul was heartbroken but he was not about to give up. Just two days after Caroline's funeral his parents were due to depart overseas on a five-year posting, and they duly left but with some extra baggage to accommodate their newly adopted little girl. Up until the actual point of departure, Paul intended to go as well, but for a variety of reasons decided to stay. His daughter, who his parents called Renee, would be safe where they were going – even the mafia would back away from the kind of security that existed in Moscow at that time. But it was Paul who would be the focus of their attention.

He did the only thing that a young rookie indestructible lad could do. He said goodbye to his daughter and enlisted in the Marines with the avowed intention of eventually tracking down the Drug barons who had been responsible for the senseless death of his young wife. Renee was ten years old by the time Paul saw her again, and he was surprised that she then knew and respected exactly who he was and what had happened to her mother. They both vowed that this was a secret that they both could keep. That would be made much easier by the fact that the mature young girl had no wish to set foot in the country of her birth. Now that his parents had found their way to New Zealand, Renee was going steady with a policeman whose size and athletic build would make most crooks cower in fear – and that was just fine with Paul.

The waitress seemed reluctant to leave as she heard Paul's story but a nod from Paul and she was on her way. Was he getting paranoid? Surely his random choice of a coffee shop had not landed him in yet another CIA meeting place. He shook his head and turned his attention to the matter of immediate concern to him. What was to become of Brad?

'How you guys' work is an absolute mystery to me. But I would have thought that, even if the so-called plot is a year away, Brads' input to the analysis would be critical even at this stage. I would find it hard to believe that the limited time we have been in Washington would be sufficient to have the whole matter, as you say, cleaned up. What the hell is going on?'

It was Paul's turn to pause. He was in the unusual position that he had been told very little of what was planned for Brad but, like Mark, he would be concerned if that source of information was to be cut off – yet again. Just because Paul was a fully paid-up member of the CIA did not mean that he knew everything there was to know. The CIA's security meant that quite often the people kept out of the loop, for sometimes but not always valid reasons, could not exactly be effective in performing their role. Add to that the fact that the security and intelligence services do get an enormous number of tips and theories all the time.

Before the original events of September 11th, 2001, there was a mountain of information in the hands of people who, had they been able to pull it all together, from disparate sources, would have revealed what was going on. But having a picture is a different thing than having a jigsaw with an unknown number of pieces. And after the events, people armed with these isolated bits of information that could only now be put into a true context once that was known, accused the authorities of being too slow and of being inept. But which of the millions of tips are they to take seriously? Hindsight is a wonderful thing, even if it is useless. On the other hand, Paul did not share Marks' faith in Brad, and therefore did Brad's absence matter?

'Did you and Brad hit it off on your trip to Rabaul?' Paul countered. 'You seem to place a great deal of faith in him, while the general opinion within the Agency is that he is something of a nerd with very little to offer.'

'Who within the Agency?' asked Mark, starting to get a little irritated 'Surely not that fuck-wit Scott – he would not be on my list of the most sensible or logical people I have met.'

Paul grinned at that comment but continued.

'You know that all bureaucratic organizations have their prejudices. Brad is firstly an African American – that puts him on the back foot for starters. Then he is a technocrat, or geek in your terms, which means that he moves in circles that most people fear. So, out of fear, they ignore him. Then he treads into other people's territory – firstly as a field agent and then as an analyst – neither of which he is specially trained for. Add to that your involvement in uncovering a cell that we knew nothing at all about. And, whether you are Special Forces trained or not, that makes professional spooks run scared. From my understanding of what you said in Wellington, you were incredibly lucky to find out what you did, and people, whether it is fair or not, resent that. You stumble apparently by pure chance into a situation which most people at the sharp end of our organization would give their right testicle to be able to uncover. What do you expect?'

Mark was starting to get mad.

'That is insane! You have got a guy – who gives a rat's arse about what is the colour of his skin – who has more brains than anyone I have met at the CIA – yourself included. And you chose to ignore him because he steps on someone's toes while trying to do his job. So, what, if we stumble onto something by pure chance? You cannot mean that intelligence gathered by chance is any different from intelligence gathered by hard graft. What a pathetic organization you work for'.

Paul did not grin this time but held his hands up in protest.

'I am simply trying to tell you how it is. I also don't give a rat's fart what colour he is either, as you very well know. But the facts are that your choice of ally worked against you. You would have been better off if I had gone to Rabaul with you.'

'And you could have done the work that Brad did?' snarled Mark. 'I don't think so. And you might like to recall, the trip to Rabaul must have been planned before I arrived on the scene – by Harold Taylor – but surely with your knowledge and agreement. Who is the fuckwit now?'

Paul pondered for a moment. He did not appear to be the least bit offended by Mark's outburst there was a hint of a smile. If only things were that simple when dealing with Harold Taylor. The decision was made in Wellington, by Harold, with Paul's knowledge. It was quite another matter to assume that Paul had agreed with the decision. The Intelligence service had more than its share of "if only we had done this and not that" scenarios. But then he became more serious, took another swig of his coffee, and seemed to come to a decision. He had to say what was on his mind, and maybe Mark would be receptive to his idea, insane though it may seem.

'There is one possibility that we have not considered – by the "we" I mean you and me, and your father and not the CIA. You want to hear it?' Paul asked but did not seem likely to accept no for an answer.

Mark just nodded – unsure of what his friend had to say – but intrigued. Paul continued.

'You remember when we were down in Colombia, and everything turned pear-shaped when we were about to get our hands on that thug Carlos—told to stand down based on Executive Orders from our Commander in Chief. Well—what say the "Cover-up" that you and Brad have been trying to work your way around emanates from a similar Executive Order—from the same office even if the personnel have changed?'

Mark could not believe what he was hearing. He remembered his experience in Colombia like it was yesterday. They had been on a top-secret mission, what was referred to in the trade as 'Black Ops', as part of a Delta Force – equivalent to the British SAS. He and Paul had been in the US Special Forces for some years, but to be promoted to the elite Delta Force was something special. The fact that being assigned to Delta Force had more than its' fair share of outright boredom is often forgotten, but the adrenaline and the pride are paramount. On this particular covert operation, not for long.

They had trudged through the forests and over mountains in the most appalling weather conditions to finally track down Carlos the man who headed one of the largest and most dangerous drug organizations the world had ever known. They had carefully planned to intercept him as he travelled between Bucaramanga north of Bogota over the mountains to Cucuta, a town close to the Venezuelan border. They had taken painstakingly careful calculated steps to make sure that they could take him without anyone knowing by who, or how or why. The Colombians would soon work out the why – Carlos had offended more people than you could shake a stick at – but not the who or the how. So covert was the operation that Marks's normal chain of command did not even know why or where he had gone. Nor would anyone know where Carlos was to be taken when he was captured. They had a helicopter with all the latest stealth characteristics and necessary electronic gear to make it almost impossible to detect ready to perform the extraction. It would have landed him on a US warship waiting off the coast of Panama where no one could get at him – other than officers of the CIA and the US Drug Enforcement Administration that is. The complete operation – the Navy, Air Force, Delta Force, CIA, DEA, and heaven knows who else—would have made a noticeably big hole in anyone's budget.

And then came that decision. Let him pass. The order appeared to be so insane that Mark had to ask that it had to be repeated and verified several times before it was finally accepted.

After they returned to the USA, Mark did some research of his own to find out why his orders had been so radically changed. The conclusion he reached was that it appeared that Carlos, despite making his vast fortune from drugs and protecting it with violent and ruthless efficiency, planned to move into politics. And the particular brand of politics he had chosen happened to suit the longer-term plans of the United States for this part of the world.

Despite its' attempts to be democratic, the country suffered from chronic corruption after over forty years of conflicts involving rebel guerrilla groups and paramilitary militias. But at the root of the problem was drug manufacture and trafficking to its' biggest customer – the USA - on a massive scale. And Carlos was going to fix that, was he? So, let him pass, and go on killing people – directly in the case of his fellow Colombians who got in his way – and indirectly in the case of United States citizens who did not care where their drugs came from. The Republica de Colombia has as its' motto – 'Libertad y Orden' which is Spanish for Liberty and Order. It could hardly be more inappropriate. This experience was the reason why Mark and Paul left the military service. Just what was the point of working for an organization that fucked up so badly?

Paul waited while Mark mulled over his thoughts, but he judged that enough of what he had said had the desired effect. He continued.

'The President has to do something about his approval

ratings – they are at their lowest level for a President in office in over twenty years. He has to justify his continued fight against terrorism, but if most of the terrorist acts are confined to places like Iraq or Afghanistan or Indonesia, or even Europe, why should the US voters care? He has to get support for more forces, and that means a whole shitload of money, at a time when public interest in the various wars is waning. What say someone conveniently sets off a couple of bombs in the United States and, for good measure, does it on the anniversary of 9/11? The President can then say – "Did I not warn you? – but you did not listen". The opposition who has claimed the risk is grossly exaggerated by the President's men would be rendered toothless. The fickle public, whose opinions change as frequently as the weather, would, in turn, say, "Of course you were right and of course, we did" and turn on the opposition for trying to mislead them. So up rocket, the ratings of our President and at a small price – say a couple of hundred citizens killed out of the population of New York City of what—eight-plus million?'

Mark found it hard, at first, to believe what his friend was saying. But then it began to make sense, both in terms of logic and in terms of the past performance of the Administration. The President not only had to worry about approval ratings. In addition to retaining public support for the "War on Terrorism," he had to somehow justify the massive financial burden that was imposed.

The cost of the "Occupation" of Iraq alone was insane, yet there was a need to spend more, not only in Iraq but also in the forgotten war in Afghanistan which, contrary to the public's perception, the US and its' allies were slowly but surely losing. The money had to come from somewhere, and no matter how his administration spun the numbers, at the end of the day, the ordinary Americans had to foot the bill. In other words, they had to forego something like healthcare in favour of a forgotten war against Who and Where? Maybe Brad's earlier analysis had made its way up through the command chain. Then the word had come back from the top – Let it pass.

This whole scenario had not been prevented from becoming exposed by some low-level bureaucrats, as Mark had assumed. The bureaucracy was working under orders! And the amorphous mass of the bureaucracy always worked on the longer-term goals and so what if a few hundred people had to die. If the numbers added to more than two, they were only statistics. If this was the case, no wonder no one had shown much interest in Mark's report at the Central Intelligence Agency. They already knew, and they knew how to deal with it – Do nothing. Holy Shit – what a screwed-up country we live in!

'What are you going to do?' Mark asked. He was not surprised by the resigned, almost defeated, look on the face of Paul Williams.

'I don't know yet. It only occurred to me this morning and I am still grappling with the issues. You are the only one who knows what I am thinking, but that is the real reason why I have to get to New York. There is no one I can talk to in the CIA. I am regarded as something of a maverick, and I would just be laughed at. That is until the Presidents security detail finds out, and then I am dead meat. The people at my level are taught to follow orders not to make decisions. If I go higher, I would be very much alone. Others may agree with me but would be too frightened to make any move. I must talk to Harold – but there are risks involved. I have to be sure I am not bugged and then I have to be sure that Harold himself is not in on the deal.'

That remark brought a smile to Mark's face.

'That is one thing on which I think you can be certain. For all his faults, my father would never be a part of it, no matter how high up it goes. He normally believes orders from on high are sacrosanct but even he would draw the line at this kind of nonsense!'

'What if they threatened his family?' Paul asked. 'And I am not talking about you – what about your mother?'

That brought another smile to Marks' face – broader this time.

'Why do you think there is so little emotion in our family? Harold Taylor is the one person that I know of that would ignore any threat. Believe me – he would accept the death of his nearest and dearest – and his own death – as part of the risks of the job. A more dedicated guy you could not imagine.'

Paul looked quite pleased with that response.

'Then we have only a couple of problems left'.

'And they are?' Mark asked, not sure he wanted to hear the reply.

'I have to try to convince him that I am right' replied Paul with a shrug. 'And then, if I do, without someone having a tracer on our conversation, I have to hope he knows someone in the hierarchy of the complex web we call our security and intelligence network, who can do something about it.'

'Does it then really matter if your conversations are tracked?' asked Mark. 'If something is going to happen it will happen in less than twenty hours. Then there is another problem – there is no way that Harry can get back to the United States in the timeframe. My guess is – you have no choice – call him – and then disappear for a day and see what happens.'

The expression on Paul's face said it all.

'I guess you are right – so here goes. If this does not work out, you will owe me one.

Paul could not know at that time – but he would never be around to collect – whether it did or did not work out.

Chapter 23

Femme Fatale

The trip from Washington to New York took about six hours. It would probably have been easier to take a commuter flight, but Mark had had enough of flying. And just wanted to be alone. Mark had rented a Chevrolet Suburban SUV and he drove.

He was desperate to get to New York City to see Annette, but he still needed to think. That needed time and space. He knew that his love for Annette was not something that should have been his highest priority. But that is the way that it was now.

The previous few days had not been so good, and he needed her if only to get the terrible thought of what would inevitably happen the following day out of his mind. And with all the nitwits running the country who did not want to listen to him, he felt he was going out of his mind.

He had done all he could and that was the end of it as far as he was concerned. He would make sure that neither he nor Annette was anywhere near any possible target. Like all people in the City of New York, he would be saddened, angry, and appalled by what was about to happen. He had done the absolute best he could and told the story to the people whose job it was to do something about it. Now he needed to bring some sanity in his life and Annette was the one person who could provide that.

As he headed out of the city on Highway 95, he rang his office. He really expected Annette to answer, but instead got Dusty again and he did not seem to be in the best of moods – he never was, but this time he was pissed.

The 'Where the fuck are you?' greeting was to be expected.

'I am driving up from Washington – should be in town by about 8:00 pm this evening. How are things going – you got everything under control?'

Mark tried to keep the conversation light. Dusty would be in an even worse mood when he learned what had happened – or what had not happened. Like Mark, Dusty had served his country in ways that would never be told, and in ways that brought into question the wisdom of the decision-makers. This was another example where the apparent lack of a coherent decision would probably cost people their lives. The decision-makers would simply move on to the next matter to be considered in their piles of mostly irrelevant papers.

'Everything is under control – what do you expect? That is apart from your girlfriend. She rang in sick. What the hell were you doing in Washington?'

Mark ignored the question about Washington. The way Dusty had said sick meant that he did not believe that Annette was sick – which was unusual for Annette. Maybe Dusty and his abrasive manner were starting to get to her, but he doubted that. Something was wrong. But what?

'I will see you in the morning – and I will bring you up to date – there is too much to talk about now. Maybe we can have lunch, but that depends on what is happening in New York City tomorrow.'

Dusty seemed oblivious to his comment about New

York and merely growled his agreement. This time, he did have the time to say goodbye before crashing the telephone onto the receiver. There was just no point in Mark telling Dusty Miller of what was expected tomorrow. He was in a foul enough mood as it was. But wasn't he in for a surprise!

Mark then rang Annette's landline number and all he got, yet again, was her answerphone. He got the same response from her cell phone. Probably asleep, or maybe gone to see the Doctor.

Wasn't he in for a surprise!

He knew he had not spent very much time with Annette. He had probably not kept her as informed of what he was up to as perhaps he should have. That was partly out of fear for her safety, partly because he just did not know whether she was what she said she was. And partly because he did not want to appear a fool.

Some of the top brains at the CIA and the FBI seemed to think he was a few slices short of a sandwich. So, they must be right. He had spent a considerable amount of time chasing phantoms on the other side of the planet. Then he had returned to Washington with what he thought was the most reasonable analysis of what was going to happen. The authorities however thought what he had to say was the most hare-brained analysis of what was going to happen. Nobody wanted to believe him.

Sure, they said that they had increased the alert level in New York. But what did that mean? So, he was returning now to New York City, and he would not share his analysis with Annette. Just keep her, and himself, out of harm's way. He was desperately tired but that did not matter in the overall scheme of things. He did not realize until he had started his journey from Washington back to New York how much he missed her and began to regret his decision to drive. It was too late now, and he had to live with that decision. Others would not.

Her apartment was nestled in the Bronx just under the shadow of the Madison Avenue bridge. This part of the city was pocketed with a wide variety of living accommodations, but Annette's was at least tidy and well maintained.

His first ring of the front doorbell was timid, almost apologetic. He wanted her, yet he didn't. He had never felt so hopelessly inadequate in all of his life. He rang again, a little more persistent this time. He knew she was home because he had seen the lights on in her apartment. Her voice, when she answered, was not quite what he had hoped for, sounding reluctant and guarded. At least she was at home, which seemed to be at variance with her failing to answer the telephone.

'Hi, it's' me, Mark.' was his answer.

There followed a brief pause. He had expected her to be surprised, pleased, and eager. But this did not appear to be going all that well.

'I didn't expect to see you tonight – is something wrong?' she asked, not sounding the least bit pleased that he was at last home from his wanderings.

'No, nothing's wrong – I just needed to see you.'

The strain must have transmitted itself to his voice, no matter how hard he tried to prevent it. The comments he added did not sound much better.

'I have not had the best of time lately. Can I come in and have a coffee or something?'

Again, the pause. Mark felt himself deflate as another thought came to him. Don't tell me she is seeing someone else! Mark's mind was beginning to play games. If she was, then that would be a bit hard to take after the days, well weeks, he had behind him of tangled plots, stories of terrorism and terrorists. And of people deceiving each other – including his father. Was it the tone of her voice? When she had spoken to him on the phone in New Zealand, she had sounded so sincere. And she had said that she missed him. Now there was—nothing!

Her final words came like a death knell – delivered in a matter-of-fact tone that sent a chill through Mark's bones.

'I am sorry, but I cannot see you tonight – I'll see you tomorrow' answered the very cold voice.

He tried to sound matter of fact with his reply, but he could not help the involuntary sob in his voice. He remembered in his youth using the sob to get around any such objections, with somewhat varied results. This time it was not planned.

'Just for a few moments – that is all I want.'

There was no warmth in her reply, just a cold 'No, I will see you tomorrow.'

The connection went dead.

Mark slumped against the door frame thinking all sorts of things. What else was to go wrong? He had set out on what was a bit of an adventure, albeit starting with deceit – from his father for heaven's sake! – and now – what?

He slowly made his way back to his vehicle, a feeling of complete helplessness beginning to overwhelm him. Glancing up at the second-floor window he could swear he saw someone watching him. He was certain it was not Annette. Who was it? Getting into the vehicle, turning on the ignition, and slowly moving out into the traffic he felt numb.

Something was wrong. She had had the odd cold moment before. But she always had a confident manner. There had never been a pause. When she spoke, particularly to Mark, and especially since – well recent events between them – she normally had a vitality and so much love in her voice. But not now. It was quite the opposite – and that did not make any sense. Something had to be wrong.

Probably against his better judgment, and his training, he decided to find out for sure. Maybe someone was in there that should not be. Or maybe she was seeing someone else. Not that he had any rights. She was single and so was he. But she had become his rock in the insanity that summed up the last couple of weeks. If he was to lose her now, he might as well find out who the other bastard was.

He turned right into the next street, and right again which brought him into what was more like an alleyway behind the rows of terraced apartments. There he turned off the vehicle lights and let the SUV cruise to a halt immediately below the fire escape that led down from her apartment. Standing on top of the SUV he could quite easily reach the first rungs of the ladder without having to lower the base. This was good because the clatter of the base coming down would have alerted the people on the second floor – not to mention half of New York City – such was the silence, except for the gentle music emanating from somewhere to his left.

Climbing the ladder up to the third-floor window, which would be the window to her bedroom, was easy. He had spent some time in a previous life dangling in places that were a little more hazardous than a fire escape. The alley was deserted, there was no traffic, and there were no streetlights, so the chances of his being spotted were remote.

He moved like a cat slowly, stealthily, and quietly. All his training in special operations came back to him quite naturally. He had every confidence in his ability to see this thing through to the logical conclusion, even though he dreaded what that conclusion may be.

The window appeared from below to be slightly open. Thank goodness Annette preferred good old fresh air to the air-conditioned crap that most New Yorkers seemed to favour. He was almost at the window, when there was a sudden burst of light from above and he could hear voices – two men talking! He remained motionless hoping that whoever was in the room above would not stay or look out the window. Or, worse still, close the window. But after what seemed like hours, but was probably only a few minutes, as he clung precariously to the ladder and as close to the building as he could, the light faded to what it had been before, and he heard the slam of a door.

Cautiously, he slowly dragged himself up the ladder until he was level with the window.

He peered inside. There was nothing to see. Getting from the ladder onto the window ledge and through the partially open window was made easier by the fact that there appeared to be no one in the room. There was a small bedside light on – there always was. The bed was in its' usual immaculately condition – neat and tidy. Just a bedroom, which was there waiting for Annette to retire for the night. That brought memories of happier days. That was a good sign – perhaps!

He eased his way over the ledge and silently stepped into the room. One of the problems with the old but fashionable apartment was the wooden floor. They tended to creek. But his years of training in the Special Forces meant his footsteps were soft and sure, easing back the weight on his feet so that any noise was minimized.

While climbing up the ladder, Mark had made up his mind that he would simply try to just make sure Annette was safe by finding out who or what was in the other room.

Then he would make his escape the way he had come in, preferably without being detected. The fact that he had heard two men eased his mind somewhat concerning Annette's affections but increased his curiosity about what was going on.

'You were very foolish to do this – don't move another inch, or you will become a dead man.'

The voice came from behind him. From behind the curtain.

A chill ran down his spine.

Why had he not checked thoroughly before blundering into the room? That was partially explainable with his tiredness and the state of mind he was in. What was not explainable was the voice. The south-east Asian accent and the arrogance were unmistakable.

'So, we meet again Asid. And what are you doing here?' Mark sighed. The irony of the situation did not escape Mark. Climbing in through the third-floor window was not the recommended form of access to the apartment. He could not avoid the laugh that involuntarily escaped his lips.

But a sickening feeling went through Mark's head at the same time. Here was Asid – one of the Indian/ Pakistanis who worked for the Augem Group and John Dubois. That meant that at least the Augem Group, and probably John Dubois, was surely involved in something. He was still unsure of what – but it had to be bad. And John Dubois's organization had recommended Annette to him! And now, here was Asid in Annette's apartment. What was going on this the eve of September 11?

It was ironic and mind-numbingly obvious that he had saved some time. His theory about someone at the Augem Group being involved in some kind of plot now began to make chilling sense. And Augem had come to him, but not in any way that Mark had planned. Was Paul correct in his assessment that Annette was part of the scheme? He had a sickening feeling that there could be no other logical explanation. Or could there?

The bedroom door was pushed open and through it came a man carrying a silenced pistol, accompanied by Annette. But the gun was not trained on Annette. It was aimed at Mark. They were followed to the door by two other men, who stayed out of sight but the reason for their presence was clear. The odds were not exactly stacked in Mark's favour. Annette appeared at first to be shocked. But she very soon gathered herself together.

'This was not part of the plan Mark, and now they will have to deal with you, unfortunately permanently. Why are you so persistent? Why did you have to get involved?'

Her words cut through him like a knife. There was a certain irritation in her voice that suggested that she genuinely could have done without this intrusion. There was a somewhat rehearsed tone to what she had to say. but gone was that calm, smiling girl who he worshipped. Here was the cold voice of someone who could be very unpleasant. She was obviously irritated by the intrusion but was equally obviously seemed quite at home with some very unpleasant men. Or was she just resigned to something over which she had no control?

Mark had to think quickly. How much did they know about what he had been up to during his recent travels?

Probably nothing. But, if they were involved in a plot, and there had been a cover-up of earlier intelligence at the CIA, the odds were that they would now know of Marks' visit to Langley.

The obvious ploy was to make light of the situation, but his various attempts at humour met with stony silence. They used tape to bind his hands behind his back. Then they bound his feet, used the same tape to gag him, and then bundled him into a chair.

The problem for Mark was there were now at least four men, all armed, and none too worried about Mark's state of health. After they had bound him in such a way that it would take a minor miracle for him to escape, two of them left the room, leaving a very edgy Asid and an incredibly stressed Annette.

Now she sat – almost provocatively—on the bed facing Mark with an almost quizzical look on her beautiful face.

'What are you doing Mark? You go halfway around the world, calling from the strangest of places, not telling me what you are doing. And then here you are, creeping into my apartment like a thief in the night. I said I would meet with you, perhaps tomorrow, but I guess there may not be a tomorrow now.'

Did Mark detect that she was trying to pass him a message? Surely not? But he could hope—even if he did not understand the message.

She leaned forward and kissed him lightly on the cheek. The aroma of her perfume filled his nostrils. His mind was racing trying to think of something to say. But then there was not much point – the tape around his mouth was so tight he could not have answered her anyway. He just looked at the lovely curve of her breasts, so warm and inviting, and thought of previous and better times.

Then she was gone, to be replaced by a man Mark who could not immediately recall seeing previously. Then it came to him. Here was the man who had accompanied the FBI's Henderson at Marks' office several weeks ago. The shape of his breasts was distorted by a bulge under the right armpit which told Mark that he was left-handed. Not that the knowledge would do him any good. One thing Mark was sure of was that the man was gay. Mark had spent too much time in the military, and he was an expert in reading body language, so he knew.

'So, you are the infamous Mark Taylor – and we meet yet again. I have wanted to talk to you, but you appear to have been on holiday!'

The laugh that followed left little doubt that the gay man did not think that Mark had been on holiday. Which was fair enough. It did not seem even remotely like a holiday. Mark just shrugged. He then added a comment that at least gave Mark some hope.

'We are a little busy dealing with other things at the moment, so you will have to be our guest for the present. Our boss wants to have a chat, but that will need to wait until tomorrow.'

It was hard to tell whether the shrug or the defiant look in Mark's eyes caused what happened next. He was hit with such force that the chair and Mark slammed against the dresser. That caused Mark's head to crash into the mirror, which shattered, as Mark and a fair amount of glass ended up on the floor.

'We will talk again later. And we will allow you to have your say – well to say what we want to hear!' he said with another laugh. And then he called out a man's name – Ted – and into the room came a large man with a bald head and wearing a suit that was at least one size too small. This one Mark definitely knew. Through the blood, which was now running down his face, he could make out the shape of his fellow passenger from that trip through New York City on what was appearing to be a fateful Friday afternoon. At least he now had a name—not that this piece of knowledge would do him any good either.

Ted gripped the chair with one hand, Marks hair with the other, and effortlessly hoisted both upright, but not before a boot from his earlier tormentor had landed in the lower mid-rift causing Mark to retch, and then choke, then spew the remnants through his nose, since there was no other way out. The gay man left the room while 'Ted' pulled a soiled book from his pocket, made himself at home on the bed, put a new toothpick between his teeth, and proceeded to read as if this was an everyday occurrence.

Mark struggled to come to terms with the predicament that he was now in. He could hardly breathe and the pain from his head and lower ribs were intense. The tape that bound his hands, feet, and mouth seems to be getting tighter. And he was outnumbered.

Well, that was a laugh. He was outnumbered and outgunned by men who at least had the use of their hands. But more to the point he had to consider the people themselves. While he may be premature to make such assumptions, had he once again by accident, found a missing link in the puzzle? That it was an Augem show was now beyond any doubt – Annette, Asid, and Ted were on the payroll. But the FBI agent's involvement was a cause for concern and not just because of his sexual orientation.

Had he stumbled upon the very people who were going to execute a part of the 9/11 plan that he had so patiently and ineffectively explained to the CIA? That explanation had been ridiculed. So here he was, tied up, watched by a gorilla, no one to talk to – well that did not matter because he could not talk anyway—no one would miss him, and now he was in sight of irrefutable proof. The only good news was that, according to his calculations, there were still about twelve hours to pass before something really bad would start to happen.

After a while, Asid came back into the room and motioned for Ted to leave. Asid reached across and ripped the tape from Mark's mouth, not worrying about the pain that it caused. Then he sat on the bed, his face close to Mark's, and he almost whispered.

'Tell me why you come into Annette's apartment in this strange way?'

The question surprised Mark because he had expected a more pertinent question. Perhaps they had no idea what he had been doing on his trip and his return from abroad after all. But the other thing that was a surprise was the way he said 'Annette' – as though he knew her as someone else. So, what was her real name? Mark decided at this stage to tell the truth. But he addressed his reply to deal with the Annette situation.

'After my trip away, I just wanted to see Annette. If you are not aware of it, we are – or rather were – a bit of an item. I did not expect to find a room full of guys. I did not realize she was into group sex – especially with one of your friend's orientations.'

The bitterness in his voice was plain to hear. But he had not seen Annette enter the room. Annette's reaction was to turn bright red and then she lashed out at Mark scrapping her nails across his unprotected face. There were tears in her eyes as she asked him.

'Why did you have to get involved?'

Again, he did not miss the strangeness of Annette's reaction. Had she lashed out at Mark to avoid a much more hostile response from Asid?

The bitterness in Mark's tone of voice could have left no doubt of what he thought.

'Well, you could enlighten me. I came into your apartment thinking you were in danger. And because I thought I loved you. And hoping to protect you from these lunatics. But now you will have to tell me—What I am involved in?' Mark asked.

There was a quick exchange of eye contact between Asid and Annette—a moment's hesitation – and then Asid recovered the situation somewhat.

'So, the jealous lover returns from his tripping around and cannot wait to get into his girlfriend's pants. So, he climbs up three floors on the outside of the building and comes in through the window, despite being told that the lady would see him tomorrow.'

Asid was enjoying himself despite the tension that existed in the room. Annette blushed again but held herself in check.

'That about sums it up' replied Mark with a shrug. 'It would not have mattered about the climbing into her pants bit, but when you think you are in love, you, or at least I, wanted to see her. I guess I got a little carried away with the moment – I promise not to do it again.'

At this, Annette could not take anymore and left the room in tears. Well, at least she seemed to care, despite the brave front, thought Mark. But what the hell was she involved in. And exactly what was her involvement?

'Well now that we have that out of the way, you and I can have a serious chat,' said Asid. 'Now tell me my friend. How come you sold the system to the Augem Group but retained some access rights for yourself. And what is more, do you continue to access our system? I am sure my boss will ask you himself tomorrow but humour me.'

Mark had to again think quickly, and carefully. Asid was talking almost fluently in English compared with how he spoke a few weeks ago – so their previous meeting had been a sham. And just how much did Asid know? Mark was confident that there was no way anyone at the Augem Group could have been able to detect the pinhole access that Taylor Software had into the Augem system. At least, that is, unless they had gone to some extraordinary lengths firstly in detection and secondly de-encryption and then finding out the who part of the equation. He racked his brain to think of who was aware of his access, but he could not think of anyone other than Brad. Surely, they had not got to Brad!

The only other people who could have had a clue were his father and maybe the US Ambassador to New Zealand. And then there was Paul and that creep called Forester in Wellington. But they were only on the periphery. He had not at any stage stated in their presence that he had access to the Augem system or stated how – just that he could get access to information. Therefore, if anyone, it had to be Brad. Or there was a serious leak somewhere between the CIA and the FBI, additional to the one that he and Brad were already aware of. Or was there?

Impulsively, Mark decided to go with his gut instinct – maybe Asid was on a fishing trip and knew fuck all.

'I do not know what this has to do with anything, but why on earth would I want to still have access to the Augem system. With the amount of money that the Augem Group paid me why should I care what the system does? After my trip down to New Zealand to visit my sick father, I am going to carry on writing software, but the Augem system is just that –it is theirs. It's a done deal and we have moved on. Why don't you Asid?'

'You mean that you have not got access?' asked Asid, a note of doubt appearing in his voice for the first time.

'Well, the only other person who could have had access, although I do not know whether he did or not, was Brad. The guy used to work for me you might recall before Augem bought the software. You might also recall he disappeared, or he may even be dead for all that I know!'

Mark was pushing his luck here, but he might as well find out just what Asid knew. He was not disappointed.

'Oh - but Brad is alive and well!' said Asid. The message slipped out of his mouth, and he immediately regretted it. But it was too late. That bit of news would make someone at the CIA pretty miffed. Brad had withdrawn from the office to avoid the Augem Group finding out who he was and what he was up to. And as far as Mark was aware the CIA still thought they were the only one's privy to that information. So, it was intuitive that there had to have been a leak. Someone was either keeping Augem fully informed—or Brad was the mole? Probably the former.

His father had said that Augem had been informed that Mark was unaware of Brads' CIA connections. Therefore Augem, or someone at Augem, had been informed of Brads' association. Consequently, Mark was safe to play the same line that he had in Wellington – treat everything to do with Brad as news.

Mark tried to look shocked by the news and responded with the mundane comment - 'Oh, is he?' and then continued.

'Well since he is, and I have not seen him since a couple of days before the deal was finalized, I suggest you direct your questions to him.'

Asid's face was a picture of confusion.

He muttered 'We have no idea where to find him and then recovered and said 'We need to talk some more about this. Unfortunately, we will be a little busy for the next evening, so I am afraid you will have to remain as our guest in the meantime. We will try not to make it too uncomfortable for you.' and he laughed.

That said he placed another piece of tape over Marks' mouth, went to the door, and summoned Ted back into the room he was gone.

That piece of the conversation had told Mark much more than the actual words said. For one thing, Asid would need to talk to someone else, and that meant he was not in charge. For a second thing, there was now little doubt that Mark's analysis of the intelligence had been spot on. The Augem Group was involved up to their armpits—he just needed to know the details and extent to which Augem was involved and more particularly who was involved. Thirdly, Asid seemed to imply that they had been tipped off about Brad rather than been told by Brad – otherwise they would know how to make contact with him.

That would be an interesting investigation! There were not that many people at the CIA who appeared to know the truth. Even less of them appeared to be acting on it. Communications were the key to any plot, and at this time communications did not appear to all that efficient in this particular group. Mark would need to take advantage of that situation, although he was not exactly in a position to do so. His reading of the situation now was grim.

Assuming the three mystery men were still involved in the so-called plot, it, therefore, seemed likely that Mark had stumbled into a cell that had very definite plans for tomorrow – September 11th. So presumably there was someone here who went by the name of Lateef, Mohammed, or Ano. That man could be sitting in the very next room being educated on how to blow up himself and his chosen part of New York. It was a pity that people on suicide missions could not do a practice run!

That said it seemed likely that Mohammed and maybe John Dubois himself were controlling two similar cells elsewhere in the city. Mark could only hope that this particular cell was not on a suicide pact, and he clung to the knowledge that he had been told that the "Boss" would like to talk to Mark tomorrow. Therefore, he just hoped that that would be after the event rather than before.

The time seemed to pass slowly. There was the occasional sound of voices from the other room. In the bedroom, Ted resumed his position on the bed and took no further interest in the goings-on. He was obviously not involved with anything other than to guard Mark or whoever else stood in their way.

Eventually, Mark began to feel the need to go to the toilet. Since he could not speak with the tape over his mouth, all he could do was grunt. After what seemed like an age, Ted finally responded with a friendly, if disinterested, 'And your problem is?'

Mark tried to indicate with his eyes but that was a waste of time. Ted reached across and told Mark that if he as much as made a squeak he would be dead and tore the tape off again.

'Now what do you want?' Ted snarled.

'I need to take a leak, and I am sure that Annette would not be overly pleased if I had it here.'

Ted did not reply. He just went to the door and said something which resulted in a good deal of shuffling before Annette came in the room. Without saying a word put a knife through the binding on his feet and indicated that Mark should follow. His feet had been bound so tightly, and for so long, that he could only stumble after her as the circulation returned. Assuming they were headed to the normal toilet, Mark was aware that it was not exceptionally large, so he laughed to himself as he envisaged what might happen next.

Someone carefully closed to door to the lounge area before Mark made his way forward. The toilet was down a narrow corridor and off to the left which meant for a few brief moments there were just the two of them. When they got to the toilet door Annette opened it, then stood aside to let Mark pass. Again, he could smell her perfume, and although she had been working with some very unsavoury people, she still had that cool charm that Mark had felt drawn to.

As he stood in the doorway he smiled and said, 'Could you please untie my hands, or this might be a little awkward.'

At this, she was about to do as he had asked when the gay man arrived on the scene and simply reached over, undid his fly and none too gently withdrew his penis from his underwear. That brought a laugh from Mark. Here he was in Annette's apartment with a gay man and Annette watching him take a leak! Neither of them seemed inclined to give him much in the way of privacy – the gay for heaven knows what reasoning went on in his twisted mind – and Annette – well there did not seem to be any logical reason why she was still there. Strange behaviour, but then the whole situation was weird – and Mark began to form a picture of an organization that was bumbling from one situation to the next and was, to say the least, amateurish. Maybe this wasn't the New York cell of some grand plan after all!

The gay man, whom the others had referred to as Gerry, became the one who volunteered to zip him back up. Mark smiled at the prospect of having Annette do the honours, but in the present company, which was hardly the time or the place. Marks' other thought was to ask if the choice of Gerry was due to his sexual orientation but thought that might get him another crack in the ribs for his trouble. However, his second choice did not do much better. His comment that they may as well leave him with his fly open was meant as a joke but brought him a stiff punch to the kidneys. He was then hustled back to the bedroom, unceremoniously dumped back into the chair and further tape applied to his feet. Before they could re-tape his mouth, he appealed for his hands to be taped in front of him, not behind, because the pain was unbearable. After an exchange of words, Ted shrugged his shoulders, untied Mark's hands, pulled them none too gently in front of him, taped them again, and then tied him to the chair with a length of cord.

It was by now getting late in the evening and Annette came into the bedroom and asked Ted to take a chair over by the window, and she simply climbed onto the bed and curled up. Mark pretended to be dozing as all this went on but through half-closed eyes saw Annette glancing at him more than once.

For a brief moment, he thought maybe Ted would go, and then maybe he could find out exactly what her role was in this extraordinary gathering. However, Ted was settling in for a long night, so he concentrated on reviewing his position.

He had established several facts about this group. Asid, while important in the scheme of things, equally clearly knew jack shit about what Mark had been up to. Or he was being very clever. But he had some source of information that was keeping him in the loop – whatever that was – and he would eventually have the gaps filled in. The guy who the others referred to as Gerry, Mark knew nothing about, other than he was gay, left-handed, and could not take a joke. He was fairly important in the scheme of things too, giving it the air of legitimacy – after all, he was from the FBI. Or was he? He would have to be watched.

Ted was just a hired thug—he probably knew nothing and cared even less.

Annette was either suffering from a split personality or was into this – whatever it was – over her head. Sure, she sounded tough in front of the boys, but was she? She appeared to be brittle and, if Mark could see that then so could Asid, who for all his faults seemed to know how to read people. She would need to be watched.

There was also a fourth man who had so far not revealed himself. Was this man Ted's mate? Was he just another hired thug? Or was Mohammed – the other Pakistani, who claimed to be Indian, gentleman from Augem – the leader of this group? Or was it no less than John Dubois himself? Or was it one of the three mysterious Pakistanis who had been recruited into the scheme? He would have to watch and listen.

Mark's reason for having them tie his hands in front, rather than behind, had nothing to do with it being more comfortable or less uncomfortable. He had noticed that they never reused any of the tapes, and while that may simply mean that they had plenty of it, he thought that he understood at least another reason why. Apart from the fact that they seemed to have an endless supply, the tape lost its' stick-ability when wet.

The one time of day or night when people appear to be less able to think coherently or act decisively, is between the hours of 3:00 am. and 5:00 am. in the early morning. It was something to do with the body clock. Even when people are stressed and unable to sleep, they still find that the body just shuts off and they do sleep – they just don't know that they do.

At this time in the morning, if people are awake for whatever reason, their mind plays silly games – basically making mountains out of molehills. Not so Mark. From his time in the Special Forces, when often work was better done in the wee small hours, and then later, when starting up his computer software business, he had worked long into the night working on his security systems. In both cases, the adrenaline and the training kept him awake. In the present case, he had more than enough adrenaline caused by the need to get the hell out of this place. He once again thanked his training in the Special Forces—concentrate, think, deduce – basically to out-think his captors.

Ted was as close as anyone could be to sleep. This Mark judged because he had not changed pages for some time. Annette, although restless, was curled up with her back to the light, as though hiding from someone or something. With his head resting on his chest, as though asleep, he chewed away at the tape, slowly, carefully, and kept up a constant stream of spit. When he finally got some leverage and there was a gap between the tape and his mouth, he dribbled onto his wrists, and very slowly the tape eased. Getting the circulation restored to his hands was quite painful but he suppressed the urge to shake them and kept on working the tape loose.

According to Annette's bedside clock, he had been working away for four hours and he was fearful that he had used up so much spit there could not be much more in the tank.

He was about to bend further down to try undoing the tape on his feet when Ted suddenly snapped his head around. But it was not a reaction to anything other than a realization that he had drifted off to sleep. He stood, stretched, and walked over towards Mark, and made a none too thorough check that he was still restrained. Mark tried to keep his breathing even and slow and made noises that he hoped would sound like someone gently snoring. That ruse seemed to work, or Ted was plain dumb. Probably the latter.

Ted then switched his attention to Annette. Because of the way she lay, he went around to the far side of the bed and bent down to take a closer look at her. Then his hand moved down to his groin, massaged it a couple of times, and it was obvious what he was thinking about. Mark almost forgot to breathe, but he could do nothing about it – he would have to watch this thug. Ted reached across touching Annette gently on the shoulder, and then when he got no reaction, moved his hand towards her breasts.

However, at the last-minute Ted thought better of it. He glanced across at Mark, let out a sigh of almost resignation, and returned to his seat by the window. Mark remembered to breathe again.

It was now 4:30 am and Mark was beginning to get desperate. Ted was sufficiently nodding off again that Mark had to take the chance. He reached down to the floor and with considerable difficulty grabbed a piece of the broken mirror. His immediate aim should have been to cut the tape on his wrists but the numbness in his legs made him tackle them first. But it was a lot quicker than dribbling. He had to keep his head down while the circulation returned to his legs, and again there was the horrible temptation to shake them to get the circulation restored, but he resisted. Then came the problem of cutting the tape on his wrists. He probably cut more of his skin than the tape.

His hands were now covered in blood and a fair amount dripped onto the carpet. But, at last, he was free.

After carefully checking that Ted and Annette were still asleep, he cut through the string that tied him to the chair. Now all he had to do was get the hell out of there.

He stood up and waited until the circulation had returned to his limbs, then slowly and carefully stepped towards the window. The position that Ted was in would make his passage back out of the window difficult but not impossible. There was nothing more certain than that he was not about to risk leaving through the front door. In the bedroom, he at least knew what the odds were. Whatever these people had gotten themselves into they could do it without him – for now. And he almost made it undetected.

He was making his last step before easing the window further open when Ted at first grunted and then stumbled to his feet at the realization that all was not well.

Mark stood quite still. The next few seconds would be critical. Ted could have yelled for help and that would have been the end of Marks' attempt to escape. And probably the end of Mark.

But Ted did not yell. Instead, he did what all other arrogant thugs and bullies try to do – do whatever had to be done by the use of overwhelming brute force against a smaller adversary. Just what Mark expected that he would do. As Ted was left-handed, he lunged at Mark leaving the right side of his face exposed. Mark just dropped under the groping hand, and then thrust up with all the force he could muster, first with his clenched right fist and then with his left, catching Ted on the side of the head and then the chin. The two enormous blows made him stagger. Then Mark hit Ted's head with a swinging pile driver that would have rendered most men unconscious.

Ted merely shook his head and then lunged forward again causing Mark to lose his balance and they both crashed to the floor. From his position on top of Mark, a nasty leer erupted on Ted's face as he threatened to plunge a fist down towards his adversary.

What is often not appreciated by people, especially of the female gender, is the excruciating pain that can be inflicted on a man in that part of the anatomy more normally associated with pleasure. And that pain tends to take the breath, and other things, away. Ted seemed to freeze in mid-stroke as Mark grabbed his testicles in a vice-like grip with his left hand, and with his right fist drove Ted into the frame of the windowsill with a sickening thud and into a state of unconsciousness.

As quickly as possible Mark grabbed Ted's gun. It was a Glock of the similar type that he had used in Papua New Guinea. He also took his cellular phone. He then turned to Annette who he had assumed would also take the one chance to make her escape from whatever was going on here. He was mistaken.

She sat up on the bed with a pistol held in both hands

and pointing directly at Mark. The look on her face was one of fear but at the same time grim determination. But she also did not yell out. Now that was strange.

Mark realized that all she had to do was pull the trigger and he was history. That was apart from the fact that her hands were trembling so much she would possibly miss, at least with the first shot. But the noise would be bad enough. All she had to do was call out for assistance, and while Mark might take someone down at the same time, he was just as likely to end up as a casualty.

At that moment he heard someone stirring in the adjacent room. It was now or never. He mouthed the words 'Come with me – please' but Annette still grimly clutched the pistol shaking her head. Body language. Mark knew that Annette would not shoot. The noise he had heard from the next room was someone going to the toilet as he heard the sound of flushing and then running water. Was their next step to come into Annette's room to check on their guest and the cause of the commotion in the bedroom? Probably.

There was only one thing left that Mark could do. He still had Ted's Glock in his hand and there was little doubt that, with all his training, he could shoot Annette before she could even blink. But he could not do that. It is at moments like these when training plays a critical part. He could have forced the issue, overpowered Annette, and then taken on the three or more men who were in the next room. But training told him that, if you do not know what you are up against, take advantage of what few things are in your favour, retreat, and regroup.

He just turned away and climbed out of the window and lowered himself onto the fire escape. He turned one last time as he slipped out of the window and looked at Annette. She was smiling through the tears that ran freely down her face. And she never said a word!

Mark vowed that he would not let the matter rest there – he would be back.

He scampered down to the alley and was about to get into his rented SUV when he realized that they had removed his car keys along with his cell phone. The loss of the keys was not of immediate concern because he did not intend to go far, but it could be a problem later. He went about a hundred yards down the alley and found a place in which he was able to hide from the overhead view and then pulled Ted's cell phone out – he would have to contact Paul or Brad or someone very quickly. He was desperately in need of help and tiring badly from lack of sleep – even ex-Special Forces operatives need sleep. And time was running out.

It was 5:23 am on September 11th.

The beauty of cellular phones is that you can store more numbers than you would ever need and by simply pressing "search" then "call" you were through to whoever you needed. The problem for Mark was that he had Ted's mobile phone and not his own. The phone would prove quite useful in ascertaining Ted's contacts – probably a mixture of his paymasters and a few local hoods and brothels. But useless for contacting anyone that Mark knew.

He now knew Ted's number but that was all. He cursed at the irony of the situation and racked his brain to try to recall the numbers that he wanted, but to no avail. The only number he could recall belonged to his lawyer - so he called Dusty Miller.

The ringing went on for some time and while it did Mark thanked himself lucky that the telephone belonged to Dusty. He would never return any messages so there was no point in the telephone having a message service.

Eventually Dusty answered with an abrupt 'Yes.'

'Hi Dusty – it's Mark.'

'What the hell do you want? It's 5:30 in the bloody morning, for fuck's sake!'

'I know – its' later than that and I have yet to get any sleep – but I need your help.'

He quickly explained his predicament and why he had to call Dusty.

'What the fuck are you up to now? How the hell did you come to lose your cell phone?' he started, but the urgency in Mark's voice must have penetrated the fog of the hangover, and he said 'Ok – give me your number and I'll get someone to call you.' and he then disconnected the call without any further preamble.

There were two things you could rely on with Dusty. Firstly - you could expect to get abused. Secondly - if he said someone would call – they would, no matter what the time, day, or night. What amazed Mark was the speed with which it all happened. The cell phone started ringing within five minutes of terminating the previous call. Mark was cautious in answering because the caller could be anyone from a local hooker to the head of the Mafia. He took a leaf from Dusty and simply said 'Yes.'

'Is that you Mark?' came the reply.

It was Paul. The words were followed by three beeps. It was not going to be Mark's best day – the battery on Ted's cell phone was about to expire.

'Paul – Listen. I am in New York City – in the Bronx – at the back of 1105-University Avenue—and we have a problem. Can you get up here? And say Yes before the battery on this phone expires.'

There was a big sigh, but Paul was not about to let Mark down.

'This is supposed to be my one chance to get some sleep, but ok – you're lucky – I came back to New York last night—precisely, where are you?' Mark told him but was not sure if he got the whole message, because the phone at some stage just went dead.

There was nothing else to do but wait. The city was already beginning to liven up but the alley he was in did not seem to be part of all the rush. Which was probably a good thing. His rental car was blocking the alley and anytime soon someone would come by and wonder why.

He did not have to wait long before there was some action on that score. A head appeared out of the window from which Mark had escaped earlier and looked both left and right, and just as quickly disappeared. Then a man reappeared from a first-floor doorway, looking the worse for wear having been rudely awakened from his sleep, got into the SUV, and simply drove away. Where he was going was anyone's guess, but it was obvious that he or they did not want any attention drawn to Annette's apartment.

Or more particularly to the missing driver.

After about a half-hour a car turned into the alley from the south end and started to cruise up towards where Mark was hiding. It was Paul. Making as sure as he could that no one saw him, Mark flagged him down and quickly got into the car.

'What the hell happened to you?' was Paul's first question.

Only then did Mark realize what a mess he was in. Apart from the blood that had dried on his hands and wrists, making the injuries look far worse than they actually were, his face had swelling. He had the making of a large bruise on the left side of his head which was steadily spreading to give him a black eye. The blood from several cuts on the right side had splattered down to cover his shirt. Bits of tape were still stuck in place. His shirt was torn although Mark could not recall how that had happened, and his hair was all over the place. Yes – he was certainly in a mess. But that did not seem all that important.

'We have to do something! I went to visit Annette, and there are other people there!' Mark started to explain. Paul rudely and abruptly interrupted him.

'Can we just get something clear in that fuddled brain of yours? The CIA has passed as much information as they can to the FBI and the anti-terrorist divisions of every security agency on the planet. Between them, they have every terrorist cell in this great state of New York under twenty-four-hour surveillance. It is tight. Some may say watertight. If they move, we move. But, although you may be disappointed, this does not include your girlfriend.'

Mark continued as though Paul had not spoken.

'I haven't got a clue what I just walked into. It has something to do with the Augem Group. At least two of the people I have spent the last few hours with work for John Dubois. And I am forming the opinion that they have something to do with what we were grilled about at Langley. There is also a man who I think works for the FBI. They may be amateurs as you called them in Wellington, but they are up to no good. I think they are something to do with "The Plot". What I do not know is, what all this has got to do with Annette? And I intend to find out between now and when the whole thing blows up, presumably sometime today. If I am reading the situation correctly, that will be sooner rather than later.'

'Fine' Paul sighed. 'But first of all, we have to get you cleaned up. If anyone sees you in that condition you could be arrested as a vagrant. You will find some clothes in my suitcase, which fortunately for you is still in the car, and we are about the same size. There is a public utility two blocks away – let's go.'

Mark wanted to protest. Paul had not looked into a mirror recently. The two of them were not even remotely of the same size! But Paul just smiled, and Mark just shrugged. They went up the road to the public toilets and Mark was in and out in next to no time. He certainly looked better for a wash and a change of clothes, although 'better' was a relative term. As he clambered back into the car, he told Paul of his plans. He was going to watch the apartment and follow Annette and whoever else had been in the apartment wherever they went.

At that suggestion, Paul got a little agitated.

'Don't you think we would do better to go and see Dubois and find out what is going on?' he retorted. He was not the least bit concerned about Mark's love life – or lack of it – or so it seemed.

Mark was about to explode but managed to hold himself in check.

'And what exactly are you going to say to Dubois?' he countered. 'Ask him what two of his staff are doing spending the night beating up an ex-supplier, apparently conspiring with his PA. And – by the way - you are aware that today is September the 11th. You would not have any plans that involve bombs and killing people today, would you?'

Mark was beginning to get fairly steamed up. Paul however got the message and sighed.

'Ok – you win. I suppose if we cannot convince the CIA based on the evidence that you and Brad presented, we would have less chance of convincing Dubois to own up to heavens knows what. But you realize the risk that we are taking, don't you? If you are right, some people will die today, and then you still have the same problem. You still have to convince the authorities that you were right about the cause. What a major balls-up.'

Now Paul was getting even more agitated.

Mark persisted.

'Look, I know you think I am distracted by Annette.'

Mark stuttered, the emotion of the moment getting to him, but he kept going.

'But see it this way. Annette knows more than we do right now. I am convinced I can get her to talk if I can get her away from Asid and the other cronies. Even if nothing happens today, she is the key. She knows me. She knows Brad. She knows John Dubois. And she knows Asid. They are all the major players in what is about to unfold. For all we know, she may be the controller!'

That was when Mark paused - he had not thought of that angle!'

'Ok – here's what we do then' said Paul, coming to an instant decision.

'I will go downtown where I can find out what Dubois is up to. No approach – just watch. My instruction from the CIA is to just be around, learn what I can, and try to spot any known or unknown troublemakers, so I am cool. You follow Annette and whoever she comes out with. But let me know what they are up to, as I will let you know what John Dubois is up to. Fair deal?'

'That is Ok with me. But how do we keep in touch? Asid has my cell phone. And Ted's is kaput.'

Paul had the answer to that too. He reached into the glove compartment and pulled out another cell phone, handing it to Mark.

'Make sure that you press only the correct buttons, or you will blow your head off!' he said with a laugh. But seeing the look on Mark's face he said realized that he had probably overstepped.

'Hey – lighten up – I was joking – but when the phone rings just answer Yes. If you don't know who is calling, just disconnect it. It has already got my cell number loaded – just speed dial 6232.'

Then Paul had another thought. He rummaged through

a bag and produced a Smith and Wesson 9mm Luger pistol.

'You may need this – not quite the model that you would prefer, but near enough.'

Paul dropped Mark down the street from the apartment and took off to go downtown. Mark got himself into a spot that was reasonably well concealed but still gave him a good view of the doorway he was watching. He was also fortunate with the choice of clothes which were different from what he had on before. His main problem would be maintaining concentration because it was now closing in on twenty-four hours since he last had any sleep.

When someone did come out of the apartment building, he almost missed them. He told himself to concentrate and recovered in time to see first Asid and then Annette appeared on the sidewalk outside the apartment. Asid was dressed in a business suit. Annette was in a coat. With the expected temperature for the day expected to be well into the seventies, she would not be needing the coat for long.

There was an intense argument before they walked rapidly to the end of the block and turned east. There was no sign of anyone else exiting the apartment, so Mark followed these two at a discrete distance. There was little chance of him being spotted in the crowds although there were not that many white people around.

It soon became obvious where they were going – to the subway station at 167th Street. They had done this before or had season tickets, because they went straight through the ticket barriers with no discernible pause. Mark was a little concerned that he would lose them as he had to get a ticket – to heaven knows where. But they were either not expecting to be followed or they were plain stupid. He caught up with them waiting on the platform, and when the train arrived, he got into the next carriage.

At least the train was heading south, so that meant – what? Annette could be going to work – at the office of Taylor Software! And Asid may also be going to work – at the office of the Augem Group. But – why was Annette not driving her car? And how was she going to get from the subway to the office? That would give Paul something to think about – thinking that Mark had at last completely lost the plot.

He pulled out the cell phone. There was no signal in the confines of the subway. Paul would have to wait.

And then things got interesting. He could see Asid and Annette through the mass of bodies, and they were very clearly not discussing the weather. Asid had a supercilious look on his face as he appeared to be whispering in her ear, and his finger was stabbing at Annette's chest. For her part, she looked terrified of Asid, or something., Her body language said she was going to comply with whatever she had been told to do, albeit reluctantly.

The train stopped at 86th Street and Annette got off. Asid stayed on. Mark got off and speed-dialled Paul. At least the phone had a signal this time.

'Asid is heading your way. I am following Annette. I have no idea where she is going. It certainly is not to work!'

Paul again exploded.

'What are you doing following Annette? What about your suspicions of a bomber? Are you nuts?'

Mark got equally aggressive.

'Paul – I cannot do everything. You have to remember that this just is not my business. If you want something else done, ring the FBI. I am going to follow Annette, and stuff the rest!'

He terminated the call.

They were both in for a surprise!

Chapter 24

Haroon Lateef

Haroon Lateef had not had the easiest of lives. When he was just a young boy, his parents, both of them Pakistani by birth, had got jobs in the Arabian Gulf. His father worked as a rigger onboard one of the many oil rigs and other paraphernalia of the oil barons that filled the gulf. His mother worked as a kitchen hand at one of the shore bases in Oman that catered for the occasional, and often violent, shore leave that the menfolk were granted.

There were masses of foreign workers, both working in and in transit to and from, the Gulf States. The Lateef family worked for long hours and Harpoon, as he was nicknamed by the other children at the school, was left largely on his own to fend for himself. The variety of children he was forced to spend his time with would have made the United Nations seem tame. Every nationality on earth was represented with their many diverse cultures – and their likes and dislikes.

But children are children. Lateef began to see a wider picture than would otherwise have been the case if he had remained in his homeland or had been educated in the presence of, and under the strict control, his family.

As he grew up in this environment, he became aware that no matter how hard his parents worked they were going precisely nowhere. They earned money – and at times exceptionally good money. Most of it was sent back home to Pakistan to support their extended family. Because of this, he developed a hatred of his extended family and his place of birth. More importantly, he began to have serious doubts about the capitalist system. Why did his parents work so hard and long in this hellhole while their 'extended family' sat on their butts in a place Haroon only vaguely knew? And why did they work so hard and perform such menial tasks while the business barons who owned everything just got richer?

There were billions of dollars being made out of oil which was simply pumped out of the ground or from the seabed, but little of that money filtered down to the people who actually did some work. The basis of the capitalist system was that you had to have continuous growth which meant more industries, more investment, more of everything. Who gained from these? The same people – the owners – not the workers. Even his young scarcely educated mind could see that it was just not fair.

Gradually he became increasingly independent. Although he still went to school, he got odd jobs around the base which gave him some money. Not much—but to a young lad, it meant a lot. There was just nothing organized for the kids to do. Everyone was always too busy, or too tired, to care. So, as boys do, they searched for something to and somewhere to go.

One day he and his friend Yasim, who was from Yemen, were sitting on the wharf—fishing. They did not know it but there were very few fish in the polluted waters, and that had been the case for the whole of their young lives. But it was something to do.

They were approached by a couple of seamen who

claimed to own a yacht. Having checked on where the boys were from and what they were doing in this place, they offered them a trip out of this hellhole to Al Hudaydah, a Yemeni port on the Red Sea. Being young and still somewhat naïve the boys were excited at the prospect. For one of the boys, it was a chance to go home. For the other, it was a chance to see something of the world that his new, yet temporary, friends had talked about.

By now the relationship with the parents of Haroon Lateef had deteriorated to that of nodding acquaintances so to go somewhere else without them was no big deal. Haroon and Yasim were also excited by the clandestine way that they had to be smuggled on board the luxury yacht that the seaman owned.

Well, it turned out that they had not been told the actual truth. For one thing, the seaman did not own the yacht. For another, it was not actually a yacht. When the boys were finally allowed onto the deck and saw the rust encrusted bucket that passed as a boat that looked as though it would sink at any moment, they realized – too late – what they had been taken on board for.

Both boys were subjected to a form of love at the hands of the two men. Some people would call it abuse. Some would call it sodomy. They were expected to perform all sorts of perverse acts that they never knew anything about before.

Eventually, after many days at sea, the two men who had taken them on board became less enchanted or were put under pressure by the rest of the crew, and many more of the crew started to share the boys. They were subjected to acts of depravity of a nature that their brief and inadequate life could not have prepared them for.

While Haroon had felt the stirring in his loins when he and his young friend had, initially and just for a laugh, crept into an area from which they could observe young girls showering. There they had learned, through trial and error, how to masturbate. But nothing could have prepared them for this kind of sexual depravity.

Haroon Lateef began to develop a hatred of men.

The port of Al Hudaydah was rapidly forgotten. The boat tramped backward and forwards between Mocha and various points in Oman and Qatar carrying anything and everything in a series of haphazard journeys that were only interrupted by the not infrequent breakdowns of the boat. The crew was constantly changing, arguing, and fighting. The captain of the boat seemed to have little or no control except in the short times they were in port tied up alongside. The boys were kept locked up when they were not at sea and there was little hope of their ever escaping, and less hope of anyone coming to their aid.

Fortunately for the two boys, the crew also drank. No drinking of alcohol was allowed in most of the ports that they visited because that was what their religion taught. However, when at sea there was not much else to do. The crew was in such a stupor after a heavy night's drinking, that when the ship had to unexpectedly call in at Aden for emergency repairs the boys slipped over the side and made their escape.

Haroon could not swim but his Yemeni friend helped him all the way to shore. Once there Lateef learned yet another one of life's hard lessons. His friend simply vanished into the rabbit warren of the slums leaving Haroon to fend for himself.

He began to develop a hatred of everyone.

There was only one way that he could survive. He had to fend for himself in the manner that he had learned on his brief terrifying life on the boat. He had to sell his body. At least he had brief moments when someone seemed to care for him. And at least he got wiser. You asked for the money upfront. You never went to a place of your choosing. And you stayed as close as possible to the few he could call associates, if not friends.

At last, someone came along who he thought he could trust – who appeared to be honest and caring – and this one owned a real luxury yacht. Lateef was taken on board, washed, and given clean clothes. And he had his own cabin – small but it was his! It was then explained to him in English, that he barely understood, that he was to work as a cabin boy. He had to fetch, carry, and serve food to the six people – three men and three women – who lived on the boat. At least he was to be kept away from the crew.

It soon became evident that the boat was not exactly on a pleasure cruise. The boat made odd rendezvous, with even odder people. There they exchanged small parcels of unspecified content for huge quantities of money. And his saviour, who went by the name of Darren Newton, turned out to be a bit of rogue in many ways. Although partnered with Hazel, the one lady who Lateef regarded as the most attractive and considerate person on the boat, he still found time to come and have his way with the young man. At times Newton would say that he just wanted to talk. But then he would lie alongside the boy. Inevitably he would become aroused. And then would either have Lateef masturbate him while he fondled the boy, or he would want full anal penetration. Or he would want Lateef to perform oral sex. Haroon had the feeling that this was not exactly how sex was supposed to be. He hated being penetrated. But at least he was not passed around as had been the case on the rust-bucket.

Newton always left the cabin with a threat of what

would happen to Lateef if his partner, or anyone else on board, were to find out about these almost nightly indiscretions. At least in his previous life, everyone knew what was going on – so what if others on this yacht happened to know? But the threat left little doubt in the young man's mind that the punishment would mean an end to his miserable, but still young, life.

Lateef began to develop a hatred for the world.

After many months at sea, when their visits to the shore seemed limited to offloading money and loading more packets, supplies, and fuel, the yacht eventually reached Florida. There, miraculously, Haroon was taken ashore to the villa that was the home base of Newton and Hazel. The place was massive and luxurious, although cut off from the world outside by high walls and vicious-looking, and heavily armed, security guards and dogs. But at least he was given a much larger room, a huge bed, his own television and play station, new clothes, and a certain amount of freedom.

He still had to endure the nightly visits from Newton– same things – same warning – just in a different place. Then the meetings, unlike his experience on the rust bucket, began to get more passionate to the point where Newton no longer seemed to care who knew, and the warnings ceased.

Finally, after a day in which he was largely left to his own devices, Lateef was surprised to see Darren come into his room wearing little more than a skimpy pair of briefs. Of an even greater surprise was that he was accompanied by Hazel who was clad in similar, if briefer, attire. They carried with them a small tray on which they had some white powder. Newton went over to the dresser and sat down with the tray and waved to Haroon to join them.

As Haroon Lateef stood next to Hazel, he realized he had never been this close to a woman with no clothes on – well hardly any. She was beautiful – small but perfectly proportioned. And she always had a mischievous smile that promised a lot to anyone who did not know she was partnered with Darren Newton. From sunning herself for days on end on the foredeck of the yacht she had a great tan, and it was obvious that she wore little on the deck because the tan was all over. The skipper would have had a magnificent view, but it would have been more than his job was worth to say or do anything about it—at least that was not an unreasonable assumption. Just enjoy! Her breasts were perfectly rounded and the provocative way she moved was so seductive that Haroon could not take his eyes off her. For the first time, he felt himself becoming aroused.

But for the moment all of Hazel's attention was focused on the white powder. And Darren was not least bit interested in Hazel or Haroon. He divided the white powder into three roughly equal piles and sniffed the first – and largest—through his nose. He then moved away and sat on the bed. Hazel could hardly wait for him to vacate the chair and sniffed up her share, and then she turned with a provocative giggle to Haroon and offered him the sniffer. But Haroon backed away.

This was something new to him and he was very unsure of what to do although it had not seemed to have done any harm to the other two. Hazel did not seem to mind his rejection of the sniffer. She just shrugged – sniffed up the remaining powder and then turned her attention back to Haroon.

She backed him onto the bed where she proceeded to undress, fondle, and kiss him all over as though she was possessed. Haroon initially tried to resist, mostly because of his fear that Darren would not like what was happening, but Hazel was getting the better of him and Darren seemed blissfully unaware and did not seem to object in the slightest.

He just sat there with a glazed smile on his face, while he watched as Haroon could not help but be further aroused.

Eventually, Darren did become involved. He reached across the bed and carefully removed Hazels' shorts which revealed her equally bronzed and very subtle buttocks. She either did not notice or did not care. She just carried on fondling Haroon, getting increasingly more excited. Then while Darren sat on the side of the bed, now completely naked, and gently stroking himself, Hazel mounted Haroon.

As she urgently and rhythmically moved on top of him, for the first time in his young life he knew what it was like, to climax with a woman.

His memory of these events had a profound effect on the young lad. That it was pleasurable was never in doubt. That these people were sick was also not in doubt. But having tasted the pleasure of women, he vowed that he would never again be penetrated by a man. Lateef did not understand how Newton could want to spend his time with him when the alternative of making love with the beautiful Hazel was so readily available and infinitely more pleasurable.

He vowed that it was time to move on and get away from these weird people.

And again, the demon booze came to his rescue. After they were both exhausted by all the sexual activity, Darren and Hazel retired to their room and peace descended on the house. Lateef was determined to escape, and he saw that this was the one chance that he had.

Later that night he crept out of his room and made it down the hallway. He had to creep as he passed Newton's room because the door was open – but Darren turned out to be sound asleep and snoring loudly. There was no sign of Hazel but from his recent experience, he knew that she could be anywhere. He made his way down the stairs and after a moment's hesitation decided to head for the rear door.

The front door was directly opposite the main gate and, while the guards would be looking outwards rather than inwards, there was no doubt that any movement from the house would have attracted their attention. That meant he had to pass by the TV lounge to get to one of the side doors. And there was someone in the lounge watching either TV or a DVD because he could see the lights coming from the set. Strangely enough, there were no other lights on.

He made his way down the hallway and stopped by the lounge and peered inside. What he saw took his breath away. What was playing on the TV was a pornographic movie. The two people on the couch were however otherwise occupied. Hazel lay back on the couch, once again completely naked. She had her eyes closed and her legs spread far apart. One hand gently stroking her breasts while the other was holding the other person's head to her lower body. Both were whimpering and moaning almost in unison. The pictures on the TV were of a man and a woman bonking away furiously and it was hardcore because nothing was left to the imagination. The real-life version on the couch was Hazel and another woman!

That brought Haroon a very nasty and rude awakening – never assume anything where women are concerned. But he could not bring himself to have a hatred of women, having only very recently experienced the pleasure that they could provide.

Although the villa was patrolled by Dobermans, the dogs seemed intent on keeping people out and did not seem to have the slightest interest in anyone who was already inside. So, he waited until the dogs had all settled down and then made his way down towards the main gate. The guard appeared to be focused on the outside of the property and was bored at that, and half asleep. But rather than take any chances, he moved along the wall for about twenty yards and found a tree with branches extending out over the wall. This he climbed and dropped down onto the sidewalk. He was free at last!

But where was he to go and how was he to survive?

Lateef made his way north by getting lifts from truck drivers who seemed extremely keen to have someone to talk to. He had gained a reasonable understanding of English – even though he could not speak it properly – but the truckers just wanted to talk and were not overly interested in any of his stories. So, he dozed most of the time – until finally, he reached New York City. There he made it into the borough of Queens where he managed to get a room with some other Pakistani people who, like Haroon, had made it into the United States illegally.

He was determined that he would not revert to his previous abusive relationships and made a living as best he could on the streets of Queens doing odd jobs for little money. It was not the easiest of lives and making friends with people of different ethnic backgrounds proved all but impossible. Of concern was that there were either fewer girls of his ethnicity or that, what few of them there were, were picked up by the white guys. Now that did not seem to make any sense, but in this complicated world where he had had some strange experiences, which did not seem to matter.

Most of the other boys he gradually got to know—most of them were from a similar ethnic background to himself – and they regularly attended the local mosque. Lateef got into the habit of going along too, originally just for the company, or just for something to do and to make him feel that he belonged. He eventually found that the language used by the Imams appealed to his sense of who or what he had become – a no-one with nothing in a land that prided itself in its' wealth for all and its' opportunities for all. At least the media and the politicians belted out a consistent message of equal opportunity for all. Except for Haroon. At the mosque, he was at least someone.

Through his study of the Koran and the teachings of the Imams he became a committed and devote Muslim. The people who ran the mosque were pleased with their new convert to Islam and eventually sent him off at their own expense to Afghanistan and even to his homeland of Pakistan where he extended his education and learned how to channel his hatred more correctly.

Well, it turned out that it was channelled against anything to do with America, his adopted country. And by a process of indoctrination – some would say brain-washing – he was strangely at peace. He was taught what every young man should be able to do—how to make a bomb—and he became very enthusiastic about the prospect of blowing something up. He was not taught how to blow himself up – well you could only do that once so there was little point in practicing—but he saw other students in explosive vests, which he found fascinating.

His various hatreds were now neatly tied to one thing – the United States of America. But that country – the land of the free – and its' inhabitants, had not exactly helped him, had it? So, that made sense.

Then came the call that his mentors had indoctrinated him into waiting for – that he had been trained for – the chance to get out of this hellhole and into the afterlife where any number of virgins was waiting for him. The fact that there is no mention in the Koran of the actual number of virgins available in Paradise escaped him. And he would have been mortified to learn that the "dark-eyed damsels" that the Koran did talk about were available to all Muslims – not just martyrs.

Had he been older and wiser he may have also been even more mortified by the Messenger of Allah having said that he could have seventy-two wives – for most people, at least in the western world - one was more than enough! Even though he was now twenty-four years of age, his only sexual encounter with a woman had been in the fantasy land of Darren and Hazel. He had longingly hoped that his life would change, and he could have a meaningful relationship with his own "Hazel"—a lady he could love and be loved by. Sadly, what he had learned along the way was that these American men and women were corrupt and decadent. And they preyed on anyone, especially anyone who happened to be an illegal immigrant, for their own good and use. But now he could have as many virgins as he would like, and he would find true love with clean people. His life was about to change, at last, for the good.

What he could not have known was the careful profiling that went on before his recruitment for the task. That he was a Muslim was a minor consideration in the scheme of things. There is nothing that ties a desire to exit this life by suicide to Islam or any other religion. But the group of people who he had got to know, and trust had developed in him a powerful sense of belonging and that is what became the important element. What he wanted to do was reward those people with something he could do for them and assure his continued acceptance within the group.

His mentor correctly judged that Haroon was in the right frame of mind and simply worked on that to motivate the young man to get himself a bomber.

Haroon developed a sense of immense pride in the fact that he was to be the first in a series of three explosions which would teach the arrogant American's a lesson and further the cause of his people. For once in his young life, he had a real purpose. The men who coached him were fastidious in their treatment of him, almost as though they were in awe of what he was about to do and what he was about to achieve in the name of Allah. They had stressed the need for absolute secrecy and that only one man, who he would not meet until the chosen morning, truly knew his target and timing. Haroon was suitably impressed and could hardly wait for his place in history.

The fellow Pakistani who was to be his final cell contact had come to the apartment at 6:00 am. They had briefly prayed together. Then his visitor commenced assembling the vest while exhorting Haroon to be strong and resolute on this momentous day. The explosive vest was much heavier than Haroon had envisaged and much bulkier. That usually meant that it was packed with enough explosives to make a noticeably big impact on someone's otherwise peaceful day.

The inner part of the vest was made up of several plastic cylinders filled with explosives – in this case, Composition 4 or C-4, a plastic-like material that had been acquired from a demolition company. Surrounding that was what is known as a fragmentation jacket which was loaded with shrapnel. In this case, shrapnel would consist of steel balls of which there was any number of suppliers who could not have cared less about what they were to be used for. The selection of the C-4 was made because of its' stability. While it did not matter if the suicide bomber blew himself up accidentally, it did matter to the planners because the timing was especially important. The use of steel balls as shrapnel simply ensured clean injuries, versus the normal nails, screws, and bits of wire – in fact, anything that could rip the target apart—that was normally used.

When faced with the vest and the final recognition of his fate, for just one fleeting moment a flicker of doubt passed through the mind of Haroon. But he fought that off by repeating verses from the Koran, and he was smiling as he received the last instructions. He received a street map of downtown New York and circled in red was the spot which was his destination. Not that it mattered. Haroon had no idea how to read a map, and anyone finding the map before the result would be equally devoid of ideas as to its' actual intent, other than it had a building marked as a target. After the event, it would not matter.

It was now 8:29 am on September 11th in New York City. His mentor had driven him into the centre of the financial district and with more words of encouragement had dropped him off in Whitehall Street and pointed him in the direction of the building that was his allocated target. He had no idea of the significance of the time that he was instructed to explode, or who would be on the receiving end of this glorious event, but those were his instructions.

His escort had said a few final prayers with him and then exhorted him to carry out this great task with all the pride that he could muster. He briefly wondered why the escort did not come with him, but the adrenaline was now pumping, and he went on alone. He had no idea why this building had been chosen, except that it contained several finance and insurance companies – pillars of western decadence. It was not that far from where he was headed to the New York Stock Exchange, but his orders were extremely specific, and he would follow them to the letter. He had been told that positioning and timing were of the essence.

He walked past hordes of people rushing to work or going about their business in a way that only a city like New York did. He smiled and said good morning, although most people were in too much of a hurry to notice. Or they did not bother to notice. Or was it because of his ethnicity? But he smiled. They did not care – but they would have something to care about real soon.

The time was 8:42 am.

He had arrived at the building. He stared up at the sheer height of it. He wondered how they could build such a thing. His mind went back to his humble beginnings in Pakistan and then in the Gulf where, apart from the massive oil rigs that his father used to work on, everything just paled into insignificance compared to this. Then he thought of the slums of Aden – there was just no comparison. Then he thought of the palace that Darren Newton and Hazel lived in – all paid for by the obvious drug dealing. And here he now was at the very centre of this decadent society and its' money machines – surrounded by users and abusers. Well, they were about to get a very nasty wakeup call. Yes! 'Allah is Great.'

He walked through the glass doors of the building and immediately ahead of him was a huge reception desk behind which sat three smiling ladies. None of them appeared to be from his part of the world but he briefly wondered whether the virgins that he would shortly meet would be as attractive.

He certainly hoped so.

He walked forward returning the smiles and then he pressed the detonator. His last view on this earth was of one of the ladies about to ask him how she could help.

Then she realized what he was going to do. Her jaw dropped in absolute horror, and she let out a scream –

except the rest of the scream was lost in the huge explosion that destroyed the reception area of the building. After the explosion there followed an eerie silence and then the whole building became an area of hysterical activity as people rushed about in a mixture of those who wanted to help the injured and those who wanted to escape.

It was 08.46 am – the exact time that the aircraft – American Airlines Flight 11—had slammed into the North Tower of the World Trade Centre on that fateful day – September 11, 2001.

Chapter 25

Aka Mohammed Khan

Mohammed Khan came from a vastly different background to that of Haroon Lateef. Like Haroon, he had become a committed and devout Muslim. Also, like Haroon, he had spent many months or years under the tutelage of some of the most revered Imams in Pakistan and Afghanistan, as well as in New York City.

But Khan was far from poor. And, unlike Haroon, he had more of a choice of what he did with his life. This was because he was born and raised in the United States of a well-to-do New England family who could trace their ancestry back to the British aristocracy who had come to this country in the immigration, and consequent military excursions of the 18th century. His real name was Denver Washington.

As a boy at school, he could not understand why he could not make any lasting friendships. He was a handsome lad and by the time he was eighteen, he stood just over six feet tall. From all the work he did at the gym he had a beautiful athletic body. And since his parents were well-to-do, and doted on their son, he had all the money to splash around and to impress people with – especially the young girls.

The ladies were initially attracted by his good looks and since money appeared to be no object he was, again initially, always the centre of attention when they went socializing. He was always to the fore at buying everyone a drink. But no sooner had he bought them a drink and started his well-rehearsed pick-up lines, they drifted away. This he could not understand.

What was wrong with them?

When he finally went to the Harvard Business School, his ability to attract the young ladies by his obvious wealth waned somewhat when faced with many competitors who could more than match him in the money stakes. He still had that attractive, if arrogant, look and a very striking body and he never missed the opportunity to show it off. Yet, the young ladies still shied away.

Even the young men seemed reluctant to become his friends. He could at least understand where they were coming from. They were quite simply jealous. But the facts of the matter were that he was an arrogant shit and a regular pain up the ass.

He began to form the view – rightly—that something was wrong with the world, and that – wrongly – he was the one who should try to put things right. All his peers were because society demanded it, pillars of the Church – at least that was what everyone wrote on their already impressive Curriculum Vitae. Denver himself was from a strict Roman Catholic family, but, like many people in the modern age, he paid only lip service to the teachings of the Church and paid all his attention first to himself and secondly to the mighty dollar.

To appear different, he started to study the Islamic faith, read the Koran, and attend the local mosque. Initially, he paid only lip service to that as well. Over several months, he formed the view that what was wrong with the world was that they had got their concept of good and evil screwed up and what was needed was a good dose of Islam which they could acquire by reading the Koran. And so, he converted to the faith and became a Muslim, and in the process changed his name to the plain and innocuous Mohammed Khan.

Still his peers seemed singularly unimpressed and at about the same rate that his beard grew his minute circle of friends diminished even further to the point that they were virtually non-existent. That is, other than his new friends from the mosque whose beliefs he now shared.

Undeterred by the fact that he was becoming more and more ostracized, and equally emboldened by the fact that he was on track to finding the correct answers to the problems of the world, he then embarked on several overseas trips to the middle east and in particular to Pakistan and Afghanistan where he learned all there was to know about the teachings of the Koran and the beliefs and practices of the Muslim faith. Unfortunately, he also met some people who were a little extremist, and so he learned about making bombs and about how to advance the Muslim cause by blowing things up.

He did not require any financial assistance from his local Islamic community because the money was never an issue. Although his parents were embarrassed to own him and by what he had become, they still fed his bank account with plenty of money, in the vain hope that they could somehow buy back their son. As a result of this, his travels did not come to the attention of the intelligence and security services, who had so very cleverly infiltrated the Islamic community to get warnings of such comings and goings. The democratic society that he was turning against was just being too clever, missed the obvious, and enabled him to keep unwittingly below the radar.

Despite this he also, and not surprisingly, began to form the view that the Western culture in which he had been raised was corrupt and evil. Well, that made sense.

A culture that could not accept him for what he was – intellectually, physically, and athletically far better than others—had to be somewhat screwed up. But the teachings of the Koran, or rather Denver's interpretation of it, fell on deaf ears among his old peers. Outside of the members of his local mosque, he lost all his western friends, and even his parents finally gave up trying to reason with him and claimed to no longer have anything to do with him. But his mother still made small contributions – well small in Washington family terms—to his bank account out of a mixture of hope and guilt

And then came the events that struck at the heart of the free world. The sickening destruction occurred in New York and Washington on September 11th, 2001.

While the rest of his fellow countrymen were both appalled and angered by the cowardly yet ruthless murder of thousands of innocent people, Denver rejoiced that someone had stuck it to the greed and decadence of the Western world, and in particular to the arrogance of the defender of the free world. He caused such a scene rejoicing at the event that he became a major suspect.

The FBI took him in for questioning on more than one occasion. There they discovered that this one-man Jihad had visited the places that would have made him a very definite 'Person of interest' had they only known about it. They grilled him on who his contacts were, what he had been doing in Pakistan and Afghanistan, and what, if any, had been his role in the events that so disturbed America and changed forever the way western society would conduct itself.

They learned very little. The facts were that he had nothing to do with those events, but he would have been a willing participant had he known about it beforehand. However, even members of the local Mosque began to steer well clear of the ranting and raving Denver aka Mohammed. The facts were that he had completely lost the plot and even the FBI wrote him off as a nutcase.

However, the events of 9/11 had a major impact on the young man and made him even more determined. He knew now that the western society was decadent and needed to be taught an even greater lesson. Having already convinced the FBI that he was mad, he then convinced his local Imam that he should go to Iraq to fight in the Jihad – whatever they or he thought that was. He did not need any money – just the contacts.

The leaders of the local mosque were keen for him to go. They could kill two birds with one stone – so to speak. On the one hand, they could get rid of this raving lunatic and on the other hand, they could be supporting their cause in the worldwide Jihad – whatever they thought that was.

But life – or death – is not always what it seems. He arrived in Baghdad armed with the Iraqi motto Allah Akbar and not much else. The translation of the motto he took to be God is great whereas the true translation is God is the greatest. It was perhaps fortunate that he did not know this since he may well have questioned it.

He was immediately assigned to Samarra, a city about eighty or so miles north of the capital Baghdad on the banks of the Tigris River. The name Samarra is derived from the Arabic phrase Sarr man ra'a, the rough translation of which is A joy for all to see. At some stage in the city's long and illustrious history the name may have been appropriate, but not now. With a population of about three 350 thousand people, the city is culturally significant to both the Shi'a and Sunni groups.

Unfortunately, the Sunni outnumbered the Shi'a by about six to one which did not make for particularly peaceful coexistence. Peace was not high on either of their agendas and there were, and still are, several prime targets that they could attack—like the al-Askari Mosque. So significant was the unease between the two groups, and so significant was this target, that al-Qaeda took an interest in the city and planned to do something about it. So, in Samarra, Denver Washington, aka Mohammed Khan, was introduced to some real terrorists.

And they scared him shitless.

Within a matter of days of his arrival in Samarra, he fled, shaved off his beard, changed his clothing to more western attire, and threw himself on the mercy of the first US soldiers that he could find. They felt sorry for this blubbering idiot and arranged for his immediate flight back home, albeit in the company of an intelligence agent in case the blubbering turned out to be a clever ploy to fool the authorities into giving him access to something that he could blow up.

When he arrived back in the United States he was placed in the hands of the Federal Bureau of Investigation and taken to Quantico Virginia for questioning by both the FBI and the Central Intelligence Agency. He came awfully close to being assigned from there to the Guantanamo Bay detention centre for further and somewhat painful investigation.

A search of their extensive and all intrusive database soon revealed that the FBI had met the gentleman previously, and the conclusions from this earlier encounter probably affected how the profilers saw him this time. The people who questioned Denver realized that he was scared, that he had just made an honest, and big, mistake. And they concluded that he would probably crawl back into some hole never to worry them again. After keeping him for several weeks, during which time several members of the FBI began to question their own sanity, they sent him on his way, his only punishment being equivalent to a slap on the wrist with a wet bus ticket.

That was a big mistake.

The switch of his name back to Mohammed Khan was quite easily made once he was out of the FBI's clutches. Since he had indeed been in Iraq ostensibly fighting alongside the al Qaeda group and had met no less a person than Abu Ayyub al-Masri in the flesh, and he had subsequently been captured, brought back to the States, then interned at Guantanamo for questioning, he had reason to view himself as something of a folk hero. He now had much more to add to an already impressive Curriculum Vitae, even if there was more than an element of exaggeration in it – as there is with all CVS.

Even so, as far as Denver could tell, no one seemed overly impressed. In the case of the people in his local mosque, they had strong suspicions that they knew the actual truth and wanted nothing more to do with him. For example, if he had been locked up in Guantanamo, why was he now back in their midst so quickly? In the case of people outside the mosque and outside of the Muslim community, very few had even heard of al-Masri, but they had heard of Guantanamo. And they simply did not believe him and were less polite than his colleagues from the Mosque – no-one gets into and out of Guantanamo Bay and out of the clutches of the intelligence services that easily! That is unless he was a fruitcake.

But then came his big chance. He would never know how they got onto him. He could only assume that his reputation as a true fighter for the cause was beginning to spread. The telephone call made him swell with pride and a certain amount of excitement and apprehension. They wanted him to make the supreme sacrifice. Yes! He would have been somewhat deflated had he known how they got his name, but that was one thing that he would never know or need to know.

The profiling in the case of Denver Washington – aka Mohammed Khan—by the people who sought to use him, was a little obtuse. He did meet the basic criteria – he had been to the bomb-making schools in the North-West Frontier Province of Pakistan and the eastern mountains of Afghanistan. The people who selected him did not have the profiling skills and resources of the FBI, so they were less encumbered by due process. There is no direct link between faith and a desire to blow something – especially yourself – into the next life. There is also a problem with a few basic elements of the profile – like age group, ethnic background, rich or poor, male, or female, and motivation.

Recent history suggests that most terrorist attacks are carried out by members of modern Islamic groups, but that does not solve the motivational and other issues. Should the profiling concentrate on the individuals who, by the time the FBI knows who they are, have since departed this life to be with seventy-two black-eyed virgins or whatever their expected rewards were. Or do you concentrate on the recruiters? In the case of Denver Washington, he was recognized as someone who just so happened to believe that blowing himself up would be cool, and who knows what motivated him? The fact that he was a somewhat discredited member of an Islamic community was all that they needed.

The fact that he was regarded as a nutcase simply made the task a little easier.

Again, the men who approached him made him feel important, not that the task was particularly difficult. Denver found himself talking to them in an equivalent manner to the top player and a coach of a basketball team – they knew what had to be done, and he would do it exactly as planned. They simply accepted him for what he was – or so he thought. The emphasis on the secrecy of the arrangement was largely wasted on Denver Washington, and that could have been a problem. But now that he had a job assigned to him, and him alone, there was no turning back. The secrecy would be absolute.

For just a moment the coaches thought that they had got the wrong man. Maybe he was just too enthusiastic. Mohammed was so sure of himself that he would go out immediately, and they had to restrain him and convince him that the precise timing and location of the event were both of paramount importance. Prancing down a city street looking like Rambo would enable Denver to show off his beautiful body. But that was not how things were done. He would need to wear a coat to cover the vest and shoulder straps and to avoid the distortion that a jacket would cause due to the bulky nature of explosives. Still, when the detonation occurred, there would be no problem removing the coat - would there?

They managed to calm him down, but never once did he question who they were or why they were doing this thing. The fact that he did not feel in any way threatened by the two Pakistani gentlemen who were his mentors sealed the deal. He was too naïve to question the why – his only interest was in the what. And of course, the how.

It is debatable whether Denver had any deep ideological reasons for his actions. At the time that the Prophet Muhammad was going about his business, the world was a vastly different place – Muslims were being persecuted and driven from their homes. So, it was not difficult for a certain amount of violence to find its way into interpretations of the Koran, and for the impression to be conveyed by those preaching from it that even martyrdom was an ok way to defend the faith. There was of course another aspect to the Muslim faith which concerned sensual activity in the life after. But to Denver Washington, also known as Mohammed Khan, these aspects did not seem to matter – he was not driven by promises of the reward of numerous virgins in the afterlife – he was quite simply a nutcase and that was that.

The date of September 10th—the day before 9/11—was his parent's wedding anniversary. In true family tradition, they sent out printed invitations to a party, most of which would be ignored. These included one to their son Denver. While his father would not have bothered, mothers have a much more paternalistic view of their errant sons. Deep in her heart she yearned for him to turn up – and provide yet another chance for them to convince him to give up his dabbling in the Islamic faith. But she would be disappointed.

On receipt of the embossed envelope, he consigned it to the rubbish bin without as much as a second glance. And 'Denver' went about organizing his last evening on this earth. He rang the local escort agency. The two young, pretty, but hard looking ladies who turned up were instructed to strip and perform, and that they willingly did for much of the night. That is what they were paid to do, and there could be worse ways to spend a night—and their host was extraordinarily generous. However, Mohammed rarely participated except to occasionally run his hands over their breasts and to encourage them to continue.

When they occasionally looked around to see what their host was up to, they found him quietly stroking himself, as indeed he had been doing for most of his short life.

He got rid of the girls at about 5:30 am before he had been visited by a fellow believer to deliver his final briefing. There was no need for any pep talk. Because it was part of the ritual, his friend read several passages from the Koran, which were somehow related to the events that were to unfold. But Denver seemed oblivious to the meaning. He also seemed oblivious to the fact that the vest that he was to wear could only have one possible outcome for him. Bring it on! And clutching a map of downtown New York he was ready and on his way!

Denver was insistent that he would drive himself to Fulton Street where his appointment was, and his mentor reluctantly agreed. It was the normal procedure for him to be driven close to the site but frankly, Denver now had his mentor scared shitless. And after-all Denver was an American, and he was also absolutely committed, so he let him go.

Now here he was driving closer to Wall Street – the very epicentre of Western decadence – China Town was on his right and the City Hall was coming up next. As he had been instructed to do, he then turned left into Fulton

Street and began looking for somewhere to park – not that he cared.

'And now who has the power!'—he cried out, to no one in particular. And certainly, no one that he knew, took the slightest notice. He checked, as instructed, that the explosive vest was secure and that the red button was correctly set.

It was 8:55 am on the morning of September 11th.

He drove further down the street and began reciting excerpts from the Koran to maintain his concentration. Unable to find anywhere else, he deliberately parked by a fire hydrant in a non-parking zone. Getting out of the car which he did not bother to lock – well there was no point was there – he strode across the street – ignoring the traffic. His target had been picked – or so he was told. It was on the other side of the financial district from where the first explosion of the day had occurred, and the dumb cops would expect any subsequent explosions to be in the same area. Well, that was nice – someone would be deeply sorry, very soon.

It was 8:59 am.

A police patrol car that happened to be scurrying by, sirens wailing, in the direction of the earlier explosion, screeched to a halt having observed the illegally parked car. The driver immediately radioed to have the street blocked off. The two policemen hit the ground running screaming at people to get away from the car. They were taking no chances after the earlier explosion. A couple of pedestrians while scurrying for cover, frantically pointed the police in the direction of Denver aka Mohammed.

It was 9:02 am.

One of the NYPD police officers ran across the street toward where Mohammed was standing in the entranceway of the building. The street rapidly cleared as people rushed to get away from the car.

'Is that your car parked over there?' he shouted, at the same time drawing his service revolver. The only reply he got was a shout in a foreign tongue that sounded something like Arabic, as Mohammed took off his coat to reveal his broad bronzed muscular shoulders and the explosive vest. The device attracted immediate attention and distracted from the body that wore it. From a distance, it looked like a crude bomb, but there was just no way of knowing what kind of explosive it was. Not that it mattered. Explosive vests were like a claymore mine. The object of the explosion was simply to launch nails, screws, ball bearings, and other shrapnel that had the effect of a shotgun blast but was far more lethal and multi-directional.

'Fuck!' was all that the cop could say. He knew instinctively from his training that he had to get people clear because people rather than property were the issue.

He knew that the only way to disable a suicide bomber was to shoot him at the base of the neck. That way you instantly disabled – well killed – the transgressor before he would have the time or the opportunity to summon sufficient force to press his detonator. You could simply shoot at the head or the chest and hope to kill the bomber without exploding the bomb. But that was not the way he had been taught to deal with terrorist events.

Then the policeman had a stroke of luck. The bomber turned to march into the building. There was no time to get properly lined up on the target. Now he had a clear view of the idiot's neck. Knowing that it was beyond the range of a normal pistol, he fired anyway – hoping.

He was too late.

The whole front of the building momentarily vanished in an explosion. And then it was as though nothing at all had happened. Except it took Denver Washington aka Mohammed Khan into the next world – be it to receive his rewards or to be consumed in the fire and pain of Hell – along with the police officer and about forty other people. Innocent victims of yet another insane act of terrorism.

The inside of the building was absolute carnage with the dead and dying scattered all over. The gravely wounded for some reason tried to crawl away from the area of the blast. The uninjured stood shocked and petrified unable to offer any help.

It was 09.03 am – the same time that United Airlines Flight 175 had struck the South Tower of the World Trade Centre on that fateful day September 11, 2001.

Chapter 26

The Third Bomber

Arif Masood was a highly educated young man. He was born in the southern United States to a Pakistani father and an Indian mother. This was unusual and was the main reason why his parents had come to the United States all those years ago. The mixture of a Muslim father from Pakistan and a Hindu mother from India would not have been tolerated in the Kashmir region where they had met—by chance and fallen in love—by fate.

Now they lived quietly and peacefully in St Louis and minded their own business. But Arif was educated so he was neither quiet nor peaceful. His knowledge of the world increased at about the same rate as his knowledge of racial discrimination. He began to resent the continual battle that he had to endure proving himself over inferior white people. The only person who seemed to have similar thoughts to him was a member of the local mosque where he used to go with his father to pray.

His father cautioned Arif that he should stay clear of the extremists and be wary of getting involved with those who had ideas of terrorism. However, the wise words had the opposite effect.

Extremists were not always terrorists. Terrorists were always extremists.

His knowledge of the Koran and the Muslim, or Islamic, faith was very comprehensive. Islam means submission to the will of God or Allah. Therefore, a true Muslim is someone who submits totally to the will of God. So, Arif declared himself to be a true Muslim.

But was he?

By the time Masood had had a couple of trips back to Pakistan and ventured north to the tribal lands, and into Afghanistan to meet up with the Taliban, he became dedicated to whatever Jihad was currently in the news. He became equally dedicated to the destruction of his adopted country and everything that it stood for.

The word Jihad is generally understood in the western world to mean a holy war on behalf of Islam. But the Muslim faith is one of peace, and Jihad could simply mean striving to live a moral and virtuous life. Masood was far from at peace. So, he did not worry too much about this distinction. Like Mohammed Khan – also known as Denver Washington – Masood became increasingly more extreme in his views. Consequently, he came to be regarded as something of a nut case.

Being well educated, he thought that he knew better than those around him, and even his closest friends became quite alarmed at the extent of his extremism.

And that is what brought him to the attention of those planning the next terrorist plot to take place on the soil of the United States.

While he was eager to serve the cause and was equally eager to be recruited into it, it turned out that he was not the ideal person for this job. Being educated and used to studying, he researched the background of those planning the attacks. He could find no reference to them. Not that that was at all unusual.

The man he had spoken with about his involvement had stressed the need for secrecy and compartmentalization so that the less each level in the organization knew of the plot and those involved in it the better. The man he was communicating with had an Indian name while in the view of Arif the gentleman was a Pakistani – now that was unusual. Given his ethnicity, he knew something about such matters, so he enquired further. But this time his poking around came to the attention of his mentors.

And it spooked the mentor's big time.

The problem, probably, was the motivation of this particular recruit. The mentors had suffered from a misconception – that Arif Masood would act out of rage and hatred. Masood was looking for a deeper meaningful relationship with the wider Muslim community and to participate in an event that would further their cause. Sure, he felt anger, and that resulted in hate, but he wanted to feel that his sacrifice was appreciated. He felt the obligation to serve the cause, but that brought a sense of belonging and fulfilment.

He also had doubts about the seventy-odd virgins that he would meet in the afterlife. There were just not that many virgins to go round, and in any case, he had learned that they were supposed to be available to all true believers so there would seem little point in making the supreme sacrifice on that basis alone.

The Pakistani, who claimed that he was an Indian, did only what he could have reasonably been expected to do in the circumstances. He met once again with Masood and they spent the evening discussing their beliefs, and the various terrorist plots and events that had occurred in places all around the world. And also consuming some of the liquor that the western infidels could not seem to get enough of. The fact that drinking alcohol was forbidden by his faith seemed to escape his sensibilities, as did the irony of it being provided, and willingly consumed, by his mentor.

Masood got progressively more vocal to the point that if anyone had been listening to them, they would have assumed that it was Arif who was organizing the next terrorist event. But Arif should have paid more attention to what and how much he was drinking.

When the Pakistani rang his boss later that evening it was to report that Masood had been eliminated as he presented a serious risk to the whole plot. He would be found dead from a heart attack brought on by high blood pressure – or so the coroner would deduce.

The Boss was of equal parts pleased and pissed. He was pleased, and very relieved, that a serious risk to his grand plan had been permanently removed. He was pissed that, after years of meticulous planning, it all could have been placed at risk, and then seriously prejudiced by the lack of the third recruit. The time for action was rapidly approaching and there just was not the time to first locate, profile, check out, and then build up another bomber.

But then he had a brainwave.

He knew just the person who could be rapidly recruited. The fact that the person was female barely mattered in the overall scheme of things. There had been many examples in recent years of females giving their lives for the cause. The boss did have some difficulty understanding how they were attracted to the cause, and its' inevitable conclusion as far as they were concerned, without the carrot of the numerous virgins. The fact that it was perfectly reasonable for a female to die for the cause, escaped the sensibilities of the "Boss" because he had never bothered to learn anything of the Muslim, faith.

And he never would.

On the morning of September 11th, the woman of his choosing entered New York Central Park from the West 90th Street entrance and made her way to a park bench where she sat down appearing to watch a couple of old ladies feeding the pigeons. She looked out over the reservoir, a look of absolute terror on her face.

Anna Lekovic was a young lady who took great care in her appearance. She was dressed in a long beige coat, a headscarf of a similar colour, and medium heeled shoes that matched the whole ensemble. It was very appropriate that the reservoir was named after Jacqueline Kennedy Onassis. Anna looked so much like Jacqueline had in her younger days – albeit that her hair was lighter. She could have been heading for a fashion show, such was the way she looked.

Except for one thing.

Out of sight, strapped to her body, was a vest in which there was enough explosive power to cause some severe damage to anyone or anything that happened to be in reasonable proximity, if or when it exploded.

Hers was probably the easiest job out of the three people who had either volunteered or had been assigned to sacrifice their lives in the name of Allah on this particular day. All that she had to do was to walk up a street block of her own choice, wander into a shop, again of her own choice. At the precise time of 09:37 am she had to simply depress the detonator that would blow her, and several other people who happened to be in that building, into the next life.

She had acquired the vest courtesy of a couple of eastern-looking gentlemen and as she left them, they had wished her well, in the name of Allah. They had appeared to be impressed that a member of the opposite sex had volunteered to make the supreme sacrifice.

At the same time, they did not care.

There were however a couple of small problems. Firstly, she was not a Muslim and did not share in the beliefs of that faith. She did not believe that this had anything to do with Allah or anything at all to do with anyone's God. She did not expect to receive any great rewards in the next life if indeed there was to be one. Secondly, she had not volunteered for the job.

As a young girl, born and raised in Serbia, Anna's life had been filled with terror. Her parents had been killed in the wars in what was once called Yugoslavia. She was too young to know which side of the conflict, if any, her parents had been on. All she knew was that one-day soldiers came along to their home. There they marched her parents out into the street and, without a word of explanation or any chance of their saying goodbye, shot them in the back of the head. Then calmly walked to the next house. And on it went.

Fortunately, at the time she was too young to interest the soldiers in anything else. Although the young girls who lived next door were not so lucky.

Nor did she know which side of the conflict Papa and Mama Milutin were on. All that she did know was that the Milutin family had, from the day of her parents' premature death, cared for her and vigorously protected her as though she were one of their own.

Many years later General Ilic Milicic, who had fought with the Serbian forces, and who was apparently on the run from NATO forces that wanted him for war crimes, had happened by and noticed Anna. She noticed him too. He was the man who had shot her parents in that horrible episode that would forever live in her memory. In the small village where they lived everyone knew what was going to happen next and knew to say nothing about it for fear of what could happen to them or their loved ones.

The very same day that the General came to town, Papa, in total secrecy and at great speed, arranged for Anna to get out of the village. He got her onto a boat which was on its' way to Italy so that she could start a new life away from these brutes and the many and varied conflicts that still occurred, yet usually went unreported, in this part of the world. But Papa did so at a very considerable personal cost. His eldest daughter was taken from the Milutin home when General Ilic Milicic realized that Anna had been spirited away. The daughter was treated like a piece of meat, raped repeatedly over several weeks, and then left to die in the cold of the Serbian winter.

Anna heard what had happened, from the comfort and safety of her new home in New York. Since that time, she carried in her heart a burning desire to see General Ilic Milicic brought to justice. She also had a burning desire to ensure that Papa would suffer no more.

Then a series of events occurred that at first seemed to be just coincidence – at least to Anna. Having made her way to the United States, she did what every young lady would do, given that she suddenly had at her fingertips all the facilities that went with life in the west – she rang Papa and Mama. The call was just to say she had 'made it' and to thank them for all they had done for her. And with tears streaming down her face, she expressed her deepest sorrow at the loss of their daughter.

To this very day, she blamed that loss on herself.

If you can transmit a shrug of the shoulders over a

telephone line, Papa did just that. And then with tears in his eyes thanked her for the good times and said how happy he was that she was safe and well. The stoicism that Papa showed in the face of nearly unbearable suffering made a big impression on Anna and she vowed that she would save as hard as she could so that she could eventually bring them out of that hell hole.

Sometime later she got a telephone call that both frightened and angered her.

'Is that you Anna?' asked the quiet voice.

'Yes' was her hesitant reply 'Who is this?'

'You do not have to worry about that Anna, you would not know me anyway. However, you do know my boss, General Ilic Milicic.'

She froze as the voice continued.

'Just to let you know we could have a small job for you to do. If you don't want to do it, that's fine, Papa and Mama will pay the price – I understand that is usually the case where you are concerned.'

The voice was so matter of fact, so cold, so confident, and so evil.

'What do you want?' she snarled into the telephone the brief mention of her past life terrifying her while at the same time pumping anger into the system.

'Oh – you will find out in the fullness of time.'

Then the line just went dead.

For a few moments, she just stared at the wall not able to think, barely able to breathe. And then the horrible, shattering truth struck her and sent a shudder throughout her body. For all the advantages of living in the age of technology, and at the very centre of it in the good old US of A, it was a trap.

Someone had traced her call to Papa. She could not know who had done this or how. Was her telephone tapped? Or was Papa's tapped? The prospect overwhelmed her, and she slid down the wall to the floor and sobbed her heart out. Exhausted from the mental stress, she curled up in a foetal position and cried herself to sleep.

A short time later, she had another call.

'I believe that you have agreed to do a small job for me.'

The voice this time was remarkably familiar.

'What job? Who said? ... What are you talking about?'

She could feel the terror creeping into her voice. It had been so long ago – still in her subconscious but long-buried by all the good things that had occurred as she settled down to her new life.

'I don't understand!'

'Oh—but you do!' came the smooth reply. 'You remember that you said you would do a job for General Ilic Milicic in exchange, I think, for the life of someone called Papa. Well now is the time. The General owes me one, so he has agreed that we will wipe the slate clean if you can do this small job for me. So, do you want to do it, or do I tell the General to go ahead and get rid of – who is it? – Oh, that's right—Papa.'

The tears started to flow again as the realization dawned on her. Since Papa had arranged her escape, he could not know that he had unwittingly handed her off into a much eviller organization, she had been set up. Everything that had happened to her had been arranged. Nothing had occurred by chance. Now the evil which she had escaped from had gotten together with the evil she had walked into and now she was trapped.

'What is it that you want me to do?' she sobbed into the telephone.'

'Simply carry a bomb. I will fill you in on the details

later. And – do not go near the police, otherwise, Papa is as good as dead.'

John Dubois hung up the telephone.

'Annette, Annette! – what is wrong?'

The question disrupted her thoughts and she realized that she was crying. Still sitting on the park bench.

Mark reached out to her to put his arms around her, then recoiled as he realized that there was something under the coat.

What kind of garment was she wearing?

'Annette – what in heaven's name are you doing?'

She looked up and saw Mark Taylors' handsome face, and in it, all that she had hoped for and that she knew she would now never have.

'My name is not Annette. It is Anna.'

Through the tears, she laughed.

'Debbie called me Annette because she could not understand my accent. And I called her Pep instead of Deb for the same reason. I guess it stuck.'

The tears again started to flow.

She looked at her watch – It was 09:01 am.

Mark was angry but he doubted that anger was going to resolve the situation now. He had heard the explosions in the distance, and he now realized that he had been closer to an answer to the riddle all along. But what the hell was Annette doing with a vest? Was she supposed to be the next?

And then the horrible truth hit him. Like everyone else, he knew the history of September 11th, 2001.

The first explosion on that awful day had been at 08.46 am when the first flight hit the Twin Towers, the second flight hit the Twin Towers at 09.03 am. The third explosion, etched into his mind forever because he was in the Pentagon at the time – was at 09.37 am when a flight slammed into the Defense Headquarters. He could not be certain, but the first two explosions he had heard were at the same time.

To maintain the symmetry there could be two further explosions although not necessarily in New York City. In 2001 the third explosion had been at the Pentagon in Arlington Virginia but that did not mean that this re-enactment had to be in the same place. There may not even be a fourth explosion since it was reasonable to assume that the crash in a field in Shanksville Pennsylvania would be regarded as a failure by the sick people who had planned that event.

All that was pure speculation.

Mark now knew that Annette was meant to be the third bomber. Someone was trying to replicate those exact timings on the same day so many years later. Were they equally sick or was there some other madness at work? Whatever the reasons for this madness, he had about half an hour to find out.

'Annette – listen to me. You do not have to do this. Tell me now, what is the problem. We can fix it.'

He pleaded with her as she sat still petrified and sobbing on the bench. He had no idea where the earlier bombs had struck, nor did he know where the target of Annette's bomb was to be. But he had a sinking feeling that it did not matter.

To the person who had planned these events, it was not a matter of how much damage was done. Rather, it was the symbolism in the timing of the events. He had been so close to reaching this conclusion in Rabaul, then in Wellington, and then again in Washington. Why did the FBI and the CIA not follow up his suspicions? He had the place right. He had the timing right. Now he had the third part of the event and that cruelly involved the lady who he loved.

The time was 09:06 am.

Paul came racing into the park, alerted by an earlier frantic call from Mark and came to an abrupt halt when he saw Mark with Annette.

She still sat on the bench looking so frightened but at the same time so determined.

Slowly she focused on Mark. Her words had a finality to them.

'I cannot let Papa die. He has been through enough and this all has nothing to do with him.'

'Annette – I do not know what you are talking about – who is Papa and why is he going to die?'

Mark looked to Paul for a clue, but Paul just shrugged.

'Annette – please help me—tell me what you are talking about?'

And then it all came out in a rush – the threat that had been issued – by of all people John Dubois, a man who had done so much to settle Annette into her adopted country.

Do this thing or Papa dies, courtesy of General Ilic Milicic.

At the mention of that name, it was Mark's turn to freeze. He knew that son-of-a-bitch.

'Annette concentrate – whereabouts in Serbia is Papa?'

Her voice was just whispered.

'In a little village called Novićević just south of a place called Novi Pazar, almost on the border with Kosovo.'

She carried on talking, but Mark had other concerns.

He got up from where he had been talking to Annette and went straight to Paul.

'Have you still got that satellite phone with you?' he

demanded of his companion. They had a shared experience from all those clandestine operations, including two in Serbia, supposedly by NATO forces—but the USA was part of NATO - wasn't it?

'Yes – it is in the car. What do you want with a satellite phone? This whole business is starting to give me the creeps.'

'You remember that British Major, Tom something —what was his second name—who was in charge of the hunt for Ilic Milicic – Dean that's his name—well I heard he was back on the Kosovo/Serbia border. Get him on your satellite phone and tell him we have a definite lead on that prick Milicic.'

'But how do we know?'

Mark cut him off.

'You CIA types always want clarification in triplicate before you will move. No wonder so many crooks are free in this world. For once in your life make a decision.'

He was starting to sound like Dusty!

Paul hesitated, but then he saw the look on Mark's face and thought better of it. In a crisis, it was funny how roles get blurred. Mark outranked Paul – well he had when they had worked together in the field all those years age – so Paul turned and rushed back to his car.

The time was 09:17 am.

Mark turned back to Annette, who was now silently sobbing.

'You must have had a fall-back position in case something should go wrong – for example, if the detonator failed to set the explosives off you would have a secondary method. What was the arrangement?'

Mark racked his brain to visualize the nature of the bomb strapped to her body and the various methods of detonation. He had left all that kind of stuff to the experts!

The tears started to flood again, and Annette was so distraught she could hardly speak. Mark tried again.

'Come on Annette—try – I know it is hard – but we must try!'

If you want to have a chance to save Papa's life - he did not add.

He knelt before her conscious of the fact that she was a bomb probably capable of blowing a rather large hole in the ground. The first responders would probably find traces of the park bench. It was unlikely that they would find any trace of Mark and Annette.

Finally, he managed to hear her response which came out as another whisper.

'None.'

Paul returned to join them, carrying his satellite phone in his hand, and thrust it towards Mark.

'He wants to talk to you.' He said in a dejected voice. Mark grasped the phone.

'Hello - Is that you Tom?'

'Of course, it is!' bellowed the very British accent.

'What is this hare-brained scheme that you have now come up with. I have been searching for Milicic for years, and then I get a call from the USA and am told to just stroll across the border and pick him up. Have you got rocks in your head? Do you know how much paperwork we have to complete for such a raid? And what proof do I have that it will be any different from the last dozen or so tip-offs? All of which produced absolute Zippo.'

Colonel Tom Dean's voice was rising so that the last words were shouted into the phone. Well, that was good. The British professional soldier and member of their much-vaunted SAS. Tom Dean was at his absolute best when he was mad.

'Tom – calm down.' Mark decided it was time to get him steamed up and decided that he would pre-empt what the NATO forces around the world would soon be made aware of.

'Tom - this is the latest news ok – we have had another al-Qaeda attack in New York City. And we are struggling to handle it. But we have very sound intelligence that your friend General Ilic Milicic is involved in some way. And we happen to also know that he will be visiting the Milutin family soon to collect a couple of debts, not unrelated to the New York attack.'

Mark had left out a few facts. He could hardly tell Dean that the story was based entirely on a young lady's ramblings. Or that she was his most recent conquest. Or that she was sitting not ten feet away from him strapped with yet another bomb.

The time was 09:23 am.

'I thought you had left the service Mark – what are you doing? Why are you involved?' Tom sounded suspicious but there was respect in his voice, which was good. He was obviously thinking about it.

'Don't get me started on that right now – I will fill you in later. Shall we say I am assisting the CIA and the FBI with their investigations? Now will you do something, or do we let the people we are negotiating with go ahead and set off a third bomb?'

'Shit! Ok – I'll get a chopper up over the border. The place that Paul mentioned is not far. But if this turns out to be a load of crap – lookout. And the next time you call remember that I am now a Colonel - so show some respect.'

'Tom – thanks. Now it is not for me to tell you how to do your job, but don't take the helicopter too close to Novićević. You don't want to give General Milicic and his cronies any warning that you are onto him.'

The time was 09:26 am.

Mark turned his attention back to Annette.

'We can do this Annette. We now know that John Dubois is behind all this. Although we have some work to do to convince the government, there is no need to blow yourself or anyone else up. Papa will be fine now we have passed the word on to the Brits. Please Annette let me take that vest off you and disarm the detonator. That way there will be no accidents.'

At first, he thought she was going to resist. Then the tears welled up in her eyes once again.

'I do not think you can. They did not trust me to go through with their plans. They rigged the bomb with a timer, so I have no control over it. And it has a tamper-proof device so that it will explode anyway.'

The time was 09:27 am.

Mark and Paul carefully examined the vest that Annette was wearing. The good news what that its' construction had been carried out by people who did not know much about explosives. The detonator that was intended to be tamper-proof was little more than a switch. The programmed detonator was not an immediate problem because that would not have any effect for another nine or so minutes. The bad news was that the bomb was so crudely put together that any little slip would mean that it would explode anyway.

With reasonably sophisticated devices it was fairly easy – that is for someone trained in the use of explosives – to see which circuits did what. As in the movies, all you had to do was cut the correct wire – was it the red one, or was it the blue one? – Times up! So, take a gamble—and puff with nanoseconds to spare we made the correct choice.

There was no such problem here. Suicide vests worn by Terrorists did not need to be all that cleverly designed. After all, once used, there was – well nothing left. There was plenty of time – well they had about eight minutes.

The time was 09:29 am.

Paul raced off back to his car to get some tools while Mark quietly cleared the curious onlookers.

'You have a few minutes to get the hell out of here before this thing explodes – your choice!' was the brief speech that he gave.

Suddenly they had this corner of Central Park to themselves.

When Paul returned, he got out a pair of tweezers and carefully lifted the edges of the vest, and peered underneath. Then he went to the electronic timer that was slowly counting down and examined how it had been set up. He then stood up and motioned to Mark that he wanted a word – in private. Mark looked Annette straight in the eyes and hoped that he did not transmit his fears and tried to assure Annette that things were under control.

'Paul knows what he is doing, so don't worry! We just have to discuss the how – I'll be back.'

Annette's eyes said 'Whatever!'

She was beginning to reconcile with the fact that she would not get out of this alive. But she still watched Mark walk away to Paul and, with a last glimmer of hope, tried to wish him to say that everything would be ok. But it wouldn't – would it?

'Well - I think we're fucked! There is no way we can do anything with the wires' said Paul, carefully facing away from Annette.

The bomb has a variety of methods to set it off. It has a timer as well as a manual detonator. That is the one that Annette was to push. But it doesn't make any difference really – it would go off anyway when the timer runs out. And I suspect it is also set for remote detonation probably by mobile phone. The clock is so crude that any attempt to cut any wire and – bang – good night.'

'But!' Mark was about to interrupt but Paul raised a hand and silenced him.

The time had rapidly advanced—it was now 09:31 am. They were just running out of time.

'There is however a way we may be able to do it. If we can take the vest off Annette—but we will need to be incredibly careful. There is a switch that is activated if any attempt is made to remove the vest. If we can hold that in place while we remove the vest then tape it down, we should be right. There will be a delay. What I do not know is whether the delay mechanism kicks in again or if the mechanism resets.' Paul said with much more confidence than he was feeling.

Mark had to concede it was a good plan. Paul was the expert and in the absence of any other plan, there seemed to be no other option. Then all they had to do was get the hell away before the vest exploded on its own accord with the elapsed time. The problem was quite simply that an explosion would scatter shrapnel equivalent to over a thousand bullets over a wide area and in all directions – so there was just nowhere to hide.

Paul looked at Mark and they both shrugged.

'If this doesn't work and I don't see you again let me just say you're not a bad sort of guy and you can borrow my harp anytime. Ok - let's go do it.'

Mark could not help but laugh. It was the same joke Paul had come up with before – and it had worked that time—hadn't it?

The time was 09:32 am.

They went back to the park bench where Annette sat

and carefully explained that they were going to remove the vest. Paul said that there would be no problem and hoped that Annette could believe him. He just asked her to remain still.

They removed her coat to reveal the entire vest. While she held her arms out to the sides Paul carefully untied the shoulder belts that held the vest in place. Now came the tricky part. They both held their breath as Mark tried to stop his hands from shaking.

He reached under the flap to locate the switch. At last, he had it! But there was no time to reflect. He had to keep the switch pressed firmly against the flap until Paul could get it taped down. Before they could do that though they had to manoeuvre the vest to get it away from Annette.

By this time Paul and Mark were both sweating profusely. Not from the physical exertion – but from the sheer nervous tension of the moment. It was relatively easy for Mark and Paul to disguise their feelings after all their experience with explosives. It was quite another matter to disguise their sweaty hands. As the time counted down Annette began to shake – from the fear that she was to be the cause of the death of two more friends. There was just not enough time.

The clock was now showing 09:35 and they had less than 2 minutes.

After what seemed like an awfully long time Paul had frantically taped the switch in place, but what was the point? They had spent so much time trying to disable it that the vest was due to explode of its own accord at any moment in any case. It was Mark who held the vest and there was just no time to think about what had to be done. Mark exchanged looks with Paul and then without saying a word it was agreed – the best thing to do was throw it as far into the reservoir as possible.

Then duck and hope.

The clock now displayed 09:36 – under a minute to go - and who could say how accurate the clock was?

Paul grabbed Annette, roughly dragged her to the ground, and covered her as best he could.

Mark summoned all his strength and flung the vest as far out into the reservoir as he could. He then dived for the ground covering his head with his hands.

There followed a huge explosion as the timer reached its critical time.

It was 09:37 am. The same time that American Airlines Flight 77 had slammed into the Pentagon on that fateful day—September 11, 2001.

Chapter 27

The Safe House

Fortunately for New York City, and more particularly for Mark, Paul, and Annette, explosives work best in confined spaces. While the explosion was spectacular, there was little damage done, and there was no loss of life. The explosive charge had been somewhat muted by the water, and although some steel balls from the fragmentation jacket had gone in all directions, they had miraculously avoided the three of them. They peered up from where they had landed checking that everyone was ok, and then they scrambled to their feet.

While Paul and Mark brushed the dirt off their clothes, Annette ran to Mark and collapsed in his arms sobbing.

'Hey now that wasn't so bad, was it?' Mark grinned. He then turned to Paul and said, 'I owe you one!'

Mark then got serious.

'So, how about making it two?'

Paul was also grinning – from relief.

'Hell, I am in enough trouble now for being here and not where I was supposed to be, so what's another one?'

Mark's grin turned to more of a grimace.

The events of the last hour had vindicated what he had been thinking all along – from the time he and Brad had analysed the data that they had discovered back in Rabaul PNG. Al Qaeda was not the force behind this the re-enactment of 9/11. And he was about to make some bastards pay, and if needs be, to hell with the CIA and the FBI.

But first things first. He had to get Annette, and for all, he knew himself, to somewhere safe and out of reach of the federal authorities. While Mark had been vindicated by the events of the morning, he felt that he could not trust anyone, at least not until everyone could cool down.

He did not expect John Dubois, in particular, to be amongst the coolest of people when he found out what had happened. And it was evident that his friends in the government would not be too happy either.

Mark turned to Paul.

'When John Dubois finds out about this explosion and the lack of any damage—and he will find out – he will be pissed. He is going to come looking for Annette. From what has been happening so far, I do not think that certain groups within the FBI would applaud what we have just done either, so they will be looking for her too. And we have the additional problem of what General Milicic is going to be told to do. But at the moment we have time on our side. Can you get a CIA safe house for Annette – preferably one that is not used very often – and one that is not known to the FBI. And then I think you and I should have an appointment with our insurance people.'

Again, Paul and Mark exchanged glances, and Paul just nodded. The last thing they needed right now was for the three of them to be swamped by authorities that would be lacking in any understanding of their situation. Even without the threat caused by some errant members, the FBI, in particular, would be looking for someone – anyone – who was even remotely connected to the events of the past hour. Since Annette was still alive then that was the logical place that they would start.

Could they trust the FBI? And for that matter, could they trust the CIA to back them up?

On recent past performance, the answer would have to be a very definite – No. But for now, a CIA safe house would be the best they could do.

Mark had not had the time to discuss the changing situation with Paul. However, he seemed to be sufficiently worried to take action.

'Ok—Follow me and just do as I say.' Paul said.

'Annette – just pretend to be injured or preferably unconscious. Mark—pick her up and follow me. Quickly! – do it now.'

As people from around the outskirts of the park began to rush forward, probably hoping to see plenty of blood and guts, a couple of police officers rushed into the park with their guns drawn, Paul rushed towards them moving in the opposite direction and away from the scene of the explosion.

When he reached the police officers, he pulled out his badge, and calm as you like told them what had happened – well almost.

'We almost had the guy – he had a vest on – he was to be the third bomber to blow himself up – we were talking him out of it and then – he just went rushing off into the pond and then, bang. These guys are scary, but from what the bomber was saying – talking quite calmly and reasonably – he is the last. This is 9/11 all over again.

Whether you will find any remains of the terrorist – I doubt it – but fortunately, no one else appears to have been killed or injured – just one of our agents—the lady—got hurt. We have to get her to a hospital. You guys take over here while I get that organized. Then I will come back, and we can see what has to be done.'

There was just too much information for the police officers followed by the instruction that they were now in charge resulting in brain overload, which is exactly what Paul had intended. The officers acknowledged the instruction and off they went looking for – well anything.

The three of them got to Paul's car and Mark loaded Annette into the back seat. Paul then produced a red light that he attached to the top of the car, Mark piled in beside Annette and they were off heading south to go around Central Park. 'I know just the place – we used to have a couple of safe houses not far from the United Nations headquarters – you can imagine in the days of the cold war we often got some people from the
UN who wanted to talk to us – in private that is. These days no one wants to talk anymore – well not to us anyway. There are still a couple of houses that the CIA have not used for years. It is probable that the bean-counters have forgotten all about them—so we should be in luck.'

He turned left into East 57th, right into 2nd Avenue and continued until they came to East 34th Street. For a moment he seemed lost, and then he saw what he was looking for and turned into a side street and stopped. 'Wait here' was all he said, and he took off down the street checking numbers and trying to relate them to what he vaguely remembered. Then he suddenly stopped, reversed a couple of houses, and then went and rang the bell of a nondescript door, and the entrance to an even more nondescript apartment.

'Is this going to all work out?' Annette sobbed.

She had not uttered a sound since they had left Central Park and now sounded both frightened and resigned.

Mark looked at her and smiled.

'Of course, it is! Don't worry. Paul knows what he is doing.' Words he hoped would reassure her, although he was not so sure himself.

'Mark – how come you know these people. And back there in the park, you were talking to someone about General Milicic as though you knew him. And then all that stuff with the bomb – you knew what to do! Who are you, Mark?'

He could see the tears starting to well up once again. She had been through a terrible time, and there was still a way to go. Now was not the time to explain either the history or the more recent past. But Mark had to reassure her. So, he laughed.

'Hey – one question at a time.' and he gave her hand a reassuring squeeze. 'Yes - I know your friend the General Ilic Milicic – a nasty piece of work—who I have had dealings with when I was younger. And the guy I was talking to on Paul's telephone is an old friend of mine in the British Army who happens to be on the lookout for the General. Paul was with me in the Adriatic when we crossed his path. Now he is just a friend who shares a desire to see your General caught and brought to justice. As for me—I am no one special Annette. But I do have some special friends. And I will keep using them until this whole thing is sorted out. We might owe a few beers by the time this is over – but hey – I can afford it.' And he laughed again.

Annette did not seem too impressed but why should

she be? She knew that there was still a way to go before this thing was sorted and right at this moment, she had no idea where they were headed.

Paul came back to the car looking worried. He climbed in and informed Mark of what he had discovered.

'I do not like what is happening – the person at the safe house – and it is supposed to be a fucking Safe House – tells me that I need to have authorization first before I can make use of it. And she wanted to know the name of the person we are delivering. Now that has never happened before. I told her I could not reveal the name – and you know what she did – she suggested another safe house to go to. You have to be joking!'

He drove away at some speed muttering under his breath.

'I know what we'll do. We will go to somewhere where no one will find us.'

Mark was beginning to get a little edgy but to keep Annette calm he just smiled and held her hand. Paul drove as though his life depended on it, switching lanes, and taking left and right-hand turns and always glancing in the rear vision mirrors to see if he could spot a tail. The business was catching and soon Mark found himself doing the same thing. Paul noticed this, said thanks, and concentrated on his driving.

They made their way over the Queensboro Bridge and then commenced again to duck and weave until eventually, they pulled up in a run-down part of Queens. Paul turned around to Mark and revealed his plan.

'This was a Safe House many years ago but hasn't been used officially for years. I have used it myself on the odd occasion, but no one knows about that. It differs from the normal safe houses in that there is no permanent resident. So, we can use it now. But you will need to find someone to keep Annette company if you intend to go out.

I would imagine that you do not want her left alone?'

'No - I certainly don't. We need to go!' replied Mark. 'We need to get her off the streets and the sooner the better.'

They got out of the car and made their way up the steps to the door of the house that Paul had pointed them towards. It was an old Brownstone dwelling, the third in a group of twelve, all of which were four stories, and all were finished in assorted colours. The front door looked innocuous enough, but all the blinds on the windows on the first floor were closed. Paul unlocked the door with a key and that led them into a hallway or parlour that had just a clothes rack on the right and ahead of them another much sturdier door that had a combination lock. After a couple of fumbles as he tried to remember the combination, he unlocked that, and the stale smell that they faced confirmed what Paul had said – the place had not had any residents for quite some time.

The door opened up into a lounge area that had several doors off to the left, every one of which was locked. The room was old-fashioned and sparsely furnished and did not appear to have any windows other than a couple of small, frosted glass blocks just below the ceiling.

Paul went to the right where there was a sideboard and produced a bunch of keys from one of the drawers which he handed to Mark.

'I will give you the combination for the main door, but you realize I'll have to then kill you, don't you?' he said with a wink.

'I have to go and report in, or I will be in even deeper trouble. Do not use the land-line – it can be easily traced – the NSA and the CIA monitor the line and, apart from the shock they will get at receiving any call on it when they hear your voice – they have voice recognition technology—they will go apoplectic. If you need to use your cellular phone, make the calls short. Don't believe all that crap about cell phones being safe and untraceable – they are neither.'

'The front door has a voice box so you can communicate with any visitors. If you let them through the first door you can watch on this video screen over in the corner. If you do not like what you see, then press this button to eject a gas that should put them to sleep for a while – at least it used to do that! The rules are – don't open the inside door until you are sure there are no unfriendly people in the outer hall, or unless you have a mask on – which should be around here somewhere. To get rid of this stale smell just turn on the air-conditioning and leave it running. I was going to say don't open any windows, but I don't think any of them open anyway. That's about it – you should be safe here – now I have to go and get you a few things and then check in with the New York office'.

Annette looked like her former self – for just a moment.

'I can do the shopping' was all she said.

The looks that she got from both Mark and Paul quickly brought her back to reality. Mark handled this situation, telling Annette that, firstly she needed to rest, and secondly that they both needed to settle down. Before there was any further discussion, Paul quickly left, leaving Mark to sort this out, but he returned within minutes with enough food and supplies to last about a week. This at least gave Annette something to keep her occupied while the two men had a serious chat.

Paul was becoming progressively more agitated, addressed himself to Mark, and ignored Annette.

'You need to explain to your girlfriend that we are in a serious predicament. Apart from the fact that your pal Dubois will come looking, or send someone looking, for Annette when he finds out what didn't happen in Central Park, you also have the FBI to worry about. They will be looking for you as well, and until we can get the situation under some kind of control you must both lay low.'

'I know' replied Mark 'But how the hell do I tell her that we cannot trust our intelligence service?'

'Well – that's your problem. Meanwhile, I have to go to a meeting to get a heads-up on the current situation, and I don't know how long I will be. I cannot stress enough – you must stay out of sight, and not talk to anyone.'

Now it was Mark's turn to be confused.

'I thought your New York office was destroyed in the original 9/11 attack on the World Trade Centre. Who are you going to meet and where?'

Paul sighed.

'Come on Mark – I cannot tell you that! Yes – the office was destroyed, but the people survived, and they set up somewhere else – that is all I will say. Just trust me. When I come back, I should know more and then we can plan what we are going to do next.'

Annette hugged Paul and said thank you. Mark just nodded his understanding. And then Paul was gone.

For the first time since the heady days before Mark departed on his trip down-under, they were alone together. Neither of them dared to take the first step. They had been apart for what seemed like a lifetime, but it would take some time for their relationship to get back to something likenormal. Annette busied herself exploring while Mark, conscious of Paul's warning, made a couple of quick calls on his cell phone.

The first call was to Brad Morgan but that was a waste of time. The answer-phone message said he was out of the area, without saying what area he was supposed to be in. The second call was to Dusty – well really the office of Taylor Software – but Dusty was not available.

They say it pays for a business owner to call his own office once in a while and get treated like any other customer. He would need to talk to someone because he was none too pleased with his reception. He had the good sense to not say who he was, and he just hung up. In fairness to his staff, and whoever was manning the telephones, it probably was not the best day for anyone working in New York City.

When they had finished getting as settled-in as was possible, they finally came together, Mark putting his arms around Annette as she collapsed sobbing. They needed some time together and for the moment Mark had all the company that he needed.

Eventually, they settled down on the couch. This time sitting close together and turned on the television tuned to CNN. While Mark was interested in what the various reporters and so-called experts had to say, he was more interested in what the reporters knew nothing about —how Annette, in particular, had got into this mess?

Mark carefully and quietly raised the question with Annette by asking simply 'Do you want to talk about it?'

The tears started to flow, but between sobs she told her story, filling in the gaps in the story she had told them in Central Park. Mark rapidly realized that the lady by his side had a conscience and that was the main reason for her attitude to him the day before, and the reason she had gone ahead with Dubois' plan when logic said – just report it to the police, or Mark, or anyone!

She had been deeply moved when Papa's daughter had been taken from him – even more deeply traumatized when she had learned about what must have been a terrifying end for that young innocent girl. And when Annette was approached by John Dubois and told that Papa would suffer unless she did as she was told, her worst nightmares had come true. She was determined that she would not have Papa suffer anymore, and this time the suffering would be hers, and hers alone.

Mark sat listening to the tale, realizing that things could very easily have been so different. On that Friday night when he had first made love to Annette, she had taken the opportunity, not to keep him from the office as he had suspected to suit the Augem Group and their devious plans, but because it was one of her last real chances for love.

If only she had told him about John Dubois' evil plans on that same Friday, he could have taken steps to both get Papa out of Serbia and to deal with Dubois. But she had no way of knowing Mark's background. She could not have known about his military service. Nor could she have known about his friends.

Very few people know what goes on in the darker side of military affairs, and the people who do, don't particularly want to talk about it. Similarly, had he told her what he was doing recently in the South Pacific, she may have realized that his contacts could have sorted out the mess long before September 11th. Instead, he had been playing at being a spook on some jaunt that as far as she was aware had nothing to do with what had unfolded in New York City.

Her attitude towards him the day before, on September 10th, had been a complex mixture of deep emotional concern and the acting out of not caring. Annette was not trained to hide her feeling, so her attitude towards him was extreme. She had to show a hard resilience that allowed no room for her love for him. When he went to escape through the window of her apartment after fighting off Ted, that was the time he should have stayed and forced her to tell him what was going on. He could have handled the amateurs that made up their little group, and the business could have ended right there. But no – he was hurt because he believed the act she was putting on. So much for his ability to read body language. On the one occasion that it mattered, it failed him because of his vanity. He would not let that happen again.

He realized that the tears were not just Annette's. Fortunately, Annette's head was buried in his shoulder. So, she neither saw the tears nor the look of grim determination on Marks' face.

The reporters droned on trying to tell their stories, while Annette finally lapsed into silence. CNN always had the latest news long before the CIA and many of the other arms of the US intelligence service – although they did not always get it right – as Mark was about to find out.

It was late in the evening when Paul finally called. He was agitated before he left. He was even more so now.

'I don't know what I am doing working for this organization!' was all he would say about his meeting, and then continued.

'I will find someone that we can trust to look after Annette – it will be in the morning. See you then.'

The line went dead.

Chapter 28

Official Comments

The CNN anchor was busy trying to explain to viewers the awful events of earlier in the day. But he was making hard work of it.

The problem was that, although everyone knew there had been several attacks on New York City, no one was certain who was responsible for it, because so far no one had claimed responsibility. The truth of the matter was they did not have even the remotest clue but that did not stop the chatter. No one seemed certain whether the security intelligence services had a hint of what was coming or not – they were saying absolutely nothing—so that could mean whatever you wanted it to mean.

The problem was that no one had claimed responsibility for the bombs. And, so far, none of the experts on such events had said anything which made sense very much. There were wide-ranging guesses delivered with all the solemnity befitting such an occurrence. And all of them were inaccurate.

There had been no official comment so that did not help.

The media, like every other organization, can suffer from shock. Their initial reaction to that is to ask someone – anyone – what the hell is going on? The bigger the shock, the higher up the bureaucratic pyramid they go, looking for official comments as a place to start their investigations. In the absence of any comment, they then start to do their research into the subject and make their own projections. The longer they have to wait for official comment, the more their projections become to have a life of their own.

Initially, they all focused on the timing of the events because that was the really big news. The almost uncanny timing of the explosions was of far greater importance than where they had occurred. And that seeming of greater importance than the people who were killed or maimed. Well, that was reasonable. You could only repeat numbers so many times and that was the end of that story. But the timings were critical. Now that was a part of this story that could be spun into endless theories based on a few known facts.

The first fact was that this had to be the work of al Qaeda. Who else would either want to or had the means to, replicate the original 9/11 so precisely?

The second fact was that this had to have been planned to just remind the entire world that al Qaeda was still alive and well and could strike at the very heart of any western democracy with ruthless and catastrophic efficiency.

But – the media had concluded.

The third fact was that the attacks had been carried out without the slightest hint of where, when, how, or who had planned them.

Mark sat on the couch with his arm around Annette while they watched CNN expecting that they would at least reveal something new, and a little closer to the truth. Mark believed that he knew who was responsible – and that "who" was not al Qaeda. He knew who had planned the whole thing, who the bombers were, how much information was in the hands of the intelligence community before the event, and who would ultimately claim responsibility. And that would not be the actual people who had been responsible.

The question that he could not answer was - What insanity was behind it? But before the next few days became were over, he was determined that he would find out.

In the absence of any official comment, CNN began to roll out any number of so-called experts on terrorists and terrorist organizations as well as conspiracy theorists, which would have confused rather than informed the public. The fact that the bombers had not caused anything like as much damage as the original attacks in 2001 led them to speculate that the attack was symbolic. Which was not a bad guess.

'Well tell that to the people who died!' murmured Mark. But the part of the discussion that interested Mark was the unanswered question of why the intelligence community appeared to have had no prior warning. On this matter, neither the National Intelligence Council, the National Counterterrorism Centre, the Director of Homeland Security nor the Federal Bureau of Investigation was 'available for comment at this time.'

The facts were, that at this time, those organizations were just as confused as everyone else. And, probably, they were just passing the buck or waiting for some comment from higher up in the command structure – be that from the Director of National Intelligence or the

the President himself.

What Mark found particularly ironic was that no one at CNN thought to ask the CIA. They, or at least a few people in the organization that Mark could name, knew all about it.

Since 2001 there had been changes in the so-called Intelligence and Security network. There was now a Director of National Intelligence who had, amongst other things, two organizations working for him that were supposed to make sure that intelligence was gathered and shared rather than locked away in any one single operational unit. The first organization was a National Intelligence Council, a strategic think tank that was supposed to produce meaningful intelligence estimates. The second one was the National Counterterrorism Centre which was supposed to integrate and analyse terrorism intelligence from all the other agencies of government and beyond. But the so-called Intelligence Community consisted of so many other agencies, some of which were a part of the bureaucracy, some which were part of the political structure, what chance was there?

Among these others were Defence, which includes the National Security Agency and at least four subgroups – Navy, Air Force, the Marine, and the Army—the Central Intelligence Agency itself, State, Homeland Security, Treasury, Justice (which includes the FBI), Foreign Affairs, Energy and several more. Add to this lot, the many Universities and other institutes that had Think Tanks that were willing to offer opinions on any subject—informed or otherwise – and usually the latter – and you had plenty of scope for endless and widely differing opinions, which depending on how the message was delivered could be interpreted as news.

On the periphery of this little lot, three men – Mark, Brad, and Paul – had gathered critical information which should have been of profound interest at least to the President. But how far up the chain through the labyrinth of the intelligence and security services had the information travelled? As far as Mark could see both Brad's earlier reports, his most recent analysis gathered from his trip down-under, Paul's analysis – which although writing the plot off as the efforts of some nut case – were nonetheless worthy of follow up, and Marks' irrefutable evidence of the involvement of Doctor Abdul Jabbar in the whole scheme of things, should have sounded a warning bell somewhere.

But it hadn't.

While it was easy for Mark to place greater reliance on facts as he saw them, he could understand why someone in a more professional position would be cautious at accepting them as the truth. But two serving CIA officers, doing what they were supposed to be doing, and reporting what they had found in the course of that? To ignore them was plain dumb.

Someone had to have killed the information.

Whoever had done that must know that the machinery of government bureaucracy, or the media, would eventually find out what had happened to that information. The only possible explanation was that they did not care whether because of what they had been paid or because of what they were. Marks' analysis of that was that money, and not ideology – be that caused by ethnicity, religion, or any one of several other things, had to be the major contributory factor.

His information now was that John Dubois was the provider of the money, as well as having some involvement in providing the people. Therefore, Mark would not rest until Dubois was made to account for his involvement.

The people who had assisted John Dubois could wait.

Annette roused him from his thoughts.

'The President is going to speak.' she whispered as she clung to his arm.

'I can tell you what he is going to say.' said Mark. 'His speechwriter probably dug up the speech from 2001 and he will repeat the same message – America is strong – we will bring the perpetrators of this evil act to account – I have today authorized a zillion dollars to search for and destroy the wrongdoers – but the priority is to help the injured – and to prevent any further attacks on our people. But deep down he must know that someone had fucked up – and he will be pissed when he finds out the who, the how, and the why.'

They sat and listened to what the President had to say. Mark was right. He could have made the speech.

Unlike the events of the original 9/11, the President was actually in the White House receiving a briefing on the goings-on in Pakistan and elsewhere, so there would be no confusion this time of who told him and what had happened. There were no school children to confuse the issue. And his speechwriter was on the job real fast.

'The United States has once again been subjected to an attack by terrorists, on the anniversary of 9/11. This cowardly act has again struck New York City whose brave citizens are still recovering from the events of 2001. Your government will immediately seek to enforce military and economic sanctions against all countries which are perceived as harbouring terrorists. Our intelligence and security forces are already assembling information on the perpetrators and will rapidly seek to bring them to justice.'

What he did not say, of course, was that he would expect an immediate increase in his approval ratings. As would all the leaders of the free world, and the not-so-free world – such is the nature of politics and life. The CNN coverage did a quick flick through the various reactions from around the world, which was a bit of a surprise given then many of the people should have been tucked up in bed.

The British Prime Minister, Gordon Brown, although not as extrovert as his predecessor, was quick to state that the British people would 'stand by our friends in the face of this act of evil'—whatever that may mean.

The Australian Prime Minister, John Howard, who would be more awake than his British counterpart, expressed a milder than would be expected 'We are all traumatized by this.' There was no point in repeating the grand statements of six years ago such as that made by the German Chancellor about the 'declaration of war against the civilized world.' or the French somewhat emotional statement that 'We are all Americans.'

The reactions from the Islamic world were equally predictable, all denying involvement just in case they were, and they would be, accused of anything. The Iranian comments, no matter how they were phrased, always came out contradictory, depending upon whether they were the words of the President, Mahmoud Ahmadinejad, or the more sympathetic ex-President Sayed Mohammed Khatami. They ranged from the brutal 'The Americans will use this as an excuse to step up their war on terrorism and their victimization of anything and anyone of the Muslim faith' to 'My deepest sympathy goes out to the American people.'

But Mark's mind was on a different subject and at a far lower level than that which the leaders of countries had to deal with. At the very start of all the troubles, there was one event that still bothered him. To what extent was Annette involved?

Sure, she had said that she had been recruited by John Dubois, and she was obviously distressed about that. But had she known about the raid on his office? He mulled over how to approach the subject – recognizing that she was still traumatized, and he could not judge what her reaction might be. But he was still angry and upset. And there were several unanswered questions.

Eventually, if reluctantly, he introduced the subject.

'If only I had known half of what I know now, this situation could have been avoided' he began. 'I should have realized that the break-in at our office was not a coincidence. It was a setup – but by who?'

The question hung in the air. Annette just stared straight ahead, deep in thought. Thinking of what? What to say? What not to say? Mark knew or thought he knew that Annette was not into the body-language thing. But even so, reading body language did have its faults – rather like a crude lie-detector test. You could sense that someone was stressed. But until you could read minds, that is all you could do.

Slowly she turned to face Mark, clutching his hand, tears welling in her eyes.

'You think that John Dubois was responsible for the break-in, don't you?' she asked.

Mark laughed at that.

'No—I do not think that. I know that! What I do not know is—how was it organized? How come I was picked up from the office – so that I had no obvious means of getting back? And then I go for a drink – and get into such a condition that I was unable to go back to the office that night. And on that night, of all nights, we get broken into.'

'You think that I had something to do with that don't you?' she asked – the tears flowing down her cheeks.

It was awful having to lie. It would hurt Mark because he was talking of a time when he had finally made love to his Personal Assistant. And there was this theory that the reality of the situation was that the reason that she had been there was at someone else's request – or was it someone else's instruction? The truth of the matter was – Mark just did not know, and did he want to know?

Mark did not laugh this time. Gathering as much composure as possible, he held her gaze, and he heard himself say what he was thinking.

'Annette – I just do not know. I do not want to think that. But all the evidence says that I should. Please convince me otherwise.'

He immediately felt guilty. She had been through so much—that is the things that he knew about. Heaven alone knew what else she had been through, and the effect on her mind would be hard to contemplate, even for someone of Mark's background who had seen so much of life's darker side. He told himself to wait – and hope. Wait to see how she reacts. Hope that it was love and not the blind follower of instructions.

They looked at each other – Mark calm and cool – Annette flushed with a mixture of anger and regret. Suddenly the words came out in a torrent – interspersed with sobs. But there was no accusation. Just hurt.

'All I know is what happened. I thought I was going to take you back to your car, but you were in no condition, so I took you home. It was not my fault – what happened at your place!' she said as the sobs became deeper. And then her tone turned to one of frustration.

'Why did you take so long to make love to me? That night meant so much to me. At first, I thought that it was just the drink – but I had wanted you so much for so long, I just took my chance.'

And then came the killer blow.

'But then I realized – you loved me too!'

And then she broke down completely.

Mark studied the tear-stained face in front of him. She fought to escape his grip, but he held on and gently pulled her to him. Then, as she buried her head in his shoulder, he knew.

She had been acting under instructions, albeit that her part in the grand scheme was minor, and she was probably uninformed of what John Dubois was really up to. She could not have known what was planned. The message that she got from Debbie was to pick Mark up, whereas the more normal thing would have been for Augem to deliver him back to his office, or wherever he wanted to go, by the same means that he had got there – by company limo. That message would have been issued by John Dubois because Matt Reynolds was with Mark.

The whole thing was planned.

Annette Covic, and Debbie Peterson for that matter, were just innocent players in the games that Dubois was orchestrating. If only Annette had dared to tell Mark on that night, while they made love, of Dubois' plans for her. That would have made a huge difference. But she could not have known of Mark's earlier life, and that Mark knew General Ilic Milicic – and that was the key.

So now John Dubois was going to pay.

Chapter 29

John Dubois

John Dubois sat in his office watching the same CNN feed that was being watched by Mark and Annette in the safe house. It was probably being watched by the rest of New York City – and the rest of the world. The Augem office in Chambers Street was sufficiently distant from the explosions that had occurred that there had been no need to evacuate that particular building.

The majority of the Augem staff, many of whom were in New York City at the time of the original 9/11 occurrence, were traumatized by what little they knew of the events of this morning. They had hurried off, either in search of friends and loved ones, or to be with their families. Or to be in their own homes where, for some reason or other, people always felt safer. Nobody knew if more explosions were to follow and they were scared, albeit grimly resolute.

But not John Dubois. He knew exactly what had happened, and when, and where. And he knew that the explosions were at an end.

Now he had to get on with the job of gaining the maximum benefit from the chaos that he had helped to create.

He strolled out of his office to the coffee machine at the far end of the reception desk and helped himself to a flat white. Something which, on a normal day, he would never do. Then he returned backed to his office and closed the door.

At the reception desk, there still sat the ever-dutiful Deborah Peterson. She had no family in New York City and at her apartment, she would not have felt safe. Debbie would only have felt more helpless and alone.

Raised in Florida, she had travelled to New York, as a young lass, to escape from a drunken and abusive father, and a drunken and beaten mother. Once in the big city, with the bright lights and 24/7 activity, and free from her abusive past, she had fallen in love with a tall handsome man who was both rich and destined to go places. She put up with his arrogance and abuse because, from her upbringing, she assumed that that was just the way things were.

Later she found out that some of the places that her handsome prince was going contained an endless supply of other girls. And that explained the mind-numbing truth that he was not actually working late at the office. So, she decided to end their relationship the next time that they met for lunch.

The events of September 11th,2001 meant that they would not meet again. He was on the 114th Floor in the North Tower of the World Trade Centre when American Airlines flight 11 came to an abrupt and somewhat catastrophic end.

Now she just sat staring at the television. Dumbfounded by the pointless savagery that had once again been visited upon this proud City. She was an emotional and caring person. Although the death of her partner in the original 9/11 was no real loss, she cried then, and she was crying now. Anyone who was in New York on that day would never forget what had happened, nor could they even now comprehend the brutal and callous savagery of the perpetrators of that horrendous crime.

While life must go on, the individuals who were affected by it would carry the traumatic and emotional scars for the rest of their lives. Debbie was therefore quite dumbfounded by the unemotional and uncaring attitude of her boss—John Dubois. She had tolerated his arrogance as part of her role as the subservient secretary. But at the moment there was something else about him that she just could not understand.

She would soon.

Dubois chuckled to himself watching it all unfold on CNN. The anchor-man, and numerous so-called experts that they had conjured up with regular monotony, tried to explain what had happened. They explained to people for the umpteenth time that there had been three explosions. And that the timing of them bore an uncanny resemblance to the timing of events that had occurred, what seemed like yesterday, but was all those years earlier on September 11th, 2001.

He watched as the cameras produced graphic pictures of the damage that had been wrought on two of the buildings, both of which housed businesses of a similar nature to the Augem Group. Although they did not show any pictures of the dead or dying, they were genuinely concerned, as reporters always are, that the toll of the dead and the injured were mounting. As people from the fire, police, ambulance, and other emergency services frantically scrambled through the rubble, the injured fought for their lives while wondering what the hell had happened.

John Dubois watched with a calm detachment that was obscene.

'At this stage, we cannot confirm the actual toll. It is expected to be several hundred dead and many more seriously injured. Both numbers are climbing as reports come in from the hospitals and medical staff, and we will inform you as soon as we have more definite figures.'

Briefly – no one had a clue. Well, that did not matter, did it? You can expect some peripheral damage – collateral damage the Central Intelligence Agency would call it—as a part of the price of progress. Or so John Dubois's insane logic told him.

The saying went something like – one death is a tragedy; a million deaths is a statistic. And when all was said and done, so Dubois thought, it was not as though the people of New York City generally had the time to care about all of the people dying of disease, starvation, and armed conflicts in other parts of the world. And al Qaeda would be blamed for the carnage, and Osama would not mind. He never did!

Meanwhile, there was money to be made and, in the process, some sacrifices had to be made. In any case, someone else was being paid to worry about the who and the why of such events.

But the television reports had not as yet shown any of the damage from the third explosion. The cameras were concentrating on what had happened down at the south end of the city where the financial centre was.

'Was not that just typical of the Americans?' Dubois mused. Concern where money was involved. No concern when just ordinary people, out for a day's shopping, were involved. The third bomb was not intended to take out any significant building in case someone put two and two together and came up with yet another theory. The only thing that mattered was the timing. That had been immaculately secured.

Dubois got up from behind his desk and went out to get another coffee, stopping by at the reception desk to talk to Debbie.

'Arrange a Board meeting for nine o'clock in the morning' he said. No, please! No could you or would you. No concern that some members of the Board might be otherwise occupied. Just his usual arrogant self.

Debbie's voice quivered and then broke into a sob as she replied. 'Do you think everything will be back to normal by then? Mr. Augem has gone to check on his friends and is terribly upset. We do not know if he will be back in the office by then.'

Translated—Debbie could have said - 'You arrogant prick! Rob has friends down there who could be dead or dying. Whatever he finds he will be in no condition to attend another verbal battle with you.' Which summed up exactly how Board meetings went these days. But she did not, being the ever-dutiful servant.

Dubois ignored her concerns and simply said 'Just arrange it – if Rob is unable to attend so be it!'

Armed with another caffeine fix, he went back into his office and again closed the door. He could have invited Debbie in to watch the horror unravel on his large screen. But then she would not understand why he was smiling. And he had important work to do.

Everything he had been planning for all this time had worked to perfection.

But, it had not.

It was just that he did not know that yet.

While he was out getting his second cup of coffee, and issuing instructions to Debbie, he had missed a critical part of the broadcast that switched to Central Park. There reporters, the NYPD, and the FBI were scratching their heads trying to fathom out what had happened.

There had been an explosion. The timing had been perfect. There was a big bang at the same time that American Airlines Flight 77 had slammed into the Pentagon on that fateful day—September 11, 2001. But there was just nothing!

Unbeknown to John Dubois, he had just given Colonel Tom Dean and his British troops the extra few minutes that would set in motion a chain of events about which he would be none too pleased. That is if he ever found out what the Brits were doing in Kosovo.

Which he would not, as things turned out.

The broadcast switched to a hurriedly called media session with the Mayor of New York City. He was understandably a very angry and confused man. Dubois nodded in understanding. He would be angry and confused, wouldn't he?

'We have this morning been witness to yet another attack on our beloved City. I ask all of you to await the Federal authorities who will at the proper time have an announcement on who was responsible for these horrific explosions. I have mobilized all available resources to attend to those who have been hurt. I am assured that no further attacks are expected, but your Police Department are on full alert, and I ask that you cooperate with them as they deal with this tragedy.'

Then the broadcast was interrupted by an announcement that they were switching to the White House where the President was about to have his say. The President came on the screen looking suitably grave. He said all of the usual things expected of him and then lowered his voice because that is what his speech notes said that he should do and continued.

'The American people can be reassured that we have allocated the full resources of the federal government to assist the local authorities to help the victims of these attacks. While this work goes on, our forces have commenced an action to hunt down those responsible for these cowardly acts. We will not be dictated to by terrorists, and they will be punished!

'Issuing the usual platitudes and pointing the finger of blame at al Qaeda and the forces of evil that his war on Terrorism was trying to deal with.,' John muttered.

But he had to laugh. The President also looked confused, as did the inevitable collection of White House staff who could find nothing better to do than to stand around in a group behind the leader of the free world looking suitably grim, important, yet impotent.

Why did so many men have to stand there not doing anything but listen to what they had agreed, or disagreed, on what their spokesperson should say? The President was a politician. He was supposed to be able to multi-task, switching between welcoming the local ladies knitting class to declaring a nuclear holocaust. That was his job. But who was running the show while they all stood there looking impotent? The net worth of the assembled "team" would have exceeded the Gross National Product of many a country, John chuckled to himself.

John Dubois smiled again and reached for the remote to turn the volume down. He never did understand politicians and had an even lesser understanding of people who sought to grovel in their presence. He had some serious plans to make so that the next phase of his scheme could be implemented.

He had heard all this political claptrap before. The Mayor and the President were expected to have views that were somehow more important than anyone else's. But they did not know anything, and they were not important except as figureheads.

The people who were supposed to know what had happened were the DNI, FBI, CIA, and the NSA. They advised the President what to think and what to say. But their advice was wrong – wasn't it?

He would expect this rhetoric to go on for some days. And then, when there was no more to be gained politically from posturing before the media, the ordinary citizens would be the only ones who continued to care – probably grieving for the rest of their lives. Such was the reality of life and politics.

Engrossed in writing up what he was going to present to the Board tomorrow he did not immediately notice the picture switch back to Central Park. But when he did, he initially froze, and then he grabbed the remote to turn up the volume again. Fortunately for John Dubois, the news was so headline-grabbing that the reporters did not want to let it go – so they repeated it. John did not believe what the reporter was saying.

'It appears that two officers from the FBI—at great personal risk to themselves—removed a vest from the third suicide bomber – and then exploded the device in the

Central Park reservoir to avoid any casualties. The suicide bomber, believed to have been a woman, has been taken into custody and is currently assisting the FBI with their inquiries. At this stage, we do not know the name of the bomber, but the FBI is expected to release the full details shortly. Stay tuned for further bulletins. I repeat – there has been no significant damage from the third explosion and – I repeat – there have been no casualties as a result of the bombing in Central Park.'

Dubois was furious. He crashed both hands down onto his desk scattering papers everywhere and knocking his coffee cup onto the floor.

'What the fuck is going on?' he yelled at the television.

Debbie heard the outburst, but she was so used to his foul temper she chose to ignore it.

'That is just not possible!' Dubois muttered almost to himself and then his temper flared again.

'Right—so now I will fix you—you bitch.'

He grabbed the telephone and punched in the number – committed to memory—never written down.

'Where are you holding her?' he demanded to know of the person at the other end of the line, without any preliminary comment or introduction.

'Holding who John?' came the calm reply.

'You know who I mean! That bitch you apprehended for want of a better word – in Central Park.' he snarled into the telephone.

'But we are not holding anyone – what are you talking about John?'

'Does your right hand know what your fucking left hand is doing?' he roared 'It was on the CNN newscast just now. Did you not see it? Why does CNN always report things before you people can say or do anything? The report said the third bomber is still alive and was assisting you people – with your inquiries. And I have no doubt who the person is. Find out where she is being held and deal with it!'

'But we have not got her John. The report that you heard or saw must be false. Or it must have been an assumption by the reporters. We do not yet know what happened. We are trying to find out. It appears that no one from the FBI was anywhere near Central Park at the time of the explosion. I repeat—We just do not know what happened.'

'Well - you had better find her – and dispose of her before she says too much!' he bellowed. He threw the phone across the room smashing it against the door – disconnecting the link to FBI headquarters at Quantico.

Debbie was just rising from her desk, concerned at the noise when Dubois burst out of his room and yelled at her to get him another telephone. She handed one to him which he snatched out of her hand and, without a word of acknowledgment, stormed back into his office slamming the door behind him.

Then he punched in a number committed to memory – never written down. This one would be a slower connection because there were security considerations, particularly at the receiving end, which did not do very much to improve John Dubois' temper.

Finally, he got through to Serbia.

'Ah! John, it is you.' General Ilic Milicic answered. 'And how are things in the great city of New York?'

The bonhomie was one-sided and short-lived.

'Kill them.'

Chapter 30

Kosovo

Colonel Tom Dean was not at all impressed with the message he had just received from his American friends. It was 3.25 pm and he had some thinking to do. Tom Dean, Mark Taylor, and Paul Williams had become very close friends because of events that only soldiers can understand. Therefore, his first thought was that he should trust them.

On the other hand, he was now on his third tour of duty in Kosovo, and throughout all three tours, he had on occasions been given good intelligence on when and where he would be able to find General Ilic Milicic and his bunch of cronies. All that intelligence had proved useless. Well not quite. That the intelligence was good was never in doubt.

What irritated Tom was the intelligence that Milicic had appeared to be far better. Either he was very clever, or very cautious, or he had excellent contacts that informed him of what the NATO forces were up to so that he simply moved on before they could get organized.

What irritated Tom far more was that he believed it was the latter. Someone from within, or very close to, the

NATO force in Kosovo, was tipping him off on an amazingly consistent, and irritating, basis.

The British forces in Kosovo were in the Pristina sector where they shared a base with the Canadian and Czech Republic contributions to the KFOR peace effort. The situation in Kosovo was difficult. The interim Government was both inept and corrupt, Serbs still lived in small pockets and had to be kept away from the Albanian Muslims, and several groups of criminals from both these ethnic entities ran the show.

The combination meant that the KFOR force was in a no-win situation. Still, they had to do the best that they could.

To get to the place where the latest piece of intelligence said that Milicic would be meant that, from the British base, they would have to fly over the Kosovska sector manned by French and Italian forces. Colonel Dean had a force of nearly three thousand men under his command. All of them were British. And all were trained for far more onerous duties than babysitting the people of Kosovo. Consequently, many in his force were irritable and bored.

A significant part of their brief was that they should be friendly towards the local population, and soldiers, being what they were and away from home, quite enjoyed at least that aspect of the job. Some more than others. So, Dean was convinced that someone was taking the "be friendly" instruction a little too far. Worse than that, he or she or they were giving information to their "friends" almost before he had it. Whether this was as a matter of just loose talk, or because of targeted information gathering, he did not know or care. If he ever found out who was responsible for such leaks, he would have his balls

– if it had any – on a platter. The Colonel was an old-fashioned soldier who could not reconcile women fighting alongside men. So, if the informant turned out to be a female – well he wasn't sure of what the female equivalent of "balls on a platter" was – but he knew that what he would do would not be nice.

While he weighed the pros and cons of the advice, deep down he knew what he was going to do. Milicic was too big a prize.

'Ok – here we go again!' he said to himself and got up out of his chair and strode out of the office. Well - it was not really an office. It was the remains of a building that used to be three stories high – but due to the exigencies of war, there was barely a ground floor.

Major Dickson was sitting outside the door reading – well looking through—a Playboy magazine. He leaped to his feet and saluted—the magazine crashing to the floor.

'More training Major?' the Colonel enquired and strode towards the door. Almost as an afterthought, he turned and said, 'I am going out for a while – can you look after things here?'

'Yes Sir!' came the reply.

The Major was quite used to the Colonels' haphazard and impetuous way of doing things. That would never happen if he was in charge!

'The pompous prick.' Tom Dean muttered under his breath. This time he would go after Milicic without his second in command. He would go without any of the officer pansies that had been assigned to him.

He made his way across the street and to a building in a similar mess to the one he had just left and entered. Well, that was also a figurative term – since there was no door to speak of. Inside four men were sitting down around makeshift table playing cards but jumped to attention when they saw who their visitor was. Dean wagged a hand in the general direction of his head by way of a salute but then told the men to sit down. He had something to talk about and protocol could fly out the window – except that there weren't any windows.

Of the men sitting around the makeshift table were Sergeant Ian McKinley, a big but gentle brute of a man going by the nickname of Mack who was the best foot soldier Dean had ever had the pleasure to serve with, and Sergeant Eric Wilkinson, the absolute opposite in terms of size, who was the pilot of the one helicopter the powers that be had decided in their wisdom to donate to the cause.

Most of his forces were either out on patrol or were on R&R, but Dean knew that firstly these two would be here, and secondly that he did not need anyone else other than the other two scoundrels making up the party. Sitting at the table there was Corporal Sean O'Brien who had previously held the rank of Sergeant. He had been demoted for refusing the orders of his Major – in the typical Irish style. Further action was pending on that – but that would need to wait. The fourth man was also a corporal, a quiet strapping lad called Roy Newton who was the best man in the force for sneaking up on people. They would be an ideal group for executing the plan, with the addition of a spare pilot which someone in Health and Safety – with nothing better to do – had decided was necessary.

'I have a job for us.' was all he had to say, and he had their instant and undivided attention.

They had something to do – at last.

What is not normally appreciated is that British SAS troops, and American Special Forces, are just ordinary people. They are just better - some would say ruthlessly - trained. They eat, shit, and fart like everybody else. They go into strange places, at strange times, and do what some would regard as strange things. They need to be hard and cold, but when the job is done, they return to as near normal a life as the services allows. So, they get up to all the usual tricks that servicemen are renowned for. They normally have officers to keep them in check, but when they have a job to do, rank does not count for much.

The Bell 212 helicopter took off at 3:48 pm and headed northwest. The crew consisted of Eric and his corporal Wendy Lennon. In an earlier life, Eric had been the pilot of British Army Attack Helicopters the Apache AH Mk 1 and had served in the Gulf, before retiring to the more sedate life driving the Bell in Kosovo. And he had proved very useful. Lennon on the other hand was theoretically unnecessary.

The Bell could quite happily function with a crew of one, but she was the navigator, and she performed every known function – well almost—including manning the machine gun, which function they were not expecting to have to use. If need be, she could fly the machine. Wendy Lennon was an enigma to the males in the Kosovo force. Her husband had been killed in an accident while serving a tour of duty in Kosovo. So, she had volunteered for the next rotation. Nobody understood why, and she never volunteered any information that would enlighten them. Any member of the force who tried to take advantage of this vulnerable young lady was soon made aware of his foolishness at some personal cost – physical that is.

The Bell 212 was designed to carry up to fourteen people so that was no problem for Dean's small band. What was a worry was that the Bell was not owned by the Army – so the commercial owners would be none too happy if it came back damaged. But that was why the Colonel had an administrative staff. All of the team were in combat uniform and full personal load carrying equipment gear which meant that they were good for twenty-four hours.

A personal call to the French commander cleared their passage through the Kosovska section, making it a relatively short flight from where they were based to a position across the at least theoretical border into Serbia. The mission though was somewhat complicated. For one thing, while the whole operation would have been better carried out at night, they did not have time to wait for darkness – Milicic would be well gone by the time that darkness arrived. For another, they could not afford to get too close to the village because the noise of the helicopter would attract attention, so they would have to do quite a bit of walking. For another, they had no idea of the direction from which Milicic would approach the village.

On this subject, they would have to make a judgment call because they had no idea at all. Their best guess was that he would not be coming from the south of the village, if for no other reason than it was closer to the area occupied by NATO troops. But that did not count for that much. The village was close enough to the border anyway. And the terrain was so rugged they could just about walk over him and have no way of knowing that they had done so.

They flew along hugging the ground, following the contours of riverbeds and streams, then hopping over a ridge and then down through the next valley. Eventually, Wilkinson hovered over a gap in the bush and pointed.

'This is as far as I should go. The village is just over that rise on our left. I could take you nearer the top but there is a risk.'

Dean was happy to rely on Wilkinson's judgment and gave him the thumbs up.

'Ok – you drop us here and then go back. But not to the base! I am sure you can think of a reason to drop down somewhere else,' the Colonel said with a wink.

'There was no point in causing any worries for Major Dickson now was there? I will radio you with a pickup position once this is all over. We will walk out so that no one else knows where we came from. It may be a different position from this one – we have a GPS so that should take care of it. Drive carefully.'

The four men jumped to the ground and seconds later they had disappeared into the woods.

There were several problems in walking over the terrain of the type they encountered. For a start, it was very easy to get lost unless you moved and worked as a team. Fortunately, they were trained for this. Another problem was that you never knew who you would run into. They were trained for that as well. Usually, that meant killing whoever they came across. Since the NATO command had yet to sanction what they were doing, and they were after all on a peacekeeping mission in Kosovo, killing people was not such a good idea. Consequently, they had to proceed with extreme caution so the trip up to the top of the ridge and down the other side took about half an hour longer than Dean had planned for.

The Colonel did not know it then, but he could thank John Dubois for the allowance of extra minutes which would prove crucial in the execution of his plan.

They steadily made their way down the ridge. It was still daylight, so they were thankful for the cover of the woods. Eventually, Dean called a halt in a position that was about one hundred yards from the edge of the woods and five hundred yards from the edge of the village. There they wrapped their SA 80 weapons in plastic and dug a small trench in which they buried them, covering the ground with a pile of leaves, and trampling down the soil so there was no evidence that they had ever been there. Then they removed their uniforms to reveal that they each had on clothes that made them locals and exchanged their helmets for cloth caps.

After putting their uniforms in their packs, they hid the packs behind rocks, and for good measure piled loose rocks on top. The only weapons they now carried were the standard-issue Browning Pistols. Their thinking was that they could hardly march into the village with more obvious armaments. All four of them felt somewhat vulnerable given the likely arms that would be carried by their Serbian opposition, but such was the reality of the situation.

They were now as ready as they could be.

Dean got the men together in a huddle and explained the next move. It was a simple plan that required careful timing.

McKinley and Newton set off in the lead, walking down a rough track that ran alongside the edge of the woods. They had the appearance of locals, but they were aware that they were still strangers coming into a small village where everyone knew everyone else. Still, it was not uncommon for odd souls to be walking in from an adjacent village usually looking for work. It was something of a paradox that Mack knew the local language very well but spoke it in a harsh Scottish accent which made him almost impossible to understand, while Roy knew very little but what he did know he spoke with almost no accent and could easily pass off as a local.

Their first encounter was with an old lady who just smiled at them as they walked towards her. Mack asked her for directions to Drina Street and she seemed to understand him perfectly.

'Niz ulieu prva levo' and pointed down the street to a position no more than a couple of hundred yards away from where another street joined from the left.

Following along behind, Dean and O'Brien had split up. The Colonel realized it was a bit of a risk of letting Sean go it alone. O'Brien knew only a smattering of the language, and he was a bit of a hothead. However, he knew the plan, and hopefully, he would stay with it. Dean had told McKinley and Newton to get as close as possible to a position where they were able to view the front door of Papa's place and then to just observe.

Once the house was located, Sean would try to find the back entrance to the property and keep that under observation. Dean's job was to try to keep both Mack and Sean in view so that he could control the situation. The Colonel had a moment when he wished he had more men at his disposal. But it would hardly be the ideal situation to have thousands of troops milling around. No matter how well disguised they were, a larger number would stand out. Milicic—the escape artist who could put Houdini to shame – would sense a trap.

Dean just shrugged and settled down to watch.

The house that Papa lived in had seen better days. Both of the windows on the first floor had cracked glass, and one of them had been boarded over with wooden planks. Just a little further on down the street from Papas' house was a bench and that is where Mack and Roy decided to sit. It had the advantage that it was on the same side of the street as Papa's place so that they could sit facing away from the house they were observing. Newton pulled out a chess set of the type people usually used when they travelled and placed it between them.

The fact that McKinley had no idea at all how to play chess was a problem. Roy did know and so they gave the impression of one man teaching the other and they commenced to play while chatting away. It was the typical conversation between chess players.

'Sean will be in position by now, and I can see Tom.' They rarely called him Colonel when they were out on a job.

'He's started playing street soccer with a couple of kids for fucks sake!'

Suddenly there was a crackle in the ear of McKinley. He heard Tom whisper.

'You've got company – watch out!'

As Mack turned, he saw two men appear around a corner and then coming down the street from the north. They could have been from Tom's force from the way they were dressed except they had that the dark craggy appearance that distinguished them as clearly Serbian—and they were carrying rifles and had a tell-tale bulge in their waistbands that they did not try particularly hard to disguise.

The few people who were out in the street, enjoying the last of the day's sun, quickly shot inside leaving little doubt in Tom's mind who these men were. The two men were on the opposite side of the street to where Mack and Roy were seated playing chess. They gave the two SAS members a long hard look. Mack looked up and just nodded his head towards them, and then returned to his game.

'Got them – looks like the advance guard.'

The communication equipment was working well.

The two men walked on glancing at the house that the British were watching, and then they did a strange thing.

One of the men walked back crossing the road and came up to Mack. Without saying who he was, or why, or giving any explanation, he said 'Mislim da vi trebz da idete

I igrate se neyde drvgo —I think you two should go and play your silly game somewhere else.'

It would have been obvious that the two men playing chess were not local or they would have done what everyone else had done already and got out of the way. Mack heard his communicator start to crackle and immediately hit the kill switch. Tom from his observation point saw the casual signal from Mack and immediately called Sean.

'You trying to communicate with someone?' he asked.

'Just wanted to let the lads know they have some company on the way' Sean replied. From where Sean was, he could not see the front of the house and therefore did not know that they already had company.

'How many men? And where?' Tom asked.

'Two groups of three – they are waiting on both sides of the street about a hundred yards north.'

Why did Irishmen always make three sound like tree? Tom thought, but their immediate problem was becoming desperate. He could handle three or four, but eight was stretching the odds with their SA-80s left behind in the woods. And which group of three was Milicic a member of – if indeed he was there at all? Would he reveal himself or just let the other members do the dirty work?

Tom was sure that Papa, and probably Mama as well, would be taken from the house and not killed until they were outside the village. Well - there would be less cleaning up to do and no explanations would need to be given. That was the way Milicic had always worked in the past and Tom was not expecting him to change his modus operandi any time soon. Tom did not have enough men to cover both groups of three, so the whole plan now depended on Milicic – just how cautious would he be?

While the General had a reputation of being arrogant,

he also had a reputation of being cunning, which made him a quite formidable foe.

Back in the street Mack got up from his seat carefully lifting the chess game so as not to disturb the pieces, shrugged his shoulders, and with as simple a look on his face as he could muster started to shuffle off back down the street towards where Tom had by now disappeared himself. Initially, Roy hesitated but then also rose and set off after Mack. The man looked at Roy almost willing him to object, but Roy just looked the man straight in the eyes with that cold emotionless stare of his and went on his way.

The man then signalled to one of the groups down the street and while, one of the men then walked towards the first two, the other two men made their way towards the back of the house. That was fine with Tom because that meant that while they now had two men heading to the back of the house, the three remaining would standpoint left, right and centre from the front. That in turn meant that when they were in place the second group of three would move towards the house.

Logic suggested that Milicic would be in that second group. The arrogant sod was so confident of there being no interference that he wanted the pleasure of telling Papa his fate himself.

What was not fine with Tom was the numbers, so he made a decision.

'Sean – it's Tom – can you speak?'

'Hi, Tom – it looks as though things are going to get interesting real soon. I have two armed men taking up positions out the back of the house. Looks like they are here just in case Papa makes a break for it – but it also looks like they will not be expecting much trouble. They have just lit up fags.'

'Ok. Do you think you can take them down, and quietly

when I give you the signal?'

'Your wish is my command Colonel Sir!' came the instant reply.

There were times when Tom wished the Irishman was not so confident – at least he could have complained about the odds. But not Sean. Tom had never asked where the Irishman had learned his trade and the truth was, he probably did not want to know. He knew from the past that he could rely on the Irishman to do the job where the use of violence was involved. What he could not rely on was the mess he would leave behind, but Tom had more important things to worry about.

The second group of three men started to come down the street. It looked quite comical. The one in the centre was obviously General Ilic Milicic. He walked down the middle of the street, while his two lieutenants strode to his left and right but a few paces behind. Rather like the commander of an invading force taking possession of a valuable asset – except that he had no force and there was no asset.

It was starting to get dark, but no lights were on except in Papa's house which indicated the locals had an idea what was going on and preferred not to have anything to do with it.

The three met up with the man standing in front of the door, exchanged a few words, and then things started to happen. There was no polite knock on the door. One of the thugs simply charged the door and booted it off its hinges. Then the three men – this time with Milicic in the rear rushed into the house.

'Now' whispered Tom into his communicator, and then without pause signalled to Mack and Roy to move. The three men remaining in the street were so busy concentrating on what was happening in the house that the two on the opposite side of the street neither heard nor saw what hit them. They were expendable and they silently slid to the ground immobilized, the life choked out of them by the skilful use of the garrotte made of catgut which compressed the jugular vein.

However, one of them let out a last choking gasp and that caused the man at the front of the house to whip around drawing his gun. Before he could sound a warning, Tom hit him with the butt of his pistol. Tom grabbed him as he fell and then expertly trussed him up with a reel of tape and gagged him with the necktie that he had been wearing as part of his disguise.

Now the odds were better. If Sean had done his job, even more so.

They cautiously entered the house. All the noise was coming from up the stairs where they could hear a female voice pleading 'Staćemo ti mi. Mi nismo uradi li ništa'—What do you want us for? – we have done nothing!' but in a resigned tone of voice that signalled that she had not much hope.

One of the Serbs – presumably, General Milicic—responded with 'Umukni kucko – Shut up bitch.'

Tom nodded toward the two doors that led off the hallway and Mack and Roy quickly each went to a door listened for a moment and then quietly opened them. Nothing. Tom nodded and signalled towards the stairs, motioned Roy to stay as a guard and he and Mack crept up the stairs.

At the top of the stairs, all the doors were open, so it was not hard to find out what was happening. But there was no time to wait.

The General was standing with hands-on-hips in the middle of the room that was immediately ahead of them. He was talking to a man of about sixty years of age who had been hit with some force because he was holding the left side of his head and blood was seeping through his fingers. This man was clearly 'Papa' and the debate seemed to be about whether Mama would accompany them. There was no doubt that Milicic and his other two cronies intended to take Papa. 'Na noge matori—Get to your feet old man' and then 'Netreba Nam tvoja žena želimo tebe—We do not want your wife—we want you.' In the end, Papa, who was sprawled on the couch issued a defiant 'Ne! – No!'

Milicic just shrugged. He levelled his revolver at Mama who was at his left although Tom could not see her from the position that he was in. 'Uredu onǒa oe umreti ovde. Štagod ti želis —So she can die here. Please yourself.'

Then things got slightly out of control. Mack launched himself through the door hitting Milicic like a Big Mac truck sending him sprawling onto the floor and pinning him under his huge frame.

'So, you want to shoot the old lady? – Well not on my watch you don't.'

Tom rushed into the room and had no choice but to shoot the thug standing to the left as he was about to shoot at Mack. The man never got the gun up to a shooting angle but as Tom entered the room, he did manage to change its position and pulled the trigger as he was thrown backward by the force of the bullet. The bullets from the Serbian just missed Tom but he heard a yell from behind him and spun round in time to see Roy take a couple just below the knee.

He had not anticipated any injuries. He took a quick look around the room and then froze. Where had the other guy come from?

'Baci oružije! Drop your weapon' the Serb said in a chilling voice. The third Serbian man had come up behind the group – Tom could not fathom out how, but he had done just that – but it was now too late.

Slowly Tom placed his pistol on the ground and stood

up. Mack, who was still pinning Milicic to the floor had at no stage drawn his weapon, so he just stayed where he was. The third Serbian seemed very nervous and more than a little unsure of what to do, but he appeared very resolute, and Tom was not about to test him out. Roy was still lying on the floor groaning in pain, and the two old people just sat on their chairs petrified and more than a little confused.

Tom turned to the Serb and steadied his voice.

'Now you don't want to do anything silly – you're in enough trouble as it is.'

He then glanced over the man's shoulder. But the Serb took that to be an attempt to confuse or distract him and he just sneered.

'Vilo pametno Ali tako me nećeś pevariti —Very clever but I will not fall for that one and motioned Tom to get out of the way so that he could get a clear line of sight to where Mack and Milicic were sprawled on the floor. It was an unfortunate error of judgment on the part of the Serb. When Tom had looked over the Serb's shoulder, he was looking for some way out. What he did not expect to see, but was very pleased to see, was Sean O'Brien.

Sean hit the man from behind with such force that he dropped straight to the floor.

'Thank you!' said Tom.

'You're welcome!' came the reply, but Sean had already rushed over to where Roy was and examined his bullet wound. However, he soon leaped to his feet, pronouncing that there was nothing life-threatening in the injury. The look on Roy's face said otherwise but he was nonetheless relieved. Meanwhile, Tom and Mack got Milicic to his feet and tightly bound his arms behind his back.

The attention of Milicic was focused on Papa and Mama 'Posetice vas moj' prijatelji —You will hear from my

friends' he snarled and spat at the old couple. For his trouble, Sean punched him right in the mouth but that did little to calm his rage. 'A ko si sad ti—And who are you?' he roared at Tom but was ignored.
Sean filled him in.

'That is my Colonel so show some respect.' and gave him another two punches, the first in the mid-rift and the second connected with his chin as he doubled over. That quietened him down somewhat. Then Sean none too gently slapped tape over his mouth. That shut him up completely.

Tom turned to Papa and said 'Mi smo iz KROR I dobili smo porrku da vam je potreba pomec. Sada birajte możete ostati ovoe ili poći sa nama nazad na Kosovo. Sta želite—We are with the British KFOR in Kosovo, and we got the message that you may be in trouble. You now have a choice – stay here or come with us back to Kosovo. What do you want to do?'

The imploring look he got from Papa was all the answer he needed – he could not answer because tears were streaming down his face, and then he said. 'Ja govorim Engleski —I can speak English.'

'Ok—gather together a few things – no more than one small bag each—and get changed into something warm and comfortable – we have a long and difficult walk.'

The three soldiers got together to plan their extraction. It was not going to be easy. Milicic was a slippery character and would need to be watched, but they were trained for that. Someone would have to help Roy who could not walk comfortably on his own – but they were trained for that also.

What they were not too trained for was babysitting the two old people and taking them through a country that they did not expect to find hospitable. But that came with the territory. No one said it would be easy when they signed up.

Sean led them out of the house. Tom had decided that he was by far the best equipped to do this despite his earlier misgivings about his hot-headed nature. By now it was dark and there were few lights on in the street. Staying close to the walls of the houses and other buildings Sean headed back south towards the woods, following the way that they had come into the village, but this time walking in the shadow of the trees on the side of the road.

Tom marched behind Milicic with his gun drawn. Then followed Papa and Mama, and the rear-guard was made up of Mack and the one-legged Roy.

They made surprisingly rapid progress out of the village and finally arrived at the place where they had hidden their gear. The fact that Sean found it so easily put him up a couple more notches in Tom's estimation. There was no evidence that their packs had been disturbed and they quickly got back into their uniforms and installed their communications gear – known as Personal Role Radios (PRR)—checked out their weapons, and then filled in the hole and scattered the surface with leaves.

It was either a stroke of good luck or simply good bushcraft, which caused Mack to go back down towards the road to make sure that they had left no signs of their extraction behind. He came rushing back into the clearing and warned.

'We have company. Looks like six men. Quick – head for cover.'

They delved into the woods for cover, Milicic simply being felled by another blow from Sean, and the old folks simply being pushed down into the undergrowth. While Roy lay alongside Milicic covering him with his SA8o series L85 the other three spread out so that they could protect the flanks as well as deal with whoever was coming towards them. The four British soldiers were well camouflaged, but their three guests were not, so Tom gestured to Papa and Mama to stay low. In the bad mood that he was already in Roy would take care of the General.

Eventually the first of the new group raised his head out of the woods on the other side of the clearing. Tom whispered into his communicator to hold their fire. This was going to get interesting. The man was in the uniform of a Serbian police sergeant and the other five were in rough mountain clothes.

It soon became evident that the Policeman was not the one in charge. They stayed in the clearing for a moment, and then, after a brief conversation, they headed towards the rough path that Toms' party had come down earlier in the day and, just as quickly as they had arrived, they were gone. The only person that they mentioned in their brief conversation, which the Brits could quite clearly hear, was Milicic. Their only purpose was to find him.

Tom's group waited for a while until all sight and sound of the men had disappeared. Then Tom motioned his group to get to their feet but to stay just off the track.

'It looks like we have to go to plan B.' said Sean in his usual cheery way.

'What is plan B?' asked Tom but knew that was a waste of time. 'Not to follow plan A.' came the reply. That caused a lighter moment, but the situation that they were now in was far more serious. They would now have to move in the opposite direction to avoid contact with the Serbian group and that meant a far harder route over the ridge. In addition, with the Serbian group now known to be in the vicinity, they would need to travel further before they could risk calling in the Helicopter.

The Bell 212 was not an attack helicopter like the Apache AH Mk1 and had little in the ways of weapons. They certainly could not risk it being shot down. The good news was that it could carry a considerable load and the extra passengers would not be a problem.

After cleaning Roy's leg, they discovered that at least two of the bullets had passed straight through the flesh just above the knee, and with the appropriate dressing and a couple of pills to kill the worst of the pain he would be relatively ok. They were on their way.

The group slowly made their way towards the top of the ridge in the same order as they had originally exited from the village. They stopped at frequent intervals to give Roy a rest, but he seemed to be keeping up, if not improving. What surprised, and pleased all of them, was Mama. Whether it was her natural stubbornness they did not know, but she turned out to be one tough old lady.

Not so General Milicic – he was a pain in the ass. Several times he fell over and refused to get up again, motioning that he wanted his arms free. He was politely told that it was not going to happen, and each time he was dragged to his feet and told to behave. Tom was beginning to think they might be better off to just shoot the guy now – especially given the problems that NATO was having bringing those with similar backgrounds to justice even after they had been captured.

He knew that he had only to give a hint of his thoughts to the rest of the team and Milicic would be confined to the history books. But he did remove the gag that Sean had put over his mouth – Milicic was having difficulty breathing and that was fair enough. Milicic could yell if he wanted to. It was made clear to him that it would be the last sound that he would ever make.

When they did reach the ridgeline Tom had to make another decision. In their climb, they had been heading north because they had assumed that their route to the south was blocked. But they could not carry on heading north because that route would take them further into Serbian territory. They had to turn south, and preferably southeast, and head back towards the Kosovo border. The longer they stayed on the present heading the longer they would be in Serbia and that was not good.

Tom calculated that they would now be about two miles behind the Serbians assuming that they had made similar progress heading south and since it was a fair assumption that once over the ridge, they also would head south-east. So, if Toms' party also headed south-east the distance between the two groups would at least remain the same and at best would widen. That was the good news. The bad news was that they still could not call for the helicopter.

While the group rested, Tom talked over what he was thinking with Mack. Tom was not the kind of Colonel to assume that because he had the rank that made him always right. But on this occasion, Mack agreed with Tom, and they went and told the other two what was planned. With a couple of nods, they were on their way again heading south and down the ridge.

The fact that they had made the wrong choice soon became clear.

They must have travelled for little more than half a mile when a bullet ricocheted through the woods narrowly missing Milicic and embedding itself in a tree close by. They all dropped to the ground. Sean came scurrying back to Tom a glint of real excitement in his eyes.

'Someone is on the opposite ridge – I saw the flash – but for him to be able to see this far and in this light, he must have a sniper rifle – and a bloody good sight.'

The L85 was an excellent weapon that replaced the rifle and the submachine gun in the British Army. But its' range was only about four hundred yards and its' accuracy over that distance was varied. A sniper rifle could easily cover about a thousand yards although at that distance accuracy would also be a problem, especially in the poor light. There is a misconception about rifles probably brought on through the old western movies. The stated range of a rifle is maybe five hundred yards or so, and with improvements in technology making them lighter and more accurate, there should be some improvement inaccuracy. But that did not mean that anyone could hit anything much smaller than a barn door over that distance.

The strange thing was that the bullet had seemed to come closest to Milicic. Was the snipers' plan to rescue Milicic or to kill him? If it was the latter then so be it, but Tom had other lives to worry about.

'Ok - this is what we do. Mack—you and Sean have got to take the sniper out. There is enough moonlight for you to see where you are. You will have to track the sniper while looking out for the other five – that is assuming this is the same bunch of men that we saw earlier. While you do that the rest of us will head straight down the ridge so that he cannot get a good sight on us. But be aware – the range of your radio is only about five hundred yards, and probably even less in this terrain – so you could get out of communications range. When we get to the bottom of the ridge, we will be heading towards you so be sure to check before you fire. The rules of engagement are, if you run into someone south of here then he is fair game. But if you are coming back to re-join the group, then be careful.'

Sean looked a bit startled.

'Any questions?' Tom asked him.

'How are you going to manage that?' Sean asked. 'We leave you with Milicic, Roy who only has one leg, and grandpa and grandma.'

'Sean – that is the price I have to pay for being a Colonel. And someone has to watch your ass, so Mack goes with you. Now away you go and leave me to sort out this lot.'

As they disappeared south through the woods, Tom turned to the group he was left with.

'Roy – you heard all that' which was obvious since Roy was still grinning at Sean's description of their rag-tag band.

'You will have to bring up the rear, Papa can you help Roy. Mama, I want you in the middle, and I will push Milicic out in front so that if we run into any more of his so-called friends, they will shoot him first. Ok—any questions?'

There were none. The person who looked more afraid than anyone else was Milicic. Now that was strange, but in a way—comforting.

They slowly made their way straight down the hill. The PRR crackled into life twice during the descent as Mack, ever the professional reported in on their progress. The canopy was thicker the lower they went. That would make it harder for the sniper to see them, but it would also make it harder for them to see where they were going.

Milicic went rolling over again at the same time that Tom heard the crack of a rifle. Tom thundered after him and caught up with him where he had become wedged against a tree.

As he approached Milicic, Tom was not sure whether the General had been hit, or if the timing had been coincidental. Or, if Milicic had dived to avoid the bullet. It appeared that whatever had happened Milicic was either dead or knocked out. The Colonel turned towards where the others were still making their way slowly down the hill and got on the radio and spoke to Roy.

'It looks as though Milicic is wedged against a tree – you keep coming while I go and...'

The blow to the back of his head knocked him off his feet. If it wasn't for the Mark 6 combat helmet, he was convinced that he would have been dead. Fortunately, he rolled to one side just as another blow came through the air and he caught a glimpse of Milicic with his hands-free whirling a large branch of wood! From his position on the ground, the L85 was nonetheless levelled at Milicic, and he felt his finger tightening on the trigger.

Milicic was about to run when Tom heard another voice.

'Just give me the bloody chance you prick.'

It was Roy looking ashen and leaning against a tree. But still, he held the gun as steady as a rock. Tom jumped to his feet and grabbed Milicic smashing him full in the mouth and then for good measure brought his knee up into his groin. The General sank to the ground, the wind completely taken out of him.

Milicic had his hands tied firmly behind his back, but Tom did not replace the gag. He sat him down with his back against a tree. Looking him straight in the eyes he said 'I am just waiting for you to give me the excuse to finish you off right here and now. It looks as though your friends up ahead want to do the same thing. So, it's' up to you now – I don't care either way.'

Tom tied his feet together he then walked back to where Roy was still standing.

'Thanks for that – now let's take another look at that leg of yours.' With all the exertion of the trip down the ridge the wound had bled profusely, and the dressings were soaked with blood. The wound had stretched from the exercise and would need a couple of stitches to fix it. He was losing too much blood. Tom removed the dressings, applied powder from his field kit, and then rewrapped it in fresh bandages using some tape to hold them in place. That would have to do for now.

He dug a hole in the ground, placed the old dressings in, covered them, and then scrapped some leaves and forest litter over the top. Old habits die hard – they were the ones doing the following – but better to be safe than sorry.

While Tom had been attending to Roy, Papa and Mama were involved in a furious argument. Just as Papa was about to start shouting Tom ran across to them and asked what was going on. Papa, his eyes blazing.

'Tell him what you just told me.'

The old woman shook her head and started crying. Papa reached out, grabbed her shoulders, and repeated his message. Still, the tears flowed so Papa turned to Tom and explained.

'The reason General Milicic had his hands free was that Mama loosened the ties.' He reached out his hand to Tom. 'She did not want to see him suffering – she did not mean any harm – she did not think – it will not happen again.' And he returned his stare at Mama – accusatory but there was a gentleness there that Tom had never seen before. 'She has been through so much!' Papa concluded with a shrug.

Tom tapped Mama on the shoulder.

'Ok – no harm done – but please – not again. Now let us find out what is going on around here.'

Tom was unsure whether Mama knew much English, but he had more important things to worry about.

When Mack and Sean had left the group, they felt somehow free of their babysitting duties, and they reverted to what they had been trained to do. Although there was a rough track through the forest, they stayed off to the left of it, Sean taking the lead.

They had travelled about four hundred yards to the south when they saw another flash from the opposing ridge. They automatically hit the ground, but the sniper was not aiming at them. And they could not tell whether, whoever he had been aiming at, had been hit. Sean sensed rather than heard a crash in the undergrowth but could not be sure. They huddled together.

'We now know where he is. One of us must take him out or it is only a matter of time before he hits someone. The other one must provide cover. Heads or tails.' Mack laughed.

'Leave the bastard to me.' said Sean, and before Mack could answer he disappeared down towards the bottom of the ridge. Mack tried to follow at a discrete distance but had no real way of being certain, Sean was so quiet. Sean whispered occasional comments into his PRR and just hoped that Mack could follow. Eventually, Sean was at a much lower level than the sniper and through the trees, he could just make him out. He was positioned about halfway up a large pine and appeared to be facing north.

Sean then studied the surrounding terrain. It was impossible to tell but there was the possibility that other people were hiding in the undergrowth. And then he got lucky. He saw the sniper signal to his right and then to his left and in the left case, he saw a man return the signal. While Sean could only speculate on what the signals were about, there were three men in the trees on the opposite ridge. What had happened to the other three Serbians that they had met earlier on the trail? Were they here or elsewhere?

Earlier than expected he had his answer.

The local Serbs were smarter than perhaps they had given them credit for. They had split into two groups – one moving steadily on the expected exit path of Tom's group and the other leapfrogging over the ridge onto the other side. When they had eventually sited Tom's group coming down the ridge, they had established a sniper to keep them busy, while the other group circled back. The other group of Serbians was now heading north on a collision course with Tom's group.

As Mack hid in the undergrowth he radioed to Scan.

'You got a plan C? Sean—I do not think you should take out the sniper – that would give our position away – and that would not be a good idea just yet. We have three hostiles moving along this ridge – back towards Tom. We are marginally out of range of the radio – but that won't last.'

'Ok – I agree. What say you follow the three hostiles? – I'll take a parallel course from where I am now – that way I can keep an eye on our sniper friend.'

It was clear that the Serbians were well organized. They had radio contact between the two groups, they were well-armed, and they knew the territory well. Also being in two groups of three they had the advantage that they could move through the forest more efficiently. If Mack had been in the Serbian group, he would have split into three groups of two as is the way the British, and American Special Forces, would have done it. That would have given them much better coverage. That is the advantage of being a professional soldier. But the Serbs did have some advantages—they did not have a prisoner, two old folks, and a soldier with only one good leg to slow them down. That was the luck of the Irish.

Mack followed at a respectful distance until they had

covered perhaps half of the distance back to Tom's group. Then he got onto the radio.

'Tom - you have three men coming in your direction and they don't look too friendly. Where are you?'

'Hi, Mack – we are at the bottom of the ridge following a stream bed. Where is Sean?'

'He is keeping an eye on the sniper and moving in your direction.'

'Ok – so it's' show time. We'll deploy as best we can and hope we can catch them by surprise.'

Tom immediately called a halt to his little rag-tag group, and staked out his position, on the eastern side of the stream. Milicic was none to gently crashed to the ground and once more had his feet tied and a gag placed over his mouth. Papa and Mama got down into the undergrowth and Tom gave Papa his Browning and putting a finger to his lips he pointed to Milicic. Surprisingly, Papa grabbed the pistol, and then very methodically checked the safety, checked that he had a round in the chamber, and nodded. He must have had an interesting life mused Tom.

He then positioned Roy at the north end of the group, himself at the south end, and waited. The next sound he heard was Sean on the radio. 'Good position you are in, but could I suggest you withdraw your weapons a little further – I can see them in the moonlight – and something is reflecting – probably your GPS.'

Ok mused Tom – the Irishman certainly had a way to make you feel incompetent – but he was right – as usual.

Then all hell broke loose. Sean let off a volley in the direction of the sniper – and it was well-aimed because he saw the sniper fall from the tree to the ground. From the way he collapsed, he would not be taking any further part in proceedings. That unleashed a volley from the two men who were hiding in the undergrowth. But Sean had fired on the run and so their aim was both sporadic and behind where he had been. The group of Serbians that had been moving up the valley immediately aimed down the slope, but now they were at a disadvantage.

Firing downhill on a moonlit night was a bit of a problem because you were effectively firing into shadow. Not so Mack, who had deliberately remained downhill from the group that he was following. He let off a burst in the direction of the flashes from the guns of the Serbs, while Sean was now hunting the other two on the other side of the valley. When Tom saw the flashes of fire - aimed, although he did not know it, at Sean - he let go a volley of fire at the Serbs. Realizing they were caught in a trap the Serbs turned their fire on Tom's group and did get off a couple of well-aimed shots. But they were outgunned.

The automatic assault rifles used by the Serbs appeared to be Heckler & Koch HK33, but they were no match for the SA 80s of the British force. Now that positions have been established both Mack from the south and Tom from the north strafed their positions with lethal fire and within seconds they were silenced. The two men who had been supporting the sniper had enough and took off, surprisingly to the northeast. Sean saw no point in pursuing them and returned to link up with Mack.

He stopped briefly to check out what remained of the bodies – which included the Serb policeman – then linked up with Tom on the stream bed.

'What the fuck happened to you?' said Mack as he walked up to Tom.

'What are you talking about?' he asked.

'Well apart from the bruise on the side of your face and the emerging black eye, your guts look shot to pieces.'

It was only then that Tom realized the seriousness

of what Mack was talking about. He groaned.

'It looks like we have a bit of a problem.'

The bullets had torn through the webbing and smashed into the GPS unit. Was it not for the GPS unit, Tom would now be dead or seriously wounded? That thought brought a shrug from the Colonel – they had other more serious problems. Now they would have difficulty establishing their precise position for the pickup.

Tom pulled out a couple of maps and under a pencil light, he tried to establish where they were and where they wanted to be. There was the main road between them and the border – well the so-called border – whichever way they went. The road itself went from Vucja—which was theoretically in Kosovo—to Rozaj which was in Montenegro. But for the majority of its' length, the road was in Serbia. To the southeast of that was the road that ran to Kosavska and that was in Kosovo. That is where they should go.

Typical of the terrain in this part of the world it was mountainous and heavily wooded. The forest cover would help them with concealment. The mountainous terrain would slow them down.

'Ok—here is our plan.' he said to the three soldiers, taking care that they were not overheard by Milicic and the old people – he was going to take no chances with them after the earlier experience.

'Our general direction will be south-east. We should try to drift near the bottom of the ridges to make it easier on you Roy. When we come to the road, we cross when it is clear to do so and then we head south. Any questions?'

Mack and Sean exchanged glances and then Mack spoke.

'Do we have a problem with our guests?' he asked –

noticing for the first time that Milicic was gagged again and strung up like a turkey. And so, Tom told the other two what he and Roy already knew – the events that led to the Milicic attack on Tom. Both smouldered.

'Why don't we kill Milicic and abandon grandma and grandpa to their fate?' Sean summed up the feeling of the three of them.

Tom could have sympathized with that feeling when he had been a corporal all those years ago. He was now a recently promoted Colonel and he had a job to do.

'Because Sean, this is not the IRA. We do not sit in judgment – that's not our job. We return with General Milicic and hand him over to the authorities. As for the old folks – I asked them if they wanted to come. They said Yes. So, we complete the job. Now – any questions?'

All three nodded. As did Papa who was sitting not too far away to not have noticed, and got the drift of, the exchange. He limited English language told him al that he needed to know. And body language is the same all over the world.

The team got wearily to their feet, undid the ties on Milicic feet – but not those on his hands or the gag, and set off. This time Mack took the lead position with Sean being assigned to watch Milicic, then followed Roy with the old couple and Tom bringing up the rear. The only problem that Tom could foresee was that the two remaining members of the group that had been following them earlier would have radioed through for further help. They would also have a fair idea in which direction Tom's force would now be heading. More importantly, they now knew the firepower they were up against. While they could not hope to match it, they could deal with it with manpower.

This time Tom had it right.

Mack came upon the road quite unexpectedly and immediately radioed the news to Tom.

'We've got company.'

They settled down in the undergrowth while Tom went forward to survey the options. The Serbs had what looked like two old ex-soviet UAZ-469 all-terrain vehicles – similar to the Jeep – of surprising reliability for soviet vehicles – and they were parked off the side of the road. The drivers were discussing something, but Tom could not hear what it was. Then one of them got into the driving seat and proceeded north but at a fairly slow speed.

Sean suggested a way to deal with the latest hold-up. The Serbs – if they were indeed working in cahoots with the ones who had been trying to find them—were expecting them to be further north than they were. So why not make them happy?

Fifteen minutes later the vehicle which had headed north, and which was now returning had its' right front tire blown apart by a single round of fire from Sean hiding in the undergrowth. At first, the vehicle carried on as if nothing had happened then suddenly somersaulted end over end and finished up in the ditch at the roadside and upside down. As one of the men tried to exit the vehicle he was pinged by another single shot and quickly retreated inside the vehicle. At that stage, the chance of the Serbs thinking it was an accident caused by a tire blow-out evaporated.

The driver of the other vehicle heard the noise and the Serbs jumped in and headed north at rapid speed. Tom's group waited a few seconds, carefully scanning the road south to make sure there were no other people around, issued a few terse instructions to his band to make it quick, then rushed down to the road and across it, Mack virtually carrying Milicic and Tom doing the same for Roy.

They almost made it undetected.

No one had the time to take care of the old folks and it was assumed that they would take care of themselves. As they plunged into the undergrowth on the opposite side of the road, Mama suddenly turned and started back across the road that they had just crossed. Roy was the first to see her and yelled to her to come back. She either did not hear or did not understand. It was too late.

A volley of fire came down the road. Mama dropped into a crumpled heap in the middle of the road. There was little doubt from the way she fell, that she was already dead before her body hit the ground.

Papa immediately rose from the undergrowth to go to her aid, but Mack grabbed him before he could take a step and held him tight.

'It's no use' he said gently. 'What in the name of heaven possessed her to do that?'

Papa's face was deathly white.

'She was checking a contact address in Albania' he said quietly. 'She had it in her hand when the Colonel said to go, and she must have dropped it. You have to understand – she does not speak much English.'

The old man could not retain his composure any longer, and he collapsed in a series of heartfelt sobs.

'Come on, we have to go.' said Tom as gently as he could.

Papa let out a couple more sobs and then rose and stuck out his chest. 'Ok' was all he said.

The look in his eyes said something different.

The emergence of Mama from the east side of the road and the gunshots that had come from the west side of the road must have confused the Serbs. After the initial shot which had caused the crash, there had only been one other shot, which caused the driver of the second vehicle to run back down the road suspecting what had taken place – they had been tricked. What he saw was someone running across the road in the opposite direction to that which he would have expected – but he fired off a volley anyway. At that short-range, and with a body in plain view, he could hardly miss.

He would not have expected to find the body of an old woman, particularly at this time of night. People often crisscrossed the border to visit relatives caught up in the dispute, but not usually at night, and not usually this old. And so, he panicked, dragging the body off the road and into the dense undergrowth. By the time he had returned to the crash scene Sean had long since crossed over the road leaving the Serbs to work out what had gone wrong as they looked west – wrongly – for the answer. If there was any advantage to be gained by Mama's untimely, sudden, and sad death, it was that she gave the rest of their group something she no longer had. Time.

Sean caught up with the group, not more than half a mile from where they had left the road.

'Where is Grandma?' was his first question. Tom quietly told him what had happened, and then had to hush him as he let rip with a barrage of profanities. He then went forward, putting his arm around Papa and squeezing his shoulders, and then went up to Milicic who was trudging along ahead of Roy, and gave him a rabbit punch that brought him to his knees yet again. He then dragged him to his feet and kicked him none too gently in the rear. That caused Milicic to stumble and then turn with a snarl on his face – but then he saw the cold stare out of the Irishman's eyes and thought better of what he was about to say – the fact that he could not talk anyway escaped them both.

They came upon the Kosovska road almost in the same way as they had the previous road. This time there were no Serbians to greet them. Again, Tom surveyed the land. About a half-mile to the west was a cutting through the hills where the builders of the road could not go around or over, so they had dug a bluff out and put the road through there. It was almost daylight so they had a clear marker which would have to do in the absence of a GPS fix. Tom brought out his radio and tuned it to the channel that he wanted.

'Good morning, Eric.' was all he said.

'Where have you been? The Major is going crazy!' was Wilkinson's response.

'Never mind about the Major.' replied Tom. 'I believe we are on the Kosovska road. And I think we are just about on the border. We would not mind a lift. Our GPS is shot so we will be unable to let you know our position. We are going to head east towards a cutting – but we will be off-road a little in case there are any more hostiles around. When you come in, land on the road. We have one prisoner and one friend who wants a lift.'

'What the fuck happened?' came the reply.

He would have to do something about troop discipline, Tom thought, especially where the language was concerned – but later.

'Could you just get that bird of yours into the air and come and get us the hell out of here. There will be plenty of time to tell you about our little walk back.' Tom was not in the mood for small talk.

'Roger that – I am on the way – I should be with you in less than thirty minutes.' and Eric cut the connection.

Helicopters do not just take off – they have to go through

pre-flight checks, otherwise, Eric would have been picking them up much sooner.

It was not his fault that the delay would prove costly.

Tom gathered the group of three together and told them the plan – they would stay about ten yards into the trees on the north side of the road so that they could see and not be seen and make their way to the bluff. As Sean was getting a little rough with Milicic, Mack took over the babysitting duties – Sean's term for it – and Sean was assigned to track ahead and between the group and the road. A truck trundled along the road from time to time but nothing of any concern, and they made good progress. They were almost at the point that Tom was aiming for when Sean came on the radio.

'We have a couple of vehicles coming east and they do not look too friendly.'

Tom immediately signalled to the group to stop and again they took up a defensive posture, this time without any instruction. Tom then responded to Sean.

'Say again – how do you know who they are?'

'They are Serbian – that's all I can tell you. There is a Jeep-type vehicle and a truck which looks like an old troop carrier. They are cruising along and looking for something or someone. Looks a bit over the top for a rabbit shoot.'

'Ok. Make sure you are well hidden. In this early morning light, we should not be so easy to spot. Let's hunker down' Tom said as he signalled to the group to keep down.

They melted into the undergrowth. Papa and Milicic were made to lie down, with Papa still hanging on to the pistol, and leaving little doubt that he would use it, whether, or not, he had to. The other three were wearing camouflage but they just hid their weapons so that the shape did not give them away. Sean was somewhere east and further towards the road, but he could look after himself.

Slowly the vehicles came down the road towards them. In the front seat of the Jeep a guy in uniform was surveying to his left through a pair of what looked like military issue binoculars—and looking to his left made sense—the terrain to his right was very steep and would offer little in the way of cover. In the following truck, the person in the passenger seat was focused on something further up the road but from Tom's position, he was unable to see what it was. As they came alongside where the British were hiding the group hardly dared breathe as the man with the binoculars seemed to have a double-take on the undergrowth to the east of where Roy was stationed but he eventually moved his search further up the road and moved on. Mack just exchanged a raised eyebrow with Tom, then whispered.

'Are you sure we are on the correct side of the border?'

Tom just smiled and replied.

'How the hell should I know?'

Then his smile vanished. They heard the steady whirring of a helicopter as it slowly came towards them – and it was coming from the east. He did not know if it was Eric, or were they indeed on the wrong side of the border, and was it a Serbian helicopter? There was such a mixture of fighting men and fighting machines in this part of the world, that it could be anyone. But the Serbians were as confused as the British. They just drove straight off the road and under the trees and killed their motors.

The standard procedure for an armed force in these circumstances would be to evacuate the vehicles and disperse. And that is exactly what they did. 'Sweet mother of Jesus – have you got room for one more where you are?' It was Sean. Tom just clicked his communicator once.

No point in replying in voice if Sean was as close to the Serbians as Tom suspected. However, a couple of minutes later Sean reappeared in the middle of the group with a big grin on his face.

‘Shit that was close! Another couple of inches and you would be attending my wake – fancy being killed in a road accident!’

They now had a problem. If it was Eric in the helicopter, they now had the Serbians between them and their means of rescue. So, they either had to wait them out and wave Eric off or become involved in yet another firefight. Tom took a couple of seconds to make up his mind.

He would warn him off.

But he never got to communicate that decision.

Things seemed to happen all at once. First Mack reported that hostiles were approaching from the east, and it was only a matter of minutes before he had to decide whether to fire. It was too late to retreat. Secondly, some idiot in the Serbian force saw the helicopter coming towards them – recognized it as KFOR machine – well non-Serbian – and started shooting at it before a degree of sanity prevailed. But it was too late to avoid the fight that was to follow.

The Bell 212 has several characteristics. It is relatively well shielded against small arms fire. It has a good climbing rate for a craft of its size and weight – and it only had a light load. It can carry L91A1 submachine guns – and it did.

It rose rapidly as Eric got on the radio to Tom.

‘Where are you? We are under fire from the ground.’

From the helicopter, Lennon let loose a blast of fire which silenced the shooter, but she was not sure whether she had just frightened him off, or whether he had simply ceased firing.

Tom answered the call from Eric.

'A couple of hundred yards east – on the other side of those who did the shooting – they are Serbians. And we are just about to engage them.' 'Bugger!' said Wendy. Fuck! Eric thought.

As a couple of volleys were exchanged on the ground between the two groups, Eric wheeled the Bell round in a wide arc from his new position about five hundred yards from the ground to just above where he judged Tom and his men were. Then he saw one of the Serbian men standing about one hundred yards from what appeared to be a truck on the edge of the woods and holding a white flag.

'Tom – what the hell is going on? A man is heading towards you with a white flag!'

Things on the ground were getting a little bit testy. After firing a withering burst of fire, one of the Serbians who had been approaching Mack's position suddenly stood up and held a white flag as he moved back towards the road. Mack called to Tom.

'Looks like a trap to me. We have hostiles moving further into the woods – seems like they are trying to outflank us while we deal with this guy.'

'Ok – whistle a couple of rounds over his head and keep him pinned.' Then he got on the radio to Eric. 'Our situation is becoming hopeless. Forget the man with the white flag and get Wendy to strafe his position. Can you land on the road as close to where we are as possible – we have got to get out of here and quick.'

'Roger that – coming in now – keep your heads down – Wendy will provide covering fire.'

The Bell dropped like a stone until it was only a foot off the road. Lennon fired off a volley down the road although she could not see a target. 'Come on – come on.' Eric muttered 'Let's get them out of here.'

But Tom had another problem. After he had spoken to Eric his idea was that he, Mack, and Sean would provide cover while they evacuated Milicic, Papa, and Roy who was by now so weak from the loss of blood he was no real use in a fight. He rushed up to where Milicic and Papa were hiding and told them to get up and run towards the road. Milicic did not move.

But this time he was not just being a pain up the ass. He was not responsive. He signalled to Mack to grab Milicic which he did in a fireman-style carry and rushed towards the Helicopter. By this time, they were under attack from the north as well as the east, and the difficulty was that the helicopter was of no use because they still could not see any target. Mack reached the helicopter threw Milicic in, turned, and pushed Papa in after him, and then much more gently helped Roy in, and then rushed back to the woods. Tom and Sean were well pinned down but were holding the Serbians at bay.

'Ok' said Tom 'here's what happens now. We hose the woods with fire while we all retreat to the edge of the road. Eric – lift about ten feet so that Wendy can fire over our heads. Then we go Sean, Mack, and then me—one at a time, and in that order. Get aboard and then provide covering fire from there. Any questions?'

Sean was about to say something but saw the steely look in Tom's eyes, and just said 'Ok boss!'

Tom replied with a grin despite the situation that they were in.

'Shit—there is always a first time for everything! An Irishman takes an order without question! Ok—let's do this – go-go-go.'

With two of them providing ground fire and the cover provided by Wendy it was not too bad. Sean made it without incident. And then Mack moved to the road and turned and dived for the helicopter leaving only Tom providing fire of any real substance. The covering fire from behind was fine but the Serbs quickly sensed that the fire from the helicopter would be too high for fear of hitting their own man. And so, they could now concentrate from three sides and Tom was under heavy fire.

'Come on Tom – come on!' whispered Mack, while trying to pick targets in the dense undergrowth. Not a good time to lose your boss – so close to rescue was criminal. The radio cracked into life once more. It was Tom.

'Eric – take her up one more time so that Wendy and the gang can strafe the trees. Quickly!'

Wilkinson's first response was to refuse. But he saw the logic. If the troops got off a withering burst of fire it was the only chance Tom had, provided Eric immediately dropped the helicopter and provided Tom withdrew in time. It was all a matter of precise timing. If Tom got it wrong, he was dead. If Lennon and the troops were still firing when Eric dropped the chopper back to the ground, then Colonel Tom Dean would be killed by his own men. And, if Eric got the drop wrong – well they were all in trouble.

The radio crackled and this time it was Eric.

'Ok – you all know what we have to do. I'll take her up then count to three and then back down. Let's go.'

As it turned out the plan worked to perfection. Almost.

As soon as the Helicopter rose, a withering burst was let loose covering the trees in a ninety-degree arc, Wendy concentrating on firing above Tom's head, and Mack, Sean, and Roy firing to both sides. Then Eric immediately dropped back down, and a deathly silence seemed to settle over the battle area apart from the steady whirring of the chopper blades.

At last, Tom ran from the woods threw his weapon to Mack and leaped at the landing rail which he clung onto and yelled 'Take her up.'

Wilkinson responded immediately taking them rapidly up and east, but not before a scare. While Mack and Sean struggled to pull Tom into the cabin the Serbs had one last burst of fire from the ground and with the sudden jerk and grimace from Tom it was very clear that he had been hit.

They finally got him on board to survey the damage. It was probable that it was only the angle of fire that had saved his life. A total of six bullets had hit him, three in the right leg, one in the back, and two in the left shoulder. The one in the back had made a mess of the uniform but then it met the body armour and was not a problem. The shoulder would also not be a problem because the bullets had passed right through and then bounced off his combat helmet. A couple of inches to the left and his head, and Tom, would have been history.

The right leg was another story. The sooner he was in the hands of the medical staff the better. He would be able to walk. But with a limp for the rest of his life.

Despite his injuries, Colonel Tom Dean turned his attention to the rest of the group. The soldiers had been fairly hyped up during the action but were now arrayed on either side of the cabin scanning the ground, firearms at the ready, but now more relaxed.

Papa was staring up ahead no doubt thinking of life without Mama – but at peace. Tom then glanced at Milicic who was slumped in a heap in the corner. Mack caught his eye, switched on his communicator since the noise made by the helicopter made normal conversation virtually impossible.

'Milicic is dead – he took one in the head during that little interchange.'

'What a fucking waste of time!' said Tom as he scanned his men.

Only Papa smiled.

Chapter 31

Deduction

Several scenarios could explain what had happened but right now none of the commentaries seemed to make any sense to Mark. As the commentators on CNN droned on it became clear that they, and the officials whose views they were reporting on, were in the same position. Nobody knew anything substantial, and they were just guessing.

Nobody had claimed responsibility, so the initial thinking that had suggested al Qaeda was beginning to wane. The whole point of a terrorist attack was to let someone know who the players were, and that those players meant business – well harm – to the people and the country that had been subject to the attack. But there had just been nothing.

Mark decided that, while Annette was asleep, he would quietly and methodically go through what he knew, or thought he knew, and then review those positions against what was coming over the news channel.

One thing was quite simple and crystal clear. Someone had organized an attempt to explode three bombs in New York City. They had succeeded in causing serious damage, injuring people, and loss of life with two of the explosions. The third bomb had exploded harmlessly over the Central Park reservoir because of the intervention by Mark and Paul. That bomb could have caused more serious damage and more loss of life if Annette had been allowed to go ahead as planned. At least Annette had survived and would no longer be consigned to a life after death with the dubious company of numerous virgins.

The timing of the explosions had been unnervingly all too familiar. They had been planned to explode at the same times as the original 9/11 events – at 8:46 am, 9:03 am and 9:37 am – albeit the original explosions had been far more catastrophic and spread between the Twin Towers of the World Trade Centre in New York City and the Pentagon in Washington.

There was no way that the events could have been random – they had been very carefully planned and timed for maximum impact, if not in their size, but certainly in the minds of the citizens of New York City. But by who?

Looking at the events from what Mark understood to be Brad's point of view this was the work of al Qaeda. While working for Taylor Software, Brad had been gathering information from the Augem Group. The very reason he was working for Taylor Software was that Taylor Software had the Augem account. And Taylor Software had commercial and valid reasons to monitor the Augem system. Therefore, it was the perfect cover. It was from the Augem system that Brad had latched onto information that tied someone in the Augem Group to communicating with someone involved in a plan to cause harm at some time, at someplace. This information Brad had passed on to his masters at the CIA. They had, or were supposed to, pass it on to the FBI, who in turn had chosen to ignore it, or had buried it, or did not think that there was a sufficient threat to take any action.

Although Mark had no way of knowing how his father had first become involved, Brad had somehow revealed to Harold Taylor that he had information. And he must have indicated that the information had not been thought of by the CIA as being particularly significant to warrant any further action.

Had Harold believed Brad and ignored the opinion of his masters at Langley?

It was not unusual in the security business for disagreements to arise, especially on whether or not to take seriously any particular threat. There were plenty of threats to choose from and, contrary to popular belief, there was not an inexhaustible supply of agents out in the field to track them all down. Many that were tracked to their logical, or illogical conclusion, would prove inconclusive at best. So why had Harold latched onto this particular threat?

The only conclusion that made any sense was that Harold also had some other information, from God knows where that confirmed what Brad had alluded to. Mark had no way of knowing why his father had dreamed up a scheme that would involve him. Mark had nothing to do with the CIA, the FBI, or any other part of the intelligence service. The only conclusion for this part of the puzzle could be that he was extremely worried about the reliability of his CIA colleagues.

Whatever the reasoning, Mark, and Brad had been to Rabaul PNG where they had discovered, much to everyone's apparent surprise, a cell that was a conduit for information and money. They had confirmed that this was the cell that someone in the Augem Group was communicating with and confirmed that the cell was part of the Jemaah Islamiyah terrorist organization. There was a connection between this group and al Qaeda, but was that a connection that made al Qaeda responsible for the horrific events that had occurred in New York City? Mark thought that this was highly unlikely.

The information gathered from this source in Rabaul was passed on to Harold and Brad's masters at the CIA. It was reasonable to assume that it was in turn passed on to the FBI. Either these organizations were too slow to react, or the information was not believed, or they chose to ignore it, or some felt that the timing was wrong, or someone chose to bury it. Mark did not know which, or which combination, of these various scenarios, applied in this case. But why, when a senior CIA officer of Harold Taylor's rank, had gone to some trouble to obtain the proof he needed, had nothing been done? That did not make any sense.

The raising of a threat level, or alert level, does not in itself do that much, contrary to popular belief. Moving an organization from a Code Green to Code Red, or from level 3 to 4 does not give that organization any more resources. Some would say they just spin faster.

Looking at it from Mark's point of view, the story was more complicated and at the same time more confusing. That complication and that confusion were caused by the involvement of John Dubois. He was not like your average terrorist. He was not the least bit concerned about money – he had more than enough. He did not appear to have any connection with Islam or any other religious organization. He had no feelings religious or otherwise. He was of middle eastern origin—but so were many hundreds of thousands of people who left or fled their homes to make the USA their future home. He was not an extremist or anything of that nature. He was simply a businessman. So why was he involved in the recruitment of at least one of the suicide bombers, and probably all three?

Well, it was not exactly recruitment – was it? It was

more like coercion.

And what was the connection with General Ilic Milicic, which in turn led to the puzzling connection to Mario Tudjman? It was of course entirely feasible that there was an experience, or a series of experiences, buried deep in the past of John Dubois. The profiling group at the FBI could do a better analysis if they had access to enough information, but to Mark, the whole thing also simply made no sense. Whatever those experiences were, they were enough to mean that he would find the opportunity to wreak havoc. But why?

There could be any one of several reasons for the involvement of Dubois, and Mark tried to puzzle his way through them. Ideology was the obvious one – it was certainly the strongest motivational force. Yet John was not religious and there was just no evidence that he was motivated by anything except money.

So – what about money? John appeared to have plenty, and it was hard to see how any amount of money could be acquired because of such an irrational act, and from who? The only people who stood to gain from this act were al Qaeda and they were not exactly flush with funds.

What if Paul had been correct in his ramblings about an Executive Order and that politics was the reason? The Presidents ratings would inevitably increase, as they always did in times of stress. But that would assume that John Dubois was working for the President and somehow Mark could not see that happening.

The other possibility was that Dubois was simply mentally unbalanced, or to use the none-PC term, a fruitcake. Again, Mark did not think so. John Dubois may be delusional and had after all recruited an unwilling Annette into his scheme, but he had the support of people who would know better and would not want to deal with him. While the events that he had been involved in were insane to the average man, there was nonetheless an amount of rationality and organization to the whole episode. And what did that leave? Ego, Prestige. Revenge, Conscience – all things that Mark could know nothing about and matters that even the top profilers at the FBI wrestled with. Was there something in Johns' past that had provoked him to organize so bizarre a response? What would this do to his ego, how would he gain any prestige when no one knew of his involvement, what event could trigger an act of revenge and against who, what event of either right or wrong could such an act salve? There was something in Johns' past – probably more than one thing – that had led to this event, or there was a combination of all of the above.

If there were to be some historical reason, one possibility was that John Dubois had been recruited into the ranks of al Qaeda and wanted to now make a statement that he was a serious player. He could have recruited three people who were extremists, or were simply mad, and planned the whole thing himself. When one of his recruits pulled out for whatever reason, then he had simply used his contacts to recruit Annette.

Not being religious, and not being emotive – Mark had long since formed the view that Dubois was almost without a soul. He would see using Annette as simply a means to an end – sick though that end may be. It had all the appearances of an operation that was not particularly professional, as alluded to by Paul in his earlier assessment. Had that been the reason why the intelligence services had chosen to ignore it? The conclusion, all things being considered, was no doubt that John Dubois was a small player and an amateur, playing a very dangerous game, in a big man's professional league.

And then there was Paul's view. Paul had changed his mind somewhat since the earlier analysis and conclusion that he had reached in Wellington. There was the scenario that Paul had alluded to in Washington—irrespective of what the cell was, or who had been responsible for it, there could have been an executive order to let the plan go ahead despite the warnings and the risks. In which case, it did not matter if Jemaah Islamiyah, al Qaeda, John Dubois, or Mickey Mouse was behind it. The damage had been done – well two-thirds of the planned damage – and now followed all the political posturing that was at least one result of such an occurrence. The President had addressed the Nation several times as different pieces came together and in response to different reactions around the world and had said almost exactly what Paul had predicted.

'Did I not warn that the battle against al Qaeda was not yet won – and this event proves that they can strike anyhow, anytime, and anywhere. The American people will not bow to such terrorist activity. We will resolutely pursue the people responsible for these acts of terrorism, with every means at our disposal, and punish them and their associates.'

But the President—any President—would have said pretty much the same thing irrespective of whether he had any prior knowledge. The question was – Was there an executive order?

Having considered all the issues, Mark thought it highly unlikely that there had been any such order. While such apparent action would cause an immediate surge in his support – would that be sustainable? Support for the War on Terrorism and support for more troops and money for the defence was commendable. But would that over-shadow the risk?

If the President's ratings in the opinion polls were low

before the event, they would certainly rapidly deteriorate if word got out that he had taken no action and had ignored earlier warnings. More so if he issued executive orders that the warnings should be ignored. In the modern age, where leaks were almost par for the course, surely no President would take such a huge risk? To cover up such an event required the knowledge and cooperation of many people from many different departments of the state. Despite the establishment of the Directorate of National Intelligence after September 11th,2001 to bring together and coordinate all the various elements of the intelligence community, that Directorate was only seen at the Presidential level.

There were still many organizations that had their own agendas, competing for limited funding and therefore recognition. Such organizations jealously guarded their territory and the original problem had been, and always would be, get them all to cooperate openly. Well, as openly as the intelligence business allowed. Imagine what could happen if just one part of this vast bureaucracy, or just one disgruntled person within that bureaucracy, had the information on a cover-up. They could wreak havoc and destroy so many people right the way up to the Boss. Would they not want to use that snippet of information to promote their own agenda? Or to get one up on their competitors. Or to just simply twist the knife into someone's back?

They did not need to have reasons that would ever make it onto the President's desk. Something as simple as the acrimonious termination of a sexual affair, or a perceived prejudice, or a missed promotion—all would do the trick. And that was only considering the people who were supposed to know! The only way to keep something secret is to tell nobody. But then – what was the point of having a secret?

The media also had a role to play, and they did not worry too much about sources, agendas, territory, or one-up-man-ship. They just reported what the public demanded to hear, even when the public didn't know about it until it was reported.

Mark was back to the original proposition. He felt that the story had not made it as high as the President or at least as high as the office of the Director of National Intelligence. Someone or some group within the two organizations that he had contact with and had himself provided information to – that was the CIA and the FBI – had sought to cover up the information at a lower level. They had either succeeded, or their purpose had been adequately met by the ineptitude of the organizations concerned. Or the bureaucracy itself was just too scared to make a decision. Or they simply passed the parcel on to someone else.

All of these scenarios were possible!

Brad Morgan had raised his concerns with his masters while he was still on the Taylor payroll – well on two payrolls. That had somehow alerted the Augem Group. And they had taken steps to deal with the problem as they saw it. Consequently, Taylor Software was no longer involved with the Augem system. Morgan was no longer involved with Taylor Software. Someone had made sure Mark was incapacitated while they checked his office. The latter was a pointless exercise, but they could not have known that.

Unless Brad was part of their cover-up!

Mark was satisfied that Brad was not. Mark's trip to Wellington and then to Rabaul had been covert and as far as he could tell, very few people knew where he had been and what he had done. It was unlikely that those responsible for ignoring Brad's earlier concerns were aware of Mark's trip or his involvement. It was highly probable that they knew of his relationship with Harold Taylor. It was unlikely that they paid much attention to it. That is until after Mark returned to the USA. Or just before his return.

In which case what was the role of Harold Taylor?

Mark and Brad had returned from the trip down-under with important new information and had reported it to the appropriate people at the CIA. At Langley, the information flow had come to a shuddering halt. The reason for this could be that Mark and Brad were quite simply not believed. Or that the people they talked to were inept. Or that these were the people involved in a cover-up.

The first reason was implausible given the nature of their information, its' origin, and the source. The second reason – based on Mark's personal experience – was proven beyond any doubt, but it still did not make much sense as a reason. Therefore, the third reason was the most obvious.

Someone, somewhere, in the complex world of the Federal government, was involved in a cover-up.

There was a common thread to the whole thing. John Dubois.

What was the role of Dubois? And how come he was able to have such a strong influence over the FBI and probably the CIA?

When Henderson of the FBI had visited Mark's office after the break-in there was something suspicious about him. Or was Mark being overly sensitive just because Henderson was an arrogant prick.

Mark was not aware of anything else that specifically involved the FBI other than the obvious – they should have been involved if there was a threat to life on American soil. Brad reported to his CIA masters but surely the FBI would get the same information. Yet nothing had happened. Similarly, surely the FBI would be immediately informed of any information coming to hand concerning a real or a perceived threat. If they had been informed of new information on Mark's return from down under then they also were either inept, or they were involved in a cover-up. Therefore, there was a group of people in both the CIA and the FBI who were involved.

The scary thought was that they had to be at an appropriate level in the organization to make it work.

Then there was the involvement of General Ilic Milicic. The General would logically have nothing to do with either the CIA or the FBI. In the case of the CIA, Milicic had nothing to do with what they were about. His indiscretions in and around Serbia were matters for NATO and the war crimes people. In the case of the FBI, Milicic had even less to do with what they were about since he was still in Serbia. That is, apart from occasions when FBI forensic experts had been invited to assist with analysis of dead bodies for which Milicic may or may not have been responsible.

It appeared that the General was an associate of John Dubois. Nothing that Mark had uncovered indicated how or why. Maybe his involvement was quite simply limited to involvement with Annette—nee Anna. This tenuous link was nonetheless significant at least as far as Mark was concerned if only, he could find the reason.

Then there was the question of the role of Mario Tudjman. Like General Milicic, Mario was a Serb. But apart from that, what on earth was the link here?

There was so much Mark did not know, and he needed to find out. Maybe the whole thing was a red herring, but it all pointed to one insurmountable conclusion.

They had to talk to John Dubois before they could hope to get any assistance from the FBI or any of the other acronym labelled authorities in this great nation.

Meanwhile, they had to stay hidden.

Now the prospect of talking to Dubois presented a couple of difficulties. Mark could hardly march into Dubois's office and accuse him of being responsible for something that everyone else seemed intent on blaming Osama bin Laden and his al Qaeda group.

He could hardly expect the CIA or the FBI to front up to John Dubois and demand answers to related questions. They had not done so thus far and did not seem likely to change their position anytime soon.

And what was Mark's position?

He had gotten into this through his father who was a world away in Wellington, New Zealand. Mark had no authority whatsoever, and any perceived authority through his father did not seem to have counted for much back here in the United States.

They had to talk to John Dubois.

Maybe Paul could think of a way.

Chapter 32

The Dubois Dilemma

They were awakened by an incessant buzzing. Mark was the first to react, reaching for the Smith and Wesson which he had in the drawer at the side of the bed.

He shook his head trying to remember where he was. Then he remembered as some clarity seeped through the fog.

They were at the safe house, and someone was at the door.

He quickly threw on some clothes and headed for the door control, picking up the telephone-style device.

He simply asked, 'Who is it?'

'That's a nice friendly greeting—Who the bloody hell do you think it is?' asked a harassed Paul.

'Ok keep your hair on! You are the one that told us to be careful! Welcome to our humble abode – come on in' Mark replied pressing the button that released the main door.

Two people entered. Paul came in first followed by a long, slim, very elegant young lady, dressed in a dark trouser suit, her long black hair obscuring her face until she swept it back with an almost arrogant toss of her head.

At first, Mark did not recognize her. It was Felicity. She looked stunningly beautiful which was not how Mark had remembered Honey, Brad's phantom partner of all that time ago—three weeks at least.

Mark unlocked the inner door and let them in. Paul's first question was to enquire about Annette, a concerned tone in his voice. The body language that Mark detected showed that the concern was genuine. But there was something else that he did not like. Something was wrong.

Mark could hear the shower starting to run so there was little danger of Annette hearing what Paul had to say. She had heard the exchange at the door and had high-tailed it to the only place where a woman found in bed with a man could retreat to.

'She is in the shower. What is wrong?' asked Mark with a fair degree of anxiety, scanning Paul's face for some clue.

'I have heard back from Tom Dean. General Ilic Milicic is dead.' he answered in a matter-of-fact tone. 'But there is more. I could not give a rat's ass about Milicic, but Papa's wife "Mama" was killed during the extraction.'

'Shit! Annette talked about Papa as though he was her father, but I do not know anything about his wife Mama. How did Tom let that happen?'

'He did not have time to say exactly, except that they were pursued during the night by some sort of Serbian militia. Papa and Mama decided to go with them, and Mama got killed before they could get back into Kosovo. It was her fault, but that does not make it any easier. Colonel Dean is on his way to Hospital – he got shot up – took a couple in the legs—but he will live.'

'Annette never really said anything about a Mama – just about Papa – but we have to tell her. Where is Papa?' asked Mark with concern, but at the same time with

'He is being held by the Brits who are trying to work out how they explain the dead body of Milicic that Tom's team brought back.' Paul replied. 'Apparently, there is some doubt about how he got shot. Tom thinks that Papa may have taken him out while they were engaged in a firefight. And who can blame him if he did? According to Tom, something about Papa being left to cover the General, and Milicic trying to escape during the confusion. So, Papa shot him. Anyway, there is a good chance that the Brits will cover it up. Papa is safe for now, and there is no chance with the General dead that they can put any further pressure on Annette.'

'I would like to have seen Milicic get his due before the courts in the Hague. However, I guess he got what he deserved. What do you plan to do now?'

'I was expecting you to have a plan' replied Paul. 'I have brought Felicity with me because I thought you might like to go out, and you would not want to leave Annette on her own. You two do know each other?' he asked, indicating Felicity, almost as an afterthought. Mark was still unsure how a lady could appear so drab in one role and so classy in another. Yes, he knew Honey. He was pleased that Paul had the forethought to bring someone who was known to both him and Annette rather than a stranger.

Felicity smiled at Mark and then went through one of the connecting doors to reintroduce herself to Annette. They had met several times in the past although Mark could draw few conclusions from that. Mark doubted that Annette would have the same problem recognizing 'Honey' despite the distraction of her looks. Women looked for different things in other women. With some benefits – with some costs.

'Well – I have been thinking – it is about time that we had a talk with John Dubois' Mark began after Felicity was out of earshot.

'Dubois seems to hold the key to this whole business. We have plenty of circumstantial evidence of the involvement of the Augem Group and we have Annette's evidence that Dubois himself was involved. The problem right now is that we only have Annette's word for it, and the FBI will be more interested in her role as a bomber, rather than her excuse. The death of Milicic just makes it that more complicated. Therefore, the next problem is how do we get to talk to Dubois, and how do we get him to admit what he has been up to? Unless we can get him to talk, and soon, this could end up getting very nasty.'

'Of more concern to us right now is how do we deal with a madman' replied Paul. 'But you are right—John Dubois is the key. We can get to see him using your contacts and my bull shit. Are you up for it?'

'I am up for it. But what about the FBI – shouldn't they be pursuing him? Is there just a chance that the FBI may believe Annette's story' Mark asked but without much conviction.

Paul gave him a doleful look, and the sheer frustration came out in his voice. Or was there institutional rivalry at play?

Felicity came back to join them, but that did not stop Paul from sounding off about the organization that paid his salary.

'That bunch of fuckwits could not pursue a tortoise if it were tied down or dead. Mark. The FBI, like the CIA, did not believe or choose not to believe, you and your theories about 9/11 repeat. They are even less likely to believe what you say about the role of Dubois. Whatever you may think of him, he is still a significant member of the financial community. His involvement in the events of yesterday would be seen as improbable without absolute proof. Part of the organization is busy trying to arrest al-

Qaeda himself for this one, and you know how much luck they will have with that. Another part of the organization seems hell-bent on covering their ass. We have got to get to Dubois and grill him with the facts that you and Brad turned up. Only then can we involve the FBI. Anything short of admission and we are wasting our time. But we have to at least try.'

Did Mark detect a twitch on Felicity's face at the mention of Brad's name as she walked back into the room? She busied herself looking at an old magazine. Her body language had changed! He made a mental note to check with Paul at a more convenient time. How much did Felicity know, or not know, about the role Brad had played in these baffling but extraordinary events?

At that moment Annette followed Felicity into the room. Her face lit up at seeing Paul and then she started somewhat at seeing the serious looks on all the faces around her. But Felicity rose gracefully from the couch and went to stand beside Annette. Paul and Mark exchanged glances and Mark stepped in front of Annette.

'General Milicic is dead. And Papa is safe.' he said in a gentle voice. But he could not keep the threat of some other fact that was still to be said out of his voice.

The relief on the face of Annette was plain to see as she collapsed into Felicity's arms sobbing. Felicity gently lowered her to the couch and Mark sat with her and let her cry it out. And then as gently as possible he added the shattering news.

'Mama has been killed.'

Her head shot up and she asked 'How?'

There was no real concern in her voice, which was puzzling.

Mark just shrugged.

'We do not know – yet.'

'But where is Papa?' she asked. This time with real

concern in her voice, and her body language. Again, Mark exchanged a glance with Paul before replying.

'He is with the British – he came out with them.'

'What will happen to him?' she demanded, clutching at Mark's arm.

'That we also don't know – yet. It is up to the Brits. He is in good hands – don't worry!' Mark replied.

It was not the most assuring language that he could have chosen, but it would have to do for now. He held Annette at arm's length and quietly added.

'Now we have to go into the city for a meeting. You will be ok here – Felicity will stay with you – despite her looks she is well equipped to deal with anything that comes up. Besides no one knows we are here – or even that "here" exists.'

'You are going to see Mr. Dubois, aren't you?' she whispered with a tremor in her voice. Neither Paul nor Felicity could have heard what she said. In the case of Paul, he knew anyway so that did not matter. In the case of Felicity, it was another moment of pure and simple luck.

'Yes – but just for a chat. We have to get a few things sorted.' Again, his voice lacked conviction. 'We will be careful.' Careful that I keep my temper and don't choke the bastard to death – he did not add.

At least with Felicity there to look after her, Mark felt that Annette would be ok. While it was easy for Mark to say it was all over, she had been through a period involving traumatic events that no young lady should ever have to face. She should now be dead.

The fact that she was not, gave her mind another set of issues to sort through. And that would take time.

Mark did not know why he said what he did next.

'Annette – do not tell anyone who we are going to see!' He raised his eyebrows so that she could clearly get the message. After all, Felicity was the only person that Annette was likely to see in the foreseeable future. The look on Annette's face was once of total confusion, but she nodded and attempted to smile.

They left the girls in the safe house and went to Paul's car which was parked in a no-parking zone. Either the police had ignored it, or Paul had some kind of badge or marker on the car. They got in and drove back across the Queensboro Bridge then turned right into 5th Avenue. They made their way down through Greenwich Village and Soho until they came into the financial district. There were still some roads blocked off and there were police and firemen everywhere. Paul just drove through flashing some form of ID that seemed to work. They turned into Chambers Street and this time Paul selected a parking building across the street from the Augem building and they walked back from there. The whole journey had been made in complete silence – each lost in their own thoughts. Mark did not ask the reason for the choice of park, and Paul did not volunteer any explanation. As they made their way towards the Augem building, Mark broke the silence.

'What is the plan?' he asked.

He already knew what the answer was going to be. If Paul had a plan, he would have discussed it instead of sitting in silence.

'I haven't got a clue' came the expected reply. 'But I know one If Dubois as much as makes a move to avoid my questions, I will rip the bastard apart.'

Paul was getting more steamed up the closer they got to the building. Then he seemed to gather himself.

'Ok – here is the deal. I cannot go in as a CIA officer otherwise the shit will hit the fan down at the FBI. So, I go in as National Security Agency – the NSA overrides CIA and FBI on matters of national security. And it usually puts the fear of God in anyone who knows a bit about the spook business. I am betting that your friend knows more than a bit. As for you, we will simply tell Dubois that you are helping us with our inquiries and that should put the fear of God into him as well. He knows that you are somehow involved. He would know that from his friends at the CIA and the FBI. I am sure he knows nothing of your trip to Rabaul. But you have been missing and I am sure he knows at least that much. He will be wary but unsuspecting.'

'Ok – you're the boss.' replied Mark as they entered the Augem building.

They rode the elevator up to the 14th floor. The building and the office seemed more like a morgue. Most of the staff were still having time out after the dramas of the day before.

Debbie Peterson was sitting at her usual spot and did a double-take as Paul and Mark came out of the lift. She appeared both pleased and confused to see Mark. But she was even more confused to see Paul.

'Mark – good morning—what are you doing here?' she asked the apprehension very evident in her voice. For the first time that Mark could recall she did not get out of her chair. She was petrified by something or someone. From the look of her eyes, she had been crying.

'Hi, Debbie – we have come to have a chat with John Dubois. Is he available?'

'Well, I am afraid he is in a meeting right now. And you do not have an appointment!'

Her response lacked conviction.

Paul had been taking a backseat to this point. Now he strode up to the reception desk and without bothering to introduce himself glared down at Debbie.

'I do not want or need an appointment. Would you kindly inform Mr. Dubois that the NSA is here for a chat, and we do not like to be kept waiting? Do it now – if you would be so kind.'

He concluded his monologue by waving an official-looking tag in such a way that Debbie had little chance of actually reading it.

Debbie almost freaked out. She grabbed the telephone, pushed a button, and after a couple of seconds they heard Dubois's voice.

'What is it?'

'There are two people at reception from the National Security Agency to see you. I told them you were in a meeting, but they asked me if you could be interrupted, Mr. Dubois.'

Debbie was not happy. She was scared. But she managed to keep the fear out of her voice.

The telephone went dead for a moment. Then John came back and simply said 'Ok—I will see them – just give me a minute.'

He sounded calm and very relaxed. Not the reaction that Paul was either expecting or hoping for. Still, John Dubois was agreeable to see them so that was progress.

'If you could just take a seat, Mr. Dubois will be with you in a moment.' Debbie attempted to be the professional receptionist.

'No thanks' replied Paul. Which is his room?'

He set off in the direction that was obviously towards door of John Dubois' office. But he did not have to wait for Debbie's frightened response to Paul's apparent rudeness. The door burst open and out came Rob Augem looking flushed and angry.

He suddenly stopped when he saw Mark and all the colour drained from his face.

'Mark! – What are you doing here?' he asked.

'Hi, Rob – How are you? – We just dropped by for a talk with John.'

'But! The NSA! What is going on?' Rob spluttered and then turned as Dubois appeared in the doorway.

'Rob – that will be all thank you. Now gentlemen – please come in.' The fact that Mark had appeared in a very different role from that which John Dubois and Rob Augem would normally have expected of him completely escaped any mention and Dubois seemed totally in control. It had been a very strange response from both men.

Dubois's office was large even by New York and Finance company standards. He had a huge desk which was remarkably cluttered with papers and a laptop computer sat on the side. But he went towards a low table which was surrounded by four double seat couches and motioned to Paul and Mark to sit.

'Can I get you a coffee?' he asked and without waiting for an answer summoned Debbie.

'And how are you, Mark? I was sorry to hear about your father. I trust he is alright now?'

The conversation was proceeding just like the preliminaries at any other meeting. But Paul was not into idle conversation.

Cutting across the pleasantries Paul introduced himself as a representative of the NSA and again flashed the same form of ID.

'John – may I call you John – these are troubled times for New York, and we would like to just clarify a couple of things concerning any possible involvement of someone in your company in the events of yesterday. You will realize that in a case like this we have to be discrete so hence we came here without any warning. I understand that you are busy so we will not take up too much of your time. Mark also is helping us with our inquiries and has just come along as an observer. I hoped his presence would set your mind at ease that this is nothing too serious – and he may be able to clear up a few things about the security on your computer system. Can I go on?'

'Sure! Anything that we can do to help.' was the calm reply.

Debbie appeared with the coffees. She knew how Dubois and Mark had their coffee but fussed over Paul with shaking hands. Mark felt sorry for her but there were other things to worry about at the present. He was very impressed with Paul's introduction, even though it did not seem to affect John one iota.

'That will be all Debbie – see to it that we are not disturbed' said Dubois as he escorted her to the door and closed it behind her.

'How do you know General Ilic Milicic? And what was his connection with the events of yesterday?' were Paul's first two questions.

It was as though he had dropped a bomb.

Mark was surprised by the questions.

John Dubois was dumbfounded.

'Who?' Dubois replied.

His body language was asking other questions.

Did Mark detect fear?

'General Ilic Milicic of Serbia. He was wanted by the War Crimes Court for crimes committed in the conflict in what was once Yugoslavia. I say he "was" wanted but the Brits' have his body now. Do you know him or not?'

'No, I don't.' Dubois lied.

The body language said 'Yes' and Dubois was shaken by the news that the General had at long last been taken. He was also shaken by the news that he was dead. Did Mark detect fear or relief?

In just those two questions Paul had changed the entire tone of the meeting.

Dubois was scared.

John Dubois, sitting in his comfortable New York office miles away from any action that may have taken place in the former Yugoslavia, had to think. And think quickly.

Life had been much easier when he had been in Beirut as a young man. There he had fallen in love with an African American girl who went by the unlikely name of Venus. In a stormy relationship that lasted less than two years they had a daughter that they named Melody but who went by the unusual, but more affectionate, name of Charlie.

Dubois followed his then-wife Venus back to the USA, but soon regretted his attempts at any reconciliation. Once back in the streets of Harlem, Venus was back into the drug scene and died of an overdose within twelve short months of her return. Charlie was fostered out with an aunt, but John and Charlie kept in touch. John Dubois's one link in what was otherwise a very lonely life, and his only link with sanity.

But it was his second relationship that did more to determine the events that inexorably led to yesterday's occurrence. This lady he met quite by chance. He chanced to be on his own in a New York bar, and she chanced to be similarly alone at the same time and in the same place. She was a reporter working for Time Magazine and between assignments. They both got very drunk and ended up spending the night in bed together at John's pad. Whether they made love or not neither of them could remember, but nine months later, almost to the day, Iraya Dubrovnik gave birth to a baby girl.

They kept in touch and met, and made love, on the rare occasions that her work brought her to New York. No commitments – just shared the company of one lonely person with another. And then Iraya asked John if he would like to come with her on her next assignment – four weeks covering the conflict in Kosovo. Her reasons were quite simple. The assignment would take her near her birthplace of Raska, a small town in southern Serbia. And she would take the opportunity to show off her young daughter to her family. What better than to show them the daughters' father at the same time?

At first, Dubois was reluctant – after all, there was a war going on and people were getting shot at – well killed. And John Dubois was a coward. But Iraya had laughed at him – patiently explaining the reality of war that she had lived with almost daily. And patiently explained that, in reality, very few people got killed. And so, he went.

Dubois spent most of his time in Serbia with her family and his daughter. Despite the warring factions that were in evidence, it was one of the happiest periods of his life. Meanwhile, Iraya was off somewhere doing what she was paid to do—reporting on the war – basically dodging bullets. But one evening when they were all together at her father's house, Iraya had just gone to check on her daughter in another room. There was a strange whoosh and then that part of the house completely disappeared in a loud explosion. The rest of the house was damaged beyond repair. In the chaos that followed only John Dubois, a visiting uncle, and his friend survived – and then only just.

The uncle had his legs trapped under a beam and his friend tried desperately to free him. They could see some NATO soldiers coming down the road towards the house – which was not unusual. But the uncle had urgently insisted that Dubois help his friend free him and equally urgently insisted that they all get the hell out of there before the troops arrived – which was unusual.

Dubois was under the impression that NATO troops were meant to be friendly – after all the USA was part of NATO—and that help was not very far away.

Here was John Dubois, in a foreign country, in the middle of a war, who had just witnessed the death of the two people in his lonely life that he loved, now on his own, and scared shitless.

He helped the uncle free himself and all three of them got out of there and into the woods, perilously avoiding the approaching but cautious troops and escaping detection. They spent the next several days trying to avoid capture while they journeyed into the Serbian hills – basically dodging bullets. During those few days, before Dubois managed to make his way out to an airport, they got to know each other very well. In that time the uncle managed to convince Dubois that it was the Americans who had killed Iraya and his daughter.

There began a hatred that would fester for a long time.

John Dubois, the big-time wheeler-dealer from New York, and the uncle, the much-wanted General Ilic Milicic of the Serbian Army.

As they shook hands and parted company the General said, 'I owe you one!'

The fact that the very existence of the General and his friend Mario Tudjman in that house and at that time was the probable reason why the house was bombed. And therefore, was the probable reason why Dubois lost his lover Iraya and their daughter—the people who were his best friends—would never be known to John.

He also would not have known that the crude missile was fired by the Albanians and was not even remotely connected to any NATO or US action. Had he known these simple facts, then things may have been different. Such is the way that fate plays a small hand in the lives of individuals, and in much larger matters that concern nations.

'**What has** a Serbian General—whatever his name is—got to do with what happened yesterday?' John countered.

'I did not say he has anything to do with what happened in New York City.' replied Paul. 'But these things have a way of being related. So, what can you tell me about Anna Leskovic? I presume you will say that you have not heard of her either?'

'No, I haven't!' John almost whispered 'Should I?'

'Yes – you certainly should. Maybe you could try her adopted name—Annette Covic – I hope you are not going to tell me you don't know that name either?'

'Of course, I know Annette. What has that to do with this Anna whatever her name is? I do not understand what all this has got to do with me or the Augem Group.'

Dubois turned to Mark as if appealing for help. John was ruffled but was so far doing a reasonable job of keeping himself under control.

'Oh well, if you do not know, let me move on to other matters.'

Mark and Paul exchanged glances – they would return to the subject later.

'What can you tell us about Doctor Abdul Jabbar?'

The pressure was beginning to tell. Dubois still managed to just keep himself under control.

'Who are you, people? I do not know who you are talking about.'

For a moment Mark began to think Dubois was on the level. What if someone had orchestrated the whole thing and that John was not involved after all? For just one scary moment Mark thought—What if Annette was the one who was lying? But Paul pressed on.

'Forgive me – I am obviously moving too fast for you. So, we will go through the three names again slowly – this time in reverse order.'

Paul took a swig of the coffee and pulled a face – this was real coffee and Paul only liked weak instant – which did not improve his mood—then he continued.

'Abdul is a kingpin in an Indonesian terrorist organization known as Jemaah Islamiyah – or JI for short. How do we know that? We know because we have access to his files and those files contain all sorts of information that associates him with JI leaders. The fact that he is a Doctor of Geology and works as a seismologist out of a little place called Rabaul in Papua New Guinea is just a cover for what he really does. But you already know all this, don't you? How do we know that you know? Because you have been communicating by email with Rabaul for quite some time. And with all due respect, we cannot see any business reason why you should do so. Therefore, we conclude that you have an interest in what the good doctor does rather than the other way around. Since there has been no seismic activity in New York City in living memory, you cannot be interested in his volcanic studies. Therefore, we conclude that you have an interest in his terrorist associates. How am I doing so far?'

Dubois sat for a moment with no expression on his face, just staring at Paul, and then tried another tactic.

'This is all conjecture on your part. What is the point that you are trying to make?'

Paul continued to apply pressure.

'We are trying to establish that you were involved with the three explosions that rocked New York City yesterday.'

'You have got to be joking. Why in heavens name would I want to do that?' Dubois replied.

Small beads of perspiration were beginning to form on his brow, and he was agitated. Body language is a terrible thing.

'Oh – we will come to that in due course.' Paul had seen the signs and knew he was getting to Dubois.

'Would you like me to continue? – you may as well hear the whole story and then you can form your own opinion.'

'What if I said I want my lawyer to listen in as well?' Dubois asked defiantly.

'Please yourself. We have not yet said that you are guilty of anything – and you are not obliged to say anything. We will leave if you like – this is just an informal chat aimed at clarifying a few things. Whatever you say we will leave when we have finished our discussion – with or without your lawyer. However, before I can do that, I will need to clear it with my boss just to be sure that he does not want you to come with us downtown. Would you like me to continue?'

A shrug was the only answer he received, so he continued.

'Let us talk about Miss Anna Leskovic. She came to the United States from Serbia to escape the troubles that have dogged that regions' recent past. She left because the man – one who goes by the name of Papa Milutin—who had taken her in when her parents were murdered – wanted to protect her from any further trouble – or rape if you would like me to be more specific. She came to New York City where somehow her benefactor turned out to be one John Dubois. Now please stop me if by any chance I have the wrong man – but I don't think so. She changed her name to Annette Covic, probably to retain some link to her heritage. Consequently, we have a clear link between you and Anna. Call it coincidence at this stage if you like. Would you like me to continue?'

Dubois summoned Debbie to replenish their coffee, to give himself breathing space from this assault and they sat in silence while she filled their cups.

Mark sat facing Dubois with a look of utter contempt on his face. It was very clear from John's body language that he was not enjoying this. But what choice did he have? It was also clear to Mark that Paul was beginning to turn the screws but outwardly it was as though he was discussing the weather.

Dubois managed to summon the resolve to say, 'If you must!'

'Yesterday morning a telephone call was made from this office to Serbia and instructions were given to General Ilic Milicic to kill Papa Milutin. Now perhaps you can explain that.'

Again, Mark and Paul exchanged glances. Paul was on thin ice here because he was making an assumption. If Annette had told them the truth, then he had to be right. The other assumption was that the NSA would have picked up the call. Now that was as good as money in the bank. The only real question was, from the hundreds of millions of calls monitored that day, why would they take note of this one call when they had no reason to be monitoring calls to Serbia?

Still—John Dubois did not know that - did he?

The reaction Paul got therefore came as a surprise. In a very angry tone, Dubois demanded.

'You spooks think everyone in this country is stupid! No one could have monitored every call from this office!'

He immediately bit his lip realizing his mistake. He was on the defensive and that was not good for him. He rushed to add 'No such call was made from this office – why would I call anyone in Serbia?'

This was the opening Paul had been waiting for.

'So, you did not make the call? Well, explain this. When our representatives called to pay a courtesy visit to Papa Milutin, who should turn up but the General Ilic Milicic himself and his thugs. Their call did not appear to be a courtesy visit. They were armed to the teeth. Our representatives then had to fight their way out of Serbia with some loss of life. So, tell me – is this another coincidence? Based on intelligence gathered here in New York, our representative turns up at the same time and in the same place as one of the most wanted, and elusive, men in Serbia. Coincidence? I don't think so.'

Dubois was not going to give in so easily.

'Yes, it is. Why would I want to have Papa whatever his name killed? – I have never heard of him. This is all absolute nonsense!'

He leaped to his feet and opened the door.

'Debbie!' he bellowed 'These gentlemen are about to leave – would you show them out.'

Neither Paul nor Mark moved, as Dubois stood fuming at the door. Debbie came towards the door but was stopped by a command from Mark.

'We are not going anywhere Debbie. John—I respectfully suggest you sit back down and hear the rest of the story. Paul has the authority to arrest you so if you like he can save us all precious time, do just that and we can continue our conversation downtown.'

Dubois looked at Mark for a long time and then almost whispered. 'You are one of them! I should have realized a long time ago. Who are you?'

Mark laughed at that.

'No John—I am not one of them.' Mark replied. 'You know what I am. I run a computer software company. I am here to try to get an understanding of why this has all happened. I am interested because I have unwittingly been dragged into it by the NSA but now it is personal. I am as interested as you are to find out what this is all about. Sit down!'

It was a long time since Mark had spoken with such authority in his voice, but it had the required effect.

Dubois sat down on his couch and muttered again.

'Why would I want this man killed.'

It was a feeble protest of innocence, but the body language was coming through loud and clear, and it was saying – 'What went wrong?'

Mark and Paul exchanged looks, and Paul nodded to Mark.

'Perhaps Mark should explain his theory – he is close enough, yet remote enough, to have an objective view.'

John just shrugged, so Mark began to talk.

'What I think happened is this. A plot was devised to have a series of explosions in New York City to exactly coincide with the events of the original 9/11. By doing so the finger of suspicion would fall on the al-Qaeda group. What is a better way to demonstrate to Americans that al-Qaeda could strike at will at any time or in any place, and had the organizational ability to make the timing exactly right? But I do not believe that it had anything to do with al-Qaeda.'

You could hear a pin drop in the room.

'Now let me speculate. Suppose you wanted to organize such a plot. The first thing you would want to do is to make sure the FBI was unaware that something was going to happen, or at least you would want to be able to cover it up. The easiest way is to find someone you can pay to keep things quiet. Drugs are usually a good motivation to start with. Then you must establish a communications link with someone who has indeed got links to al-Qaeda.

More than that, someone who has all the required knowledge on how these things are done. But you do not want the other security services to find out too much, so you improve the security on your systems.'

'Then you must recruit people who will carry out the plot. The advice you receive is that you should recruit vulnerable people with a hatred of all things American but who have had no direct links to any local terrorist organization. Why? Because the local terrorists would be mightily angry if they were to discover that their raison d'être was being used to the advantage of someone else. How am I doing so far?' No one answered so he continued.

'So, you recruit three people who come recommended to you by your overseas contact. They are nut cases that even local terrorists think is too mad to recruit. Otherwise, they have all the qualifications. Why three? Because there are three events to be timed for 08:46 am, 09:03 am and 09:37 am. Forget the fourth explosion – that was a failure because some brave Americans gave their lives to make sure the flight crashed and could not cause any damage. The chosen method for the events this time is by a suicide bomber.'

The atmosphere in the room was tense, as Mark sat forward in his seat, his attention focused on the evil man who sat before him.

'Let us give them names just so we can identify them. Haroon who we think is – correction was – a Pakistani. Mohammed who we think was a US-born and bred convert to Islam. And Arif another Pakistani.'

He was getting to John in a big way. He was by now sitting slumped with a look of disbelief on his face. His expression said, 'This has nothing to do with me.'
His body language said, 'How the fuck does he know all this?'

Mark continued.

'For some reason, your friend Arif pulled out. Probably because he found out that the plot was not after all being organized by al-Qaeda. So, what do you do? You panic – that's what you do. After all this organizing over many months, even years, including I might add making sure that your friends in the FBI kept a lid on things, your plot may unravel before it can even be executed. Arif is probably dead. I say that for two reasons – firstly, you could not afford anything to leak out about your crazy scheme – secondly, what's another body? But then you have a brain wave – or explosion – or whatever you like to call it. You have contacts in Serbia who can put pressure on a young lady from those parts that would enable you to make her the ideal third bomber. That way the connection to al-Qaeda becomes irrelevant and the risk factor at so late a stage in your planning is nullified.'

'Now we come to the events of the last few weeks. Let us deal with your computer system first. Someone in the FBI, or maybe higher up the security chain, finds out something I did not know – that the CIA had infiltrated your security. What do you do? You panic – that's what you do. Your overseas friends send you two Indian gentlemen – who we believe were actually from Pakistan —who can take over the system and you set out to buy me out. Price is no object – just get control.'

'Just to make sure, you raid my office while I am out celebrating the deal and steal a copy of all the source code so you can be certain you are not being short-changed. Make absolutely sure that no one can get wind of your schemes. Just to be sure that you have all bases covered, your FBI pals get involved which has a strange side-effect. It causes my guy – well the CIA's guy – to disappear. Very clever, except that the software you stole was incomplete to put it kindly. Useless to be more accurate. But your Indian friends are so clever. Meaning they did not have a clue what to look for—that they don't tell you. That was probably another mistake – and a fatal one.'

'So, what happened yesterday? The first two explosions went according to plan. The timing was perfect and, although deaths and casualties were significantly less than the original 9/11, al-Qaeda was the only suspect. But then we come to the third explosion. That did not exactly go according to plan. A petrified young lady was intercepted before the bomb could go off. And she told the people who stopped her about you, and your friend General Milicic, and her friend Papa. When you heard about the third explosion – or lack of – what do you do? You panic – that's what you do. You pick up the phone and call Milicic. We do not know what the nature of your connection is, but his instructions are to kill Papa Milutin. And he duly seeks to carry out those instructions. But the British arrived in time and instead of being witness to yet another crime, Papa survives, and they capture your friend Milicic. He talks and the circle is complete.'

'But you said Ilic Milicic was dead!' Dubois blurted out before he could stop himself.

'Thanks, Mark. Now I will take over.'

Paul leaned forward to look Dubois straight in the eyes.

'We do not know yet about the fate of the General – that is not important at this stage. Now let's look at what we have here. At the very least we have you communicating with one of the most wanted criminals in Europe and commissioning a murder – the punishment? – well more years in a penitentiary than you have left to live. We also have you implicated in arranging a suicide bomber who did not want to commit suicide and had nothing to do with al-Qaeda or anyone else in the terrorism game. The punishment for you? – more years in the penitentiary. We also have ample evidence that you have contact with people in the FBI who for money, or whatever other crazy ideas they may have, have deliberately interfered with the course of our investigations. The punishment for you? – more years in jail.'

Paul paused for a sip of his coffee – or so it appeared. He was letting the reality of what he had said sink in, before continuing.

'Then we have you communicating with a man who, now that we know where he is and what he has been up to, would be one of the most wanted terrorists in the world. The punishment for you? Probably a lock-up in Guantanamo with the key thrown away forever. We could go on. The fact that Mark thinks the whole scenario yesterday has nothing whatsoever to do with al-Qaeda does not concern me a rat's ass. Right here and now we have more than enough to declare that you are a terrorist and, if you want to go down this line, we will declare that you are the controller of an al-Qaeda cell. And do not doubt for one minute that we can make it stick, no matter what your friends at the FBI may have told you. The only piece of the puzzle that we don't have is—why in heavens name you did all these things and what you could hope to gain from it?'

'I think I can answer that.'

The soft but firm voice came from the doorway that John had left open. It was Rob Augem. He walked in and sat down on the fourth couch, glaring at Dubois.

'Get out of my office!' shouted Dubois rising from his seat. Mark reached across and rather more firmly than was necessary deposited him back in his seat.

'This might not be your office for very much longer.' Mark said. 'Let us hear what Rob has to say.'

Rob summoned as much control as he could muster.

'John you are insane!' he said, almost spitting the words out, then he turned to address Paul.

'I do not know how much you know about our business, but we are into Insurance and in particular, we arrange the underwriting for a number of the leading Insurance companies in New York City and beyond. One clause is sacrosanct in all our policies and every other company in the insurance business—particularly since 9/11 – the exclusion of any damage caused directly or indirectly as a result of terrorist activity. Apart from the fine print, there is nothing really to choose between one policy or the next, one underwriter or the next. Then along comes John Dubois who knows next to nothing about insurance. He asks—Why not cover people for terrorist activity? Just up the premium, arrange the underwriting via a fund that all insurance companies contribute to, and you are set. By itself it sounds quite logical – there are not that many terrorist events – and by raising every premium you are into a customer pays situation – which seems fair on the customer but much more profitable for the insurer. The Risk Management people – those are the people who assess the risk in any insurance event – or possible event – were looking into it. But John had other ideas. He was determined to launch a new product.'

John once more began to leap to his feet but was shoved back by Mark.

'He decided – and I stress it was him and not the Augem Board that decided – to move things along. He came up with the hair-brained scheme whereby there would be another terrorist event, following which he would immediately announce a new product. His theory was that we would increase our business exponentially almost overnight, leaving everyone else in catch-up mode. Then he added a twist that I only realized yesterday. Why not knock out a couple of our strongest competitors at the same time. So, if you are looking for a reason for the selection of targets yesterday – look at the occupation of the businesses that suffered most. Both of the buildings hit contained competitors of ours and they are both virtually out of the game for some time – because they have lost some of their key people. And despite the competitive nature of business, they were my friends. John is insane!'

Rob Augem finished and was visibly upset. Mark reached across to calm him down. Taking advantage of Mark's distraction and before any other reaction was possible John leaped out of his seat and rushed out the door.

Paul and Mark took off after him. Once in the reception area, there was no sign of him. Debbie, who had heard most of the recent conversation and was crying, pointed to the stairwell. They rushed to the door onto the landing, but he had vanished. Paul paused.

'He probably went down so that is where I go – could you just check that he has not gone up?'

He was away down the stairs taking them two and three at a time. Mark took off up the stairs. Fortunately, there were only two levels to climb. He flung open the door on the 15th floor startling a secretary and yelled at her to ask whether anyone had entered that floor. She looked terrified but shook her head in the negative and he was gone again. He repeated the same thing on the 16th floor and again the response was negative.

That just left the service entry onto the roof. It was only barred as a fire exit and Mark crashed through it.

On the top of the Chambers Street building was a helicopter pad and parked there was a Bell Jet Ranger. John Dubois stood leaning on the door trying to open it and turned around, as Mark came out of the door, with a look that was more of a sneer than anything else.

'Why did you have to get tied up in this? Why not stick to your computers – did we not pay you enough money? – I would have thought that 10 million dollars would do.'

Mark moved slowly towards Dubois. While John was well built and despite his rotund appearance kept himself reasonably fit, he would not be a match for an ex-Special Forces officer, especially one with a Smith and Wesson in his hand, and that superiority was reflected in the way Mark spoke.

'Give it up John. It's finished. If you had not involved Annette, I might have taken a different view, but you did, so let's go. Who knows? You may be able to plead insanity – I could not care less. I am not a judge – but you have to answer for your actions and God help you when you do.'

A strange smile covered John's face.

'Well, you did alright out of it didn't you—10 million dollars! Far more than your system was worth. Not bad for a small-time computer guy. So how about we make it another 10 million dollars if you let me go.'

'Do you ever know when to stop?' Mark asked. 'I said give it up. Now come away from that helicopter and come and face the music. Money will not buy your way out of this one.'

Mark was almost within arm's length of Dubois. A crash behind him announced the arrival of a very breathless Paul who immediately drew his weapon and shouted.

'Hands on your head – now! You should know that private flights around New York are banned at the moment – thanks to you. So, don't be silly – if you take off, you're as good as dead.'

That just brought another strange smile.

Then John Dubois just rushed to the edge of the building and somersaulted over the rail.

Mark, who was easily the closest, grabbed him as he went over the edge. He almost had him. But Dubois simply shrugged off the jacket that Mark had grabbed onto, and he plunged down the side of the building, crashing into the public walkway roof of the second floor.

There was no way anyone could survive such a fall.

John Dubois, the architect of the second 9/11, was dead.

Paul slid down the wall of the outside of the lift shaft and summed up the events of the morning so far in one word.

'Fuck!'

'We have to call the police – why don't you do that? I have something I want to attend to.' said Mark as he rushed to go down the stairs. But Paul held up his hand and stopped Mark.

'It is better if I am not involved – get the old guy to ring the NYPD. We cannot yet adequately explain what the hell is going on, and for all we know, someone may have alerted the FBI, who may be on their way here. We had him! I never expected John to commit suicide. Now we are right back where we started – this only leaves Annette to back up our story. I cannot be involved. Otherwise, the CIA and the FBI will go ballistic. And that's only talking about the people who are on our side. We have to get back to the Safehouse and leave others to sort this lot out while we come up with another plan.'

Mark hesitated, but he could see the logic of what Paul had just said. But he still had something to do, and Paul nodded his agreement when Mark explained.

They rushed back inside. Debbie and Rob were waiting in the reception area as Paul and Mark came back to the fourteenth floor. The grim look on Mark's face told the story that they had yet to hear. It was Marks' sense of purpose that they did not understand.

He rushed straight past them into Dubois' office while Paul took Rob to one side, told him what had happened and what he wanted him to do. Then he immediately left.

If Rob Augem was in any way disappointed at the news of the demise of John Dubois it certainly did not show on his face. He appeared only mildly surprised at the turn of events.

Debbie rushed after Mark and as she came into Dubois' office, she saw him already sitting at Johns' laptop computer on the desk.

'What are you doing Mark – no one is allowed to touch Mr. Dubois's computer?' she asked, not sure whether to be indignant or scared. Almost as an afterthought she asked. 'Where is John?'

'John is dead Debbie – he dived into the side of the building. I tried to stop him, but I couldn't.' he replied as gently as he could. But the effect on Debbie was nothing like as mild as Rob's reaction. She collapsed onto the couch, the horrible truth too much for her to absorb, and burst into tears. Mark was shocked at Debbie's reaction, but he had a critical task to perform. Debbie would have to wait.

'Don't worry Debbie – I will only be a minute.' Mark said. 'Something on this machine should tell me why – why a guy wants to commit suicide?'

He worked furiously at the machine, alternatively looking puzzled then enlightened, and then he found what he was looking for. The folder was password protected and well hidden, but not from someone with Mark's skills. It was a set of accounts for a shell company whose role appeared to be to receive money and then disperse it. It was the list of payments that Mark was interested in – that would tell him who was on Dubois's payroll and at a cursory glance, it looked as though he had found exactly the right information. Most of the payments were to foreign bank accounts. There was just one minor problem. Included in the transactions were two payments each of five million dollars – to Taylor Software. If the rest of the payments in this schedule turned out to be suspicious, then these two would also be treated as suspicious. The payment of a total of 10 million dollars for the software was a bit over the top – so someone would ask what was the purpose of the pay-outs? This would make it look as though Mark was also on the Dubois payroll. And ridiculous though such an association may appear to be, there were enough twists to the story so far that Mark did not need this possible connection.

Mark made a rapid decision. He logged on to the Internet, connected to his own office. He then logged onto his system. He then set up the connection to download the entire folder from John's machine to the machine at Taylor Software. When the download was complete, he then carefully encrypted it and password protected it, burying the folder deep in the Taylor system. The security on the Taylor Software system was far more secure than that used at the Augem Group or by Dubois. He then disconnected and erased all evidence of the fact that he had been using the machine. And then he erased two transaction records from Dubois's machine that concerned payments to Taylor Software. It was crude, and a careful audit of the machine would reveal that 10 million dollars had gone missing.

The only good news was that amongst the other transactions on this particular computer the amount was only petty cash.

He then went across to Debbie, who had spent the entire time sitting on the couch quietly sobbing, and she cradled her head against his chest. She cried uncontrollably.

Mark realized that Debbie was an emotional person. Despite the rudeness that John had shown towards her, Rob Augem, and many others, she was still concerned enough for the loss of life.

A few weeks would pass before Mark fully understood.

It would not be the last time she cried.

Nor would it be the last time that he held her in his arms.

Chapter 33

Despair

The police did not have that much to do on the fourteenth floor of the Chambers Street building. John Dubois had fallen from above the sixteenth floor, and the NYPD had very rapidly formed the correct conclusion that he had committed suicide.

It was not exactly an unusual event in this part of the city or this particular industry, even if the reasons, in this case, might cause a few eyebrows to be raised. They had confirmation from Mark that he had tried to prevent the fall and from the other witnesses who claimed to have seen the whole scenario unfold. Mark was something of a hero – holding onto the jacket that he had gripped in the forlorn attempt to stop Dubois's fall.

Mark did not feel like a hero. He had not attempted to save the life of John Dubois. All he had attempted to do was stop him from falling so that Dubois could face the wrath of the United States justice system and the anger of the people who had lost loved ones in the events in the city. His trial would have brought some peace. Instead, he left a massive hole that somehow Mark, and Paul would have to find their way around.

After talking to the three people who had witnessed the event as far as Augem was concerned – Mark, Debbie, and Rob – the police formed the impression that they were all deeply saddened by the affair. They were—but for different reasons. Except that is for Rob—he was elated – but then, at his age, he was hardly likely to have thrown anyone from a building. And it was hard to tell the difference, again because of his age, between tears of joy and tears for any other reason. Debbie would have a similar view to Rob, except that she was naturally an emotional person and so genuine tears flowed. Mark could not have cared less about the death, except that he had a whole range of new problems to deal with. He had lost the one person who could provide the truth to support Annette's story, and the other link in this insane occurrence was also dead.

On a less emotional side, the good news was that the death would bring the whole sorry affair to an end. The man who had masterminded the plot was no more. All they had to do now was to sort out the scum in the intelligence and security services who had, for reasons unknown, supported John Dubois in this mad affair. And that had nothing to do with Mark.

The NYPD still took an extraordinary amount of time to bring the situation under control, but at least they did not appear to bring the FBI into it. Nor was anyone as dumb as McGuire from Marks' last encounter with the NYPD involved. They had a job to do, but since it appeared that half the residents of New York had witnessed the body, and the media had temporarily forgotten yesterday and concentrated all their unwanted attention on this latest death, they took their time in the full glare of publicity.

It was therefore quite late in the day that Mark, already somewhat weary after the events of the morning, made his way back to the car hoping that Paul had not left. He had not—Paul sat patiently waiting. They eventually made their way back to Paul's safe house as quickly as the traffic would allow. They both realized that they now had yet another set of problems to deal with and, on reflection, Mark could not leave Paul to sort that out.

Their conversation with Dubois had not been recorded so that, while they had effectively got the next best thing to a confession – if jumping off the roof of a sixteen-floor building could be called that – they still had the problem of getting the story accepted with only a body for proof –two bodies if you were to include one half a world away – that of General Ilic Milicic. In addition, they were still no closer to finding out who it was in the FBI and the CIA who was pulling strings although Mark hoped that the folder, he had extracted from John Dubois' machine would help them with that part of the problem. If they were not on John Dubois' machine, then they could have some explaining to do.

The parking in the street did not allow them to park alongside the curb so Paul pulled out another key and asked Mark to open a garage door about half a block from where they were headed. Mark jumped out of the car and did as he was asked – how many more surprises was Paul going to pull he asked himself? Paul reversed into the garage using the good old service maxim – be ready for a quick getaway.

Little did Paul know at that point that he would not be using the car again. Mark locked the garage and they moved off down the street.

As they walked up to the door of the safe house, Mark thought about what he should tell Annette of the events at Augem and decided that he would say as little as possible. At least for now.

They were certain that they now knew exactly who had orchestrated the events of the last few days. But, although they had Rob's story, they still did not know jack shit about what was going on. Of major concern now was to find out why anyone at the FBI and in the CIA would want to be a part of this crazy scheme. If they did not find out – and soon – they, and more particularly Annette, were in trouble. Any person with that kind of power and influence was not likely to let other members of the establishment, who knew the truth, live for very long. Whether he liked it or not, Mark realized that he was part of that establishment, and although he had been conned into involvement in the first place, that small issue would not be of major concern to those at the business end of a gun.

Paul touched the communicator to announce their return and was immediately answered by Felicity.

'Hi – it's Paul and Mark – we are back.'

'Ok – come on in!' was her calm cool reply.

Paul temporarily froze. He motioned to Mark to go in first and for no reason that Mark could tell, gave him a sign that they had used long ago in a far-off forgotten place. He was to say nothing. Mark was about to ask what the hell was going on now but saw the cold steely look in Paul's eyes. 'Just make sure you distract the video camera – it is just to the left of the inner door' he urged in almost a whisper. 'I don't remember telling Felicity how the security system worked, and so I would have thought that Annette would have answered, and I am not about to take any chances.'

They entered the door when they heard the locking

mechanism disengage, and they closed it behind them. Mark immediately swung to his left and sure enough, the video camera followed him. He turned to see Paul doing a strange thing – he was straightening his tie in the hall mirror – Paul never did that, even though he was about to enter a room in which there should be two rather stunning ladies. Paul turned away from the mirror, shrugged, and went towards the inner door, winking at Mark as he did so. Mark just shook his head. Once again, he had no idea what was going on, but Paul did, so that was good enough.

Mark would soon find out in any case.

They assumed that the inner door would be opened for them. But it wasn't. Paul had to use the access code.

They entered the lounge area. It was not quite the welcome that they, or at least Mark, had expected.

'Very clever – you could have saved us a lot of trouble if you hadn't disconnected the gas—but I am afraid that's not good enough. Now – both of you – let's have your weapons on the table nice and easy – and no heroics – I have got neither the time nor the patience.'

Mark just stood there absolutely dumbfounded. It was the FBI agent Clive Henderson who was holding a Berretta pointing straight at them, only wavering slightly to show that he had both Mark and Paul covered. An even greater shock was the position of Felicity. She had one hand resting on Annette's shoulder and the other held a similar weapon to Henderson's but this one was pointing at the back of Annette's head. Understandably Annette was petrified. She looked at Mark almost beseeching him to do something – but what could he do?

'What the fuck is going on?' said Paul, reaching for his weapon. Those were his last words. The Berretta seemed so quiet. The shot to the head was so well-aimed and precise. Paul just dropped like a sack and was probably dead before he hit the ground, a bullet hole in the centre of his forehead.

Marks' initial reaction was one of shock and then anger as he stared at the body of his friend. They had been through so much together, in some very tight corners, but to see him so brutally and callously shot and on the floor of his own safe house – dead! The bitterness he felt towards Henderson at that moment was indescribable.

He looked into those cold eyes and vowed, if he lived through this, he would kill the man with his own hands. A moment later he would have even more reason to do so.

Henderson kept his eyes and his Berretta trained on Mark, while he asked Felicity to check that the visitors were alone. She re-holstered her gun then went through the door out onto the street and returned moments later to confirm there was no one else out there. Then Henderson turned his gun on Annette.

'You seem to have outlived your usefulness too – you should have ended it all yesterday.' he said to her as she slowly rose to her feet, a look of absolute horror on her face.

Mark launched himself across the intervening space between Henderson and the place where he had been standing. It was no use trying to protect Annette – that would just delay the inevitable. His one chance was to get to the gun before Henderson had the chance to fire it, disable Henderson, and then turn the gun on Felicity before she had the chance to draw her gun again.

Being a hero twice in one day was a bit much, but he had to try.

And he almost made it.

In the split seconds that followed there were two shots presumably one from the gun that Henderson held and the other from Felicity. He never knew who fired which shot, but he saw the look of disbelief on Annette's face as her hands covered the hole that had punctured her chest.

Mark tried to cry out in anger as he crashed into Henderson.

But everything just went blank.

Mark shook his head to try to get rid of the pain and blinked to try to clear his eyes. He did not know whether he was alive or not.

He had visions of entry into an afterlife that so many of his fellow countrymen said they believed in. All had different grades of doubt about whether it existed or not. Mark was either an atheist or an agnostic, but he was beginning to wonder if he had made a terrible mistake. He tried moving his arms, and then his legs. Nothing would move. He then tried to roll – nothing. Gradually full consciousness returned, and the fog began to clear from his head but not the pain. No! He was not moving into the afterlife. He was not moving anywhere. Because he couldn't.

Mark could discern to his right a straight vertical line of light. Eventually, he worked out that he was in a cupboard, but where, the cupboard was he had no idea. He was trussed up like a turkey and gagged. The reason he could not roll was quite simply because he was wedged into a space that was if anything a little too small for a man with his frame. There were other things on the floor that made for less room, but no one seemed to have bothered about his comfort.

He was very awkwardly positioned but no matter how he tried to squirm he could not get into a more comfortable position. It would have helped if the other objects on the floor moved, but they did not, and they were too heavy for Mark to shift given his own lack of mobility.

He had a thumping headache but during the occasions when the pain lessened, he could feel another pain just over his right temple. He would have smiled at the irony except that he could not move his face, so tight was the gag. He now had injuries to both sides of his head. He was also aware from recent experience that he would be in much more pain when, or if, the restraints on his arms and legs were removed.

He wondered about what time it was. He had no way of knowing how long he had been tied up in this position. He had no visual reference to give him a clue, save for the thin line of light.

He must have dozed for some time before he heard a voice and then footsteps coming closer. The door to the cupboard was pulled open, immediately he was kicked on the side of the face, and before he could see who the visitors were, a piece of cloth was roughly tied around his eyes. He was then dragged by the feet out of the cupboard and dumped in the middle of what was a room. There followed a good deal of activity and then he was lifted by two men. They had to be men, and big ones at that because Mark weighed more than two hundred pounds.

They trundled him outside. That much he knew because of the breeze and the change in the temperature.

He was dumped on what felt like the floor of a vehicle, and that was confirmed almost immediately when the vehicle started up and the vibrations went through his body. What concerned him more than the noise and vibration was the smell.

For a while, he could not quite make out what was causing the nauseating smell. Then the horrible truth dawned on him. He was being transported alongside a couple of corpses! And he had a fair idea who the corpses might be.

One would be Paul Williams. The other would have

to be Annette Covic.

His position seemed hopeless. He felt himself being dragged into the depths of despair. What he did not know was – why was he still alive while his two friends were dead? The first shock hit him like a rifle bullet. Annette – the lady who he had barely got to know in an intimate sense – had been taken from him so quickly and so brutally. He realized now that he had been very much in love with her, despite all that had happened in the recent past. And her young life had been so violently and abruptly cut short. Mark was once again alone, and fearful. He had just rescued her from one form of certain death only to have her life taken in another.

The tears started to flow and for once in Mark's equally young life his mind dragged him down into a pit of depression. He thought about Paul but that could not mask his sorrow at the loss of a beautiful friend. Paul had been at his side in many a skirmish and life, or death was a part of the deal. But not Annette – so young, so loving, and as far as he knew, so innocent.

Then anger started to take over. Who were these people who had ended her life, and that of Paul, so callously? In those moments, the grief was almost unbearable. But from it came the resolution to get even. He struggled with the cords that bound his hands and feet and the frustration built up inside him.

Although the anger and frustration began to bring him to the point of despair, he realized that he had to try to concentrate and to keep emotion out of it. For now.

He could hear two people talking so that meant that there were at least five people in the vehicle – two in the drivers' and passenger's seats, Mark who was still trussed up like a turkey, and the two bodies.

He tried but could not make out what the driver and his passenger were saying because of the noise. The conversation however did not last long before they lapsed into silence. All he could hear was the engine, the noise of the wheels on the road, and the drumming that went on in his head from being near the floor.

This was the first time he had the opportunity to think about what had occurred. It was fairly clear that they had killed his two friends. But why? And why then was he still alive? The frustration and the remorse got the better of him and he sobbed, partly from the grief, partly from the hopelessness of his situation, partly from the incredibly uncomfortable position that his arms and legs were tied in.

The journey seemed to last for hours. The drumming of the wheels, the vibration that resulted from his being on the floor, and the rumble of the exhaust combined into a continuous and monotonous din that sent him numbed him into a fitful sleep.

He became more awake when eventually the noise made by the wheels changed as did the motion of the vehicle. Mark was tossed from side to side as they travelled over the uneven surface of what was clearly a dirt road and one that was not particularly well maintained.

Finally, they came to a halt. The engine was switched off and he heard the doors slam as they – whoever they were – got out of the vehicle. Nothing happened for quite some time and then the rear door opened, and someone climbed in. There was a good deal of grunting and cursing as the two men struggled to get what was one of the bodies out of the vehicle. There was a period of silence and then the same process was repeated over again. Mark felt helpless as the confirmation came to him then that he had been transported alongside the bodies of his friends Paul and Annette, probably to their final resting place.

He vowed that if he ever got out of this one, in one

piece, someone was going to pay. However, that hope appeared to be wishful thinking. What he did not know was why he was still alive, and if it wasn't for his wish for revenge, he would not have cared if he were also dead.

The men finally returned to the vehicle and from the noise, it sounded as though they were now removing some tools. Then, without warning, he was grabbed and roughly dragged to his feet. and miraculously the ties were undone, the gag and the blindfold removed. It was night-time but there was some moonlight, and compared to the situation Mark had been in, it was like being in broad daylight.

Standing before him was Clive Henderson, this time holding a Glock 19 semi-automatic pistol. And grinning.

'Well now, if you would be so kind, we will get you to dig a hole—since you have had the pleasure of resting for a while.'

Henderson was enjoying himself.

'Just to give you an idea of the size of the hole we want, Paul Williams was about the same height as you – so your length and the width enough for the two of your friends. I am sure Paul would like to be as close as possible to Annette, though it is a pity it is not in better circumstances. As for the depth – well you do not need to go too deep – after all, we will be back to dig them up again real soon.'

Mark looked at Henderson with bitterness and loathing that he could hardly contain. But said nothing. He was too shocked at the realization of what was happening. In the depth of his despair, he had hoped and prayed that Annette had somehow survived. He now had confirmation that this was not the case. They wanted him to dig their graves – just make enough room for Paul and Annette. And he was more than a little surprised to notice that the vehicle that they had travelled in was the SUV that he had hired in Washington a couple of days ago.

He just shrugged and thought that he must remember to send the FBI the bill for the additional mileage – if he lived long enough to do that. He noticed about one hundred yards further up the track was another vehicle but could not see clearly enough what it was or how many people were in it. Suffice to know that Henderson was armed, was not alone, and that Mark had a snowflake show in hell of escaping.

He was resigned to his fate and shuffled off in the direction indicated by Henderson. Because his legs had been bound so tightly for so long, walking was a bit of a problem. Henderson did not attempt to help him. They came to an area in which there were two bodies wrapped roughly in blankets, a couple of spades, and a pickaxe. Another man who went by the name of Grant, who Mark had not seen before, threw a spade to Mark and without a word commenced digging. Henderson sat down with his back against a tree and watched.

Mark had been in many tight spots before, against far smarter and more heavily armed foes, but he could not see a way out of this one. The problem was that he was alone and out in the open. If only he could distract Henderson, he was confident that he was more than capable of disabling Grant. They were working so close together – and his only weapon – a spade – would be quite lethal at that range. But how to distract Henderson? – bearing in mind that they would be expecting some kind of reaction from Mark, and therefore watching his every movement.

As the hole began to reach the specified size Mark began to lose energy and to give up hope.

He had to try something if only to find out why he was still alive. 'So, tell me Henderson – Why am I not dead? You surely have not just kept me alive to dig a hole. Since the hole will only fit two, you have other plans for me. What gives?'

Henderson stood and stretched, and then came over to the side of the hole, grinning down at Mark.

'You should not underestimate your value – albeit temporary' he began. 'My boss would like to have a chat with you, so we will dispose of these bodies, and then go see him. You have been a busy boy in recent weeks, and I am sure the two of you will exchange some interesting information. That is unless you would like to spill the beans so to speak now, and then we can bury you as well.'

Mark glared up at the FBI man and spat out his reply.

'If you think I am going to talk to anyone - either you or your boss, after what you have done to my friends - think again. And as for your boss – I assume you are referring to John Dubois and not someone at the FBI – I have some news for you – John is dead.'

If Mark intended the piece of information to have any effect on the man from the FBI, he was hugely disappointed,

Henderson just smiled.

'Mark – you are a very brave man and your loyalty to your friends is admirable. I already know about your friend Dubois. That is sad. But we move on. We are more interested in what you might be able to tell us. Interrogation techniques have changed a bit since your time in Special Forces especially when you consider you will be dead at the end of it. You will talk and help us. Like unscrambling that computer of yours, revealing the secrets of Taylor Software. And tell us what you have been up to these last few weeks – that kind of thing. So, you see

– you have immense value at the moment. And – here is the bit that seals the deal – you will be accused of the murder of your two friends – not that you will live to argue the case – so you're fucked either way.'

Mark felt sick. The whole plot that he had ascribed to John Dubois' greed was more complicated than he had assumed.

Never assume!

He had thought that John Dubois's death would bring this whole business to a rapid conclusion. That was not to be. Dubois had been used just like the rest of them. There was another level to this thing, and he shuddered as he contemplated that thought. That level was higher than anything he had been involved with so far, and that level would have access to resources.

As part of his training with the Special Forces, he had been put through several unpleasant experiences in the guise of fitting him to handle interrogation by enemy forces. But he knew it had all been a waste of time. They were not exactly dealing with people who played by the rules – and if nobody knew where you were or who had you, they were even less likely to care. While he had heard about the goings-on at Guantanamo, the CIA and other intelligence operators had other methods of interrogation that had not seen the same level of media attention.

They would just inject drugs and let matters take their course. If the victim happened to die in the course of the interrogation, then so be it. If he happened to live, after giving them everything from the name of the person who changed his first nappy to the full encryption algorithm of his software, he would be a vegetable for the rest of his natural life.

Mark was in a hopeless situation, and began to think – What the hell? He could tell them all they wanted to know without having to go through all that misery, and did it matter? But – and it was a big 'But' – they would probably kill him anyway. And Henderson was right about the outcome. The FBI could soon spin a story that Mark, or virtually anyone they cared to name, was a murderer, and kill him in the act of trying to escape, so to speak. There was just no means of escape. There did not seem to be an abundance of witnesses.

His position was hopeless.

Then his chance came unexpectedly and for all the wrong reasons. Grant got out of the hole and said he was going to relieve himself. Instead of just standing to one side, whether out of vanity or shyness that some men inexplicably feel, he went further into the scrub, out of sight of Mark and presumably out of sight of Henderson. Which meant he could not see them. As Henderson turned to direct some joke towards Grants' back Mark seized the only chance he would have to escape.

He flung himself at Henderson bringing the spade up towards his head with all the remaining strength that he could muster. The spade made a sickening sound as it connected with Henderson's head and the FBI agent collapsed under the sudden unexpected and vicious assault. The Glock sprang from his grasp and shot off to his right before Mark could prevent it or retain it for his own use.

Grant heard the noise, turned, and yelled asking what was going on. Again, that few extra seconds were critical, and were all that Mark desperately needed. Grant finished what he was doing and zipped up before turning.

Mark raced off as fast as his legs would allow in the opposite direction to where he knew there were people, keeping low to the ground – away from the dig and away from the other car.

The moonlight was now both his friend and his enemy. While he had to be able to see where he was going, the men behind would be able to see him. The problem with trying to escape, even at night, was that the human eye is attracted to movement. And he had to move and quickly. They would know where he was headed.

Unfortunately, he had no idea where he was or where it was safest to head.

He came fairly quickly to the edge of either a river or a lake. He was about to creep into the water when a couple of shots rang out. At least one of the shots barely missed him, and in his haste to avoid any others, he dived into the water making much more noise than he would have planned.

Mark was an excellent swimmer. He immediately immersed himself completely, and slowly, but powerfully and deliberately stroked away from the bank or shore. Then he turned left behind a tree stump that had presumably been washed to shore and, gasping for breath, he surfaced to peer towards the bank through the mangle of roots and branches.

On the shoreline, Grant searched the water looking for any sign of Mark. He was immediately joined by two other men and someone else who from where Mark was hiding looked like a woman and could have been Felicity. She had a very powerful torch that she swept out over the water. The light slowly arched in Marks' direction and as it came closer Mark slowly slid under the water once more, careful to not ripple the water with either movement or bubbles.

All the old skills learned in Special Forces came back to him quite naturally. They were now playing his game, by his rules. He had been given the chance because of one man's silly vanity. If he could help it, he would not make the same mistake and give his pursuers the same opportunity.

It soon became obvious that there were more people

in the vicinity than Mark had realized – probably to make sure that no one accidentally stumbled on the site while they were burying the bodies. The team, some of them clearly FBI and others could have been anything, rapidly came together and then split into three groups. Two of the groups moved in opposite directions along the banks. The other group brought a vehicle to the water's edge with its' headlights on full beam.

Mark was protected by the tree stump but that had its' problems. If the FBI knew anything about searching on water, they would look for areas of concealment, and they did. Mark had no option but to retreat from the shore, and he did.

A guy got out of the driver's seat of the Jeep and plunged straight into the water and headed out towards the tree while being covered by his rifle-carrying colleagues on the shore. He certainly had to give them credit for being thorough. The FBI guy just drove on out into the water until he reached the tree and then – nothing. He gave an all-clear signal to the agent standing on the bank, looked around, and then headed back to the shore. They must have been in radio contact with the others, and they gathered again on the shore, as Mark slowly, imperceptibly crept back to his position behind the tree stump.

The voices of his pursuers carried clearly over the water. The first thing that Mark noticed was the absence of Henderson. Whether he had killed him in the vicious attack with the spade he neither knew nor cared. His interest was in what the others would do now. The agent named Grant was quite adamant that he had shot Mark. There was blood on the ground which he took as proof. The others seemed to take Grant at his word and effectively gave up their search.

Mark had not been hit. As far as Mark knew the blood must have come from a head wound that he had suffered earlier because he had not been hit by any bullets. Grant opined that their course of action now was to complete the burial, leave a skeleton crew to keep a lookout and return in daylight for a full search of the shoreline to retrieve Marks' body.

The lady, who Mark took to be Felicity, was the only one who was not so sure. But she was either outranked or took the view that it just was not her problem. They decided there was no point in continuing and the search was abandoned.

Not the decision that Mark would have made. Until you have a body you should never assume that you have made a kill. The FBI was not in the business of killing people or at least was not supposed to be, so they were trained differently. That is unless they were bent – and these people were – but it is hard to change a habit even if you swapped sides. The other worry for Mark was that – just maybe – these guys were so confident that they did not care.

Hiding out in the water Mark was starting to feel the cold. It was only September, but the water was already beginning to chill. Now was the time that he needed some help. But who could help him now?

Paul was the ideal accomplice when you were up to your ass in alligators – but he was now dead. The beautiful and innocent Annette would have been useless – at least she would have kept him warm. She was also now dead. Floating in the water the dampness on his face could quite easily be explained. Mark did not care as the tears began to flow, out of frustration or out of grief, his emotions were so mixed up.

There was no one around to see or to know.

But his training had taught him to wait and watch, keeping movement to an absolute minimum.

So, that is what he did.

Chapter 34

Chesapeake Bay

It was ironic really. Mark had been dragged into this whole business as an unwilling participant – as an outsider—and now he appeared to be the only one left in the game. At least on the side of the good guys. That is apart from Brad Morgan, and he was not answering his telephone – and not for the first time in the period of the last few weeks.

Mark had no wish to become a hero or to bring anyone to account for what had happened because that was nothing to do with him – had it? Nor did he wish to sort out the bad apples in the Central Intelligence Agency and the Federal Bureau of Investigation. He was neither qualified nor equipped to deal with them. Nor did he wish to account to anyone for the events of the last few days – greater forces than him would have to unscramble that mess. It just was not his business.

However, he was involved in a very personal way, and he was pissed off. For whatever reason, they had taken his best friend and the lady he loved. He was not done yet. The grieving would have to wait.

Mark was now on his own, and under no illusions as

to what that meant. He had been to the movies and seen how one man could, without thought for life or limb, against insurmountable odds, save the world. While some people sat spellbound while the plot unfurled, Mark just enjoyed the impossible drama for what it was— entertainment. But this recent experience certainly was not entertainment, and the fact of the matter was, one man on his own could achieve fuck all, even with the help of mysterious and equally incredible accomplices.

Mark was pissed off because they had taken the lady that he cared about and taken her for no sane reason that he was aware of. They had also cost him a long-time friend with whom he had been in many a close scrap, each one of them at some stage or another probably responsible for saving the other man's life. And they had killed him in cold blood – and again for no sane reason to do so. So – no – he was not going to let things lie.

But first, he had to think.

He realized that the whole mess could be his fault. A small thing that he had overlooked. Why had he not reported the fact that his rental car had been stolen? The fact that the FBI had used it to transport a bound and gagged Mark Taylor was probably explainable. They could be heading for Quantico with the perpetrator of some crime a prisoner in his own vehicle. Strange, but still plausible.

But how would they have explained the two bodies? It is not normal FBI procedure for bodies to be removed from "the crime scene" and transported anywhere in a Hertz rental SUV in the dead of night. Had he reported the missing vehicle there at least would be people looking for it – but there had just too much going on. Still, while that was a mistake on Marks' part, it could not bring back his two friends.

The killing of Annette had some logic to it, insane though it may be. She was supposed to blow herself up, but since she survived that little episode, she was an obvious threat to those who had orchestrated the plan. She knew who they were. The fact that one of the planners – John Dubois—was himself dead had to be countered by the fact that, so far, few would be aware of that.

The death of Paul Williams was another matter. There would only be some logic to that if he was a threat – but to who? Were the FBI, through Henderson, and the CIA through Felicity, still working under some executive order? Had Paul been identified as a threat to the Administration? Mark still thought that this was implausible but then why had Paul been eliminated in such a brutal and callous way? He had to find out, but at this very moment in time, he had other things to worry about.

In the cold of the water, and the early hours of the morning, the mind plays tricks. He was supposed to be somewhere tucked up, warm and snug in his bed, but he wasn't. At such times, the mind makes every minor event a catastrophe and the "if only" scenarios plague every thought process.

If only Mark had made an effort many months ago to get closer to Annette – then he would have realized that something was not quite right – and people talk about things, that they otherwise would not, between the sheets. But he was a wimp, or he was too shy. If only when they returned to the safe house, they had announced that John Dubois was dead. That should have been an end to the matter. But they were too shocked by finding Henderson there and finding Annette being threatened by Felicity. If only Brad Morgan had realized that Felicity was on the other side – surely there must have been some hint, even if they did not consummate their relationship.

However - what if Brad did know? Or was Felicity just too clever? What if Mark had been conned? What if Brad was not on his side after all?

The death of John Dubois did not seem to have changed anything. That meant that the CIA and the FBI each had someone or some group working within their ranks who was playing at a higher level in some corrupt, if insane, game. This should narrow the field down a little. Both organizations had very strict methods of vetting their people. But that did not prevent the occasional bad apple from sneaking through, so the intelligence and security services had their own office manual about that. The manual did not say how they would be dealt with when caught. What it did say was that they would be trusted and loyal friends, so it was likely that their reception would not be nice. Then was the question of how to find them.

Mark recalled going through a similar analysis in trying to fathom out the role of John Dubois, and how wide of the mark he had been on that! He felt that this case should be much simpler, but still impossible to reach any logical conclusion. Since all the trick-cyclists that the government employed would claim to have sorted out all the ego, prestige, revenge, political, historical, and other crap, that left just two motivational things to look for – Money, which was quite simple if you knew who you were investigating, and Ideology, which made things difficult or impossible to resolve.

Deep down Mark thought it doubtful that ideology was a factor so that left Money – and in Marks's experience that meant drugs. Was the simple answer that John Dubois had provided money for drugs in exchange for cooperation?

If only? Mark shook himself – get back to the present! The first thing he had to think about was getting himself cleaned up – for the second time in as many days he was a mess. And he had to find somewhere to do that without revealing himself to anyone, especially in the police or any other organization that represented the federal authorities. It did not matter what he thought of the people who were after him. They were the FBI – and that would count for far more in the eyes of anyone who was on his trail than a mere software programmer.

He turned his attention to the environment. The water that he was in was saltwater, not river water, and by the currents he had felt, first going one way and then the other, he had to be in some kind of bay or an inlet of the sea. After studying his surroundings and remembering the length of the journey in the back of the SUV, he guessed that the most likely place he could be somewhere on the Chesapeake Bay estuary. There would be many weekend holiday homes scattered around this vast area that most of them were likely to be vacant – that was the good news. The bad news was that the Chesapeake Bay probably had more than eleven thousand miles of shoreline – a distance equivalent to almost halfway around the world. That meant that his chance of being able to find Henderson and Felicity again, and more importantly the bodies of his two friends, was remote. That is if the agents did not find him first.

Think! – What would they expect him to do?

After a long period of contemplation hiding in the water, he made a decision. The agents had gone back to the burial site and then, after what seemed like hours, they had all moved in a direction that looked northwest by Marks' crude judgment based on the stars. Therefore, to journey south would take him deeper into the Bay, and eventually, he would have to swim or find a boat or a runabout. They would surely also expect him to travel north-west, following the track and back to the relative safety of people and more open space. Not that Henderson would be in much condition for a while to follow anyone, but Mark had to assume from their conversation that they would summon some more people – and sooner rather than later.

The fact that away in the distance to the north-west he could now see some vehicle lights, and they appeared to be getting closer, made his decision more or less inevitable. It was a fair assumption that a guard detail would occupy the area overnight. At least that is what would be a logical conclusion – not that there was much logic in the recent events as they had unfolded.

So, he swam and crawled slowly and carefully south, and then got out of the water and headed south-east going deeper into the Bay.

He finally came across what he was looking for. The cottage was old and looked to be in a state of disrepair, either from a lack of use or because the owners just did not care.

That was of no concern to Mark. He reconnoitred the dwelling, looking for any sign that it was occupied. There was nothing—no noise, no light, nobody. It was a ramshackle place with numerous rooms that looked as though they had been added with very little thought for architectural elegance.

Gaining entry was not an issue – what Mark assumed to be the front door was not locked. There was nothing inside worth keeping, or few people came this way, or the owners figured those thieves would break in anyway – so what was the point?

Mark went in and soon discovered he had the story slightly wrong. There was light, put out by a vintage oil lamp. It had been masked by the heavy curtains that hung over the windows and it was just sufficiently bright to enable him to peer around.

An old man, wrapped in a blanket, was asleep in a chair, gently snoring away, and judging by the number of assorted bottles scattered around the place, he was not about to wake up any time soon. There was another oil lamp on the table, but it had either never been lit or switched off or the oil had run out.

Mark's initial thought was to leave. But, on second thought, he did not know where he was and this could be the only place, and he had to get out of his wet clothes and cleaned up. If the old man woke up, he was confident he could handle the situation. He circled the man and entered what was an underused bathroom. There was running cold water. That did not worry Mark because he was relatively cold anyway and in fact, he was suffering from slight hyperthermia.

He stripped off his wet clothing, quickly cleaned up, and dried himself on what he took to be a towel. Then he went into what was a bedroom and found an amazing collection of shirts, trousers, jerseys, and assorted underwear that seemed a little out of place. The clothes were all too large to fit the old man asleep in the next room, so Mark surmised that the cottage had another resident. So where was the other man?

Mark decided to get dressed as quickly as possible before anyone interrupted his activity. The neck size of the clothes was a little on the large size, yet the trousers were a little short, but Mark soon found a set of clothes that were more or less the correct size, and he changed into them.

He was about to leave the room when he heard a banging coming from the door through which Mark had entered the cottage earlier. In the room that Mark found himself in there was no way out of it other than back to where the old man was asleep or through a window. From Marks' cursory examination of the place, it did not look as though the windows had been opened in his lifetime, so that option was a no-brainer. Remembering the layout of the place he could not recall seeing another easy exit.

He had no other choice than to wait and see what happened.

After the second set of bangs, a voice yelled 'Hello? Is anybody home? FBI!'

That greeting was met with silence. There came a loud crash, and the front door was smashed in. It all seemed pretty pointless since even a casual look would have proved that the door was not locked. But it certainly got the attention of the old man.

He jumped to his feet with amazing agility, and to Mark's surprise, he held a mean-looking rifle which added weight to his demand to know what the fuck was going on.

The first man who entered was dressed in black trousers and a dark blue windcheater which had "FBI" emblazoned on the top left pocket. He held his hands outward showing that he was only carrying a torch, and not holding a weapon, but no doubt carrying one.

'Ok—cool it – we are FBI – we're looking for a fugitive.'

This did not seem to impress the old man who had an unmistakable authority in his voice as he replied to the intruder.

'That does not give you the right to break into my home. Now leave your card so I can claim to get the door fixed – and clear off!'

He reached down to the table, struck a match, and lit the lamp. The man in the FBI windcheater looked all embarrassed as did his identically dressed colleague who had followed him in.

'We are very sorry to bother you, and we will not take up much of your time. We just had to check that he was not here – and we were not aware there was anyone at home. We will be on our way shortly. And your name, Sir?'

The old man looked at the FBI agent with something close to contempt and gave the impression that this was not his first meeting with officials, but he did reply.

'Shannon – Elliott, you can have my rank and serial number, social security number, date of birth, and what I had for breakfast if you like.'

The FBI agent was not the least bit concerned by the old man's attitude, simply replying.

'So, you are Elliott!' and left it at that.

Despite the reaction of the old man, his lethal-looking weapon, and his explanation that he had seen no one, the FBI agent came further into the room. He shone his powerful torch and headed towards another door and out into another part at the back of the cottage where Mark could hear him rummaging, none too quietly, around. The other man first went into the bathroom where Mark had cleaned himself and then came into the bedroom. Mark had only seconds to react. He got down on the floor and squeezed under the bed. Not that there was much room. The bed was old, heavy, and fairly low to the ground. Underneath it was all manner of things that had just been stored there, or kicked there, out of the way.

Mark could see the agents' feet as he moved around the bed, and it was only a matter of time before he came around to the side where Mark was hiding. Only good luck, and probably the agents' apparent total disinterest in what he was doing, is what probably saved Mark. The search was fortunately only cursory and the light from the man's torch reflected off the junk. When the FBI agent bent down to look from the opposite side of the bed, it was like a wall. Mark was just glad when the guy left because breathing would have caused the bed to lift if ever so slightly off the floor. They searched the rest of the house, but it was rapid and not very thorough, indicating that they did not expect to find anything.

Finally, the senior FBI agent went back to where this Elliott had lit the oil lamp and asked the old man one final question.

'Is there anywhere down here where you think anyone could hide?'

The old man just laughed.

'There certainly would be no point in going any further south than here – unless he has webbed feet and he is a bloody good swimmer. No – if anyone had been this way I would know – and there hasn't—so I don't.'

'Ah well – he may be dead and floating in the river —if you come across a body, please let us know.'

'Why come looking for your fugitive in here, if you think he might be floating in the river? You are not making much sense young man – is he or isn't he dead? In any case—if he were floating as you say, you are heading in the wrong direction – the tide is coming in now so you should head north not south. Don't they teach you anything at Quantico?' said the old man with nothing but contempt in his voice.

We will leave you in peace Elliott. Thanks for your help and understanding.' the young FBI agent muttered, as he and his accomplice sought to get the hell out of the cottage.

As the two FBI agents turned to go, they were stopped by a barked command from the old man. It seemed a fair assumption that they knew who this guy was or had been. It also seemed a fair assumption that they were not going anywhere without leaving a card. As they left the old man muttered something along the lines of 'What is the Bureau coming to?' which gave Mark the startling clue that the man was ex FBI, or ex-CIA or at least an ex-policeman, or possibly ex-military.

Shaking his head as the agents left, the old man, picked up a book, dumped his feet on the coffee table, and commenced to read as though this kind of thing happened every day.

Mark now had another dilemma – how to get out? From his cursory examination of the outside of the building, there had been no visible evidence of any form of transport, power, or telephones. The old man was very confident and fit, but he doubted that he had walked here, so that was a puzzle. Mark now had the unfortunate confirmation that he could go no further south, and it appeared that the FBI, although they did not know it, had him trapped.

After about 10 minutes the FBI made a return visit. This time they knocked timidly on the door, but still walked in uninvited.

'Your boat – I assume the boat at the jetty is yours —I see it has a security alarm on it – but is it set? And if not, is there any chance someone could be hiding on board?'

The old man let out another big sigh, but this time remained in his seat, before replying.

'What would be the point of having a security alarm if it was not set? So it is, and no! If your dead man was able to defeat the alarm, which I doubt, he would have sailed away long ago and not be waiting around for you idiots to find him.'

For Mark, this piece of information answered the question of how the old man had got here. Also, he now had a means of escape. He would have very little trouble with the boat alarm, despite the old man's opinion to the contrary. He just had to wait until the place was less crowded. And the FBI agents quickly helped him in that regard. They left looking humbled, disappointed but pleased that this little escapade was over.

After a while, it became evident that the old man was not about to fall asleep again anytime soon and Mark had to do something. He decided it was worth the gamble. The FBI agents would now be well on their way – back to the north and well out of earshot. His original thought that Elliott was some kind of crook, and known to the FBI, had been mellowed by his reference to the Bureau. A genuine crook would have referred to them in far less polite terms. So, he just got up and walked in on the old man who went by the name of Elliott.

The old man got his second shock of the night and again leaped to his feet, gun in hand.

'Hands where I can see them and stop right where you are!' the old man barked.

There was not even a hint of fear in his voice. There was authority and coldness, which made Mark think that revealing himself had been a mistake.

Mark held his hands out in front of him.

'I am not who you think I am – I don't mean you any harm.' began Mark, but he had no chance to elaborate. The rifle butt swung up expertly and caught Mark right on the temple – the same one that had been grazed by a bullet earlier in the day – or was it yesterday? His immediate reaction was one of intense pain but then he collapsed in a crumpled heap on the floor, and everything again went blank. For the second time in the space of twenty-four hours, Mark was out cold.

Not bad for an ex-Marine with all that experience in the Special Forces and Delta.

When Mark came to, he was lying on the floor trussed up like a turkey although he did not appear to have been blindfolded or gagged. Again – for the second time in as many days – it was getting to be something of a habit! There was a deep throbbing in his head that would not go away. His legs felt numb. He squirmed around to look at them and he immediately saw the problem. He had been bound so that his legs were doubled up. Then he was glad that they were numb because the way he had been tied up would have caused him excruciating pain in that position if he had been able to feel anything.

He was not looking forward to the binding coming off but then reflected he probably would not know. Was this finally the end of the road? He had luck very much on his side when he had escaped from Henderson. And he had been extremely lucky that the FBI search of the cottage had been little more than cursory. Now he had been expertly tied up by a man who had to be at least twice Mark's age, and his luck seemed to have come to a somewhat abrupt end. For someone with Mark's military experience, he was not having a good couple of days. And what did this tell him of the old man whose residence he had stumbled into?

The old man must have noticed the movement. He put down the book and stared at Mark. There was no more than a moments' hesitancy, then he sat forward, his right hand never far from the rifle, cool but intelligent eyes studying the man who lay before him.

The confidence in the old man's voice that Mark had sensed before was still there.

'And who exactly are you and what would you be doing here?'

Deep down Mark detected an Irish brogue. There appeared to be no automatic assumption that Mark had anything to do with the FBI's claims of a fugitive, even though the three visits, late at night, miles from anywhere, had occurred only minutes apart. There was no comment on Mark's clothing so the old man either did not know or did not care, that Mark had stolen them from one of his bedrooms.

'Mark – Mark Taylor' he said as he looked around the room in the forlorn hope of finding some improbable means of escape or some equally improbable source of assistance.

'And what would Mark Taylor be doing out in the middle of the Chesapeake, in the middle of the night, being chased by the FBI?' the old man asked, sounding as though he did not expect much in the way of a response that would make any sense.

Marks' response did engender some interest.

'I am with the CIA!' was all that Mark could think of to say. He was not about to say he had recently, probably, almost decapitated an FBI agent, and eluded a female CIA agent with the unlikely name of Felicity, to escape from the burial site of another CIA agent, only to be captured again by this old man.

It sounded very unlike the CIA, particularly since the CIA does not normally run from the FBI. But those were the only words that Mark felt would at least buy him some time, and after all, it was close to the truth. He was right.

'Just give me a minute while I ring the President and find out what mission he has the CIA working on – in the Chesapeake' the old man responded, clearly enjoying himself.

'Let me remind you – just in case you are a bit slow – the CIA works overseas – this is about as close to Washington DC, the White House, and all the other trappings of the good old US of A as you can get. Try some other explanation.'

'I have just returned from overseas and was just tying up a few loose ends.' Mark offered but without much hope.

He would have shrugged his shoulders except that, his arms were so tightly bound behind him, he could not.

'Taylor? Mark Taylor? I know that name, but you are a little on the young side.' Then almost as an after-though 'What is your father's first name?'

Mark was surprised by the question, which was completely out of the leftfield but answered anyway.

'Harold – Harold Taylor.'

The old man moved closer to the edge of the seat.

'Where is he stationed at the moment – you could have just saved your ass – and don't give me any shit about confidentiality – where is he stationed?'

'Wellington – Wellington New Zealand. That is where I have just come back from.'

That answer seemed to strike a chord with the old man. He stroked his chin thoughtfully staring at Mark. Then a smile spread over his face as he came to a decision.

'Well, I'll be darned. You don't remember me, do you? But then—again, why should you? Are you still into reading people by their body language?'

He laughed out loud as Mark racked his memory to think. Who is, or was, this guy? He obviously knew Mark.

Mark had, from a very early age been able to read what people were like, just from looking at them. That could be a pain up the ass at times. The problem that it presented was that he had made up his mind about whether he liked or disliked a person before they even spoke. Communication between human beings is always a two-way process. It meant that he found that people did not like him, in his view because they had realized that Mark had read them, and the next step from being "discovered" is to resent the discoverer. The other problem was – it did not always work, or it got masked by other issues – as was the case with Annette. But now he was in the presence of a guy who Mark thought was ok, and if you extended the perverse logic of human relations a little bit, could assume that the guy liked him.

He got his answer. Elliott abruptly got to his feet and grabbed an evil-looking knife from the side of his chair. Mark cringed not knowing what to expect, but with a couple of swift cuts, the old man freed Mark from the tethers. The old man then laughed long and hard as Mark fought the pain as the circulation returned to his now freed limbs.

Eventually, Mark restored something resembling full circulation as he regained the use of his legs. He reached out a hand across the table. The old man took the hand and responded 'Elliott Shannon.'

The handshake was strong, the dark blue eyes piercing. Elliott was about five feet ten, and although he was beginning to develop a pot, he was well muscled. His hair was dishevelled, grey, and receding, but his face was still handsome, and there was evidence of a ready smile.

Mark relied on body language.

'I am the guy that the FBI is looking for, except that they were not the real FBI.' Mark said in a matter-of-fact voice. 'I am just trying to avoid being killed before I have the time to tell someone who cares the truth about what happened in New York City.'

'Yes – I heard about that – nasty business. So, you are another one of the conspiracy theorists who thinks only he knows the truth.' Elliott chuckled, but his eyes never left Marks. And there was a certain coldness behind the smile. Mark wondered about how Elliott could have heard about New York. There was no evidence of any form of communication, no television, or radio, no telephone. Then Elliott continued.

'Do you want to talk about your theory? There is plenty of time – you cannot go anywhere until it's light – and that is still a couple of hours away.'

Mark hesitated, not knowing what to do or expect. And what did this old man mean by not going anywhere? He decided that innocence and honesty were now his best policy, but before that, he had to find out where Shannon was coming from.

'Am I right to assume you are ex FBI?' he asked, not expecting an answer. But at that Elliott Shannon laughed out loud again before he replied.

'Not bloody likely! But – Yes! You are on the right track—CIA – I was the most promoted agent the Company ever had – and the most demoted – until they finally retired me.'

He continued laughing for some time, lost in his own thoughts and memories. But then he recovered.

'Yes – I worked for the CIA – not for that prissy New York field office where our FBI visitors were from.'

The expression on his face told Mark that he was none too pleased with the visitors, but it was unclear what the significance of that was.

Since he was alone and had few ideas as to how to proceed from here, he figured that there was no harm in telling at least part of his story, so Mark did just that - told it in reverse – the most recent events first.

'Those FBI visitors, as you call them, may have been fine, but they were working under instruction from someone who is bent – the guy who is responsible for the deaths of a lady and my best friend – who incidentally also happens to be – sorry happened to be – a CIA agent. The FBI officers and another CIA agent had their bodies not far from here and were intent on burying them once I had dug the graves. There is nothing remarkable in my still being alive. The so-called "Boss" of the operation wants a word with me before they planned to kill me too and pinned the murder of my two friends on me. I had a bit of luck and managed to escape.'

Mark made it all sound so matter of fact, but it was so incredible – no one would seriously believe that story. But Elliott did and by now was looking serious.

'Why would they want to do that? Who was the lady? What has the CIA got to do with all this? Who the hell are you?' The questions came flooding out, but the look on his face was one of concentration and intrigue rather than one of disbelief.

'Whoa – slow down!'

Again, Mark decided to deal with Elliott's questions in reverse order. 'I am an ex-Marine - Delta Force, but nothing special. My friend the CIA guy – Paul—who got killed was also an ex-Special Forces buddy of mine. We had just travelled to the South Pacific to gather evidence on a terrorist plot for the anniversary of 9/11. Except that it wasn't a terrorist plot. I can explain how I got dragged into this thing if you like – it reads like a kids' adventure story and almost defies belief. I believe that can wait. The lady was the third bomber and, if you know what happened in New York, the third bomb failed. It failed because Paul and I talked her out of it.'

'As for your question of - Why the CIA was involved? – the FBI and the CIA had at least two opportunities to react before the events took place on September 11th, but someone blocked the information. I believe I now know at least two names – one at the FBI and the other at the CIA – who were involved. As for the 'Why' people got killed? – I can only assume that it was to silence the remaining players. The other theory you don't want to know about.'

'Try me' said Elliott as he sat forward, obviously intrigued, but also his brain was working overtime.

'Well, it was an alternative theory that Paul Williams came up with. He suggested that there was a cover-up at the highest level—instructions came down from on high to just let the plot proceed, and then the Commander-in-Chief could claim "I told you so – al Qaeda can strike us anywhere any time." Mark replied with a shrug.

Again, Elliott laughed.

'Your Paul Williams has been watching too many movies.' He considered the information for no more than a few moments, and then asked, 'When you say it was not a terrorist plot – how do you know that?'

'I know that because the day after the event, the guy who orchestrated the whole thing – an American businessman called John Dubois—committed suicide by jumping from the 16th floor of a New York City building. Not the kind of thing your average successful CEO, of an equally successful finance and insurance company does – unless too many things had caught up with him.'

The expression on Elliott's face changed instantly to one of shock. 'I know that name!' he grimaced. Without saying another word, he got up and walked to what was the back door to his ramshackle property, across a yard and into a lean-to shed. Mark followed, his head still throbbing and his muscles still aching, but caught up with Elliott's enthusiasm.

In the shed, Elliott started up a portable generator, and almost immediately lights came on in the cottage. He then walked back into the cottage, Mark trailing along behind like someone forgotten, into another room and unlocked a very old bureau-style desk. Sitting on the desk was a laptop computer, which was far from very old, which Elliott proceeded to fire up.

He turned to Mark and, almost as an afterthought, apologized for the fact that the battery for the laptop had long since died. It was fairly clear to Mark that Elliott's computer keyboard skills were fairly limited, but he eventually got through to some network that looked suspiciously like an FBI one. It was doubtful that even an ex-CIA man was supposed to be in there.

Shannon did not indicate that he cared and typed 'John Dubois' into the search engine. After a few moments, it came up with a message—Not Found. He then tried another database but got the same result – Not Found.

'Ok – that at least tells us something!' he almost muttered to himself.

'What does it tell us?' Mark asked, beginning to get a little impatient with his new associates' slow ponderous computer keyboard skills.

'This is a low-level database where virtually anyone – well anyone at the FBI and some of our other agencies – can go to look up some persons of interest. I doubt whether John Dubois would have been deleted so soon after his death by any legal means. That is quite impossible. But someone has deleted him – at least under the name of Dubois.' Elliott mused.

'Do you mind if I have a go? I know a fair bit about computers and databases.'

Elliott looked a little apprehensive but moved aside and they swapped places. Mark immediately began typing at a speed that Elliott could only wonder at and certainly one that he could not keep up with. Very quickly Mark was into another database and typed Dubois and then a whole variety of miss-spelled versions – but again—nothing.

After a moment's thought, he typed Henderson into the search engine. The screen presented a list of nine Henderson's. There was one in New York, so Mark clicked on that, and brief details appeared around the FBI career of one Irene Henderson. That made no sense. He went back the database, selected terminated, and typed the full name – Clive Henderson. That got a reaction and an even sharper reaction from Elliott Shannon.

'You know this guy too? You certainly have some very interesting friends.'

'No – I wouldn't exactly describe him as a friend. He was the FBI agent who was burying bodies not far from here.' Mark responded. 'But how do you know him – apart from the fact that he is or was with the FBI?'

'During an investigation at the time of the original 9/11, I was assigned to look at contacts between the CIA and the FBI that occurred both before and after the event. During that investigation, there developed a strong suspicion that your friend Clive Henderson was somehow involved in withholding information. Nothing was proven, and the investigation was eventually dropped. Something about too many assumptions being made was the story. They teach us in spy school not to make assumptions – but how the hell you are supposed to analyse without assuming something is a mystery to me. However, the case was dropped and in fact, Henderson came out of it smelling like roses. For my trouble, I got a back-office desk job counting paper clips. So how did you get to know him?'

Mark tried to remember how much he had already told Shannon, but in the end decided that the guy seemed to have such clarity of thought, despite the physical evidence to the contrary – he had lost count of the bottles around the place – he would catch up.

'I first met him after my office had been broken into a few weeks ago – and he was as useless as tits on a bull. We never found out anything about the break-in, or what happened to a work colleague who went missing. The second time was at a CIA safe house yesterday. He was the guy who shot my two friends Paul and the lady who was the third bomber – Annette was her name. He certainly gets around and seems to turn up whenever there is trouble. But according to this file, his employment was terminated fifteen months ago!'

'You are about to say that your office break-in has something to do with the events in New York City the other day?' Shannon asked in a voice that was at the same time incredulous and disbelieving.

'I cannot discount that. It was a strange day. John Dubois certainly had something to do with it – so I found out later. And a CIA guy who was working for me at the time was the one who simply disappeared.'

The look on Elliott Shannon's face was a picture. Mark held up his hands in supplication. 'It is a long story. – the CIA guy was a plant in my company, but the plant was supposed to have been an FBI agent, they just screwed up – yet again.'

This new piece of incredible information was ignored. Shannon got up and paced the room. Mark just waited. Eventually, he came to a decision.

'I think you are right. There are too many coincidences, both in your story and in my experience with the Company. I cannot remember the details, but John Dubois – incidentally, that is not his original name – was always bad news and now I realize why the investigations never went far – he was being protected. And Clive Henderson – while I have a prior interest in nailing that bastard – as you say he turns up at the most convenient – or inconvenient – times. Not only that, but he is also apparently still claiming to be FBI. That means one of only two things. Either he is a rogue but still being controlled by someone at the FBI or he is running a deep undercover operation. Ok—you can count me in – so what do you plan to do?'

The offer of assistance came as a complete, but welcome,

surprise. Mark had barely thought more than one step ahead during the last few hours, but he knew he had been alone, and he needed all the help that he could get. He smiled at the thought.

'I suppose it is out of the question to walk up to the J Edgar Hoover Building and make an appointment with the Director?'

Shannon sighed but smiled.

'It is out of the question for me – but there may be a way we can do something similar. What do you think Henderson and his accomplices will do now? Well, let me tell you.' He carried on talking as though to himself. 'They will stick with a story that says that you were responsible for the murder of your two friends and that is why you are a fugitive. They will have an all-points bulletin out to have you apprehended dead or alive – and they will hope that one of their own finds you first. That way they can assure the former rather than the latter. Make you feel good about yourself? – having the whole country on the lookout for you?'

Shannon laughed at that too. Mark did not.

Mark however saw the logic of the argument, and he was not fazed by it.

'I agree with your assessment – but they are not going to get away with it. There must be something we can do – and you indicated that there may be a way – so what is it?'

'Well, how is this for a plan?'

Shannon spent the next half hour outlining a possible plan. Mark was impressed with the confidence his new associate showed but was unimpressed with the story so far.

'Are you saying that we tell both agencies what has

transpired so that they can in effect cover their ass?' Mark retorted.

He looked at Mark as though he were from another planet, but then mellowed.

'How else do you think this is going to work? If you think that either Agency is going to admit involvement – think again. And at this stage, we do not know how many Agency and Bureau people are involved, or how high up the organizations this has infiltrated. And you must know how the bureaucracy works. If you think that either organization is going to admit that Americans, and not al Qaeda, was responsible for the deaths of our citizens in New York City– again – think.'

Mark sagged in the chair.

The logic of what Elliott had said was crystal clear and he knew deep down that he had to be correct. He would need to pick himself up off the deck and at least ensure that the Agencies took action against the key rogue players. Not quite as good as total public humiliation but it would have to do. For now.

Mark still had a couple of cards to play. The involvement of the Serbian General Ilic Milicic which was hard to equate with al Qaeda, and the involvement of Doctor Abdul Jabbar who would be none too pleased with the botched bombing and the cutting off of funding with the suicide of his source. Mark had also given quite a bit of information to Peter in Australia, and he did not expect that the information would be idle for long. He decided to say nothing at this stage about these three subjects and instead went along with the Shannon plan.

'My father – sorry Harold Taylor - knows the Chief Executive Officer of the Washington Post – something about meeting him at the tender age of twenty-two in Vietnam – and they have stayed in touch ever since. I know one of the sub-editors—Charles Coll – he was in Bosnia covering the war in 1993 and we became friends. He may remember me.'

'Ok – we need to move – but first, you need to get out of those pansy clothes and into something a little classier.'

Mark suddenly remembered about the clothes.

'I am sorry – I stole them from you.' which statement caused Elliott again to laugh out loud.

'Those will be from my son's collection – incidentally, you did not think that all the bottles around the place were mine, did you?' The look on Mark's face told the story and Shannon laughed again.

'My son is with the DIA – US Special Forces – De oppresso liber – to free from oppression - and all that. So, you are in good company. He comes and goes – don't ask where from or where to. Last night he had a few drinks before heading off on another assignment. As for myself – I don't drink. Surprised Huh? Not for me the same fate as so many ex-CIA bodies. Most drink themselves into oblivion within a year of retirement. They claim they miss all the cloak and dagger stuff, while in reality—no one wants them anymore. There is not a huge demand in the market for ex-spooks. But not for me. And as for this ramshackle place I call home – I started house sitting for an associate several years ago. He disappeared from the face of the earth a year or so back, probably dead in some God-forsaken backwater. But we live in hope. And rent-free.'

'Now come on. We have things to do. But first, let's get you fixed up.'

When Shannon had finished, Mark had to say he was impressed. Gone was the curly hair that since leaving the military he had so fastidiously grown – in Elliott's theory those who put on false beards and false hair by way of disguises were delusional. He was now back to the haircut he had when he was in the military. Elliott's logic was that in Washington every second person had a military haircut, and that included the residents at Langley, although the CIA was, in fact, a civilian organization. The dark grey suit – also from his sons' collection – together with a white shirt and neutral tie – made him look – well ordinary, and that was the purpose.

Elliott gave him a pair of thick rimmed lightly shaded glasses that had no effect on his sight but served to cover the worst of the various injuries around his head. Mark could walk the street, and few would recognize him. He changed out of the suit and returned to the more casual wear that he had been in before, although even that had been purloined from his host. The change was necessary – it would look a little stupid if someone saw him traveling in a boat on the Chesapeake Bay dressed up as a funeral director – however appropriate that may have seemed.

The sun, such as it was, was beginning to light the sky. Shannon scurried around filling a bag with all manner of bits and pieces, and then led Mark out into the early morning air and off into the bushes where there was no discernible track. To Mark's surprise, they came to a small jetty, and there tied up alongside was a very racy-looking boat.

They climbed on board, Mark standing around like a loose goose, while Elliott first switched off the alarm and then busied himself with checking and preparing the boat for their trip down the Chesapeake.

Finally satisfied with the preparations, Elliott fired up the powerful engines and after letting them run on idle for a few minutes, cast the lines off the jetty. The contented smile of a man who knew exactly what he was roared into the wind.

'Ok—Let's go and whip some ass.'

For the first time in several days, Mark began to feel a degree of confidence in what they were about to do.

He sure felt that it was about time things started to go his way. He had been very lucky so far – well he was still alive. It was about time things started to happen because they were planned that way, rather than by pure chance or by just plain old dumb luck.

In some ways, he was going to be somewhat pleasantly surprised.

But not in the ways that he may have expected.

Chapter 35

Media Frenzy

It was a beautiful morning for a cruise on the Chesapeake Bay. There was very little wind, other than a gentle offshore breeze that they both found invigorating. The Chesapeake was always busy with boats and ships of all nationalities and sizes. The banks of the Bay were a strange and confusing mixture of the residential and industrial sprawl, interspersed with acres of wilderness. It seemed a fitting backdrop for what they were about to do – it was certainly cheeky, but they had nothing to lose.

They cruised south at a good speed until they came to the mouth of the Potomac River. Shannon then slowed the boat and checked for other boats in the vicinity, then turned west to go up the river.

He continued through Washington itself until he came to a small marina – small that is in the number of boats that it could accommodate. The facilities there were second to none and the boat that they were in seemed tiny alongside the other boats in the marina. Shannon knew exactly where he was going and skilfully brought the boat alongside the jetty, tied up, and then shut off the engines.

He quickly attached several cables and pipes to fixtures

on the jetty and then came back into the cabin where Mark was waiting. He then removed the cover from a TV and tuned in to the CNN news channel.

'Ok – now to get in touch with the radio people!'

Shannon dialled the number for the WTOP – one of two all-news radio stations serving metropolitan Washington. It was soon clear that Elliott was as good as his word. He obviously knew the people who he was contacting very well – a little too well, but that did not matter. The man he was talking to was Douglas Curtis who was WTOP's morning news Anchor. His shift normally finished at ten o'clock but like many in the media, there were more pressing things to worry about this morning than taking time out. After an exchange of pleasantries, Elliott got down to business.

'Hi, Doug – I think I have a story for you—I am onto something big. It concerns what happened in New York City a couple of days ago on September the 11th. There would appear to be more to those events than has been picked up so far. I have had contacts with some people – and they are genuine—who say that they know who planned the whole thing. They also say that the FBI knew beforehand that it was going to happen.'

The story that Elliott delivered was in an even tone – no drama—no excitement. Just a matter-of-fact explanation. It had the desired effect. Doug Curtis was the man in charge of the news service that several stations broadcast at half-hourly intervals throughout each day, and like many in the city of Washington DC, he was looking for a new angle on a story that was already beginning to lose some of its news-worthy-ness.

The hot news of the day – and several days to come – would be the events in New York City. They had to keep broadcasting the same regurgitated stories, albeit from different angles, because their listeners had an insatiable appetite for more information – the more controversial the better. But listeners are fickle and would soon switch channels if the newsreaders did not come up with something new or different.

'Just how reliable is your source?' Doug asked. He was already examining the outline of the next rather bland bulletin and hoping that he could spice it up.

'Well, it is early days. But I would say that it is rock solid. I am currently with a guy who was at the scene of the third explosion. Someone is trying to kill him now so I guess that means his information must be pretty much correct.'

Curtis could hardly resist the bait that Elliott had dangled before him but was not quite ready to bite.

'Why come to me, Elliott? – Why radio? With a story like you say – why have you not gone to CNN or the Washington Post? If it is true – and don't misunderstand me – I know you have never given me a bum steer in the past. The story could be worth a fortune. We don't have that kind of budget.'

One of the things about the Media, worldwide and whether involved in radio, TV, or print, was that there were a few unwritten rules that most, although not all, complied with. Reporters did not, contrary to popular belief, creep around individually getting a thousand views on the same story. They shared information. If a story came to the attention of one, unless there was a Pulitzer Prize beckoning, he or she usually talked to other reporters.

That was not especially generous. There was no point in publishing a scoop if everyone already knew about it. There was no point in raving about something if it turned into a damp squib. And of course, there was the chance that something good would come out of such cooperation – others may be able to add to the story, if not on the current story, then on future stories. The art of journalism was in the way the story got presented. One part of the art was knowing who to present it to, and you did not need to be involved in the game to know that.

Most people at work, contrary to the view put out by the very media themselves, did not sit there watching TV. They listened to the radio. But before any of this could happen the story had to be verified.

The skill with which Elliott handled the man was something to behold. Elliott laughed for not the first time today.

'You know me Doug – money does not interest me. The Post and CNN are working on a similar story. It should break later today. But I owe you one. Do you want to meet this guy? – I can arrange it if you want. But you will need to be quick.'

Doug Curtis was hooked.

'Where are you? It would take me hours to get to that ramshackle cottage you call home!'

'No problem! We are at the Columbia Island Marina on the Pentagon lagoon. The usual spot. Why not pop down? But three things before you come. First—how about a snippet on the news before your leave? Second—don't tell anyone any more than you need to for the moment. Third – make sure you are alone, and you are not followed—I don't want to get my ass blown off just yet. I don't care about yours – but you should.'

Doug got the message loud and clear – and he had taken the bait – hook, line, and sinker. He had almost been told the truth, except that they had yet to get CNN and the Post involved – but everything was relative. He had the added thrill that he could be followed and in a strange sort of way that made him feel as though he was already involved.

Shannon hung up the telephone and laughed.

'If you hire a Labrador as Product Tester in a pet food factory – you will get the result that you wanted.'

Mark just raised his eyebrows. Elliott Shannon should be taking this much more seriously than appeared to be the case. But what choice did Mark have?

They turned the radio to WTOP.

Mark had to somehow do the same thing as Elliott had just done but dealing with the print media involved a different set of rules. The problem was to get the Washington Post to move at the same speed. While they had good reporters, and they would just love the story, there was the question of reliability, trust, ethics, and all the other matters that would be raised before they would run with it. So, he rang Harold Taylor on his cell phone.

The call which presumably went to Wellington took forever to connect. Eventually, the stern voice of Mark's father came on the line.

'Hi, Dad – it's Mark.'

The reaction he got was not quite what he expected but was nonetheless along the right track.

'What the hell has been going on in New York? I thought you would have had the whole thing sewn up.'

It was typical of his father to blame his son even though Harold was already aware that all had not gone well with Mark's visit to the CIA at Langley. It was also typical for him to forget that his son was also a very small cog in a very big wheel. And his son was not being paid by anyone.

'Well, we thought so. But, as usual, they did not believe the story. Or they were too slow to react. Or we did not have the full facts as it turned out. Or some combination of all three. That analysis can come later. Now we have a much more pressing problem. We need to get in touch with someone at the Washington Post – I believe you know the Chief.'

Mark was about to get irritated, as always seemed to happen when he talked to his father but kept himself under control.

'Who is "we"? Is Paul still with you?'

'Dad – Paul is dead – courtesy of our friends in the FBI –we now are me and Elliott Shannon.'

That got a reaction.

'Shit!' Mark was certain he heard his father saying.

'How did you let that happen?' but ignored the jibe. Harold was not thinking straight.

'Ok – I am on my way back to the United States as soon as we end this conversation and tie up a few loose ends – this thing has got to stop. I think I know Elliott Shannon. He retired from the Company a couple of years ago. A good man. How did he get involved?'

'Oh – I met him quite by chance early this morning – he is helping me sort out a few things – in the absence of anyone else I can rely on this side of the world.' was Mark's response, immediately regretting the outburst.

'Father – good to hear you are coming back – but we have to start moving now. Can you ring your contact in the Washington Post and tell him we are contacting one of his editors – Charles Coll. All we want is someone who will listen – your contact could help make sure that he does.'

'It would make more sense to contact someone at CNN' came the response from Harold.

Mark was about to lose it when Elliot grabbed the telephone.

'Harold! – Elliott here. We are working on the CNN thing, but right now we need the contact at the Washington Post – do you know the Chief Executive Officer or don't you? If you do, ring him right fucking now, tell him what Mark just told you, and stop pissing us around.' And he disconnected the link.

'Your father is a good man, but he surely can be very frustrating at times like these.' Then Elliott grinned.

'We will call him back later when he is a bit more amicable.'

Mark had never heard anyone speak to his father so dismissively, but he deserved it, so he grinned too. He got out the telephone book, while they listened to the news from WTOP.

'We have just had some breaking news from our sources here in Washington DC about the events in New York City. Our sources have been contacted by people who, they claim, know who was responsible for the planning of the bomb attacks. There is also news from a reliable source in New York City that the FBI and other authorities knew about the planned bombings before the event but failed to take any action. We will have further news as it comes to hand Meanwhile in Washington.'

There was also a snippet of information flashed across CNN:

'News is coming in that the FBI is on the trail of a man who is alleged to have been responsible for two further deaths, following the bombings in New York City. It is not yet clear who the dead people are, but our sources indicate that one of them was a government agent investigating the tragedy and the other a woman who was high on the list of suspects that the FBI wished to speak to about the bombings as they continue their inquiries. We will have more on this breaking story in our eleven o'clock news roundup.'

'What the fuck are they talking about?' Mark said to the TV.

'They are talking about you.' Elliott replied, with a laugh. 'It looks as though your friends at the FBI are playing the same game. Not to worry, they spin, we spin.'

'Could I speak with Charles Coll?' Mark said to the cheerful voice that answered the telephone at the Washington Post.

'I am afraid Mr. Coll is out of the office at the moment. Could I have him call you back?' came the efficient, if uncaring, response. This was not going so well but the situation could have been anticipated. Mark replied by asking for his cell phone number and the girl eventually patched him through, although it did take a while for Charles Coll to respond.

Charles sounded more than a little bit irritated as he answered.

'You are speaking with Charles Coll.' as though the mere act of being able to make the contact was a privilege, the act of answering it condescending.

'Charles – this is Mark Taylor – it has been quite some time since we last met—how are you?'

'Mark who?' asked Charles. He was beginning to sound even more irritated. About half as much as Mark. Mark repeated his name and after a long pause, Charles's memory kicked into gear.

'Bosnia – 1994 – Yes, I remember now. I am good thank you, but a little busy at the moment. It is nice to catch up, but could we do this some other time. I am tied up with this business in New York City.'

Charles – never Charlie—always was the sort of man who expressed the view that he was always intimately involved with whatever story he was working on at the time. As a reporter, he was among the best, while to those who knew him in a more personal environment, he was both pompous and arrogant. But Mark knew that was all a show. Beneath the external bravado though was a very insecure personality and after a few drinks, he became a different being. Even without a few drinks he could be fairly easily manipulated. All you needed to do was to point him in the right direction.

In telling Mark that he was busy, and he was working the New York case, he had given Mark the lead that he needed.

'I know that you are working on the New York story. That is why I called. I wanted to bounce off some very interesting information that has just come to hand. If you are busy, perhaps you could point me in the direction of someone else I should talk to at the Post? Your CEO probably now knows a little.'

He was beginning to sound just like Elliott. But at least he had told the truth – well more or less. The events in New York City were the biggest story of the moment, so it stood to reason that the Washington Post would have one of its' top reporters working on it. Since Charles was fairly high up the totem pole it was therefore probable that he would be involved. But first and foremost, he was a newspaperman, and the thought of any other reporter getting very interesting information from a 'Charles' contact was an enigma.

'When can we meet? I just have to finish this briefing session at the Bureau.' Charles asked maintaining his persona.

'I presume by "the Bureau" you are talking about the FBI. Why don't you ask them a question while you are there? Ask them if there is any truth in the news story that the attacks had nothing at all to do with al Qaeda?'

'What story? I haven't heard any such thing!' Charles

was beginning to sound apoplectic. But Mark knew he had his interest, and the rest would be plain sailing.

'You should not spend so much time watching CNN. There are other sources of intelligence in the world.' Mark laughed adding another barb.

'What story?' Charles shouted into the phone.

When he got excited, his voice took on the timbre of a youngster who had just lost all his toys.

'Oh – the story is out there and gaining momentum. However, the facts are—I am probably part of the small select group who know the truth.' Mark spun along with the story. It was going to end soon either by Charles having a heart attack or by Charles smashing his cell phone.

'Who are you working for now?' a note of suspicion crept into Charles' voice. But Mark knew – or thought he knew – his target well. He was looking for even more intrigue to feed his rapacious appetite. He wanted Charles to ask almost any question of the FBI – it did not matter if it was based on fact or fiction. Every network in town and beyond would be at the briefing, and those with their ears closest to the ground would be aware by now of the breaking news on radio WTOP. Backed up by a question from a senior Washington Post reporter who pointed in the same direction, all the networks would be salivating.

'Let us just say I was working undercover with the CIA. Look – I have to go. My associate will give you directions.' and he handed the telephone to Elliott.
He did a good job of sounding like a PA, but if Charles could have seen the twinkle in Elliott's eyes, and the suppressed laughter, he would not have been quite so impressed.

The next place Mark called was Sydney Australia.

He only had a mobile telephone number but since the Aussies used the same GSM network that should not have been a problem. Again, there was a delay while his call battled with systems and bureaucracy, but eventually, he was connected after convincing the various operators that he was from the CIA. 'G'day Peter. How are things in Australia?'

'Who is this?' came the stern reply.

'It's Mark – Mark Taylor – we met briefly in Sydney and again in Brisbane—I am calling from Washington DC.'

The recognition was instant, and Peter sounded quite pleased to hear a friendly voice.

'G'day, Mark – how you going? Bad news that business in New York. I guess they could not find the right people in time. You have our sympathy, but I suppose that is not your problem. What can I do for you now?'

'Peter – how are you getting on with the notes I left with you on Doctor Abdul Jabbar?' Mark asked, hoping for a positive response. He got more than he had bargained for, and that suited him just fine.

'Ok – we have the guy under surveillance 24/7. The Papua New Guinea police are playing along. Because the doctor seems to have been involved in all the goings-on in Bali, we were thinking we might pick him up and hand him over to the CIA. We certainly have enough on him to do just that.'

'That is just fine Peter. What we need to do is to tie your surveillance, or preferably the arrest of Doctor Jabbar, to a tip-off you received from someone in the CIA.'

'I can do that!' he replied immediately. 'Let me guess – you are having problems convincing the powers that be that they should have already known about the attacks but wouldn't listen – Yes! – I like your style. You wouldn't like a job with us, would you? – we could use someone like you.'

Mark chuckled at that.

'Any chance of my getting further involved in the spook business is decreasing rapidly. I now have the FBI looking for me and if they have their way I won't be around long enough! Anyway – don't you have to clear this whole thing with your superiors? I am getting quite used to bureaucracy stuffing up the plans.'

'Don't you worry about that mate – I will have to talk to the ADG – sorry the Assistant Director-General – but No Worries! Watch CNN – that is where you Americans get most of your information from.' and he cut the connection.

The next stage of the plan was not so easy to implement. That was because, in thinking through the various interactions, Mark began to realize he should have told Elliott about the Serbian connection. Nonetheless, it had to be done.

'Can I speak with Colonel Dean?' Mark had almost exhausted his patience by the time Tom answered. He had expected that the number Paul had called him on a couple of days before would work, but he had not counted on two things – firstly on Colonel Tom Dean now being at a field hospital, and secondly on Major Dixon being a complete idiot. It was not as though the British were involved in World War III in Kosovo, but the Major made a big thing of just making things difficult. After all the Major was temporarily in charge of things during Tom's absence. If it was not for a chance conversation with a Sergeant McKinley Mark would never have got through.

'Colonel Dean speaking – who is this?'

'Hi, Tom – it's Mark Taylor – 10th SFG'.

'Oh, Shit! I am in hospital following the last madcap mission you fellows sent me off on. What is going on in New York? What do you want now Mark? Or are you ringing on behalf of that mad bastard Paul?'

'Tom – Paul is dead.'

The resulting silence on the telephone made Mark wonder whether the connection had been cut. Then Tom came back, the shock evident in his voice.

'Paul – dead – How?'

'He was shot – by someone who was supposed to be on our side. They also killed Annette Covic. She is the lady who gave us the tip-off about your General Milicic. Tom— we have serious problems here and we need your help – but nothing too onerous. Can you talk to one of the British reporters in Kosovo? Tell them where you got the word on Milicic – that you got it from the CIA?'

'Why not just talk to a CNN reporter yourself – or are you Yanks not talking to each other?' came the inevitable response.

Mark bit his tongue. Even the Brits thought that CNN was tops, but they were wrong. The British Broadcasting Corporation's BBC News provided a much wider coverage than CNN and tended to have a more detached style of reporting. This meant that people tended to pay more attention to what they reported. So, if the BBC said the CIA had tipped off someone, people tended to listen. Especially if they were CIA and did not know the first thing about the subject until they heard the BBC report. And the CIA did watch BBC News.

'Tom – do me just this one favour and I will never ask again – well not until next time.' Mark encouraged.

There was a big sigh and then Tom made another decision.

'Ok – I'll do it. Let me know when Paul's funeral is – I might come over.' And he disconnected the call. Perhaps a good job. Mark did not want to mention the fact that at this stage of proceedings they did not have a body!

'What has a British Colonel in Kosovo got to do with the goings-on in New York?' Elliott wanted to know. So, Mark told him. And that got a reaction.

'You are learning fast – that should piss someone off big time—you sure you are not working undercover with the Company?' That comment brought a cringe from Mark. Elliott laughed again.

Doug Curtis, the news anchor-man from the WTOP, arrived but did not stay long. Just long enough for Elliott to introduce him to Mark and fill him in on at least a part of the story that they wanted to get across. Mark was a little unsure of the man who started his day with a double scotch and kept drinking at every opportunity. Elliott was still laughing. They were using Doug and the fact that he would become less coherent as the day progressed was fine. The radio stations in Washington, as in most cities, used a common news reporting service. The story would be covered by those interested, which meant all the networks and it would rapidly spread to different parts of the country, and that was all they needed.

Charles Coll, on the other hand, was a very different kind of a man. He took any news story very seriously—as though it was his own personal property – and now was not the time to take advantage of him. They told him who had organized the events in New York – well almost. They told him enough about a Doctor Abdul Jabbar to have him seriously interested in the theory of Indonesian involvement. They did not tell him anything about the Serbian connection. He would be pretty pissed off when he connected the dots himself but that was all part of the intrigue. Elliott planned to feed so much information out there that there would be a media feeding frenzy as people fell over each other to get at the truth – well the story so far – it did not matter whether it was the truth or not.

There were two more news flashes on CNN during the next hour as well as news items from the BBC and WTOP.

CNN Newsflash – 10:46 am – Thursday, September the 12th.

'Our sources in Sydney Australia report that the ASIS – the Australian Secret Intelligence Service which is the equivalent of the CIA—has taken a senior scientist into custody. This man, who goes by the name of Doctor Abdul Jabbar, was working at the Rabaul Volcano Observatory in Papua New Guinea. He is alleged to have been involved with the Bali bombings and is believed to be a member of the Jemaah Islamiyah terrorist organization. It is also believed that the CIA provided the information that led to his arrest. We are currently trying to assess whether this event has any connection to the recent events in New York City.'

BBC News – 11:00 am Eastern Standard time.

'BBC News has reported that British forces in Kosovo have apprehended General Ilic Milicic, wanted for war crimes in the Bosnian conflict. It is not yet known where the General was captured or where he is being held. Our sources are reporting that the CIA provided the vital piece of information which led to his being located and.'

WTOP News – 11:00 am Eastern Standard time.

'Stories are coming to our attention that a further conflict is developing between the FBI Counterterrorism Division and the CIA, this time over the recent events in New York City. It has been reported that the FBI had prior warning of the attack but failed to share this information with other agencies other than the CIA. A spokesman for the National Counterterrorism Centre, the agency responsible for coordinating intelligence, would not comment. Spokesmen for the FBI and the CIA said that there would be no comment at this time while the allegation was being investigated. In breaking news – at least one CIA agent is believed to have been killed.'

CNN Newsflash – 11:05 AM

'News is coming to hand that the most recent bombings in New York City may not have been planned by al Qaeda. Our sources have also indicated that the FBI may have had prior warning of the events and who was behind them but failed to act in time. In addition, it is being reported that the CIA may have passed the information on to the FBI some weeks ago but that this information was not passed on to the office of the Director of National Intelligence. No one from the FBI or the CIA is available for comment at this time, but this points to further problems that are known to exist between our two principal intelligence organizations. No one from the office of the DNI would make any comment on these allegations. We will bring you further news as this story unfolds.'

'**Well – I** think it is time we rang the CIA – if anyone there can come down off the ceiling long enough to talk to us.' said Elliott after watching the last of the stories being produced on CNN.

'They must be scratching their heads.'

He dialled a number from memory. It again took an

inordinate length of time to get to the person he wanted – everyone must be very busy today!

'Hi Stephen – it's Elliott Shannon – how are things at the Company today?'

The voice at the other end of the line sounded strained but sounded as though he was not averse to the call.

'You still poking your nose around?' came the response. 'You are as aware as anyone that we have a few problems to deal with. To what do I owe the pleasure of this call at this time?'

'Well – I thought you might like me to come in and have a chat – that is unless you already know all the answers – and bring a friend of mine who should be able to shed some light on what is going on.' said Elliott, actually enjoying the obvious discomfort of the guy at the other end of the line.

'What makes you think we have things that need light shed on them?' came the cautious response. 'And who is your friend – I didn't know you had any left after the chaos you caused around here.'

But Rodriguez did not have his heart really in it. Sure, Elliott had caused chaos for the very simple reason that he had very little respect for the bureaucratic structure. And the CIA was after all a bureaucracy and a large one at that. Consequently. it was divided into two distinctive groups—one of the people who strictly followed the protocols – the majority, and the other of people who wanted to get something done—a minority. The majority tended to be administrative and accounting staff. The minority is operational.

Both Stephen Rodriguez and Elliott Shannon came from the latter group. Unfortunately, the higher you rose up the ranks the more you had to be aware of all the crap that went on under the disguise as protocol. So, Rodriguez was forever trying to control an operational mob who reckoned that promotion had in effect recruited him into the ranks of the bureaucratic majority.

'Well now, how about I write it all up in a report, in duplicate?' Elliott continued oblivious to the implied criticism. 'Then I can give one copy to you and the other to CNN or the Post. But no – there is no point in doing that – is there? CNN is already onto the story – you can have both copies. As for my friend – well I have not had time to piss him off yet – only met him earlier this morning. Incidentally, some guy from a sister organization of yours was trying to bury him – and a couple of other people that they killed along the way. One of them will eventually turn up on your list of agents killed in action – that is if you can ever find the body.'

'What the fuck are you talking about Elliott? What does CNN know? Who is this guy? What agent?'

The tone of Rodriguez's voice had changed. Shannon could sense his change in attitude and that caused Rodriguez to quickly come to a decision. His voice became very quiet and measured.

'Ok – you are right. We need to have a chat and urgently – can you come into Langley?'

'Now that is what I like to hear – a decision. We can come in, but only on one condition. You must guarantee the safety of my friend. Can you do that?'

'What are you talking about? Nothing is going to happen to him. Who would want to harm him?'

'Your sister organization – the FBI – that's who.'

Chapter 36

Consultations

At the CIA headquarters in Langley Virginia, the Assistant Deputy Director of Intelligence, Stephen Rodriguez, was not a happy man. He had called together those senior members of his staff who were in the building at the time, thumped the conference room table, and demanded answers.

'Someone in this room must know – or is going to find out before this day is over. What in heaven's name is going on out there?'

He glared at the assembled staff, but none of them was going to be the first to speak. They quite simply did not know, or they were not prepared to say, or they were too scared to say anything with a senior member of the CIA in this kind of foul mood.

In the spook business, they were supposed to know everything, but they were also supposed to know when to keep quiet. The only thing that gave them individually a little confidence was that they were all in the same boat. Or was one of their number guilty of hiding something?

Rodriguez continued talking and the more he said the worse his temper got.

'I have at least got a source that may shed some light on some of the issues. I had a call from one of our past employees – someone who retired a couple of years ago – and he claims that he knows everything. And knowing this guy I would say that he does. Meanwhile, we either know fuck all or else someone in this room knows something and is not saying. Therefore no one leaves this room until I know what you know.'

As if to emphasize what he was saying he waved his left hand towards the door. Clearly outlined through the frosted glass was a guard and from the shape of the outline, it was clear that he was armed. It was also clear that he was not alone.

'The people out there are a Rapid Response squad from the Metropolitan Police Department, nor the FBI – for reasons that, if not already clear, will soon become so.'

'Does your source, who claims to know everything, say where he is getting his information from?'

The question came from a man sitting at the far end of the table. John was dressed like all the others – grey suit, white shirt, red tie –innocuous – except for the odd shape of his face. He was well over six feet in height and almost impossibly thin. Although nearly fifty years old he still had a bad case of acne. He wore small circular glasses with thick lenses which made his eyes look about twice their normal size. He had a petulant and arrogant air about him that appeared to irritate Stephen and several of his fellow workers. But he was a brilliant analyst.

'No!' came the answer.

'I am about to have a meeting with him and his associate in the hope that they can shed some light on that issue.'

Stephen Rodriguez looked at his watch.

'I was rather hoping that someone in this, the principal

intelligence agency of the United States, would provide me with a few clues first.' The sarcasm in Stephens' voice was not feigned.

'Your words were 'him and his associate.' Who is the associate?' asked John.

Rodriguez had been in the business a long time. He had developed many skills in those years. One of them was a skill similar to that developed by Mark – he placed a lot of reliance on his ability to read body language. He was not at the moment receiving very good vibes. But since he expected that the people working for him would have the same or similar skills as his own, there was no point in lying to them or in trying to mislead them.

'I have yet to meet the other guy, so I don't know.' The reply was delivered leaving no doubt that any further questions on that particular subject would not be tolerated.

'Now, it appears to me that there are several stories that the press has gotten a hold of. And that causes me to raise the following questions.' He pulled a scrappy piece of paper from his top jacket pocket and began to read from it.

'The first question is – who gave the Australians the tip-off about an Indonesian gentleman who goes by the name of Doctor Abdul Jabbar. Apart from his being a Doctor of Geology—Who and What is he. Where does he come from and what are his connections? Does he appear on any of our watch lists? If he was involved in this Bali thing, and subsequently involved in what happened in New York City the other day, how come I have never heard of him? So how could someone who is working for the CIA have tipped off our colleagues in Australia?'

Rodriguez paused but got no reaction from his audience, so he continued.

'The second question is – Who in our esteemed organization tipped off the Brits in Kosovo about the Serbian

General by the name of Ilic Milicic, who is wanted by our European friends for war crimes, and what has he got to do with anything?' The last words were almost spat out.

Still, there was no reaction from the group of senior analysts.

'Third – who tipped off CNN and the Radio stations that we have yet another turf war with the FBI? And what is the turf war supposed to be about this time?' That question at least got a reaction. Everyone grinned. The many "turf wars" that go on in any bureaucratic structure are not usually a problem for the people who actually do some work, otherwise known as the operational level. There is a job to be done, each one has his or her own part to play in that job, so they just get on with it. Nor do they seem to be a problem at the opposite end of the organizations, otherwise known, at least in FBI and CIA circles, as the command level.

The problem lay in the middle, which therefore included the vast majority. Of all the bureaucratic organizations, the military had a slight advantage with its' system of more clearly defined ranks plus the constant movement of personnel. However, that advantage was only one of perception rather than fact. Consequently, Rodriguez did not expect to get much response to his question. He would not be disappointed,

'Fourth—who is our CIA agent who is going to turn up dead anytime soon?'

That got a more serious reaction and the grinning ceased.

Up until this time his audience – apart from the analyst called John - had sat in silence, either absorbing what was being said or simply dreading the next question. This fourth question caused several people in the room to gasp, and exchange looks of bewilderment.

If Rodriguez had not had his eyes down reading from

his bit of paper, he would have observed that one person did not show the least surprise.

'Fifth – and, despite the serious situation that these four prior questions represent, most important of all – who knew before the event that New York City was to be attacked, and on, of all days, September 11th?' This question got no reaction either.

'And lastly, the reason why we are here now, the sixth question is – Why were these bits of apparently unrelated intelligence not passed on up the chain? Did this make it as far as the office of the Director of National Intelligence or the National Counterterrorism Centre? If so who by? If not – why not. I could mention the fact that they did not reach my level, but we can talk about that later.'

Rodriguez waited for a few seconds for his words to sink in. Some people in the room had been making notes while he spoke. He hoped that they were not just doodling. Not that it mattered. None of the sheets of paper that they were making notes on would be leaving the room when their meeting concluded. He continued.

'Ok folks – those are the questions. I am going to leave you now to mull them over. The only people missing from this room are Tim Cochrane who is our expert in South America and Melissa Calabresi our resident expert in the Middle East. Tim should not be a problem – no one has mentioned his area – at least not yet – so he should not be missed. Melissa may be a problem – if you need any help in this area then sing out and I will consider getting her deputy. But for now, the discussion is confined to this group at this level, and you will see to it that it stays that way. Everything that I have said is to be kept within these four walls and I would advise you not to discuss these matters with anyone outside. Do I make myself clear?'

Whether it was the glare, or his words, or the enormity of the task that he had set, the normally confident staff merely nodded as one. And that done, he left, returning to his own office.

As he left, John hit the send button on his cell phone, and a text message went out advising his contacts to look for two men entering the building seeking an appointment with Stephen Rodriguez. Unfortunately for John, they were already in the building and sitting patiently waiting for him.

The two men – Mark and Elliott—were waiting for Rodriguez in his office, attended by an ever-watchful secretary . She was dressed in a suit and the lady looked more like a man than a woman. And she had an expression on her face, and the body language, that suggested she was not in the mood for any nonsense. There was certainly no attempt at conversation and that was fine with Mark.

Shannon had done his best to dress for the occasion, but it did not seem to matter. He still managed to look untidy. Mark on the other hand was very neat, albeit wearing the suit which was at least one size too large, and one size too short.

When Rodriguez came back into his office he greeted Elliott Shannon, dismissed the secretary with a nod, and then introduced himself to Mark. His attitude was cautious but brusque.

'You must be the source of Elliott's information – I am not sure that I want to talk to you or not! You seem to be a bit of a mystery man!'

The body language said otherwise. He was obviously very anxious to talk, and that was fine with Mark. Elliott was not so accommodating.

'Stephen – if I may call you Stephen since I am retired

– the information Mark has is likely to cause a few ripples through this and some other establishments – so I suggest that you listen to what he has to say – and this time act on it.'

'What do you mean—this time?' asked a seemingly rather puzzled Stephen Rodriguez.

'I was in this building a couple of days ago.' Mark began.

'I was interviewed by one of your guys named Scott. He never ventured his second name, so I cannot help you there. My friends Paul Williams – should I say the late Paul Williams – and Brad Morgan – who has subsequently disappeared from the face of the earth, for not the first time I may add – were interviewed by others. The net result of those interviews was Zilch – Zippo – Nada, and you know the rest. New York City does anyway.'

Rodriguez sat looking at Mark for a full minute. No one spoke or moved. Then he cleared his throat and asked a question that he already knew the answer to.

'You told this Scott—that the attacks were going to take place – and on the anniversary of 9/11?'.

The words were spoken almost in a whisper, the terrible significance of what Mark had said slowly sinking in.

'That is exactly what I told him on several occasions.' Mark replied. 'And that is exactly what Paul and Brad would have told the people who interviewed them. I have no idea why it was necessary to interview us separately—we would have all told pretty much the same story. At least Paul confirmed that he did. As for Brad—I would not know because I have yet to speak to him. As I said, he has disappeared. And I might add – not for the first time in our brief association.'

Rodriguez gave the appearance of being annoyed, but his mind was on other things.

'It is normal practice for us to interview people separately.' He replied, more or less talking to himself. 'Now - Paul Williams, the man that you described as the late Paul Williams. He is one of ours! How do you know him? How do you know he is dead?'

'I knew him because we were in the Special Forces together. I assume you would know that piece of history. As for how I know he is dead—because I was present when he took a bullet in the head.'

The anger in Mark's voice was obvious. The cold, clinical attitude coming from the other side of the desk did nothing to improve things. Mark could appreciate that Rodriguez had no doubt had to deal with many similar situations. But they were talking about Paul Williams – his friend. Mark seethed, Elliott Shannon watched, Stephen Rodriguez thought.

Then Rodriguez reached a decision.

'I have just tasked a group of our top analysts to find answers to six questions that I have posed for them. Do you mind if I ask you the same six questions?'

'Go ahead!' replied Mark with a shrug that belied his interest. He would be fascinated to see if anything had changed at the CIA in the course of a couple of fairly eventful days. And it would be interesting to see what kind of question could be raised at this esteemed level. Presumably, the questions would be a synopsis of what had been and was continuing to be, regurgitated through the media. This was probably not the best way to run a country. But, after all, it was a democracy - wasn't it?

Rodriguez consulted the piece of paper again. Mark and Elliott noted that the paper was scrappy and handwritten, which would be unusual for someone in the position of ADDI. That meant that the meeting of analysts was either off the record, or he wanted to keep things tight, or things were just happening too fast. Probably the latter Mark thought – incorrectly.

'Ok – Who tipped off the Australians about this Doctor Abdul Jabbar? And who is he?'

Mark did not even have to think about that one.

'Doctor Abdul Jabbar is a conduit, or if you like a cog in the wheels of the Jemaah Islamiyah. He operates out of a Volcanic observatory in Rabaul – Papua New Guinea. As for who tipped off the Australians? That is quite simple – I did.'

'How did you do that? Who are you?'

Mark gave an ironic smile at the second part of the question. It was getting to be a habit of bureaucrats.

'I just happened to meet a gentleman from Australian Intelligence on my way back from a visit to Rabaul. As for who am I? I am a guy who is getting pissed off by the question. I am nobody. I did not want to be involved. I did not ask to be involved. But I am. What's your second question?'

'But how did you get involved with all of this? We had never heard of Doctor Abdul Jabbar until CNN picked up the story from Australia. Yet you appear to not only know of the guy. You know precisely where he was operating and what he was doing. How did you know that?'

Mark looked at the confused face in front of him. The body language said that Rodriguez was confused. But confused by the news? Or confused about how to deal with the news? The worst-case scenario was that he was confused about how to deal with Mark – permanently. The immediate problem for Mark was just who could he trust?

His immediate decision was – he could trust no one. His more immediate problem was – this man Stephen Rodriguez, was Harold Taylor's boss! Consequently, his answer to Rodriguez's question came as a surprise to the other two in the room.

'I am sure the questions that you posed for your analysts were not this complicated. So, either you ask me the same questions, or I am out of here!' said Mark, his voice cold and uncompromising.

The look of shock encouraged him to continue.

'I do not trust the Central Intelligence Agency, and therefore that means I do not trust you. But you don't need to feel so bad about that. I would say the same in similar circumstances with the Federal Bureau of Investigation. All I am interested in is bringing the people, who killed two close friends of mine, to justice. If that means talking to you then so be it. But I only have Elliott's word for it that you can be trusted. I have only known Elliott for less than twenty- four hours, so you will understand my concern.'

Elliott Shannon chuckled at that comment and entered the conversation for the first time.

'I know you Stephen, but Mark does not. The decision he must make is to either talk to the CIA, and possibly the FBI, or to let things take their course in a very public arena. He has already taken precautions so the story will unfold whatever you say or do, and, if he should disappear, you will have even more serious problems, if you get my drift. So, his concern now is quite a simple one. Who was responsible for the goings-on in New York? That is unless you are in on the cover-up?'

The look that Elliott and Mark got from Stephen was one of profound shock. People in his position were not used to being treated this way by a retired employee and a civilian. He sat silent for several minutes. You could cut the air with a knife, but neither Mark nor Elliott said anything further. The person with the problem now was Rodriguez.

The problem of there being a cover-up was always an issue with all people involved in the security and intelligence business, especially on a national or international scale. While the CIA was used to working in the underworld where few facts ever made the light of day, they were also conscious of the power of the media. Usually, like everyone and everything else, the media could be manipulated by misinformation or by other means. But to be able to do this, you had to start from a position of confidence. Confidence that you knew more about the subject than they did, and at this moment the CIA, at least officially, knew less.

Slowly Rodriguez re-gathered his composure. And then it was his turn to surprise his guests.

'What has become of the Company?' He was looking at Elliott, but his eyes were looking far beyond anything or anyone in the room.

'There was a time when to serve your country was sufficient reward. Probably because some of us still feel that way, we do not put sufficient effort into checking what goes on – or in this case, doesn't go on.' Stephen Rodriguez seemed to have noticeably aged. He shook his head and then he sat forward in his chair and addressed himself to Mark.

'I am not in any way, shape, or form, as Elliott terms it in on the cover-up. To prove that to you, when I have finished listing my questions, I am going to suggest a course of action that is unprecedented in the history of this office. I am going to invite you to attend the meeting of analysts.' That startled Elliott – it was more than unprecedented, it was an absolute no-no. But slowly he nodded in understanding. What Stephen was effectively saying was that the truth would eventually be found in that room. Mark and Elliott exchanged looks.

Rodriguez appeared to be on the level – at least for the moment.

'Ok' Mark said, 'What is the next question?'

Rodriguez consulted his handwritten notes again.

'Who tipped off the British about the Serbian General Ilic Milicic?'

Mark struggled with his emotions to answer that one.

'We got the information from the third bomber in New York – a lady called Annette Covic. Apparently, General Milicic took a fancy to her, did not have things go his way, and then threatened her family if she did not cooperate. Why? — I do not know. It is a long complex story.'

Mark paused. It was only a couple of days ago that he had lost her, and he still had not had time to grieve. A few days that seemed like a lifetime and he had been sort of busy during that time. Now he struggled to recover his composure – he made it but only just.

'Paul Williams and I both talked to the British and you should know the rest.'

'What has a Serbian General wanted for war crimes got to do with the goings-on in New York City – that is apart from the fact that there is a sort of connection – Muslims and Kosovo?'

Rodriguez started to ask more of himself than anyone else. But he just got a cold stare, and then a dismissive shrug of the shoulders. Mark got out of his chair and headed towards the door.

The emotion was finally too much for Mark. He could no longer face going through it all again. Elliott leaped to his feet, held on to Mark's arm, and turned to Stephen.

You have to get yourself under control Stephen' he began. 'You may be the ADDI of the CIA, but remember, Mark is a civilian and he couldn't give a rats' ass what or who you are. This is not an "interview" – it is a chat – supposedly between friends. Now can we all sit down and try just one more time?'

'I am just trying to understand.' Rodriguez began, but Elliott cut him off.

'You have got to understand. I say again—Mark does not trust the CIA – you and I included. I would imagine that he wants to know what questions you have asked your so-called "team" and then, and only then, will he be able to judge whether he should go on. That about sums it up?' he asked Mark.

Mark just nodded in the affirmative, but he remained stubborn and silent, staring at Rodriguez. They stayed where they were for several minutes – the Assistant Deputy behind his desk, Mark still half-turned towards the door, and Elliott standing now with hands-on-hips. Finally, Stephen broached the icy standoff.

'Ok – you're quite correct – I was out of line. I am sorry Mark – you have been through a lot – and I was being insensitive. Please can we return to where we were? I will tell you the other two questions I have posed.'

Stephen bit his tongue at the error, really a misjudgment, as he realized that Mark had instantly noted the difference. Well, it wasn't an error. The last two questions had nothing to do with Mark - did they? But a sickening feeling filled his whole being as he realized, these questions were fundamental and probably the reason why Mark was here.

'Sorry – four questions.'

Mark sat back down in his chair but still did not say a word. It was as though this whole business had gone too far with questions but not far enough with answers. Mark looked as though he was beginning to feel claustrophobic, the effect of being in the inner sanctum of a secretive and influential government institution – hemmed in by the bureaucracy and surrounded by so much power. Elliott's plan to stir up the media was a good one, but Mark was not so sure about the next part of the plan. His shoulders were now stooped, his eyes dead, the body language said it all – he was about to give up.

The two CIA men had seen it before. After days of endless questions, detainees under intense interrogation often adopted this pose. After that, the CIA usually got the information it was after. But this situation was supposed to be quite different. Slowly the truth dawned on Stephen and Elliott at about the same time. The Miss Covic had been closer to Mark than they had realized – and now she was dead. Add to that the simultaneous loss of his close friend Paul Williams and you could find a reason to break any man. Was that why Mark looked so defeated?

From Mark's perception, they had completely misread the situation. And that was fine with him. He was fed up with playing their games. They would now have to play his game by his rules, or not at all. He had to be certain that Rodriguez was not going to kill the story – and the longer this went on, the less certain he became of that. But first, he had to be sure of Elliott. While he had taken Elliott more or less at face value, there was another view. It did seem a little too convenient that an ex-CIA agent happened to be on hand when Mark had escaped from his FBI captors. This was the thought that Mark grappled with, and it was not therefore difficult to simulate the body language that the CIA was reading. Yes – he was mortified by Annette's passing and the senseless killing of Paul. But—No – he was not going to rest until those responsible paid a very dear price – with Stephen and Elliott's help or otherwise.

Rodriguez started to speak again and aroused Mark from his thoughts.

'Is it ok with you if I read the other four questions – exactly as I put them to the analysts?'

Mark just nodded. Rodriguez was unsure what that

meant but he continued anyway.

'Question three was – Who tipped off CNN that we had a turf war with the FBI and what is the so-called turf war about? Well, we are always involved in turf wars, so what is one more – apart from the timing. Question four – Who is the CIA agent who is dead? Question five – Who knew that New York City was to be attacked on the anniversary of 9/11? Question six – Why were these unrelated bits of intelligence not passed up the line – for fucks sake!?'

Rodriguez was not happy, and Elliott could well imagine delivering the last message in the same tone to his staff. That gave Elliott a clue. The level at which the information had been held up had to be below Assistant Deputy Director Intelligence level, and that meant it was as Stephen had alluded to – it was one or more of the senior analysts gathered in the conference room. But who and why? The idea of presenting Mark to the group was therefore a brilliant ploy by Stephen as shock tactics go, albeit that Mark would be unaware of his role. And albeit that Mark would be involved in some risk. If no conclusion came from the session, that left Mark unknowingly exposed to someone who would hardly be averse to getting rid of him permanently.

On the other hand, Mark knew nothing of CIA protocol. All that he did know was that the organization that he had come to intending to unravel what had happened in New York and why, seemed inept.

'Surely the CIA is the lead agency in these matters and must have some powers?' Mark asked, not able to believe the impotence of the organization.

Rodriguez laughed, the bitter irony of Mark's comment evident to him and Elliott.

'The CIA might be perceived as the lead agency in the spook business, but the truth is somewhat different.

Over eighty percent of the money allocated by the Government of the United States for intelligence matters goes down the road to the Pentagon, and God only knows what they do with it. The Pentagon has about ten different organizations in the intelligence game – if you allocate one each to the Army, Navy, Air Force, and I guess the Marines, which leaves six others doing fuck knows what. The rest is unevenly shared between Justice, State, Homeland Security, Energy, Treasury, and heaven knows who else. We don't have the power – and we have even less than we used to have. Our director used to brief the President. Now he briefs the DNI – sorry the Director of National Intelligence if he can get beyond the two subsidiary organizations. However, all is not lost. We still talk to the FBI and that is what I am about to do. But first I need to know—who in the CIA fucked up and why?'

'To just answer your questions first.' Mark began, not the least bit concerned about the CIA funding problems, intriguing though they were. 'I don't know about your problems with the FBI, but I doubt whether they have much effect on the present issues, apart from the fact that the information should have been passed on and probably was not. Someone has his knickers in a twist about that – who cares? As for who tipped of CNN about a turf war – they were probably just on a fishing expedition – you are not on the FBI's Christmas card list from what I hear.'

At that comment, Elliott started to laugh. That earned him a glare from Stephen, but that did not make much difference.

Mark continued. 'The fourth question – you already know the answer to that – my good friend Paul Williams – and just for your information I know who killed him. And it wasn't me. I believe the agent responsible goes by the name Clive Henderson, and I hope someone gets to him before I do. The question of who knew there was to be an attack – the answer would appear to be everyone except the people appointed to do something about it. As for the sixth question – you have to look at your own organization – the message was delivered in this building several days before the events and in plenty of time to do something about it. I would have thought someone would have reacted.'

'The only reason we could have had for not passing your story up the line was that they did not believe you. There was an increase in the threat level—That is standard procedure.'

Rodriguez was uneasy but was still wanting to defend his staff despite, at least as far as Mark was concerned, the overwhelming evidence to the contrary.

'Well, you could start by talking to Brad Morgan.' said Mark. 'That is if you can find him. I have not seen Brad since we last arrived in this building. Since then, he has not responded to any of my calls. The only other person who can verify my story is your agent—Paul Williams – but he is dead. Sorry, there is another—my father – Harold Taylor.'

That got a reaction, but not the reaction that Mark would have expected.

'You are Harold's boy! Son of a bitch!'

Rodriguez grabbed his phone, issued some instructions, and then replaced it. The ability to read body language can be a real bitch at times. You could never be certain that the tone of someone's language was exactly what you took it to be. And when you were dealing with the CIA, these guys were experts at the nuances of deception. But Mark was none-the-less certain. Stephen Rodriguez knew all about his relationship with Harold. He was more convinced by how this revelation was absorbed with only a mild comment, as Stephen continued.

'So that is how you got involved?'

His phone rang and he snatched it up. After listening for a few moments, he replaced the receiver and sat back – frustrated.

'So, Harold Taylor is on his way back to the United States – he must be angry!' he said, more to himself, but worried about it. Nonetheless, he continued as though he was now on a mission.

'Ok – back to this Mr. Morgan – I have to find out where he is.'

He jumped to his feet, pulled the door open, and yelled to his assistant to come in. She was not the same lady who had earlier played guard, but he still did not bother with any introductions. The secretary must have been about forty years old but certainly, she carried the years well. Take away the almost brutal way her hair was tied and the official secretarial uniform of long black skirt, white starched shirt, and black jacket, and she could have been some looker. That is if she smiled.

'Where is Brad Morgan?' was the simple question Rodriguez asked.

'He has been reassigned from the Directorate of Technology to Operations Group Central America. He leaves from Andrews for Panama this afternoon' his secretary answered as if reading but she had no notes. Mark began to worry. This piece of information was news to Mark – it was not news to Stephen Rodriguez. He already knew – so why the play-acting?

'Well would you be so kind as to change his orders – and have him report to my office as soon as convenient!' replied Rodriguez.

'Do I inform his department of the change?' she asked. It was obvious to Mark that the answer would be No. Rodriguez just smiled and winked. She had her answer and left. He continued smiling.

'If you ever want to know who runs this department, you have just witnessed proof. That lady has the most incredible mind – there are times when I think she should have my job!'

Neither Elliott nor Mark commented.

He then turned his attention back to Mark. 'Can I ask you? – What can you tell me about Brad, and how come you seem to have so much faith in him and not in his parent organization?'

So, Mark told him – about the theatrical, if comical, way that Brad had come into the employment of Taylor Software – about his original disappearance – how he had reappeared in Wellington – about their trip to Rabaul – their return journey to the USA. Well—it was a highly edited version of what happened.

When Mark had finished telling his partial story, Stephen sat for a while absorbing and observing. He then sat forward in his chair

'What has this organization come to?' he murmured. 'That is the most incredible story I have heard. Do you want a job?'

It was now Mark's turn to laugh.

'No thank you!' was his emphatic reply, then he continued.

'The important thing is – do you believe that there is ample evidence that this story was told to your officers, and if you do, then what are you going to do about it? Do you believe me about the deaths of my two friends? — and will you do something about that?'

'Oh Yes! – It all makes sense.' He pushed a button on his desk and spoke.

'Miss Trembath – could you please ask Mr. Barton if he could spare me a few moments? Thank you. Yes – I know—I will take responsibility. Is he? – Ok—good. Thank you.' And he terminated the connection.

'Well—Brad Morgan is on his way – now to deal with our friends at the funny farm.' This time he grabbed his telephone and punched the keys with a number that was committed to memory and was in frequent use. After a none-too friendly conversation, he hung up, just as his secretary opened the office door, ushering in Peter Barton.

At the sight of a familiar face, Mark smiled, stood, and shook hands with the familiar figure who entered the room. He had not seen Peter since he was in Brisbane. What a member of the Australian Security Intelligence Service was doing in Washington was anyone's guess. But more to the point, Mark had talked to him less than a few hours ago and had assumed that he was in Australia. What was going on now?

'G'day, mate. I hope the CIA is paying attention for once!' Peter drawled, then shook hands with Elliott, just nodded to Stephen, and made himself at home on the couch. Mark noted that Peter was much better presented than he had been on the previous two occasions that they had met. It was hard for Peter to disguise the casual way he dressed and the informal way in which he conducted himself. Mark had underestimated this Australian. He was, also obviously, either fairly high up in his organization, held in high regard by the CIA, or both. Peter roused Mark from his thoughts.

'Shit – what happened to your head?'

He had noticed for the first time the bruising and other injuries that were evident on Mark's face.

'Do you mean the haircut?' asked Mark with a laugh. 'No – I've had the odd rumble since I got back – but nothing that time won't heal. So, what brings you to Washington, and in so short a time? Mark asked with a more than puzzled look on his face.'

Barton just laughed.

'The wonders of modern communication!' he said with a wink. 'I have come over here to try to shed some light on the goings-on in Rabaul and the activities of our friend Doctor Abdul Jabbar. Someone else will have to accompany him.' he added with another laugh. The joke was an inside job because the significance of it completely escaped Mark.

'He is about to be transferred now into the hands of the CIA, so we hope they can do something with him.'

Again, Barton winked. What the wink meant Mark had no idea, but he assumed that Barton had not talked to Rodriguez about their conversation of a few hours ago. So, neither would he. He skipped that subject and raised another question.

'I thought you were with the Australian domestic security service?'

Rodriguez abruptly cut into the conversation.

'Peter is Deputy Chief of ASIS. Mark – you certainly seem to move in high circles for someone who is not part of any security organization.' He then turned to Barton.

'So, from what you know, what Mark told us is all true? Have we fucked up or what?' He then turned to Mark.

'Please do not get upset – the spy business has so many twists to it that it is a miracle any of us wakes up in the same bed that we went to sleep in. Peter would have told you he was with the Australian intelligence organization because, like the CIA, the Intelligence Service is not supposed to operate any domestic operations.'

Barton just nodded in the affirmative. It was funny how Mark took the subterfuge of the Australians for granted. It was practical and honest. It was also obvious that Rodriguez knew more about Mark's recent history than he had previously acknowledged. But being practical, Mark could see the reasons for that.

Rodriguez was correct – the CIA had fucked up— big time.

'So, how did you get on with Tudjman? I never could work out where he fitted into things.'

Mark's question was directed at Peter Barton whose body language said this was a sensitive subject. It may not have mattered judging by the reaction from Rodriguez and Elliott Shannon. Mario Tudjman was a matter of little concern to the CIA. Barton just shrugged and said that was an ongoing inquiry.

He got up to leave. Again, the wink – which Barton assumed that Mark would know the significance of. He didn't.

The atmosphere in Rodriguez's office suddenly became more business-like as Barton left with an assurance to Mark that he would stay in touch. It became especially so as Brad Morgan was ushered in by the secretary.

He looked somewhat hurried, harassed, and confused. He was even more confused by the presence of Mark, but the way his face lit up, he was obviously pleased to see him. And he was soon placed at ease by Rodriguez.

'It looks like you have been kicked around a bit!' Rodriguez started off as he addressed himself to Brad.

'That will cease – now. Just tell me in your own words what the hell is going on? How long had you known about 9/11 mark II? What happened the other day here in this building? When did you get reassigned? And—more to the point—by whom?'

So, Morgan told them while the other three sat in silence.

The person interviewing Morgan had seemed more concerned with how he and Mark had found the source –

first the emails and then the laptop computer belonging to Doctor Abdul Jabbar—and then how he had extracted the information than he was with what was contained in the information or their analysis of it. While Brad told his story, it became clear to Mark that Brad had not revealed to the agency that he had a copy of the information on his laptop. That in itself gave Mark some confidence. However, it did not mean that the CIA had not taken a look anyway. That was why the data was encrypted, and if the CIA was still trying to break that encryption without asking for some help, good luck to them. A simple error or mistake in their attempt to break the algorithm would render the information even less accessible. The CIA would know that. But Mark knew that the CIA would know that, hence the extra protection that his code provided.

They would assume that unauthorized attempts to access the data would trigger a virus of some sort. So, the first thing they would have done was to sweep the data to remove any kind of virus. They were very good at that kind of thing. Hence, they would be puzzled that this action made no difference. At the end of the day, they would fathom it out. Now Mark would need to change his algorithm yet again as the computer business continued to play cat and mouse in this never-ending game. In Morgan's favour was firstly the thought that the CIA would assume that Mark was responsible for the encryption, and secondly, they were treating Morgan as an office boy who did not know shit. Why someone with Brads' knowledge and undoubted skill chose to work for the Company was a mystery to Mark. In due course, that view would change.

At the end of Brad's recounting the events, Rodriguez sat there contemplating for several minutes. Then he came to a decision.

'We would normally call the FBI in if we were going to apprehend one of our own, but from what Mark has told me, who do you trust? So, we do it ourselves. Brad and Elliott – could you please stay here – there are just too many people who will recognize you both. Mark Taylor on the other hand – no one should recognize him – so he and I should go and see how our analysts are progressing. I would predict zero progress, but you never know. Mark if you wouldn't mind coming with me – I think you might enjoy this little exchange.'

They went out of Rodriguez's office. Mark noted that the silent man-sized female secretary and an armed guard resumed the role of watchdog in the office. They made their way past the armed police officers outside the conference room and entered.

The room was already quiet and assumed complete silence as the two entered. Rodriguez took a seat at the head of the table, while Mark slid into a chair by the door. The ADDI surveyed those present, and then in a very quiet voice asked whether any progress had been made. From the head shaking that went on around the room Stephen's prediction of the degree of progress had been spot on. Nonetheless, the representatives of the World's leading spook organization did a reasonable job of reporting very little.

The spokesman, Tim Wilson, was obviously the least senior of those present but he equally obviously had the job of assembling the bits of information that they had.

'We had no information on Doctor Abdul Jabbar until we were advised by the ASIS just recently. Before that, we did not know of anyone operating out of Papua New Guinea that was of interest. We were aware that Wellington had someone down there, but we have not yet had any confirmation of that.'

The notes were delivered in a monotone with a total lack of emotion or even interest. To Mark, the notes told a different story which was of interest. The first statement told him that Barton has done his job in informing the CIA that they had a problem. But the last two statements told Mark that someone was lying.

'Turning to the events in Kosovo.' the spokesman continued. 'The British mounted a covert operation in southern Serbia three days ago. The operation was so covert that nothing was reported to our sources until after the event. We understand that they successfully captured General Ilic Milicic, but he was killed in an exchange of fire during the extraction. The British Colonel who led the raid was injured and we have been unable so far to find out where he got his information from.'

Well, wasn't that convenient? The CIA did know nothing. One of the problems with a bureaucratic organization was that it was filled with people who were adept at avoiding answering questions, out of fear that they would be proven wrong. The situation did not improve as Tim continued.

'The turf war issue we should skip because we need more time to analyse the chain of events which lead up to the current situation.'

In other words – who cares? But since the ADDI had asked a question then someone had to appear as though something was happening. There was a hint of laughter from several of the analysts, which was rapidly suppressed by a glare from Rodriguez.

Wilson continued as people in the room suddenly became tenser. 'On the question of one of our agents missing, we are checking to see who has not reported in. At this stage, those inquiries are continuing. As you know we had several CIA people on covert assignments, and we cannot easily trace them all in the timeframe.'

That statement made Mark angry. He was about to say something but was stopped by Rodriguez.

'Go on.' was all he said. So, Wilson did – never changing his tone, his eyes never leaving the papers in front of him.

'We have received many messages over several months indicating that there would be an attack timed for the anniversary of September 11th. Most of these were tracked down and analysed but turned up nothing of any value. Some weeks ago, we had a source that was tracking the activity of a previously unknown group believed to be based in New York, but that information also lead to nowhere. We had some information that was tracked out of New Zealand, but again that information was not taken any further. There was just nothing to indicate that an attack was planned – no organization, no plan, no people, no weapons.'

At this stage, Wilson felt that he needed to defend his superiors, though heaven knows why, as he added an ad-lib comment, which strangely he directed at Mark.

'We get millions of messages, the vast majority of which are eventually discarded, and we concentrate on known terrorists.'

The final comments from this illustrious group were even less enlightening.

'The reason why these various pieces of information did not trigger a higher threat level was that they were never associated with each other until now. Most of these questions are raised after the main event on September 11th and there has just not been the time to properly analyse what occurred and why? And we still do not know exactly who was responsible.'

In Mark's opinion, the group had done a reasonable job given the time they had at arriving at a statement that would keep the bureaucrats happy. They had just listened to what the best-known intelligence organization the world had to offer, and that was about as good as anything you had been hearing and seeing on CNN. It indicated two things about the counter-terrorism aspect of the organization. Firstly, they did have a mass of information from disparate sources, and they did need a clue – like two or three explosions – to help tie things together. Secondly, they were after all a bureaucracy, and of paramount importance to them was to ensure their backsides were adequately covered.

At the conclusion, Wilson sat back placing his notes on the table. He did not anticipate having to take any further part in the discussion. But other people in the room would not be so lucky.

'Ok – let me help you out with a couple of things that you do not know.' said Stephen, obviously in control but at the same time totally unimpressed.

'I now know who Doctor Abdul Jabbar is and I will want to talk some more about him later. Suffice to say for the moment that the Aussies beat us on that one, and even they were beaten by someone best described as an amateur. Are you with me so far?'

There were murmurs from around the room, but no one spoke, except John.

'We are not in competition with the Australians. So, they failed to pass the information on. We are not the only organization in this intelligence business who fail to share information' John said with a shrug. 'Is that not typical? And who is the "amateur?'

'We'll get to that later. I take it that no one here has heard of our not-so-good Doctor. Is that correct or not?' Stephen replied with a question of his own.

This time no one replied but there was a general, if imperceptible, shaking of heads. So, he carried on.

'The second question I left with you concerned General Ilic Milicic who, as all of you should be aware of, was one of the most wanted men in Serbia – for war crimes.

Well, I can now tell you who tipped off the British. We did. And what has the General got to do with anything? He has, or rather had, friends in New York City. Exactly how he became involved we do not know except that he was responsible for the provision of the third bomber. Sobering, isn't it?'

Rodriguez paused, but the room was so quiet you could hear a pin drop. He continued.

'I will skip the third question that you all find so amusing until I have had a chance to talk with the FBI. The fourth question concerned a dead CIA agent. I can now tell you who he was. He was a member of special operations on temporary assignment to Australasia, along with John Forster. He was the man who tipped off the British. Now that presents a small problem. He died in New York City, and I intend to find out why. The British did not kill him – why should they? I doubt whether the General did because by that time he was dead. So, how could he?'

He looked around the room and saw stunned looks on all faces except one. The exception stared at the table. Rodriguez continued.

'I have reason to believe that the agent, whose name I cannot release just yet, was killed by someone in the United States security service. That someone will have some explaining to do!'

The cold way this latter comment was delivered sent a chill through the room. But for one of those in attendance, he felt more than a chill. Mark froze. The comment that someone will have some explaining to do was not delivered in the manner of a man who felt any emotion at the loss of one of "His" men. And he should have done. Rodriguez again continued while Mark contemplated whether he had once again stumbled into a situation where he would be a party to another cover-up.

'The fifth question was—Who knew? The answer is we did. One of the most important things about intelligence gathering – especially since 9/11 – is that information is shared but on a "need-to-know" basis. So, someone knew but decided either that the information was irrelevant or that someone higher up the chain did not need to know. Before this day is over that "someone" will also have some explaining to do.'

He just let that threat hang over the meeting. The trouble with western bureaucracies is that such threats do not mean much – getting passed over for promotion does not have the same connotation as a similar threat issued in countries in more eastern locations with less concern for human life, or the niceties of interrogation.

'The sixth question, which follows on from question number five – why was the intelligence not passed up the chain? Perhaps I should ask for some help on that one. But first – I have another problem and that concerns the whereabouts of our agent, Brad Morgan.'

That got a reaction. There was an exchange of looks between the representative of the directorate of Science & Technology and the agent in charge – Central America. But there was also a reaction from the agent in charge – Africa. The latter who went by the name of Vincent was, like Brad, an African American. He was a man well over six feet in height and a body like the back of a bus. He had an easy smile, but right now his face was like thunder.

'Brad is dead?' he asked, sitting forward in his chair – all aggression. Rodriguez held up a hand to calm Vincent and assured him that Brad Morgan was not the dead agent he had referred to. But his attention was on others in the room.

The agent for Central America went by the name of Lopez. He was about the absolute opposite of Vincent. He barely made five and a half feet in height and his body was wiry. He looked more confused than anyone else, but at least had the guts to speak.

'Brad Morgan put in a request for a transfer to operations citing irreconcilable differences with the personnel in his present position.' Lopez began, and then added with a tired smile. 'I understand that it concerned a woman – he wanted out immediately – we had an urgent vacancy with someone of his experience – so we grabbed him.'

'That woman would not have gone by the name of Felicity by any chance?'

They turned as one to the source of the question. The question, spoken so quietly, had come from Mark. They looked from Mark to Rodriguez waiting for some indication of who the stranger was. Rodriguez was not about to inform them. He focused his attention on Lopez.

'And the answer is?'

'I have no idea.'

'Well perhaps someone else can answer the question – how about you answer the question Arran?' he asked of the directorate of S&T.

'I do not know.' came the reply.

'Ok – wait here a minute.'

Rodriguez marched out of the conference room, and almost immediately returned with Brad Morgan and two armed guards.

'Right! Now Brad – I understand you have requested a transfer – Is that correct?' The answer surprised everyone except Mark.

'No Sir.'

'Ok. John. Can you shed some light on this? You have been strangely silent!' Rodriguez asked in a quiet but measured tone. No reply was forthcoming as all in the room stared at the irritating man at the end of the table.

'Very well. The operative who is dead is Paul Williams.

Both Paul and Brad were on assignment – the same assignment as you John.' he said indicating the man at the end of the table.

'So, how come of the three, one is now dead, and one was rapidly and conveniently transferred?'

Rodriguez's voice had become brittle, as he continued.

'I would like to thank you all for coming. Remember – everything that you have heard in this room must not be discussed with anyone. You may go now except for two things. Firstly—all your papers and cell phones – place them on the table before you leave. The cell phones will be returned to you later in the day. Secondly – John – a quiet word with you if we may.'

The assembled officials took their leave.

Mark turned to Rodriguez with a look of loathing. Stephen was a little confused about who the loathing was directed at until Mark spoke. 'So—John is his first name – John Forester – the gentleman who was assisting my father in Wellington. No wonder!'

His voice trailed away, as he now focused his gaze on Forester.

'So, you are the mole – I hope you rot in hell.'

Rodriguez moved in quickly and quietly.

'Officers would you be so kind as to place John Forester under arrest – the charge sheet can begin with aiding and abetting the commission of a felony – including falsification of documents. Later we can add other things including one of accessory to murder or murder itself.'

'So, that is where I have seen you before – in Wellington!' Forester said with a sneer.

'Hang on to your day job – your disguise is not the best – although you look as though you have been roughed up – not part of the disguise, is it?'

It was all that Mark could do to restrain himself from hitting that insipid man. But he controlled himself and just shook his head. The bitterness welled in his throat.

At last, Mark had got the very core of the problem. Forester was the CIA mole. If it was not for Harold's gut feeling in Wellington, that resulted in Forester being unaware of the trip to Rabaul, then Forester could have made things very difficult indeed.

This was progress but the nagging thought was that Forester had known all along and he just did not care.

The other nagging thought revolved around why Stephen had enabled Mark to come into the meeting. There did not seem to be much point unless it was to enable him to see Forester. Or was it so that Forester could see him?

Those thoughts would have to wait.

They had to talk to the FBI and find out who their mole was.

Wasn't that going to be fun?

Chapter 37

Federal Bureau of Investigation

The Deputy Director of the Counterterrorism Division of the Federal Bureau of Investigation, Nicolas Gagarin, was not used to being called away to attend meetings at the CIA headquarters in Langley. Especially at such short notice. And especially by an Assistant Deputy. But he had to do something given the nature of the call.

It concerned the happenings in New York City. And that was the current top priority for his division. There was also the implication that someone in the FBI was involved. That was of an even higher priority – at least for Gagarin.

In the insane logic of bureaucracies, the good news was that he outranked the person he was going to see. The bad news was that he had no idea what had prompted the meeting. The no-so-bad news was that he would soon find out – and finding out for him was also a top priority. At least he had been advised that he should not tell anyone in the building where or why he was going. So, while he would normally have received a briefing, he said nothing – well almost—and therefore received nothing.

Bureaucracies are strange things. By the time he made it to his car, several people in the FBI knew where he was going. At least one person had a pretty fair idea why.

He arrived at Langley and the office of the Assistant Deputy Director Intelligence and was a little nervous as he took a seat. Nervous because he too had heard the stories doing the rounds about a turf war between his organization and the one that he was now visiting. Not that turf wars were unusual. They were the norm. It was just that at this particular point in time he was working very well with certain members of this organization, it was just that few knew about that.

Gagarin knew Stephen Rodriguez quite well from previous meetings and, at least in his view, they got along fairly well. He had in the past found him to be a very relaxed and cheerful fellow. However, he was far from relaxed now and not at all cheerful.

'Thank you for coming over at such short notice Nicolas. We have been in meetings all morning over here trying to get to the bottom of a dilemma. We believe you will be interested in what we have come up with.' Rodriguez began but was not so sure where to finish.

He was always wary of people who insisted on being addressed by their full name. If he could just get that one extra step and call the guy Nick, he would have felt much better. Not that he had ever heard anyone call Nicolas by anything other than his title. A further problem was the fact that irrespective of the current spat, there was just no love lost between these two organizations. So, any conversation would be subject to the usual smiles and politeness that was normally reserved for lawyers in a divorce court. They would each say what they were expected to say leaving all the important stuff, like agreeing, to others further up or down the scale depending upon just how important they thought it was. Not that they would agree on that either.

'Always glad to help!' came the response, assuming

that he was here to help.

'Like you, I have heard stories in the media, but I am sure you have not invited me over to talk about them.' being equally sure that was precisely why he was here, Nicolas continued, while looking at the two gentlemen who sat in silence on one of the couches.

Rodriguez turned towards Mark Taylor and Elliott Shannon and simply introduced them by just their surnames as part of 'his team.' He then continued as though Gagarin had not spoken.

'We are trying to get to the bottom of a riddle. One of our agents is missing and we believe he is probably dead. We have some information that suggests he was killed by one of your agents?' Rodriguez began.

Mark cringed at the none too subtle introduction to the subject matter. Elliott just sat placidly twiddling his thumbs. Gagarin looked like he was going to explode.

'That's a rather presumptuous statement – you have proof?' Gagarin blustered. But before he could get any further, Rodriguez continued.

'And according to the same source, he had a CIA agent helping him – now that's another twist to the riddle – and, as you can imagine, a matter of serious concern for the CIA! So, as you see, it is a sensitive issue.'

'I thought you said in our telephone conversation that this meeting had something to do with the happenings in New York City. What has a presumed dead agent got to do with what happened in New York?' he asked.

'That is what we hoped you would be able to help us work out. Our inquiries must be closing in on the identification of your agent, but we need some help to find him. After all, that is the FBI's responsibility despite the apparent conflict of interest.' said Rodriguez, more in hope than anything else.

'We have a report that an FBI agent got into a shooting

incident at one of our safe houses and tried to kill – and probably succeeded—one of our agents. Neither the alleged FBI agent nor the alleged CIA agent has been seen since, either dead or alive.'

He then turned to Mark.

'Why don't you tell Nicolas how you came to be here?' he suggested.

Mark was not about to tell a Deputy Director of the FBI that he had arrived at CIA headquarters after clouting, probably nearly killing, and then escaping from, one of his own agents.

He was also not about to say that he had been present at the alleged shooting. Otherwise, he would have to explain why he was still alive – and it was too early for that. In any case, he was not that sure himself why he was still alive. Also, Mark did not like the body language emanating from this Nicolas Gagarin guy—so he seized the opportunity to try another angle.

'We can get to that later, but before we do— yesterday in New York, in Chambers Street, at the office of the Augem Group, the Chief Executive Officer, who went by the name John Dubois—committed suicide by leaping off the 16th floor of the building. I was present when he did, so that much we know to be true. I was also in his office both before and after his fatal leap.'

Mark paused as Gagarin tensed. His body language was saying that he did not like the direction the conversation was headed.

'There must have been something in his office, perhaps on his computer, which would give you a clue as to what he had been up to. You see, I think that the events in New York City were funded by John Dubois and not by al Qaeda. I also think he had help from someone in the FBI to cover his tracks. And help from someone in the CIA to keep the plot, which was hatched with overseas help, under wraps. The only reason he would get such help from your organization would be for money, blackmail, or ideological reasons. I have enough confidence in your screening procedures to discount the latter two reasons. Therefore, we are looking for some records of payments made by Dubois. We follow the money – and we have your "rogue" agent. At least that seems a logical approach. But then I don't have access to the resources of the FBI.' Mark concluded with a shrug.

'Do you have a name for the agent?' Gagarin asked, directing his question at Rodriguez.

It was as though Mark's comments were either of no interest to Gagarin, or he already knew, or he was just plain dumb. Body language said that he already knew. And you do not get to be a Deputy Director by being dumb.

'Henderson – Clive Henderson.' Rodriguez replied.

That got a reaction.

Gagarin sat there deep in thought, and deeply worried, for a few moments. Rodriguez and Shannon were not sure where this would lead. Mark could not have cared less where it would lead because his reading of body language told him that they were about to watch true bureaucratic bullshit in action. All three held their peace and waited. Eventually, Gagarin got to his feet.

'I have to call the ADIC in New York. Will you please excuse me for a minute?' It was not a question for he just walked out of the door fishing out a cell phone. All three of them stared at the telephone on Rodriguez's desk and shrugged. All for different reasons.

They sat in silence, also for different reasons.

A few minutes later Gagarin came back into the room, looking even more worried than he had when he left. He sat down this time on the front edge of the seat.

'Clive Henderson no longer works for the FBI. You are either mistaken or someone is using his ID. We are onto it.'

Then he looked from Rodriguez to Mark and decided to address himself to Mark.

'The FBI New York office has seized a computer from the Augem office of a Mr. Dubois as part of their normal procedure. They are looking for a suicide note or something of that kind. But they say there is nothing on the computer that looks anything like what you are suggesting. Do you have any evidence of any such payment records, or are you just speculating?'

The latter question was accompanied by a shift in his body language – arrogance probably adequately described it. Mark should have felt put out by the attitude, but he had come too far over the last few weeks. He was beginning to harden up and just looked at the FBI man with contempt. Gagarin was lying.

The question was – was he lying about Clive Henderson? Or was he lying to protect his sources - as was more common in inter-agency affairs than the public realized? Or was he lying to protect someone? Or was he lying to hide the fact that he simply knew jack shit?

Mark told Gagarin what he would eventually find out if indeed he did not already know.

'Some people would describe me as an expert in computer systems, although I would have to defer to the experts who work for the FBI. Suffice for me to say however that your people who looked at John Dubois' computer don't know shit. Or they are lying – probably the latter.'

Sensing the increasing tension in the room, Rodriguez decided on another change of angle.

'The fugitive that the FBI is on the lookout for, as of last night, is supposed to have done what? And what do we know about him?'

The questions came as a shock to Mark, but he hoped

that Gagarin did not notice. The question also came as a shock to Nicolas, but he at least seemed more confident in handling this. He quickly got on his cell phone again, but this time he did not leave the room. His call went through to a David Reid, but Gagarin did not indicate what organization, or what department if he was part of the FBI, he represented. By the tone of the conversation, Reid was a record keeper and was reading from a computer. Finally, Gagarin disconnected the call and resumed his composure.

'The man is believed to be a Mark Taylor who is the owner of a company called Taylor Software. The man is alleged to be involved in a couple of murders. He is armed and dangerous, so our agents have a "dead or alive" status on him. The last report we have is that he is probably now dead – shot while attempting to escape. We are currently looking for a body somewhere out in the Chesapeake Bay.'

'Escape from where?' Mark asked, pleased that his "body" could carry on a conversation with apparent impunity.

'What was he doing in the Chesapeake Bay in the first place?'
Gagarin looked his arrogant best as he replied.

'Our agents followed him from New York and found him hiding up north in the Chesapeake. He escaped, but one of our agents shot him, and we believe his body will turn up floating somewhere in the estuary. We have an SUV whose records show that was hired by Taylor in Washington four days ago. Our forensic experts are going through it now, but the early indications are that this was the vehicle used to transport two bodies both of whom had been shot, and it contains evidence of blood. Again, we are working on the analysis of the blood, but at this stage, it looks like there are three types. I guess that the blood belongs to his two victims, and the third type will again point us to this Mark Taylor.'

This chilling explanation told Mark that either the whole of the FBI was involved, or those that were had managed to convince the rest. It was now official. Either way, Mark Taylor was dead meat. That was a sobering thought.

'And the bodies of the dead are of whom and, where are they?' Elliott Shannon asked.

'That we don't know for sure yet, but we believe they are buried somewhere in the Chesapeake, and somewhere in that area could take a while to check—as you know, since that is where you live. We believe that one of the bodies is the woman who should have been the third bomber – you heard that the third bomber did not die at the scene?' he said almost with contempt. 'The other is the man who talked her out of it. What we suspect is that Taylor was part of the al Qaeda plot and was just tying up loose ends. Terrorists don't take too kindly to a failed suicide bomber and are even less enamoured by people who interfere.' he concluded.

Mark was stunned by the logic of it all. But even more stunned that Gagarin obviously knew where Elliott Shannon lived, and therefore probably knew who Elliott was.

He exchanged glances with the CIA people. Shannon was neutral. But he did not like what he saw in the eyes of the ADDI. Rodriguez was performing mental gymnastics because he had a simple choice. He could believe what Gagarin had described, and then he did not have to go far to resolve the issue—Mark Taylor was after all sitting not more than a few feet away. One part of this ever-increasing riddle was that Gagarin had failed to recognize Mark despite the apparent notice to apprehend or kill him – he had only shaved his head which was hardly a disguise despite what Elliott had said—Why?

On the other hand, Mark had walked into Rodriguez's office of his own free will. That would hardly be normal for someone on the run from the law. Gagarin had said there were two bodies, but he could not produce them. Or was that another angle on the inter-agency lack of cooperation? Mark had said there were two bodies, and he knew where they were. Or he at least where they had been. Gagarin had not said who the second body was. Mark had identified one of the bodies as Paul – a CIA agent – but that was still to be confirmed. The only major dispute seemed to be who had shot them.

Elliott Shannon, on the other hand, was quietly seething. That the FBI knew that he lived on the Chesapeake was not an issue. They knew or at least claimed to know, everything about everyone. His issue was why a Deputy Director would have such instant recall of the location of a retired, and not very important ex-CIA guy, who he had met for the first time within the last half an hour. Who had told him, and then what had he been told about Mark? He certainly did not appear to know who Mark was, but then he had no idea what game that Gagarin was playing.

Rodriguez seemed oblivious to these concerns.

One of the problems with bureaucracies is that they tend to reach the obvious conclusions – the easiest ones. They also tend to rely on the opinions of fellow bureaucrats – that way there is always the chance that the blame can be shifted elsewhere if something goes wrong. Rodriguez wavered, then he reached a decision—based apparently on the simple fact that he regarded Gagarin as an arrogant prick.

'It seems to me that we have to find some bodies. Your forensic experts should then be able to find out what these people were shot with and that should tell us which weapon, or weapons, fired the shots.' Rodriguez concluded, handing the conversation over to his visitor.

'Ok – I agree – let me get on to that!' Nicolas said. 'You do understand that this is an inter-divisional matter within the FBI – and one normally outside my area. But in the circumstances, I will take an interest.'

'I thought that you were remarkably well informed already!' said Rodriguez, as they shook hands, and Gagarin took his leave.

'Well that certainly was interesting.' said Rodriguez, almost to himself. Then he turned and focused on Mark.

'So, the FBI now has the problem. Gagarin is an arrogant prick, but I think we shook him up. He will get to the bottom of it very quickly. It seems to me that Henderson is moonlighting rather than covert and the FBI will want to stamp on him fairly quickly. We have the matter under control. Thanks to you Mark. So – what now?' Stephen Rodriguez asked of his amateur and retired guests.

'Thank you for not referring to me by name.' said Mark. 'I guess we have to let things take their course, and I can get back to running a software company.'

Although Elliott had other thoughts, he kept quiet, and the two of them left the office of the ADDI, with a reminder from Rodriguez that they should keep in touch. Elliott waited until they were back in the car, and well away from Langley, before breaking the silence.

'So, what do you think of Stephen?' Elliott asked while navigating through the Washington traffic.

'I like him.' lied Mark, who had already dismissed any thoughts of help from the CIA and was more interested in what his plans would be from this point forward.

'If you could drop me off at a rental car office – anything

other than Hertz, because I do not think I am in their good books right now—then I'll be on my way. Thanks for your help.'

'And what do you plan to do now? – Are you going to drop the subject and leave it to the FBI?' Elliott asked, looking at Mark as if he did not believe what he was hearing.

'Well, no! From what I've seen and heard I would not want to leave things in the hands of Nicolas Gagarin. I am going to try to find the place where I last saw Henderson and the bodies of my two friends and take it from there.'

'And you don't think you need any help with that? Have you any idea how big Chesapeake Bay is?' Elliott asked with more than a hint of sarcasm in his voice.

Mark had to think about that, but not for long. On reflection, he had no idea where he had been, and his first real starting point was the ramshackle cottage that was the Shannon residence. So, like it or not, he was stuck with Elliott Shannon.

'You don't mind being involved – it could get nasty?' Mark asked of his newfound Irish friend.

'Well, my first reason for wishing to be involved is – we are being followed. I am not sure who by, but I would suspect CIA rather than FBI. I can lose them, or we can just let them tail along.'

Elliott switched lanes as he spoke and then dived down a side street. He laughed as the following car almost crashed as it sought to keep on their tail.
But keep on their tail it did.

'All the more reason for you not to be involved.' replied Mark, as he scanned the street behind them and located the car.

Elliott just laughed out loud.

'You couldn't keep me out of it if you tried. I might

have retired, but I am still loyal to the CIA. If someone wants to mess with our people, I want to find out who it is. And I could start with that arrogant shit Gagarin.' That surprised Mark, but he looked at Elliott with renewed respect. They were on the same wavelength – even if Elliott did not know why – yet.

'Ok' said Mark 'I think we need to return to your cottage and track back from there. However, I think we need to be armed and undercover. I would suspect that Henderson or the FBI will try to remove the bodies, if indeed they are still there, for fear that we know more than has been said so far. I would expect that they will not make a move until after dark for fear of their being spotted – not so much by a member of the public, because they can easily be kept out of the way – but by other FBI people who are not part of their plan. They will be armed, and ready to use them, so we need to get ourselves something a little more powerful than sidearms and some camouflage gear. I don't suppose you have anything like that, and do you have a GPS locator apart from the one on your boat?'

Elliott laughed again 'Is the Pope a Catholic?'

Mark grinned and asked Elliott if he would happen to have a telephone number for Fort Bragg. He looked at Mark with some scepticism.

'Are you planning on starting a third world war?' But then he just shrugged. 'Everything that I think you will need – arms and gear—is back at the cottage and any numbers you need to call are on my laptop. But first I think we need to change boats.'

When they arrived back at the marina Elliott made for the office. He obviously knew the Manager well, an ex-Navy Seal who went by the name of Max Clarke but was referred to as The Chief. He quickly explained what he wanted.

Although the "what" would have sounded a little weird, the Chief simply waved to a couple of men who were working on an outboard motor to come inside the office. They had a similar demeanour and Mark assessed that they were more than just roustabouts. After a few words with the Chief, they just grinned. One of the men wandered down the marina with a tool bag in his hand until he reached Elliott's boat. There he proceeded to check all manner of things before, with the obvious air of a job well done, sauntered back to the office. The tool bag now contained Elliott's laptop. The two men next took the outer garments from Elliott and Mark, put on beanies, and they were gone – heading back for Elliott's boat.

The car that had been following Mark and Elliott earlier was parked in a "No Parking" area, but the occupants did not seem to care. They sprinted from the car to a nearby mooring and leaped on board a powerful-looking boat.

'That's an FBI boat!' remarked the Chief, in the same tone in which he might describe the weather. That comment caused a frown to appear on Elliott's face.

'I do not like this.' Elliott mused. 'It looks as though we have been fooled. Something is going on. The CIA and the FBI are not usually so cooperative. Still, we can worry about that later. Now, where is this boat of yours Chief?'

The Chief's boat was a brute of a machine. Not particularly pretty to look at from the outside, but it belonged to someone who knew all there was to know about boats. Mark and Elliott dressed in dark blue windcheaters and blue caps that any casual observer would take to be uniforms of the US Coast Guard. After a short instruction from the Chief, Elliott very quickly got the boat underway. They were soon sailing at a fair clip down the Potomac. Very rapidly they came within sight of the FBI boat and further ahead was Elliott's boat. Unlike the FBI boat which turned to starboard in pursuit of Elliott's. Elliott turned to port and the distance between them increased rapidly.

While all this was going on, Mark had a conversation with someone at Fort Bragg. That got him patched through to someone at the Pentagon. He did not volunteer any information on what the calls were about, and Elliott did not ask. Mark was very pissed off with the FBI but what that had to do with the 7th, 10th, and 20th Special Forces Groups Elliott could only wonder.

Mark's next call was to Dusty Miller. It was not going to be an easy conversation, but if ever Mark needed any help – Dusty was the man.

'Hi, Dusty – I need a little help!' was Mark's opening comment. The providers of the communication service would have been non-too impressed with what Dusty had to say in reply. There are laws against using foul language over a public network. But that was the least of Dusty's worries.

'What the fuck is going on? What have you gotten yourself into this time? The FBI and the NYPD are looking for you everywhere. You are responsible for a couple of deaths – not to mention blowing up half of New York City!' Dusty was in fine form, but eventually, he calmed down. Mark explained over the continuous interruptions and objections what he needed.

The various conversations that Mark had with people in the Special Forces, the Pentagon, and with Dusty Miller, were with people he knew, and who he felt he could trust. They were however almost entirely lacking in enthusiasm for what he had in mind. He had felt that if the CIA and FBI were not to be trusted, then the military would come to his aid. But he was dealing with the Government of the United States, and they all seemed to run for cover when he mentioned turf wars. They just did not want to be involved.

In his disappointment, Mark decided to say nothing to Elliott. Well, he had not told Elliott what he planned, so because this particular line of attack seemed to be a total failure – there did not appear to be much future in telling him of his failure to impress.

They were on their own – yet again.

Eventually, they turned further to port and began to make their way further up the Chesapeake. The trip took just under three hours, by which time the sun was beginning to set. Elliott seemed to instinctively know his way around the Chesapeake and turned the boat in towards his jetty. Then he did a strange thing – he kept on turning and waved. At first, Mark was confused. Then he saw the reason – or reasons. There were two men, not particularly well hidden, at the shore end of the jetty.

'So, we play a game of double bluff, do we?' Elliott laughed. 'The FBI, or whoever they are, has staked out the cottage. Well, let's play your silly games!'

Mark was not impressed and certainly did not think the situation was at all a laughing matter but decided he would leave the matter in Elliott's capable hands. He nonetheless had to ask.

'So, what do we do now?'

'Have you ever killed or immobilized anyone from the FBI?' Elliott asked while continuing to laugh.

Mark did not answer. He was not certain about the killing part.

The boat drifted in towards the jetty, and then Elliott began a series of hand signals pointing to the south. He then gunned the engines and the boat smoothly proceeded in the same direction. They would have travelled about a mile when Elliott again cut the engines and drifted in towards the shore, nudging the bow through the reeds until it rested against the shore. Almost in scripted fashion, the two men, who were FBI, appeared through the reeds looking both flushed from the exercise and confused. Elliott simply threw a stepladder over the side, and like lambs, to the slaughter, the FBI agents climbed on board.

It is funny how in real life people do some stupid things – especially relatively inexperienced officers, faced with a very imposing Coast Guard boat, which was on the same wavelength as they were. They realized how stupid they had been seconds after arriving onboard. Being ex-Navy, the Chief had a brig, and that is where the two FBI men ended up suitably bound and gagged.

Elliott became serious for a moment.

'They were not expected to do much. Just watch and report, so their silence would mean – nothing is happening. But we had better tread very carefully.'

Elliott eased the boat out of the reeds and returned to his jetty further up the Chesapeake Bay. Cutting the engines, he grabbed his bag and stepped ashore.

'What we need to find out now is whether our two friends were alone, or do we have another reception committee. The FBI has concluded that this is where we would head, but why they should be so interested is anyone's guess. After that, the first thing we have to do is eat. I have a feeling it could be a long night' he said cheerfully as they made their way up the track.

They were just about at the cottage when Elliott held up his hand. 'Someone has definitely been here.' he said while withdrawing a Glock from his bag.

Mark immediately took out his favoured Smith and Wesson and crouched beside Elliott. There was no sign of anyone, but Mark had little doubt that he was right – such was the level of trust developing between the two men. They had, after all, known each other for almost twenty-four hours. Mark grinned at the thought.

Elliott was oblivious to why Mark was grinning.

'Ok - you take the right – I'll take the left—we meet at the other side—if you don't get killed on the way.'

Mark had a distinct impression that Elliott was enjoying himself. A better plan was for one of them to stay right where they were, covering the rear exit, while the other one circled around to the front. But no matter. They had two men well wrapped up and whoever else had been here had long since left. Mark would be able to smell if people were around and there were no people.

He went along with the Elliott plan, Elliott creeping through the undergrowth like a new recruit on live-fire training, while Mark just walked around the other side.

Finally, Elliott burst through the front door like Rambo on steroids announcing his arrival.

There was no one there.

However, he was right. Someone had been there. They had been looking for something or someone, but nothing appeared to have been stolen. Except that is for the wet clothing that Mark had discarded the night before.

The only reason that Marks' clothing could have been taken would be to eliminate any evidence that he had been there. Therefore, it had to be the FBI, and they had a plan. That plan would involve a short lifespan for Mark if, or when, they caught up with him. What was also now evident was that their plans now included Elliott, and someone had good reason to presume that their plan would be successful. Mark was at a stage where he no longer cared about his own safety, but Elliott was another matter. He turned to his host very concerned.

'Are you sure you want to be a part of this? It is not your fight, and you could be dead before the day is over!'

It must have been the Irish in him. Elliott just grinned and shook his head.

'And leave you on your own! No chance. Mark – just allow a retired old man to have some fun. Come on – we have some work to do.'

Mark should have argued. But Elliott was right. They were talking about the might of the FBI, and it did not seem like an even contest.

Elliott rustled up some food and they both ate in silence. Then he rummaged around in his sons' bedroom and came out with some camouflage training gear which they both donned. The clothes were a bit on the large side for Elliott, but once he had belted himself up, he looked quite the part. Next, he led Mark into the office where he had used his laptop the night before and pushed the desk to one side. He then removed a couple of floorboards and after rearranging numerous planks he came out with two rifles, and with a smile described what he had.

'These are US Army M14's semi-automatic 7.62 millimetre – but I am sure you know all that. As for how they come to be here – well it's a long story. I want it back when we are finished – can't have them falling into the wrong hands – can we?'

They were now physically ready to go.

Mark sat down and poured over a map to try to work out where they should go. The map was an aerial photo and like all aerial photographs, you first had to find something that you knew existed before you could get your bearings. Elliott pointed out his cottage and jetty, and then to the north Mark could make out a rough track. Three tracks were starting further north which eventually merged into one, then that one finally petering out. There was no obvious track to the cottage.

From his memory of the night before, aided by the map and prodding from Elliott, Mark calculated that he must have travelled about four miles from his hiding place in the water to the place where he had met Elliott. That placed the site where Henderson had planned the burial close to the end of the track.

'We will have to be careful. They will be as nervous as a bride on her first night. Expecting something, but not sure what. They will also be expecting some communication from our two friends, and when they don't get any, they will be suspicious. And they will also be in contact with the men on the FBI boat which by now should be somewhere in the Caribbean.'

Elliott again laughed. 'Ok – Let's go and whip some ass.'

Mark did not say a word. It was Elliott's battle cry, but Mark felt nervous. Elliott was proving to be a little gung-ho. Mark was not sure that the tactic of charging in with all gun's blazing was quite the way to go about things. That was not the way he had trained with the Special Forces.

He was to be proved right.

Not that it made that much difference.

Chapter 38

Burial Ground

They set off through the undergrowth towards the beginning of the track. For a man who must have been well into his late sixties, Elliott moved very quickly and efficiently. In addition to that, he had had similar experiences, albeit in foreign countries and probably not quite so close to the seat of his government. Mark again got a distinct impression that Elliott was enjoying himself. That feeling would not last long.

Mark had tried to get some assistance from his contacts in the Special Forces. On his side was the fact that he had been one of their numbers and members of that elite group were forever loyal to each other. On the other side was the fact that Mark's story was barely plausible. Still, he had tried. Unfortunately, Mark could not wait. He was convinced that something was going to happen to the bodies of his two friends, sooner rather than later. And, while the FBI was large, supremely efficient, and therefore scary, he doubted that more than a few were involved in what was after all criminal activity.

The fight may be uneven, but by calling on all the skills that he had learned through intensive training, and honed through a couple of overseas exploits, he convinced himself that he could pull this off. Or at least die having given it his best shot.

Elliott used the GPS device to check where they were in relation to the coordinates on their map. That was because they did not want to blunder onto the site where they believed the bodies of Marks' friends were buried without scouting it out first. Elliott had an amazing ability to work out where the burial ground was most likely to be and set his search accordingly.

Mark had the scary thought that, just maybe, Elliott knew more than he was telling, but they had come this far, and they had to press on. It was just possible, in fact highly probable, that they would not be alone.

It was also possible that someone had tried to contact the FBI people who had been near the cottage. Getting no response from them, they may venture south to find out why. So, Mark and Elliott could not travel in a straight line. In addition, Mark had a suspicion that it was rare for Elliott to stray this far north. Mark suspected he had never been there – there was just nothing to see or do. Fortunately, a GPS locator was far more reliable than human memory.

The ground they were traversing was uneven and covered with an assortment of decaying or dead vegetation. This slowed their progress as the noise their feet made could warn anyone of their progress, especially anyone who was in their path. After a couple of attempts at walking side by side, Mark signalled that he would take the lead and that Elliott should follow in his footsteps. He had plenty of experience from his various missions overseas, particularly in Columbia, where he had trained himself to travel through this kind of country unseen, unheard, and virtually invisible.

They soon fell into a rhythm and were able to increase

their speed. But they did not go too fast. Although it was unlikely that they would meet anyone other than the FBI in this part of the Chesapeake Bay, and at this time of the evening, they did not want to take any chances.

As they came closer to where they believed the site to be, they could begin to make out some lights and they could also hear a motor running. They got closer still and it became evident what the lights were for. Henderson had said to Mark the night before that they would soon be digging the bodies up again – and that was exactly what they were doing. The lights were coming from a black Jeep that was parked on the track, and it had its motor running to maintain the charge in the battery.

That told Mark that the dig had been arranged in a bit of a hurry—otherwise, they would have brought a generator and other lighting gear.

As they crouched in the undergrowth, Mark whispered to Elliott.

'I think these people are Henderson and his cronies. There is no way that Gagarin could have got organized and found this site in the time he had. Therefore, Henderson must have found out what was going on and is going to remove the bodies before the real FBI come along. Do you agree?'

Elliott studied the scene before committing but finally nodded his head.

'It sure seems that way. Let's go and disrupt their little party!'

'No – wait!' said Mark. 'This is no time for heroics – they are digging up two bodies – we don't want to take their place – I've been through that scenario once already!'

For a brief moment, Mark thought of splitting up so that they could approach the site from opposite sides but rapidly discounted that thought, at least for the time being. He had no idea how many men there were, who they were or where they were, so their first mission was to find that out. And quickly.

What he did know was that they were outnumbered. He also knew that the firearms that Elliott had produced were more than a match for the side-arms that the FBI had, so it was just a matter of getting into the right position.

He could see two men digging in the spot where Mark had been the night before, while another two were continuously scanning the terrain to the north. Mark thought that was rather strange. He had no means of knowing what they were thinking – but he could guess. They obviously thought that any interruption would come overland, and they thought that anything from the south would be dealt with by the men positioned near Elliott's cottage. They did not know about the Chiefs' boat that Elliott had borrowed, and therefore assumed there was no threat likely to eventuate from the south – either from Mark or from the legitimate FBI. To be so confident in that they had to be in communication with the boat that was following Elliott's boat – further down, not up, the Chesapeake Bay.

If it was an FBI boat, manned by the CIA, Henderson sure had some interesting friends.

The people at the scene had at least three vehicles including the Jeep, and on the assumption that there were at least two people per vehicle, which made six. So where were the other two? Before Mark and Elliott could make a move, they needed to be certain where all the people were, and also who they were. The four people that Mark could see were all wearing FBI jackets. As were the two who appeared behind them.

'Drop your weapons—nice and slow – then hands in

the air where I can see them—then move forward into the clearing. Do it now, or I will kill you.'

Mark and Elliott froze. They both recognized the voice. How could he have managed to creep up on them?

With a certain amount of bitterness, Mark realized that he had been out of action for about five years, and now he knew why they trained so hard, and so repetitively, all those years ago. A two-man team should never get into such a mess – and it was no use blaming Elliott. Mark was the one with the training. And the skills that he had acquired had failed him, not for the first time within the last few days.

Slowly they placed their M14 weapons on the ground making it clear that they were complying with the instruction. They exchanged looks, but Mark's eyes had an equally clear message for Elliott.

'Don't do anything foolish!'

They first stood stepping forward into the clearing.

One of the men holding a gun behind them was Nicolas Gagarin.

'Well, isn't this interesting?' Gagarin asked as he re-holstered his weapon – his companion maintaining the cover.

'Elliott Shannon and Mark Taylor – you two certainly seem to get around. Now I wonder why you would be here. Let me guess. You want to retrieve two bodies. So why don't you do just that?'

He motioned to the two men who were digging to hand their shovels over to the new arrivals. Having done that the two FBI men drew their weapons with a smile and stood on either side of the hole.

Desperately, Mark looked around. He could see no means of escape. And now the odds were stacked heavily against them.

It was becoming something of a habit, but this time there was to be no easy way out. Mark had to laugh. During the last twenty-four hours, his efforts had exercised the minds of the two leading intelligence organizations the country had. And he had got the media steamed up in the most incredible story. All for what? He was back where he had started, and seemingly no further ahead.

As he grabbed the spade that was thrust into his hands, he saw two other people approaching them from up the track. He recognized one of them as Henderson. The other person was the Secretary who had so impressed Stephen Rodriguez with her knowledge of his organization. Now wasn't that convenient!

There was at least some good news. Mark had finally got to the two people – one in the CIA and the other in the FBI who seemed to be responsible for the whole fiasco. It was a pity that Mark had assisted these very people in filling in the gaps. And it now became agonizingly clear that while Stephen Rodriguez had said nothing to Gagarin about who Mark was, that gap in his knowledge would have been quickly filled by the ever-efficient Secretary.

If indeed Gagarin did not already know.

Rodriguez had known exactly who he should call at the FBI, and he had quite rightly judged that the problems would be taken care of. But it was this lady who would make sure that Mark's story was killed off once and for all. All the drama about having the team investigate the various points in contention was a load of crap. It would get lost in the mix which was the bureaucratic jungle of the CIA. Mark, and even Elliott, had swallowed the whole story hook line and sinker in the expectation they were talking to an organization that could make things happen.

Well, he had certainly achieved that. It appeared that they had been out-thought, out-foxed, and were out of hope. The bureaucrats knew exactly what Mark would do. Apart from the additional inconvenience of having Elliott along for the ride, they could now continue with their plan. Then the thought again entered Marks' head. Was Elliott a part of the deal? If he was, that made Mark an even bigger fool.

The fact that Elliott had just so happened to be available when Mark had most needed some help was a little too much of a coincidence. That this assumption was wrong would come as a pleasant surprise, but it did not help the immediate position. There was to be no fairy-tale ending – just an ending in which an amateur would prove no match for professionals – albeit bent ones.

When Henderson recognized Mark, he came straight across and without hesitation struck him a hefty blow to the head and followed that up with one to the midriff. Mark defiantly stood his ground and glared at Henderson. He stood expecting further blows, but the fracas was interrupted by the lady, who went by the name of Hilary Trembath.

'Now Clive – that is no way to treat our guests. Why not wait until he has finished this little task? – then you can do what you like to him – before we leave him in the hole.'

The fact that the message was conveyed in a tone of some authority, should have made Mark think, but it did not. He would come to regret the omission.

'This is the fucker who did this!' he said pointing to the stitching on his chin and the huge bruise to the side of his head. The bruising had extended to his left eye, which was blood red, swollen, and partially closed. It would rapidly turn into a fully closed black eye. Mark had to admit that Henderson did not look so good. But Trembath and Gagarin were unmoved by the drama and seemed little interested in Clive's medical problems.

'So, Mr. Taylor has been giving you problems, has he? Well not for much longer. Let's get the job finished, then we will work out how to deal with him.' Gagarin added with a smile.

'How did you know who I was?' asked Mark, pretending to be puzzled by the interplay between the two. 'And how come Henderson is with you? When I first met Henderson, we thought that we had stumbled onto a drug cartel!'

That brought a reaction from Henderson – at least his body language changed markedly. Mark inwardly grimaced. So, that could be what it was all about! This particular collection of CIA and FBI people was into drugs. Had they just been playing games and in that process getting money from Dubois to buy drugs? They were not interested in Islam, al Qaeda, or any other links with terrorism. They were in it purely for the money. Mark felt sick.

Although he had played only a minor role in this whole shamble, Dusty had been closer to the truth right at the very beginning.

Gagarin returned Mark's cold stare.

'You have just signed your own death warrant. As for Clive—he and I go back a long way.' he laughed. 'And I knew who you were the moment I walked into Stephen Rodriguez's office. I should congratulate you Elliott – you paid some attention to the courses that we ran for the CIA. But I am afraid you are not good enough. As for how I recognized Mr. Taylor – well it was not too hard. He disappears one night in the Chesapeake Bay not more than a few clicks from your home, and then you turn up with a guy who has virtually no hair – obviously shaved off the same day otherwise his skin colouring on the fringes would be consistent—the right build, the right age, looks like an ex-Marine – and saying all the things we would expect a guy who has been where Mark Taylor has been recently. Not to mention the fact that he looks as though he had just completed twelve rounds in the ring with Joe Frazier. Do you honestly think you could fool the FBI? Typical CIA!' he laughed and so did Trembath.

'Now get to work!'

Elliott had been watching and listening to the interplay, becoming more and more agitated, and a vicious sneer came on his face. He turned to Stephens' secretary and spoke as though the stuffing had been kicked out of him.

'You of all people!' he said, and at that moment, Mark knew there was at least one person still on his side.

'Mark was right not to trust the CIA – it is just that he could not have anticipated how high up the organization you vermin had crept. In a position of absolute trust – how long have you been Stephens' secretary? What on earth can possess someone in your position to be a part of all this? No amount of money can compensate for such despicable action. You are insane!'

That just brought a smile from Trembath.

'The organization is fucked – if you will excuse the unladylike expression – just get over it.'

She brought her pistol up suddenly and crashed it into Elliott's head sending the ex-agent staggering backward, blood oozing from a gaping wound around the temple on the left side of his head. Mark started forward to protect his new friend, but Trembath was far too quick and brought the gun up into his face.

'Now let's not be silly Mr. Taylor – you've had a tiring day. Let us just try to end the day relatively peacefully.'

Mark looked at her with loathing.

'You will not get away with this – whatever your insane plans are. There are now too many people who know of the CIA's involvement and your part in it will soon become clear – that is if the rest of the CIA isn't infested.'

Trembath just smiled and shrugged.

'You think so? Well, you will not live long enough to find out. I did not buy into Elliott's story that you had all bases covered. You are just an amateur in a big boy's league – and now you will pay the price for your meddling.'

She turned to Gagarin and issued a command.

'Get this lot cleaned up quickly and let's get out of here.'

It became obvious to Mark that Trembath was in charge. The FBI was simply providing the labour. No wonder it had been hard to pick where the trouble in the United States security and intelligence service was. The problem at the CIA was in the bureaucratic jungle, instead of the more logical Directorate level. And the CIA had infiltrated, or at least were being assisted by, their sister organization, the FBI! There was no hope. The CIA and the FBI people, whichever side they were on, held all the cards and it looked like they were going to get away with things – not for the first time.

A couple more agents came down the track and again Mark recognized one of them. Felicity first walked up to Trembath and whispered something to her that brought a smile. Again, it was the body language. No wonder this Hilary Trembath had looked so brutally male – Felicity was her girlfriend!

It was ironic that Felicity had been paired up with Brad Morgan not so long ago and Mark had failed to pick up the anomaly!

Mark carefully chipped away with the spade, slowly uncovering the shroud-wrapped body while his mind wandered through the various interplays. He was constantly being cajoled and abused by the so-called FBI agents encouraging him to speed up. But he did not. For all, he knew the body that he was uncovering could be that of Annette and she had been subjected to enough rough treatment. He was not about to add any further indignity to that even though in death she was beyond caring.

The mood seemed to be contagious because Elliott worked at the same slow but deliberate pace, handicapped by his head wound that would not stop bleeding. But they could only maintain this charade for so long. b.

Eventually, both of the body bags were fully uncovered to the point that they could be removed. They were rapidly hustled off to the waiting Jeep by four other agents who Mark had not seen before. That made a total of twelve agents in the vicinity and that did not make for very good odds. They were doomed. Just for something to do Mark proceeded to fill in the hole that was left in the ground.

That process was brought to an abrupt halt on the command of Gagarin.

'Now don't be silly Mr. Taylor. You seem to forget that we have a body to take their place. You still have some talking to do – we need to get into your laptop, and I am sure you will show us how to do that. Not willingly, but you will nonetheless do it. So, for now, we will excuse you. However, your friend Elliott has reached his use-by date. I understand from Hilary that he has been a constant pain up the ass for the CIA, but thanks to you we can relieve ourselves of any further misery. Welcome to the real world of terrorism.'

Gagarin stood at the edge of the hole with his revolver pointing directly at Mark, and Henderson stood at the other side of the hole covering Elliott. Trembath returned to the scene and stood to the side impatiently waiting.

Mark could see no way out and there was no sign that

any help would be coming their way. It looked very much as though this was the end of the line. But he had to try to extend the time before Elliott was shot, in the forlorn hope that some opportunity may present itself.

'You won't get away with this Gagarin.'

It sounded so much better to refer to people by their surname when you had no wish to sound friendly.

'When you said at Rodriguez' office that the FBI could not find any evidence on Dubois' computer I knew you were lying. There was evidence on that computer. And I downloaded a copy of the relevant folders to my office computer. Welcome to the real world of computing.'

Nicolas Gagarin again just laughed.

'We know all about your computers Mr. Taylor.'

He checked his watch and then in his true arrogant style dropped the bombshell that would certainly end it all.

'Even as we speak your computers are all being destroyed. Something about an electrical fault I believe the fire department report will say – aided by the storage of highly flammable materials in your building. Of course, you did not know about those – but the paperwork all exists to show that you did. So, your insurance company will reject your claim. Not that it will matter to you. Welcome to the real world.'

Mark looked at Gagarin with hate in his eyes. But that made no difference.

Gagarin continued to gloat.

'I am told that you were responsible in a roundabout way for the death of my uncle, a General by the name of Ilic Milicic. And then you were present when our mutual friend John Dubois was killed – and tried to pass that one off as a suicide!' he sneered. 'Well, you will learn a hard lesson today but too late to make use of it—Don't mess with professionals. Now say goodbye to Elliott as he says goodbye to this world.'

Gagarin eased the safety catch off his gun.

'You mean that General Milicic is – or was—your uncle? And John Dubois, or whatever his name was, is – or was—your friend?' said Mark almost to himself – almost unable to believe what he had just heard – but then it all made sense!

'Well, you certainly have one weird circle of friends – how do you plan to get away with this? Surely the real FBI will find out.'

'Oh, I don't think so.' replied Gagarin, obviously enjoying the exchange. 'This whole business would never have raised its' head if you had kept your nose out of it. But never mind. You have seen what the spin doctors can do – so we must invent another story. Unfortunately, you will not be around to hear it. Say goodbye Elliott!'

'Now everyone can just stay cool. Mr. Gagarin— Sir – would you place your gun on the ground – and no sudden movements. The same for you Ms. Trembath and Mr. Henderson.'

The words were spoken in a soft voice. But it had the timbre of one that would not tolerate much and left no doubt that it meant business. They all turned to see a soldier in full camouflage uniform and wearing on his left sleeve the insignia of Special Forces Airborne and carrying a mean-looking semi-automatic rifle.

Gagarin earnestly looked back to where his men had parked their cars, looking for help. They were surrounded by Special Forces troops all looking equally well-armed and equally meaning business. Gagarin still reacted like you would expect – the man's arrogance was almost unbelievable.

'Who are you, people? What is the meaning of this? Can't you see that this is an FBI operation? You have absolutely no authority here. Put down your weapons.'

At that moment, Mark saw the bureaucratic nonsense that was ingrained into people of his type. Nicolas Gagarin was the one issuing all the bluster because as an FBI official, he was the one who was calling the shots in this domestic matter. But Mark knew that Hilary Trembath was really the boss. Who would have thought that a lady could be in charge of such events? But none of this seemed to phase the member of the US Special Forces group.

'I frankly really don't give a rat's ass Sir' the soldier replied. 'For the record, we are a part of the 7th Special Forces Group – two ODA's to be precise. Also, for the record, this is a US Army M14 that I have pointing at you, loaded and ready to fire. That gives me all the authority I require for now. What I have just witnessed is you threatening these two gentlemen and that is not normal for the FBI that I know, and not recommended. And you very conveniently confirmed – if we needed any confirmation – that you are into this up to your armpits. As the saying goes – When you are up to your ass in alligators, it is hard to remember that you went in there to drain the swamp. Now place your weapon on the ground. Do it now. This order will not be repeated.'

At first, Gagarin just stood there in disbelief. Beads of nervous perspiration started to form on his forehead and his hands. But he still did not release the weapon that he held pointing towards Elliott. The silence of the Chesapeake Bay was suddenly ruptured by a single blast of gunfire. The hand that had been holding the weapon was shattered. Nicolas Gagarin stared at the bleeding stump for a moment and then he turned towards Elliott. The pain must have been excruciating but he still managed to talk between clenched teeth.

'I suppose you arranged this little gathering through

your son. Well, he is a dead man. My people will find him and then come after you.'

Elliott got out of the grave and hit Gagarin with such force that he winced from the pain of the connection. Nicolas reeled back but was kept upright by one of the soldiers who had come down the track to join his colleague. On the other side of the grave, Trembath and Henderson made a desperate attempt to get away while the attention was focused elsewhere, but there was to be no escaping the true professionalism of the US Special Forces. They were very rapidly rounded up by a couple of other soldiers. Still, Gagarin continued to utter threats, so Elliott began hitting him again to the point where the Special Forces soldiers had to restrain him. There was a lot of hate in every blow.

Mark thought that he must talk to Elliott about that later but now was not the time. He turned to the soldier who had by now removed his helmet – he had a look that was somehow familiar to Mark. But then it dawned on him who he was.

He was Elliott's son – Brent Shannon!

The next soldier to join the group looked like someone who had turned up at a fancy-dress party ill-prepared. He was a huge powerful black man, and the uniform was at least two sizes too small, except for the boots. And he was perspiring as though he had been on an exercise for which he was unprepared.

The smile on Dusty Miller's face said it all.

'You sure know how to arrange a party!' as he gripped first Mark's and then Elliott's hand.

'Sorry we were a little late – next time a bit more notice and a little more information would not go amiss.' he added with a grin.

Mark held out a right hand to Brent and the grip was firm and friendly.

'Why don't we four just wander back to Elliott's cottage for a beer and a chat?' the big soldier said.

'I did not expect to meet my father again so soon and in these circumstances. I'll need a beer in my hand while you explain what the old fool has been up to this time.' he added with a laugh.

'But what about this lot? Won't there be some explaining to do?' asked Mark.

That also brought a laugh.

'You either have some very powerful friends, or you are very good at convincing people.' replied Brent. 'I was at Fort Bragg when your call came through and you know how to make things happen. We were in the air twenty minutes after your call. That CIA mate of my dad's – Harry Taylor – rang at about the same time. He was pretty pumped. He just said that you and my dad may need some help. And then we get a call from Dusty here – and that certainly put the cat amongst the pigeons.'

Mark had to think about that. He did not know whether the concept of a turf war between the CIA and the FBI had any bearing on events. But it sure seemed a good opportunity to have a sort out between rivals, and he did not think that those in the Pentagon, who had probably made this decision, needed much to encourage them to have a go.

Still, Mark was not concerned about that. He had looked into the eyes of those responsible for the deaths of his two friends, Annette Covic, and Paul Williams and at last, he had seen defeat.

It was little consolation, but at least he had seen it through.

'So, who do you represent in this bureaucratic quagmire?' Mark asked.

'We work for the Pentagon, and I understand that they have had a gut full of the bickering that goes on between the CIA and FBI. We would like you to talk with the boss, but tomorrow will do. Let's go have a drink. My men know what to do with this lot.'

'What will happen to the bodies of my two friends?' Mark asked in a whisper.

'They will be taken good care of.' Brent replied in a gentle voice. 'The best thing your friends can do for you now is to reveal how they were killed – that is a job for the coroner.'

'That will not be the FBI coroner I hope!' Mark replied, with some feeling.

Chapter 39

Decisions

They settled in front of the log fire. The day had taken its' toll on all four of them albeit for quite different reasons. But the adrenaline was still pumping and so, despite the late hour, the only things to do after being on a mission of this kind were to eat, drink, and think.

And to talk.

The Special Forces soldiers had taken away the two agents that Mark and Elliott had met and tied up at the quay near the cottage earlier in the day. They had no way of knowing whether they had been involved with Nicolas Gagarin and his cronies or just been two innocent pawns. The way that they were treated by the Special Forces left little doubt as to what the soldiers felt, and that may have been unfair. No one else in the little group that sat around in Elliott's cottage could have cared less.

It was over at last.

Tomorrow Mark would go back to Washington and give his version of the events to what he hoped would be a much more receptive audience than he had recently received in that City. There was now no doubting the proof, so this time they would have to listen. Or that was Mark's assumption – wrong as it turned out.

He had already had a brief telephone conversation with the Deputy Director of National Intelligence. The tone had been friendly, if apologetic, and almost fearful. The Deputy Director apologized for the fact that Mark should have talked to the Director himself if he had not been otherwise engaged on urgent business. Mark was getting used to bureaucratic speak. For one thing, the Director had a reputation for shunning the limelight, and in this particular case limelight was the last thing that he would want. For another, he would expect his minions to sort out this extraordinary mess.

There were still some serious unanswered questions, and they would need some serious answers before the Director of National Intelligence could get involved. A turf war between two of the principal government intelligence and security agencies was one thing. To have two agencies cooperate on a mission of this bizarre nature was quite incredible, unbelievable, and certain to grab the attention of the powers that be. And the media.

Above all else, the Director had a far more important job of advising the President, at least as much as he dared while covering his backside, about what had occurred. Mark did not envy him that job although it would no doubt be a concoction of fact and fiction, with the emphasis very much on the latter.

As they settled down, the four men had very different perceptions of what had been going on and used a different set of values in their assessments.

Brent Shannon did not even ask what his guests would like to drink. He just appeared with a case of beer, ripped the top of it, and proceeded to hand out bottles. He then turned to Elliott and demanded to know how the hell he had got himself involved in such a mess.

That just got a shrug, a smile, and an exchange of looks between Elliott and Mark that turned the smile into a laugh. As far as Brent was concerned, he had been given a job to do by the Pentagon, and he had carried it out with ruthless efficiency and expedition. His group had been due to go out on a night-time exercise anyway, so they were set to go. Not to the Chesapeake, and not so close to home, but a slight change of venue was a trivial matter.

Brent was a solidly built man of just under six feet, always ready to smile, but behind the smile was the coldness that came with his job. Brent sat back and watched the strange mixture of people that these events had brought together and shook his head. He could only speculate at the influence the likes of Mark, Harold and Dusty had on what had transpired. But such was the way things got done. He had done his duty—so now it was time to move on – what's next? He had long since given up trying to fathom out the idiosyncrasies of the bureaucrats so there was no point in worrying any further. Neither could he understand what went on in the sick minds of the likes of Gagarin, Trembath, and Henderson. That was not his problem either. Just move on.

Elliott Shannon had been on an adrenalin rush from the moment that the FBI, and then Mark, had burst unscheduled and uninvited into his otherwise peaceful existence. He had been through the hoops before – many times—and nothing surprised him. Except that is, this young man from the Taylor family.

He sat in what was his favourite chair and could only stare at Mark and wonder at the doggedness and resolution that had brought this business to a conclusion. Sure, at the end of this little exercise Elliott was within a hair's breadth – a single squeeze on a trigger—of being shot.

But he had volunteered, so you took the risk. On the other hand, he knew that Mark's involvement had been entirely involuntary, and Mark should never have had so rude an introduction to the failings of "The Club" as the US security services were generally referred to. With pride and affection by those on the inside. With scorn and loathing by many of those on the outside. It frightened him to find out that someone so high up the bureaucratic ladder had been turned and he wondered whether, if he had risen as high as say, Stephen Rodriguez, he would have been able to spot the rotten apple.

He did not envy the task now facing his old master to explain how this had all happened – further stress on an already badly damaged organization. But it was finished as far as he was concerned, leaving someone else to sort out the mess that had been left behind. If people in Washington still wanted to play their political games, then so be it. The thing was at an end. Clean up the loose ends, move on, and let me get back to a life away from all the bureaucratic nonsense.

For Dusty Miller, the situation was a little more complicated. While he had stepped in to help his friend when he had to take off to see his ill or dying father, at this stage he did not have clue about what had subsequently really happened. He knew that his close friend Mark was hurt, both physically and mentally – and it was the mental part that was the most worrying. Dusty obviously knew Mark far better than either Elliott or Brent and, in some respects, better than Mark knew himself.

At some stage, he knew that Mark, probably over a few beers, would tell him the full story. But now was not the time. Dusty knew that Mark needed to rest and sort out what he had buried deep in his mind. He had lost two close and very good friends. He had been through similar situations throughout his time in the Marines, and more so when he moved to the US Special Forces. But this was different. This was cold-blooded murder. And Dusty knew that deep-down Mark had a burning desire to beat the living shit out of those responsible.

He also knew that Mark would have to move on – but at what cost? This was different from the combat situation that they had been in during a previous life. This was personal and Dusty could not know how his good friend Mark may react. Best to let him do it in his own way, in his own time. Dusty would be there when needed, and if Mark wanted to beat the living shit out of those responsible for his grief, Dusty would be there for that as well.

To Mark, the day had felt like the longest day he could remember. And at the end of it, came the pain. Now that the adrenalin rush that he had been on had ceased came the full realization of what had happened. He had been robbed of a close friend – the kind of friend that only those who had served in the elite forces of your country whose mission was to protect their fellow citizens could comprehend. He had been to hell and back with Paul, and for all their respective faults, they had never faltered in their respect for each other. And then came that senseless shot – out of the blue, and from someone who was supposed to be on the same side!

Paul Williams was now dead. But that was only part of the story. The same people that had removed Paul, had also killed his other close friend, the beautiful and innocent Annette, in cold blood, and for no sane reason. Well, there was a reason wasn't there. It appeared that irrespective of the other reasons, they wanted money so that they could buy the drugs that they could not otherwise afford from their normal salaries. In this environment, there was no logic or control. They just blindly did whatever their paymaster asked them to do. It was insane.

He had tried to save Annette in that desperate but

forlorn dive across the room to try to get at the gun that Henderson was about to use for the second time in as many minutes. Should he have dived towards Annette and taken the bullet instead of her? But they would have killed her anyway, so his decision at the time was the correct one, even though at the end of the day, it achieved nothing.

There was still some work to be done to bring those thugs to justice. And he was determined to see to it that it happened. Mark had originally thought that John Dubois was the instigator of the plot, and therefore the person ultimately responsible for his tragic loss. But now he knew differently. He could feel no sympathy for Dubois having been used as part of someone's much grander scheme. Dubois knew or thought he knew, what it was all about. Greed.

But Dubois had been dealing with people who had access to the kind of resources – material things, people, political influence, and power – that he could only dream about.

Mark could only speculate about what motive, or collection of different motives, for money or political ends, could drive people to disregard life so callously. The problem it seemed was that the higher up the political or bureaucratic pyramid these people came the less likely they were to care too much about what they euphemistically called collateral damage. At the other end of the scale, real people died. And their friends and loved ones had feelings too.

Life without Paul would be manageable. They had lived a life where death just happened and there was always that chance that one, or even both, could die while pursuing their chosen career. But life without Annette – that was a very different story, and some bastard was still to pay, and pay he should and would.

Mark would forever have the emotion of hate in his guts for both the perpetrators and the facilitators. It would only be eased by the punishment of those responsible.

It would never go away.

He was rou74sed from his thoughts by a concerned Dusty.

'Come on man – it's over now – have a drink and then you need some rest. You've earned it!'

Mark had not realized that while he sat clutching his beer, tears were streaming down his face. But he managed to laugh.

'That's the politest thing you have ever said to me – Are you feeling, ok?' Mark replied, easing the tension.

Dusty appraised his friend with a look of sadness on his face, and that sadness extended to his eyes.

'I can only guess at what you have been through – and this thing is not yet over is it? When you go to talk with the Deputy Director tomorrow, how will you manage to keep things in perspective? It is obvious that you have been let down by the intelligence people – yet again – I would not blame you if you told them to shove it up their combined asses and walked away.'

Mark became very calm as he studied Dusty's face. The man sure knew how to handle people. Despite his rough language, his somewhat untidy appearance, his aggressive attitude, and his outward could not care less attitude, Dusty was amongst the very best men he knew.

'Well – I guess you will have to come along as my lawyer and make sure that I do.'

Dusty was the one man on the planet who knew of the bond between Mark and Paul, and he realized now that he would somehow have to fill the gap. And somehow, he would. But Annette Covic was another story that he could do nothing about except to be there when needed.

Mark woke up and peered around wondering, for not the first time in his recent past, where he was. Someone had placed a couple of blankets over him when he had apparently succumbed to sleep but had otherwise left him where he was. Pots were clanging together in the kitchen and from the language, it was obvious that Dusty had recovered from his sentimental interlude. Elliott was trying to help, but when it came to making breakfast Dusty had it down to a fine art.

Mark got up offering to help but was ushered towards the bathroom and told in no uncertain terms to get himself smartened up.

'You will be the star attraction in Washington, so don't let the side down, now fuck off and get cleaned up.' was about as politely as Dusty could put it.

Mark and Dusty journeyed to Washington courtesy of a helicopter – and it was a Sikorsky VH-3 Sea King of the type used in the Presidential fleet. Elliott and Brent took a more sedate pace back to Washington in the Chief's boat.

The meeting with the Deputy Director took place at a so-called safe house, but who owned the safe house was not revealed. The reason given for this arrangement was that there was so much going on in Washington at the moment that there was just no room. Dusty felt this explanation was crap and said so. Mark was beyond wondering about the bureaucrats, with their insane logic, and just went along with it.

The truth of the matter was, without any doubt, that they were hell-bent on keeping Mark, and indeed the whole sorry business, away from the prying journalists and all the other media paraphernalia that would have been alerted if they had met at headquarters. Again, there were explanations for the Director not being present – but it was reasonable to assume that meetings with the President and of the National Security Council took priority over a meeting with Mark Taylor.

In Mark's view, what they had been privy to, should have at least exercised the mind of the President. If the intelligence community was as fucked up as had been proven by recent events, there was probably no-one left in Washington for the Commander-in-Chief to listen to – or trust.

It was a pleasant surprise to find no CIA or FBI people present – at least none admitting to any such association. Except that is for one, Harold Taylor.

Harold was introduced as the Assistant Inspector General of the Central Intelligence Agency, and it was briefly explained that he would be conducting a thorough investigation into what had transpired. Mark did not ask, as the thought occurred to him that the CIA was only a part of the problem, but then, what did he know about the working of the Washington bureaucracy? Harold Taylor looked very much like he was totally out of his depth in this new role – having rushed back to the USA in time to miss everything. He was tired but otherwise his normal self – lost in the new job which he had now held for at least a half-hour. But he greeted Mark like a son for about the first time in living memory and showed due concern at Mark's battered appearance, and genuine sympathy for his loss of his two close friends.

The Deputy Director, Rick Herbert, was not as friendly as they had expected, which puzzled Mark for a while. And then made sense when put in context. Herbert was here to ensure that none of the essential details of what had happened made it into the real world. Nothing was to be said about the role that the FBI or the CIA had played in the events before, and after, the second 9/11.

Nothing was to be said about the role played by John Dubois. Nothing was to be said about the deaths of Paul Williams or Annette Covic. Nothing was to be said about the connection with General Ilic Milicic, although deep down Mark felt that this twist in the tale had a much greater significance than it had been given weight to.

Marks' mind drifted back to the events in Colombia. After the order came through to let Carlos pass, Mark had assumed that they would use the same helicopter that had been assigned for the extraction of Carlos for the return of his men to the real world. But that was not the way it was to be. They were told to make their own way across the border into Venezuela where they would be collected by the support crew that was waiting for them. Why they should have to go into Venezuela was one of the mysteries of clandestine operations.

The logical path would have been into Panama but since that border was monitored more so than the others, and the CIA did not trust the Panamanians, another route had to be found. So – why not use Colombia's vast and lawless coastline on the Caribbean? Probably because there was a risk of running into a FARC militia group – the "Fuerzas Armadas Revolutionaries de Colombia"—and the secrecy attached to Mark's little group would be compromised.

The choice of using Venezuela was not exactly based on the logic of using a friendly country. The President of Venezuela was about as far left as was possible, about as unfriendly as could be, and made no secret of his criticism of the USA. At least in the public arena. But who would know what logical or illogical reasoning went on in the minds of those who had planned this mess?

The most illogical thing was that their source of information was cut off. Their GPS systems still worked, but they were only good for telling you where you were. To find out what was around them, they had been receiving irregular updates via the various satellites that occasionally covered this part of the world, and with very good reason. Drugs. They had now been advised that the satellites were being reoriented, whatever that may mean, and their regular feed of information was, therefore, to be 'discontinued until further notice.' They were in a country, where they were not supposed to be, and had to move to another country where they would not exactly be welcomed and would receive absolutely no assistance from the people who had asked them to go there.

They were given additional instructions – well really, they were instructions that they had received before the trip into the jungle – they were to 'Strictly adhere to their Rules of Engagement.' This idiotic instruction was perhaps the single most significant reason that had resulted in Mark's resignation from Special Forces. Why had the people in Washington sent a force with enough firepower and skill to start a third world war, and tell them they were not to shoot anyone?

The support crew was originally designated as a backup team but now that was not required - was it? So here they were, in a country that they were not supposed to be in, doing things that they were not supposed to be doing, and having been instructed not to do what they had intended. Now they were to make their way into another country that they were also not supposed to be in, to be rescued by a support crew that was also not supposed to be there.

Getting to the border proved even more difficult than expected. As they made their way down into the forests they discovered, more by good luck than good judgment, that an ambush had been set up for them. At first, they thought that they had been set upon by one of the many FARC guerrilla bands that roamed this part of the world and were not overly concerned – professional soldier versus bandits – there could only be one winner, no matter what the odds. Well usually.

The US task force disbursed into the undergrowth outflanked the ambush and finally managed to reassemble about two miles to the east of the ambush site. That is four of them did. The other two of their group never turned up and there was only silence from their communicators. That could have meant that they were holed up and did not want to give away their positions – but that turned out to not be the case. They were dead.

A radio call was made to their 'support' team who immediately sent their helicopter to assist, and the four survivors barely made it to safety before their foes pounced on their new position. Eugene, the senior sergeant in charge of this extraction, was a very angry man.

'What are you doing picking a fight with the whole Colombian Army.' he demanded to know as he dragged Mark on board.

'How do you know that?' Mark asked in obvious surprise.

'Because they were supported by Colombian Army vehicles, helicopters, all the latest weapons and fuck knows what else—and in case you don't know I'll tell you, who else has that kind of gear in this area? Either you picked the fight, or you were set up. What a fucking mess!'

Yes – the senior sergeant – who went by the name of Dusty Miller—was far from happy.

Mark had a couple of questions that he kept to himself. His first question was—Why did the authorities insist that Mark's team had to go to the trouble of trekking over a hundred miles through that kind of terrain when the simple thing was to stay with the original plan – albeit without Carlos in tow? His second question was more worrying. Who had given the tip-off to the Colombians? The logical answer to the first was that their masters did not want to have any more to do with this whole business, so they simply withdrew to a position of denial. To the second, he always had a suspicion that the CIA, or whoever had sanctioned the original plan, would rather Mark's team did not survive to tell the tale. If this was not a high-level denial, it sure involved some fairly important people.

Mark looked across the room at Richard Herbert and wondered what kind of man he was. Rick was a short, thickset man, probably in his early fifties who had the appearance of someone who could handle himself in a street fight. He had been a CIA field agent for several years, mostly working in Eastern Europe, which was regarded in the trade as a soft assignment these days. The Cold War had long since ended so there was not much happening there. Bored, he had returned to the USA and was going to embark on a career in a private security company. Then came 9/11, the formation of the Directorate of National Intelligence, and a new career for Rick. Had he now succumbed to the rigors of being employed in the bureaucratic nightmare that was Washington?

Mark knew the kinds of issues and problems that an ex-field operative would face. He was now working within the inner sanctums of a political animal that had more spin-doctors in Washington than the whole CIA Operations Division had officers gathering the data that they had used for their spinning.

At the time of the first Gulf War, in which Mark, Dusty,

and Paul had all played their part, the Administration had it right. They pushed the Iraqis back out of Kuwait in rapid time and proved beyond any doubt that the USA would not tolerate the bully-boy tactics of the likes of Saddam Hussein and his cronies. The USA probably missed a trick in not completing the job – leaving Saddam to run Iraq was not exactly the brightest idea – but there were, and still are, mixed views on that issue.

Then followed the events of September 11th, 2001, after which the United States administration, both military and political, really lost the plot. The incursion into Afghanistan was originally a success, but then rapidly deteriorated into an almost forgotten war with no apparent end.

The second Gulf War had immediate success. They got rid of Saddam in a matter of days – at least he disappeared and was no longer in control of his vast and totally useless army. But then that deteriorated into the most expensive occupation in the history of the planet. Washington had orchestrated a campaign to focus public opinion on a problem and a solution, and on that basis, they went to war. But the problem was a lie.

Even the briefest study of history would have told them that there is a difference between a minor squabble and an argument between the Sunni and Shiite groups, not to mention the Shi'a and Kurdish movements. The real curly one was that the USA had at various times in its' history supported Saddam Hussein who was a Sunni Muslim, and for that matter, it had supported Osama bin laden who is also Sunni, in the subtle and varied manoeuvres of the foreign policy of the supposed leaders of the free world. But the whole business was really about oil. And now they were playing similar games again.

'Why do you not want the truth to be told?' Mark asked, rousing himself from the meanderings of his mind.

'The truth should be told about this mess if only to put the ordinary citizen's minds at rest. Why not tell them that you have identified, captured, and will bring to account corrupt officials in two of your leading security organizations? Why would the administration want to cover that up? That is assuming that the same administration was not involved in the original cover-up?'

Dusty was in an even meaner mood. He did not need to wonder about the kind of man Rick was. He knew – he was a "Yes" man – sucked into a bureaucracy that never delivered a straight answer, or that provided so many options that it was hard to know what they had said. Dusty retained an unusual control as he looked at the man with loathing and contempt. 'So, you are going to hide the truth from the public, because you fear that their faith in the system of national security would be so badly shaken? Well, do you not think it needs to be?'

The Deputy Director looked from one to the other unsure which to answer first. Then he made probably the only decision he could. He sat back and raised his hands in supplication. He too had known circumstances in which executive orders perplexed him even when explained in all their political mumbo-jumbo. He addressed himself to Mark, who seemed like the one he had to convince, despite Dusty's obvious contempt.

'Look – I know this is hard for you – but hear me out' he began. 'I know the CIA and the FBI are in a mess. But they are still the lead agencies in this country in this war on terrorism. If the public loses faith in them, we have got nowhere to turn. Both agencies are being given a massive shakeup, and we will get to a position where heads will roll. But that has to be out of the public's view. As for Dubois – revealing the involvement of one of our financial institutions would have massive implications for our financial markets – which are already under pressure.'

'On the subject of General Ilic Milicic – the involvement of the Serbian General in all of this – could you imagine the twist that would be put on the story if it were revealed that the only time the CIA shares information with our allies is when the USA itself is threatened? It is not about politics – you must believe me – it is about trying to retain public and international confidence in the whole democratic process.'

'You mean confidence in the Administration, don't you? And what confidence have we got?' Mark enquired. 'Once again, the system fails to protect innocent civilians, and, worse than that, it is seen as protecting those who were complicit in enabling this mess. Apart from my two friends who were murdered by fully paid-up members of our intelligence service—for no sane reason – what about the hundreds killed or injured in New York? Aren't their friends and loved ones entitled to some explanation and some form of closure?'

'Yes of course they are!' Rick replied. 'But consider the cost. Right now, they can blame al Qaeda – an organization they probably already hate anyway. If that blame was turned around and pointed at our institutions – what good would that achieve? That would not be closure. That would open up a whole bag of worms – and God only knows where that would all end up. Surely you can see that.'

'Try me!' was Mark's answer, as his father sat facing him across the lounge, cringing at every word, but surprisingly staying silent.

'You have made a couple of statements but not backed it with facts. It is just political hogwash. So - the public doesn't have confidence. What's new? At this point, they cannot have much faith in our ability to protect them from al Qaeda. So why not relieve that and say – "Yes we can" – and this latest mess was caused by our own people.

But we found them, and here they are, and this is what is now going to happen to them!'

'Because public confidence is not the only issue' answered Rick. 'The issue is the international markets. It would not matter who gets the blame, the damage would be done. If confidence is lost in the US Administration, people will take their money elsewhere. That means the market will collapse and so will the US dollar. We are already under enormous pressure from countries who are supposed to be on our side. But money talks – so right here and now they will be sympathetic – but only for half a second. Then imagine the glee that would be felt in Moscow, Beijing, Teheran, and all the other not-so-friendly cities around the world. If confidence is lost, we could see the end of the USA as we know it. Is that what you want?'

Mark sat quietly regarding the DNI man. Herbert did have a point albeit erroneously conceived. Mark knew what he was trying to do, and he was on a mission that no man should have to undertake in a real democracy. It did not matter what the truth was. Rick Herbert had stated the case on behalf of the Administration and that was, quite simply put, an end to the matter. Both Mark and Dusty were ex-Special Forces and had sworn allegiance to their country and all it stood for. Both Mark and Dusty both knew that at the end of the day the matter could be taken no further. But would it?

'So, what do you want to do about the copy of the data from Rabaul that when analysed shows quite clearly the involvement of people other than al Qaeda, not to mention the huge quantities of money, most of it emanating from here in the USA.' Mark began, knowing that with this statement he now had Rick's undivided attention. He could not have cared less about the reaction of his father, which was one of horror, or the reaction of Dusty which was one of extreme amusement. He continued.

'And then there is the copy of John Dubois' system that when analysed shows equally clearly the involvement of members of the FBI and the CIA – at least they were on the Dubois payroll for reasons you, or anyone else, would have difficulty explaining. How do you intend to keep that out of the public forum?'

'Who has a copy of that?' asked a now extremely tense Rick, looking from the elder to the younger Taylor as though watching a game of tennis.

Mark laughed, having observed Herbert's mental gymnastics.

'There is no need to blame my father – after all, he cannot know everything – and there are certain facts that he does not know, for the simple reason – he was not told! But to answer your question – in both cases—I do.'

'Why was that never revealed to the authorities? You have no right to withhold that kind of information!' Herbert almost shouted.

The reply he got to that surprisingly came from Dusty.

'What do you expect?' Dusty began. 'Think about what actually happened and then tell me that Mark Taylor did not do the right thing. He presented his analysis of the data to the CIA. And what did they do? I'll tell you what they did – fuck all! – that's what they did. All the talk about the increased alert level in New York was just crap. I was in New York at the time, and I know all about alert levels. And you should check with the CIA because they have a copy of everything from Mark's computer. Mark then told the FBI about the data on John Dubois' computer, although they had the actual computer – and what did they do. I'll tell you what they did – burned the office of Taylor Software to the ground – that's what they did. Now tell me Herbert – what do you intend to do now? Believe me—all this data is still intact thanks to Mark – in places that you will not find by your usual methods. Now just try to force the issue of him not revealing it to you and I will cause you and your masters so much trouble you would wish you had never been born!'

It was as though Dusty had not spoken, and it was Mark who had responded. Herbert was focused on Mark.

'If the FBI did burn down your office as you allege, how can you be so sure that the data that you allude to is still intact?'

This question was delivered with almost an air of triumph. It was almost as if Herbert would be more than happy if it proved that he had successfully called their bluff. Mark had to think about how to respond to that. Whatever he said now, Richard Herbert was going to be mightily disappointed.

He could not know about Mark's longstanding, and secret, arrangement with Dusty that assured the system was fully backed up off-site. More to the point, he had still not revealed the extra copy of the original data that he had on a memory stick to anyone. The CIA's various attempts to unscramble the encryption on his laptop, while no doubt they had finally succeeded, was only a part of the issue. Only Brad in the CIA and Peter Barton in the Australian Security Intelligence Service knew of the original content. Even if they revealed what they knew, it was of doubtful value without or until the two sets of data were analysed together. He had to assume that they had eventually worked their way around the encryption on Brad's copy – that was a matter for Brad to deal with as he saw fit. But, even if the CIA had now got access to all the data, and done their analysis of it, that was not to say that they had informed anyone else in the complex bureaucracy that was the Intelligence and Security Service of either their possession or their analysis.

Based on the performance thus far, the odds were that

the Deputy Director did not know. He decided to continue to keep Herbert guessing,

'You may not know.' began Mark, knowing full well that Herbert should have known. 'The FBI had access to John Dubois' computer which had the same information that I copied down to my computers. So - all you need to do is go and have a look, although I suspect that our FBI friends may have deleted it. My system on the other hand is backed up off-site, so if you still need a copy all you need to do is ask. I suspect that your new Assistant Inspector may be very interested. As for the information we acquired in Rabaul, a copy of which I am sure the CIA has, a copy of that was placed in a secure location before we came back to Washington. We thought the data was valuable. Apparently, it is not.'

That statement caused Harold Taylor, who had hitherto remained silent, to enter the conversation.

'You did not tell me that!' he almost whispered. Rick Herbert in the meantime was beginning to turn ashen.

Mark again smiled.

'That was probably an omission on my part. We were so busy in Wellington, and you were so anxious that we return to the States in a hurry, it slipped my mind. Anyway – a copy of the data we were working on is also in the hands of your Australian friends.'

That news brought a smile from Harold – did Mark detect a look of triumph, or were they back to just playing inter-agency games? But Harold was a pro, and Mark could do nothing but admire his old man.

'That makes sense – you were after all working in their territory – and I had to ask for their cooperation. But that also means that when they detained the Doctor, they also probably got a copy of his computer records. So irrespective of what we do or say, the Australians have effectively got us by the short and curlies.' The old man was smiling.

Mark continued. 'Yes – I have a copy, and so do the CIA. I understand that they have had some difficulty with it because it is encrypted, and they have not asked for the algorithm. Something to do with them stealing the copy so they were reluctant to seek help, but that is another story. Anyway, what is the point of handing the encryption algorithm over now? The damage has been done and the CIA has probably by now made a mess of their various copies. Still, no one in our weird and wonderful intelligence community seems particularly interested in doing anything other than a cover-up, so the only purpose to be served by giving you another copy would be so that you can destroy it. But the critical thing about this whole business is that the CIA had all the information that was needed to prevent what happened on September 11th. The FBI had sufficient information to establish who the players were in your own security services after the event. Neither did anything with that information and now you are telling me that the Director of National Intelligence, as the principal adviser to the President of the USA wants to cover up that incompetence. Does that about sum up the position?'

Dusty leaned forward and glowered at Herbert and added.

'And, knowing how you people think, you can rest assured that we have taken steps to ensure that, should anything happen to Mark, the whole sorry story will be immediately released by the press. You, or at least the CIA, have already seen what we can do.'

At least Mark had given the CIA a way around any problems they may have with what was effectively their parent organization. He had effectively said that the CIA may have stuffed up their copy, hence they had not reported anything to their superiors. But at the same time, had left the impression that there were enough copies of the data in existence to mean the story would not go away anytime soon.

Herbert was now completely on the defensive.

'I have told you that we cannot afford to let the full details get out. The damage to our economy and our whole democratic structure could not take such a hit. As ex-serving officers, you have certain ongoing responsibilities when you took the oath to serve your country. We are only asking that you respect that – there is no threat either made or implied.'

At least at this stage, he did not add.

Mark noted the comment but the look on his face said all that was needed.

'So – Was Paul's analysis right after all?' asked Mark.

'Paul's analysis?' Herbert asked as he looked from Mark to Dusty.

Mark sat forward in his chair.

'Paul Williams was the CIA agent, and my friend, who got himself killed by the FBI. He had a theory that there was a cover-up of the whole plot at the chief executive level. He did not suggest that the whole plot was engineered by them – heaven help us if that was the case – but having been made aware of it, they decided to let it go ahead. His theory was that the President would get a boost to his support for the war on terror. It had been a while since anything happened, at least on this side of the pond, so what better than another terrorist attack, not as spectacular as 9/11, but with such similarity in timing that all the memories would come flooding back?'

'You surely cannot believe that!' yelled Herbert, almost losing his hitherto relatively controlled attitude.

'It is not a matter of what I believe' Mark replied and continued in a more cynical tone. 'You will be, or should be, aware of our involvement with operations in Colombia not so many years ago – your masters left us to fend for ourselves and we were lucky to come out of that one alive. Don't talk to me about what I can believe or not believe. For once in your life tell us the truth about what happened a couple of days ago. Did any such order come from the White House? Did the President effectively authorize the deaths of all those people in New York because the collateral costs were acceptable in the grander scheme?'

'Of course not!'

'Well, we have our answer then.' said Mark as he and Dusty got up and took their leave.

The answer was—Richard Herbert was lying. However, they could not know what he was lying about?

Was there a cover-up or was it just one big cock-up?

And the truth of the matter was – Richard Herbert probably did not know either.

Chapter 40

Moving On

It started very much like any other day. Well, it was Friday—so that made it different in a way.

Mark still had some residual unease and misgivings over how the authorities had handled the aftermath of 9/11 version two. More correctly said – he was totally and utterly pissed off, even though he knew that the real truth would probably never be told.

The statements that appeared in media reports seemed so bland and inaccurate – despite the efforts of CNN and other channels to spice them up:

'A spokesman for the FBI has informed our reporters that they now know who was behind the extraordinary events in New York City and how it was organized. They have arrested several people in connection with the incident and they believe that they have tracked down all the terrorists involved. They now know that three suicide bombers carried out the attacks and that they were trained in Pakistan and Afghanistan. The plot itself was hatched overseas by people with strong links to the al Qaeda network. The spokesman said the FBI was satisfied with the speed with which their agents had been able to arrest those responsible, and there was no evidence of any further terrorist activity being planned in the United States.'

No mention of any United States government agency or other people being involved. No mention of any failure on the part of the United States security and intelligence organization. No mention of any failure on the part of either the CIA or the FBI. No mention of Mark Taylor or Elliott Shannon. There was no mention of the related deaths of Annette Covic or Paul Williams. There was nothing to relate the event with the deaths of General Ilic Milicic or John Dubois. Such was the nature of politics.

The statement put out by the Director of National Intelligence was drafted by the CIA, and it was not hard to guess why they had not released it themselves. Before it was released it had been through the hands of several "media'" experts, and the original authors would not now have recognized their own work. Every person who vetted press releases put out by a branch of the bureaucracy had something to contribute or had a particular view on what should, or should not, be released to the innocent public. Not that their joint efforts added much to the story.

'An Indonesian-born doctor, Abdul Jabbar has been transferred to the Guantanamo detention centre, where he is being questioned by the CIA and other United States authorities. The Doctor was arrested by the Papua New Guinea police shortly after September the 11th, handed over to the Australian security service, and was subsequently transferred to the CIA. The CIA has reason to suspect that he has strong links to the Jemaah Islamiyah terrorist group and that he was involved in planning the events that occurred here in New York City. This is the first time the Jemaah Islamiyah group is suspected of having been involved in terrorist activity outside of Southeast Asia, and in particular in the USA. Several members of this group are believed to be hiding in the Philippines but are still actively involved in terrorism, The US security intelligence services and the government and security services of the Philippines have stepped up their surveillance of this group.'

Well, wasn't that nice! Doctor Abdul Jabbar was to be seen by the civilian population as the main instigator of the atrocities. And what the PNG police had to do with his apprehension was anyone's guess.

Even the President of the United States – the so-called leader of the free world – came out with a bland and carefully worded, if equally inaccurate, statement:

'Our forces are once again bringing those responsible for this cowardly act to justice, and they are to be commended for the speed with which they have resolved the matter. I have instructed my Director of National Intelligence to take all possible steps to improve our intelligence gathering and analysis techniques and to ensure that any future threat to US citizens is minimized. Those who threaten us will be tracked down, no matter where they seek to hide, and they will feel the full might of the international justice system. I have previously stressed the need for vigilance in the ongoing battle against the forces of evil. The actions taken by my administration should be a warning to all those who seek to attack our people anywhere they may be.'

Well, who could blame him? So bland, and yet so predictable, were the comments made by the President. But that had to be. The facts may or may not have been made known to him, but he still had a country to run. So, he would hardly say that the Security Services of the government of the United States of America had once again failed to protect its' citizens. Rick Herbert was correct in that sense. And, given the multitude of often crank calls that were received every day, the security services were in a "Damned if we do, Damned if we don't" situation.

Mark thought back to the recent views expressed by Paul Williams. While Paul had more or less discarded the theory in the heat of trying to sort it all out, now in the cold light of day he was also probably right. For those few who knew what had truly happened, the statement was just political hogwash—trotted out by some speechwriter more concerned with how it was received rather than what is described. But the world had to move on, looking forward not backward. What's done is done. Like the President, Mark had a business to run. A decision had been made – no one would ever hear the truth of this story from the few remaining participants—so move on!

The silence on the role of the FBI in the past events was certainly not reflected in the way Taylor Software was placed rapidly back in business. The original building and all its' contents were a complete write-off as a consequence of the fire, caused by the storage of highly flammable products, orchestrated by the crooks in the FBI. But it is surprising how fast things can happen when there is an ulterior motive, and when powerful people are lubricating the wheels.

The Department of Homeland Security just so happened to have some surplus accommodation in a much better building than Mark would ever have thought of using. They had rapidly outgrown it and had moved on, so it was available and at a very affordable rent. This suited Mark because the whole building was significantly more secure than his old one and far less likely to be burnt out. It also had more than ample power and telephone connections already in place – enough to drive a small town and then some.

He had a similar experience when it came to the replacement of his computer equipment. The National Security Agency, which is a part of the Department of Defence, just so happened to have some surplus equipment that more than fit the bill. The fact that it was delivered to the new premises in its' original packing meant that it was not surplus—by the serial and model numbers it was very recently purchased as new. But that was not Mark's concern, was it?

The people who came to unpack and install the new machines were also not your average computer installation technicians. These guys talked the same language as Mark. The only problem anticipated by Mark was removing the various hooks they left behind. Even though Mark was friendly and was an embarrassment to the government having been stuffed up by their own people, did not mean that the government agencies would miss the chance to place discrete monitoring on his systems. He had a thought that he may even choose to leave some of their monitoring systems in place just to give them something to do!

The reinstallation of the software was fairly straightforward and in no one else's domain other than Mark's. Unlike systems that are processing data, the recovery of software is easy so long as you have a copy of the source code. The backup procedures at Taylor Software were both simple and subtle. The system, or rather the changes that had occurred since the last time, was backed up several times per day. There was a backup tape on site which was then taken offsite each day – very much the traditional backup procedure. Any software changes were noted and backed up as well so you could restore the system from almost any date. But Mark had other backups that were electronically taken off-site – to somewhere different – namely Dusty Miller's office – just in case. And an event that qualified as a 'just in case' had just recently occurred.

The stuff that Mark had copied down from John Dubois' laptop had been recorded by the system as a "change" and therefore backed up automatically, and therefore restored in its' original state. Eat your hearts out, Nicolas Gagarin and Rick Herbert!

The Insurance Company must have been given a serve from someone on high because all claims were met almost immediately. Mark was doubtful whether the whole exercise of restoration of his systems had cost him anything, but then again – why should he care? The fact that he could afford the costs – well as long as they stayed within ten or so million – did not seem to concern officialdom. The attitude was – get him off our backs at any cost.

The office was therefore now a very different place from what it had been.

Brad Morgan resigned from the CIA immediately, and who could blame him? There was no need for someone with Brad's particular skills in Taylor Software, but he came on board anyway – and the price was quite fair. As it transpired this turned out to be a good move, for reasons that they were both to find out very shortly. Mark had also recruited a marketing graduate. He had long had the view that the Chief Executive Officers of most United States businesses paid only lip services to their IT budget for security. But that had to change – the increased use of social networking, cloud computing and other forms of communication meant that cyber-crime was on the increase and would get worst – and rather rapidly. And Mark was in a position to do something about it and, so far, it seemed to be working out well, albeit that Scott – same name but not the same person who Mark had met at the CIA—was almost always out of the office doing the rounds.

That left, for the most part, just Mark and his Personal Assistant in the office. And that PA was Debbie – a Miss Deborah Peterson—the lady who used to work for the Augem Group.

It turned out that Debbie had a history that she had kept well hidden. But gradually she had opened up. And Mark, in his usual sentimental way, became determined that no one would ever get to harm her again. She lived on her own and did not appear to have any close friends. She took the subway to and from work and never seemed to go anywhere socially. Consequently, it was inevitable, after a long trying day at the office, that Mark had offered her a lift home.

Once there, she had invited him in, and since he was not going anywhere else, and had nothing else to do, they ended up having a home-cooked meal and sharing a bottle of wine. Neither of them was prepared to talk about work, or the events that had led them to this situation – they were just content to be together alone in their own little world.

Loneliness can be a terrible thing. By definition, you are on your own – and even one more lonely person in the same room, the same place, and the same space cannot know what you feel. For Mark, the shattering loss of Annette caused him to feel heartbroken. For Debbie, there was an even deeper and darker secret.

Late in the evening, when Mark came back into the lounge after a visit to the bathroom, he found Debbie seated on the rug leaning back against the couch, staring into the fire, lost in thought. He quietly sat down beside her and gently placed an arm around her shoulders. She was small, especially alongside Mark, but she also seemed very vulnerable and alone.

They sat there in silence, neither of them saying anything until she turned to Mark and gazed up with those large brown eyes. Body language is a wonderful thing, and the eyes tell the full story. Eventually, she brushed her lips against his. At first, it was tentative, almost reluctant, but when she realized that Mark was receptive then it became more intense and more meaningful. Then satisfied, she snuggled into his arms.

Mark did not know what to do, but he decided that he would just let matters take their course. Debbie was a very beautiful woman, and it was a surprise to Mark that she had not settled down to married life. From his point of view, although it was not long since they had buried Annette, he regretted that he and Annette had had an association that was largely unfulfilled. He longed for someone to take her place in his life.

On the other hand, Debbie had been hurt by a relationship that had gone wrong many years before and she simply did not trust men. Except for Mark.

He caressed her body gently almost fearing to touch her with too heavy a hand in case she rejected him. But she did not. He was again in a space where he felt vulnerable. His only sexual experiences of any consequence had been first with Helen – his ex-wife – who at the prospect of sex was stripped naked and lying on her back within seconds. Then he had a brief experience with Annette who had been taken from him so soon and so abruptly. So, Mark did not have a clue of what to do, and how far he should go.

Very slowly they explored each other and then by mutual consent her blouse and Mark's shirt was eased away. Eventually, he found himself caressing her breasts for no other reason than that Debbie had unfastened the clasp of her bra and invited him to do so. Her breasts were small but perfectly rounded and before long she raised herself and Mark found his lips kissing her small but protruding nipples. Their caressing of each other seemed to go on forever.

He had no idea how he came to be laid out on the floor or whether Debbie or he undid his trousers, but she climbed on top of him with an urgency that both surprised and excited him. When he finally slowly and gently entered her, she let out a gasp, and he was fearful again that he had let this whole thing go too far. But she continued to kiss him and moved slowly and rhythmically on top of him, then buried her face in the hairs on his chest as she lurched in the throes of an orgasm that seemed to go on and on.

Mark wanted to let her just go on, and he held himself in control as she continued to gently move above him. But he could not hold himself in check much longer. It seemed to rise in him like an exploding volcano and they reached a climax at the same time. They gripped each other in excitement and desperation, as though they both wanted to hang on to the moment for as long as possible.

Then they just lay there in front of the fire, clutching each other, content in each other's arms. They had found a bond of love and an end to their loneliness – in Mark's case initially as a replacement, in Debbie's case for the very first time.

Mark looked up as Debbie Peterson came into the

office and smiled. Gone was the tension that always seemed to hang around her when she had worked at the Augem Group. She looked more alive, vibrant, and always smiling. Because none of the other staff had known her in a previous life, they did not notice. But Mark did.

He had been able to convince her to do away with the rather stern dress style that she had always worn at Augem. Now she was relaxed in her blouse and trousers, and when she walked into the room, the place lit up. He owed this one to Matt Reynolds.

Funnily enough, it arose from what had happened at Annette's funeral.

The day was wet and grey as it always seemed to manage to be on funeral days. It was planned as a small private occasion. Very few people in New York City knew Annette, and outside of work, she did not appear to have many friends. But they still turned out in numbers that surprised Mark. Brad Morgan was there, as were other representatives from the CIA and the FBI. At least Mark assumed that was where they were from. Elliott and Brent Shannon were there – even if they did not know Annette. They felt that she had somehow, for the very briefest of moments, touched their lives in a way that they could not forget. Several of the staff from Taylor Software were there, as were a number from the Augem Group, including Matt Reynolds, Debbie Peterson, and Rob Augem.

When the Augem group had arrived, Debbie came running to Mark, clung onto his arm and the tears started to flow long before the service had begun. She clung on, and Mark, who felt so alone despite the presence of the ever-faithful Dusty, was glad that she did.

Mark's mother and father were also at the funeral. His mother was tense as she watched her son grapple with the emotions of burying someone that he loved and conscious of the fact that this was a part of Mark's life that she never knew. His father had the sense to leave Mark to grieve. While he was an old-fashioned CIA bureaucrat and had been a stern father, almost lacking the ability to allow Mark the space he needed, on this occasion, he took a back seat.

His son was hurt. The sad grey eyes still missed nothing and misted over as he watched Mark moving amongst the guests and maintaining a very dignified presence.

There was a moving moment just before they went into the church for the formal part of the funeral. A US Army vehicle trundled up the path and parked off to the left side of the church. Out of the vehicle stepped Colonel Tom Dean resplendent in his best dress uniform. Although somewhat inhibited by the crutches, he strode over to where Mark was standing and held out his right hand.

'They filled me in on what happened – You have had a hard time of it for a civilian – are you ok?' he enquired in his typical clipped very British accent.

'Yes, I am fine – thanks, Tom. And thanks for taking care of that business in Kosovo. Annette was the one who gave us the tip-off. I think all the loose ends are now tied up, apart from a total reorganization of our fucked-up intelligence service. How is the leg?'

'Oh - I will be good as new in a few weeks. Just a few nicks.' Tom said in a typical understatement. Then half turning he introduced the old man who had accompanied him.

'Mark—I would like you to meet Papa.'

Mark had barely noticed the old man who had also got out of the Army vehicle.

Papa was a relatively small man with a face that looked as though it had seen its fair share of strife. But the deep brown eyes had both a look of intelligence and a look of understanding. There was a twinkle, which suggested this guy had some unfinished business, even after all he had been through. He grasped Mark's hand and his eyes started to water. For a moment he said nothing. Then he just said 'Thank you. Thank you for caring. Tom has told me all about you, and it is my privilege to be able to meet you.' His message was delivered with dignity and came from the heart. Mark looked into those deep brown eyes and nodded.

They understood each other.

That meeting made Mark's task of delivering a eulogy at the funeral more difficult because it brought into brutal relief all his pent-up emotions. It is easy to talk about someone who has died when no one present knew that person intimately. Mark knew Annette intimately but for so short a time. Now here was Papa, who had given so much so that Annette could have a better life, and it turned out all for nothing. So, during his eulogy Mark looked, and continued to look, directly into Papa's eyes, knowing that he was the one person in attendance who understood.

When delivering a eulogy, it is always best to try to visualize the person in happier times. But for Mark, he could not drag his mind away from the awful, inevitable day when he had been called to the morgue for identification. Whether some unknown person thought it would be easier on Mark if he did both Annette and Paul at the same time, he did not know. What he did know was that the event had left an indelible stain on his soul. All the compassion in the world did not make Mark's task any easier.

He could handle the death of Paul ok. He always knew that someday this may happen. But Annette was different. Her body lay there looking so beautiful and in peace, it was as though at any moment she would arise as though from a dream. Mark looked at her and could have sworn there was an expression that asked – "Why me?"

Mark cried then. And on this day, at the final laying to rest of Anna Leskovic, both Mark and Papa cried.

Both men would never forget.

After the service, Matt Reynolds took Mark to one side. His body language said that he was unsure of how Mark would feel. He was correct on that count. But he sighed and forced himself to speak in as level a voice as he could muster.

'I know it is probably the wrong time, and you have every right to tell me to piss off, but I want to ask you for a favour.' he began, his tone guarded and fearful.

Mark was still unsure of how he should deal with any of the Augem Group. In fact, at times he wished he had never heard of the organization. But as far as he could tell Reynolds had not been a party to the underhand goings-on at the Augem Group and it was probably unfair to lump Matt in with the work of the late John Dubois.

He was still intrigued at the prospect of being able to do Matt a favour. In the circumstances, it might have been more appropriate if the offer had been the other way around. But he was very surprised when Matt explained what he wanted.

'Debbie has resigned from the Augem Group. She was so traumatized by the recent events that she is going to move on. Rob is upset and does not want her to go, but he understands. Now I know that you and Debbie have always got on well. I thought you might like to take her on as a secretary in your company.'

Reynolds was pleased that he had managed to avoid using the words new or personal assistant, but he still stumbled as he tried to find a way to explain that Mark would need someone to replace Annette. In the end, Mark saved him the trouble.

'If Debbie would like to come and work with me, that's fine. Just as long as there is no baggage and no ulterior motive.' Mark said with a certain amount of bitterness in his voice. He inwardly cursed himself for making the last comment and let out a somewhat sardonic laugh. But he did not apologize for it.

Matt seemed to understand. He just held out his hand, which Mark took, and they shook.

The funeral for Paul Williams was held on the following day. The first plan for this event was that the CIA would arrange the funeral, but with some gentle persuasion from Mark, and a not so gentle 'You've got to be fucking joking.' from Dusty, it was decided that Paul would have a full military send-off.

It was arranged by the Special Forces Group, and it had all the solemnity and dignity befitting such an occasion.

Paul had not had an easy life. When he enlisted in the Marines, following the death of his young wife, he went through boot camp at the Marine Corps Recruit Depot Parris Island – a military installation near Beaufort, South Carolina. Boot Camp is always hard work. Much harder than the training that Mark had to endure at the United States Naval Academy. But Paul both amazed and annoyed the people at Parris Island with the sheer determination and aggression he displayed in every aspect of his training. By the time Mark, then a Captain, and Paul, then a Sergeant OR-5, met in the elite Special Operations Force commonly known as Delta, he had calmed down somewhat.

The years of training, and then recruitment into the Special Forces ensured that he did, although the same dogged determination was still there. That determination was to be the best he could be, and all who worked with him knew they could depend absolutely on Paul Williams. And now he was to be buried, leaving so much unfulfilled, because some shithead wanted him out of the way, for no reason that bore any resemblance to the high ethics and integrity that Paul had displayed in life.

The CIA was represented by the Deputy Director of Intelligence and his assistant, the Stephen Rodriguez that Mark had met to sort out the trouble at CIA Langley. Marks' father would have been there anyway, so he had two roles to fill and neither role was easy for him. The FBI was represented by no less than the Director himself. Other members of both organizations were present, but they kept very much to themselves and in the background, and with very good reason.

The funeral was conducted with all the solemn dignity that only the military can provide. It was hard for Mark, being held so soon after the funeral for Annette, but it had a different set of emotions. Mark recognized that he was not the only one mourning. Paul's daughter Renee came to the service and was presented with the Stars and Stripes that had adorned the coffin. At first, she seemed quite overwhelmed by it all—burying a father who she hardly knew – but one that she loved and was loved by. The tears flowed when the Marine cadet tried to present the immaculately folded stars and stripes flag to Renee and as usual Dusty was there, placing his huge arm around her shoulders and shedding a tear himself.

What a waste of a good man was the thought that went through Dusty's head as he stood resolutely beside Paul's daughter. And someone in attendance at this funeral must have known the people responsible for his death, and apparently, the political reality of the situation prevented their being known!

There were two distinct groups of men who watched

the scene unfold. One group contained the CIA and the FBI representatives who all looked and felt subdued. And almost embarrassed. The other group contained the Special Forces personnel and among those the Delta Force personnel, who looked bitter, grim, and angry. The latter group would not forget the loss of one of their own, and the tragedy that this innocent girl was facing for not the first time in her young life.

Now it was a fortnight after the funeral and Friday was coming to an end. The telephone rang and Debbie answered it in her usual efficient manner. Then she seemed to get a little flustered. Eventually, she patched the call through to Mark.

'It is Mr. Reynolds who would like to speak to you.'

Mark picked up the nearest telephone and said, 'Hi Matt – how are things? – you cannot have your secretary back if that is what you are ringing about.'

But his voice was light as he was beginning to move on from all the drama of the last month or so. Matt chuckled as he realized the significance of Marks' tone.

'Nothing quite as important as that.' he said, back to his confident self. 'I know you would probably tell me to get stuffed if I asked you to come to a meeting at the Augem Group' he began. 'But how about you come and have dinner with Rob and myself – I think we can make you an offer which would interest you. You can say "Yes" to the offer now if you like – and still, come to dinner.'

Matt certainly had a way of getting around difficult situations, by not saying what the hell he was talking about.

'What is the offer?' Mark asked – alarm bells starting to ring. The alarm must have transferred to his voice. The last time he could recall a telephone call from Matt on a Friday, which led to an offer that turned out to be almost too good to be true, he had got into unbelievable strife. The last thing he needed was to go through a similar experience again.

Reynolds again chuckled.

'Nothing like what you would expect. Rob and I have been discussing where we are going with the business, and a few changes are under review. For a start, Rob is severing his relationship with the CIA – no more clandestine funding arrangements. He said you would understand, but I do not know why he said that. Also, with Dubois no longer – err – with us – we are going back to our more traditional business. The problem we have is with the computer system. No one in our organization knows five eights of fuck all about it. We would not know how to fix it when things go wrong, and we need someone to take ownership of it – and fast.'

'You paid ten million dollars for it!' Mark re-joined. 'And what happened to our two Indian friends who were supposed to know everything there was to know?'

Mark had not pursued the fact that at least one of them had been complicit in getting Annette into the whole sorry mess and saw no reason to educate Matt on that score – well at least not yet. He also knew that neither of the two had been seen since the death of John Dubois, and the probability was they were both now holed up. Probably somewhere in Pakistan. And probably in the northern tribal territories – anywhere where Mark could not find them. Because if he did – they would not be long for this world.

'They have not been seen since the day Dubois decided to go for flying lessons.' replied Matt. He certainly had a way with words.

'As for the 10 million dollars – there is no record that I can find in the Augem accounts of any payment—to you or anyone else. The agreement that your lawyer had us sign is nowhere to be found either. That means you still own it.'

Mark laughed but was nonetheless deadly serious in his reply.

'No – the Augem Group owns it. The record of the payment is in our accounts, and a copy of our agreement is in our files. That is a done deal, so you will need to somehow fix that. I have no intention of returning the 10 million dollars.'

What Mark did not say was that he had the proof of payment, but that was not in a copy of the Augem accounts - was it? It was in the folders from John Dubois's machine, which presumably Matt knew nothing about. Thanks to the instructions issued by Richard Herbert it seemed very unlikely that those folders would ever see the light of day. And the Augem Group was also unlikely to learn about them unless they ended up in court and took on the overwhelming power that Mark had faced in the wash-up in Washington. And lost.

All this appeared irrelevant to Reynolds and Mark realized the truth. The Augem Group had quickly written off their association with Dubois. It was as though he never existed!

'So, we own the software!' Matt replied, also laughing and oblivious to any issues that may arise.

'What is to stop us contracting you to look after it for us?'

Mark had to think about that. But only for a few seconds.

'Well, nothing – I suppose.' Mark answered, but still cautious as he continued.

'You may not know, but Brad Morgan has returned and joined Taylor Software on a more permanent basis, so it should be business as usual from our point of view.'

And his job would now be much easier without the

dual role of working for both Taylor Software and the CIA, Mark did not add.

'Yes – we heard about that.' Matt continued as though discussing the weather.

'So, here is the deal. We will pay you the same rate per month that we used to pay – that is unless you have some other figure in mind?'

Reynolds, in normal circumstances, would not make such an offer. That meant that he had been told to negotiate, and that meant upwards. But not at the cost of what was now a very tenuous friendship. And why should Mark care? The original price that Augem paid Taylor Software for their services included support, but the bulk of the amount covered the cost of the software. That meant that the Augem Group would effectively be paying twice since the agreement that his lawyer Dusty Miller LLB had originally drawn up said that they already owned it!

'No – that's fine.' Mark said in as managerial a voice as he could muster, to avoid laughing. 'You will just need to get some more paperwork drawn up to reflect our new role.'

'Mark – why don't you get Dusty Miller to draw up the papers? We will want a document that if you like settles the previous deal that you did with Dubois, as well as a new contract. We will pay for his time plus the normal charges that lawyers seem to invent to pad out their bills – and apart from a legal opinion from our side – there should be no problem. Shall we say a five-year agreement, with an automatic annual adjustment of the rate, and an automatic renewal clause?'

Mark was more than a little surprised at this offer. It was generous, to say the least. And like the original deal made with the Augem Group over two years ago, there was not a tremendous amount of negotiation. But what the hell – if he knew Dusty, this agreement would be bulletproof –

with perhaps another buy-out clause should Augem chose to terminate the agreement early.

'Ok – Where's dinner? – and is it ok if I bring a friend?' was all that Mark could think of to say.

'Let's say Marcelino's at seven-thirty – and we would be pleased if you would bring a friend with you. Rob would like to catch up with Debbie.'

Now how did he know that Debbie was the one who Mark would bring?

Chapter 41

Marcelino's

Marcelino's Restaurant was very busy, but it had been designed in such a way that no one group of diners encroached on any other. That it was Italian would have been made obvious from the constant screaming and shouting that came from the kitchen, but the restaurant still managed to produce excellent cuisine and served it with the very best of Italian wines.

The table that the Augem Group had been allocated was towards the back of the restaurant and in an alcove, so that it had an air of both intimacy and privacy about it. Mark could not have cared less, but he was not too sure whether the other guests cared, apart from Debbie. He was certain that Matt was still married although he had never delved into the details, yet he had brought his daughter as his guest – Ivory—or to use her more correct name—Virginia.

The last time Mark had met Ivory he remembered with bitterness the events that had followed. But that was not her fault, was it? He would have met her again, had he gone to the funeral of the father of her friend Ebony – or to use her more correct name, Charlie. But he could bring himself to do that, much as he would have enjoyed the prospect of witnessing John Dubois gone forever from this life.

He did not know of Rob's marital status either but there was no Mrs. Augem at the dinner. Instead, Rob had invited Renee who was still in New York following the funeral of her father Paul, sorting out the estate of a very private and lonely man. That she wanted to get as far away from New York as soon as was possible, and back to the relative peace of New Zealand, was very apparent.

Still, the three girls from very different backgrounds got on just fine and Mark supposed that that was the intention of his hosts.

There was initially some light-hearted discussion and debate on which wine to choose, but that was as close as the group got to any sort of disagreement. The business side of the gathering was over very quickly with a toast proposed by Rob towards a long and successful association. As the conversation meandered along in the relaxed and pleasant atmosphere, Mark could not help thinking about recent events that had been very dramatic and, in his view, had never been brought to a satisfactory conclusion.

At first, he had been surprised at Rob's obvious interest in Renee and then pleased in a way. Here she was in New York, a city that was both vibrant and frightening, alone and with no known family, and along came Rob. He was far too old to have any romantic interest in the girl, yet he was hell-bent on ensuring that her every need was met. And he always had a concerned and caring look about him that said no one would harm this girl again.

But why?

What was the connection between either Rob and Renee or, more likely, between Rob and Renee's late father, Paul Williams? Was the untimely death of her father the primary reason for Rob being so concerned about her welfare? And if it was, it was not too much of a stretch to think that the reason was pure guilt. Did Rob feel guilty that Renee has lost her father, and of course, Mark had lost a close friend, and that Rob had somehow been involved?

And then the horrible truth dawned on Mark, something he should have been able to work out long ago but had not. He could have been persuaded by Rob's helplessness given that the late John Dubois had so ruthlessly taken over his company. But when he thought about the subject of Augem and Rob slightly differently, there had to have been another reason for the fact that Dubois had wielded so much power.

Why had Rob Augem been retained by John Dubois when the more obvious course of action would have been to put Rob out of his misery and retire him? More importantly, why had Rob stayed on, in an atmosphere and an environment that appeared to suit neither of them – even more so—Rob?

Then there was the episode at Augem when Paul and Mark had visited John Dubois on that memorable day. Rob had looked shocked at the illusion that Mark was somehow tied to the NSA. Mark had taken Rob's reaction to mean that he was more than a little surprised. But was there something more sinister?

He waited until Rob had to excuse himself to go to the bathroom – which, given his age and the number of drinks he had consumed, would happen quite frequently – and Mark followed him.

When they got there, Mark turned and locked the door into the bathroom, and with his back to the door, he addressed Rob in a quiet voice.

'So, why don't you fill me in on the bit of this riddle that I am missing? What was your role in recent events that I need to know about?'

Rob had been standing at the urinal and turned sharply spraying his water all over his grey, immaculately pressed trousers, at Marks' question. 'What are you talking about?' he inquired, in a voice that revealed more than the discomfort of his wet trousers.

'Oh, you know alright!' replied Mark.

'I have been somewhat puzzled by your befriending Paul's daughter Renee. I know that you cannot harbour any amorous desires for the girl. I think it has something to do with Paul's death, and I am picking that you feel guilty about that. So, how can that be?'

'I don't know what you are talking about!' Rob burst out.

But it was the body language that said that he did know, that answered Mark's question.

At that moment, all the pent-up emotions of rage, anger, and heartbreak that Mark had felt since the deaths of his closest friend Paul, and his beautiful and innocent partner Annette, were too much. He grabbed the old man with both hands around the throat and pinned him hard against the wall.

'You have a minute to tell me the truth, or else, God help me, I will kill you here and now!' in a tone of voice that would have left little doubt that he meant it.

As he waited for a response, Mark relaxed his grip, the initial burst of anger, but not the emotion, dissipating as quickly as it had come. But his spontaneous action and his display of anger had a remarkable effect.

Rob Augem was not the type of person who could withstand this kind of physical violence but there was more to his reaction than could be explained by fear. Rob slid down the wall and put his head in his hands. Then he looked up at Mark with tears streaming down his face, a look of shattered resignation on his face, and it all came pouring out.

'I got caught up in the market crash in the 1980s, as you well know, and I stole some money. It was not as though I planned to keep it – it was just a short-term fix. We had our backs to the wall – before we were approached by John Dubois. We had no money—except that is for the funds that came through the CIA and any number of other people in the intelligence business. And I made a mistake – I shifted some funds into my own accounts – just to survive. You must believe me—it was not as though I intended to keep it – it was just a short-term thing.'

Rob blundered on repeating himself as though that one thought was locked in his mind.

'Rob – I do not care about your money problems.' interrupted Mark 'Just tell me what happened!'

Rob's eyes focused on some indefinable spot on the wall and began a monologue, talking almost to himself.

'Well, someone from within the federal government got wind of what I was trying to do and approached me.' Rob began, talking even more slowly and quietly than he normally did.

'The man said he knew all about what I had done, but everything would be fine – he would make some arrangements—and I thought no more about it. And along came John Dubois with all his money and bailed us out. It was not until later that I realized – too late – that John Dubois was put forward by this someone who, as it turned out, was with the Central Intelligence Agency. You must believe me – I did not know at the time. The CIA officially did not know about these deals either – it was done by people who, as it transpired, had their own personal agendas. It was not until recently that I realized what Dubois was really up to. When I approached him to have it

Augem paused to gather his thoughts. Mark hoped that the pause was not so that Rob could invent some other story to disguise what he had done. But the look of distress on the old mans' face suggested otherwise.

'The guy from the CIA then rang me again – all these years later – and warned me to back off or else he would reveal the whole sorry mess and my involvement. He said that the easiest way to do that would be to have me removed, and then I could posthumously take the blame for a number of their nasty little schemes! I was scared— the guy had been promoted to a fairly high position, he had more than enough power and influence, and he left me in little doubt that I could be in real trouble. But if I had known the trouble it would subsequently cause for so many people, I would have owned up and taken whatever was coming.'

'You have to believe me – I never intended that people would die, and certainly never envisaged that you or any of your friends would get hurt! When I met Renee, the whole world seemed to come crashing down. I realized that the things we do can have an indelible effect on peoples' lives. My actions had resulted in that innocent young lady losing her father, in a world in which she was already alone. I have tried to show remorse, but that is not good enough, is it? I know the FBI and the CIA have some questions to answer, but I thought in the mess that followed the events of that horrible day, and with John Dubois gone, I could now forget about my transgressions. But I cannot forget. And Renee seemed like something I could cling onto.'

The tears flowed down the old man's face. Mark initially thought of letting Rob carry on, but he was looking at a broken man. He sat on the floor next to Rob as someone tried to enter the bathroom area.

Mark ignored the interruption.

'You are blaming yourself for the involvement of John Dubois.' Mark began, and then the truth became clear. 'And therefore, you are blaming yourself for the death of Paul Williams and Annette Covic, not to mention countless other innocent people?' Mark added as though talking to himself.

'All this would not have happened if I had only stuck to my principles.' Rob almost shouted. That resulted in someone again hammering on the bathroom door and yelling for it to be opened.

But Mark continued to ignore them.

'What was the name of the guy from the CIA who contacted you?'

When Rob whispered the man's name, Mark's blood turned icy cold.

While the hammering on the door continued, and while Rob tried to clean the mess off his trousers, Mark took out his cell phone, hit the 'Names' button, and scrolled down to Harold Taylor and then pressed the Call Key. His father's answerphone kicked in almost instantly.

'Hi dad – it's Mark. You are not going to believe this, but I think you have some work to do!'

Mark left the message at that. He thought that this business was all behind him but now another piece of the puzzle had been revealed.

Mark shook his head.

'Come on Rob – Let me tell you now – I do not blame you for the loss of my two friends. You were sucked in like the rest of us. And we can deal with it – but right now, we need a drink.'

Mark helped the old man to his feet and helped him straighten his clothes. He then unlocked the door and was met by an irate man who proceeded to demand to know what was going on. But Mark's cold stare, and the dishevelled state of Rob, soon caused him to shuffle past in embarrassment.

They returned to their table where their absence was barely noticed, except for the anxious look which Mark got from Debbie. She was getting fairly good at reading body language.

Both Mark and Rob laughed as Rob explained the reason for their delay.

'I had a slight accident, but Mark helped me clean it up so, apart from my pride, it is all cleared up now.'

'A slight understatement!' Mark thought.

The evening continued to its' logical conclusion. Mark was quieter than he had been previously, but no one noticed. Rob managed to consume more than his fair share of wine which everyone assumed was the reason why he excused himself before the dessert arrived and bundled himself into a taxi.

After another hour or so, Matt finally decided it was time to call it a day and took Virginia and Renee home leaving just Debbie and Mark to have a last coffee.

Mark hated himself for lying, but what else could he do?

Debbie had known Mark for several years. She had always liked him, but now in changed circumstances, she realized she loved him, and she hoped and felt that the love was reciprocated. She was correct on that score.

Looking into his eyes she asked with concern in her voice.

'There is something wrong isn't there? What happened when you and Rob went out?'

'Oh – it was just a minor matter.' Mark said. 'I wanted to pick up the tab for tonight – after all, I can afford it – and the deal we now have is a further bonus. And despite the air of all being well, the Augem Group have some serious problems to deal with. What is more, Marcelino's is not exactly the cheapest place in town – is it?' Mark added with a laugh and a wink, as he held Debbie's hand across the table.

Debbie smiled and the smile was genuine. Mark also smiled and hoped that Debbie was not as good at reading body language as he was. He would eventually tell her the truth but now was neither the time nor the place.

Mark was unsure what Debbie's reaction might be. To a certain extent, he was conditioned by his marriage to Helen. In that case, it had become a waste of time to talk about problems for the simple reason that Helen had always assumed there was a simple, valid, and therefore obvious explanation for everything, and therefore there was no problem at all.

If only life was that simple.

They decided to go to Mark's apartment for the night. It was a two-bedroom place and Debbie made herself at home in the second bedroom because, she laughed as she explained, Mark snored when he had been drinking and she wanted some sleep. On this occasion, Mark did not object, and after a long and passionate embrace, he retired to his own room.

When he was certain that Debbie was asleep, and snoring, which they would laugh about in the morning, he again called his father. This time Harold answered despite the lateness of the call.

'What have you been up to that requires my attention?' Harold inquired of his son.

'Let's talk about who was responsible for the shambles that we believed was sorted.' Mark began, before his father cut him off, the panic obvious in his voice.

'What do you mean? The people are identified thanks in no small part to your efforts. They will go before the courts, and I have no doubt they will be found guilty. We can do no more now. Let the matter rest!'

Mark did not quite know how to say it.

'What about Stephen Rodriguez?'

It was amazing how body language could be transmitted over the telephone, as Harold gulped. 'What about Stephen?'

'Well—he is not as lily white as he would have us believe.'

The cold reality of what Mark had said hung in the air.

Harold Taylor hesitated, but then it was a simple request.

'I think I might need your help.'

That involved another decision.

The US Review of Books
– Book review by Nicole Yurcaba

'Mark had been in many tight spots before, against far smarter and more heavily armed foes, but he could not see a way out of this one.'

Readers follow Mark Taylor, a US Army Special Forces soldier turned computer guru, as he ventures from New York City to places like Kosovo, New Zealand, and even Papua New Guinea as he fights to clear his name after the aftermath of a deal gone wrong with a client known as The Augem Group. Readers join Mark as he begins questioning the intelligence and security infrastructures and bureaus that he once served and worked with during his Special Forces career, and they follow his calculated strategies to protect himself, a city, innocent people, and possibly the world, as he uncovers a potential terrorist attack that could bring New York, once again, to ruins. As readers follow Mark's adventures, they encounter a cast of corrupt, yet slightly relatable, characters with whom they will develop love-hate relationships, and they will experience first-hand the complex world of cybersecurity, international terrorism, and clandestine, mercenary-like operations that are probably closer to fact than fiction in today's unpredictable world of political and technological upheaval.

This book details the intricate workings of operations like cybersecurity, government agencies, and even individuals that people, in their everyday lives, remain ignorant of or take for granted. With its fast-paced adventure, this book will engage readers as its main character globe-trots in the name of justice, protection, and peace. This book will also enlighten readers on the struggles that ex-military personnel, especially those in the Special Operations realm, face in adapting to civilian life. And in its main character, readers will find a hero-villain that defies their wildest imaginations and expectations. Readers with an interest in covert operations and espionage will enjoy this book, as will those who have an interest in the ever-changing faces of national and international securities, technologies, and the influences of technology on societies.

Pacific Book Review
– by Anthony Avina

Trust in the government is a hotly debated issue for many reasons across the world. As Thomas Paine once said, "Government, even in its best state, is but a necessary evil, in its worst state, an intolerable one.' To trust in the government takes a major leap of blind faith, yet often a knowledgeable citizen is one who keeps one eye open. In author Donald Peters book Covert Decisions, one computer software developer and analyst discover this harsh truth as he uncovers a heinous plot.

In this book, Mark Taylor retired from his career in the United States Special Forces and took a job in security software for a computer company. After an unusual client offering a large cash offer creates a dangerous situation, Mark finds himself uncovering and international terrorist plot and unable to convince the government of its existence. He'll have to combat the FBI and CIA to show the plot is real and stop this terrorist act before more lives are lost.

This is a well written, lengthy and powerful read that captures the intensity of an international action/ military thriller with the complexities of fully fleshed out characters. The author did a brilliant job of creating a narrative which would draw the reader in for the slow burn as the intense plot uncovered by the protagonist slowing begins to peel away the layers surrounding it, leaving a series of twists and turns that will keep readers on the edge of their seats.

This is a novel for anyone who enjoys drama, action, international intrigue, mysteries, and thrillers. As a fan of the genre, the story was intriguing and inviting as the story began to unravel before me. The lengthy read was a fantastic addition, as it fully realized this story into the complex reality of international terrorism and the justice system overall, especially when dealing with government agencies in the process.

This was a great read overall. A protagonist that was complicated and identifiable as they sunk further and further into the plot and a story that keeps the reader guessing at every turn make author Donald Peters' book Covert Decisions and incredible ride that will thrill readers. Be sure to grab your copy today!